"One historical mystery series that never gets boring or dull."
—*Midwest Book Review*

WHAT WOULD SCOTLAND YARD DO
WITHOUT DEAR MRS. JEFFRIES?

Even Inspector Witherspoon himself doesn't know—because his secret weapon is as ladylike as she is clever. She's Mrs. Jeffries—the charming detective who stars in this unique Victorian mystery series. Enjoy them all . . .

The Inspector and Mrs. Jeffries
A doctor is found dead in his own office—and Mrs. Jeffries must scour the premises to find the prescription for murder.

Mrs. Jeffries Dusts for Clues
One case is solved and another is opened when the Inspector finds a missing brooch—pinned to a dead woman's gown. But Mrs. Jeffries never cleans a room without dusting under the bed—and never gives up on a case before every loose end is tightly tied.

The Ghost and Mrs. Jeffries
Death is unpredictable . . . but the murder of Mrs. Hodges was foreseen at a spooky séance. The practical-minded housekeeper may not be able to see the future—but she can look into the past and put things in order to solve this haunting crime.

Mrs. Jeffries Takes Stock
A businessman has been murdered—and it could be because he cheated his stockholders. The housekeeper's interest is piqued . . . and when it comes to catching killers, the smart money's on Mrs. Jeffries.

continued . . .

Mrs. Jeffries On the Ball

A festive Jubilee celebration turns into a fatal affair—and Mrs. Jeffries must find the guilty party.

Mrs. Jeffries on the Trail

Why was Annie Shields out selling flowers so late on a foggy night? And more importantly, who killed her while she was doing it? It's up to Mrs. Jeffries to sniff out the clues.

Mrs. Jeffries Plays the Cook

Mrs. Jeffries finds herself doing double duty: cooking for the inspector's household and trying to cook a killer's goose.

Mrs. Jeffries and the Missing Alibi

When Inspector Witherspoon becomes the main suspect in a murder, Scotland Yard refuses to let him investigate. But no one said anything about Mrs. Jeffries.

Mrs. Jeffries Stands Corrected

When a local publican is murdered, and Inspector Witherspoon botches the investigation, trouble starts to brew for Mrs. Jeffries.

Mrs. Jeffries Takes the Stage

After a theatre critic is murdered, Mrs. Jeffries uncovers the victim's secret past: a real-life drama more compelling than any stage play.

Mrs. Jeffries Questions the Answer

Hannah Cameron was not well-liked. But were her friends or family the sort to stab her in the back? Mrs. Jeffries must really tiptoe around this time—or it could be a matter of life and death.

Mrs. Jeffries Reveals Her Art

Mrs. Jeffries has to work double-time to find a missing model *and* a killer. And she'll have to get her whole staff involved—before someone else becomes the next subject . . .

Mrs. Jeffries Takes the Cake

The evidence was all there: a dead body, two dessert plates, and a gun. As if Mr. Ashbury had been sharing cake with his own killer. Now Mrs. Jeffries will have to do some snooping around—to dish up clues.

Mrs. Jeffries Rocks the Boat

Mirabelle had traveled by boat all the way from Australia to visit her sister—only to wind up murdered. Now Mrs. Jeffries must solve the case—and it's sink or swim.

Mrs. Jeffries Weeds the Plot

Three attempts have been made on Annabeth Gentry's life. Is it due to her recent inheritance, or was it because her bloodhound dug up the body of a murdered thief? Mrs. Jeffries will have to sniff out some clues before the plot thickens.

Mrs. Jeffries Pinches the Post

Harrison Nye may have had some dubious business dealings, but no one expected him to be murdered. Now Mrs. Jeffries and her staff must root through the sins of his past to discover which one caught up with him.

Mrs. Jeffries Pleads Her Case

Harlan Westover's death was deemed a suicide by the magistrate. But Inspector Witherspoon is willing to risk his career to prove otherwise. Mrs. Jeffries must ensure the good inspector remains afloat.

Mrs. Jeffries Sweeps the Chimney

A dead vicar has been found, propped against a church wall. And Inspector Witherspoon's only prayer is to seek the divinations of Mrs. Jeffries.

Mrs. Jeffries Stalks the Hunter

Puppy love turns to obsession, which leads to murder. Who better to get to the heart of the matter than Inspector Witherspoon's indomitable companion, Mrs. Jeffries.

continued . . .

Mrs. Jeffries and the Silent Knight

The yuletide murder of an elderly man is complicated by several suspects—none of whom were in the Christmas spirit.

Mrs. Jeffries Appeals the Verdict

Mrs. Jeffries and her belowstairs cohorts have their work cut out for them if they want to save an innocent man from the gallows.

Mrs. Jeffries and the Best Laid Plans

Banker Lawrence Boyd didn't waste his time making friends, which is why hardly anyone mourns his death. With a list of enemies including just about everyone the miser's ever met, it will take Mrs. Jeffries' shrewd eye to find the killer.

Mrs. Jeffries and the Feast of St. Stephen

'Tis the season for sleuthing when wealthy Stephen Whitfield is murdered during his holiday dinner party. It's up to Mrs. Jeffries to solve the case in time for Christmas.

Mrs. Jeffries Holds the Trump

A very well-liked but very dead magnate is found floating down the river. Now Mrs. Jeffries and company will have to dive into a mystery that only grows more complex.

Mrs. Jeffries in the Nick of Time

Mrs. Jeffries lends her downstairs common sense to this upstairs murder mystery—and hopes that she and the inspector don't get derailed in the case of a rich uncle-cum-model-train-enthusiast.

Mrs. Jeffries and the Yuletide Weddings

Wedding bells will make this season all the more jolly. Until one humbug sings a carol of murder.

Mrs. Jeffries Speaks Her Mind

When an eccentric old woman suspects she's going to be murdered, everyone thinks she's just being peculiar—until the prediction comes true.

Mrs. Jeffries Forges Ahead

A free-spirited bride is poisoned at a society ball, and it's up to Mrs. Jeffries to discover who wanted to make the modern young woman into a postmortem.

Mrs. Jeffries and the Mistletoe Mix-Up

There's murder going on under the mistletoe as Mrs. Jeffries and Inspector Witherspoon hurry to solve the case before the eggnog is ladled out on Christmas Eve.

Mrs. Jeffries Defends Her Own

When an unwelcome visitor from her past needs help, Mrs. Jeffries steps into the fray to stop a terrible miscarriage of justice.

Visit Emily Brightwell's website
www.emilybrightwell.com

Also available from Prime Crime:
The first nine Mrs. Jeffries Mysteries in three volumes
Mrs. Jeffries Learns the Trade, *Mrs. Jeffries Takes a Second Look*, and
Mrs. Jeffries Takes Tea at Three

Berkley Prime Crime titles by Emily Brightwell

THE INSPECTOR AND MRS. JEFFRIES
MRS. JEFFRIES DUSTS FOR CLUES
THE GHOST AND MRS. JEFFRIES
MRS. JEFFRIES TAKES STOCK
MRS. JEFFRIES ON THE BALL
MRS. JEFFRIES ON THE TRAIL
MRS. JEFFRIES PLAYS THE COOK
MRS. JEFFRIES AND THE MISSING ALIBI
MRS. JEFFRIES STANDS CORRECTED
MRS. JEFFRIES TAKES THE STAGE
MRS. JEFFRIES QUESTIONS THE ANSWER
MRS. JEFFRIES REVEALS HER ART
MRS. JEFFRIES TAKES THE CAKE
MRS. JEFFRIES ROCKS THE BOAT
MRS. JEFFRIES WEEDS THE PLOT
MRS. JEFFRIES PINCHES THE POST
MRS. JEFFRIES PLEADS HER CASE
MRS. JEFFRIES SWEEPS THE CHIMNEY
MRS. JEFFRIES STALKS THE HUNTER
MRS. JEFFRIES AND THE SILENT KNIGHT
MRS. JEFFRIES APPEALS THE VERDICT
MRS. JEFFRIES AND THE BEST LAID PLANS
MRS. JEFFRIES AND THE FEAST OF ST. STEPHEN
MRS. JEFFRIES HOLDS THE TRUMP
MRS. JEFFRIES IN THE NICK OF TIME
MRS. JEFFRIES AND THE YULETIDE WEDDINGS
MRS. JEFFRIES SPEAKS HER MIND
MRS. JEFFRIES FORGES AHEAD
MRS. JEFFRIES AND THE MISTLETOE MIX-UP
MRS. JEFFRIES DEFENDS HER OWN
MRS. JEFFRIES TURNS THE TIDE

Anthologies

MRS. JEFFRIES LEARNS THE TRADE
MRS. JEFFRIES TAKES A SECOND LOOK
MRS. JEFFRIES TAKES TEA AT THREE
MRS. JEFFRIES SALLIES FORTH

MRS. JEFFRIES
SALLIES FORTH

EMILY BRIGHTWELL

BERKLEY PRIME CRIME, NEW YORK

THE BERKLEY PUBLISHING GROUP
Published by the Penguin Group
Penguin Group (USA)
375 Hudson Street, New York, New York 10014, USA

USA I Canada I UK I Ireland I Australia I New Zealand I India I South Africa I China

Penguin Books Ltd., Registered Offices: 80 Strand, London WC2R 0RL, England
For more information about the Penguin Group, visit penguin.com.

MRS. JEFFRIES SALLIES FORTH

Berkley Prime Crime Books are published by The Berkley Publishing Group.
BERKLEY® PRIME CRIME and the PRIME CRIME logo are registered trademarks of
Penguin Group (USA).

Berkley Prime Crime trade paperback ISBN: 978-0-425-26934-3

An application to register this book for cataloging has been submitted to the Library of Congress.

PUBLISHING HISTORY
Berkley Prime Crime trade paperback edition / October 2013

PRINTED IN THE UNITED STATES OF AMERICA

10 9 8 7 6 5 4 3 2 1

Cover illustration by Jeff Walker.

ALWAYS LEARNING   PEARSON

CONTENTS

MRS. JEFFRIES TAKES THE STAGE

CHAPTER 1

"What's that blackguard doing here?" Albert Parks muttered under his breath as he watched the small man in elegant black evening dress march down the center aisle of the Hayden Theatre.

Parks's heartbeat raced, beads of sweat popped out on his forehead and his hands started to shake. He dropped the velvet curtain, letting the material close so he wouldn't have to look at that hated face. What in the name of God was he going to do? The bastard wasn't even supposed to be in England. The last Parks had heard, Hinchley was in New York savaging careers and giving the theatre people of London a well-earned rest from his vicious pen.

Now oblivious to the hustle and bustle going on around and behind him on the stage, Parks peeked through the curtain again. He spotted the critic taking a seat in the third row center. Damn. His eyes hadn't been playing tricks on him. It was Hinchley all right.

"Mr. Parks," the wardrobe mistress called from the back of the stage. "Mr. Swinton wants a word with you before the show starts."

Parks nodded dully and stepped away from the side curtain. "All right, Agnes. Tell him I'll be right there."

He wondered if Tally Drummond still kept a bottle of whiskey in the bottom of the prop box. With Hinchley here, they'd probably all need a drink by the end of the evening.

Trevor Remington, the leading man, saw Albert Parks wander off the stage. Parks's shoulders were slumped and his face was pale. Remington, always curious, dashed over to the spot Parks had just vacated and inched the curtain apart. The house was full. Remington couldn't see an empty seat, so what was wrong with dear old Albert? Fellow was a bit on the high strung side, but then again, most good directors were, Remington thought.

He started to step back when a man in the third row suddenly stood up. Remington's breath left him in a rush, his ears rang and he felt his face flush with remembered shame. What was he doing here? Remington leapt back from the curtain so fast he almost tripped over his feet. Dear God in heaven, what was he going to do? Ogden Hinchley was in the audience. Ogden-the-ugly wasn't in America; he was sitting right out front! Swearing softly, Remington stalked off the stage, brushing rudely past Edmund Delaney without so much as a word.

Edmund Delaney watched the actor stomp towards the back of the theatre. Must have a bad case of opening-night nerves, Delaney thought, then dismissed the man in favor of curiosity. He stepped up to the curtain on stage left, pulled it apart and peeked out. He smiled. Not an empty seat in the house. Quickly, he scanned the first few rows, wondering which critics had bothered to come. He hoped the *Gazette* and the *Strand* were here. Both papers were quite sympathetic to new playwrights. Then he spotted the man in the third row. Delaney stared hard for a few moments, hoping his eyes were playing tricks on him. But they weren't. The devil. In the flesh. Delaney's hands clenched into fists, a red mist of rage floated in front of his face and for a brief moment, he thought he might be sick.

"Five minutes, everyone." Delaney heard Eddie Garvey, the stage manager, call the warning.

Delaney, his face set like a stone, turned and walked stiffly off the stage without so much as a glance at the stage manager or the wardrobe mistress. He was too sunk in his own misery to notice anyone.

"Well, what's got into him?" Garvey asked. But Agnes had already hustled off to make sure the first scene changes were ready, so he ended up talking to himself.

"What's got into who?" Willard Swinton, the owner of the Hayden Theatre, said from behind Garvey.

"Mr. Delaney." Garvey nodded toward the curtain "He was having a peek at the house and then he walked off like he'd seen a ghost."

Swinton, a balding man with a huge mustache and an infectious grin, laughed. "He probably saw one of his former mistresses in the front row. No doubt that would give a man pause." Swinton wandered over to the curtain, eased it apart and looked out. "I wonder which of his former lovelies has turned up to torment the poor man . . ." His voice trailed off as he saw a familiar figure sitting in the third row. "Blast and thunder," he cursed softly under his breath.

"What'd you say, Mr. Swinton?" Garvey asked curiously. "Who's out there?"

Swinton quickly dropped the curtain and leapt back. "No one," he said hastily. "No one at all. Go on, Garvey, get about your business. We've a play to put on and I don't want any mistakes tonight."

"Yes, sir." Garvey hustled off. But he wondered just who was sitting out front. This was the fourth person now who'd looked like they'd seen the devil himself out front. The director, the playwright, the leading man and now Mr. Swinton had turned pale as curdled milk when they'd peeked through that curtain. Eddie Garvey decided he'd take a gander himself as soon as he got Mr. Swinton out of his way.

"What time's the inspector's train due in?" asked Wiggins, the footman. He settled himself in his usual spot at the kitchen table and reached for one of the apple turnovers Mrs. Goodge had baked early that morning. Wiggins, with his round, innocent face, fair skin and chestnut brown hair that no amount of pomade could keep plastered to his head, was the youngest in the household of Inspector Gerald Witherspoon of Scotland Yard.

"Half eight," Smythe, the coachman, answered. "But he said he'd take a hansom home. He doesn't want me to bother gettin' the carriage out to collect him from the station."

Smythe was a big, muscular man with dark hair, heavy, almost brutal features and brown eyes that generally twinkled with good humor. Unless, of course, he was annoyed, as he was now. He turned his head and frowned at Betsy, the pretty, blonde maid. The lass could get his dander up quicker than anyone, but by the same token, one smile from her could brighten his whole day.

But Betsy wasn't in the least intimidated by the coachman's glare. She knew him too well ever to be afraid of him.

"It's no good you giving me those dark looks," she said tartly. "My mind's made up. Tomorrow I'm going to Whitechapel whether you or anyone else likes it."

"Then I'm goin' with you," Smythe shot back. "I'll not have you over there on your own. It's too ruddy dangerous."

"That woman was murdered in the middle of the night," Betsy said irritably. The last thing she wanted was Smythe tagging along with her. Not that she didn't like his company—she did. Lately they'd been keeping quite a bit of company together. But this time, she had a special errand to do. She didn't want to be explaining herself to anyone else from the household. "I'm going to be there in broad daylight. Besides, murders happen all the time in the East End. I don't know why everyone's makin' such a fuss over this one."

"'Cause this one's different," Wiggins chimed in. "This lady were out and out butchered. I know, I over-'eard Constable Barnes talkin' to Constable Griffith when they brought the inspector's reports round this mornin'" He was glad he'd had the good sense to dally about the hall when the constables had come by that morning. You could pick up quite a bit of news if you kept yourself quiet and took plenty of time polishing a banister.

"What'd he say?" Mrs. Goodge, the cook, asked eagerly.

Wiggins's eyes grew as big as egg yolks. "Constable Barnes 'eard that the constable that found that woman's body was so sickened 'e lost his stomach. And it's not just one person that's been done in, accordin' to today's *Penny Illustrated*. The police think there might 'ave been two more ladies killed as well."

"Two others?" Mrs. Goodge exclaimed. "What nonsense."

"It's what was in the paper," Wiggins argued.

"Since when have you taken to reading that rubbish?" the cook scoffed. "Radical nonsense, if you ask me. And where did you get a copy? We don't have it here."

"I buy it," Wiggins replied. "It's not radical, it just prints the truth. Not like the borin' ole *Times*. They don't even 'ave pictures."

"I like the *Illustrated* too," Betsy said hastily. She'd much rather talk about newspapers than her proposed trip to the East End. "The drawings are ever so clever."

"Goin' over to Whitechapel isn't bein' very clever," Smythe snapped. He wasn't about to be sidetracked by a discussion of the literary merits of London's daily newspapers. He narrowed his eyes and gave Betsy his most intimidating frown. It had no effect whatsoever.

"You got an itch on your face," Betsy asked bluntly, "or are you just glaring at me?"

For a few moments, they had a silent contest of wills. Smythe capitulated first. Though he was twice her size and outweighed her by two stone, he knew he was helpless against that stubborn set to her chin and that determined glint in her blue eyes.

"You're daft, girl." Smythe slumped back in his seat and looked at the woman sitting at the head of the table. Keeping Betsy safe was worth appealing to a higher authority. The housekeeper. "You tell her, Mrs. Jeffries. Tell her it's not safe to be runnin' about that part of London now."

Hepzibah Jeffries, a plump, middle-aged woman with dark auburn hair liberally streaked with gray, a kind face and sharp eyes that seemed to see everything, only smiled. She'd deliberately stayed out of this particular debate. Though she could see Smythe's point, she rather thought he was being a bit overprotective. Betsy had a right to both her privacy and her time. "It is Betsy's day out, Smythe," she said gently. "If she wishes to go to Whitechapel, it really isn't any of my concern. Though I do understand your trepidation and to some extent, I share it. This murder was particularly brutal. But I'm sure Betsy will be very careful." She smiled at the maid. "Won't you?"

"Of course I'll be careful. I'm not stupid. I know there's a killer about," Betsy replied eagerly. "I'll not be gone long. Just a couple of hours in the morning. Do you think the inspector will get that awful murder case?"

"I sincerely hope not," Mrs. Jeffries said soberly.

"But why don't you want him to get it?" Mrs. Goodge exclaimed. "We haven't had us a murder in months. I mean, it's not a very nice murder, but still, it's better than just sitting here doing nothing."

Mrs. Jeffries tapped her finger against the handle of the tea cup. She needed to explain things carefully. It wouldn't do to have the others thinking she didn't believe the inspector was capable of solving the crime:

"I have an awful feeling about this one," Mrs. Jeffries replied slowly. "It's going to be very political. The radicals won't hesitate to use the poor Nicholls woman's murder for their own purposes. They want to call public attention to the conditions in the East End and this murder is a good way of doing that."

"And about time, too," Betsy muttered.

"I agree," Mrs. Jeffries said quickly. "It's shocking the way the government has conveniently ignored the plight of those poor unfortunates living in abject poverty and misery."

"Then 'ow come you don't want the inspector to get this one?" Wiggins asked. "A man as kindhearted as our inspector would do his best to see this poor lady's killer brought to justice."

To give herself a moment to think of exactly how to say what she thought ought to be said, Mrs. Jeffries reached for her teacup and took a sip. "Please don't misunderstand. You're right, Wiggins, Inspector Witherspoon would do his best. But I've a feeling in this case, it wouldn't be enough. He is a wonderful man and an excellent detective, but in many ways, he's very, very naive."

"Innocent like," Smythe added with a nod. He understood what the housekeeper was saying.

"This murder, with the radical press following it and using it, is going to be mired in politics from top to bottom," Mrs. Jeffries continued. "I'd hate to see the inspector subjected to that. He's far too honorable a person to know how to protect himself in those kinds of situations. They always get terribly complicated. Furthermore, it's not the kind of case he'd be much good at, I'm afraid."

"Why not?" Betsy demanded. "He solved our last case all on his own." That was still a sore point with the staff, but in all honesty, she had to give credit where credit was due.

Mrs. Jeffries held up her hand. "Don't mistake my meaning, Betsy. But frankly, I'll be surprised if anyone solves this murder. There was something so savage, so awful about it, that I rather suspect the murderer is more like a mad dog than a human being. I've a feeling there won't be any clues or any connections or threads for the police to follow. It was an act of madness as well as murder." She shivered. "The inspector is well out of this one. It's fortunate that he had to pay a duty visit to his cousin. Otherwise, considering his record of success at the Yard, no doubt he'd have been dragged into it."

"I don't reckon any of us could suss this one out," Wiggins said. "None of us would 'ave the stomach for it."

"Speak for yourself," Betsy said. "I'd like to get my hands on the animal that did it."

"That's why I don't want you anywhere near Whitechapel," Smythe exclaimed. "You don't need to be pokin' into this one, girl. It's too dangerous."

"I'm not goin' to be pokin' into anything," she snapped. "I've got a personal errand. But that don't mean I'd lose my stomach for catching the killer. Just because the Nicholls woman was a prostitute don't mean she doesn't deserve justice."

"No one said that," Mrs. Jeffries said softly. "Of course she deserves justice. But Smythe is correct. Whoever killed that woman is dangerous.

Very dangerous. I hope none of us gets involved. Something like this could scar one for life."

"Seems to me that we're not likely to get involved in any murder." Mrs. Goodge snorted delicately. "Not with the way the inspector was carrying on before he left to visit that wretched cousin of his."

Everyone stared at the cook in shocked silence. She'd said what all the others had been thinking, but hadn't wanted to actually say.

Mrs. Goodge folded her arms across her ample bosom. "Well, I'm right, aren't I? Just because Inspector Witherspoon solved that last case all on his own, he's been strutting about like the cock of the walk. It's not like him. Maybe the next time there's a murder, I'll just not help at all. Then see how he likes it."

Mrs. Jeffries's heart sank. This situation had been brewing since June. Since Gerald Witherspoon had solved their last murder completely on his own. Oh, they'd helped as they always did. But they'd been completely wrong. They hadn't even come close to figuring out who the real killer was. "I wouldn't say he's been strutting about," she said. "But I will admit he's been quite proud of himself and justifiably so."

"I know, I know." The cook waved her arms impatiently. "But if I have to listen to him go on and on about how he solved the whole thing from one little clue . . ." She broke off and sighed. "Well, it's enough to drive a person mad."

"He does rather go on about it," Betsy agreed.

"Of course he does," Mrs. Jeffries said. "He's very proud of that particular case. But it's not as if he realizes what he's doing. Remember, the inspector has no idea we've ever helped out on his investigations. So it isn't as if he's . . ."

"Lording it over us," Wiggins suggested. "I read that in a book. Good, huh?"

"Excellent, Wiggins." Mrs. Jeffries always took the time to encourage education. But she also wanted to get this problem aired out too. "Furthermore," she continued, "the inspector's behaviour hasn't been objectionable." She wasn't so sure that was a correct assessment at all. There had been several times in the weeks following their last case in which she'd definitely heard a very patronizing tone in his voice when she and the inspector were having one of their chats over a glass of sherry. But really, she mustn't be silly about it. Inspector Gerald Witherspoon was the best of men. Truly one of nature's gentlemen.

He'd spent years in the Records room at the Yard. It was only after he had inherited this house and a fortune from his late Aunt Euphemia that his skills as a detective had really blossomed. Of course the fact that he'd also hired Mrs. Jeffries had much to do with that blossoming.

As a policeman's widow, Mrs. Jeffries had a keen interest in justice. She'd taken one look at the others in the household of Upper Edmonton Gardens and realized that all of them were intelligent, loyal and utterly dedicated to Gerald Witherspoon. Naturally, they'd taken to helping him surreptitiously with his cases. They took great pains not to let him know they were helping him.

"He's not been objectionable," Betsy agreed, "but I agree with Mrs. Goodge—he has been a bit full of himself. I'm not so sure I want to help him anymore either. Not after all those nasty things he said about the idea of women police constables."

"He were only sayin' he didn't think it was a safe thing for a woman to be doin'" Smythe defended his employer. "Catchin' killers is dangerous work. He's a gentleman, is the inspector, wouldn't want to see a woman in 'arms way, that's all."

"He was full of himself," Mrs. Goodge said firmly. "And whether he knows it or not, he needs us. But if he don't change his attitude a bit, the next time round, I just might tend to my cookin' and leave him to it."

Two days later, Inspector Gerald Witherspoon came down the stairs and into the dining room. "Good morning, Mrs. Jeffries," he said brightly. "Is breakfast ready yet? I'm in a bit of a rush this morning."

Mrs. Jeffries put the pot of tea she'd just brought up from the kitchen on the table. "Betsy's just bringing it, sir. Shall I pour your tea?"

"Thank you." He sat down and laid his serviette on his lap. "That would be most kind."

As she poured his tea, she could feel him watching her expectantly. Silently, Mrs. Jeffries sighed. She knew he wanted her to ask why he was in a rush this morning. But before she could get the question formed, Betsy, carrying a covered silver tray, came in with his breakfast.

"Thank you, Betsy," Witherspoon said. "It's very good of you to be so prompt; I'm in a bit of a hurry this morning."

"Something interesting going on at the Yard?" Mrs. Jeffries asked. She glanced at Betsy, who rolled her eyes heavenward. The staff already knew what was going on at the Yard. The inspector had told them at least a dozen times.

"Why, yes, now that you ask." Witherspoon picked up his fork. "Ever since I solved that last murder, the Chief Inspector has kept me dreadfully busy. I've another one of those lectures to give this morning. You know what I mean, a group of police constables get bundled in and I tell them about my methods."

"Do you tell 'em about your inner voice, sir?" Betsy asked, her voice seemingly innocent.

Mrs. Jeffries gave her a sharp look. But Witherspoon hadn't heard the laughter in the girl's tone.

"Well, not precisely," the inspector said. "That's a difficult idea to get across."

"Do you tell them about . . ." She broke off as they heard the pounding of the brass knocker. Betsy smiled apologetically and went to answer the front door.

They heard voices in the hall, and a moment later Betsy came back followed by a tall, gray-haired man in a police constable's uniform. "Constable Barnes is here to see you, sir," she announced.

"Good morning, Inspector. Mrs. Jeffries." Barnes smiled and took off his helmet. "Sorry to interrupt your breakfast, sir."

"That's quite all right," Witherspoon said. "Do have a seat. Have you eaten?"

"I've had breakfast, sir." Barnes pulled out the chair next to him and sat down. "But I wouldn't say no to a cup of tea."

"I'm already pouring it, Constable." Mrs. Jeffries handed him a cup.

"Ta." Barnes's craggy face relaxed a little as he took a long, slow sip. Then he put the cup down. "There's been a murder, sir."

Betsy, who'd been on her way toward the door, stopped dead.

Mrs. Jeffries sat down at the end of the table.

"Oh, dear," Witherspoon replied. "Not another one of those poor women in Whitechapel, I hope."

"No, sir. Nothing as grisly as that." He grimaced. "But bad enough. This one's a man. They found him floating in the Regents Canal late last night. Fully dressed, too. It looked like an accidental drowning, except that Dr. Bosworth happened to be at the mortuary when they brought the body in. Sharp fellow, that Bosworth. He noticed there was lavender soap under the victim's fingernails."

"Lavender soap?" Witherspoon looked puzzled.

"Yes, sir." Barnes took another sip of tea. "That got the doctor curious so he had a good look at the man. There's indications he didn't drown in the canal at all. Bosworth thinks his head was held under in a bathtub. There's marks around the fellow's ankles."

"Marks around the ankles?" the inspector repeated. "Gracious, how could that indicate someone had drowned in a bathtub?"

As puzzled as the inspector, Barnes shrugged. "I don't know, sir. Dr. Bosworth said he'd explain it to you when you get to the mortuary."

"Perhaps the marks were caused by the fall into the canal?" Witherspoon suggested. He really didn't believe in going about looking for a murderer when there was a chance that the man's death had been accidental.

"Bosworth doesn't think so."

Witherspoon tapped his fingers against the tablecloth. He had a great deal of respect for Dr. Bosworth's opinion. "Has the victim been identified?"

"That was the easy part, sir." Barnes grinned. "Dr. Potter identified him."

"Potter?" Witherspoon's eyebrows rose. "But I thought you said that young Dr. Bosworth examined the corpse."

"He did." Barnes chuckled. "But you know what an old busybody Potter is. He stuck his nose in to see what Bosworth was up to. Seems the victim was one of Potter's acquaintances. Fellow was a theatre critic. According to Potter, he's quite well known. Name of Hinchley, sir. Ogden Hinchley."

"How dreadful," Witherspoon murmured.

"Gave Potter a bit of shock, sir. Especially as Hinchley was supposed to be out of the country, not dead and floating in the Regents Canal."

"Did Bosworth have an estimate on how long the body's been in the canal?"

"He said he'd know better after he finished the postmortem, but his best guess is about forty-eight hours."

"How can he tell?" Betsy asked. "Oh, excuse me, sir." She smiled apologetically at her employer. "It's just, you know how we all like hearin' about your cases."

"That's quite all right, Betsy." Witherspoon smiled kindly at the girl. He was such a lucky man; his staff was so very devoted. "I'm curious myself."

Barnes picked up his helmet. "I'm not sure. Potter asked the same thing.

Bosworth said somethin' about water temperature and fluid in the lungs, sir, and some new tests he'd read about. I really couldn't follow it all that well. Frankly, I don't think old Potter could either, but he pretended he knew what Bosworth was talkin' about. Didn't seem to believe it though; you know how Potter is, scoffs at anything he don't understand." He grinned again. "Finally, after they'd argued for a few minutes, Potter stomped off in a huff. I told Dr. Bosworth to go ahead and do whatever tests he needed to do. I hope that's all right, sir?"

"Of course it is," Witherspoon said. "Even if Dr. Bosworth's ideas aren't readily accepted by the courts or the medical establishment, I've found his insights to be quite useful in the past. If he thinks it's approximately forty-eight hours since the man was killed . . ." He broke off and frowned in concentration. "That would make it . . ."

"Saturday night, sir," Mrs. Jeffries finished.

"Right. Was he reported missing from his home?" Witherspoon asked Barnes.

"I don't know, sir. There hasn't been much time to check. Dr. Bosworth had a word with the Chief Inspector and he sent me along here to fetch you."

"So I'm getting this one," Witherspoon said thoughtfully.

"Probably, sir. If it turns out that Bosworth is right and Hinchley's death wasn't an accident. The Chief didn't say much, only to fetch you along to the hospital mortuary and get the inquiry started. Just between you and me, sir, with the papers full of that awful murder in Whitechapel, I expect the Chief isn't taking any chances. He'll want an investigation whether Hinchley was really murdered or not."

"Do we have an address for the victim?" Witherspoon asked.

Barnes dug his notebook out of his pocket and flipped it open. "Number fourteen, Avenue Road. St. John's Wood."

The inspector absently popped a bit of toast into his mouth.

"I haven't been round there, sir," Barnes continued. "I came here straight away."

"Not to worry, Constable. We'll call round Mr. Hinchley's residence as soon as we've been to the mortuary. Which hospital is it?"

"St. Thomas's, sir. That's why Bosworth was on hand."

Witherspoon tossed down his serviette and stood up. "Right then. Let's get cracking."

"Will you be home for lunch, sir?" Mrs. Jeffries asked.

"No, I don't think so. If young Dr. Bosworth is correct, we've a murder to solve."

Mrs. Jeffries walked her employer and Barnes to the door. As they reached the front door, she glanced back down the hall and saw Betsy dart out of the dining room, walk casually to the top of the back stairs and then disappear in the blink of an eye. Good girl, the housekeeper thought. She had no doubt that Betsy had gone to tell the others. They had a murder to solve. Thank goodness.

And this time, she was going to make very sure that they solved it properly.

"Good day, Mrs. Jeffries," Witherspoon called over his shoulder as he closed the front door. "Don't be alarmed if I'm home later than usual."

"Yes, sir. I'll have Mrs. Goodge do a cold supper, sir." She smiled broadly. With any luck, he wouldn't be home for hours.

She closed the door, took a deep breath and then ran for the back stairs. Coming into the kitchen she wasn't surprised to see Mrs. Goodge hurriedly clearing up the last of the breakfast dishes and Betsy heading for the back door.

"I'm just off to get Smythe," Betsy said. "He's at Howard's playing about with those ruddy horses. I've sent Wiggins for Luty Belle and Hatchet. I hope that's all right."

"That's fine, Betsy," Mrs. Jeffries replied. "I'll help Mrs. Goodge clear up, and by the time everyone's returned we'll have tea ready. But do hurry."

The two women worked quickly and efficiently. By the time they'd washed up and brewed a large pot of tea, Smythe and Betsy were back.

"Betsy says we've got a murder," the coachman said.

"I said we *might* have one," the maid replied with a grin. She looked at the housekeeper. "How much longer do you think the others will be?"

"Not long now," Mrs. Jeffries replied. She was glad to see that Smythe and Betsy seemed to be speaking civilly. Ever since the girl's mysterious errand to the East End they hadn't been comfortable with one another. Mrs. Jeffries was fairly certain that the coachman wasn't annoyed that Betsy had disobeyed him. Smythe wasn't stupid enough to think that just because he was paying court to the maid, his word was law. Rather, she thought Smythe was hurt because Betsy hadn't confided in him. Now that they had a murder to solve, perhaps the two of them could iron out their difficulties. If, indeed, Dr. Bosworth was correct and they did have a homicide and not a case of accidental drowning.

"I suppose we have to wait for them," Betsy said. "But perhaps . . ."

"No buts, Betsy," Mrs. Goodge said firmly. "We'll wait. It wouldn't be fair to start without them."

"You're right." Betsy laughed. "I'd be annoyed if you started without me."

From outside the back door, Mrs. Jeffries heard the sound of a carriage pulling up. "Let's get the tea poured, Mrs. Goodge," she said. "I think I hear them now."

A few moments later Wiggins came into the kitchen, followed by two others. "Good thing I got there when I did," he announced as he hurried to take his usual seat at the kitchen table. "They was fixin' to go out."

"Oh, dear." Mrs. Jeffries smiled apologetically at the newcomers. "I do hope our summons didn't interrupt something important."

Luty Belle Crookshank and her butler, Hatchet, had helped on several of the inspector's cases. They would have been most put out if they weren't immediately summoned when a murder was afoot. Co-conspirators, they were trustworthy, intelligent and extremely well connected.

Luty Belle, an elderly American woman, waved her parasol impatiently. "Don't be silly, Hepzibah," she said, using the housekeeper's given name. "Nothin's as important as our investigatin'."

Luty was dressed, as usual, in an outrageously bright day dress of buttercup yellow. A matching yellow hat decorated with plumes, lace and brilliant blue peacock feathers sat at a jaunty angle on her white hair. Beneath the wispy vail, her dark brown eyes glowed with enthusiasm. The wealthy widow of a self-made English millionaire, Luty had plenty of time on her hands and liked nothing better than spending it catching killers.

"Please don't concern yourself," Hatchet, Luty's tall, white-haired butler said. "We were only going for a drive. Madam was bored."

"Good. Let's get started then." Mrs. Jeffries took her place at the table.

"Who's the victim?" Hatchet asked. He sat his black top hat down on the empty chair next to him.

"A man named Ogden Hinchley . . ."

"The theatre critic?" Wiggins exclaimed. Everyone turned to gape at him.

"How'd you know he was a critic?" Betsy asked.

"Gracious, Wiggins, you do surprise one," Mrs. Jeffries said.

"I like to read," Wiggins said, somewhat defensively. "And he's famous. I've read some of his reviews in the papers. Funny, but nasty, too. Says the most awful things about people when 'e don't like a play."

"That's very good, Wiggins." Mrs. Jeffries smiled proudly at the footman. "How clever of you to recognize the name. Obviously, then, if he's as nasty in print as you say he is, he probably has plenty of enemies."

"How was he killed?" Smythe asked.

"I'll tell you everything I know." Mrs. Jeffries launched into the tale. "Therefore, I expect the first place to start is where we usually do, with the victim."

Mrs. Goodge cleared her throat. "Excuse me, Mrs. Jeffries. But that's what we did the last time and look what happened then."

"The inspector solved it!" Betsy cried.

"We was completely wrong on that one," Smythe muttered.

"Perhaps it would be best to take a different approach this time," Hatchet suggested.

"Fiddlesticks," Luty cried. "What's wrong with you people? Just because the inspector got lucky the last time don't mean our methods are wrong. Seems to me you all are forgettin' all them other cases we solved."

"Thank you, Luty," Mrs. Jeffries said primly. "I couldn't have said it better myself."

"I still think we ought to do like 'atchet says and try something different," Wiggins muttered. "It couldn't 'urt."

"No one's stoppin' ya, boy," Luty said tartly. "But I'm goin' to do what I always do. One piddly loss out of a whole bunch of wins ain't goin' to dampen my spirits. Anyway, enough of this chest bleatin'. Let's get on with it. We've got us a killer to catch." She smiled eagerly at Mrs. Jeffries. "Well, come on, Hepzibah, time's a wastin'. Where do we start? What do you want us to do?"

Mrs. Jeffries thought for a moment. "Do you have any connections in the theatre?"

"I've gone to a lot of plays." Luty frowned. "But I don't really know any actors or people like that."

"I do," Hatchet said quickly. "I've several acquaintances who have some connection to the thespian world. Should I start making inquiries of them?"

"Who the dickens do you know?" Luty asked, irritated that her blasted butler had the jump on her.

Mrs. Jeffries hurried to nip any incipient rivalry between these two in the bud before it had a chance to flower. "That's a wonderful idea, Hatchet. Luty, dear, if you wouldn't mind, I'd like you to begin making inquiries about Hinchley's financial situation. You've more sources in the financial community than the rest of us."

"Humph," she snorted. "Hatchet gets to talk to actors and interestin' people and I get to talk to bankers. It ain't fair, but I'll do it." For good measure, she shot her butler a glare. But he only grinned wickedly in response.

Dismissing Luty's good-natured grumbling, Mrs. Jeffries turned to Betsy. "You know what to do, don't you?"

"I'll get right to it. If I'm lucky, maybe I'll be able to get round to Hinchley's neighborhood before the Inspector does. It'd be nice to get the jump on him."

"Take care the police don't see you," Mrs. Jeffries warned. Betsy would do as she always did when they were starting an investigation. She'd talk to all the tradespeople and shopkeepers and learn as much as she could about the victim's household.

"I'll do the hansoms and the pubs," Smythe said. "Maybe I'll get lucky and find out who came and went on Saturday night."

"Excellent, Smythe." Mrs. Jeffries nodded in satisfaction. They were falling back into their old routine very nicely.

"I'll get round there and see if I can find a servant," Wiggins said. "But I'll be careful, Mrs. Jeffries. Fred and I'll lie low until we sees that the inspector and the rest of the constables is gone."

"I have no doubt you will, Wiggins." She glanced down at the black and brown mongrel dog lying by the footman's chair. "If you take Fred with you, make sure he doesn't see the inspector." Fred, hearing his name, raised his head and thumped his tail on the floor.

"The last thing we need is for the inspector to catch us," Mrs. Jeffries continued. She glanced at the cook. "You know what to do."

The cook nodded. She had a veritable army of people she called upon when they were investigating a murder. Without ever leaving her kitchen Mrs. Goodge used her very own, very sophisticated network of street boys, fruit vendors, chimney sweeps, delivery people and former acquaintances to suss out every morsel of gossip about the victim.

Gossip, Mrs. Jeffries had always found, was immensely useful in a murder investigation.

CHAPTER 2

Inspector Witherspoon hated mortuaries. He hated looking at dead bodies too. But as it was an integral part of his job, he did it without complaint. He stared at the corpse lying beneath the gray sheet on the wooden table and braced himself. "Right, Dr. Bosworth. We might as well get on with it."

Dr. Bosworth, a tall young man with red hair and an earnest, intelligent face, gazed at the inspector sympathetically. "He's not as bad as many victims, Inspector. By my estimation, he'd only been in the canal a couple of days, not long enough for too much decomposition to have set in."

Witherspoon smiled weakly, reminded himself of his duty and stepped closer to the table.

"Actually, the water in the canal was quite cold for this time of year," Bosworth continued chattily. "Kept the fellow very well preserved, especially as he hadn't sunk."

The inspector made himself watch as Dr. Bosworth pulled the sheet away. The body was fully dressed in formal evening clothes—white shirt, proper black tie, black and gray vest and black longcoat. But the face was ghastly white, the eyes open and staring lifelessly up at the ceiling. They were hazel and bulging wide, as though the poor fellow was surprised to find himself lying on a mortuary slab. His hair was brown and thinning on top, his lips thin and his nose long and aquiline.

"Excuse me, Dr. Bosworth," Witherspoon said hesitantly. "I'm not trying to tell you your business, but isn't it usual to conduct a postmortem with the clothes off?"

"I left them on for a reason," Bosworth said. "They could well be evidence."

"Evidence?"

"Yes. Have a good look at this, Inspector." The doctor leaned over and pointed at the vest. "The buttons are fastened incorrectly. See, the top button goes into the second hole, not the first. But that's not all." He quickly undid the vest and pulled it apart, exposing the shirt. "Have a look at this."

Witherspoon noticed the shirt hadn't been buttoned right either. But he didn't quite see what that had to do with anything. "It's not done up properly either," he said.

Bosworth nodded. "That's what I noticed when the fellow was brought in. I asked the constable who pulled the body out of the canal if anyone had tampered with the victim's clothes. They hadn't. You do see what this means, Inspector."

"It could mean the victim had been dressed after he was already dead," the inspector guessed, hoping his reasoning was along the same path as the doctor's.

"My thoughts exactly." Bosworth leaned down and pointed at the man's shoes. "And look here. Brown shoes. Day shoes. No one wears brown day shoes with evening dress. It looked most odd to me. So I had a good look at the chap's feet."

Witherspoon gaped at Bosworth, who was busily working the victim's right shoe and sock off.

"See." The doctor pointed to a pronounced bluish imprint angled at the bottom of the man's shinbone. The discolored flesh was approximately the size and shape of a withered sausage. "Look at this mark here." He quickly grabbed the other leg and shoved the sock down. "And here, there's another one. Equally pronounced and lying in almost the same position, only reversed." Bosworth looked at him expectantly.

Baffled, Witherspoon could only mutter, "Yes, it's most odd."

"There's more," Bosworth said excitedly as he yanked the right foot up again and stuck it under Witherspoon's nose. "See, there's a bruise on this heel."

The inspector stumbled back, almost tripping over his own feet to get away from the hideous dead foot the doctor thrust at him. But he did see the bruise. "You're right, Doctor," he mumbled, "it's . . . it's very much a bruise."

"Of course it is," Bosworth agreed. "But there isn't one on the other foot. I checked. Well, naturally, as soon as I saw this, I immediately notified the authorities that this might very well be a homicide rather than an accidental death."

"I see." Witherspoon didn't really see at all. What on earth was Bosworth getting at? But he wouldn't for the world admit that he couldn't follow the man's reasoning. His inner voice told him that Bosworth might be on to something. "Would you mind explaining how you came to that conclusion? Just so I have it clear in my own mind."

"Not at all," Bosworth said enthusiastically. "It's quite simple, really. From all indications, someone drowned this poor fellow in a bathtub, stuffed him back in his clothes and then dumped his body in the nearest body of water, which just happened to be the Regents Canal. Your killer, Inspector, was hoping to make it look like an accidental death."

For a moment, the inspector couldn't think of what to say. "Er, why do you think those marks on his ankle proved he was drowned in a bathtub?"

Bosworth looked surprised by the question. "I think it's rather obvious, Inspector."

"But wouldn't the killer have just shoved his head under?" Barnes asked. "Shouldn't there be marks around the neck, not the ankles?"

Witherspoon nodded gratefully at the constable, relieved that Barnes apparently didn't get it either. "That's right, if he was drowned in the tub, there should be some kind of bruises about the poor chap's neck."

Bosworth shook his head stubbornly. "Not necessarily, Inspector. If someone has his head shoved under, he might be thrown off balance for a second, but he could use his legs and arms to fight back against the hands holding him under. Unless, of course, he was in a such a huge tub his legs didn't reach the end. And neither of the victim's arms had any bruises or abrasions at all. If someone was holding the poor chap's head under, unless the hands were tied, he'd have been flopping about and fighting back for all he was worth." Bosworth suddenly scurried down to the end of the table and grabbed the dead man's ankles. "However, if you walk up to someone in a bath, reach in and quickly jerk their ankles straight up"—to Witherspoon's horror, he jerked the corpse's legs straight into the air—"the entire upper torso and head gets pulled under quickly and the legs cannot be used defensively," Bosworth explained eagerly. "The arms are almost useless because in most of the new baths, the sides are so high it would be hard to grab them to lever yourself up. Plus, if the killer acted quickly, the victim's mouth and lungs would be filled with water so fast, they literally wouldn't have time to react." Bosworth put the poor chap's limbs down.

Witherspoon sighed in relief. For a moment there, he'd been afraid that in his enthusiasm, the good doctor was going to yank the fellow off the slab. He glanced at Barnes, who was staring thoughtfully at the body.

"Too bad we don't have a bathtub handy," Barnes mumbled. "It could easily have happened like that."

"That would be a rather interesting experiment," Bosworth said cheerfully. "Perhaps I'll try it at home."

Scandalized, the inspector gasped. "You're going to take the body home?"

"No, no." Bosworth grinned. "I wouldn't be that disrespectful, Inspector. However, I'm sure my landlady's son will give me a hand with it. He's helped me conduct some other experiments. Of course I will promise not to drown the lad."

Witherspoon smiled weakly. He wasn't sure this theory made sense but he made a mental note to have a good, hard look at the victim's bathtub. "So you think the killer held him under by grabbing his ankles? Right?"

"Yes," Bosworth said. "That would explain these bruises." He leaned over and gripped the dead man's ankles again. This time, he carefully placed his thumbs over the bruises at the bottom of the shins. They fit perfectly. "See. That could be what made these bruises. I'd have to hold tight to keep him under the water, but it could certainly be done."

"What about the bruise on the heel?" Barnes asked.

"Probably from the top of the tub." Bosworth stepped back. "Even under water, the victim would have had some fight left in him. I expect the killer had a bit of a hard time hanging on to him. With all the other evidence, I think it's quite clear, don't you?"

"Other evidence?" Witherspoon wasn't sure he wanted to ask.

"The soap under his fingernails." Bosworth lifted one of the lifeless hands. "Here." He shoved the extremity toward Witherspoon's nose. "Take a sniff, you can still smell it. Lavender soap. Luckily, whoever dumped the body didn't realize it landed on top of a carriage wheel someone had tossed in the canal. This hand wasn't in the water at all and the soap didn't get washed away. Believe me, Inspector. One doesn't find much lavender soap in the Regents Canal. From the way the soap's caked under the fingernails of the hand, I'm rather led to believe that the victim must have been washing when the killer grabbed him. Too bad he didn't have a better defensive weapon at hand. You can't do much damage with a bit of soap. More's the pity." Bosworth smiled sheepishly. "Mind you, Dr. Potter doesn't necessarily agree with my analysis of the situation. But considering the evidence, I'd wager the family silver, if I had any, that you've a murder on your hands."

Impressed, Witherspoon gazed at the young doctor. "Are you doing the postmortem?"

"Yes. Potter didn't think it would be fitting for him to do it." Bosworth grinned. "Slicing into an old friend, you know."

"So, Dr. Potter *was* a friend of the victim," Barnes said.

"Not really. More of an acquaintance, I'd say." Bosworth pulled the sheet back up. Witherspoon smothered another sigh of relief. "But it did give the poor fellow a shock when he came barging in here and saw who was lying on the table. That's how we identified the victim so quickly. Well, what do you think, Inspector?"

Witherspoon wasn't sure what to think, but he did have a great deal of respect for the doctor. "You've made a most compelling case. Most compelling, indeed. But isn't it possible that the buttons got mangled from being in the canal? Currents, that sort of thing?"

Bosworth shook his head. "No. The buttons on the vest are extremely small and quite difficult to undo. The shirt buttons are even tinier. I had a good look at the size of the holes too. No current is strong enough to worry the material out of shape so much that buttons could slip out then slip themselves back in again in a different order.

"Besides, as I said, the body was actually caught on a carriage wheel some fool had tossed under the canal bridge. I should have loved to have had a go at the poor chap before they fished him out. I've a theory you can get an awful lot of information about the crime if you just take the time and trouble to look at the body before people start mucking about with it."

"Yes, yes, I'm sure." Actually, Witherspoon thought that was a rather silly notion. Dead was dead. Furthermore, most police surgeons did have a look at the corpse before it was moved. He didn't see what good it would have done Dr. Bosworth to stare at this poor fellow while he was flopped over a wheel in a canal. But there was no point in being rude.

"There's the shoes as well," Barnes added. "I'd say that's good evidence of a murder."

Witherspoon glanced at the feet again. "True. One doesn't usually wear brown shoes with full, formal evening dress."

"And don't forget the soap, sir," Barnes persisted.

"Thank you for reminding me, Barnes," Witherspoon said. He looked at the doctor. "How sure are you about the time of death?"

Bosworth looked doubtful. "Not as positive as I'd like to be. I should have a better idea once I cut him open."

Witherspoon shuddered and glanced at the shrouded body. "Poor chap. I wonder where he'd been?"

"I know," Dr. Bosworth announced proudly. "At least, Dr. Potter knew where he'd been on Saturday evening. He saw him, you see."

"Saw him? Where?" Witherspoon hoped that didn't mean that old Potter was going to end up being a suspect. He didn't much like the doctor but he couldn't quite see him as a murderer.

"The Hayden Theatre. They were both there. Not together. Dr. Potter was with his wife. But he said he saw Hinchley there and actually spoke to the man. A new play was opening. Potter said that it was duller than a rusty scalpel."

"It were a right surprise, Mr. Hinchley coming back the way he did," said Maggie Malone, proprietress of Malone's, a grocer's shop at the end of Avenue Road. She flipped her duster over a row of tinned sausages. "Saw him Saturday afternoon when I was sweeping the stoop," she continued. "Told Mr. Malone he ought to go round to Hinchley's house right away and collect what's owed to us, but Mr. Malone said we'd wait until Monday. Had a bit of a row over it, we did. We're only a small shop, now, aren't we? Can't be waiting forever for our money. But Mr. Malone says Mr. Hinchley's a good customer, so he had his way. Blast, now the man's dead and who knows if we'll ever get paid?"

Betsy nodded sympathetically. She'd struck gold on her first try this morning. "Can't you talk to this Mr. Hinchley's solicitor and get them to pay it out of the estate?"

"That'll take forever." Maggie tossed the duster under the counter and began straightening a row of tinned ox tongue. She was a tall, rawboned middle-aged woman with frizzy brown hair and a ruddy complexion. "Once you get solicitors and such muckin' about, you're lucky if you get a tuppence for your trouble."

Betsy nodded in agreement. "How long had he been gone?"

"Almost three months." Maggie tugged at the tight bodice of her gray broadcloth dress. "He were supposed to stay gone for six."

"How come he went there?" Betsy asked.

Maggie shrugged. "Who knows? Took it into his head to go and so up he went. He was an odd duck, if you know what I mean. I think he might have been writin' for one of them American newspapers but I expect the Americans didn't like his nasty pieces any better than anyone over here does."

"Nasty pieces?" Betsy prodded gently. She wasn't worried about this one shutting up on her. The minute Betsy had mentioned Hinchley, the shopkeeper's tongue had taken off like a greyhound after a rabbit. "Was he a newspaper reporter, then?"

Maggie shook her head. "Not a reporter, a critic. For the theatre. He wrote reviews of plays and such for some of the newspapers. Seems a silly thing for a grown man to do, if you ask me. But he liked it well enough. Mind you, the people he wrote about didn't like him much. More than once Lilly's been round here telling tales about some actor or writer raising a ruckus with the man. Not that Mr. Hinchley cared what people thought of him. Rather hard sort of man, if you get my meaning."

Betsy thought it sounded like Lilly liked to talk as well. She made a mental note to try and find the girl. "Some men are like that," she agreed. "Don't care if half the world hates them."

"Hinchley certainly didn't." Maggie broke off just as the shop door opened and a well-dressed woman stepped inside. "Good morning, Mrs. Baker. I'll be right with you." All business now, Maggie looked inquiringly at Betsy. "What was it you wanted, miss?"

"A tin of Le Page's Liquid Glue, please," she replied. Drat. If that woman hadn't come in, she'd probably have been able to get a lot more information out of the shopkeeper. But Mrs. Baker had a list in her hand and didn't appear to be in any hurry. So Betsy paid for her glue, which would make a nice gift for Wiggins, smiled at Maggie Malone and left. She could always come back.

The late Ogden Hinchley had resided in a large, beige brick townhouse at the very end of Avenue Road, only a few hundred feet from the canal where his body had been found. From the outside, nothing about it looked extraordinary. But the inside was quite another story.

Inspector Witherspoon gazed curiously around the drawing room. Voluminous sheer fabric had been draped artfully across the ceiling, giving one the effect of standing in a rather opulent tent. The floor was covered with a huge, intricate and boldly patterned oriental rug. Gigantic red and white pillows were tossed willy nilly around the room and several low tables, all draped in elegant red and gold fringed silk were ringed about in strategic places next to the pillows. The air smelled faintly of incense. Tapestries, mostly Indian in style, and a bright brass plate completed the decorations on the wall. The far end of the room was dominated by a low day bed covered with a white silk spread and canopied in sheets of sheer cream. At the foot of the bed was a chair, ornately carved and covered with a deep maroon velvet.

"Place looks like the throne room of a heathen king," Barnes muttered, staring at the chair.

"It certainly does," Witherspoon agreed. "Do you think the whole house is like this?"

"No, sir," a low voice said from behind him. "Only this room and the master bedroom and bath. The rest of house is quite ordinary."

Witherspoon and Barnes both whirled around. A tall, dark-haired man with brown eyes, sculpted cheeks and exceptionally pale skin stood just inside the doorway. "I'm Rather, sir. Mr. Hinchley's butler. Lilly said you wanted a word with us."

"Yes, I'd like to speak to the entire staff, if I may," Witherspoon replied.

Rather smiled faintly. "There's only Lilly and myself, sir. Mr. Hinchley sacked everyone else when he left for New York."

"He wasn't planning on returning then?" Barnes asked.

"Yes, sir," Rather replied. "He was planning on coming back."

"You don't mean he expected a house this size to be managed by only two servants?" Witherspoon asked. Odd-looking room and all, it was still a big house.

Rather's lip curled. "I wasn't privy to Mr. Hinchley's expectations, sir. Perhaps he was planning on hiring new servants when he returned. I wouldn't know. I'd planned on leaving well before he got back."

"You didn't like Mr. Hinchley?" the inspector probed.

"It wasn't a matter of liking or disliking." The butler shrugged negligently, as though the matter were of no consequence. "I simply felt I could better myself somewhat by seeking employment elsewhere. Lilly was planning on going as well. Ogden Hinchley wasn't the kind of employer to inspire loyalty amongst his staff."

Witherspoon thought that most interesting. "Is there somewhere else we can talk?" This room was getting on his nerves. Perhaps it was that sickly, cloying incense smell. But he didn't much like being in there.

Rather looked at him for a moment and a flash of amusement flitted over his face. "We can go into the butler's pantry."

The man led them down a long, wide hall toward the back of the silent house. Their footsteps echoed eerily on the polished wood floor. At the last door, the butler stopped. "In here, gentlemen. Should I call Lilly?"

The room was small and ordinary. A tiny fireplace, an overstuffed settee and two wing chairs.

"We'd like to speak with you first," Witherspoon said. "Do you mind if we sit down?"

"Please do." Rather nodded at the settee, but remained standing himself.

As soon as they were seated, Barnes whipped out his notebook while the inspector started the questioning. "You do know that your employer was found dead last night?"

"Yes. A police constable came round and told us this morning."

"Mr. Hinchley's body was found in the canal. Have you any idea how he got there?" Witherspoon asked.

"None, sir."

"When was the last time you saw your employer?" Barnes asked.

"Saturday evening," Rather replied. "He left for the theatre at half six. He told me he was going to a new play that was opening at the Hayden Theatre."

"He left at half six?" Barnes asked.

"Yes."

"Why so early?" the constable persisted. "The theatre usually starts at eight. Was he going to stop and have supper first?"

Rather shook his head. "He ate a light supper before he left."

"Then why did he leave so early?" Witherspoon asked. "Even in traffic it doesn't take an hour and a half to get to the Strand."

"I've no idea." Rather said calmly. "It wasn't my place to question the man."

Witherspoon leaned forward. "Weren't you concerned when he didn't return home that night?"

"I didn't know he hadn't come home, did I? I was asleep."

"But when you saw he wasn't here on Sunday morning, weren't you alarmed?"

Rather hesitated. "Not really. Sometimes he'd go off for a few days on his own. He'd done it before. As his clothes were still packed, when he didn't come down to breakfast, I thought he'd come home, grabbed a few things and gone off with a friend."

"Did he have a lot of friends, then?" Barnes asked softly.

The butler smiled slyly. "Not really."

"So the last time you saw Mr. Hinchley was early Saturday evening," Witherspoon mused. "Tell me, how long would you expect him to be away without communicating with his household?"

"Lilly and I were thinking that if we didn't hear from him by tomorrow, we might go to the police. But I honestly thought he'd simply gone off with a friend."

"And you didn't wait up for him on Saturday night, then?" Barnes asked.

"No. I was under my usual instructions. I left the side door unlocked and went to bed at my normal time."

"Mr. Hinchley had you leave the door unlocked?" Witherspoon pressed. This was most curious, most curious indeed.

"Yes. That's the way he liked things done," Rather said firmly.

Witherspoon drummed his fingers against the settee. "Did Mr. Hinchley have enemies?"

"If you're looking for people who wanted him dead, you'd best try the Hayden Theatre." Rather laughed nastily. "The last person any of that lot wanted to see in the audience that night was Ogden Hinchley."

"Took 'im to the Hayden, guv," the cabbie told Smythe. The big burly man whipped his hat off and wiped beads of sweat off his forehead. "That's a theatre over on the Strand."

"What time did ya pick 'im up?" Smythe asked and glanced up the road, keeping a wary eye on the corner. He didn't want the inspector or Constable Barnes to come barreling round and catch him chatting with a hansom driver. Finding the cabbie that had picked Ogden Hinchley up on

Saturday had been a stroke of luck, but Smythe didn't believe in pushing good fortune too far. He wasn't one to take advantage of Lady Luck.

The man shrugged. "'Bout half six, I reckon. Might 'ave been a bit later. I wasn't watchin' the time. Why you so interested in this bloke, mate?"

"Doin' a bit of snoopin' for a lady," Smythe gave him a man-to-man grin. "She's sweet on 'im and she don't trust 'im much. Wants to make sure he minds himself, if you know what I mean."

The cabbie's eyes glittered greedily. "This lady pay good?"

Smythe wiped the smile off his face and replaced it with a scowl.

Unlike Betsy, the driver was immediately cowed. "Don't get narked, now," he said quickly. "I was only askin'. Can't blame a feller fer tryin' to pick up a bit of coin now and then. I'm round these parts lots. I wouldn't mind doin' a bit of watchin' if the pay was good. That's all I'm sayin'. Times is tough, you know. Hard to make a decent livin', what with fares bein' set by the bloomin' council and people stealin' lifts on the back instead of payin' properly."

"I've already paid ya all you're going to get," Smythe snapped. He hated doing this. But sometimes, if you weren't careful, you'd get fleeced faster than a green boy at a racecourse. "And I've paid ya well too." One thing the coachman didn't have to worry about was money. He had plenty of it. He felt just a bit guilty that he could buy his information when he needed to, while the others in the household had to dash about all over London to pick up clues. But it weren't his fault he had more money than he knew what to do with.

"Never said you didn't," the cabbie said quickly. "Anyway, I took him to the Hayden and dropped him off. That's all there was to it. He were just a regular fare."

"Did you see if he talked to anyone when he got out?"

"Didn't 'ang about to notice," the cabbie replied. He began to stroke the horse's nose. "As soon as we pulled up, another fare got in."

Witherspoon and Barnes walked slowly down the center aisle of the Hayden Theatre. The auditorium was horseshoe shaped. Boxes, stalls and galleries, each of them catering to a different class and different price level, layered themselves toward the large stage.

"What's that?" Barnes asked, pointing to the giltframed moulding flush with the front of the stage. "It looks like a giant picture frame."

"I think it's called a proscenium," Witherspoon replied. "I believe it's used to help stage the play. I say, do you think there's anyone about?"

He peered down toward the stage, but saw nothing in the poor light. However, he could see that the backing on the seats in this part of the theatre was aged and fading. On the boxes to his left, he noticed the paint was chipping.

"Can I help you gents?" someone called. Just then a head popped up from one of the front rows.

Witherspoon was so startled by the man's sudden appearance he didn't answer for a moment. "Uh, could we see someone in charge, please?"

"You coppers?"

"Yes, I'm Inspector Witherspoon and this is Constable Barnes."

"I'll get Mr. Swinton for you," the man said. "He's the guv."

"Odd sort of place, isn't it, sir?" Barnes commented as they waited. "For some reason, it makes you want to whisper. Like church."

A bald man with a huge mustache appeared at the front of the stage. He squinted at the two policemen. "I'm Willard Swinton. You want to see me?"

"If we could have a word, please," Witherspoon shouted. Swinton nodded and disappeared behind the proscenium. Witherspoon, alarmed that he'd lost his prey, hurried toward the stage. Constable Barnes was right on his heels.

By the time they reached the front, Willard Swinton had reappeared in front of a door tucked neatly to the left of the stage.

"This way, gentlemen," he called, waving them over. "We'd be more comfortable in my office." He led them through the door, down a long corridor and into a small room at the very end. Gaudy playbills decorated the walls. There was a huge rolltop desk in the center, a gas fire in the hearth and several overstuffed chairs. "Have a seat," Swinton invited, sitting down behind his desk. "Now, what can I do for her Majesty's boys in blue?"

It took a moment for Witherspoon to understand he meant the police. "Ah, we'd like to ask you a few questions if you don't mind. About Saturday evening."

"Great night it was, sir." Swinton beamed proudly. *Belvedere's Burden* was an absolute smash! We're sold out for the next three weeks."

"I take it that's the name of the current production?" Witherspoon asked.

"That's right. Saturday night was our opening. The house was sold out." Impossibly enough, Swinton's smile broadened even further.

Witherspoon asked, "Do you know a gentleman named Ogden Hinchley?"

Swinton's smile evaporated. "I know him," he sneered. "He was here Saturday night, sitting right in the third row."

"Did you speak to him?" Barnes asked.

"Not bloody likely," Swinton snapped. "I haven't spoken to that man for two years. The only reason I didn't throw him out when I spotted him was because I didn't want to create a fuss in front of the audience."

"I take it you didn't like Mr. Hinchley?" Witherspoon said.

Swinton's eyes narrowed suspiciously. "What's this all about, then?"

Witherspoon realized he didn't have to break the news gently to the man. "Mr. Hinchley's dead. His body was found in the Regents Canal. We've reason to believe the death wasn't an accident."

Swinton's jaw gaped. "Dead? Hinchley? That explains it then. We wondered why his review wasn't in the paper."

The door flew open and a tall, fair-haired man came charging in. "For God's sake, Willard," he cried, "you promised you'd take care of those wretchedly old lime-lights . . ." He broke off as he saw the two men, his deepset eyes widening when he noticed Constable Barnes's uniform. "Oh, excuse me. I didn't realize anyone else was here. Do forgive me for intruding." He started backing toward the door.

"Don't go, Edmund," Swinton said. "These gentlemen are police. They've just given me the most shocking news. Ogden Hinchley's been murdered."

He stopped. "Murdered? My God, you are joking?"

Swinton shook his head.

Witherspoon quickly introduced himself and Barnes. "And who are you, sir?"

"Sorry, Inspector." Swinton belatedly remembered his manners and introduced the newcomer. "This is Edmund Delaney, the author of the play."

"Did you know Mr. Hinchley, sir?" Barnes asked quickly.

Delaney didn't speak for a moment. "Yes," he finally replied so softly that Witherspoon had to strain to catch what he was saying. "I knew him. Everybody in the theatre knew him."

"Why don't you sit down, sir?" Witherspoon invited. He usually liked to interview people alone, but it might be interesting to try it a bit differently this time.

Delany sat down in a chair next to Swinton's desk. He clasped his hands together. "How was he killed?"

"He was drowned," Witherspoon said. It wouldn't do to give too much information away. From the reactions of both these men, it was obvious they had strong feelings about the victim. "And he was last seen alive right here at this theatre on Saturday night."

"What do you mean by that?" Swinton blustered. "Are you trying to imply this theatre had something to do with Hinchley's death?"

"I'm implying nothing, Mr. Swinton," Witherspoon replied calmly. He directed his attention to Delaney, noticing that the man's face had gone pale. "Did you know Mr. Hinchley well?"

"He was a professional acquaintance," Delaney muttered.

"Did you like him?" Barnes asked.

Delaney appeared surprised by the question, but he recovered quickly. "No one in the theatre liked him. He was a critic. Quite a nasty one too. Hinchley ruined a number of careers both here and in America." He laughed harshly. "I understand Americans are quite a violent people. Perhaps Hinchley's vitriolic pen didn't sit well with the New York theatre crowed. Maybe one of them followed him back and killed him."

Surprised by such a silly statement, Witherspoon's eyebrows shot up. "Are you suggesting he was murdered by an American?" he asked incredulously.

"Not really." Delaney smiled apologetically. "This is a bit of a shock, Inspector. I'm just babbling nonsense." He stopped and took a deep breath. "Hinchley wasn't loved by any of us here in England, but he had been gone for rather a long time. None of us even knew he was back."

"Mr. Swinton did," Barnes said.

"Here now, what are you saying?" Swinton snapped. "I wasn't the only one who knew he was back. Half of London saw him sitting big as a ruddy toad. And I wasn't the only one in the theatre who'd seen him either. Remington and Parks were both peeking out at the audience that night. They could've seen him too."

"Please, Mr. Swinton, don't excite yourself." Gracious, the man's face had gone so red, Witherspoon was afraid he might burst something. "We're merely trying to ascertain Mr. Hinchley's movements on Saturday evening."

Swinton seemed to calm down. "His movements have nothing to do with us. As far as I know, he watched the play and then left."

"I see," the inspector replied. "And what time did the play end?"

"Around eleven o'clock."

"It's three hours long?" Barnes exclaimed. Blimey, he thought, that would flatten your backside.

"Of course not," Delaney said. "But it was late starting and we had quite a long intermission." He tossed a quick frown at Swinton. "We had a bit of trouble with some of the limelights and that delayed us a good fifteen minutes."

"So the play ended at approximately eleven," Witherspoon said.

"Closer to ten-fifty than eleven," Swinton interrupted.

"All right," the inspector said patiently, "ten-fifty. What did you gentlemen do after the play was over?"

Both men appeared surprised by the question. Delaney answered first. "I went for a walk, Inspector. By the Thames."

"How long did you walk?"

"I'm not sure," Delaney replied. "An hour, maybe more. Try and understand, Inspector, I was quite excited. This is my first play. I guess I was in a bit of a state. I knew I wouldn't sleep so I went down to the river and walked. Then I went home."

"And you, Mr. Swinton?" Barnes asked.

"I came in and counted the receipts," Swinton replied. "Good take that night."

"What time did you leave your office?" Witherspoon glanced over to make sure the constable was getting this down in his notebook.

Swinton stroked his mustache. "I wasn't watching the clock. It took a couple of hours to count out and do the books. By then it was late, so I went home."

"Did anyone see you leave?" Witherspoon asked.

"No. The place was empty when I locked up."

The inspector turned to Delaney. "Did anyone see you by the river?"

"Lots of people saw me, Inspector," Delaney replied sarcastically. "But unfortunately, I doubt any of them knew who I was."

Mrs. Jeffries spotted Dr. Bosworth the moment he left St. Thomas's Hospital through the side door. She darted forward and planted herself directly in front of his path.

"Good day, Dr. Bosworth," she said brightly.

Bosworth stopped and cocked his head to one side. "Why am I not surprised to see you?"

"Because you're most intelligent." she smiled confidently. "And you know I'd want to hear every little detail of the postmortem on Ogden Hinchley." As one of her "secret sources," Dr. Bosworth had been most helpful on several of the other of the inspector's cases.

"Of course." He offered her his arm. "Let's stroll while we talk, Mrs. Jeffries. To be perfectly frank, I'm very tired. But I think I can manage to stay awake long enough to give you the essentials. Has the inspector got this one, then?"

"It seems so," she said as they walked toward the bridge. "I understand you don't think this is a case of accidental drowning."

"Absolutely not," Bosworth replied. He repeated everything he had already told Witherspoon. "And when I opened the fellow up, there wasn't any debris in the lungs."

"I'm sorry, I don't quite follow you."

Bosworth yawned. "If he'd drowned in the canal, there would have been dirt and filth from the canal in his lungs. Now, there was debris in his mouth, but not in the lungs, if you follow."

"So if he drowned in his bathtub, then someone would have had to move his body and take it to the canal," she said thoughtfully. "How big a man was he?"

"Quite small, really," Bosworth replied. "Very slender, with very poorly developed muscle. But even a small man would be quite difficult to move. Dead weight and all."

"Was there anything else, Doctor?" Mrs. Jeffries asked. Poor Dr. Bosworth did look very tired. She really mustn't keep him too long. "Anything else that might be useful to us?"

Bosworth thought for a moment. "I don't believe so, but honestly, I'm so tired I'm not thinking all that clearly. Tell you what—if I remember anything else, I'll send you a note."

"What about the time of death?"

Bosworth hesitated. "It's only an educated guess, but my estimate is late Saturday night or the very early hours of Sunday morning."

"But someone tried to make it look like he was murdered Saturday night as he walked along the canal?"

"That's how it appears to me," Bosworth yawned again. "But I'm only a doctor, Mrs. Jeffries. I leave the real detecting to you."

CHAPTER 3

Inspector Witherspoon arrived home for dinner that evening much earlier than expected. Luckily, as the weather was still quite warm, Mrs. Goodge had been able to whip up a cold, light supper, which the inspector ate quickly.

"I wish I had time to sit and talk with you, Mrs. Jeffries," he fretted, pushing the remains of his beef and cheese to one side. "Discussing the case does give me a better perspective on the whole matter. But Constable Barnes was quite tired this evening and as we couldn't interview any of the others involved in this theatre production until after this evening's performance, I told him to pop along home and take a rest. I'm meeting him at the theatre later. I only hope I can make sense out of what these people actually say. They are quite a dramatic lot, even the theatre owner. One would think he, at least, would be a businessman first and foremost."

"You always make sense of things, sir," she said kindly. She hoped Smythe and Wiggins would be back by the time Luty and Hatchet arrived. They had much to discuss. "So according to both Swinton and Delaney, a goodly number of people didn't like Hinchley."

"Yes. He certainly wasn't very popular. Even his servants didn't care for him. Both of them were planning on leaving before Hinchley got back from America. But"—he sighed—"we've no evidence that anyone at the theatre or his own household murdered him. Yet I can't help thinking that it must have been done by someone from the Hayden."

"Why, sir?" she asked curiously. This time, she promised herself silently, she wouldn't be so quick to ignore the inspector's ideas about the murder. After all, he had solved the last one. "Surely someone that unpopular would have many enemies."

"True. But he'd been out of the country, Mrs. Jeffries. According to what Lilly, his maid, told us, he'd arrived back only on Saturday afternoon." Witherspoon took a sip of beer. "He'd had no visitors, hadn't gone out and hadn't sent any messages. Regardless of how many people in London disliked the man, most of them wouldn't have known he was back. Besides, I've got a feeling about it. You know, my inner voice."

She cringed inwardly. Sometimes she wished he'd never mentioned that particular concept. "Yes, sir, your voice. It tells you that the killer is someone from the production of this play?"

"*Belvedere's Burden,*" he said. "That's the name of the thing. I suppose I really ought to watch a performance. It's melodrama. Something to do with murderous rages and all sorts of hidden emotions. Can't say that it's the kind of thing I much enjoy." He sighed. "But yes, in answer to your question, I do think it's someone involved in the production. Essentially, they were the only people in London who knew Hinchley had come back unexpectedly from America."

"But wasn't he in the audience?" she asked. "Couldn't the killer have seen him there?"

"True." Witherspoon frowned thoughtfully. "But I've got to start somewhere, and just amongst the people involved with the play there's enough animosity toward Hinchley to warrant starting there. If it turns out that the killer isn't one of them, I'll look elsewhere."

"You obviously heard quite a bit today," she said pleasantly.

"Oh, I did," he said enthusiastically. He told her everything he'd learned, all about Bosworth's theory, the visit to the Hinchley house and how he'd gotten a good look at Hinchley's bath. "It was a jolly large tub," he concluded as he glanced at the clock. He got up. "I'd best be off, then. It's getting late."

"Surely the play isn't over this early," she said, getting to her feet and starting to clear the remains of his dinner.

"It's not. But I'm going to pop round to the Yard to do some background checking," he said, stifling a yawn. "By the time I've finished, it will be time to meet Constable Barnes. Don't wait up for me, Mrs. Jeffries. It'll be very late when I return."

Mrs. Jeffries and Betsy got the supper things cleaned up in record time. By the time the last plate was being put in the cupboard, the others had arrived.

Mrs. Jeffries took her usual seat at the head of the table. "Inspector Witherspoon's gone out," she began, "but we managed to have a nice chat before he went off. He had a number of things to report."

"Lucky for us, I had the rest of that beef joint left over from last night's dinner," Mrs. Goodge muttered. "Otherwise, we'd have had some explaining to do. Tied up all day with my sources, I didn't have time to cook a proper meal."

"Did ya find out anything?" Wiggins asked the cook.

"Found out plenty," she replied. "Not that it's fit for decent ears."

"Would you like to start, then?" Mrs. Jeffries said.

Mrs. Goodge shook her head. "Let's hear what you got out of the inspector first. After our last muck-up, I don't want to get sidetracked."

"She's right," Betsy said quickly. "This time we've got to keep right on top of what the inspector's doing."

Faintly alarmed, Mrs. Jeffries frowned. "Do all of you feel that way?"

"Yup," Luty said firmly.

"'Fraid so," Smythe agreed. "Don't want to waste my time chasin' my tail instead of the killer."

"Perhaps it would be in the best interests of justice if we did pay proper attention to Inspector Witherspoon's investigation," Hatchet said. "We certainly don't want a repeat of our last performance."

Mrs. Jeffries couldn't believe her ears. Had they all completely lost confidence in themselves? "Nonsense," she said stoutly. "We've solved a number of cases and just because we didn't solve the last one is no reason to change our methods. I'm surprised at all of you. Have you completely forgotten how many successes we've had in the past? I'm not saying we ought to ignore the inspector's investigation; we don't do that in any case. However, I won't have all of you sitting here on your hands too frightened to tell what you've learned because you're afraid you might be wrong. Is that clear?"

She spoke with the authority of a general addressing his troops. For a moment, no one said anything.

Luty broke the silence. She laughed. "Turnin' my own words back on me—that's a good one, Hepzibah. You're right. We're all actin' like a bunch of greenhorns too scared to get back on a horse that's thrown us. Well, we're danged good at what we do and I'm glad you reminded me of it. Seein' as everyone else is still skittish, why don't I go first? I learned a bit today. To begin with, Ogden Hinchley's got plenty of money. Family money, all inherited."

"Who gets it now that 'e's dead?" Smythe asked.

"I don't know yet. Thistlebottom only handles his money, not his will. But I've got another source . . ."

She was interrupted by a loud, derisive snort from her butler. "Source. Why, that man's a senile old solicitor," Hatchet muttered. "You can't rely on a thing he says. Furthermore, the fellow's so indiscreet it's a wonder he's still allowed to practise."

"Stampton ain't senile," Luty snapped. "He's a drunk. There's a difference, ya know. But drunk or sober, the man knows his facts. Now, as I was sayin' before I was so rudely interrupted, Hinchley never had to worry about earnin' a living. He started out as an actor and a playwright, but couldn't get anyone to hire him or produce his plays so he started writin' pieces for some of the newspapers. That's how he become a critic."

"Was he ever paid for his writing?" Mrs. Jeffries asked curiously.

"Not at first," Luty said eagerly. "But after he got so mean and nasty, his reviews started to help sell papers. That's when they started payin' him."

"So he was a failure as an actor and a playwright, but not as a critic," Mrs. Jeffries mused. "That's quite interesting. Wealthy too. Excellent, Luty."

Luty shot Hatchet a smug smile. She was pretty sure he hadn't found out a danged thing.

Smythe said, "I'd like to go next if nobody cares. I found a hansom driver who picked Ogden Hinchley up on Saturday night. It was half past six and he took him to the Hayden Theatre. That's all I learned. Not much, I'm afraid."

"I think it's quite good, considerin'," Betsy said, giving the coachman a bright smile. It bothered her that things weren't right between the two of them yet and she was getting tired of walking on eggshells around the man. "We've only just got this case. It's still early yet."

But Smythe obviously didn't mind that they were still at odds because he simply stared at her with that closed up expression he'd been wearing since she got back from the East End.

Flustered, she babbled on. "I didn't learn much either. Just that one of the shopkeepers saw Hinchley on Saturday and was surprised to see him back from America. He was supposed to be gone another three months. But he came back early. But I did find out that Hinchley's maid is a real chatterbox. She was always coming in to the grocer's and gossiping."

"Did you talk to the maid?" Mrs. Goodge asked eagerly.

Betsy shook her head. "I hung about Hinchley's house, but the only person who set foot out the door was a man. I think it was Hinchley's butler. He took himself off in a cab so I waited a bit, hoping the maid would come out, but she never did."

"Did you find out what the girl gossiped about?" Luty asked.

Betsy grinned. "The shopkeeper said she was always going on about the actors and theatre people comin' round to Hinchley's house and raising a ruckus over some of the nasty things he wrote about them in his reviews. I'm going to try and talk to the girl tomorrow."

"Good idea, Betsy." Mrs. Jeffries looked at the footman. She rather suspected Wiggins hadn't had a good day. He hadn't asked one question since they'd sat down and he looked a bit down in the mouth. "Did you learn anything?"

"Not a ruddy thing," he replied glumly. "No one I talked to knew anything about Hinchley."

"Don't take it so hard, lad," Mrs. Goodge said kindly. "We all have our bad days. The only thing I found out was that Hinchley wasn't any better than he ought to be." Disgusted, she made a face.

"Go on," Mrs. Jeffries prompted.

"Give me a minute," the cook said. "I'm tryin' to think of how to put it so it doesn't sound so . . . so . . . indecent . . ." She waved her hands in the air. "Oh, bother, I might as well just say it and get it over with. Hinchley frequented brothels."

Betsy giggled. Luty laughed and Wiggins blushed a bright pink. Smythe looked down at the tabletop to hide a grin.

Mrs. Jeffries, who was trying not to smile herself, said, "There's no need to be embarrassed, Mrs. Goodge. We all know that such places exist. Your information might become quite useful." Considering that probably a huge number of men in London frequented brothels, she didn't think this particular bit of information was noteworthy, but one never knew and she didn't want the cook to feel left out. "Do keep on digging. Now, let me tell you what I got out of the inspector." She told them everything she'd learned and, more important, she shared Witherspoon's contention that the murder was related to the play at the Hayden Theatre. "I'm inclined to agree with the inspector," she concluded.

"Why?" Smythe asked. "Sounds to me like this 'inchley were the sort of man who prided 'imself on makin' enemies."

"Yes, but it would have been a very lucky enemy who spotted him in a crowded theatre that night," the housekeeper said. "And Swinton told the inspector that half the cast had seen Hinchley in the audience that night. Besides," she said honestly, taking another leaf from the inspector's book, "it's at least a place to start."

"Names, Hepzibah," Luty said eagerly. "Did ya get any names for us?"

"There's Willard Swinton, the producer and the owner of the Hayden," she said. "And the playwright, Edmund Delaney. The Inspector was quite certain both those men hated the victim. He also mentioned that tonight he'd be interviewing Albert Parks, the play's director, and the two leads, Trevor Remington and Theodora Vaughan. All of them knew Hinchley as well."

"That's a good start," Luty said. "I'll dig around and see what I can learn about Swinton. If he owns a theatre, some banker'll have the goods on him."

"I'll take Delaney," Hatchet said. "As I mentioned earlier today, I've a number of contacts in the theatrical world."

"Do you want me to take Remington?" Betsy asked. "It won't take long tomorrow to talk to Hinchley's housemaid."

"That'll be fine, Betsy," Mrs. Jeffries said.

"I'll go over to the theatre tomorrow and see what I can find out about all of 'em," Wiggins said enthusiastically. "I like theatres."

"I can do the pubs round there and see what I can pick up," Smythe said. "And maybe talk to a few more cabbies as well." He frowned. "There's something botherin' me about that cabbie who took Hinchley to the Hayden on Saturday."

"What?" Betsy asked and then could have bitten her tongue.

"Well, he picked Hinchley up at half six, but the theatre's no more than a couple of miles from Hinchley's house. Why'd he take 'im so early?"

"I see what you mean, Smythe," Mrs. Jeffries said slowly. "The play wouldn't have started till eight o'clock. If the cabbie picked Hinchley up at six thirty, they would have been at the theatre by seven o'clock . . ."

"What if there was a lot of traffic?" Wiggins interrupted excitedly.

"Even then they should have been there by seven fifteen, seven-twenty at the latest," Smythe said. "That means that Hinchley would have had a good half hour to forty-five minutes to lark about and make himself known to anyone who happened to be about." He looked at Mrs. Jeffries.

"Which means that the killer isn't necessarily someone from the play. Cor, Hinchley had time enough to be seen by anyone at the ruddy theatre that night."

"Dag blast it," Luty exclaimed. "That means anyone could've killed him."

Smythe slumped back in his chair. "It'll be like lookin' for a needle in a 'aystack."

"Not necessarily," Mrs. Jeffries said quickly. "Before we jump to any conclusions, I think Smythe ought to talk to that cabbie again."

"I'm thinkin' the same thing," the coachman muttered. "I think I'd best ask the bloke what time they got to the theatre. I never asked the cabbie if they stopped anywhere along the way."

"You mean you didn't ask him that when you had the chance?" Betsy said.

Smythe kept a tight leash on his temper. The lass was just trying to rile him because he was still annoyed with her. He'd ignored her bright smiles and her overtures to make up because he was hurt. He gave her a cocky grin, the one he knew infuriated her. "I know it's hard to believe, girl," he said slowly, relishing the way her eyes narrowed angrily, "but even I can make a mistake. But not to worry, I'll hunt 'im up again tomorrow. This time, I'll make sure I ask the right questions."

"Do sit down, Inspector." Theodora Vaughan, the star of *Belvedere's Burden* and the loveliest woman Witherspoon had ever seen, gestured gracefully at the overstuffed settee.

Witherspoon, staring like a schoolboy, tripped over his own feet, caught his balance before making a complete fool of himself and stumbled toward the settee. Constable Barnes, following at a more leisurely pace, couldn't quite hide his smile of amusement. "Thank you," the inspector gushed. "This is quite comfortable. Your dressing room is lovely, Miss Vaughan, absolutely lovely."

Barnes gave the inspector a puzzled glance. The room was nice. Freshly painted cream walls, a colorful oriental dressing screen in one corner, long-stemmed roses on the vanity table and decent rugs on the floor, but it was hardly Buckingham Palace.

"That's very kind of you, Inspector," she replied. "Willard wanted me to be comfortable. He insisted on redoing this room before we opened. Not that I cared one way or the other. But it is quite nice."

"I'm awfully sorry to trouble you . . ." he began.

"It's no trouble at all, Inspector," she interrupted, tilting her head to one side and giving him another dazzling smile. "I'm sorry you had to wait while I took off my makeup, but if I don't get it off right away, it does horrid things to one's complexion."

Witherspoon didn't see anything horrid about her complexion. In the soft light of the dressing room, her skin was creamy white and utterly flawless, as was the rest of her. Her hair was a deep auburn, reminding him of a blazing sunset on a summer's day. Her eyes were a dark sapphire color, set deep in a sculpted face beneath perfectly formed brows.

Awed by her beauty, Witherspoon gaped at her. Barnes cleared his throat. The inspector, still gawking, didn't seem to hear him. Barnes did it again, loudly this time.

"Oh." Witherspoon shook himself slightly. "Yes, yes, indeed. Now, where was I?"

"Apologizing for troubling me," she said with a laugh. "But as I said, it's really no trouble at all. Though I'm afraid I won't be of much help to you. I haven't seen or spoken to Ogden Hinchley in months. I didn't realize he was back in London until I heard of his death."

Witherspoon nodded. His mind seemed to have gone blank because he couldn't think of one single, solitary question to ask this lovely creature.

Barnes glanced at his superior, but the inspector was still staring at the actress with a rather glazed look on his face. "You didn't know that Mr. Hinchley was in the audience that night?" Barnes asked.

"No. I thought he was still in New York."

Witherspoon started. Really, he must concentrate on his duty. But gracious, it was difficult. Every time she looked his way his thoughts tended to muddle. "Er, I take it that neither Mr. Swinton nor any of the other cast members mentioned to you that they'd seen Hinchley in the audience?"

"Absolutely not," she said fervently. "It was opening night, you see."

"I'm afraid I don't quite follow."

"I'm an artist, Inspector." She emphasized the words with a graceful sweep of her arms. "I don't see or speak to anyone before a performance until the first curtain call. Naturally, I had to concentrate on my role before I went on. I'm afraid my dressing room is completely out of bounds for everyone. The entire cast knows that. I don't see anyone, not even the stage manager or the director. So even if someone had wanted to tell me that Hinchley was out front, they wouldn't have been able to."

"What about after the play?" Barnes asked.

"I left right after the performance," she said. "I was exhausted. I'm on stage for virtually every scene. As soon as the curtain went down, I had one of the crew call me a hansom and I went home."

"Hearing about Hinchley's death must have been a dreadful shock to you," Witherspoon said sympathetically.

She clasped her hands to her chest. "It was a terrible shock. Absolutely terrible."

"It's a wonder you were able to go on tonight," the inspector said earnestly. "You're obviously most sensitive. Otherwise you wouldn't be such a wonderful actress."

Barnes glanced at Witherspoon sharply. What was the inspector up to now? Was he trying to lull this woman into talking? He knew for a fact the inspector had never seen the woman perform.

"How very kind of you to say so, Inspector," Theodora said, giving him another blazing smile. "I am sensitive. All great performers must be. But then you probably know that. From what I hear you're quite an artist in your own right. Scotland Yard's most successful detective."

Flattered, Witherspoon blushed. "Really, Miss Vaughan, there's nothing artistic about solving murders."

"Don't be so modest, Inspector." She leaned toward him and laid her hand on his arm. "I've heard about some of your cases. You were brilliant. Absolutely brilliant. In your own way, you have to be as creative as I am. And much braver."

"You're far too kind, Miss Vaughan," Witherspoon replied.

Again, Barnes waited for Witherspoon to ask a question. But the inspector only smiled at the woman like a smitten schoolboy. "Were you and Mr. Hinchley good friends?" Barnes finally asked.

"Friends? No, not really." She gave the constable the benefit of her smile.

But he, being older and a bit cranky at having to be out this late, wasn't in the least moved. Stone-faced, he stared back at her. "Then why was his death such a shock to you, ma'am?" he asked.

Thedora Vaughan's brilliant smile faded and was replaced by a look of offended dignity. "The London theatre world is a rather small community, Constable. Even though Mr. Hinchley and I weren't well acquainted, his death was still a terrible blow. One doesn't normally hear that one's acquaintance has been murdered. I was quite shocked when I heard the news."

"But of course you were, dear lady," Witherspoon said quickly. He flicked a disappointed look at his constable. "No doubt having to carry on and perform tonight has made you dreadfully tired."

"It has, Inspector. You must indeed be the most perceptive of men, for I pride myself on hiding my feelings well." She gazed at Witherspoon in admiration.

Barnes thought he just might be sick. He hoped Theodora Vaughan was a better actress on stage than she was tonight. This performance wouldn't fool a deaf mute. He glanced at his superior again, hoping to see a knowing gleam in the inspector's eyes. But instead, Witherspoon was getting to his feet.

"Then we shan't keep you, madam," Witherspoon said briskly. "You must have your rest. I'll call round tomorrow to ask the rest of my questions. Will that be all right?"

"Thank you, Inspector." She clasped her hands to her bosom again. "Rose, my maid, is right outside. She'll give you my address and I do thank you for being so astute. A performance exhausts me. It'll be far better for me to answer your questions tomorrow afternoon than tonight."

Barnes couldn't believe his ears. They'd come here at this god-awful hour of the night to question the rest of the cast and now the inspector was getting snookered by a pair of blue eyes and a few flashy smiles. Surely not? Barnes refused to believe the man he so admired for his detecting genius could be such a fool for a woman. The inspector must have a reason for what he was doing.

Witherspoon bowed formally. "Until tomorrow afternoon, madam. Good evening." With that, he turned on his heel and left.

As soon as the door of Theodora Vaughan's dressing room had closed behind them, Barnes said. "You think you'll get more out of her at her home, sir?"

"Oh, no, Barnes," Witherspoon said. "I just thought the poor lady looked tired. She's magnificent, isn't she?"

Barnes's jaw dropped in shock. But the inspector didn't notice as he charged for the dressing room down the hall.

"Let's go see what Mr. Remington has to say for himself. I believe his dressing room is here." He rapped sharply on the door.

"Who is it?" a man's voice shouted irritably.

"The police," Witherspoon yelled. "We'd like to speak with Mr. Remington."

"Just a moment, please."

They waited in the hall for quite a few moments. Barnes had just raised his fist to knock again when the door opened. A tall man, his hair mussed and his face shining with some greasy substance, stuck his head out. "Police? What do you want?" he asked rudely.

Witherspoon straightened his spine. "We would like to speak with you about the murder of Ogden Hinchley."

The man stared at them, then reluctantly opened the door. "Swinton told me you'd been here. But I honestly don't see why you're bothering me with this matter. I've nothing to do with it."

"Nevertheless, we'd like to ask you some questions," Witherspoon said.

Remington sighed dramatically, like a king condescending to speak to a stupid peasant. "Come in, then. But I don't know why you need to see me. I haven't talked to Hinchley in months. I didn't even know he was back from New York."

The room was identical in size to the one they'd just left. But size was the only thing the two rooms had in common. Remington's dressing room was dark and dingy, with bad lighting, ugly green walls, a bare floor and a scraggly hanging curtain on one end instead of a dressing screen. In place of a nice overstuffed settee, Remington had two disreputable balloon-backed chairs.

He sat down in front of his vanity table and gestured toward the other seats. "Sit down, please." He turned to his mirror, picked up a cotton cloth and began wiping his face.

Witherspoon took a moment to study the actor as he and Barnes sat down. The man's hair was dark but there were a few strands of gray sprouting at his temples. His nose was aquiline, his jawline firm and manly and his bone structure excellent. But there were more than a few age lines at the corners of his dark brown eyes, and the brackets around his mouth marked his years as numbering closer to forty than thirty.

"Mr. Remington," Witherspoon began, but the actor interrupted him.

"Is this going to take long?" he asked. "I've a supper engagement soon and I don't want to be late."

"We'll be as quick as possible," the inspector replied. "You were acquainted with Ogden Hinchley?"

"Everyone in the theatre knew Hinchley." Remington tossed the cloth down and turned to look at them. "What of it?"

"When was the last time you saw him?"

"Three months ago at the Drury Lane Theatre."

"Did you know that he was in the Hayden last night?" Barnes asked.

Remington shrugged. "I didn't know it at the time. Only after the play was over. Albert Parks told me he'd spotted him sitting down front."

"Albert Parks is the director of your play?" Witherspoon asked.

"That's right. Albert took a peek out the curtains before the lights went down and spotted Hinchley. But he didn't tell me until after the play was over."

"Was Hinchley here to review your play?" Barnes asked. He didn't have a clue what the inspector was up to, so he decided to put his oar in the water as well. He could always shut up if need be.

Remington's mouth flattened into a grim line. "Probably. Not that I cared one way or the other. No one took Hinchley's reviews all that seriously anymore."

"Had he reviewed any of your earlier performances?" the inspector asked. "I mean, had he ever reviewed you in another play?" He'd no idea why he was asking the question, but it seemed to him that perhaps the victim's being a critic might have been important to his murder.

Remington lifted his chin. "I am rather well known, Inspector," he said stiffly. "Hinchley had reviewed me a number of times."

"Good reviews, sir?" Barnes asked.

Remington lifted his chin a notch higher. "Some were quite good, others weren't. He was a failed actor himself, you know. When he couldn't make it on the boards, he turned to writing reviews. And not writing them very well, I might add. Just read a few of his reviews and you'll see why there won't be many tears at his funeral."

"So you didn't know he was out in front until after the play was over," Witherspoon mused. He tried to remember exactly what it was that Swinton had told him. Surely the man had said that Remington and Parks had peeked out the curtain before the play. "What time did Mr. Parks tell you about seeing Mr. Hinchley in the audience?"

"It was quite late," Remington said. "Around eleven, I think, right before I left the theatre."

"Did you go straight home?" Barnes asked. They might as well start checking alibis.

"As a matter of fact, I did. Opening nights are always exhausting."

"Where do you live, sir?" Barnes continued.

"I've taken rooms in Sidwell Lane. I went straight there right after I left here."

"Did anyone see you?" Barnes persisted.

"No, I live alone."

"What about your servants?" Witherspoon asked.

Remington sighed loudly. "Really, Inspector, this is most tiresome. I don't have a house full of servants and if I did, I wouldn't keep them up that late to wait on me. My landlady doesn't keep late hours so she was already asleep when I got home. I saw no one and no one saw me."

"If the landlady was asleep," Barnes asked, "how did you get in?"

"She rents rooms to many in my profession. She gave me a key." He got up and began to pace the room. "This is most intolerable. I didn't even know Hinchley was back from America until late Saturday night and now I'm being questioned in the man's murder. It's absurd. Why would I want to kill him?"

"No one's accusing you of anything," Witherspoon said soothingly. "We're merely trying to eliminate as many people as possible. By the way, are you absolutely certain you didn't know that Hinchley was in the audience until Mr. Parks mentioned it?" He didn't know why that point seemed important, but it did.

"Of course I'm sure. Why do you ask?"

"Because you were seen looking out at the audience before the play began," Witherspoon said. "And I wondered if perhaps you'd spotted Hinchley. He was right in the third row center. I believe he would have been difficult to miss."

"I didn't see him," Remington snapped. "I may have glanced out but I didn't see Ogden Hinchley."

Witherspoon decided to try a different tactic. "Did Hinchley have any enemies that you know about?"

"He had dozens of them," Remington cried. "Virtually every actor in England hated him, and I dare say, by now most of the ones in New York loathed him as well. But egads, Inspector, if actors murdered every critic that had ever given them a bad review, there wouldn't be any left on either side of the ocean."

• • •

Smythe leaned against the doorjamb and watched Betsy put the teapot back in its proper place on the sideboard. She moved with the grace of a dancer and he sighed inwardly, wondering if he'd ever have the nerve to tell her his true feelings.

She turned and gasped, startled by his presence. "I wish you'd stop doing that," she snapped.

"Doin' what?" he asked innocently, knowing he shouldn't irritate her now that he was wanting to make peace. "I was just standin' 'ere."

"You come sneakin' up on a body like that and it's a wonder you don't scare them half to death," she fumed. She was embarrassed because she'd been thinking about him. "I thought you said you were going up to bed."

"I was." He walked to the table and pulled a chair out. "But Wiggins is still readin' all them wretched newspapers and I didn't 'ave the 'eart to make 'im turn out the lamps yet. Besides, I wanted to 'ave a word with you."

She gazed at him suspiciously. "About what?"

"About what you was doin' over at the East End the other day," he shot back.

"That's none of your concern," she replied.

Smythe opened his mouth and then clamped it shut again. Arguing with the lass would only put her back up. He decided to take another tactic. "I thought we was friends, Betsy," he said gently. "I thought you trusted me."

Betsy felt her resolve melting. She didn't want to tell Smythe what she'd been doing. She didn't want to tell anyone. She was too ashamed. "I do. But sometimes people have things they'd rather keep private. I had some old business to take care of, that's all. But it's over and done with now."

Old business. The words sent a shiver up Smythe's spine. He'd run into some of Betsy's old business before and it liked to put the fear of God in him. On one of their other cases, they'd run into an old acquaintance of Betsy's from her days of struggling to survive in the East End. Raymond Skegit. Blast, Smythe thought, he hoped this latest trip over there didn't have anything to do with the likes of someone like him. Protecting Betsy was all he cared about. How could he protect her if she wouldn't talk? But pressing her wasn't going to get him any answers; that was certain. "All right, Betsy. I'll not bother you on the matter again. It's your secret."

"It's not a secret," she protested. "You're not always telling me what you're up to, either." She glanced over her shoulder at the clock. "It's getting late. I'm going up."

Smythe said goodnight and watched her leave. Her words had hit home. He too had a secret. But he fully intended to share it with her one of these days. When she was ready. When she could hear the truth without wanting to box his ears. He smiled wryly, thinking that the promise he'd made to the late Euphemia Witherspoon, the inspector's aunt, had caused him nothing but trouble.

Euphemia had known she was dying and she'd begged him to stay on at Upper Edmonton Gardens and keep an eye on her "naive nephew," at least until he'd settled in. Smythe, not wanting to upset his old friend, had agreed. One thing had led to another. Soon, Mrs. Jeffries and Betsy had arrived in the household and before you could say Bob's-Your-Uncle, they'd been investigating murders. Acting like a family.

Smythe turned and started for the stairs. But what would his "family" think if they knew that he was rich as sin and too scared to tell them? Would they think he'd lied to them all this time? Would they hate him? Smythe grimaced. The idea of Betsy or any of the others hating him was too awful to think about. One of these days he'd tell them the truth. One of these days. In the meantime he'd continue on the way he was and do his best to keep that silly banker of his from letting the cat out of the bag. Besides, he told himself as he started up the stairs, the fact that he was rich didn't change who he was. It wasn't as if he'd been born that way.

Mrs. Jeffries stared at the black night outside her window. She hadn't even tried to sleep. It would be pointless with her mind still so much on this case. Who had hated Ogden Hinchley enough to murder him? More important, who had gone to so much trouble to try to make it look like an accident? And why had they botched it so badly? Or maybe she was wrong.

If Dr. Bosworth hadn't been in the mortuary that night, they could well have gotten away with it being ruled an accidental death. It was Bosworth's sharp eye that had noted the buttons on the man's clothes and the fact that the shoes were all wrong. Of course the marks around the man's ankles should have been a signal to any physician doing the postmortem that it hadn't been an accidental death. But Mrs. Jeffries knew that there were many doctors who would have dismissed those bruises altogether, if they'd even noticed them at all. Or perhaps the killer hadn't realized he'd left those marks on the victim's body. Or perhaps the killer hadn't cared. Perhaps he was so arrogant that he felt absolutely sure he'd never get caught.

He? Mrs. Jeffries sighed. At least they knew one thing for certain. The killer was a man. No woman could haul a dead body even the short distance between Hinchley's house and the canal.

CHAPTER 4

"Miss Vaughan is a superb actress, Mrs. Jeffries," Witherspoon enthused. "She's so graceful, so accomplished. She fairly lights up the stage when she makes her entrance. It's no wonder the dear lady was so tired when I tried to interview her. Giving such a performance must be extremely taxing on one's strength."

"Excuse me, sir, but I didn't think you'd actually seen the play."

"Well, I didn't actually see her performance," he admitted, "but one could tell from just speaking with Miss Vaughan that she's a true artist."

"I'm sure she is, sir," Mrs. Jeffries said dryly. "No doubt Mr. Remington is an artist as well, yet he managed the interview."

"His part isn't nearly as complex or intense as Miss Vaughan's." Witherspoon waved his fork dismissively. "It's the sort of role a professional actor could do in his sleep. Why, he was only offered the part because Miss Vaughan interceded on his behalf."

"Did he tell you that?" Mrs. Jeffries eyed her employer suspiciously.

"Constable Barnes picked up that tidbit when he was interviewing the stagehands," the inspector replied, forking up another bit of bacon. "Mind you, none of them had any pertinent information to report, but all of them knew who the victim was and they'd all heard about his murder. But back to Miss Vaughan. I tell you, Mrs. Jeffries, I can't remember when I've ever met such a captivating woman. She is utterly superb."

Mrs. Jeffries said nothing. Silently, she sipped her tea, watching the inspector over the rim of her cup. He'd been singing Theodora Vaughan's praises since he'd sat down to eat his breakfast. That was fifteen minutes ago. Surely the inspector wasn't getting hoodwinked by this actress? Gracious, the woman was a suspect! But then she remembered the conclusion she herself had come to last night. The killer was a man. Witherspoon, obviously, had come to the same conclusion. Maybe well before she had.

Suddenly, her own high spirits plummeted. Mrs. Jeffries put her cup down and stared at the tablecloth. Perhaps the household wasn't as clever as they'd always thought. Maybe the inspector *Could* handle all his cases on his own. He continued wittering on about Theodora Vaughan as he finished his breakfast. Mrs. Jeffries, fighting off a sense of failure totally alien to her nature, stopped listening.

Perhaps if they really worked hard, they could find some useful information, she told herself. Surely they weren't totally unnecessary to the investigation. Surely there was something important they could contribute.

"I say, Mrs. Jeffries." Witherspoon raised his voice.

With a start, she looked up to see him staring at her curiously. "I'm sorry, sir. I was woolgathering. What did you say?"

"I asked you if you had any ideas," he repeated.

She stared at him blankly. "Ideas?"

He smiled kindly. "Why, yes. You've been ever so helpful in the past."

As she hadn't a clue whether he was talking about the household or about the case, she hesitated.

"Now, really, Mrs. Jeffries," Witherspoon encouraged, "you mustn't be so modest. You know very well that I rely on you for this sort of thing."

"Rely on me, sir?"

"But of course. Who else could I possibly ask to advise me on such a delicate matter?"

Now she really didn't know what he was talking about. "Yes, sir, it is a delicate matter."

"I mean, what is one supposed to do in a situation like this?" He drummed his fingers on the table. "Somehow, accepting the invitation seems a bit odd. After all, this is a murder investigation and even though I personally think the dear lady is probably quite innocent . . ."

"Probaby innocent," Mrs. Jeffries interrupted, her spirits lifting a bit. "But wouldn't the murder have had to have been committed by a man?"

Taken aback, he gazed at her. "Not necessarily. I don't see why a woman couldn't grab someone's ankles as easily as a man could. It might be a bit more difficult for a woman to hang onto the chap," he mused, "but certainly not impossible."

"But what about getting the body to the canal?" she asked. It was rare for her to be so confused, but that's exactly what she was. "Unless a woman had extraordinary strength, how could she possibly do it?"

"She probably couldn't." Witherspoon smiled slowly. "But she could have had help."

"Two people?" Blast. Why hadn't the idea occurred to her? Of course he was right. Conspiracies to commit murder were rare, but not impossible. From what little they knew of the victim, there were plenty of people who hated him. But did two of them hate him enough to conspire in murder? From her observation of life, if it were two people, why not more? Perhaps the whole lot of them had gotten together to kill him.

"It's highly unlikely that Miss Vaughan has anything to do with Hinchley's murder," Witherspoon continued. "But the possibility does exist. So you can see my quandry."

"No, sir, I'm afraid I don't."

He drew back, a puzzled frown on his face. "Really, Mrs. Jeffries, I'm surprised at you. Do you honestly think it's fitting to accept a social invitation from the lady when she's a suspect in a murder I'm investigating? Then, of course, there's Lady Cannonberry to consider. I realize there's nothing formal between us, no understandings or anything like that. But I shouldn't like to offend her." A slight blush crept over his cheeks. "She's become quite . . . er . . . important to me."

Mrs. Jeffries decided that she couldn't bluff her way out of this. She hadn't been listening and she might as well own up to it. "Inspector, please forgive me, but as I said a few moments ago, I wasn't listening properly when you were speaking. Precisely what invitation are you talking about?"

"Miss Vaughan's invited me to a dinner party next Monday evening," he said patiently. "She had her maid bring me a note before I left the theatre last night. But I feel I really must decline. Suspect or not, accepting the invitation seems a bit disloyal to Lady Cannonberry."

Ruth Cannonberry, their neighbor and a very dear friend, was off in the country visiting relatives. She and the Inspector were becoming quite close.

"I understand." Mrs. Jeffries nodded in agreement. "Well, sir, then if I were you, I'd politely decline Miss Vaughan's invitation. I'm sure she'll understand that under the circumstances it would hardly be appropriate."

"Yes, well, I certainly hope so. I quite admire the lady, but I wouldn't hurt Lady Cannonberry"—he reached for his teacup—"for all the tea in China, as they say."

"Did you discover anything else yesterday?" Mrs. Jeffries prodded. She decided to worry about her own abilities as a detective later.

Witherspoon told her about the interviews he'd conducted at the theatre and the background information he'd gotten from the the police constables.

"What did you think of their alibis?" she asked when he'd finished speaking.

He looked thoughtful. "I don't really know what to think. The problem is, unless we know precisely when the man was killed, we've not much to investigate when it comes to alibis?"

"But you said you're fairly sure it was late Saturday night or in the very early hours of Sunday morning?"

"Yes, but we don't know for certain." He sighed. "As most people are well asleep in their beds by the time Hinchley was probably murdered, it's difficult to break the alibis of our suspects. Unless we come up with a witness or a cabbie or someone like that, we've really very little hope."

"I see your point, sir." She nodded in agreement. "Then don't you think it might be useful to find the last person who did see the victim alive? But, of course, you've already thought of that."

As he hadn't, it sounded like a jolly good idea. Witherspoon smiled broadly. "Mrs. Jeffries, I do believe you ought to take to the stage yourself. Perhaps as one of those mind readers at the music hall. That's precisely what I'd decided to do. I'll get the uniformed lads working on it straight away. The man had to get home somehow. Someone must have seen him."

"Why, thank you, sir," she replied, genuinely pleased by his words. "And of course you're instructing the constables to ask about the neighborhood to see if any of them saw anything suspicious on Saturday evening?"

"We've already done that," Witherspoon said. "Yesterday. But no luck there, I'm afraid. No one saw any bodies being trundled off to the canal and tossed off the bridge. We even inquired at the Regents Park Baptist College, in the hopes that one of them might have been out and seen something." He sighed. "But no one had. The Baptists were a bit put out that we'd even asked, too."

His words had given Mrs. Jeffries an idea. Hinchley, though a small man, had been dead weight. She wondered how long it took the killer to move the body. "I expect you'll also be walking the route the killer must have taken from the victim's house to where his body was actually found. Am I right?"

"Bravo, Mrs. Jeffries," Witherspoon cried. Egads, that was a wonderful idea. He was amazed he hadn't thought of it himself. "You've done it. That's exactly what I'm going to do this morning. Frankly, I want to know precisely how long it would take to move a body. After all, the longer the killer was outside the house, the more likely it is that someone might have seen him."

Wiggins licked the last of the sticky bun off his fingers, pulled out his handkerchief and then wiped his chin. He leaned against the base of the huge, shepherd's hook—shaped lamppost and watched the front entrance of the Hayden Theatre. He'd been hanging about for an hour now and hadn't seen anyone go in or out. He was almost ready to give up.

Despite the heavy foot traffic on the Strand today, none of those feet had turned toward the theatre. "Blimey," he muttered under his breath, "this 'as been a waste of ruddy time." He straightened and crossed the road to the pedestrian island in the center. The walk in front of the theatre remained empty.

Then he saw the front door open, and a young, dark-haired girl dressed in a plain brown dress darted out. She turned and said something to a man standing in the doorway. Then she hurried off, making for the corner.

Wiggins was after her like a shot. He skidded to a halt as he came round the side of building and saw her opening the door of an opulent black carriage. A moment later, she tugged a square wicker case out, heaved it awkwardly under her arm and started right toward him.

"Can I 'elp you with that, miss?" he asked, moving quickly and blocking her path. Up close, he could see that her face was long and thin and her eyes hazel.

She stared at him suspiciously for a moment. Her gaze raked him from head to toe, taking in his neatly pressed trousers, his clean white shirt and his new boots. She smiled flirtatiously. "That's right kind of you. It is a bit heavy." She dumped the box into his outstretched arms. "I'm just taking these things round the corner to the theatre."

"My name's Wiggins," he said, falling into step next to her.

"I'm Rose," she said.

Wiggins pretended to stumble. "Sorry." He caught the box. "Cor, what's in 'ere? Feels 'eavy."

"It's just a few costumes," the girl replied. "My mistress is Theodora Vaughan."

"The actress?" Wiggins couldn't believe his luck.

"That's right. She's in a play at this very theatre," Rose said proudly. "Plays the lead. She's a star, she is."

"You're lucky to work for someone like that," Wiggins enthused. "Must be ever so excitin'"

"Oh, I am," Rose agreed. "I'm Miss Vaughan's personal maid. It's not like I scrub floors or do any heavy work."

"Is she nice then?"

"Nicest mistress I've ever had," Rose replied. "Training me proper too. I've learned to do hair and take care of all her clothes . . . "

"Like these? Are you bringin' 'em to the theatre for her?" he asked, trying desperately to keep her talking.

"Those are old costumes." Rose waved her hand in dismissal. "She doesn't need them anymore so she's giving them to the Hayden."

"Just old costumes?" He contrived to sound disappointed.

"You needn't say it like that," she snapped. "It's right kind of Miss Vaughan to be giving away these things."

"I'm sure it is," Wiggins said quickly. They were almost at the door. He couldn't lose her, not now. She worked for one of the suspects.

"Thank you ever so much for carrying this for me," Rose said as they came close to the entrance. "It was heavy."

Wiggins pretended to trip. The case flew out of his arms and landed right in front of the door. The lid popped open and a mass of black velvet and silk spilled out onto the pavement.

"Oh." Rose dropped to her knees in alarm. "Garvey'll 'ave my head if these things get dirty."

"I'm sorry." Wiggins dropped down beside her. "Tell this Garvey person it were my fault. I'm a big, clumsy oaf. My guv's right. I'm too dumb to be let out without a leash." He gave Rose his most pathetic, poor-little-me expression.

Her anger immediately evaporated and was replaced with a look of pity. "Your employer talks to you like that?"

Dumbly, wishing he could cry on cue, he nodded. "Yeah. He only keeps me on because I work real cheap."

"Why, you poor thing," Rose cried.

"Oh, it's all right." He made his lower lip tremble. "I'm used to it and my guv don't mean no 'arm. That's just the way 'e is."

"That's no excuse for treating you like dirt," Rose declared. "I'd not put up with it."

"But you work for a kind mistress." Wiggins, who was quite enjoying himself by now, pointed to the velvet trousers that Rose was folding. "Generous, she is."

"She has her moments," Rose said chattily. She put the clothes back in the case and slammed the lid down. "Mind you, she's no saint. She can be a bit . . . what's the word Mr. Delaney always uses . . . temperamental. Yes, that's it. Like all actors, she can be temperamental," she repeated, obviously proud of herself for learning such a posh word. "Came back from the country house on Saturday in a right nasty mood. Complained about the train, complained about the weather, complained about the crowds at the station. 'Course she were probably just het up because it was opening night."

"Well, it's nice of her to be givin' away 'er costumes," Wiggins said.

Rose laughed. "She's only donating these things because she doesn't want to do pantomime or trouser roles anymore. Claims those kind of parts is beneath her now." She jutted her chin toward the door. "And this place can use all the help it can get."

"What' da ya mean?" Wiggins got up and helped Rose to her feet.

Rose flicked a glance at the front door. "Well," she said softly, "this isn't the best theatre on the Strand. They haven't had a successful show here in ages. I don't know what Miss Vaughan was thinking of, agreeing to play here. She could have her pick of parts if she wanted to. Of course, this was probably the only place that would agree to produce Mr. Delaney's play. Not that it's a bad one, mind you. But if you ask me, it is a bit dull."

"Then why does Miss Vaughan want to be in it?"

Rose laughed gaily. "Because she's in love with him, that's why. She'll do anything for Mr. Delaney. Anything at all. Not that I blame her . . . but still, some say it's not right."

"What's not right," Wiggins asked, "her bein' in love with Mr. Delaney?"

Rose yanked open the heavy wooden front door and stepped inside. "Shhh . . ." she cautioned. "You've got to be careful what you say around here. People are always running about carrying tales. Eddie, are you about, then? Blast!" She stamped her foot and looked around the huge foyer. "I told that man I'd be right back. Where's he got to, then?"

"I'm right here, girl." Eddie Garvey, holding a hammer in his hand, frowned suspiciously as Wiggins popped out from behind a pillar. "Just leave the costumes there, girl," he instructed the maid. "I'll get them to the back."

Rose nodded and flounced out the way she'd come. "It wouldn't have hurt him to say 'thank you,'" she muttered. She stalked toward the corner. "Ruddy stage manager. Thinks he's too good to bother thanking the likes of someone like me."

Wiggins desperately wanted to get her talking about Theodora Vaughan again. But he couldn't think how to bring the subject up. Cor, he couldn't lose her. Not now. "Uh, excuse me, Miss Rose."

She whirled around. "What?"

"If I may be so bold, miss. Would you like to 'ave a cup of tea? I mean, if you're not in a great 'urry to get back. There's a Lyons just up the road."

"I'm in no rush to get back." Rose cocked her head to one side. "Tea, you say? Cakes too?"

Wiggins put his hand in his pocket. He had plenty of coins. "Cakes too," he agreed quickly. "And sticky buns as well if you want 'em."

Lilly Coltrane wasn't a very pretty girl. With her round, pudgy face; frizzy, dull brown hair and bulbous, watery blue eyes, she looked dim-witted, but Betsy had realized after only a few moments of speaking to the maid that she was as sharp as they come.

She'd deliberately cornered the girl when she'd spotted her leaving the Hinchley house, a shopping basket tucked under her arm. Getting Lilly in a conversation was as easy as snapping your fingers. "So did you like working for Mr. Hinchley?" Betsy asked. She leaned against the railing on the bridge over the canal.

Lilly shrugged. "Just as soon work for him as most. Of course, the last three months has been dead easy, what with him being gone to America. Quite a shock it give Rather and me when he turned up all sudden like on

Saturday afternoon." She laughed. "Luckily, the house was turned out proper, excepting for the rooms we'd closed off."

"I heard that Mr. Hinchley was a real nasty sort," Betsy ventured. Though Lilly dearly loved the sound of her own voice, she hadn't said much that was useful.

Lilly shook her head. "He weren't that bad. He weren't the sort to forget a slight, I'll say that for him. But he could be quite kind. When my mum took sick last year, he gave me the money to make sure she had a proper doctor and all. I was quite grateful."

"Then how come all them actors and such hated him?" Betsy persisted. She was going to get Lilly talking about this if it was the last thing she did.

Lilly waved her hand. "Oh, them. They was always coming round and having a go at him. Silly sort, aren't they? I mean, take that actor—Remington, his name is. Almost came to blows with Mr. Hinchley."

"Did this Mr. Remington actually strike Mr. Hinchley?"

"And risk being hit in the face?" She laughed. "Not blooming likely. All he did was scream and carry on loud enough to wake the dead."

"Guess this Mr. Remington didn't like Mr. Hinchley's review."

"It weren't about a review," Lilly said eagerly. "It were about money. That's what was so odd about it. Seems this actor claimed Mr. Hinchley owed him some money and he wanted to collect it before he went off to America. Well, they got so loud with their shoutin' and all that Mr. Mickleshaft, our next door neighbor, he come over and told them if they didn't quiet down so he could get some sleep, he'd have the police on them for disturbing the peace. So Mr. Remington left."

Betsy's mind whirled with the information. "That's not very smart, having a row in the middle of the night like that."

"It weren't the middle of the night. Mr. Mickleshaft doesn't sleep at night. To hear him complain about it he doesn't sleep at all. He's one of them silly types that's always ailin' but hasn't really been sick a day in his life. Insomnia—who ever heard of such a thing!" Lilly snorted derisively. Then she started toward the other side of the bridge. "Well, I can't stand here chattin' all day. I'd best be getting back. Even with Mr. Hinchley dead there's things that need doing."

"So you're staying on, then?" Betsy asked as she hurried to keep up with the girl's quick steps.

Lilly smiled widely. "This is the easiest position I've ever had. Especially now that Hinchley's dead. I'm staying until that ruddy solicitor sells the house and tosses me out. I hope it takes a long time. They're going to be selling off his house and furniture, not that they'll get much for some of that silly stuff Mr. Hinchley had about." She snorted again. "Looks like something out of a picture book, the stuff in the drawing room does."

"Oh," Betsy said quickly. "Really? Strange tastes, had he?"

"Not just in furnishings, either." Lilly smiled slyly. "If you know what I mean."

Betsy could guess. "At least you didn't have to worry about him trying to paw you," she said, giving the girl a knowing woman-to-woman look. "Not like some households."

Lilly nodded. "Of course, the footman, he used to lead him a merry chase. Oh, well, live and let live, that's what I always say. And like you said, it kept him from bothering me that way. Give me a bit of peace. As long as I minded myself and pretended not to notice all his silly ceremonies, he left me alone to do my work."

"What ceremonies?" Betsy asked. She noticed that despite Lilly's protests that she had to get back, the girl dawdled so she could continue talking.

They'd come to the other side of the bridge. Lilly stopped and gazed at Betsy thoughtfully. "You're asking a lot of questions," she said.

Betsy gave her a wide, innocent smile. "Sorry if I'm nosy. It's just that you've such an interesting way of telling things, I can't help myself."

"I do have a way with words," Lilly agreed. "Everyone says so. My mum used to say I could tell a tale better than anyone."

"And it's dead boring where I work," Betsy said earnestly.

"Most houses is when you're a maid," she replied. "I always liked working for Mr. Hinchley, even though sometimes he could be nasty. He left me alone as long as I minded my own business and did me work, and his house was a lot more interestin' than most places."

"Tell me about his secret ceremonies," Betsy said eagerly.

Lilly looked a little sheepish. "Well, he didn't have all that many," she admitted. "Just the one, and then only on the nights when he was reviewing a new play."

"What'd he do then?" Betsy prompted.

"He had a complete routine," Lilly said. She started walking again. "It never varied and he was right strict about it, too. First of all, he always left the house at exactly the same time, half past six. We was under instructions that once he was gone, we was to carry on, have our dinner and then go to bed. He didn't want no one waiting up for him. Right before we locked up for the night, Rather was to unlock the side door and make sure the boiler was fired so there'd be plenty of hot water for his bath."

"Is that it then?" Betsy was disappointed. "He took a bath when he came home from the theatre?"

Lilly giggled. "He took a bath all right, but he made sure he had someone there to scrub his back. That's why he insisted the side door be kept unlocked. He wanted his friend to be able to slip in without anyone seeing."

Betsy steeled herself to keep asking questions. But she had a fair idea where this was leading and it made her half sick to her stomach. She knew from her days in the poverty-stricken East End the kind of sick, ugly games the rich could buy for themselves. The fact that a side door was kept unlocked and the servants instructed to go to bed told her one thing. Whoever came to Hinchley's house wasn't a real friend; it was someone who was being paid. Probably someone who hated it and probably hated Hinchley as well.

Lilly gave Betsy a sharp look when she kept silent. "I'm not makin' this up, you know. I seen it with my own eyes. One night I had to get up and go do my business, you see, and there right in the hallway was this young man. 'Course I knew if Mr. Hinchley knew I'd spotted the fellow I'd get sacked, so I flattened meself against the shadows at the top of the stairs. A few minutes later I heard Mr. Hinchley call out that he was through writing the review and the lad could come in and help him get in the bath." Lilly broke off and stared in the distance, her giggling brightness suddenly gone. "Upset me, it did. The idea of someone being about to buy another person like that. Don't know why. God knows, us poor people don't have much choice—it's either sell your labor if you can or sell your body."

"Are you absolutely sure it was Mr. Hinchley you saw getting in the hansom?" Witherspoon asked the man. "You couldn't have been mistaken, Mr. Packard?"

"Know his face as well as I know me own," Packard replied. "Everyone that works in the business knew Hinchley. That man had closed more shows than a smallpox epidemic."

"Really?" Witherspoon found that quite odd. He could understand that actors and playwrights might know the critic, but he was quite amazed to find a limelighter who did. "Everyone?"

Packard grinned, revealing several tobacco-blackened teeth. "Hinchley had a lot of influence, Inspector. But even if he didn't, we would have known who he was. Mr. Swinton made sure we all knew who he was. We was under orders to make sure Hinchley didn't get backstage."

"Goodness, Mr. Swinton gave you those instructions Saturday night?"

"Nah," Packard replied. "He give us those instructions months ago. Different play here then, but that didn't make any difference to Mr. Swinton. Hated Hinchley. Didn't want him nosing about the place."

"Did he say why?"

"Didn't say and none of us asked," Packard said with a casual shrug.

"But surely you've some idea?"

Packard glanced over his shoulder toward the stage. It was empty. "Well, my guess is he didn't want Hinchley having a close look at the scenery or the props. We cut a few corners here and there, you know. Got to make ends meet."

"The theatre is in financial difficulties?"

Packard laughed. "That's a polite way of puttin' it. There hasn't been a money-makin' production here in five years. Part of that's due to Hinchley's bad reviews. Part of it's due to the fact that this theatre ain't what she used to be. Don't attract the top drawer anymore, the cream, so to speak."

"That's interesting," Witherspoon said. "But back to your identification of Mr. Hinchley. You're certain you saw him getting into a hansom right after the performance, is that correct?"

"Right." Packard pointed toward the side of the auditorium. "It were right out in the alley. I'd gone out and gotten a hansom for Miss Vaughan and was seein' her off when all of a sudden, Hinchley comes strolling out the side door, saunters up the alley and hails a hansom. Well, blow me for a game of tin soldiers, I thought. If Mr. Swinton had seen Hinchley comin' out that door instead of the front, there'd be some heads rolling around here. I were only glad it weren't going to be mine."

"So Hinchley must have gotten into the backstage area," Barnes said. "Otherwise he couldn't have come out the side door."

"That's right. 'Course when I asked round in here, no one would admit to seein' him." Packard crossed his arms over his chest. "They might have been telling the truth too; everyone's pretty busy right after the curtain goes down. But my guess is Hinchley slipped into the back, had a good gander at the scenery and whatnot and then took himself off without so much as a by-your-leave."

"And this was directly after the performance?" Witherspoon wanted to be absolutely, positively clear about the time.

"Not more than five minutes. Miss Vaughan asked me to get her a hansom right after she come off the stage. By the time I got him round to the side, she was waiting there to go."

"Packard, I told you to fix this ruddy door." The director's sharp voice boomed from the side of the stage. "What are you doing larking about? We've got a performance in a few hours and I don't want this thing sticking again in the first act."

Witherspoon stared at Albert Parks as he stepped into view from the side of the stage. "Mr. Packard is speaking to us," he called out. "Please don't be angry with him. He's answering a few questions."

"I'd best get back to work," Packard muttered as he edged away.

"Thank you for your assistance, sir," Witherspoon said. "You've been most helpful." He turned back toward the stage. "Mr. Parks, may I have a word with you?"

"Me?" Parks's eyes bulged. "Why on earth would you want to speak to me?"

"It's merely routine, sir," the inspector assured him. Gracious, how on earth did people think the police actually solved murders if they didn't ask questions? "We won't take too much of your time."

Parks stared at them sourly. "Oh, all right, if I must. I'll be with you in a moment."

"Too bad Mr. Swinton and Mr. Delaney aren't here," Barnes muttered softly. "This one doesn't look like he wants to tell us anything."

"Very few people do, Constable," Witherspoon said. "And I'm a tad annoyed that the other gentlemen are gone. We told them we'd be back this afternoon to ask more questions."

Parks, pointedly looking at the watch on his waistcoat, came hurrying toward them. "Do please make this quick, sir. I've not much time."

"But it's hours before tonight's performance," Barnes pointed out.

Parks tucked his watch in. "And there's an enormous amount of work to do yet. Just because the actors aren't emoting all over the stage doesn't mean I'm not busy."

"Mr. Parks," Witherspoon began, "we'll try not to inconvenience you too much. But we've a few questions we must ask. How well did you know Mr. Hinchley?"

Parks thought about it for a moment. "I knew of him, of course. Everyone in the theatre did. But I didn't know him all that well. Not personally."

"Did you like him, sir?" Barnes asked.

"He was a critic." Parks sneered the last word. "Of course I didn't like him."

"Had he reviewed any of your previous productions?" Witherspoon asked.

Parks hesitated. "He reviewed my production of *Hamlet*. He didn't like it overly much. But Hinchley was kinder to me about it than to Remington. He actually said Remington's performance in the title role was so bad that if Shakespeare were alive to see it, he'd have died of apoplexy on the spot."

"Did you know he was in the theatre on Saturday evening?"

Again, Parks hesitated. "Well, I believe I heard someone mention they saw him out front."

That was a lie, Witherspoon thought. They'd already been told by Trevor Remington that Parks had spotted Hinchley sitting in the audience. Drat. Why did people persist in lying to the police? "And you were unhappy that he was here?"

"He was a critic. Inspector," Parks drew himself up straighter. "I'm neither pleased nor displeased to know they're in the audience. It's simply a fact of life that one has to put up with."

"What time did you leave the theatre?" Witherspoon asked. He remembered his discussion with his housekeeper.

"Right after the performance," Parks replied. "I was in a hurry to get home. I wanted to make some notes on some changes I'm doing for the first act."

"Did anyone see you?" Barnes asked.

"When I got home?" Parks lifted one shoulder in a casual shrug. "My housekeeper might have heard me come in. It was after eleven-thirty so I didn't see her, of course. But I noticed the light on under her door when I went upstairs."

Witherspoon asked, "How did you get home?"

"I walked, Inspector," Parks said impatiently. "I live on Pope Street. It took ten minutes to get home."

"Did anyone see you walking home?" Barnes prodded.

Parks shook his head. "Not that I remember. It was quite late at night. The streets were fairly empty. I went home, let myself in, wrote up my notes and went to bed."

"Where are they, sir?" Barnes asked.

"Where are what?" Parks asked irritably.

"The notes, sir? I'd like to see them."

Parks's eyes narrowed. "Well, you can't. I put them down backstage and now I can't find them. I don't know what you're implying. But if I were you, I wouldn't waste my time questioning innocent people. I didn't like Ogden Hinchley but I certainly didn't kill him. Ridiculous. There wouldn't be a critic left in all of England if they were murdered because they'd given a bad reviews. If I were you, I'd start talking to people who had personal reasons for hating Hinchley."

"Who would they be, sir?" Witherspoon asked.

"A number of people, sir." Parks's smile was slow and sly. "To begin with, you might ask Edmund Delaney what he did after the performance. He hated Hinchley and his reasons were personal."

CHAPTER 5

"I've a dreadful headache, Mrs. Jeffries." The inspector rubbed the bridge of his nose. "Absolutely dreadful. I say, is there time before dinner for us to have a glass of sherry?"

"But of course, sir," she replied as she got up and went to the sideboard. "With all this heat, it's only a light supper. Mrs. Goodge will send it up whenever we're ready. I believe a glass of Harvey's will relax you. Perhaps help your headache." She poured two small glasses of the amber liquid and, smiling sympathetically at her dear employer, handed one to him. "Oh, really, sir. It's quite awful how you exhaust yourself on these cases."

"One must do one's duty." He took a sip and sighed softly. "Today was quite trying. Theatre people are so . . . so . . ."

"Melodramatic," she finished for him. "That's what you called them this morning, sir."

"And I was right too. Not only are they a melodramatic lot, but they're rather cavalier about the most important matters."

"Really, sir?" She took a sip from her own glass and waited for him to continue. As Luty would say, he'd come home with a bee in his bonnet, and she'd decided it would be best to let him unburden himself at his own pace. "In what way?"

"Humphhh." He snorted delicately. "They're not very good at keeping appointments, I can tell you that. Do you know that neither Swinton nor Delaney were at the theatre today? They knew perfectly well we were coming back to talk with them and neither of them could be bothered to show up. I say, Mrs. Jeffries, that's not good. Not good at all."

"So you didn't learn much today, sir?" she queried.

"I wouldn't say that," he replied, tossing back another mouthful. "Actually, we had quite an interesting interview with Albert Parks. He claims he only knew Hinchley in a professional capacity. Of course, that's what all of them say."

"Do you believe him, sir?"

"I'm not sure." Witherspoon thought about it for a moment. "I think so, but then again, it's difficult to say."

"Why is that, sir?"

"Well, I'm fairly certain he told us one lie today," he replied. He told her about Parks's claim that he thought he heard someone mention Hinchley's presence in the audience. "But we know that Parks had actually seen the man out front. So I'm wondering why he'd bother to lie over a trifle like that? I mean, if he was going to lie, why not tell us that he didn't know Hinchley was in the theatre at all?" It was most puzzling for the inspector. He hoped his housekeeper might have an idea about it.

"Does he have an alibi, sir?" she asked.

Disappointed, Witherspoon sighed and pushed his glasses back up his nose. "Not exactly. He claims to have gone home right after the performance to make some notes on changes he wanted in the first act. But when Constable Barnes asked to see them, he said he couldn't find them. I find that odd too, but not as odd as that silly lie." Really, didn't Mrs. Jeffries have any thoughts on the matter?

"I see," Mrs. Jeffries replied.

The inspector stared at her. "Don't you find Parks's behaviour odd?" he finally asked.

"I do, sir," she said calmly and then went back to sipping her sherry.

"Well, don't you have any thoughts on the matter?" he asked.

Mrs. Jeffries shrugged. "It seems to me, sir, that he wasn't really lying. He never said he didn't know that Hinchley was out front; he merely didn't mention that he'd seen the man. It could well be that in his own mind, there was no need for him to tell you the circumstances of how he came by the information." She could tell this point niggled the inspector, but she honestly didn't see how it could matter. "Did you see Miss Vaughan today?"

"Not exactly," he replied. "I think sending my regrets to her invitation might have offended her. She sent a note along to the theatre today saying she was indisposed."

"Excuse me, sir," Mrs. Jeffries said. "But that doesn't mean you're not going to question her again, does it?"

"Oh, no." He laughed. "Of course not. I'm a policeman, Mrs. Jeffries. I must question her again. However, I do believe that it can wait until tomorrow. I know that she left the theatre right after the play ended on Saturday evening."

He went on to tell her everything. Mrs. Jeffries listened calmly, asking questions where appropriate, clucking her tongue sympathetically and generally learning every little detail of his day. One never knew what might or might not be important.

An hour later, with dinner over and the inspector firmly ensconced in his room writing a letter to Lady Cannonberry, Mrs. Jeffries hurried down the kitchen steps.

Luty Belle and Hatchet had just arrived, Mrs. Goodge was putting the teapot on the table and Fred was jumping about, wagging his tail and generally making a nuisance of himself.

"Good, we're all 'ere, then," Smythe said. He was already seated at the table.

"Give us a minute," Betsy said as she shoved the last of the dinner plates into the cupboard. "Some of us have work to finish."

Luty, frowning thoughtfully as she watched Betsy and Mrs. Goodge bustling about the kitchen tidying up, said, "maybe I ought to send Effie over to help out when we're on a case."

"There's no need for that," Wiggins said quickly. The thought of Effie, one of Luty's homelier maids, hanging about Upper Edmonton Gardens, sent cold chills down the footman's spine. Effie was a maid whom Luty had taken in because the girl had lost her position when they were investigating an earlier case. She was sweet on the footman. Wiggins hated to hurt Effie's feelings and he was afraid that if she were here, dogging his footsteps and watching him like a lovesick calf, he just might have a slip of the tongue.

"We'd never get away with it," Betsy agreed breathlessly as she dropped into the chair next to Smythe. "The inspector would notice if there was a new maid about the place. But it's right nice of you to offer." She smiled at Luty.

"You look right ragged, girl." Luty shook her head as she took in the maid's disheveled appearance. Stray locks of hair had slipped out of Betsy's topknot, her apron was wrinkled and there was a tight, worried set to the girl's face.

"I'm just a bit rushed today," Betsy explained quickly. She could feel

Smythe boring a hole in the side of her head with his steely stare. The man was overprotective enough as it was; she didn't want him nagging at her to take things easy. "I was late getting back, that's all."

"But Luty does have a point," Mrs. Jeffries said thoughtfully. "The rest of us can put many of our tasks to one side when we're on a case, especially in the summer months. But you and Mrs. Goodge can't. It doesn't seem right."

"We 'aven't been 'elpin' enough," Smythe said softly. "You'll run yourself sick if you're not careful. From now on, I'll nip in early and 'elp Mrs. Goodge with the supper things."

"You will not," Betsy exclaimed. "How would we explain you washing up or setting the table if the inspector came down to get Fred for a walk?"

"But Mrs. Jeffries is right," Smythe protested. "I can put off a lot of my duties and so can Wiggins."

"I wouldn't say that," Wiggins interrupted. "I've still got to see to things about the place."

"Why don't we discuss this at another time?" Mrs. Jeffries interrupted. "It's getting late. We've a lot to cover tonight. Who would like to go first?"

"I believe you ought to speak," Hatchet said. "It is vitally important that we know what the inspector has learned."

Mrs. Jeffries sighed silently as she scanned the faces at the table. They were still skittish and afraid that the inspector was going to solve this case before they could. "As you wish." She spent the next fifteen minutes telling them what she'd gotten out of Witherspoon. They all listened carefully. Even Wiggins paid attention. "That's it, then. He's going to try to talk to the rest of them tomorrow. Who'd like to go next?"

"I 'ad a bit of luck today," Wiggins volunteered. "I managed to meet Theodora Vaughan's maid. I was actually right clever, got 'er to come out with me and 'ave tea. Her name's Rose, and a right nice girl she is too."

"Get on with it, Wiggins," Mrs. Goodge ordered.

"You can sing this girl's praises some other time. But right now, tell us what you learned."

Wiggins, annoyed that he wasn't going to have the chance to brag about his cleverness, frowned but did as he was told. He started at the beginning, and, as Mrs. Jeffries had taught him, mentioned every single detail of the meeting.

"But I really struck gold when we was 'avin' tea," he said. "That's when I found out about Miss Vaughan and Mr. Remington. They're not divorced."

"Divorced?" Mrs. Jeffries repeated. "You mean they're married?"

"Didn't I just say they was?" Wiggins replied and frowned thoughtfully. "Sorry, I meant to. They've been married for years. They was supposed to have gotten a divorce a couple of years back when they was tourin' in America. But they didn't. There was some kind of a legal cock-up and they're still married. But everyone in London thinks they got the divorce, ya see. For the past year, Miss Vaughan's had her solicitor tryin' to sort it out, but he can't. But that's not the important bit. The reason Miss Vaughan's been tryin' to get it all sorted out is because she's in love with Mr. Delaney. They've been together for almost a year. She wants to marry 'im, but she can't 'cause she's still married to Mr. Remington. Rose told me that Miss Vaughan is desperate to make sure no one finds out she ain't divorced from Mr. Remington."

"Because she's living in sin with Mr. Delaney?" Mrs. Goodge asked, her face set in disapproval.

"She's not livin' with 'im," Wiggins replied. "But he's round at 'er 'ouse all the time."

"What else did Rose tell you?" Betsy asked.

"She didn't say much more than that," he admitted.

"She sort of dried up. I don't think she meant to tell me as much as she did."

"That's very interesting, Wiggins," Mrs. Jeffries said thoughtfully. "Did you manage to find out if Rose could vouch for Miss Vaughan's alibi?"

He shook his head. "All Rose said when I brought it up was that she'd slept like the dead on Saturday night."

"That's too bad." Luty drummed her fingers on the table. "Seems to me if we can't find out what everyone was up to that night, we'll never solve this case."

"We'll solve it," Mrs. Jeffries said firmly. She glanced at Mrs Goodge. "Were any of your sources helpful today?"

Mrs. Goodge made a face. "Not really. The best I could do was a bit of information on Albert Parks and it weren't much. Seems he got run off from a theatre in Manchester because there was some that thought he had sticky fingers. The receipts kept disappearing when he was in charge. But it was a long time ago, and from what I could learn, that bit of indiscretion doesn't have anything to do with Hinchley's murder."

Mrs. Jeffries wasn't so certain. But she wasn't sure she ought to ask the cook to investigate it further. She debated the matter to herself. The whole lot of them were already second-guessing their every move. It wouldn't do to imply they weren't doing the best they could. But on the other hand, on many of their other cases, things from the suspects' past had been very important.

"Excellent, Mrs. Goodge." she smiled brightly. "Do keep on digging. Your contributions are always so very helpful. But you know, it might be useful to find out a bit more about Parks's past," she ventured, watching the cook's face to see if she was offended.

"You might be right." Mrs. Goodge nodded eagerly.

"You never know when something from someone's past turns out to be the clue that we need. We've proved that more than once. I've got people coming by tomorrow. I should find out more then and I'll get my sources diggin' up more on who was about when Parks got run off from Manchester."

Hatchet cleared his throat. "If no one has any objection, I believe I'd like to speak next. As you all know, I've a number of connections in the theatrical world." Luty snorted faintly, but he ignored her. "And I must say, I do think I've learned something quite important today." He stopped, picked up his tea and took a sip.

"Are you goin' to tell us or do we have to guess?" Luty snapped.

"Do be patient, madam." He put the cup down. "I found out that Edmund Delaney and Ogden Hinchley aren't merely professional acquaintances. They were once very good friends. Up until about a year ago, Delaney actually lived in a small house in Chelsea that Hinchley owned. The gossip was that he was paying little or no rent on the place. The two men had gone to Italy together. Hinchley was paying, of course. Delaney hasn't any money. All of a sudden, Delaney shows back up in England, packs up his stuff and moves out of the house in Chelsea."

"I wonder what happened?" Mrs. Jeffries murmured. Hatchet coughed. "I believe, madam, that it was a woman who caused the breach in the friendship. It was shortly after Delaney returned that he was seen squiring Miss Vaughan about. The gossip about them is equally interesting. It's being said that Miss Vaughan has provided Mr. Delaney with financial support since his return from the continent."

There was a shocked silence. Wiggins's eyes were boggling, Mrs. Goodge was shaking her head in disapproval and even Smythe looked disgusted.

"Why's everyone so quiet?" Betsy asked.

"Because it's awful," Smythe said. "From what Hatchet's sayin', Edmund Delaney's a kept man."

"So?" Betsy persisted. "None of you would be shocked if it was the other way around."

"We're not shocked," Mrs. Goodge declared. "Just disgusted. A kept man, indeed. What's the world coming to?"

"Did you learn anything else?" Mrs. Jeffries asked. "Not that what you've told us isn't enough," she amended hastily. "It's excellent . . ."

Hatchet laughed. "I didn't take offense. I'll keep at it, of course, and see what else I can find out."

"Is it my turn yet?" Luty demanded.

The housekeeper tried to hide a smile behind her teacup. Luty and Hatchet were arch rivals when it came to ferreting out clues. "Please, Luty, go right ahead."

Luty sat up straighter in her chair. "Well, I didn't have much luck findin' out who's goin' to get Hinchley's estate; Stampton wasn't available. But I'll hunt him down yet. I did find out that Willard Swinton's in hock up to his neck over that theatre."

"He's got it mortgaged?" Smythe said.

"To the hilt." Luty grinned. "And that ain't the best part. Guess who's holdin' the bulk of the note?"

"That's easy, madam," Hatchet said smoothly. "It's obviously Ogden Hinchley."

Luty glared at him. "Was you eavesdroppin' on me?"

"One wouldn't have to eavesdrop to guess that particular point of information. You were so pleased with yourself it had to be Hinchley."

"Humph."

Mrs. Jeffries decided to intervene before this got out of hand. Honestly, between worrying about keeping their confidence up and worrying about their competitiveness on gathering information, it was a wonder her wits still worked at all. "That's very interesting, Luty," she said hastily.

"And that ain't all. Supposedly, Swinton got the mortgage from some sort of middleman, he didn't have any idea until recently that it was Hinchley who held the note. My source told me that when he found out, he was so mad, he almost had a conniption fit."

"When did he find out?" Betsy asked.

"That's the best part." Luty's eyes twinkled. "Swinton found out on Saturday, the day Hinchley came back from America."

"How did he find out?" Mrs. Jeffries asked.

"From the middleman. He'd come around to the theatre late Saturday afternoon to collect his payment, and somehow he let it slip that Hinchley held the note on the place."

"That's most intriguing," Mrs. Jeffries murmured.

"Especially if he was angry."

"Yeah," Luty agreed, "but was he mad enough to kill Hinchley? That's the question. 'Cause even with Hinchley dead, his estate would still have the note on the Hayden."

"But Hinchley wouldn't benefit from it," Hatchet said.

"It's too bad you haven't been able to ascertain who does benefit from Hinchley's estate." He smiled smugly at his employer.

"Don't you worry about that, Hatchet," Luty said confidently. "By tomorrow night, I oughta know."

"Good. We mustn't close our minds to all the possiblities in this case." Mrs. Jeffries looked at the only two who hadn't spoken yet. "Who'd like to go next?"

"I will," Betsy said. She wanted to get it over with. Slowly, she told them about her meeting with Hinchley's maid. By the time she'd finished, she knew her cheeks were flaming and she was practically cross-eyed from staring at the same spot on the table.

Mrs. Jeffries deliberately kept her voice matter-of-fact. "So according to Lilly, Hinchley's habit when he reviewed a new play never varied."

"That's what she said."

"If the side door was unlocked," Luty put in, "anyone could have come in and killed him."

"But how would they know the door was unlocked?" Mrs. Goodge asked.

"Betsy found out easy enough," Wiggins said. "Sounds to me like this Lilly told anyone who'd stand still for a few seconds anything they wanted to know."

"Meaning that if someone wanted to find out about Hinchley's habits, they wouldn't have to work very hard at it," Mrs. Jeffries agreed.

"I think lots of people knew about his . . . er . . . habits," Betsy said. "From the way Lilly spoke, he'd been carrying on like this a good while."

"For the last year," Smythe said.

Mrs. Jeffries looked at him sharply. "What did you find out?"

"I tracked down that cabbie that took him to the Hayden," he grimaced. "You were right. Hinchley did make a stop."

"Where?"

"At a house on Lisle Street."

"Who lives there?" Wiggins asked.

"No one really *lives* there." Smythe stumbled over the words. Cor blimey, saying it out loud in front of a roomful of decent women wasn't going to be easy. "It's more like people work there, if you get my meanin'"

"A workhouse?" Betsy muttered. "On Lisle Street?"

Smythe cleared his throat. Blast, he was going to have to explain it. "It's not a workhouse."

"Then what in tarnation is it?" Luty demanded.

"I believe," Hatchet said, "that Smythe is referring to a brothel."

Luty's head jerked sharply as she looked at her butler.

"How the dickens do you know that?"

"Really, madam." Hatchet clucked his tongue. "You ought to be ashamed of yourself for the ideas that are popping into your head. Surely you know me better than that? At my age and with my experience of life, there's little about London that I don't know—and certainly not because I'm a frequenter of such places. Now, if I may continue. If Smythe is referring to the place I think he is, then it's one that caters to anyone with . . . shall we say, unusual tastes."

"Unusual tastes, huh," Luty said, shaking her head. "Well, what of it? He isn't the first man to do it and I expect he won't be the last."

"'Inchley didn't stay inside long, at least not long enough to do . . ." Smythe broke off. There were simply no words to say what he needed to say.

"Maybe it don't take him long," Luty muttered.

Wiggins looked confused and Mrs. Jeffries deliberately kept her expression blank but the others couldn't help themselves. Betsy giggled. Mrs. Goodge snickered. Even Hatchet cracked a grin.

"He didn't stay long enough to patronize the establishment at that particular time," Mrs. Jeffries suggested quickly. "Is that what you're trying to tell us?"

Smythe nodded. "But since he didn't do anything, why'd he stop?"

Luty opened her mouth but Hatchet, fearing his mistress wouldn't bother to mince her words, spoke before she could. "Perhaps he stopped to make arrangements for later?"

"The side door," Betsy murmured. "That's it. That's why he stopped at that . . . place. He was buying someone for later. For after he wrote his review."

"Cor blimey, that's probably who killed 'im." Smythe shook his head. "This case doesn't 'ave a ruddy thing to do with the Hayden Theatre."

"I don't think so," Mrs. Jeffries said.

"Why not?" Luty demanded. "Maybe they got in an argument over the money. Maybe Hinchley didn't want to pay what he'd promised."

"Hinchley would have taken care of the business end of things when he stopped to make the arrangements," Hatchet said.

"I agree," Mrs. Jeffries said. "Besides, professional . . . uh . . ."

"Prostitutes," Luty supplied blandly.

"Right, prostitutes," Mrs. Jeffries continued, "don't generally make it a habit to murder their customers. From what Betsy has told us, Hinchley indulged in this behaviour quite often. I don't think it was a prostitute who murdered the man.'

"Neither do I," Mrs. Goodge said. "I don't think this killing was done by some poor soul who was sellin' Hinchley his body. Seems to me if that were the case and they'd killed someone, they wouldn't bother wasting time getting the man dressed, dragging him to a canal and making it look like an accident. Seems to me, if it was someone like that, they'd have cleaned him out good and scarpered for the coast."

"Precisely my thoughts," Mrs. Jeffries said. She looked at Smythe. "We've got to talk to someone at that brothel before the police do."

Smythe glanced at Betsy, who was resolutely looking past his shoulder at the far wall. "Uh, you want me to do it?" he asked. "Go back to that place?"

"Well, we could send Wiggins," Mrs. Jeffries suggested dryly, knowing precisely how the overprotective coachman would react.

Wiggins shot up from his seat. "Really?"

"Down, lad." Smythe laid a restraining hand on his arm. "I'm not lettin' you go wanderin' into a place like that."

"I wouldn't mind," the footman said eagerly. "Not that I want to go to a place like that. But this is right important. You know 'ow devoted I am to solvin' our cases."

"That would hardly be appropriate," Hatchet said quickly. "But perhaps I . . ."

"I'll go," Smythe interrupted bluntly. He shot a quick glance at Betsy

and saw that her eyes were now flashing fire. Blast, he'd have to smooth
her feathers later. But at least the lass cared enough to get good and narked
at him. "No offense meant, Hatchet," he said to the butler, "but you're
not likely to get anyone to loosen their tongues too quickly, and like Mrs.
Jeffries says, we've got to talk to this er . . . person before the police do."

Hatchet's eyebrows rose. "I believe I'm quite good at getting information out of people," he said loftily.

"Yeah, but we need it fast," Luty put in. "And we ain't got time to
come up with a good story for ya. Let's face it, Hatchet. You look too
much like a preacher to get any fallen angels to spill their secrets to you.
Smythe is right; he's the one that ought to go."

Smythe nodded. He did have a way to get folks to loosen their tongues.
His way was quicker and more effective than any story Hatchet could
come up with. He looked around the table. "Someone's got to go there
and it's goin' to 'ave to be me."

The house on Lisle Street was easy enough to find. Smythe paused in front
of the door. From inside, he could hear laughter and the faint sounds of a
piano. He raised his hand to knock, lost his nerve and stepped back into
the shadows of the overhanging eaves. It wasn't that he was scared. He
was thirty-five years old and he'd lived hard in Australia for a good number
of those years. Brothels didn't shock him. But he wasn't going to think
about his past and it wasn't his past that was keeping him from pounding
on the front door.

It was Betsy. Her face. The way she'd watched him as he got ready to
leave, her expression as shut and locked as a bank vault. What had she
been thinking? That he *wanted* to go out to visit a place like this?

Oh, blast it all anyway, he thought, raising his fist and pounding on
the wood. The quicker I get in there, the quicker I can get out.

A heavy-set, middle-aged woman with frizzy red hair and rouged
cheeks stuck her head out. She raked him with a long, appraising glance,
decided he looked like he might have money and asked, "What can I do
for you, big fella?"

"Ya can let me in for a start." He shoved at the door, but she blocked
it with her ample hips.

"This ain't a church," she said. "You got any money?"

In response, he reached into his pocket and pulled out a roll of bills. "Enough."

Her eyes gleamed greedily as she stared at the bundle between his fingers. Her painted mouth split into a welcoming smile. "Then come on in, handsome. We've got anything you want." She took his arm and he had to restrain himself from shaking her off. "And I do mean anything."

Smythe tried not to think about that. She tugged him down a narrow hall and into a large room. The windows were covered with heavy red velvet, the floor with a gaudy Persian rug and the walls were covered with paintings, most of them voluptous nudes. People, some of them well-dressed businessmen with their collars undone and no jackets, were sprawled on various settees and chairs. Women, many of them wearing nothing more than diaphanous wraps, were entertaining their customers. Smythe was torn between pity and revulsion. The women probably had no choice. Hunger and poverty could drive a body to do just about anything to survive. So he refused to sit in judgment on these poor girls, but the men were a different matter altogether. They sickened him. Bloated, wealthy and thinking solely of their own pleasures, they sprawled about the room like little kings. But he tried to keep his feelings from showing on his face. No point in making anyone suspicious.

"See anything you like?" the madam asked. She swept her arm in a great arc. "Have a wander around and take a good look. There's more girls in the other room."

He started to tell her he didn't want a girl, caught himself, nodded and started towards the inner room, the one where he could hear the piano. Women, some of them no more than girls, smiled and preened as he walked past. He made a show of studying the "merchandise" as he went, but he was actually looking for something quite different from womanly charms. He spotted a pale-haired young woman sitting slumped in the corner, almost as though she were trying to hide. Something in her posture and the wary look in her eyes convinced him she hadn't been on the game long.

The madam, who was coming right behind him, saw where he was looking. "That's Janet. She's new here."

"She'll do." He turned to the madam and took care of the business end of things. A few minutes later, another girl, this one a maid, led him up a wide staircase and showed him into a bedroom. "Janet'll be right up," the girl said as she lit the lamp. "You want anything else? There's gin, ale or champagne; I can bring some up."

"Maybe later," he said. If cold hard cash wouldn't loosen Janet's tongue, maybe gin would. But he'd try money first.

He sat down on the bed, wincing as the bed springs creaked dangerously under his weight. The maid went out and Janet, her eyes wide and frightened, came in. "Hello." She forced a smile, put her hands on her painfully thin hips and started towards him.

Blast, Smythe thought, up close she couldn't be more than sixteen. "What's your name?" he asked gently, even though he already knew.

"Janet." She stopped in front of him and her fingers went to the buttons on the top of her pink robe. "And I'm to do whatever you want."

"How old are you?"

She looked surprised by the question. "Nineteen." She undid the top button.

Smythe leapt to his feet and clasped his hands over her fingers. "You don't have to do this," he explained.

"You want me to keep my clothes on?"

"No. I mean, yes," he stuttered. "I mean, I just want to talk to you, lass."

Puzzled, she said, "You just want to chat?"

"Come on, lass, sit down." He eased her down on the bed and sat down beside her. "How long 'ave you been at this?"

She looked down at the floor. "I know what I'm doin', if that's what's worryin' ya."

Smythe sighed. "Look, I'm not worried about your . . . er . . . uh, whatever. I'd just like to talk, that's all."

She eyed him suspiciously. "About what?"

Smythe wondered how best to put it. "Well, I need some information."

"You're not a copper, are ya?"

"No, I promise. I'm willing to pay fer my information," he said quickly. "Pay ya directly, I will. You've no need to be tellin' anyone else."

She thought about if for a moment. "What do ya want to know?" she asked, glancing at the closed door.

"Was ya workin' on Saturday evenin'?"

"I work every evenin'," she sighed. "It's the only way to make a livin'"

"Around seven o'clock, did ya see a man come in?"

She laughed. "Lots of men come in 'ere."

"I mean a well-dressed man, small like and done up in evening clothes," Smythe explained. "He didn't stay long; my guess is 'e 'ad a word or two with the madam and then left."

She frowned slightly. "He's the one that come in for Rupert." She broke off and blushed. "Rupert only does the special one's like. I mean, he's a . . ."

Smythe stopped her by raising his hand. "I think I know what 'e does. Anyways. This man who come, did 'e make arrangements for Rupert to come to 'is 'ouse later that night?"

"That's what Rupert said," Janet shrugged. "Mind you, he were right upset when he found out the whole thing 'ad been called off and 'e weren't to go. He'd been there before, you see, and knew this bloke were a big tipper. Some of the men like to give little presents on the side." She glanced quickly at the closed door again. "I mean, what she don't know won't 'urt 'er, will it? It's not like they pays us all that much."

"So Rupert was told he didn't have to go?" Smythe prodded. "How was 'e told? Did the man come back 'ere?"

"Here, what are you askin' all these questions for?"

Smythe pulled out his roll of notes, thanking his lucky stars he had more money than he'd ever spend. "I said I'm willin' to pay for information," he said, waving the roll under the girl's nose. "And I'm not a copper, so you don't 'ave to watch what ya say."

"How much you willin' to pay?" she asked. She seemed more curious than greedy.

He pulled off three five-pound notes and handed them to her. Her eyes got as big as Mrs. Goodge's scones. It was probably more money than she made in a month. "Here, you tell me what I need to know and I'll double this."

Janet stared at the bills for a moment, almost as though she were afraid to touch them. "All this?"

"Take it, lass," Smythe encouraged. "I know you need it."

Janet grabbed the money, rolled it tightly and stuck it up her sleeve. Then she looked at Smythe and blushed. "Sorry, I didn't mean to act like such a greedy cow, but things 'as been 'ard lately. Me brother's been sick . . ."

"It's all right, lass," he said softly. "I know what it's like to be poor." He wondered if Luty could use another housemaid. "Now go on, answer my question. How did Rupert know that 'e wasn't to go to the man's house?"

"A lad came round with a note," Janet said. "Rupert almost had a go at him. Poncy little fella all tarted up in velvet and silk. Mind you, some of the others was laughin', thinkin' that Rupert 'ad lost out to a street boy, but this weren't no street boy that come 'ere with the note. He was too well fed for that. Not that 'e was fat or anythin'. But he 'ad a nice rounded backside and carried himself all nice like. Made Rupert right angry, it did."

"What time did the lad show up?"

"Right before Rupert was goin' to leave himself, around eleven forty-five. If the boy had been five minutes later, Rupert would 'ave already been gone."

CHAPTER 6

Betsy glared at the clock. What was taking him so long? He'd been gone for hours now and if he didn't come walking through that back door soon, she'd ruddy well go out after him.

She got to her feet and started to pace, thankful that Mrs. Goodge and Mrs. Jeffries had gone to bed, sparing her the need to come up with some feeble excuse as to why she was sitting here in the blooming kitchen in the middle of the night.

She stopped dead as she heard the familiar sound of the back door opening. A second later, heavy footsteps moved in the hallway and a relieved smile curved her lips.

Betsy dashed toward the back stairs. Now that she knew he was home safe, she could go to bed and get some sleep. Worrying about someone certainly was hard on the nerves, she thought as she skipped quietly up the stairs. The only thing worse would be him finding out she'd worried and waited.

"The inspector's just gone," Mrs. Jeffries announced as she dashed into the kitchen the next morning. "He's going to interview Theodora Vaughan, Trevor Remington and Willard Swinton again this morning."

"What about Delaney?" Mrs. Goodge asked. She picked the empty pot off the table. "Seems to me after what that Mr. Parks said, this Delaney fellow needs a bit more looking into."

"I agree," the housekeeper said as she picked up the last of the dirty breakfast plates. "But there really wasn't time to drop any hints in that direction, so we'll have to look into Delaney on our own."

"I'll get my sources working on him," Mrs. Goodge said. "I've got a few of them dropping by this morning."

Betsy, stifling a yawn, trudged into the kitchen. "I've finished up the dry larder," she said.

"Gracious, Betsy," Mrs. Jeffries exclaimed. "Are you all right? You don't look like you slept well."

"I'm fine." Betsy yawned again. "Just a bit tired is all. It was too warm to sleep much last night."

As Mrs. Jeffries knew perfectly well that Betsy had sat up waiting for Smythe until well after two A.M., she decided not to press the subject. "Try and take a rest this afternoon if you can," she advised. "Smythe and Wiggins ought to be here any moment, and then we'll have a brief meeting."

"Aren't we going to wait for Luty and Hatchet?" Mrs. Goodge asked.

"Luty was planning on ambushing one of her legal sources this morning. She's bound and determined to find out who Hinchley left his money to," Mrs. Jeffries explained, "so she wants us to go ahead without her."

"And no doubt Hatchet is so worried she'll get more information than him, he's probably out snooping too," Betsy said with a grin.

Smythe came into the kitchen, followed by Wiggins. "Mornin' all," he said cheerfully. "Sorry we missed breakfast, but we 'ad to take a quick run over to the stables."

"Are you hungry?" Mrs. Goodge asked.

"We 'ad us some buns from the bake shop," Wiggins replied, "but I could do with a cuppa."

"So could I." Smythe dropped into his seat. He still didn't quite have the nerve to look Betsy in the eye, even though he knew he'd not done a ruddy thing to feel guilty about. Cor, it wasn't as if he'd *wanted* to go to that place.

Mrs. Goodge put a fresh pot on the table. "Come on, then," she said, "let's get cracking. My sources'll be here any minute and I want this kitchen to myself."

Wiggins, who'd been trying to teach Fred to roll over, hurried to the table. Mrs. Jeffries quickly took her seat, and Betsy, without so much as a glance in the coachman's direction, sat down in her place.

"Why don't you tell us what you learned," Mrs. Jeffries said to Smythe.

She wanted him to give his report quickly and matter-of-factly. Betsy's nose was already out of joint and it wouldn't do to torment the poor girl needlessly.

Smythe, keeping his voice casual, quickly told them what he'd learned at the brothel. "So you see," he finished, "we're no better off than we were before. We'll probably never find the lad that brung the note around."

"Did you get a look at it?" Mrs. Goodge asked.

Smythe shook his head. "Janet said she'd seen the madam toss it in the stove. No reason for anyone to keep it, was there?"

"But we do know that the, er . . . person who was supposed to go to Hinchley's never went," Mrs. Jeffries said. "Which once again leads us right back to the Hayden Theatre."

"Maybe the lad that brung the note did the killing," Wiggins suggested.

"Don't be daft, boy," Mrs. Goodge said impatiently. "Why would some lad want to kill Hinchley? It's got to be someone from the Hayden. Seems like we've got plenty of people right there to worry about without bringing anyone else into it."

"Yes, indeed," Mrs. Jeffries interjected. "We do have a sufficient number of suspects and more important, Hinchley had only returned from overseas. Whatever other enemies he may have had wouldn't have had time to know he was back, let alone plan his murder. But we should try to find the boy."

"Why?" Betsy asked. "All he did was bring a note."

"Because," Mrs. Jeffries said slowly, "I don't think that note was from Hinchley."

"Then who sent it?" Wiggins asked.

"The murderer." Mrs. Jeffries nodded as she spoke. She was sure of this; she could feel it in her bones. "It was from the murderer."

"How do ya figure that?" Smythe asked softly, his words echoing what the rest of them were thinking. "Couldn't Hinchley 'ave sent it?"

"No. He didn't have time," Mrs. Jeffries replied. "Besides, why would he? According to what Hinchley's maid told Betsy, he was very routine in his behaviour. Nothing we've heard about what he did that night leads me to believe he'd changed his plans. I think the murderer sent that note to the brothel. As a matter of fact, it's the only thing that makes sense."

"But how would the killer know what Hinchley had planned for his evening?" Betsy asked.

"Simple." The housekeeper clasped her hands together. "According to what Smythe said he'd learned from, the, er, young woman at the brothel, Hinchley was a regular customer who always behaved precisely in the same manner. Add that to the information that Betsy got from Hinchley's maid, that his routine never varied and was well known to everyone, and I think we may have found the way our killer managed to commit the crime. The killer knew that Hinchley had gone to the house on Lisle Street because that's what he always did. The killer also knew that the side door would be unlocked and the servants in bed. Therefore, all he had to do was send a note to the brothel telling them that Hinchley had changed his mind and his field was clear. No servants, no locked doors and a bathtub full of water."

Smythe nodded. "So if we can find that boy, 'e'll be able to tell us who gave 'im the note."

"Precisely." Mrs. Jeffries smiled confidently. She hoped she was right. Her interpretation of the facts seemed to be correct, but one part of her was quite worried. What if she was wrong? She straightened her spine, refusing to give in to self-doubt. "So I think your first task," she continued, looking at Wiggins and Smythe, "is to find the lad who brought that note."

"What are the rest of us going to do, then?" Betsy demanded.

"You must forgive me, Inspector," Theodora Vaughan gave Witherspoon a wan smile. "But I was entirely too distraught to see you yesterday. This dreadful business has put a terrible strain on my nerves."

"Of course, Miss Vaughan," the inspector replied. "I quite understand. Do you feel up to answering a few questions today?"

She sighed and clasped one hand to her bosom. In the soft morning sunlight filtering through the gauzy curtains of the sitting room, she looked frail and vulnerable. Dressed in a pale blue-and-mauve day dress, she sat on one end of the settee, a lacy hankerchief clutched in her hand. "One must do one's duty," she said.

Barnes, who thought she had a fair amount of color in her cheeks for someone whose nerves were strained, asked, "Why did you leave the theatre so soon after your performance on Saturday evening?"

She gave him a quick, sharp look. "Who told you that?"

"A number of people mentioned it," the constable replied. "Why? Was it supposed to be a secret?"

"Of course not, Constable," she snapped, then caught herself and gave him a gracious smile. "But I don't like knowing that I'm being gossiped about behind my back."

"It was hardly gossip, Miss Vaughan," the inspector interjected. "We were asking questions, you know. Please don't be angry with any of the stage workers. They were merely doing *their* duty."

"We know you left in a hansom not five minutes after your last curtain call," Barnes continued. "Wasn't that a bit odd, ma'am?"

"Not at all," Theodora replied smoothly. "I was very tired. Opening night is always a bit of a strain. I wanted to get right home."

"Did you take your stage makeup off?" Witherspoon asked. He wasn't sure where this was leading, but the constable's query was well taken.

"No." She smiled brightly. "I should have, of course. But I was so dreadfully tired and frankly, I was afraid if I stayed too long, I'd get caught by someone."

"Caught by someone?" Witherspoon echoed. Whatever did she mean?

She laughed. "I was afraid Trevor or Albert would get their hooks into me. Oh, Inspector, you've no idea how theatre people love discussing the performance. I knew if I went to my dressing room, one of them would come barging in insisting on going over every little detail of the night. Frankly, I just wasn't up to it so I nipped right out as soon as I could."

"I see," Witherspoon said. "Did you happen to notice anything unusual as you left?"

"Unusual?"

"Did you see Mr. Hinchley hanging about backstage?" Barnes asked.

"No. In any case, I wasn't paying much attention. All I wanted to do was go home."

"Did your maid see you come in?" Witherspoon asked.

Theodora smiled benignly. "I'm not a slave driver, Inspector. I don't expect my maid to wait up for me. I imagine she was sound asleep. But do feel free to ask her yourself. Shall I ring for her?"

Witherspoon nodded. Theodora gracefully got up, went to the bell pull by the door and tugged it gently. The maid, who was probably just outside, immediately appeared. "Yes, ma'am," she said, looking at her mistress.

"Rose, these gentlemen would like to ask you a few questions." Theodora gestured at the two policemen.

"The police?" Rose asked, shaking her head in their direction.

"Yes, Rose, and you must answer all their questions." Theodora smiled.

"If you'll excuse me, gentlemen, I really must go and deal with my correspondence." With another beautiful smile, she swept out of the room.

Witherspoon gestured toward the settee. "Do sit down, Miss Rose. We'll not take up too much of your time, I promise."

The maid sat. She didn't look in the least nervous. "Go ahead, then, ask your questions."

"Er, uh, did you happen to notice what time Miss Vaughan came home from the theatre on Saturday evening?"

Rose shook her head. "No, sir. I was dead asleep, I was. Miss Vaughan don't like me to wait up for her."

"Then who helps her . . . uh . . . with her toilette?"

Rose frowned. "Toilette? You mean who helps her get undressed?"

"Yes." The inspector hoped he wasn't blushing. "That's what I mean."

Rose shrugged. "Not me, that's for certain. Miss Vaughan never did like me fussin' over her when she's gettin' dressed. She's right self-sufficient; she can hook up her own buttons and everything. I reckon it comes from back in the days when she was just startin' out. Actresses in the theatre have got to be able to change and undo themselves quickly. Mind you, she's got a proper dresser at the theatre now, but she didn't always have."

Witherspoon was no expert on female articles of clothing, but he did know that undoing a fancy evening dress—or for that matter, most day dresses—was a time-consuming and complicated matter. Gracious, that's one of the main reasons ladies of a certain station had maids. "So, you're not in the habit of waiting up and helping her . . . er . . . disrobe."

"Sometimes I do." Rose shrugged. "But mostly, considering the late hours she keeps, I go on to bed. Now I do her hair for her." She smiled proudly. "That's why she hired me on; I've a deft hand with hair. And I take care of her clothes and all, see that they're laundered proper and hung just so in the cupboards."

"I see," the inspector tried to think of something else to ask. If the girl couldn't help confirm the time Theodora Vaughan had arrived back from the theatre, there wasn't any point in questioning her further. The maid wasn't likely to be acquainted with Ogden Hinchley. But perhaps he ought to ask anyway. "Were you acquainted with Mr. Hinchley?"

Rose nodded eagerly. "Not really acquainted, sir. But I knew who he was. Everybody in the theatre did. Most hated him too."

"Was Miss Vaughan closely acquainted with him?" Barnes asked softly.

"She knew him. Actually"—Rose glanced at the closed door—"I think she was relieved when he went off to America. They all like to pretend he wasn't worth fretting over, but the truth is, he had ever so much power."

Witherspoon looked at her sharply. "What do you mean by that?"

"Just what I said," Rose replied stubbornly. "They was all scared of him. Mr. Remington, Mr. Parks and even that toff of a theatre owner. They was all round here a few days before Hinchlely left for America. I was bringin' in the tea and I couldn't help overhearin' what they was saying. Mr. Parks was going on and on about how he hoped one of them gunslingers blew Mr. Hinchley's brains out—"

"Excuse me," Witherspoon interrupted. "I thought Hinchley had gone to New York?"

"He did." Rose grinned. "I forgot to mention that they'd had several bottles of wine before I brought in the tea. Mr. Parks was drunk. But he was dead serious. He hated Hinchley."

"And the others who were there that day, what were they saying?" the inspector pressed. He wasn't certain this conversation had any connection whatsoever to this case, but one never knew. The girl seemed to be quite bright and obviously had a good memory.

Warming to her tale, Rose plunged straight ahead. "Well, Mr. Delaney was trying to be casual like and pretend it didn't matter to him, but he was so excited that Hinchley would be gone when his play opened he all but danced. Mr. Remington"—Rose smiled broadly—"didn't make any bones about it, said Hinchley had single-handedly tried to ruin his career and he hoped the blighter never came back."

"Why were they here?" Witherspoon asked. "This must have been several months ago. Hinchley left for New York the first week in June."

Rose looked surprised by the question. "They was here about Mr. Delaney's play."

"Oh." Witherspoon nodded wisely. "Yes, yes, I see. Doing the casting and that sort of thing."

"No, sir," Rose contradicted. "They didn't do that till the middle of July. They was drawing up the agreements, sir."

Puzzled, the inspector stared at her. "Agreements?"

"Yes, sir. Agreements. The royalties and such off the house take on receipts."

"I would have thought that would have been between Mr. Delaney and Mr. Swinton," Witherspoon said slowly.

"Mr. Swinton was here that night too," Rose agreed. "But they was all involved in the money end of it, sir. I mean, the business side of things."

"I'm afraid I don't quite understand what you mean," Witherspoon said.

"What don't you understand, sir? Mr. Parks has a share in the play and Mr. Remington's got a bit, but their shares aren't very big. Of course, Mr. Swinton'll get a share of the receipts because it's his theatre."

Witherspoon scratched his chin. "Are you saying they all put their own money into this play?"

"Yes, sir." Rose smiled broadly.

"Is that a usual practise?" Barnes asked.

"I wouldn't rightly know, sir." Rose flicked a piece of lint off the arm of the chair. "But I do know one thing for certain. If Miss Vaughan and the others hadn't ponied up the cash, Mr. Delaney wouldn't ever have had that play of his produced."

Trevor Remington had taken rooms in a three-story townhouse on Farley Street, not far from the theatre. The house was quite well kept; one could almost say it was opulent. The front walkway was lined by flowering shrubs, the stairs were freshly painted white and the brass lamp and door knocker glittered brightly in the sunlight.

"Do you think the maid knew what she was talking about?" Barnes asked the inspector as they reached the front door.

Witherspoon thought about it for a moment. "I don't think she was lying. She'd have no reason to. But I do think it might be possible she was mistaken, confused perhaps, about what she'd really heard that day. It was over three months ago." He banged the knocker against the wood. "On the other hand, she seemed quite certain."

"I thought so too," Barnes said quickly as the door opened.

"Yes? May I help you?" A round, dark-haired woman wearing a brown bombazine dress stared at them.

"Good morning." He smiled brightly. "I'm Inspector Witherspoon and this is Constable Barnes. We'd like to see Mr. Remington if we may."

She held the door open wider and stepped back. "Of course; please come in. I'm not sure that Mr. Remington is awake yet, so if you'll go into the drawing room, I'll let him know you're here."

She nodded toward an open door down the hall and then started for the flight of stairs.

"Excuse me." Witherspoon stopped her. "But are you the landlady?"

She turned and nodded. "Mrs. McGraw. I own this house."

"Do you mind if we ask you a few questions?"

"Is it about Hinchley's murder?" she asked eagerly.

Taken aback, Witherspoon could only nod. Gracious, the woman seemed keen to talk to the police. How very refreshing. "Yes, I'm afraid it is. Did you know Mr. Hinchley?"

She laughed. "I know everyone, Inspector. I've been renting rooms to theatre people for forty years. Some of the best in the business have stayed in this house. Pinero, Irving, Ellen Terry—they've all been my guests at one time or another."

Witherspoon was rather embarrassed that the names meant nothing to him. Mrs. McGraw did seem rather proud of them. "Yes, of course. Uh, have you ever met Mr. Hinchley?"

"He's never stayed here." She grinned. "He wouldn't have to. He's rich as sin, that one."

"Yes, so I understand." Witherspoon racked his brain to come up with another question. "Mr. Remington, uh . . . he says you were asleep when he came home on Saturday evening . . ."

"Don't be ridiculous," Mrs. McGraw replied. "Of course I wasn't asleep. I'd gone to the Hayden to see the play."

"You did?"

"Naturally. I always go and see every new play," Mrs. McGraw explained. "These people make my living for me; it's the least I can do. Besides, I adore the theatre. That's the main reason I decided to let rooms to actors. Such an interesting lot, aren't they?"

"Er, yes," Witherspoon replied.

"What time did you get home that night, Mrs. McGraw?" Barnes asked.

"Well . . ." She thought about it for a moment. "Let's see. I stopped outside the theatre and had a bit of a chat with Maisie Duncan, but we didn't talk for more than five minutes. So, by the time I flagged a hansom and got here, it must have been close to eleven-thirty."

"Did you hear Mr. Remington come in later that evening?"

"No," Mrs. McGraw's mouth flattened into a thin line. "I didn't and

I was bit annoyed. My tenants know I like to be in bed by a reasonable hour. I'm quite tolerant, but there are limits. When he wasn't here by half past twelve, I woke the tweeny and told her to listen for him."

"You hadn't given Mr. Remington his own key?" Witherspoon asked.

"Certainly not," she replied. "I don't give any of them a key, Inspector."

Barnes and Witherspoon exchanged glances. Then the Inspector asked, "May we speak to the tweeny?"

Mrs. McGraw stared at them in a surprise for a moment, then turned on her heel and marched down the hall toward the back of the house. "Just a moment. I'll get her." She gestured toward an open door as she went. "Go on into the drawing room and make yourselves comfortable."

"Remington lied to us," Barnes said softly as they went into the drawing room.

"Indeed he did." Witherspoon stopped just inside, took one look at the elegant furniture and furnishings and understood why Mrs. McGraw didn't hand out keys to her tenants. "And I'm wondering why. Remington doesn't strike me as a stupid man. Surely he realized we'd check."

"You wanted to see me, sir?"

Witherspoon whirled around to see a young blonde girl wearing a maid's uniform standing in the open doorway. He introduced himself and the constable.

"I'm Elsa Chambers," the maid said. "Mrs. McGraw said you needed to ask me some questions."

"I understand you waited up on Saturday evening to let Mr. Remington in?" Witherspoon said.

"Yes, sir." Elsa replied. "I mean I let him in, but I was dozing off a bit in the chair in the hall."

"Did you notice what time it was that he came in?"

"Oh, I did, sir," Elsa said eagerly. "I mean, I didn't see the time so much as hear it." She pointed to a huge grandfather clock by the drawing room door. "The clock had just chimed three when he come home."

"How did he look?"

Elsa stared at them blankly. "Look, sir?"

Witherspoon smiled at her. "I'm sorry. I didn't phrase that correctly. I meant to ask was there anything unusual about him when he came home?"

Her thin face creased in concentration. "Well, I was sleepy sir, but Mr. Remington seemed the same as usual to me."

"Did he say anything to you?" Witherspoon asked.

"Just said hello and apologized for keeping me up so late."

"He didn't mention where he'd been?" Barnes pressed.

She shook her head. "Not to me. Just gave me his coat and hat and went on upstairs to his rooms."

Witherspoon tried to think of another pertinent question but couldn't. "Thank you, Elsa. We appreciate your help."

She dropped a quick curtsy, smiled and turned to leave. "Oh, excuse me, sir, I didn't see you come in," she gushed, stumbling backwards to keep from ploughing into Trevor Remington.

"It's quite all right, Elsa," Remington said, but he wasn't looking at the maid. His attention was on the policemen. She bobbed another curtsy and dashed out.

Remington said nothing for a moment. Then he sighed loudly, ran his hands through his hair and dropped onto a large ottoman at the foot of the settee. "I know what you must be thinking. But I assure you, Inspector, though I may have lied about coming straight home, I had nothing to do with Ogden Hinchley's murder."

"Where were you on Saturday evening?" Witherspoon asked. "You didn't come home right after the performance. Both Mrs. McGraw and Elsa have told us that."

Remington dropped his head into his hands. Finally, he looked up. "Would you believe me if I told you I went for a walk?"

"You went for a walk? Where?" Barnes asked.

"I walked along the embankment for a good while, then I went over to Theodora's. But I didn't go inside."

"The embankment?" Barnes repeated. "You mean you walked along the river?"

Remington nodded.

"Till three in the morning?" the constable persisted. As Delaney claimed he'd been walking along the river that night too, Barnes was beginning to think it must have been getting blooming crowded.

"No, of course not," Remington said. "I'm not a fool, Constable. With that awful murder over in Whitechapel, I realized it would be foolish to stay out there too long. But there were a few people about, and I saw a policeman or two."

"Did they see you, sir?" Barnes interrupted. That would be easy to check, and Remington, with his actor's looks and graceful carriage, would be easy to remember.

He shrugged. "I assume so. I wasn't trying to hide. But as I was saying, I walked along the embankment for a while, until it began to get quite late, and then I went over to Theodora's. But her lights were all out and I thought she'd probably gone to bed so I didn't knock or anything. I was still quite upset. Despite what the others may have told you, I don't think the play's going to be much of a success." He closed his eyes for a moment. "Add that to my seeing Hinchley in the audience and I knew I couldn't possibly get to sleep."

"So what did you do?" the inspector asked.

"By this time it was fairly late and I realized that it was foolish to be wandering around alone that time of night. I tried to find a hansom but I couldn't. I finally walked back towards the Strand and caught one close to the theatre."

"What time was this, sir?" Barnes persisted.

"About two forty-five or so." Remington flung out his hands. "I don't know. I was upset and to be perfectly honest, very alarmed. The play wasn't perfect, but if we got lucky and had a decent review or two, we might be able to keep the house filled and turn a profit."

"And that was important, wasn't it?" Witherspoon said softly. "Your own money's invested in the play."

Remington's eyes widened. "So you know that, do you? Well, it was bound to come out."

"How much did you invest, sir?" the inspector had no idea whether it was important or not, but he thought it might be.

"Invest?" Remington laughed. "It wasn't exactly an investment. I put a thousand pounds of my own money into this play. It was the only way they'd give me the lead."

Witherspoon stared at him. "I see."

"Do you?" Remington sighed deeply. "I doubt it, Inspector. But suffice to say, I wanted to play that part. Wanted it badly enough to be hood-winked into putting up a good portion of the production costs myself."

"Why did you lie to us?" Witherspoon asked. "Surely you must have realized we'd try to verify your statement."

"Because I was frightened you'd think I killed Hinchley if I told you the truth. I had no alibi and I hated him. Everyone knew I hated him. I'm sorry, Inspector, I wasn't trying to do anything but give myself some time."

"You knew Hinchley was in the audience that night, didn't you?" Barnes said.

Remington nodded. "Yes. I'd peeked out the side curtain and saw him take his seat. It was quite a shock. Here I'd thought I was safe from him and that wicked pen of his. When I looked out and saw him there, I almost fainted. I was so rattled I almost forgot my lines in the first act."

"Why did you hate him so much, sir?" Barnes asked.

"Hate isn't exactly the right word," Remington mused.

"Actually, I feared him more than anything else."

"But why?" Witherspoon pressed. "Surely as an actor you're used to coping with critics."

"Ah, but he wasn't just a critic." Remington laughed harshly. "He was a monster. One bad performance and you were marked for life."

Witherspoon frowned slightly. "I'm afraid I don't understand."

"Hinchley, odious as he was, was very influential with other critics, Inspector." Remington shrugged. "I don't know why, but he was. If you got a bad review from him, you could be bloody sure that the other critics, mindless sheep that they are, wouldn't give you a decent one either. Hinchley never forgot a performance or an actor. I had the misfortune of playing in a rather shoddy production out in the provinces a while back. It was right after I'd come back from a tour of America." He laughed derisively. "I only took the role to do a favor for a friend. But Hinchley came to one of our performances. I wasn't feeling well that night, but I did the best I could. Hinchley pilloried me the next day in the local newspaper. I didn't mind that; I knew I hadn't done my best. What I hated was the fact that no matter what I did after that, he never saw it."

"Was he like that with everyone?" Witherspoon asked.

Remington shrugged. "More or less. Ogden Hinchley was a very strange man. I admit I hated him, but I didn't kill him."

Witherspoon thought Remington's voice had the unmistakable ring of truth to it, but then he reminded himself that this man was an actor. Maybe a much better actor than Ogden Hinchley had ever thought. "Would you say that a bad review from Hinchley would have the power to close a production?"

"Perhaps." Remington got up and walked toward the fireplace. "Perhaps not. I do know that he had enough power to almost ruin my career, Inspector. Why do you think I was so desperate for a lead part that I was willing to put up my own money for the chance at it? My career had virtually come to a stop since Hinchley pilloried me."

"Could you give us a guess on that question, sir?" Barnes pressed. "Not that I'm doubtin' you, sir. But it's one thing to ruin an actor, and quite another to close down a play."

Remington hesitated. "Well, all right, I suppose he could. As I said a moment ago, he'd a lot of influence."

"I think I understand," Witherspoon said slowly. "So if Hinchley was in the theatre on Saturday evening, you were fairly certain he was there for the sole purpose of reviewing the play?"

"Why else would he have come?" Remington asked. "He certainly wasn't there to provide moral support for his old protégé."

"Protégé?" Barnes said. "And who would that be?"

Remington's mouth curved into a mirthless smile. "Edmund Delaney. He and Ogden were once good friends. Very good friends."

Witherspoon wasn't sure he completely understood what Remington was getting at. But he was the second person to mention animosity between Delaney and Hinchley. "So you don't think Hinchley might have come to the theatre just to see his old friend's play?"

"Hardly." Remington laughed nastily. "Ogden Hinchley hated Edmund. What's more, he hated everyone else involved in that production. Why do you think I was so depressed when I realized he was back in London? Hinchley was there for one purpose and one purpose only: to ruin us."

"Mr. Remington," Witherspoon said quietly, "You said you invested a thousand pounds. That's quite a bit of money."

A strangled, high-pitched hysterical sound that might have been a laugh came out of the actor's mouth. "I know how much it is, Inspector. It's virtually every penny I had in the world."

CHAPTER 7

"It's so good to see you, Mollie," Mrs. Goodge said. She forced herself to smile at the prune-faced woman sitting like the Queen of Sheba at the head of the table. Mollie Dubay wasn't really a friend. But Mrs. Goodge thought she might be useful. The tall, gray haired woman was the house-keeper to Lord Fremont and she never for one blooming moment let you forget it.

Mrs. Goodge wouldn't even have bothered contacting the stuck-up old thing, but she was worried about making a mistake in this investigation. She'd put her pride to one side and sent Mollie an invitation to tea. Mollie might be a housekeeper for a peer of the realm now, but Mrs. Goodge could remember the days when she was scrubbing out stalls at the Lyceum Theatre.

Mollie was also the worst gossip on three continents and even better, she never forgot a face, a name or a bit of dirt.

"I was ever so pleased you decided to accept my invitation."

Mollie smiled faintly and brushed an imaginary crumb off the sleeve of her severe black bombazine dress. "Lord and Lady Fremont are in France at the moment. He's on a most delicate diplomatic mission for Her Majesty, so I'm not pressed for time. Normally, of course, I've such a large household to attend to I don't dare even take my day out." She glanced around the kitchen, her gaze sharp and calculating as she scanned the large, cozy room.

"Well," Mrs. Goodge said chattily, "then I'm very pleased Lord and Lady Fremont are gone."

"Is that Wedgwood?" Mollie jerked her chin toward the pale blue-and-white china on the dresser.

"Yes," Mrs. Goodge replied, stretching the truth a bit. One of the pieces was a Wedgwood.

Mollie's heavy eyebrows drew together in disapproval. "Really, don't you think good china ought to be locked in the china room? You do have one, don't you?"

"Of course," Mrs. Goodge replied smoothly. She was fairly sure that Mrs. Jeffries hadn't the faintest idea where the key to the china room was. As a matter of fact, the last time the cook had glanced in the tiny room off the housekeeper's bedroom, the only thing in there had been some old suitcases and other odds and ends.

"Then I don't know what can your housekeeper can be thinking, leaving it out here where it could be so easily broken."

"Mrs. Jeffries thinks that beautiful things ought to be used, not locked up."

"One must maintain proper standards." Mollie sniffed. "But perhaps this household isn't very strict. Not at all like Lord Fremont. We do things absolutely correctly in his house."

Mrs. Goodge clamped her lips together to keep from saying something rude. She took a deep breath and promised herself she wouldn't lose her temper. At least not until she got what she wanted. "Inspector Witherspoon lives quite simply, considering, of course, how very wealthy he is." She smiled in satisfaction as she saw Mollie's eyes widen.

Mollie recovered quickly. "Really? I hadn't realized Scotland Yard policemen were so well paid."

"They're not." Mrs. Goodge was careful to speak properly. "But then again, he doesn't really need his wages. Inherited wealth, you know. He only stays with Scotland Yard because he's such a brilliant detective. Why, I don't know what they'd do without him. Perhaps you've read of some of his cases in the papers."

"Murders? Hardly." Mollie stuck her chin in the air. "I've no interest in reading about such horrid things."

Mrs. Goodge decided she'd had enough of tweaking Mollie's nose. She didn't want the woman too annoyed. The whole point of putting up with the silly biddy was to get some information out of her. With that end firmly in mind, she smiled broadly. "Oh, but you really should take an interest. Murder can be quite fascinating."

She got up and bustled toward the cooling pantry. "Now, you just make yourself comfortable, Mollie. When I knew you were coming, I baked a seed cake. Oh, and I've bought us a bottle of Harvey's as well." When she got to the hall, she turned to make sure Mollie wasn't going to bolt.

Mollie was staring at her, her expression pleased and a bit puzzled. "You baked a seed cake? Why, how very nice. It's kind of you to go to so much trouble."

Mrs. Goodge felt a flash of guilt. Some of the starch had gone out of her guest. As a matter of fact, the woman looked almost pathetically pleased that someone had done something special for her. Perhaps Mollie wasn't such a snob. Maybe she was just one of those lonely women who spend their lives in the service of others and forget that they have a right to want something for themselves.

"It's no trouble at all," the cook lied graciously. Baking that seed cake had taken hours, and the only reason she'd splurged and bought the sherry was because if she remembered correctly, Mollie couldn't hold more than a glass or two before she lost control of her tongue. "I've a tray made up in the pantry. I'll just go get it and we can have a nice, long chat."

Wiggins reached down and pretended to wipe a bit of dust off his shoe. The girl was just ahead of him and twice now, he'd caught her looking back at him, like she knew she was being followed.

A second later, his worst fear was confirmed. She turned away from the shop window and charged toward him. "'Ere, are you followin' me?"

For a moment, he was struck dumb. He hadn't had a good look at her face when he'd seen her coming out of the Parks house; he'd only dashed after her as she set off down the road toward the shops. But even with an accusing frown on her face, she was the prettiest girl he'd ever seen. Her eyes were widely spaced, deep brown in color and framed with the longest lashes in the world. A small, turned-up nose, skin the color of pale cream, an adorable rosebud of a mouth and perfectly shaped winged brows came together to from a perfect face. Her hair was tucked under a maid's cap, but it was the color of dark honey and curling tendrils escaped to dance around her long, slender neck.

Without thinking, Wiggins blurted out the truth. "Uh, yes. I was."

For a few seconds, she eyed him suspiciously. Then her mouth curved in a slow, satisfied smile. "So, you admit it then?"

He could feel the blood rushing to his cheeks. "I'm sorry, miss. I didn't mean no 'arm. It's just that . . . that . . ." What? His mind was completely blank.

"You're not the first to follow me." She laughed. "And you look harmless enough."

"Thank you," he mumbled, not sure if being called "harmless" was a compliment or an insult. "May I carry your shopping basket?"

"What? You're wantin' to follow me about and carry my shopping? Is that it, then?"

"Well, I've nothing else to do today," he replied truthfully. "It wouldn't be any trouble and I do 'ate to see a delicate lady like yourself 'aving to trundle this great basket around."

"You've a glib tongue on you." She laughed again and shoved it into his hands. "This thing does get heavy. I accept. Come on, then." Turning on her heel, she started toward the butcher shop on the corner. Wiggins grimaced at the sight of the hanging carcasses in the open air front. But the girl stalked on past the butchers, turned the corner and went toward the grocer's. "Come on," she called over her shoulder. "Hurry up. I've not got all day."

"Sorry." He dashed up to her and reached for the handle of the door. "Didn't mean to dawdle."

She gave him a dazzling smile. "That's all right. I shouldn't have snapped. But I've got a lot to do today and I want to get this ruddy shopping done. It's not even my job. But the housekeeper quit all sudden like, and if we're going to eat, I've got to get some food in. If I waited for Mr. Parks to remember to buy it, we'd starve to death."

Wiggins opened the door for her. "Is that who you work for, Mr. and Mrs. Parks?"

"Just Mr. Parks," the girl said in a low voice as they went toward the back of the shop. A stern-faced woman wearing an apron stood behind the counter, watching them.

"Have you got your list, Annie?" the woman asked, holding out her hand.

"Right here." She handed it to the shopkeeper.

The proprietress scanned the list with a frown. "Quite a bit, here, Annie."

"It's not all that much," Annie said. Wiggins could hear a note of desperation in her voice. "Only a few things to get us through till the end of the week."

"And will Mr. Parks be coming in to pay last month's bill?" the woman asked.

"He said he would. He said he'd be in to settle up sometime this week."

She tapped the paper against the top of the counter. "All right, then. But you tell Mr. Parks that if he doesn't come in and pay up by Saturday, there won't be any more credit. Do you understand?"

"Oh, yes," Annie said quickly. "I'll make sure I tell him." She grabbed the basket out of Wiggins's hand and shoved it on the counter. "Just put the things in this. I've got to go to the fishmongers and then I'll be back for it." With that, she turned and flew towards the front door, a puzzled Wiggins right on her heels.

"I hate going in that place," she said as soon as they were outside.

Wiggins could understand why. "Then how come you shop there?"

"Because it's the only shop that'll give Mr. Parks credit," she said. "Oh, I shouldn't have said that, and I shouldn't have let you carry my basket. Mr. Parks will have a fit if everyone in town knew he weren't payin' his bills." She bit her lower lip and Wiggins watched in horror as her beautiful eyes filled with tears.

"Here now." He stepped closer, using his body to shield her from the interested stares of pedestrians. "Don't cry."

"I'm sorry." Annie covered her face with her hands and sobbed. "But I can't seem to stop. You saw what happened in there," she chocked out. "It's like that everywhere and it's so ruddy embarrassin'"

Panic hit him. What should he do? He couldn't stand to see a woman cry. Suddenly, he remembered Mrs. Jeffries and the sensible, kind way she always dealt with weeping and wailing. Wiggins straightened his spine and glared at an elderly woman who was openly trying to peek around him at the sobbing girl. "Look, Miss Annie. You'll make yourself ill if you carry on like this. Things is never as bad as ya think."

"Yes, they are," she wailed. "And they're gettin' worse too. What's goin' to happen when Mr. Parks doesn't pay the bill? We'll bloomin' starve to death, that's what."

"There's a tea house just up the road," Wiggins said. "Let's nip up and 'ave a nice cuppa."

"I don't have any money." She sniffled. "Mr. Parks hasn't paid me this quarter."

"I do." Taking her arm, he led her toward the corner. Wiggins thanked his lucky stars that he'd had the good sense to put some coins in his pocket before he left this morning. Mind you, he thought, without their mysterious benefactor he probably wouldn't have had any coins. But for the past year, someone in the household at Upper Edmonton Gardens had been buying them all useful presents. Nice things like note paper and shoe polish and even brand new shirts. So much so that when he got his quarterly wages, he put most of it in the post office account the inspector had opened for him. Consequently, he always had a few coins to jingle in his pocket. He was pretty sure he knew who their benefactor was; after all, he was getting pretty good at investigating. But Wiggins wouldn't say a word to anyone. Not one word.

"This is very nice of you." Annie hiccupped gently. "I'm right pleased to do it," he replied. "I 'ate seein' a nice girl like you so upset." He held her arm protectively as they reached the tearoom. Guiding her inside, he led her to a table and pulled out a chair for her. "You sit down and 'ave a rest. I'll go get us some tea and cakes. Would you like that?"

She nodded mutely and then looked up and gave him an adoring smile. "I haven't had proper tea cakes in ages."

"You're goin' to 'ave some now," he boasted. "As many as you like. What's your favorite?"

"I think you're the nicest man I've ever met," she said softly.

Wiggins's heart melted.

"Madam," Hatchet hissed at Luty Belle, "you cannot go in there. It's the St. James. Women aren't allowed." He shuddered as he thought of his employer hurtling through the doors of the most exclusive men's club in London.

"Then how the dickens am I gonna git my information?" Luty started towards the stately club. "Stupid goldarned rules anyway. No women allowed. Humph! What woman worth her salt wants to go in and watch a bunch of fat geezers sittin' around tidding whiskey and flapping their lips? But that old fool's been in there for hours and I need to talk to him."

"Madam." Hatchet grabbed her arm. "Please go wait in the carriage. I'll go in and tell Mr. Stampton you wish to speak to him."

Luty's eyes narrowed suspiciously. "That's all you'll say? You wouldn't try pumpin' the old goat yourself?"

Hatchet glared at her. That was precisely what he'd planned on doing. Now, of course, he couldn't. "Certainly not," he replied huffily. "I wouldn't dream of doing something so crass."

She snorted. "Pull the other one, Hatchet. You know danged good and well you ain't found out diddly about this case. I can see you chompin' at the bit to get your hooks into my source."

"I'll have you know, madam," Hatchet said pompously, "I've found out a great deal more than you have about this murder."

"Oh, yeah?"

"Yeah . . . I mean yes," he snapped. "However, I'm waiting until our meeting tonight at Upper Edmonton Gardens before I share any of it. Now, if you'll stop making a spectacle of yourself and go wait in the carriage, I'll ask Mr. Stampton to step outside."

Luty weighed her choices. She could either try charging the St. James and get tossed out on her ear or she could send Hatchet in to fetch the man. The third choice was to wait out here till the old buzzard stumbled out himself. That wasn't much good either. If someone else was buying the drinks, Stampton might be in there till the cows come home. And she had to see him. Blast it! Much as she hated to, she'd just have to rely on Hatchet. In any other situation, she'd trust Hatchet with her life. She had trusted him with it on more than one occasion. But when it came to digging up clues and investigating murders, Hatchet was as sneaky as a polecat creeping up to the chicken coop. Especially when he wasn't getting anywhere with his own sources. Still, she really didn't have much choice here.

"Okay, Hatchet," she said reluctantly, "you go get him. I'll be in the carriage. But if you're not back in ten minutes, I'm coming in."

"You do realize what this means," Witherspoon said to Barnes. He grabbed the door of the hansom as the cab hit a particularly large pothole and almost jolted him off his seat.

"Well, sir, I reckon it means that all of them had a reason for wishing Hinchley had stayed in New York," Barnes replied. "From what Remington said, they all had put up money in the production, and if Hinchley closed it, they'd get worse than just a bad review. They'd be ruined financially. At least Remington, Parks and Swinton would."

"Precisely, Barnes." Witherspoon nodded. He wasn't sure himself what to think about the information they'd received. It was reassuring to hear that the constable had come to the same conclusion. "But what worries me is whether or not one review from a critic could have such a devastating effect."

"I don't reckon the truth of that matters all that much, sir. They believed it could," Barnes pointed out. "That's what's important, and one of them believed it enough to kill him." He cleared his throat. It wasn't his place to be telling Inspector Witherspoon what to do, but in light of what they'd gotten out of Trevor Remington, he thought he ought to point something out. "Inspector, I think we ought to have another look at everyone's alibis, sir. We know that Mr. Remington didn't go straight home like he said before. It seems to me the others might be lying as well."

Witherspoon nodded. "I've had the same thought. Really, Barnes, I don't know what's come over me. I ought to have checked the alibis more thoroughly right away."

But the inspector did know what was wrong. It was that wretched last case. The one he'd solved by listening to his instincts and his "inner voice." He'd been waiting for his "inner voice" to start talking to him on this case too. But so far, the wretched thing had been stubbornly mute. He sighed inwardly and resolved to talk to Mrs. Jeffries more frequently. There was something about his chats with her that helped clarify his thoughts. He wished now he'd taken the time to have a longer conversation with her at breakfast. But he hadn't and now he felt totally lost and at sea. Drat. Perhaps he'd go home early today for tea. "Why don't we start with the cabbies at the Hayden? We know that one of them took Miss Vaughan home right after the performance, so let's find out if Parks, Swinton or Delaney got one as well."

"Delaney claimed he'd gone for a walk by the river and Swinton was supposed to have been in counting the receipts until after one in the morning," Barnes mused "But they might be lyin'"

"That's what I'm afraid of," Witherspoon said slowly. "But if one of them is lying, we'll find out. Whoever killed Hinchley would have had to have left the theatre district sometime that night. Hopefully, in a hansom."

"Unless they walked there, sir," Barnes pointed out. "It's not quite three miles."

"I hadn't realized it was quite that far." Witherspoon stared out at the heavy traffic on the Strand. Drat, that was another point he should have checked immediately. Gracious, he must get a hold of himself; he was forgetting to take care of even the most elementary aspects of good policing. Perhaps it would be best if he retired his 'inner voice' altogether. It certainly wasn't doing him any good on this case. "However the killer got to Hinchley's house, I think we can safely assume that he probably went there quite soon after the performance ended."

"He might have gone home first," Barnes said.

"True. We don't know exactly when Hinchley was murdered. But I'm betting that whoever killed him did it as quickly as possible and then hurried home himself. After all, you're far more likely to be noticed by a policeman or a night watchman or even someone who can't sleep and is looking out their window if you're wandering the streets or catching hansoms at three in the morning rather than at midnight."

Barnes nodded. "That's true, sir. Back when I was on the streets, I always took care to notice them that was out in the middle of the night. So you're pretty sure Hinchley was murdered, say, before two in the morning?"

Witherspoon pursed his lips. "Not absolutely, Constable. It's just, you see, these people strike me as being so . . . excitable, so dramatic. I've a feeling that if one of them did it, they did it quickly and without thinking. I could be wrong, of course, but somehow, I don't think I am."

Barnes scratched his nose. "And all of them probably knew about Hinchley's private . . . er . . . habits."

"You mean about the door being unlocked"—the inspector hesitated, then reminded himself this was a murder case—"and a male prostitute being expected?" He looked away, sure he was beet red.

"Everyone knew about Hinchley and his habits, and according to Remington, it wasn't a secret. The way he tells it, everyone in the theatre district laughed at the man behind his back."

"We've only Remington's word for that," Witherspoon reminded the constable. "But it's certainly something we can easily check."

"Let's say Remington was tellin' the truth and everyone did know about Hinchley's little habit on the nights he reviewed a play," Barnes continued. "Wouldn't the killer have expected Hinchley to have company?"

"That's why I think he acted quickly. Remington also said that Hinchley wrote his review before the person arrived. He was most strict about that"—again Witherspoon could feel his cheeks flaming—"so I'm quite sure that the murderer got there right after Hinchley got into his bath. As a matter of fact, that would explain why we didn't find a copy of the review when we searched the victim's house. The killer took it."

"Then why didn't the prostitute"—Barnes didn't even stumble over the word—"raise the alarm when he arrived and found the place empty?"

"Come now, Constable, someone in that profession must be discreet," Witherspoon explained. "I expect when this person got there and found the place empty, he turned and left, assuming that the customer had changed his mind." He coughed. "After we finish at the Hayden, we'll have to go to Lisle Street."

"I know the place, sir." Barnes's mouth curved in distaste. "High-class brothel. Caters to men with lots of money and some with unusual habits."

Witherspoon sighed. "Let's hope we can get them to talk with us, Barnes. I don't think places of that sort are all that keen on the police."

"I'd say not, sir." Barnes turned his head so Witherspoon wouldn't see his smile. Sometimes he forgot that for all the inspector's brillance at solving homicides, he'd spent most of his years at the Yard working in the records room. For a copper, he was amazingly innocent about some aspects of life.

"Let's hope we can make some progress on this case, Barnes."

"You'll suss it out in the end, sir," Barnes said cheerfully.

The hansom pulled to a stop and they got out. Barnes paid the driver and then followed Witherspoon to the front door of the Hayden Theatre.

Inside the theatre, Witherspoon stopped a limelighter and asked, "Is Mr. Swinton here?"

"The guv's in the office," the man replied, yanking his head toward the auditorium. "You want me to show the way?"

"We know our way, thank you," the inspector replied. They went into the darkened theatre and down the aisle.

Two men were on the empty stage and from the sound of their raised voices, Edmund Delaney and Willard Swinton were having a heated argument.

Barnes and Witherspoon stopped. They were far enough back that neither man had seen them.

"I tell you, just because he's dead doesn't mean we're out of the woods," Swinton snarled. "He wasn't the only critic in town. If you don't change that first scene in the second act and put a bit more life in it, we'll be shut down by the end of the month."

"I'm not changing a bloody thing." Delaney threw out his arms. "I didn't write a music hall review . . ."

"More's the pity," Swinton cried. "If you had, we might actually be making some money."

"You told us we were sold out for the next three weeks," Delaney charged. "Or was that just a lie you told for the convenience of the police?"

Swinton's hands rolled into fists, but he didn't raise them. "It wasn't a lie, you idiot. We are sold out. But that's only because of Theodora. She's a star. People come to see her, not your play. But even her drawing power won't keep them coming in if the play gets panned by every critic in England."

"The critic from the *Gazette* loved it," Delaney cried passionately.

"He was the only one," Swinton yelled. "And if you don't make some changes in this ruddy bunch of rubbish I got hoodwinked into producing, we're going to all be stone broke in two months. And that, my friend, includes our illustrious star and your patron." Swinton stepped back, a satisfied smile on his face. "I think you'll find that Theodora won't be quite as amenable to your charms once she's bankrupt."

"You despicable cur." Delaney took a step closer, his face contorting with rage. "How dare you imply . . ."

"Gentlemen, gentlemen," Witherspoon called. He would have liked to have heard more, but he couldn't in good conscience let a situation become violent. From the look on Edmund Delaney's face, the inspector was sure he was only seconds away from throttling Swinton.

Startled, both men reacted. Delaney's whole body jerked. Swinton stumbled backwards. The playwright recovered first. "Who's there?" he called, squinting into the darkened auditorium.

"Inspector Witherspoon and Constable Barnes." They moved closer to the stage. "And if you don't mind, we'd like to have a word with both of you."

Smythe desperately wanted to talk to Betsy alone. Things hadn't been right between them since they'd rowed about her mysterious errand to the East End a few days ago. Matters hadn't improved any when he'd gone to the house on Lisle Street, either. But he wasn't one to let a wound fester. Better to have a frank talk with the lass and get everything cleared up and out in the open.

He stopped at the head of the back stairs and listened to the hubbub from the kitchen. Mrs. Goodge, Betsy and Mrs. Jeffries were below, getting things ready for an early tea. Everyone was due back for a quick meeting, and after that he'd probably be back out at the pubs doing more digging.

But if Betsy did what she often did, she'd pop up to her room to tidy her hair before tea. He'd have a chance to talk to her in private. He waited a few more minutes and then his patience was rewarded as he heard Betsy say, "I'll be right back. I just want to tidy myself up a bit."

Smythe turned and raced for the back stairs. By the time Betsy got to the third floor, he was leaning against her door. "I'd like to have a word with ya."

"Now?" She stared at him like he'd gone daft. "But the others will be here any minute. Can't it wait?"

"No," he said patiently. He was always patient when something important was at stake. "It can't. And Luty and Hatchet aren't due for another fifteen minutes. Besides, this won't take long."

"Oh, all right," she said peevishly. "But I don't see what's so important it can't wait until after supper." She crossed her arms over her chest. She wasn't going to invite him into her room. The inspector and Mrs. Jeffries ran a very liberal household, but even they would look askance at her entertaining men in her bedroom. "What is it?"

Smythe cleared his throat. "It's about us."

"Us?" She raised her eyebrows.

His heart plummeted to his toes. Then he decided she was just being contrary. She did that when she was annoyed. "Yes, us," he insisted, "so don't go pretendin' you don't know what I'm on about. You and I 'ave been keepin' company."

"All right," she capitulated, "so what if we have?"

"Things ain't been right between us," he stated, his expression daring her to argue that point. "Ever since we' ad that little tiff about you flouncin' off the East End on yer own . . ."

"Little tiff," she yelped, outraged. "You were tryin' to boss me about. Tell me what to do. I'll not have that, Smythe."

He raised his hand in a placating gesture. "I weren't tryin' to boss you about," he said. "I was worried because there's a murderin' maniac on the loose and I didn't want you to get' urt."

Betsy relaxed a little. Blast the man, anyway, he did make it hard to stay annoyed with him. "I know that," she said bluntly. "But I do have some sense. I know how to take care of myself."

"Never said you didn't," he replied. "But that street woman that got 'erself butchered thought she could take care of 'erself too."

"She was out in the middle of the night," Betsy protested. "I went to Whitechapel in broad daylight."

Smythe decided he'd better change tactics. This was old ground they were covering. Best to move on. He touched her arm. "I don't think I could stand it if anythin' 'appened to you, Betsy," he said sincerely. "You're right important to me."

Her heart melted. She couldn't think of what to say. He was important to her too. "Oh, Smythe," she murmured.

"And I didn't like goin' to that brothel, either," he continued as he watched her soften. "I could tell that put your nose out some . . ."

"It didn't bother me at all," she snapped, wanting to box his ears for bringing that subject up. It was one she preferred to forget. "But you certainly stayed there long enough that night."

"How do you know how long I was?" he asked. "You were asleep. Besides, I had to find out . . ."

"Betsy, Smythe," Wiggins yelled up the staircase. "Are ya comin'? The others is already 'ere and Mrs. Jeffries wants to get things started."

"We'd better get downstairs," Betsy mumbled. She started for the staircase, but he grabbed her elbow and stopped her.

"We'll finish our talk later," he promised. "There's still a few things we need to clear up."

"All right," she agreed quickly, annoyed with herself for letting it slip that she knew what time he'd come in. She hoped that he wouldn't press her about why she'd gone to the East End. She didn't like the way things were between them now, either. It wasn't that she didn't believe him; she was female enough to realize that he was telling the truth. He had been worried about her. But he was also very adept at whittling away some of the walls she'd erected between her past and her present. Betsy had shared much of her past with him, but she wasn't sure she could share all of it. One part of her was still afraid that if he knew exactly where she'd come from, exactly how bad it had been, maybe he wouldn't hold her in such high esteem.

She couldn't stand that thought. Smythe, in truth, had become very important to her as well.

As soon as they were all seated at their usual places, Mrs. Jeffries plunged right in. She'd spent most of the day fruitlessly tracking down clues that hadn't led anywhere, talking to people who knew nothing and trying to think of each and every possible solution to this murder. She sincerely hoped the others had had a better day than she had.

"I'll start," Mrs. Goodge announced in a tone that brooked no argument. "I had an old acquaintance of mine around this afternoon . . ."

"Is she the one that ate all the seed cake?" Wiggins demanded.

"I'll thank you not to interrupt," the cook said tartly. "And she didn't eat it *all*."

"Then why aren't we 'avin' some now?" Wiggins persisted. He'd been looking forward to that cake all day. Ever since he'd spotted Mrs. Goodge baking it that morning.

"For goodness' sake, don't you ever think of anything but your stomach?" Mrs. Goodge glared at him. "I'm savin' the cake for some more sources I've got comin' by tomorrow."

Wiggins opened his mouth to protest, but Mrs. Jeffries, seeing another tempest in a teapot, quickly intervened. "Please, Wiggins, do let Mrs. Goodge have her say. We haven't much time today; the inspector might be home early for supper."

"Yeah, and I want to go next," Luty said. She was busting to tell them what she'd found out. "Go on, Mrs. Goodge," she encouraged, knowing full well that none of the others had a patch on her today.

"Thank you." The cook nodded regally to Luty. "As I was saying, an old acquaintance of mine came around for tea today. This person doesn't have any theatre connections now, but she did at one time. I found out the most extraordinary thing from her. It seems that when Edmund Delaney suddenly left Hinchley and more or less took up with Miss Vaughan, Hinchley was so upset that he publicly vowed vengeance on Delaney."

"Publicly? How?" Mrs. Jeffries asked.

Mrs. Goodge smiled. Normally, repeating what she was about to say would have made her blush, but Mollie Dubay wasn't the only one who'd had a couple of glasses of sherry that afternoon. "Hinchley accosted the couple right outside the Empire Theatre on Leicester Square. Silly man made a fool of himself in front of dozens of people. He told Delaney he'd make him sorry he left him for, as he put it, 'a has-been actress like Theodora Vaughan.' Delaney was furious with Hinchley, and from what my source told me, they had more than a few words. It ended with Delaney yelling that if Hinchley came near Miss Vaughan, he'd kill him." Satisfied, Mrs. Goodge sat back.

"A death threat," Mrs. Jeffries murmured. "Exactly when was this?"

"It would have been a little over a year ago, just after Hinchley came back from Italy."

"So Delaney could well have thought that Hinchley was going to have his vengeance against Miss Vaughan by giving her a terrible review," Mrs. Jeffries said. "I wonder if that's motive enough for murder?"

"It wouldn't be the first time a man's killed to protect 'is woman," Smythe added.

"Well, fiddlesticks," Luty cried. "That don't make any sense at all."

"Excuse me." Mrs. Goodge straightened up in her chair. "It makes perfect sense to me."

"Not in light of what I found out today," Luty charged.

"Really, madam," Hatchet said quickly. "Mr. Stampton's information might not be true. The man was in his cups when we talked to him this afternoon."

"It is true," Luty snapped. "Drunk or sober, Harold don't have the imagination to make up tales."

"Make what up, Luty?" Mrs. Jeffries asked.

Luty, her face set in a frown, shook her head. "That Edmund Delaney is Ogden Hinchley's heir."

"His heir?" the cook repeated.

"He inherits?" Betsy said. "But Hinchley hated him."

Luty nodded and a slow grin broke across her face. "Hate him or not, Edmund Delaney is now a rich man. He stands to inherit over a hundred thousand pounds."

Mrs. Jeffries looked from Luty to Hatchet and then back. She didn't wish to offend Luty, but this was one point they had to be absolutely sure about. "Was your source absolutely certain of this?"

"Harold might have been drunk as a skunk," Luty said, "but he don't get things like that wrong. Hinchley redid his will right before he left for New York. Edmund Delaney gets the whole kit and caboodle. The estate, the house and all Hinchley's money."

CHAPTER 8

"This case is getting very confusing," Mrs. Jeffries admitted. She didn't doubt that Luty was telling the truth, but she wondered if Luty's drunken solicitor could be trusted. "Why would Ogden Hinchley leave a fortune to a man he'd come to hate? A man he'd threatened to ruin?"

"Stampton didn't know." Luty shrugged. "But he was sure about it. His firm has handled Hinchley's affairs for years. It wasn't the first time Hinchley'd changed his will."

"But he changed it after Delaney left him for Miss Vaughan?" Mrs. Goodge murmured. "The man must be daft. Sounds like he's got a few ingredients missin' from his cupboard."

"Cor blimey," Smythe interjected. "I wonder if Edmund Delaney knew he was goin' to inherit a ruddy fortune?"

"Stampton didn't know that either," Luty replied. "Useful fellow is Stampton—pour a couple of drinks down his throat and he'll tell you anything."

"For a solicitor he certainly isn't very discreet," Hatchet agreed. "It's a wonder he hasn't been tossed out of the legal profession on his ear."

"You're just bellyachin' cause I found out somethin' important." Luty grinned.

"Oh, really?" He arched an eyebrow. "For your information, madam, I too have something to report."

"So do I," Wiggins added.

Mrs. Jeffries glanced at the clock and saw that it was getting late. "Please, Hatchet, tell us what you found out. Then Wiggins can go. As interesting as Luty's information is, we must get on. The Inspector will probably be home soon."

Hatchet put down the teacup he'd been holding. "Willard Swinton lied about his alibi the night of the murder. He wasn't at the theatre counting receipts. He waited until everyone had left and then left himself. Furthermore, according to my information, he didn't get home until after three in the morning."

"So he doesn't have an alibi either," Betsy said eagerly. "I wonder why he lied?"

"Most people lie' cause they don't want to tell the truth," Wiggins said somberly.

"Well, of course that's why they do it," Mrs. Goodge said impatiently. She was rather annoyed that all the information she'd worked so hard to drag out of Mollie Dubay was being overshadowed by everyone else.

Wiggins shook his head. "That's not what I meant. I mean, I know people lie' cause they don't want to tell the truth, but there's lots of different reasons for not wantin' to tell the truth, if you see what I mean. Take Annie, fer instance, she's been fibbin' a bit, but it's not because she's done something wrong."

"Who's Annie?" Smythe asked.

"Albert Parks's maid," Wiggins replied. He leaned forward eagerly. "I had a nice long chat with 'er today. Mind you, I did 'ave to take 'er fer tea." He glanced quickly at the cook. "You're right, you know. People do tell you ever so much more when you're feedin' 'em."

Mrs. Goodge "humphed" softly. She wasn't all that sure she wanted the others to be using her methods. But she could hardly complain about it now. "Well, get on with it, boy. What did this Annie tell you?"

"She told me plenty." He grinned. "Seems Albert Parks is in a bad way with money. He don't 'ave none. His housekeeper quit yesterday 'cause 'e ain't paid this quarter's wages and 'e was late payin' last quarter's. Poor Annie's been 'avin' to go round to the shops and all and get credit just to buy food. She's ever so embarrassed about it too. It's right 'umiliatin' for the poor girl. It's digustin' the way people get treated just because they've got to 'ave a bit of 'elp. Sometimes I think the radicals are right . . ."

"Get on with it, lad," Smythe said sharply. "We don't 'ave time for one of yer political speeches."

"Yes, Wiggins." Mrs. Jeffries intervened quickly. "Do go on and finish telling us what you got out of Annie." She didn't want to let him digress. Wiggins had a very soft heart. He could spend ages harping on how badly the working classes were treated in this country. Mrs. Jeffries had noticed that his political opinions had sharpened somewhat since their neighbor, Lady Cannonberry, had taken to spending so much time visiting. Underneath her upper-class facade, Lady Cannonberry was a bit of a radical. Not that Mrs. Jeffries didn't agree with most of her attitudes—she did. The poor in this country were treated abominably. But Smythe was right; they didn't have time for the luxury of a political polemic right now. Unless one guided Wiggins firmly, he was very likely to stray off the point.

Unabashed, Wiggins took a quick gulp of tea. "Well, Annie told me that Albert Parks 'as been skint ever since he invested in Edmund Delaney's play."

"If Parks were broke, why'd he invest in the first place?" Smythe demanded. "Did ya find that out?"

"'Course I found out." Wiggins looked offended. "Parks didn't 'ave no choice. 'E wanted to direct the play and the only way the others would take a chance on 'im was to make 'im put up some money. 'E took a loan out on 'is 'ouse."

"From a bank?" Luty asked eagerly. She knew lots of bankers and she was pretty darned good at getting them to talk too.

Wiggin's face fell. "I, uh, didn't ask that."

Disappointed, Luty said, "Find out, will ya?"

"I'm seein' Annie again tomorrow," Wiggins said, looking doubtful. "But she might not know 'ow Parks got the loan."

"Why didn't the others want to take a chance on Parks?" Luty asked curiously.

Wiggins made a face. "I didn't think to ask."

"Why is this Annie staying on with Parks if he's not paying her?" Betsy asked.

Wiggins brightened. He did know the answer to that one. "She don't have anywhere else to go," he explained. "And at least it's a roof over her head. Besides, the play's doin' well. She's pretty sure Mr. Parks is goin' to be able to pay her next week. She's just hopin' there'll be enough money for 'im to pay off the grocers. If he don't settle up with them, they're goin' to stop givin' him credit."

"Did you learn anything else from her?" Mrs. Jeffries prompted. "What about Albert Parks's alibi? Did he come right home on the night of the murder?"

Wiggins nodded eagerly. "I asked Annie that and she didn't know. She were asleep. But I'll see what else I can get out of 'er tomorrow."

"Good, Wiggins; you do that," Mrs. Jeffries said. She looked at Betsy and Smythe. "Who wants to go next?"

Betsy shrugged. "I didn't learn anything useful today. I talked to a footman from Theodora Vaughan's household, but he didn't know anything." The lad had been more interested in trying to get to know her better than in answering questions. After listening to him complain about the mountain of luggage that the actress traveled with, and dodging his quick hands, Betsy had decided to try elsewhere for information.

Mrs. Jeffries smiled kindly. "There's always tomorrow, my dear. You mustn't let one bad day dampen your spirits."

Betsy gave her a strained smile. Truth was, not only hadn't she learned anything worthwhile, but her conscience was bothering her too. Even putting the money in the collection plate at St. Jude's hadn't completely washed away her guilt. Every time she looked at the coachman, she just knew he was hurt to the bone because she wouldn't tell him the truth.

Smythe said, "Don't take it so 'ard, lass; I didn't 'ave much luck today either." But he fully intended to have plenty tomorrow. It was time to make contact with one of his sources, Blimpey Groggins. Someone had to know something about this ruddy murder. And if there was any information about the city, Blimpey was sure to find it. "The only thing I learned was that except for the 'ansoms that Hinchley took back to his 'ouse and the one Theodora Vaughan took that night to go 'ome, no one else took one. Least of all, none of the drivers I talked to could remember pickin' up a fare and takin' 'em to Hinchley's neighborhood."

"Maybe the killer didn't take a hanson," Hatchet suggested.

"I thought of that," Smythe said, "but unless they walked, 'ow else would they get there? All the suspects live close to the Hayden. Hinchley lived almost three miles away. That's a fair walk."

"Maybe the killer took the Underground," Wiggins said.

Smythe shook his head. "There's not an Underground station close to Hinchley's and even if there were, the trains don't run that time of night."

Mrs. Jeffries thought about it for a moment. Smythe did have a point. How did the killer get there? She had a feeling he wouldn't have walked;

that was too risky. People tended to be noticed when the streets were deserted. The killer wouldn't have wanted that. Also, with that awful murder in the East End, she knew the police had doubled their street patrols all over the city. The killer would have known that as well. That fact had been in every newspaper. "Do any of them have private carriages?"

"Theodora Vaughan has one," Betsy said. She'd forgotten she'd found that out. "But it's at her cottage in the country. Oliver was ever so put out because they had to come up to Victoria by train on Saturday because the carriage had a bad wheel."

"Who's Oliver?" Smythe asked quickly.

"The footman," Betsy replied.

"So the carriage definitely wasn't here on Saturday evening?" Mrs. Jeffries asked.

"It still isn't." Betsy reached for a slice of bread. "Oliver told me that too." More like he'd bent her ear for ten minutes complaining about the fact that without the carriage, he had to accompany Miss Vaughan all over London to carry her ruddy packages. She smiled at the memory. She couldn't really blame the lad for being put out. Theodora Vaughan liked to shop. The only day she didn't head for Regent Street was Sunday.

"So once again, we're back to our original question," Mrs. Jeffries mused. "How did the killer get there that night?"

There were dozens more questions that needed to be answered, but focusing on this one at least gave her a place to start. She knew she needed to think about this case more thoroughly. But if the truth were told, she was almost as nervous about her abilities as the rest of them were. Quickly, she squashed that notion. She refused to think they were finished. They'd had far too much success in the past to be completely wrong now.

"What do we do next?" Betsy asked, her words echoing everyone else's thoughts. "I mean, do we keep on as we are or try somethin' a bit different?"

"I think we ought to keep on as we are," Wiggins declared. "I'll 'ave another go at Annie tomorrow and the rest of ya can keep right on doin' what you've been doin'. We're learnin' lots of things."

"But are we learnin' anything that's goin' to lead us to the killer?" Luty asked bluntly. "Or are we just chasin' our tails?"

No one said anything for a moment. Mrs. Jeffries looked at the others. Mrs. Goodge was eyeing the plate of bread on the table as if she expected it to talk to her. Smythe was staring off into space; Luty's mouth was set in a flat, thin line. Hatchet's eyes were worried and Betsy was biting her lower lip. The only one who didn't look concerned was Wiggins. He was leaning back in his chair, a dreamy expression on his young face.

"We're not chasing our tails," Mrs. Jeffries said firmly. "We're solving a heinous and horrible murder. We are serving justice, and I, for one, am going to keep at it till the killer is caught. If any of you feel that you can't, or that it's too difficult, you've a perfect right to bow out now."

That got their attention.

"But what if we're wrong?" Betsy said. "What if it's like the last time . . ."

"It won't be," the housekeeper declared. "We're far too good at this to be wrong again. Now, we've got to get cracking. As I see it, someone slipped into Hinchley's house sometime after midnight on Saturday night, found him in the bathtub, drowned him and put his body in the Regents Canal." She paused for a moment to gather her thoughts. The others were watching her carefully, their expressions a mixture of hope and fear. "We know who our suspects are and we know that one of them is probably the killer. So here's what I propose we do now."

Mrs. Jeffries, her mind working furiously, began issuing orders like a general. She had no idea whether she was on the right track or not, but she knew that activity, any activity, would be better for them the constant doubts about their own abilities.

"As soon as the inspector gets home this evening," she finished, "I'm going to relay the information you've all gathered to him."

"Be careful, Mrs. J.," Smythe warned. "We don't want the Inspector gettin' suspicious."

"I intend to be," she promised, getting to her feet. "I won't tell him everything this evening—that would be a bit too much. But I've breakfast tomorrow to work on him. Now, I want all of you back here tomorrow for lunch."

"But that's in the middle of our day," Wiggins whined.

"I know, but it's important. I've got to pass on to you what I get out of the inspector tonight and tomorrow morning. Don't worry; you'll have plenty of time for gathering information. If any of you are right in the middle of something, then, naturally, you'll be excused from attending. But do try to be here."

True to her word, Mrs. Jeffries pumped the inspector ruthlessly before he went in to dinner that evening. She also kept him well supplied with sherry.

"Have a bit more, sir," she urged, topping up his glass for the third time. "It's been a very warm day and you could do with a bit of relaxation. Mrs. Goodge is making something special this evening, so there's no hurry."

"Thank you, Mrs. Jeffries," he said with a grateful sigh. "This is so very nice. I will admit it's been rather a tiring day."

"You work too hard, sir," she replied sympathetically. "I must say, you were particularly clever today." She laughed delightedly. "But then, you always are."

Witherspoon, who'd already unburdened himself and felt much better for it, straightened his spine. "Oh, thank you, Mrs. Jeffries. It's good of you to say so. Er . . . uh, I'm interested in which of my methods you thought clever."

"Really, sir"—she poured herself a glass—"now do stop teasing. You know very well what I mean. It was uncanny how you managed to get Remington to 'spill the beans,' as Luty would say about the others."

As Remington had spilt quite a few beans, Witherspoon wondered which ones she meant. "Could you be a bit more specific?"

She contrived to look surprised. "Why, the information about how virtually everyone involved in the play had to put up money. That's most important, don't you think?"

Witherspoon sincerely hoped it was, but the truth was, this case was so muddled it was difficult to understand what was important and what wasn't. That was why he was so glad he had his housekeeper to talk with. She was rather good at helping him clarify his ideas. "Yes," he agreed eagerly. "I believe it is. Then you don't think the information about Remington not having an alibi is important?"

"But of course I do, sir," she exclaimed. "It's vitally important. I'm so glad you're going to be checking into the others' alibis as well." She hesitated. This part was going to be tricky. "Take Mr. Swinton, for instance."

"What about him?" Witherspoon looked at her expectantly.

"Well, he claimed he was in the theatre, counting the receipts. But from what you said about that dreadful row he was having with Mr. Delaney today, I think it's very possible he might have had more than a passing interest in making sure that Hinchley didn't have a chance to give the play a bad review. From what you overheard, Swinton doesn't think much of the production in the best of circumstances. Wouldn't you agree?"

"That's true," Witherspoon said. He wondered what she was getting

at. "But that doesn't mean Swinton killed him. Besides"—he sighed—
"Swinton's alibi will be very difficult to verify."

"Perhaps for an ordinary detective, sir," she enthused, "but not for
you."

"Really?"

"Really, sir. Why, of course you know how to verify it." She smiled
serenely. "You're going to check with all the watchmen and constables on
patrol in the area. If Swinton was indeed sitting in his office adding up
receipts, someone will have seen the lights." It was weak and she knew it,
but after thinking about the matter, it was the best she could come up
with.

Witherspoon brightened. "Yes, yes, of course, that's exactly what I'm
going to do." He'd already decided to check with the police constables,
but it had never occurred to him to question the night watchmen in the
area. It was a commercial area too, so many of the businesses and buildings in the neighborhood had both watchmen and porters.

"And you'll do the same for Delaney, I'm sure." She hoped he would
take the hint. She didn't want to have to go into too much detail. But
honestly, with half of the London police on foot patrols because of that
wretched East End murder, it had finally occurred to her that if Edmund
Delaney had indeed been walking by the river, someone—probably a police
constable—would not only have seen him, but would have remembered
him. She'd bet her housekeeping money that every face a constable passed
was etched in his memory. "Goodness, sir, I almost forgot."

"Forgot what?"

"Oh, I know I shouldn't bother you with such trifles, but I did promise
the old dear I'd pass it along . . ." She broke off and gazed at him anxiously,
waiting for him to take the bait.

Witherspoon, who was still trying to determine how many porters or
watchmen might have been awake that night in the vicinity of the Hayden,
realized that his housekeeper had said something. "Trifles? You never
bother me with trifles. What is it?"

She looked embarrassed. "This is so awkward, but Mollie so insisted
we mention it."

"Mention what?"

"Well, sir"—her face flushed slightly, an effect she'd achieved by holding her breath for several seconds—"one of Mrs. Goodge's old acquaintances dropped by yesterday. It seems you're quite famous, sir. This person,

a Miss Mollie Dubay, had some information about one of your suspects. Naturally, Mrs. Goodge told her we couldn't possibly interfere in one of your cases, but Miss Dubay was quite insistent we tell you."

Flattered, Witherspoon's chest puffed out a bit. "I'm hardly famous, Mrs. Jeffries. But please, do go on and tell me what Mrs. Goodge's friend said."

Mrs. Jeffries took a deep breath and plunged right in. In the course of the conversation she not only told him everything Mrs. Goodge had gotten out of Mollie Dubay, but she also managed to mention the rumor that Edmund Delaney was Hinchley's heir.

Spellbound, Witherspoon listened. From the expression on his face, Mrs. Jeffries could see that he was taking in every single word.

Mrs. Jeffries sat staring out at the London night. A wispy fog drifted in off the river, softening the glow of the gas lamp across the road. She liked sitting in the dark when she was trying to think.

Sitting back, she let her mind drift for a moment. Sometimes, putting the puzzle together began with nothing more than letting the bits and pieces float about aimlessly until, all of a sudden, a piece or two would fit together.

The inspector was fairly certain that Hinchley had been murdered soon after the play ended. That piece might be important. Mrs. Jeffries was inclined to agree with Witherspoon's reasoning. Whoever did it wouldn't have wanted to be found roaming the streets at three or four in the morning. With the police out in full force all over London, the killer wouldn't have risked being stopped by a constable.

Then there was the argument the inspector had overheard. She frowned because it really didn't make sense. If Swinton thought Delaney's play was that bad, why had he agreed to produce it in the first place? Even with Theodora Vaughan as a draw, it was obvious that the owner had realized that wouldn't keep the show open long if the play was awful. Yet he'd not only produced the play; he'd invested his own money in it as well. Why? Then she remembered the inspector telling her that the theatre was in a bad way, that they hadn't had a success there in years. She nodded to herself. Perhaps Swinton hadn't had a choice. Perhaps even producing a bad play with a big star was better than letting the theatre sit empty.

For a long time, she sat in the darkened room, her mind going over and over all the pieces of information. Had Hinchley come back early from America for a reason? Could he have come back for the express purpose of destroying Delaney's play with a bad review? Where was the review? The police hadn't found it when they searched his house; Mrs. Jeffries had asked the inspector that this morning at breakfast. She thought not finding it might be important. If what they'd heard of the victim's habits were true, then that meant the killer must have either destroyed it (she made another mental note to ask Witherspoon if there'd been a fire in the grate) or taken the review with him.

Finally, unable to come to any conclusion except that she needed more facts and information, Mrs. Jeffries got up and went to bed.

The next morning at breakfast, Mrs. Jeffries managed to feed the inspector the remainder of the information. It was hard work; she couldn't use Mollie Dubay this time. In the end, she couched everything in terms of "possible" and "maybe" and "didn't the Inspector think." By the time Witherspoon left with Constable Barnes, Mrs. Jeffries felt she'd spent the morning walking on egg shells.

As soon as the door closed behind the two policemen, she hurried upstairs and put on her hat. The others had already gone out. Pausing only to tell Mrs. Goodge that she would be back before lunch, she dashed out the front door and down to the end of the road. Going out to Uxbridge Road she debated a moment, wondering if it would be faster to take an omnibus or a hansom to St. John's Wood. But her mind was made up when a hansom pulled up just then. She smiled at the elderly woman alighting from the cab, waited till the fare was paid and then hopped in herself. "Avenue Road, St. John's Wood, please," she called to the driver.

She had the hansom drop her at the North Gate of Regents Park. The day had dimmed, and a layer of yellowish fog had crept in to cover the sun. Mrs. Jeffries glanced across the intersection of Avenue Road. Time enough to get a good look at the victim's house later. She turned and walked slowly into the park, towards the canal. Towards Macclesfield Bridge.

When she got to the edge of the bridge, she took a moment to study her surroundings. Down the path to her left was the entrance to the Zoological Gardens. The water in the canal was a dark wine color. Cool looking and deep, it reeked slightly of damp and rotting vegetation.

Stepping onto the bridge, she walked until she came to the middle and then peeked over the side.

The drop wasn't very far. Only a few feet. Leaning further, Mrs. Jeffries craned her neck until she could see under the bridge. But all she saw was the dark water lapping against the sides of the supports. The carriage wheel that the body had landed on was gone. Taken away, probably, by the police.

Mrs. Jeffries turned and walked back the way she'd come. Crossing Albert Road to Avenue Road, she found herself in front of Hinchley's house. His was the last one at this end of the street. She edged closer to the house, her eyes darting from the front door to the side. A cobblestone walkway veered off from the walkway and led round the side of the tall building. It took only a second to realize that the killer must have used the side door, which was flat against the pavement, or been as strong as an ox. There were six steps leading up to the front door. Carrying a body down them wouldn't have been easy. She studied the side of the house for a few more minutes, trying in her mind's eye to imagine what the area would have been like in the dark of the night. Glancing over her shoulder, she noted that on the corner there was a gas lamp. Across the intersection, just outside the North Gate entrance, was another one. The were small gaslamps, not like the huge ones on Oxford Street or the Strand, but they would have been lighted. The killer could have avoided the lamp on the corner by veering out into the darkened street. But he would have had to pass the one by the park entrance.

Then she turned and slowly began to measure just how far it was to the bridge. She pretended she was carrying a dead weight over her shoulder and slowed her steps accordingly.

Then she did it again.

And again.

Each time, she mentally ticked off the passing seconds in her head. By her estimation, the killer must have been visible, out where people could see him, for at least a minute and a half.

"'Ow much you willin' to pay, mate?" Blimpey lifted the pint of beer Smythe had just paid for and took a long, greedy sip.

"That's what I like about you, Blimpey," Smythe replied, taking a sip from his own glass, "you don't waste time askin' a lot of questions."

"Just takin' care of business, mate. No offense meant. After all, snoopin' about in a murder could be dangerous."

"All you've got to do is ask a few questions, Blimpey. You're not riskin' life or limb. Besides, don't I always pay a good price?" Smythe replied. "You can trust me on that."

Blimpey wiped his mouth with the cuff of his dirty, checkered sleeve. He grinned and slapped the glass on the counter. "Yer good fer it, mate. Just tryin' to rattle ya a bit. Now, what's them names again?"

They were standing at the bar of the Baying Hound Pub on Wapping High Street. The place was old and dark and smelled of rotting wood, stale beer and unwashed bodies. It was Blimpey's favorite pub and the one place he could ususaly be found during the daylight hours. During the night hours he worked. His job was an odd one, and Smythe had found it useful on several occasions.

Blimpey bought and sold information. He also did other things. Things that occasionally skirted the law a fraction, but as long as Smythe didn't know the details, he didn't ask questions. But for all Blimpey's criminal associations, and Smythe knew he had plenty, he was a good sort. Once you paid him, he got what you needed and then kept his mouth shut. He wasn't one to sell out a friend, either. Not for any amount of money.

"You want me to write 'em down for ya?" Smythe asked.

Blimpey shook his head. "What'd be the point? Can't read now, can I?" He laughed heartily at his own wit. "Is there anythin' in particular you want me to find out?"

Smythe thought about it for a moment. He didn't doubt that Blimpey could find out most anything. But he wasn't sure himself just what it was that he was looking for. Blast a Spaniard, he felt a bit of a fool, not even able to say what it was he wanted to know. "No, just general stuff. Anythin' about the night of the killin' and anythin' about them names I give ya."

Blimpey's eyebrows rose so far they almost disappeared under the brim of his filthy pork pie hat. "What da ya mean, general stuff? Come on now, mate, I'm good, but I can't get blood out of a bleedin' turnip. These people ain't crooks. It's not like I'm goin' to be able to tap my usual sources."

Irritated with himself more than Blimpey, Smythe answered harshly. "Look, I've given you the bloomin' names. Just find out if any of 'em' as come into a bit of money or is plannin' on leavin' town or . . . or . . ."

"Or anythin' else," Blimpey finished. He took another swallow of beer.

"This is gonna cost you. Thems a lot of names, I'll 'ave to spread the lolly about a bit to cover 'em all."

"Spread as much as ya 'ave to," Smythe retorted, then caught himself and quickly picked up his own beer. Bloomin' Ada, he'd forgotten for a moment that Blimpey only thought of him as a coachman. When he glanced at the other man over the rim of his tankard, Blimpey was staring at him with a long, speculative gleam in his eye. "What are you lookin' at?"

Blimpey smiled slowly. "Nuthin'. Just wonderin' where a coachman gets that kind of lolly."

"I told ya before, I play the 'orses."

"Then we'll 'ave to go to the races together sometime," Blimpey said amiably. "The way you spread the stuff about, you must be bloomin' good at pickin' winners."

"So what if I am?"

"You was out in Australia a while back, wasn't ya?"

Smythe blinked, surprised by the abrupt change of subject. "Yeah, what of it?"

"Nuthin', just chattin'" Blimpey pointedly looked down at his now-empty glass. "I could use another."

Smythe nodded at the barman, who hustled over with another glass of beer and slapped it down in front of Blimpey.

"Seems to me, even if ya play the ponies a bit, you're always ready with the cash," Blimpey said softly. "Not that I'm askin' any questions, mind ya. Just curious like."

"Good, 'cause I'm not answerin'" Smythe wondered if Blimpey was going to raise his price now.

"The price is the same," Blimpey said, as though he could read the coachman's mind. "But ya know, if I 'ad the kind of money I think you 'ave, I wouldn't be 'angin' about drivin' someone else's 'orses. I'd be buyin' my own."

"You're talkin' daft, man," Smythe retorted. But he knew then that Blimpey knew the truth. Cor blimey, he'd been a fool to think the likes of Blimpey Groggins wouldn't get curious about him. Especially considering the kind of money he'd tossed Blimpey's way for information—and in one case for a little more than information.

He'd no doubt that Blimpey knew to the penny exactly how much money Smythe had.

"I'm daft?" Blimpey laughed. "Look, Smythe, you're a good sort and

I owe you one. So don't think I'm goin' to be spreadin' any stories about you. If someone as rich as you wants to go on livin' in a policeman's 'ouse and drivin' a team of ruddy 'orses, that's yer business."

Puzzled, Smythe stared at him. He didn't remember doing Blimpey Groggins any favors. "You owe me one?"

"Forget I said that," he said quickly, slamming his glass on the counter. "I'd best get crackin'" Blimpey was obviously flustered; he hadn't even finished his beer. "I'll get back to you in a day or two." He turned and started for the door. Smythe grabbed his arm. "Come on, Blimp, what'd ya mean?"

Blimpey blushed.

Smythe gaped at him as a red flush climbed Blimpey's cheeks and spread all the way up to his dirty forehead. "I didn't mean nuthin' by it," he protested. "Now leave off and let me git to work."

But Smythe had to have his curiosity satisfied. "Oh, no, ya don't. Tell me what ya meant."

Blimpey glared at the hand on his sleeve for a moment and the shrugged. "Oh, well, if you must know. There was a woman . . . a friend of mine, like."

"Yeah?" Smythe encouraged. For a talker, Blimpey had sure got tongue-tied quick enough.

"Ya 'elped 'er, that's all."

"What woman?" Smythe asked. He couldn't remember helping any friends of Blimpey's. "What's 'er name?"

"Abby," Blimpey replied.

"Abby?" Smythe looked at him blankly.

"Sometimes she uses 'Abigail.'"

Then he remembered. It had been back at the beginning of the case in which the inspector had been a suspect in those businessmen's murders. Oh, yes, he remembered all right.

"Ya 'elped 'er out a few months back," Blimpey continued. "She wouldn't come to me."

"Why?" Smythe asked. "Why wouldn't she come to ya?" As he recalled, his helping sweet Abigail had caused a few problems between him and Betsy. It didn't do to let a woman see another woman throw her arms about your neck. Even when it didn't mean anything but a bit of gratitude. Betsy's nose had really been out of joint when she'd seen Abigail's hug of thanks.

"'Cause we'd 'ad words over some triflin' matter," Blimpey said irritably. He wished he'd never brought the bloomin' subject up, but he owed Smythe. "And she weren't speakin' to me. Silly woman, rather go 'ungry than give in to 'er pride. She come to you at the stables and you lent 'er a few quid. It were enough to keep her off the streets. I'm grateful for that. She means somethin' to me. Now leave off and let me go. I've got work to do."

Amazed, Smythe watched as Blimpey stalked off. He couldn't believe it! Blimpey Groggins was in love.

CHAPTER 9

"Did we have any luck on the brothel?" Witherspoon asked as he and Constable Barnes waited at the pedestrian island for a dray to pass. He felt a flash of guilt when he thought of the house on Lisle Street. He really should have gone there himself, but he simply hadn't had time.

Barnes brightened. "We did, sir. It seems that Hinchley had been there that night, before he went to the theatre. He'd made arrangements for later in the evening. But then he cancelled and the . . . er . . . person never went."

"Cancelled?" Witherspoon queried. "How'd he do that?"

"He sent a lad round with a note." Barnes checked the traffic and started across the road. "The message said that he'd changed his mind and no one was to come to his house that night."

"Was the police constable sure they were telling him the truth?" Realizing how awkward that sounded, the inspector quickly amended his words, "I mean, is he sure the people at the brothel aren't lying to protect a member of their establishment?"

"Oh, yes, sir. Constable Giffith questioned everyone at the brothel himself. He's sure no one's lying. The maid and half a dozen other people swear that Rupert Bowker never left the premises that night." Barnes chuckled. "Bowker was the one scheduled to go to Hinchley's. Seems this Bowker was quite put out about the whole thing. I gather the madam kept the money and as he'd not gone to the client, she wouldn't pay him."

"I don't suppose the message was in writing?" Witherspoon turned the corner.

"Yes, but the madam burned it."

"Burned it?"

"She tossed it in the stove with the rest of the waste paper the next morning."

"Drat." Witherspoon would have liked to have had a look at that note. "What time did the messenger get there?"

"About eleven forty-five, sir," Barnes replied. "Just a few minutes before Bowker was set to leave."

"Eleven forty-five, huh?" Witherspoon mused. "Barnes, remind me to have another chat with Rather."

"The Hinchley butler? Why?"

Witherspoon really didn't know. But he had to say something. "Well, the note had to be written somewhere," he said. Aware of the constable's quizzical gaze, he hastily asked, "Did we get a description of the lad who brought the message around?"

Barnes grimaced. "Not much. But the madam told Griffith he was small, dressed well, had black hair and wore a cap pulled low over his face."

"So it wasn't a street arab?"

"The madam thought it was Hinchley's footman."

Witherspoon sighed. Drat. Now they'd have to try and track down this footman. "But all Hinchley's staff had been let go, so it couldn't have been one of his footmen."

"It could have been someone from the theatre district," Barnes ventured. "An actor or someone like that. Hinchley could have hired someone to take the message round for him."

"Yes, I suppose that's what must have happened. Have you had any reports back on the hansoms?" Witherspoon asked Barnes as they stopped in front of Theodora Vaughan's town house.

Barnes held open the wrought iron gate for the inspector. "According to the reports, the only two of the suspects they can determine actually took a cab that night were Miss Vaughan and the victim."

"Let's keep at it, Barnes," Witherspoon said bracingly. He might still be a tad confused about a few aspects of this case, but all in all, he felt ever so much better. It had been a most enlightening morning.

First, he'd gone to the Yard and sent out the word to the constables on patrol. Then he and Barnes had gone to pay a visit to Mr. Hinchley's solicitor. That conversation had been quite enlightening.

"Excuse me, sir," Barnes said as they reached the front door, "but why are we comin' here to see Edmund Delaney? Won't he be at his own home?"

Witherspoon banged the brass door knocker. "I believe"—the inspector dropped his voice to a whisper—"he spends rather more time with Miss Vaughan than he does in his rooms. If you'll remember, his landlady said he's rarely ever there."

The door opened, and a few minutes later Witherspoon and Barnes were ensconced in Theodora Vaughan's delightfully feminine drawing room.

The walls were a pale ivory and the carpet a deep, rich red. A crystal chandelier hung from an intricately paterned ceiling. Delicate rose velvet settees and wing chairs were scattered artfully around the room. But it was the painting hanging over the mantel that caught one's eye.

Drawn to the picture, Witherspoon wandered toward the fireplace, his gaze fixed on the portrait of Theodora Vaughan.

Her hair was loose and flowed like a deep auburn cloak over her shoulders, spilling over a deep blue gown. Her hands were clasped demurely together, and her head angled slightly to one side.

"Beautiful," Witherspoon murmured.

"Juliet," Edmund Delaney said from behind them.

"Juliet?" the inspector repeated. "Oh, you mean the play. Shakespeare. *Romeo and Juliet.*"

Delaney smiled and crossed the room to join them. "She was twenty-six when she played that part. This portrait was done at that time. She was superb. All of London was at her feet. She went from being a poor, struggling actress stealing apples for supper and sneaking lifts off the backs of cabs to being the toast of the town."

"She is a remarkable actress," Witherspoon agreed. "I'm privileged to have met her."

"Goodness, Inspector, you make it sound as though I'm retiring," Theodora said from the doorway. She was dressed in a pale yellow day gown, her hair was elegantly arranged in a mass of brillant curls and her face wreathed in a charming smile as she advanced into the room.

"Forgive me, dear Miss Vaughan." Witherspoon felt like he ought to kiss her hand or bow, but wasn't quite certain how one did that sort of thing. "It will be a great tragedy for the stage when that dreadful moment comes."

"How very kind you are, Inspector." She gestured gracefully toward the settee. "Please sit down. Shall I ring for tea?"

"No, thank you." Witherspoon sat down. Barnes took one of the wing chairs and Delaney, all the friendliness gone from his face, sat down on the love seat next to Theodora.

"Why have you come, Inspector?" Delaney asked bluntly.

Witherspoon silently debated the wisdom of asking his questions with both of them present, then he decided it really didn't matter. No matter how delicate or diplomatic he was, the next few moments were going to be rather painful and embarrassing for both of them. "I've a few more questions to ask," he said.

"But we've answered all your questions." Delaney got up and began to pace. "Really, sir, this is beginning to be annoying."

"It's all right, Edmund," Theodora said soothingly. "The inspector is only doing his duty. Please, ask me anything you like."

Witherspoon took a deep breath. He was surprised at how difficult it was to form the words properly. "How well did you know Ogden Hinchley?"

"He was a critic," she said, looking surprised. "I've known him for years, but I didn't really *know* him, if you understand my meaning. Not socially."

"So you would say you have merely a professional relationship with him?" Barnes asked.

Theodora glanced at Delaney. "For the most part," she replied.

Witherspoon watched her carefully, reminding himself that this woman was an actress. "Are you aware that Hinchley had threatened to ruin you?"

"Yes," she replied, her expression hardening just a bit. "I am." She kept her gaze on the inspector, not on Delaney, who had stopped by the mantel. "I didn't take it seriously."

"But he had the power to do it," Barnes put in. "Weren't you worried?"

"Not at all," she said, folding her hands in her lap. "He's only one person, Constable. Admittedly, Ogden Hinchley was the most powerful critic in London, but his word was hardly law."

"I see." The inspector thought her attitude most sensible. He waited a moment, hoping that Barnes would carry on and ask the next question. But the constable was busy scribbling in his notebook.

So Witherspoon cleared his throat and tried and failed to make himself look at Theodora Vaughan. "Were you aware of why Ogden Hinchley wanted to ruin you?" he asked gently as he stared at the carpet. His head jerked up when he heard Delaney's exclamation of disgust.

"For God's sake, Inspector," Delaney snapped.

"It's all right, Edmund." She smiled slightly, as though she were amused by the inspector's obvious discomfort. "Of course I knew why Hinchley wanted to ruin me. Half of London knew. He was ridiculously jealous of my relationship with Edmund," she said calmly, "but I naturally assumed he'd get over it."

Witherspoon looked at Delaney. This one wasn't an actor. His face was showing strain. He'd gone pale around the mouth. "Mr. Delaney, forgive me for bringing up such a delicate matter, but . . . er . . . would you mind telling us what your relationship with Hinchley was? I mean, before the two of you quarreled."

Delaney's lips tightened. "We were once good friends. At least, it was friendship on my part."

"You weren't"—Barnes coughed—"more intimately involved?"

"No," Delaney said fiercely. "I'd heard the rumors about Ogden, of course. But he never approached me in that way." He began to pace back and forth across the room. "Try and understand. I was a poor, struggling playwright when we first met. I was flattered that he took an interest in me, that he wanted to be my friend."

"When did he start paying your rent on the house in Chelsea?" Barnes asked bluntly. He didn't much like this kind of questioning, but he figured he'd do better than the inspector at getting at the truth.

Delaney sighed. "You make it sound so ugly, Constable. It wasn't like that at all. I paid Hinchley rent on the Chelsea house."

"That's not what we've heard, sir."

"I know what all the rumor mongers said," Delaney replied wearily, "but it simply isn't true. I've got rent receipts. You can see them if you like."

Barnes glanced at Witherspoon, who nodded encouragingly. "I would like to see them, sir," the constable said. "You can bring them by the station."

"Fine," Delaney agreed grudgingly. "I will. Ogden didn't charge me very much, but nonetheless, I did pay rent. He knew I didn't have much money, just a small income that had been left to me by my father, and that I was trying to write. So he lowered the rent because we were friends. It was only later, when he invited me to Italy, that I realized his feelings for me were much deeper than mine for him. By that time, I'd met Miss Vaughan and we'd . . . we'd . . ."

"Fallen in love," Theodora finished. "As a matter of fact, Inspector, congratulations are in order."

"Really, Theodora," Edmund said quickly. "I don't believe this is the time . . ."

"Oh, nonsense." She laughed gaily. "I'm too happy to keep this all to myself. Edmund and I are going to be married."

Witherspoon was totally at a loss. Questioning people who'd just announced wedding plans seemed a tad churlish. "Er, congratulations—to both of you. When is the happy event taking place?"

"As soon as possible, Inspector," Theodora replied, smiling broadly. "We've waited long enough. But I've just had word that the difficulties surrounding my divorce from Trevor Remington have been resolved. By the time Edmund and I can get a license and make the arrangements, I'll be free to marry him."

"All the very best to both of you," Barnes muttered. He cleared his throat and looked pointedly at the inspector, who was staring at Theodora Vaughan.

"Excuse me, Miss Vaughan, did I just hear you say you're married to Mr. Remington?" Witherspoon asked incredulously.

"*Was* married to Mr. Remington," she replied. "I received word from my American lawyers while I was at my country house that our divorce had finally been obtained." She got up, walked over to Delaney and linked her arm with his. "We've waited a long time, Inspector."

Barnes's head was spinning, but spinning or not, he had a few more questions to ask. Especially since it looked as if the inspector was too shocked to do anything but stand there gaping at the happy couple. "Mr. Delaney," he said quietly, "is it true you threatened to kill Hinchley?"

Delaney gasped. "For God's sake, that was over a year ago."

"Nevertheless, you admit you did it?"

"I lost my temper, Inspector," Delaney cried. "He accosted us in public. I tell you, he was out of his mind with rage and jealousy. He went on and on about how he was going to ruin us. Kept screaming that I'd never see one of my plays on the boards and that he'd make Theodora a laughing-stock. I didn't mind so much him having a go at me, but when he turned his venom on her, I lost my temper and told him if he came near her, I'd kill him. But I hardly think you ought to put any credence in something that happened so long ago. If I was going to kill the man, I'd have done it then, when I was good and angry."

As they'd planned, Wiggins met Mrs. Jeffries by the Serpentine in Hyde Park. "How did it go?" she asked.

"I found out the name of Parks's 'ousekeeper," Wiggins replied. "Mind you, it weren't easy. Annie was lookin' at me funny when I started in askin' all them questions again."

"It's never easy, Wiggins." Mrs. Jeffries patted his arm. "But you are very good at it. Now, what's the house-keeper's name and where does she live?"

Wiggins grinned broadly, delighted by the praise. "Her name is Roberta Seldon and she lives with her sister in Clapham. Number six, Bester Road."

"Excellent." Mrs. Jeffries already had an idea about how to approach the woman. "And did Annie know where Parks had gotten the loan on his house?"

"No," he said. "She said Parks never told her and she never asked. So what do I do now?" After his success with Annie today, he was raring to have at it again.

The housekeeper thought for a moment. She still had no real idea about the solution of this case, but she felt that keeping everyone busy was very important. "I think you ought to have another snoop around the victim's neighborhood," she said. She didn't think there was much more to learn there. The police had questioned the neighbors thoroughly and no one had seen anything that night. But it was something for the boy to do and one never knew—sometimes the police overlooked things.

"Sounds fair enough." Wiggins grinned. "You takin' off for Clapham now?"

"Yes, I want to find out precisely why this Mrs. Seldon left Parks's employment."

"But Annie said it was because they 'adn't been paid."

"I know, but sometimes there's more to a situation than meets the eye."

Betsy couldn't believe her eyes. What was Smythe doing with someone like that? She dodged behind the oak tree in the center of the communal gardens behind the inspector's house and peeked out. Smythe, his back to her, was standing at the far end of the garden talking to a short, chubby man in a checkered coat and a porkpie hat.

She wondered if she ought to call out, to let him know that she was here. But there was something about the way the two men stood close together in the shadows of the wall, almost like they were hiding, that kept her silent.

Besides, she told herself firmly, it wasn't like she was spying on him deliberately. Could she help it if just when she'd followed him out here to tell him the truth about her trip to the East End, he'd decided to have a visitor?

Guilt pierced through her like an arrow. She ought to call out and let him know that she was here. Or better yet, she ought to nip out from behind this tree and go back into the house. Smythe had a right to his privacy. Goodness knows, she'd harped on that subject herself to know enough to respect it for others.

But she couldn't bring herself to move.

As she watched, she saw the fat man's mouth moving a mile a minute, his hands punctuating the air as he talked. Smythe was leaning towards him, like he was listening with his whole body.

From his vantage point at the other end of the garden, Blimpey Groggins had seen the girl slip behind the tree. He grinned.

"You took a chance on comin' 'ere," Smythe said. "Cor blimey, I only give ya the job this mornin'"

"I 'appened to be passin' this way," Blimpey said conversationally. "And as I'd learned a thing or two, I thought I'd stop round. You said you needed this information right quick. Make up yer mind, man. Do you want it or not?"

"'Course I want it." Smythe cast a quick glance over his shoulder. "I just didn't expect to open the back door and find you standin' there like a ruddy statue. What'd ya find out?"

"A couple of things." Blimpey decided to wait until after he'd finished and gotten some of his pay before telling Smythe about the girl spying on them from behind the tree. No point in making the big man angry over trifles that couldn't be helped. "First of all, the servants left at the Hinchley 'ouse is doin' fine now that the old geezer's gone to his reward. Hinchley's solicitors ain't inventoried the estate yet, so the two of 'em are 'aving a fine old time sellin' off some of his smaller treasures."

"They're stealin' from the dead man's 'ouse?" Smythe asked incredulously. "Cor blimey, that takes a bit of nerve." But it was hardly a motive for murder.

"Not really." Blimpey figured the dead man was probably getting what he deserved. Not that it mattered now. "If there's no family about to see to things, you'd be surprised how often things like that 'appen."

"But won't the solicitors notice that things is missin'?"

"So what if they do?" Blimpey shrugged. "By then the maid and the butler will be gone. The solicitor went round there yesterday and told them to start lookin' for other positions. The maid was right annoyed about that too. Ranted and raved about what bastards lawyers are to every shopkeeper on the ruddy 'igh street." He chuckled. "Mind you, she were also narked that they weren't gettin' anythin' from the dear departed, the solicitor made that clear enough. She's started lookin' for another place. God knows where she'll end up. And the butler's already booked passage on a steamer for America."

Smythe's brows drew together in a fierce frown. Stealing from the dead just didn't seem right.

Blimpey, correctly interpreting the coachman's expression, quickly said, "Look, don't you be gettin' on yer 'igh 'orse because two servants is 'elpin' themselves to a few bits from the old bastards 'ouse. From what I 'eard about Hinchley, 'e's gettin' what 'e earned in life. As ye sow, so shall ye reap; that's what my old gran used to say."

"Don't worry, I'm not goin' to be blatherin' to the police about what you've told me," Smythe said. "Anythin' else?"

"I found out where that Swinton fella was on last Saturday night," Blimpey said. "Fella's got a nasty 'abit."

"How nasty?"

"Likes to smoke opium." Blimpey scratched his nose. "Showed up at a den down by the river at around midnight and stayed until almost three in the morning."

"Swinton was in an opium den?" Smythe knew such places existed, but he'd never actually known of anyone who frequented them.

"That's right. Accordin' to my sources, Swinton's a real regular. That's why 'is business 'as gone to pot, so to speak. Spends what money 'is theatre brings in on blowin' smoke up 'is nose."

No wonder Willard Swinton claimed to be in the office, counting receipts on his own, Smythe thought. That was a better alibi than admitting you were in an opium den. "Anything else?" Smythe pressed. He was beginning to get nervous about being out here with Blimpey. Mrs. Jeffries or Wiggins or even, God forbid, Betsy might come home any minute and come looking for him.

"Not much. I'll keep workin' on them other names you give me," Blimpey said.

"What about the theatre?" Smythe pressed. He'd asked Blimpey to see if anyone had seen anything suspicious at or around the Hayden on Saturday evening. "Did any of yer sources 'ave any luck there?"

Blimpey made a face. "Nah. Most of 'em was pickin' pockets that night, not watchin' the crowd."

"So that's it, then?" Smythe started to reach in his pocket for his roll of bills.

"'Ang on a minute," Blimpey warned, his gaze fixed on a point over Smythe's shoulder. "I wouldn't be flashin' that wad of yours unlessin' you want people to see it."

Smythe dropped his hand. "Are we bein' watched, then?"

Blimpey grinned broadly. "Right, mate. And she's a pretty little snoop, she is. Blond 'air, slim, got a right graceful way of dodgin' behind a tree, she 'as. Been there ever since you come out. Matter of fact, I'd say she followed ya out 'ere."

Blast, Smythe thought. Betsy. "All right, then, Blimpey. You go on and keep yer ears open. I'll meet ya at the pub tonight around ten to see what else you've got for me and to pay ya."

Blimpey tugged nattily on his filthy porkpie hat and, whistling a merry tune, sauntered off toward the gate.

Smythe whirled around. From the side of the tree he could see a bit of light blue fabric sticking out.

Betsy froze. She hadn't had the wits to make a run for the house when she had the chance and now she didn't dare move. Smythe was charging toward her hiding place. Lifting her chin, she stepped out from behind the tree before he got there and caught her hiding like a thief in the night.

"I've been waiting for you," she said boldly. "And who was that funny man you were talking to?" She'd decided it would be best just to brazen it out.

Surprised, he stopped. Then he put his hands on his hips. "Seems to me that you're askin' a lot of questions," he said, remembering how she'd refused to tell him about her mysterious errand the other day. "Aren't you the one that's always goin' on about 'ow everyone has some things that are private?"

"It couldn't be too private with you and him out here in broad daylight," she sputtered. "Besides, I was just asking. It's none of my business. I was only bein' friendly."

"Friendly? You was hidin' behind a ruddy tree and spyin' on me," he yelped.

Embarrassed, she took refuge in anger. "I wasn't hiding, I was waiting for you," she snapped. "I wanted to talk to you, but if you're too busy, I won't bother." She started to stomp past him but he caught her arm.

"Betsy," he said. "Let's stop this. We've been pickin' at each other for days now and I can't stand it."

"I don't like it either," she admitted, relieved that he wasn't going to be angry over her watching him. "And that's why I followed you out here. I wanted to tell you about why I had to go to Whitechapel."

"Go on," he urged.

She glanced back at the inspector's house. "This might take a few minutes, and I don't want the others coming back and interrupting us."

"They're not due for a bit yet," he said soothingly. "We've got time." It was ten minutes until one o'clock. Smythe hoped that, for once, everyone would be late.

"Let's sit down." She nodded toward a wooden bench under one of the other trees. "I'd feel better talkin' about this if I was sitting down."

Taking her arm, Smythe led her to the bench, waited till she was seated and then dropped down next to her. He wanted to reach for her hand, but she was holding herself as stiff as one of them mummies at the British Museum, so he merely waited.

Betsy swallowed heavily. There was only one way to do this. "I went over to Whitechapel because I wanted to put some money in the collection plate at St. Jude's," she said. "Five pounds. I gave them five pounds."

Smythe waited for her to continue. But she was staring straight ahead, her gaze blank and unfocused. He was going to have to coax the story out of her. "Why'd ya give 'em so much?" he asked gently.

"I owed it."

"Owed it?"

She nodded stiffly. "Yes. Would five pounds pay for a broken window?" That had been worrying her. She hoped she'd put in enough.

"Depends on how big the window was," he admitted honestly. "But unless you smashed a great painted-glass one, I'd say you give 'em enough."

She looked relieved. "Well, that's why I went to Whitechapel." She started to get up, but he put out his arm and gently pushed her back down. "That's not all of it, lass, is it?"

"No." She sighed. "But it's such an ugly story. I'm ashamed, Smythe. I want you to think well of me, and once you hear what I did, I don't think you will."

"There's nothin' you could 'ave done that would make me think less of you," he said honestly. And he meant every word too. "I know what it must 'ave been like for you tryin' to survive in the East End."

She looked up at him, her eyes shimmering with unshed tears. "Survival's one thing. Bein' deliberately wrong is something else. What I did was wrong, and even worse, I did it to the house of God."

"Tell me about it," he urged softly. "I don't want there to be any secrets between us, lass." Maybe if she shared all of her past with him, he'd find the courage to tell her about his secret.

"It was years ago," she began. "I told you, I had two sisters."

"Yeah, I remember."

"And I told you that one of them got sick and died of a fever—do you remember that as well?"

"I remember everything you told me," he assured her.

"Well, when my sister got sick, we knew she was real bad off. Mum wanted to take her to the doctor, but she was only workin' as a barmaid and it took every penny we had just to pay the rent and buy a bit of food." She drew in a deep breath as the memories came flooding back. "So Mum went over to the parish church, St. Jude's. The vicar that was there had been known to lend a hand every now and again. But they had a new one, a Reverend Barnett and his wife. He didn't believe in givin' the poor money, said it only made the problem worse. So he turned her away with nothin'. Ann died two days later." She swiped at a tear. "We was heartbroken. A few weeks after that, a crowd had gathered in front of the church. I don't know why they was there: I expect I knew at the time but I don't remember. But it wasn't the first time crowds had come round there and caused trouble. A scuffle broke out and before you knew it, people was pickin' up stones and bricks and hurling them at the church." She closed her eyes. "I don't know what come over me; maybe I was half out of my mind with grief. But I picked up the biggest brick I could find and I hurled it right at one of the windows. Broke it too."

"Then what 'appened?"

"About that time someone called out that the police were coming, so I ran off."

"How old were you, Betsy?"

"Thirteen, maybe fourteen." She shrugged. "Old enough to know better. But I was so angry . . . they wouldn't help my mum. They wouldn't part with a few pennies to buy medicine or get a doctor for a dying child. And we'd not done anything wrong. We were just poor."

Smythe reached for her hand. "Betsy, why didn't you tell me this?"

She looked at him, her expression incredulous. "Don't you understand? I broke a church window. Deliberately. I sinned against the house of God. I was part of a mob . . ."

"You were a child still 'urtin' over losin' your baby sister," Smythe said angrily. He couldn't believe she'd risked herself goin' all the way to bloomin' Whitechapel to make up for something she'd done years ago. She'd spent her hard-earned money to boot. "And all you did was break a window in a buildin'. If it'd really been God's 'ouse, that old preacher would 'ave 'elped your mum. I can't believe you went all the way back there to give 'em the money. Cor blimey, it's not like the Church of England is poor, lass. They've got more ruddy money than the Queen."

Mrs. Jeffries stood in front of the last house on a row of terraces near Clapham High Street. She wondered for a moment precisely what approach to take and then decided that she'd make up her mind when she had a look at Roberta Seldon.

She walked up the walkway to the front door, noting that though there were cracks in the paving stones, the small lawn was neatly tended and someone had planted several rose bushes under the front window. The house was neatly painted too.

Taking a deep breath, Mrs. Jeffries climbed the two steps and knocked.

A moment later, she heard footsteps coming down the hall.

A short, dark-haired woman who appeared to be in her mid to late thirties stuck her head out. "Yes?"

"Mrs. Seldon?" Mrs. Jeffries smiled brightly.

"I'm Roberta Seldon. Have we met?"

"No, but I do hope you'll be able to help me." She wanted to get inside and talk to the woman. What she needed to know about Albert Parks couldn't be obtained by standing on a door stoop.

"Help you how?" Roberta Seldon replied. "Are you collecting for a charity?"

"No, no," Mrs. Jeffries said quickly. "I'm actually seeking some information for my employer. I'm sure you'll understand when I tell you it's most confidential, most confidential indeed."

"What kind of information?" The woman was still wary, but Mrs. Jeffries could see that she was interested too.

"About Albert Parks," Mrs. Jeffries replied, deciding to go for the direct approach. "I believe you used to be in his employ."

Roberta Seldon said nothing; she simply stared at her. Mrs. Jeffries was afraid her bold approach had failed.

Finally, she said, "You'd better come inside, then. I've got quite a bit to say about Albert Parks."

CHAPTER 10

———⋄⋗∞⋖⋄———

Wiggins couldn't make up his mind what to do. If he went back to meet the others at Upper Edmonton Gardens, he'd lose her. He hesitated at the corner, keeping one eye out for the omnibus and the other on the clock over the bank. Across the street, he could see the girl from Hinchley's house tapping her foot impatiently as she waited at the bus stop.

The omnibus came around the corner. Wiggins made up his mind and sprinted across the street. The girl's head swiveled as she heard his footsteps pounding towards her.

"Didn't want to miss it," he explained, jerking his chin toward the omnibus and giving her his most charming smile.

She wasn't impressed. She turned her head and went to pick up her case.

"Let me," he said quickly as the vehicle drew up and stopped.

Startled, she drew back, raked him with a swift, calculating gaze. Apparently finding him harmless, she said, "Go ahead, then."

They climbed aboard and Wiggins, though he dearly loved riding up top, dutifully followed her inside the bus. She took a seat by the window. Wiggins put the suitcase down in the aisle and dropped down next to her. "You don't mind, do ya?" he asked.

She shrugged. "It's all the same to me where ya sit. Thanks for carryin' my case. Thing's heavy."

The conductor came and they paid their fares. Wiggins noted the girl paid all the way to Victoria Station. He cursed himself for not letting her pay first, as he'd only paid to Hyde Park.

"Goin' on a trip?" he asked.

"Wish I was." She snorted delicately. "It's all right for some. But the rest of us has got a livin' to earn."

"My name's Wiggins." He tried again. If this girl was Lilly, the one Betsy had talked to, then she'd changed in the last couple of days. Betsy had claimed that girl would talk a fence post deaf. "What's yours?"

She kept her gaze straight ahead. "That's not your concern now, is it?"

"Sorry." He cringed. "I wasn't tryin' to be bold, miss. Just friendly."

The girl turned, looked at him for a moment and then gave an apologetic shrug. "My name's Lilly. I'm not in a very good frame of mind, if you know what I mean."

"Is there somethin' wrong?"

"Well, I've had better days, I can tell ya that." She turned and gazed out the window again.

Wiggins wondered what to do. Something had happened at the Hinchley house—he was sure of it. But he sensed that Lilly's mood was as changeable as the weather. Women were funny creatures. You never knew when you'd say the wrong thing and they'd shut up tighter than a biscuit tin. He didn't want that. Then he remembered how Mrs. Jeffries often got people to talk. He dropped his voice slightly. "I 'ate to see a pretty lass like yourself lookin' so sad," he said sympathetically.

"You'd look sad too if you'd put up with what I've 'ad to lately," she retorted. "Bloomin' solicitors."

"You've 'ad a bit of a rough time." He patted her arm. "Maybe it would 'elp to talk about it some? Make you feel better."

She sighed. "Don't see what good talkin' about it will do; won't change things none. But as I'm stuck on this ruddy omnibus all the way to Victoria, I might as well."

By one-fifteen, Inspector Witherspoon had finished his lunch and gone to meet Constable Barnes at the Yard. As soon as the door had closed behind him, Mrs. Jeffries hurried down to the kitchen.

The others were already seated around the table. Mrs. Goodge had put out plates of bread, cold roast beef, buns and turnovers for the household's meal.

"If you don't mind, Mrs. Jeffries, we'll eat as we talk," she said as the housekeeper took her seat. "I'd like to get this kitchen cleared as quickly as possible," Mrs. Goodge explained. "I've got more people droppin' by this afternoon."

"That's a splendid idea," Mrs. Jeffries agreed. "We are a bit pressed for time and I, for one, have quite a bit of information to share."

"So do I," Luty said, helping herself to a turnover. "Are we goin' to wait for Wiggins?"

"I wouldn't," Smythe said. He helped himself to a slice of brown bread. "'E were goin' back over to the Hinchley neighborhood to snoop about. As 'e's not back yet, 'e's probably on to something."

Mrs. Jeffries nodded and reached for the teapot. "Then I'll start." She told them everything she'd gotten out of the inspector at lunch. "He was quite shocked, poor man. I don't think he'd ever met a woman quite like Theodora Vaughan. As he put it, 'in one breath she announced she's divorced and a moment later, she's announcing her engagement.' Poor man. He was quite taken with the woman too—until this afternoon."

"Actresses," Mrs. Goodge muttered darkly. "And her older than him by a good ten years!"

"But Rose told Wiggins that the divorce was off," Betsy exclaimed. "There was some sort of legal muck-up."

"Apparently, Miss Vaughan's American lawyers straightened it out."

Betsy shook her head. "But why wouldn't her personal maid know that?"

"From what I gather," Mrs. Jeffries said, "Theodora Vaughan only found out herself last week. Maybe the maid didn't know."

"And now the woman's fixin' to marry Delaney," Luty said incredulously. "Some women just don't learn. She finally sheds one husband and now she wants another one."

"Really, madam." Hatchet clucked his tongue. "That's rather a cynical point of view. Marriage is an honorable estate . . ."

"If it's so honorable, how come you ain't ever got hitched?" she shot back.

"Or maybe she was keepin' it a secret," Betsy murmured, then flushed when she glanced up and saw Smythe grinning knowingly at her. She resisted the impulse to stick her tongue out at him. Cheeky devil. But she felt ever so much better now that they'd cleared the air.

"Was that all you got out of the inspector?" Mrs. Goodge prodded. She really did want the lot of them to get a move on. None of her sources would say a word if they walked in and found half of London sitting at the kitchen table.

Mrs. Jeffries added a few more details about the inspector's morning and then plunged in with her own tale. "I managed to get Roberta Seldon, Albert Parks's former housekeeper, to tell me quite a bit," she continued. "Apparently, she did quit. As Wiggins said, she hadn't been paid. But, and this is the important part, she also told me that Parks didn't come home right after the performance on Saturday evening. She was still awake at half past eleven. As a matter of fact, she heard him come in at around two A.M."

"Don't tell me 'e was out walkin' along the ruddy river too," Smythe said disgustedly. "Cor blimey, there's more bloomin' foot traffic on that embankment than there is on Oxford Street."

Mrs. Jeffries shook her head. "Mrs. Seldon had no idea where he was, only that he didn't come home that night when he claimed. There's something else too. I'm not sure if it's important or not. Mrs. Seldon said that when she went into his study to tell him she was leaving, he was locking something in his desk."

"What was it?" Hatchet asked.

"She wasn't sure; she only got a glimpse of it," Mrs. Jeffries explained. "But she thinks it might have been a note of some kind. All she saw was a flash of white. It struck her as odd because Parks jumped ten feet when she walked into the room. Furthermore, he'd never locked that desk before. Mrs. Seldon said he kept the keys right out on his desk all the time, so she was quite surprised when she suddenly found him locking it up tighter than the Bank of England. When Parks saw that she'd seen him, he gave her specific instructions not to touch it. Not that it mattered to her; she'd come in to tell him she was leaving his household."

"Did he leave the keys out?" Hatchet asked.

"No," Mrs. Jeffries replied. "He put them in his pocket. Mrs. Seldon was rather annoyed. She thought he might have been locking up an envelope of money and he did owe her her wages."

"So he was lockin' somethin' up and he ain't got an alibi," Luty muttered.

"None of them have an alibi," Betsy pointed out.

"One of 'em does," Smythe said. He passed on the information Blimpey had given him about Willard Swinton.

"An opium den!" Mrs. Goodge's eyes were as round as saucers behind her spectacles. "I can't believe it. A respectable businessman like that."

"It's true," Smythe said. "My source was sure of it. That's one of the reasons the Hayden's been doin' so poorly the last few years. Swinton's addicted. Every bit of money that comes in goes right up his nose. And I learned something else too," he said, reaching for a another bun. In between bites, he told them about Hinchley's servants. "Stealin' from a dead man, they are," he concluded.

"Shocking," Mrs. Goodge said indignantly. She hadn't enjoyed herself so much in days. "Absolutely shocking."

Mrs. Jeffries cleared her throat. "Actually," she said, "I've got more to tell you about Parks."

"Sorry, Mrs. J.," Smythe said hastily. "Didn't mean to steal yer thunder."

"That's quite all right; your comments were pertinent to the subject at hand," she said. "But as I was saying, Mrs. Seldon asked Parks when she could expect to be paid her wages. She claims he got a 'funny little smile' on his face and then told her he fully expected to come into money very soon. Enough to pay her and the rest of his debts."

"I don't suppose he told the Seldon woman how or why he was comin' into this money?" Luty asked.

"No," Mrs. Jeffries replied. "He didn't."

"I think I know," Betsy said. "From the theatre. The inspector said the play is sold out for a number of weeks."

"I asked Mrs. Seldon that," Mrs. Jeffries said. "And she was positive that wasn't it. The day after opening night, Theodora Vaughan, Trevor Remington and Swinton had a meeting at Parks's house. Mrs. Seldon overheard them talking. They were discussing what they were going to do if the play failed. They were fairly certain it would too."

"Delaney wasn't there?" Smythe asked.

"No, he wasn't," Mrs. Jeffries answered. "I find that most signficant."

"They was sure that Ogden Hinchley was goin' to give the play a bad review and kill it," Luty murmured.

"But Hinchley didn't give it a bad review," Betsy pointed out. "At least not that any of them knew about. He was already dead by then. No one ever saw the review."

"Oh, I believe someone did, Betsy," Mrs. Jeffries replied. "The killer saw it."

Mrs. Goodge cast a quick, frantic glance at the clock. "I've got a bit to say too, and as we're still talking about Albert Parks, I'd like to get on with it." She forged right ahead. "Remember how I told you that Parks had been run off from a theatre in Manchester? Well, guess who it was that was behind gettin' rid of him."

"Ogden Hinchley," Smythe said.

She nodded. "That's right. Hinchley was only an actor back then, but he was a rich one. He put up most of the money to produce the play. Accordin' to what I heard, he was so bad at it, that's the only way Hinchley could ever get a part. But as he'd put up the money, he took quite an interest in the business end of things. When the money from the receipts didn't match the head count at the door, Hinchley got suspicious. Parks was only a stage manager at the time, but he was the one that got the blame for the shortfall between the receipts and the head count. Hinchley run him off and what's worse, every time the man tried to get another stage manager's position, Hinchley would make sure whoever was fixing to hire Parks knew that he'd been accused of theft. As you can imagine, Parks's reputation wasn't worth much after that. That's how he came to be a director. He couldn't get work here in England, so he went to Germany and fell in with a theatre there. That's where he learned this directin' business. He was there for a goodly number of years."

"Pardon me, Mrs. Goodge," Hatchet interrupted smoothly. "But how did Parks end up owning a home and having a staff? From what you've told us, he was unemployed and broke."

"That's why he come back to England," she replied. "His granny died and left him the house and a bit of an income. Not really enough to live on—he still needed to work. Especially as he'd taken a loan on his home and put cash in Delaney's play. He was hoping this play would be his . . . his . . ." She hesitated, trying to think of the right word. "Entry back into the British theatre."

"Looks instead like it might be 'is entry to the Old Bailey," Smythe mumbled.

"Yes, it's beginning to look that way," Mrs. Jeffries agreed. Some of the puzzle pieces were starting to fit together. Or were they? From the back of her mind, something niggled her, but she firmly ignored it. This time, she wasn't going to think the situation to death.

"You think he might be our killer?" Luty asked eagerly.

Mrs. Jeffries didn't want to commit herself, but on the other hand, not committing herself might make the others believe she lacked confidence in them and her own powers of deduction. "I think we can assume that Hinchley was killed because he was a critic. He had the power of life or death over a play. The evidence against Parks is quite substantial. He, more than the others, appears to have had more to lose if Hinchley gave the play a bad review, and consequently, the play failed. It wasn't just his reputation that was at stake anymore, it was his entire future."

"But what about Mr. Delaney?" Betsy challenged. "He'd got a lot to lose."

"Yes, but he wouldn't be ruined financially," Mrs. Jeffries pointed out. "He is marrying Miss Vaughan. She's quite a wealthy woman. Furthermore, there's a long and honorable tradition in the theatre of playwrights having both successes and failures. In other words, one failed play wouldn't necessarily mean he'd never write another, more successful play. Especially if he was married to Theodora Vaughan."

"And Willard Swinton's got to know that no matter 'ow much money 'e gets, as long as 'e's addicted to opium, it'll never be enough," Smythe said thoughtfully.

"Remington's a pretty successful actor," Luty added. "One bad play wouldn't kill him. Even though he'd invested all his money, it wasn't like he'd never be able to work again."

"He could always tour the American West again," Hatchet put in, just to annoy Luty. "I believe that in many of the more barbarian and desolate villages, the population is desperate enough to watch anything."

"What d'ya mean, 'again'?" Luty asked. She'd take him to task for that barbarian remark when she got him back in the carriage.

Hatchet smiled. "One of the bits of information I wanted to share today was that I learned that Miss Vaughan and Mr. Remington had toured the western part of the United States eighteen months or so ago. According to what I heard, they quarreled publicly through six states, two territories and several major cities. Apparently, by the time they reached San Francisco, they hated each other so much that Miss Vaughan, in a fit of rage, shot Mr. Remington. Luckily, she's a better actress than she is a marksman, and she only wounded him slightly in the shoulder." He shrugged. "A nice bit of gossip, I'm afraid, but hardly pertinent to the problem at hand."

"Do you really think Parks might be the one?" Betsy asked Mrs. Jeffries.

"I'm not sure. But if the inspector manages to find a constable or a watchman that saw Delaney and Remington walking along the river on

the night of the murder, then I don't think there's anyone else it could be."
She honestly didn't know what to think. On the last case, she'd ignored
the obvious and run herself in circles without coming up with the right
answer. She didn't want that to happen again. "But sure or not"—she got
to her feet—"we've got to keep at it."

They all looked at her expectantly. For a moment, her mind went blank.
But she recovered quickly. "Betsy, why don't you have another go at Rose
and find out why Theodora Vaughan kept her divorce a secret." She looked
at Smythe, but he was getting to his feet as well. "I've got a few things to
chase up," he said. "There's still a few pubs I need to do over near the
'ayden."

"I've got a banker or two I need to pester," Luty added. "I'm determined to find out about that loan Parks got on his house."

"I'll help you, madam," Hatchet said.

Mrs. Goodge breathed a heartfelt sigh of relief as they all got up. Then
the back door opened and pounding footsteps sounded in the hall.

"Sorry, I'm late," Wiggins yelled breathlessly, "but I was on to
somethin'"

"What is it?" Mrs. Jeffries asked.

"Is there any tea left?" Wiggins dashed toward the table. "I'm parched."

"Listen, boy," Mrs. Goodge snapped. "You pour yourself a cup and
then clear out. I've got people comin' and I don't want you hangin' about
puttin' your oar in."

"But I'm hungry," he protested. "I didn't 'ave time to eat."

"Here, then." The cook slapped a slab of beef between two slices of
bread and handed it to him. "Now, get off."

"But I want to tell ya want I learned." Unable to help himself, he
jammed a bite of the sandwich in his mouth. "It's about Hinchley's servants. I think they've been robbin' the man blind, or they would be if 'e
wasn't already dead . . ."

"We already know about that," Smythe said kindly.

"But . . . but . . ."

"It's all right, Wiggins." Mrs. Jeffries wanted to go out to the garden
to have a good think. "You've done quite well, but we are in a bit of a
hurry. Mrs. Goodge needs the kitchen."

"But what about . . ."

"Go up and have a rest," Betsy advised. "We'll fill you in later on what
all we've learned."

• • •

Mrs. Jeffries sat on the bench and gazed blankly at the grass. Her conscience was bothering her. She wondered if the others had observed what she'd done on this case. So far, none of them had said anything, but then again, perhaps they wouldn't even if they'd noticed.

It hadn't been intentional. Had it? Had she deliberately kept information from the inspector so that she could solve the case first? She honestly didn't know. She hadn't realized she'd even done it until today at lunch when he'd told her about how shocked he was to learn that Remington and Theodora Vaughan had been husband and wife.

She'd known about the marriage. She hadn't passed that bit on to him. She'd meant to, she really had. But somehow the time hadn't been right.

She forced herself to think back to the beginning, to try to remember what she'd told the inspector and, more important, what she hadn't.

But it was no use. She was in such a muddle, she simply couldn't remember. She thought she was getting worse too. Just a few minutes ago she'd forgotten to tell the others something else she'd done today. She'd talked Roberta Seldon into going to Scotland Yard to see Inspector Witherspoon. Why hadn't she told the others that? Was it because she was afraid that if she told everyone everything and then didn't solve this case, she'd be humiliated?

But surely she wasn't that smallminded. That petty. Surely she was more interested in justice than in gratifying her own sense of importance. Or was she? She pushed the idea out of her mind. She hadn't deliberately kept anything from the others. They'd been in a dreadful hurry today and she'd simply forgotten. She'd tell them tonight.

She'd also have a nice, long chat with the inspector. If there was something else she'd forgotten to tell him, he'd learn it right after supper.

"Hepzibah." Lady Cannonberry's voice jolted her out of her reverie. "How nice to find you out here."

"Gracious, Ruth, I didn't expect you back until next week." Mrs. Jeffries smiled at the fair-haired, slender middle-aged woman walking toward her.

"I came back early." Ruth Cannonberry sat down next to her and gazed out at the peaceful garden. "This is so lovely, so quiet. The train station was an absolute madhouse today."

"You came back by train?"

"Yes. I'd forgotten how crowded the trains are this time of year. The crush was awful. But it still amazes me that even in such a huge crowd, one always manages to run into someone one knows." She laughed.

"That does happen."

"I did something terrible, Hepzibah," she confided. "Jane Riddleton was at the station too. She must have come up on the same train as I did. But naturally, she'd have ridden in first class. No mixing with the masses for Jane. God forbid the woman actually speak to someone who might work for a living. I ducked behind a pillar so she wouldn't see me."

"Is she not a nice woman, then?" Mrs. Jeffries asked politely. Lady Cannonberry's late husband had been a peer of the realm, but Ruth Cannonberry was a vicar's daughter with a social conscience and political opinions that bordered on the radical. But she rarely said anything nasty about someone. She was simply too nice a person. If she made negative comments at all, she generally reserved them for the government, the church, or a variety of other institutions that she believed oppressed people, especially the poor.

"She's a terrible gossip," Ruth replied bluntly. "I knew if she caught me, I'd have to listen to her make catty remarks about my sister-in-law, Muriel. Muriel is behaving like an idiot, but I didn't particularly want to listen to Jane go on about it."

"Oh, dear."

Ruth sighed. "That doesn't make any sense, does it? I'm annoyed with Muriel too. More than annoyed, actually. I'm furious."

"What on earth has she done?" Mrs. Jeffries queried.

"Muriel is making a complete fool of herself over some young man and the whole county is talking about it," Ruth replied. She crossed her arms over her chest. "That's one of the reasons I came home early. My tolerance for the intrigues and excitements of picnics, balls and dinner parties just isn't what it used to be."

Mrs. Jeffries gazed at her curiously. "Gracious, you do sound like you've had an interesting visit."

"More tiring than interesting, I assure you. Because I'm a widow, Muriel decided I could act as chaperone for her. She apparently exhausted her mother some time ago. The silly girl dragged me to every social event in Sussex. Besides, if I hadn't left, I'm afraid I'd have done something unforgiveable."

Surprised, Mrs. Jeffries said, "You?"

"Yes, me." Ruth grimaced. "Muriel's following the poor young man about everywhere, pestering him mercilessly and even going so far as to try to discredit the young lady Thomas is in love with. Isn't that despicable? She's telling terrible tales about a perfectly nice young woman just so Catherine will be humiliated and come back to London. I was very much afraid I was going to lose my temper and box Muriel's ears. Goodness knows, she certainly deserved it. Honestly, what some people will do to win back a suitor."

"Win back?"

"Oh, yes, Muriel and Thomas were engaged. But he broke it off when he met Catherine. Muriel, instead of acting with any dignity about the whole affair, has instead behaved like a shrew. Thomas absolutely loathes the sight of her. Even if Catherine came back to London, he certainly wouldn't have a thing to do with Muriel." She paused to take a breath, then closed her eyes briefly. "Oh, forgive me, Hepzibah, I'm wittering on like a magpie. It's terribly rude. I haven't even asked how you are."

But Mrs. Jeffries didn't hear her; she was too busy thinking.

"Hepzibah?" Ruth prodded as the housekeeper stared straight ahead. "Is everything all right?"

A dozen puzzle pieces clicked together in Mrs. Jeffries's mind. She leapt to her feet. "Ruth, you're a genius. Thank goodness you came back. Thank goodness. I've got it now. I'm sure of it."

"Got what?"

"You must forgive me," Mrs. Jeffries cried as she dashed toward the house, "but I've got to get Betsy before she goes out. Do come by later on and I'll tell you all about it."

"Is it a murder?" Ruth asked excitedly.

"Yes."

"Can I help?"

Mrs. Jeffries laughed. "You already have."

"You want me to what?" Betsy asked.

"I want you to find this Oliver person who told you about Theodora Vaughan's broken carriage." Mrs. Jeffries explained. "And I want you to find out several very specific things."

She gave Betsy detailed instructions. When she was finished, Betsy said, "I understand, but what if I can't get to him? He's likely to be in the house."

Mrs. Jeffries thought about that problem for a moment. "Go to the back door and tell the cook you've a message from Oliver's mother. If you have to, lie. Make up a sad tale of some sort and get that boy outside so you can question him away from the house. It's imperative that no one, especially Mr. Delaney or Miss Vaughan, overhears you talking to him."

"I'll do my best," Betsy said doubtfully.

"You're a very intelligent woman, Betsy," Mrs. Jeffries said honestly, "and if I had time, I'd explain everything to you. But the truth is, I don't have any idea how much time we do have. If I'm right, Inspector Witherspoon may be on the verge of arresting the wrong person."

Betsy straightened up and lifted her chin. "I'll get the answers, Mrs. Jeffries. You can count on me."

"Good. I knew I could. Off you go, now."

As soon as Betsy had gone, Mrs. Jeffries hurried upstairs to find Wiggins. By the time she reached his room on the third floor, she was breathless. She knocked and then shoved the door open.

Wiggins was sound asleep. Fred was curled up at his feet. The dog woke first, spotted the housekeeper and thumped his tail in apology for being caught on the bed. But Mrs. Jeffries had far more important matters to worry about than a bit of dog hair. "Wiggins." She shook him by the shoulder. "Wake up this instant."

"Huh?" Wiggins mumbled groggily. "What's wrong?"

"Nothing's wrong," Mrs. Jeffries said. "But I need you to do something right away. It's urgent."

"Urgent? All right," he mumbled. It always took him a moment or two to wake up.

Mrs. Jeffries waited patiently for his eyes to focus. "Are you awake yet?"

"I think so."

"Good. I need you to go out and find Smythe."

"Where do I look?"

"Try the area around the Hayden Theatre, but find him and tell him to get back here as soon as he can." She wondered if she was going to make a fool of herself in front of everyone and then decided that it didn't matter. She'd take her chances. "As soon as you find him, go over to Luty's and tell her and Hatchet to get here right away."

Wiggins stumbled to his feet. "What do I tell 'em?"

"Just tell them to get here as quickly as they can. I think I may have figured out who killed Ogden Hinchley."

The later it got, the more Mrs. Jeffries's nerves tightened. She'd no idea why she had such a sense of urgency, but she did. As afternoon faded into evening, she almost wore a hole in the drawing room carpet. Mrs. Goodge's sources were in the kitchen and she didn't want to disturb the cook.

Finally, though, she heard footsteps on the back stairs. Betsy popped her head around the corner. She grinned. "I did it. I found out just what you wanted."

"Excellent, Betsy. Does Mrs. Goodge still have guests downstairs?"

"The butcher's boy was just leaving when I came in," Betsy replied. "Should we go down?"

"Yes," Mrs. Jeffries said. "With any luck, the others will be here soon."

Mrs. Goodge gazed at them curiously when they came into the room. "Is everything all right?"

"No, Mrs. Goodge," Mrs. Jeffries replied. "It isn't. But hopefully, when the others get here, it will be."

"Should I make us a pot of tea?"

"That would be a wonderful idea," the housekeeper replied.

Despite the curious looks from Betsy and Mrs. Goodge, Mrs. Jeffries refused to say anything more until the others arrived. It wouldn't be fair. She'd no idea whether or not Wiggins would be able to track down Smythe, but considering how guilty she felt about the way she'd conducted herself on this case, she'd wait till they were all here to say what was on her mind. It was the least she could do.

Smythe came in first. "Wiggins'll be here soon with Luty and Hatchet," he announced. "What's up? The lad said it was urgent."

"Why don't we wait till the others are here?" Mrs. Jeffries said as she sat a pot of tea on the table. "I'll explain everything then."

Smythe nodded and, as soon as the housekeeper's back was turned, glanced at Betsy. She shrugged to indicate she didn't know what was going on either. But they only had to wait a few moments before they heard the back door open. "I've got 'em," Wiggins called out from the hall.

Luty and Hatchet hurried into the room. "What's goin' on, Hepzibah?"

Luty demanded. "I was on my way out to corner old Mickleshaft when Wiggins come flyin' in sayin' ya needed us."

"Sit down everyone," Mrs. Jeffries commanded. "And I'll explain everything."

Something in her tone brooked no argument or questions, and without another word, everyone took their seats.

Mrs. Jeffries looked at Betsy. "Tell me what you learned from Oliver."

"Who's Oliver?" Smythe asked.

"Theodora Vaughan's footman," Betsy said quickly. "He told me that he'd accompanied Miss Vaughan from her country house up to Victoria Station last Saturday. You were right, Mrs. Jeffries. She did run into someone she knew. It was a man."

The knot of tension in Mrs. Jeffries's stomach began to ease. "Did Oliver remember what he looked like?"

"He was small and well dressed," Betsy continued "He and Miss Vaughan talked for a good fifteen minutes. Oliver said the man must've said something to upset her because she was in a real rage by the time he hailed a hansom and got her in it."

Mrs. Jeffries closed her eyes as relief flooded her whole body. She was right. She had to be. It was the only answer. "Thank you, Betsy. You did very well, my dear."

"Hepzibah, what in tarnation is goin' on?" Luty demanded.

"I'm sorry. Do forgive me for being so mysterious. But you see, I had to be sure."

"Sure of what?" Hatchet asked.

"The identity of the killer."

"But I thought you said it was Albert Parks," Mrs. Goodge complained.

"Until I spoke to Lady Cannonberry this afternoon, I was sure it was Parks," she admitted honestly. "But she said something to me that made me suddenly realize that we—that I," she hastily amended, "was making a big mistake. You see, I'd assumed that Hinchley was killed because he was a critic. But his being a critic had nothing to do with his death."

"Then why was he killed?" Wiggins asked.

"For love, Wiggins. Love and money." She realized that time was getting on and she had to get busy. Witherspoon might be getting ready to arrest Parks. "I don't have a lot of time to go into it right now. If we don't act quickly, the inspector will be at the Hayden Theatre soon, probably arresting the wrong man."

"The inspector'll 'ave to find 'im at 'ome, then," Smythe said. "Theatre's dark tonight. Closed."

"Are you sure?" Mrs. Jeffries asked him.

"Positive. I was just over there."

She frowned. This was a problem that hadn't occurred to her. But before she could think of what to do next, Wiggins spoke up.

"Seein' as yer all 'ere, can I tell ya what I learned today?"

"I'd rather know who the killer is," Mrs. Goodge said testily. "If it's not Albert Parks, then who is it?"

Mrs. Jeffries took a deep breath. If she was wrong, she'd give up snooping about in the inspector's cases. "Theodora Vaughan," she said firmly. "She killed Hinchley to keep from losing Edmund Delaney."

No one said anything for a moment, then Hatchet cleared his throat. "Mrs. Jeffries, how did she get the body to the canal? Hinchley was small, but as you yourself pointed out, he was dead weight."

"She had an accomplice," Mrs. Jeffries replied. "Rather. Hinchley's butler."

CHAPTER 11

There was an ominous silence from the others. Mrs. Jeffries began to understand what an actor felt like when the play ended and the audience booed and hissed. Not that any of them would do that; they were far too polite. But from the incredulous expressions on their faces, she was going to have talk hard and fast to convince them.

"Rather?" Hatchet finally said. "May we ask why?" Mrs. Jeffries wasn't sure how to persuade them she was on to something, but at least no one's life was at stake at the moment, so she had time to make her case. "Because he lied to the inspector. Rather told him that both he and the housemaid had planned on being gone well before Hinchley came back from America. But Lilly, Hinchley's maid, told Betsy that working at the Hinchley house was the easiest position she'd ever had and she'd had no plans to leave."

"But that was after the murder, Mrs. Jeffries," Betsy said softly. "When she knew he definitely wasn't coming back."

"I know, Betsy." Mrs. Jeffries couldn't think of how to express what was really more a feeling than a fact, but she was sure she was on to something. "But I got the impression from you that the girl had never had plans to go anywhere. Isn't that what you thought?"

"Well, yes," Betsy agreed, somewhat reluctantly. "But I don't see how Rather telling one fib to Inspector Witherspoon makes the man a murderer."

"Not a murderer, an accomplice," she corrected. "All he did was carry Hinchley's body to the canal." They were still staring at her like she'd lost her mind, so she plunged straight on, telling them some of the other reasons that led to her conclusions about the killing.

"So you see," she concluded, "we've got to get the inspector to keep a watch on Rather. I suspect that before he leaves London, he'll be contacting Theodora Vaughan. He'll want money for his silence."

"How sure are you about this?" Luty asked.

Mrs. Jeffries glanced around the table. Luty's doubts were mirrored on several other faces. For a moment, she wasn't sure at all about it. What if it was like the last case and she was completely and utterly wrong about everything?

"We'd best get crackin', then," Wiggins said as he stood up. "The butler's plannin' on leavin' tonight."

"Tonight?" Smythe exclaimed. "Well, why didn't ya tell us?"

"I tried to this afternoon," Wiggins cried defensively, "but everyone told me to get out of the kitchen and go 'ave a rest. I didn't know the man was an accomplice, did I? Rather's plannin' on takin' a night train to the coast tonight—that's what Lilly told me when we was on the omnibus today."

"You spoke to Lilly?" Betsy said.

Wiggins nodded excitedly. "It were 'ard work too, gettin' her to talk. Lilly was right upset about the solicitor tossin' 'er out on 'er ear. Would 'ave been really narked only she's got another position. You'll never guess where she's goin'" He paused dramatically. "Theodora Vaughan's country house. Lilly said the offer come right out of the blue. Miss Vaughan sent 'er a note this mornin', tellin' her to go down there and see 'er 'ousekeeper if she were interested in a position. Well, Lilly 'adn't been, but then Rather and the solicitor put their 'eads together and before Lilly knew it, she was out of work and Rather was packin' his trunks. He's goin' to America on a ship."

Smythe flicked a glance at the clock as he got up. "What time's is train?"

Wiggins shrugged. "She didn't say."

"Should I go find the inspector?" Smythe asked Mrs. Jeffries.

"Yes, but give me a moment." Her doubts about the case had vanished. She knew she was right. But she didn't understand why Theodora Vaughan would offer Hinchley's housemaid a position. "Wiggins," she asked, "why did you say you thought Hinchley's servants were robbing him blind?"

"Because when I was carryin' Lilly's case out to the platform, the latch sprung open on one end. When I put it down to try and shove it back in, she got all nasty and pushed me away. Told me she'd fix it 'erself. I got suspicious about the way she was actin', so I 'ad a good look inside." He grinned at his own cleverness. "She couldn't put the latch back in without poppin' open the other end, and when the lid tipped open a bit, I saw all sorts of bits and pieces in 'er case. There was a silver candlestick and a bit of crystal inside. You know, things no 'ousemaid would own. Why? Is it important?"

"I'm not sure," she said, frowning slightly. "But I did wonder."

"So Rather's got the place to himself," Mrs. Goodge said derisively. "He's probably filling his cases with Hinchley's belongings right this very minute."

As soon as the words left the cook's mouth, Mrs. Jeffries understood. She couldn't believe she'd been such a fool as not to see it sooner. "Rather's there alone. Oh, my goodness, we've got to hurry," she exclaimed. "Gracious, I've been so stupid about this. I only hope we're in time."

"What's the rush?" Luty asked. "Theodora Vaughan ain't goin' nowhere. Just this butler feller. The inspector can send a wire to have him picked up before he boards his ship."

"He won't be boarding that ship," Mrs. Jeffries said. "If what I suspect is true, Rather won't be going anywhere." She turned to the footman. "Wiggins, go and get me some of your notepaper and then I want you to go and find the inspector. But you must listen carefully. It's imperative that you follow my instructions to the letter. Otherwise, someone else is going to die tonight."

"Too bad Parks wasn't at home," Barnes said to Witherspoon. He grabbed onto the strap hanging from the ceiling of the hansom as the cab suddenly dipped. "After hearing what that Mrs. Seldon had to tell us, if I was a bettin' man, I'd say Parks has a lot of questions to answer."

"He most certainly does," Witherspoon replied. "It was good of Mrs. Seldon to come forward. Er . . . Constable, you don't think we're on a wild goose chase, do you?" He was a bit concerned that the note that Wiggins had brought around to the Yard had been written by a crank. "I mean, there were spelling errors in the note. It suddenly occurred to me that it might be some prankster having a bit of fun with the police."

"I don't think so, sir," Barnes assured him. "Young Wiggins said a girl brought it round to Upper Edmonton Gardens herself. A prankster would've sent it by post, not shown up on your doorstep and risk bein' identified later."

"But this girl didn't give Wiggins her name," Witherspoon protested. "She simply shoved the note in his hand and ran off. That's most odd."

"Not really, sir," Barnes replied kindly. Sometimes the inspector was so innocent. It was as plain as the nose on his face why the girl hadn't wanted to come to the police station and make a statement. "The lass didn't want to risk being questioned, but her conscience was botherin' her because she'd seen Rather on the night of the murder."

"But why wouldn't she want to be questioned?" Witherspoon said.

"Because she'd probably slipped out to be with her young man in the park, Inspector," the constable explained patiently. "You know, to be alone . . ." he looked at Witherspoon meaningfully.

It took a moment for him to get it. "Oh," he exclaimed. "You mean they were . . ."

"Most likely, sir," Barnes grinned. "Now, the girl couldn't come forward with what she'd seen, not if she'd been playin' about with a man in the middle of the night, could she? She'd lose her position."

"Yes, yes, I see." Satisfied with the explanation, Witherspoon sat back and patted the pocket containing the grubby, wrinkled message. He glanced out the window and saw the North Gate entrance to the park up ahead. "Driver," he yelled. "Pull over in front of the park entrance, please."

The hansom bounced one last time, then pulled up and stopped. They got out, paid the cabbie and then waited until it pulled away. Witherspoon pulled the note out of his pocket, unfolded the paper and held it close to the lamplight. Squinting, he read it through one more time.

Inspector. You should ask Mr. Hinchley's butler why he was in Regents Park at two in the mornin on Saturday night. I'd ask him quick if I was you, the blighter's gettin reidy to scraper off to America.

"Ready, sir?" Barnes asked.

"Yes. Let's see what Rather has to say for himself." They started across toward Avenue Road. There wasn't much pedestrian or vehicle traffic on Albert Road and none at all that Witherspoon could see on Avenue Road. As they crossed the intersection, their footsteps echoed heavily in the silent evening. Witherspoon felt the back of his neck tingle, as though he was being watched. He whipped his head around, but saw nothing but an empty street.

"Something wrong, sir?" Barnes asked as saw the inspector looking behind him.

The inspector felt a tad foolish. Gracious, he was getting silly. Of course he wasn't being followed. "No, Constable."

They turned up the walkway leading to Hinchley's house. Barnes stopped. Witherspoon, thinking something was amiss, stumbled to a halt next to him. "Look, sir"—the constable pointed at the house—"the door's ajar."

"And not many lights on," Witherspoon mused. He could only see the faintest of glows from inside the house. "Let's hope that Rather hasn't already scarpered off and left the place wide open . . ." He broke off as a loud, ear-splitting bang filled the air.

"That sounds like a gunshot, sir. It came from inside." Barnes leapt toward the front stairs and took them two at a time. Witherspoon was right behind him.

They bounded into the house and slid to a halt. Inside, it was eerily quiet. The front hall was dark but there was a dim light from the far end. "The butler's pantry," Witherspoon yelled, hurrying in that direction.

They raced down the hall. From the pantry, they heard a soft groan and the sound of scrapping. The inspector thought he heard the front door slam behind him, but he didn't stop to look. Flying into the room, Witherspoon stumbled over a large object on the floor. Barnes, seeing the inspector stumble, jumped over it.

"Egads," Witherspoon cried. "It's Rather." Rather moaned softly.

Simultaneously, both men dropped to their knees. Even in the poor light, they could see blood seeping out of the butler's shoulder. Barnes pulled the man's coat away from him. "He's bleeding, sir. But it doesn't look too bad."

Rather lifted his hand and gestured toward the door. "Go after her. I'll be all right. Hurry. In the park. Go, go. I'll be fine."

Barnes and Witherspoon looked at each other for a split second and then raced out. They flew back the way they'd come. Witherspoon was behind the constable by a nose as they sprinted down the steps and leapt onto the pavement. Their prey had reached the entrance to the park by the time they cleared the walkway and dashed into the road.

"Halt in the name of the law," Witherspoon cried. But the figure kept on running, hurtling through the gate and heading straight for the bridge.

"Stop, I tell you," the inspector cried. His breath was coming in short, hard gasps and beside him, he could hear the constable wheezing as they gave chase.

She was fast, so fast that Witherspoon was afraid they'd never catch up and the suspect would make it across the canal bridge and into the park, disappearing into the night.

All of a sudden, another figure leapt out from the shadows of the bridge and hurled itself at the fleeing criminal.

There was a scream of rage and pain as the two shapes merged for an istant before crashing against the pavement with a loud thud.

Witherspoon and Barnes skidded to a halt beside the struggling bodies. "Ow . . ." one of them cried just as the constable waded in and grabbed him by the scruff of his neck. With surprising strength, he flung him toward the inspector, who surprised himself by getting a grip on the fellow's arm. Then the constable yanked other one to his feet.

"Egads," Witherspoon cried as he drug his captive closer to the lamplight. "Wiggins?"

"Blow your whistle, sir," Barnes cried as he lugged his struggling prisoner toward the lamp. "We need help. There's coppers on patrol in the park."

"Yes, right." The inspector pulled his whistle out of his pocket and blew hard on it several times. Immediately, the answering call of another whistle rent the air and the faint sound of pounding footsteps echoed in the night.

Barnes finally managed to manuever his captive into the small circle of light cast by the lamp. Witherspoon gasped. "Good gracious. It's Theodora Vaughan."

Dressed in an ill-fitting pair of trousers and a man's jacket, she glared at him coldly from beneath the porkpie cap pulled low over her head.

"This is an outrage, Inspector," she said haughtily. "Can't one take a walk in a park without being set upon by ruffians?" She jerked her head toward Wiggins and then slapped at the constable's hands as he reached into her jacket pocket. "Stop that, you idiot . . ."

"I'm not a ruffian," Wiggins yelped. "And you was runnin' from the law."

"Here's the gun, sir," Barnes said, holding up a derringer he pulled out of her jacket. "It's still warm."

They heard footsteps pounding across the bridge. Two police constables were coming towards them at a fast run.

Witherspoon didn't quite understand what was going on, but he did know that this woman whom he'd so admired had tried to murder a man tonight. "Theodora Vaughan," he said somberly, "you're under arrest for the attempted murder of Mr. Rather."

"I bet she killed Mr. 'inchley too," Wiggins added.

Theodora Vaughan said nothing for a moment. Then she smiled slowly, triumphantly. "Try to prove it, Inspector."

"I don't think that will be very hard, Miss Vaughan," he said. "Your bullet hasn't killed the man. I'm sure he'll be quite able to testify against you."

She laughed. "Then it will be his word against mine, won't it? Remember this, Inspector: I'm Theodora Vaughan, one of the greatest actresses of the English theatre, and I can assure you, when I'm in the dock at the Old Bailey, I'll make you look a fool. I shall give a performance of a lifetime."

"All this waitin' is goin' to drive me plum loco," Luty snapped. "It's been hours since them three left. What the dickens is takin' so long?"

"I don't know," Mrs. Jeffries said, her expression worried. She prayed she hadn't been wrong. But as the clock hands moved, she was beginning to think she'd made a terrible mistake.

Betsy leapt to her feet as they heard the back door opening. "That's them now," she cried, dashing to the stove and putting the kettle on to boil.

Smythe and Hatchet hurried into the room. Fred jumped up, wagged his tail a few times and tried to butt Smythe on the knees. "Down, boy," the coachman said, giving him a quick pat.

"What happened?" Mrs. Jeffries cried.

"Where's Wiggins?" Mrs. Goodge yelped.

"About time someone got back here," Luty grumbled.

"Are you all right?" Betsy asked anxiously, her gaze fixed on Smythe. "I've got the kettle on for tea."

"We're fine," Hatchet assured them as he sat down. "So is Wiggins"— he grinned—"but I expect the young man will have to do some fast talking when he gets to the station."

"You mean the inspector spotted him?" Luty snapped.

Hatchet grinned broadly. "You could say that. He was instrumental in capturing Theodora Vaughan. One could also say, had it not been for Wiggins, she might have made her escape."

"Oh, dear." Mrs. Jeffries frowned. "Tell us what happened. Were we in time?"

"Almost," Smythe said. "She did shoot the butler, but like Luty said, she's not a good shot and she only wounded him. The coppers were takin' 'im to 'ospital when I left to come back 'ere. I overheard one of 'em say it was only a flesh wound. 'E'll be all right. He'll be able to testify against Theodora Vaughan."

Mrs. Jeffries sagged in relief. "Thank God." She'd never have forgiven herself if that man had been killed.

"I did like ya said, Mrs. J.," Smythe continued, "and we was lucky you sussed it out when ya did. I got to the Vaughan 'ouse just in time to see her nippin' out the back door. She was dressed in boy's clothes." He paused to toss a quick smile of thanks at Betsy as she set a mug of tea in front of him. "I followed 'er to 'inchley's house, saw her go inside and then a minute later, I 'eard the shot. Bloomin' Ada, I didn't know what to do! But just then, the inspector and Constable Barnes showed up. They 'eard the shot too and went barrelin' inside. Then, just a few seconds after they'd gone in, she comes flyin' out and takes off across the road toward the park."

"I, too, didn't know what to do at that point," Hatchet added. "As Mrs. Jeffries had instructed, I was keeping watch on the Hinchley house from across the street. I saw her go in, and before I could gather my wits about me, I saw a hansom draw up and the inspector and Constable Barnes got out." His brows drew together. "At that point, I'd no idea what was going to happen. About then, the shot rang out and everything moved so quickly after that I didn't have time to do anything."

"But she was arrested?" Mrs. Goodge asked.

"She were nicked, all right." Smythe grinned. "You'da been right proud of Wiggins. If 'e 'adn't come flyin' out of the shadows and brought 'er down before she crossed that bridge and disappeared into the park, there's a good chance she'd have gotten away."

"Good fer Wiggins," Luty cried. Then a worried frown crossed her face. "I hope he's got enough sense to spin some kind of yarn for the inspector. Otherwise, we're all in trouble."

Mrs. Jeffries had the same concern. "He's a very bright young man," she said. "I'm sure he'll think of something."

Mrs. Goodge leaned toward the housekeeper. "Before the inspector gets back, are you goin' to tell us how you figured it out?"

"There may not be time," Mrs. Jeffries said uneasily.

"You've plenty of time. The inspector will be tied up for hours," Hatchet interjected.

"All right." She took a deep breath and tried to force herself to relax. Thank goodness she had been right about this case. "As I said," she began, "it was when Lady Cannonberry made those remarks about her sister-in-law this afternoon that I realized the truth. We'd all assumed the motive for Hinchley's murder was to stop him from publicly reviewing Edmund Delaney's play. Yet as Ruth talked, I realized that there was another motive that had been apparent all along."

"Doesn't seem that apparent to me," the cook complained.

"Nor to me until today," Mrs. Jeffries agreed. "But as Ruth told me about the outrageous things her sister-in-law had done to try to get her young man back, I saw the similarities between that young woman's behaviour and the way Hinchley acted. Then I realized the truth. Hinchley was still infatuated with Delaney. That's why he changed his will naming Delaney as heir before he left for the United States. He might have hated Delaney for rejecting him, but the sad truth was he had no one else. Hinchley still loved Delaney enough so that he wanted him to have his property in the event something happened to him while he was away. Once I looked at the case from that point of view, it was quite simple."

"I still don't get it," Betsy said, echoing the confusion the rest of them felt. "Even if Hinchley was in love with Delaney, why would that make Theodora Vaughan hate him enough to kill him? Delaney had left Hinchley over a year ago."

"I know," Mrs. Jeffries replied. "That's one of the reasons I didn't see it until it was almost too late. Theodora Vaughan didn't kill Hinchley because she hated him, though I expect she did. She murdered him for money. The money Edmund Delaney was going to inherit when Hinchley died. Remember, she planned to be Delaney's wife. I expect she realized that once she and Delaney were actually man and wife, Hinchley would finally give up and disinherit Delaney. She didn't want to lose over a hundred thousand pounds."

"Money?" Luty exclaimed. "But how did she know that Hinchley had left his fortune to Delaney?"

"Hinchley told her," Mrs. Jeffries explained. "According to what Oliver told Betsy, Theodora Vaughan was in a rage after talking to a small man at the train station on Saturday. That man was Ogden Hinchley. He wasn't a subtle person; I expect he told Theodora Vaughan quite plainly that he'd made Delaney his heir and that he was going to do everything in his power to win Delaney back. More important, I suspect he tormented her about Delaney's play. You see, I'm quite sure he'd come back for the sole purpose of reviewing it and I'm equally certain he knew it wasn't very good. But most important, Theodora Vaughan had invested a goodly amount of money in that play. If Hinchley managed to close it down, not only would her lover be disgraced, but she'd be quite poor. Perhaps even bankrupt. Beautiful as she is, she's a number of years older than Delaney. With no money of her own, I expect she was worried that she wouldn't be able to keep Delaney."

"But how would Hinchley know that the play was so awful if he was in New York?" Hatchet asked.

"From Trevor Remington. Remember, supposedly Remington and Hinchley had a quarrel about money before Hinchley left for America," Mrs. Jeffries clarified. "Lilly told Betsy that. I'd quite forgotten it until yesterday."

"Ah, I see." Hatchet nodded in understanding. "You think that Hinchley's been paying Remington all along."

"Correct. I also think the reason there was a problem with Theodora Vaughan obtaining her divorce from Remington might have also been Hinchley's doing."

"How could 'e do that?" Smythe asked. "They got the divorce in America."

"He coulda done it," Luty interjected. "We don't know what state issued the divorce decree. All Remington woulda had to do was claim he lost the papers or not signed something. Some states have a waitin' period between goin' to court and gettin' the divorce."

"But what was Remington gettin' paid for?" Mrs. Goodge wailed. "I still don't understand."

"For keeping Hinchley informed," Mrs. Jeffries said. "As long as Delaney and Theodora Vaughan weren't married, Hinchley had hopes of winning him back. But when her American lawyers managed to get the decree despite Remington's lack of cooperation, Hinchley took the first ship back from America. By this time, Hinchley had probably learned from Remington that Delaney's play was being produced and that it wasn't very good. As luck would have it, Hinchley ran into Theodora Vaughan at the train station. Actually, I'm not so sure that meeting was accidental or whether he arranged to run into her. We don't know for certain precisely what day he arrived back from New York, but it's not particularly important whether he met her accidentally or on purpose—he accomplished what he'd set out to do. He couldn't stop himself from taunting the woman, thereby sealing his own death warrant."

"But 'ow did you suss out the way she'd done it?" Smythe asked.

Mrs. Jeffries smiled. "I didn't, not until it was almost too late. But the evidence was right there. Remember when Wiggins told us about Rose, Theodora's maid, taking that case of clothes to the theatre? There were boys' clothes inside. Velvet and silk, the same kind of clothes the lad who'd brought the note to the brothel on Lisle street wore. Rose also told Wiggins that Theodora didn't do 'trouser parts' anymore."

"What's that?" Mrs. Goodge asked grumpily. She was a bit put out that she hadn't figured any of it out and she still wasn't sure she understood it.

"It's a woman playing a boy's role in a play," the housekeeper explained. "Theodora Vaughan got rid of those clothes because they were evidence. She'd worn them the night of the murder. She'd dressed as a boy to take that note to the brothel . . ."

"But how did she get to the Hinchley house?" Luty interrupted.

"She took a hansom."

"But Smythe talked to all the cabbies and none of them remembers pickin' up a boy that night."

"I know 'ow she did it." Smythe grinned. "The same way she did it tonight. she hitched a ride by 'angin' on the back. Bloomin' good at it she was too—hopped right on like she'd been doin' it all 'er life."

"Precisely," Mrs. Jeffries agreed. "Anyway, she knew all about Hinchley's . . . uh . . . habits, so when she realized he was determined to ruin the play and in turn, ruin her, she decided to kill him." She shook her head in disgust. "I should have realized it when the inspector told us she'd left the theatre right after the performance that night. She hadn't even taken off her makeup. Instead, she went home, put on boys' clothes and a dark-haired wig. Dressed as a boy, she went to Lisle Street. The last thing she wanted was for a male prostitute to show up while she was committing murder. Then she went to Hinchley's and let herself in the side door, which she knew would be unlocked. I expect his being in the bathtub was sheer luck."

"You don't think she planned on drowning him?" Betsy queried.

"No, I think she was going to shoot him. But unluckily for him, he was in the bath. She walked up, grabbed his ankles and pulled him under. Unfortunately for her, Rather hadn't gone to bed. Instead, he came in and caught her red-handed."

"But why did he carry the body to the canal?" Hatchet asked. "Why didn't he call the police?"

Mrs. Jeffries shrugged. "From what the inspector told me, Rather wasn't particularly fond of his employer. I expect Theodora Vaughan offered him money. Probably the money to go to America and start a new life."

"I wonder whose idea it was to toss the body in the canal?" Luty asked.

"Probably Theodora Vaughan's," Mrs. Jeffries guessed. "Once Rather did that, once he willingly participated, he was then an accomplice. I think she was hoping that act would buy his silence."

"But if she'd paid him," Betsy asked, "why did she try to kill him tonight?"

"Because I expect he wanted more. By this time, she'd realized that accomplice or not, Rather could blackmail her for the rest of her life."

"So she did it for money," Luty muttered. "Greed."

"And for love," Mrs. Jeffries added. "I think she really did love Edmund Delaney. Even knowing his play wasn't very good, she helped him get it produced on the stage."

From outside, they heard the rattle of a hansom pull up in front of the house. Fred leapt to his feet and ran for the stairs. "That'll be the inspector and Wiggins," Mrs. Jeffries said.

Luty and Hatchet were already up and scurrying toward the back door. "We'll be back tomorrow for the rest of the details," Luty called over her shoulder.

Smythe, Betsy, and Mrs. Goodge started to get up too, but Mrs. Jeffries waved them back into their chairs. "No, stay here. Wiggins might need a bit of moral support. It'll look better if the inspector sees we were all concerned for him."

The inspector and Wiggins came into the kitchen just as the back door shut behind Luty and Hatchet. Fred, who'd followed them into the back hall to say goodbye, trotted in, spotted the newcomers and bounded over to greet them, his tail wagging frantically as he bounced between his two favorite people.

"Gracious," Witherspoon said as he took in everyone sitting at the table, "you shouldn't have waited up for me."

"We were concerned, sir," Mrs. Jeffries said. "When that girl arrived here with the note and then Wiggins didn't come right back from taking it to you, we feared something was amiss."

"Well, I'm very touched," the inspector said. He spotted the teapot. "I say, is there more of that?"

The housekeeper quickly poured him a cup and put it in front of the chair that Luty had just vacated. "Do sit down and tell us what happened, sir."

"Thank you, Mrs. Jeffries." Witherspoon sat down. "Now, sit down, Wiggins, and stop your sulking. I didn't mean to be sharp with you earlier, but you could have been hurt tonight. You were very, very brave and I'm quite proud of you, but still it was a foolish thing to do. I'd never forgive myself if something happened to you."

"What happened?" Mrs. Jeffries asked, though she knew perfectly well exactly what had happened.

"Well." Witherspoon told them what they already knew. But all of them played their parts perfectly as he spun his tale.

Mrs. Goodge clucked her tongue, Betsy shook her head in disbelief, Smythe occasionally mumbled something under his breath and Mrs. Jeffries vacillated between sympathetic glances and stern frowns.

When he'd finished, Mrs. Jeffries asked, "Does she really think she'll convince a jury she's innocent?"

Witherspoon shrugged. "She'll try. But with the physical evidence against her and Rather's testimony, I don't think she'll succeed."

"What about Rather, then?" Betsy asked. "Is he bein' charged?"

"No, he's agreed to turn Queen's Evidence," Witherspoon explained. "In exchange for testifying against her, he won't be charged as an accomplice."

After a few more questions, Betsy, Smythe and Mrs. Goodge excused themselves. Wiggins took Fred out for a brief visit to the gardens. As the boy and the dog disappeared down the hall, the inspector turned to Mrs. Jeffries, a concerned frown on his face. "Honestly, Mrs. Jeffries, I don't know what to do. I didn't like to be sharp with Wiggins, but he took a terrible risk tonight."

"He only wanted to help you, sir," she replied hesitantly. As she didn't quite know what story Wiggins had cooked up to explain his presence at the Hinchley house, she wasn't sure what to say.

"That's why I feel so responsible." Witherspoon clucked his tongue. "Gracious, the lad jumped on the back of our hansom, followed me all the way there and then leapt upon an armed killer. It was very brave of the boy, but I'd never have forgiven myself if he'd been shot. Gracious, what if she'd been holding that wretched derringer instead of carrying it in her jacket? Egads, it could even have gone off in the struggle."

"Did he tell you why he'd followed you, sir?"

"That's what I wanted to talk to you about." Witherspoon glanced toward the back hall to make sure Wiggins was still out. "I really must ask you to be more careful about loaning him books, Mrs. Jeffries."

"Books, sir?"

"I think it's wonderful the way you're encouraging him to read. He is, after all, quite a bright lad. But some of them have the most dreadful effect on him. He told me he'd been reading some poem by that American fellow, Mr. Edgar Allan Poe."

"Edgar Allan Poe?"

"Yes, some poem about a blackbird . . . no, no, I tell a lie, it's not about a blackbird, it's a raven. Anyway"—Witherspoon waved impatiently—"the point is, I gather it's quite a gloomy piece with this bird carping on and on about 'nevermore' or some such thing. There's a dead woman in it as well and the bird's going on and on and on about this 'nevermore.'" He shrugged helplessly. "Poor Wiggins told me this poem so upset him that when he brought that note around to the Yard this evening, he was quite sure he'd never see me again. That's why he followed me. Honestly, Mrs. Jeffries, I've no idea what to do. I'm touched by his devotion, but he mustn't ever, ever, take such risks. You will speak to him, won't you? Tell him not to take poetry so seriously." He yawned and rose slowly to his feet.

"I'll have a word with him in the morning, sir," she promised. She'd fix him a special breakfast too, she told herself. "By the way, sir, Lady Cannonberry's back from the country."

Tired as he was, Witherspoon positively beamed. "That's wonderful. Shall we invite her round for tea tomorrow?"

"I expect she'll be happy to drop by," Mrs. Jeffries said as she got to her feet and picked up the teapot. Ruth would probably be here before breakfast demanding to know everything. "You'd better get some rest, sir."

"Good night, Mrs. Jeffries, and do see that Wiggins is all right, will you?"

"Of course, sir," she called as he headed for the stairs.

Wiggins and Fred came in a few minutes later. He stopped by the door and grinned at her.

She arched an eyebrow. "Edgar Allan Poe?"

"I was right pleased with myself for thinkin' of that so quick. Good thing I'd read that poem."

"Wiggins," she replied, "you missed your true calling. You should have been an actor. You convinced him completely."

"Nah, wouldn't want to be one of them," he said. "Too borin' by 'alf. But I do think maybe I'll try my 'and at spinnin' tales. I think I might be right good at it."

"I think," she replied sincerely, "you'll be excellent at it. As a matter of fact, you'll do us proud."

MRS. JEFFRIES
QUESTIONS THE ANSWER

This book is dedicated
to Amanda Belle Arguile.
The sunshine of my life.

CHAPTER 1

Hannah Cameron smiled slyly as she stepped into the darkened room. Good, she thought, it's black as sin in here. No one would be able to see a thing. That should make the surprise even better. Hannah patted the pocket of her emerald-green velvet gown, making sure the box of matches was still secure on her person. It wouldn't do to let a small detail like forgetting the matches cause her to ruin the plan. No, she'd waited too long for this night, planned too hard to let it go awry now.

Moving cautiously, she edged further into the darkness, toward the French doors on the opposite side. Her heart pounded and her dress rustled loudly when it brushed against the settee as she eased past. She stopped, turned and looked toward the closed door through which she'd just come. It wouldn't do for one of the servants to come snooping about now. Not when she was so close to achieving her goal. But she heard nothing. Most of the servants should be fast asleep. That was one of the reasons the little tart felt so safe. The silly minx didn't realize anyone was on to her tricks. But by heaven, she'd find out differently tonight.

Her eyes adjusted to the darkness and through the faint light filtering in from the balcony, she could see the outline of the lamp she'd carefully placed on the table. Next to the table was the balloon-backed chair she'd put there earlier that evening. She wanted to be comfortable while she waited. Who knew what time the little tramp would actually come home? Reaching into her pocket again, she pulled the matches out and set them down next to the lamp. Then, wanting to be certain that everything was going according to schedule, she went to the French doors and peered out into the night. Across the garden, she could see the faint glow of a gas lamp rising above the high walls. She squinted, trying to see if the lock was still disengaged as it had been earlier. But there wasn't enough light to see. She had to be sure. Holding her breath, she eased the door open and shut it again. The door made the faintest of noises in the quiet house. But she was satisfied. It was still unlocked.

She giggled softly and then her laughter died abruptly as she heard a faint creak. She whirled around and peered through the blackness to the door leading to the hall. No sign of light there, so it must still be closed, she thought. But Hannah wasn't taking any chances. She glanced to her left, squinting hard to make sure the only other door in the small sitting room, a door that led to a rarely used guest room, was still closed. Nothing there either. Hannah shrugged, decided the creak she heard must have been the house settling and turned back toward the window to continue her vigil. She concentrated on staring out into the garden, watching the shadows and wondering when her quarry would arrive.

The thick carpet masked the sound of the footsteps creeping up behind her. Suddenly, she gasped and made a strangling noise deep in her throat. But the knife that had been plunged into her back had struck true and deep. Her heart stopped pumping. In an agony of pain, she couldn't find the breath to scream for help. She wheezed and choked, her hands flailing wildly in the air until finally, her knees buckled and she collapsed upon the floor.

Hannah Cameron wouldn't be surprising anyone tonight.

"I tell you, it's just not convenient now," Mrs. Goodge grumbled. The cook nodded her gray head emphatically, pushed her spectacles back up her nose and gazed around the table at the rest of the household of Upper Edmonton Gardens, home of Inspector Gerald Witherspoon of Scotland Yard.

"But Mrs. Goodge," Mrs. Jeffries, the housekeeper, said softly, "I don't think you've any choice in the matter. Your Aunt Elberta will be here tomorrow." She was a plump, kindly looking woman with dark auburn hair liberally sprinkled with gray at the temples, intelligent brown eyes and a fair complexion that contrasted nicely with the bronze-colored bombazine dress she wore.

"I could send her a telegram tonight," Mrs. Goodge said quickly. She glanced at the clock. "Wiggins here could nip out and get one off . . ."

"That might 'urt the lady's feelin's," Wiggins, the footman, pointed out. "She's already done 'er packin' and all. Not that I mind goin' out fer ya. I don't. But ya told us a fortnight ago she'd be comin'" The footman was a sturdy young man of nineteen, with dark hair, blue eyes and round apple cheeks that blushed easily.

"Why don't you want her to come and visit?" Betsy, the pretty blond-haired maid, asked. "The inspector's already said he doesn't mind. There's plenty of room in the house for her."

Smythe, the black-haired coachman, crossed his arms over his massive chest. His brown eyes twinkled with amusement. His features were heavy, almost brutal looking, belying an easygoing nature and a kind heart. "What's all the fuss, Mrs. Goodge? I thought you liked your old auntie."

"I do like her," the cook shot back, "but it's just not convenient for her to come visiting now. We've got that dinner party for the inspector coming up and we've got. . . . we've got. . . ." She broke off, for in truth, except for one dinner party a few weeks hence, there was nothing else of any importance coming up for the household. Inspector Witherspoon, one of Scotland Yard's foremost detectives, was an exceptionally easy employer. Having not been born with a silver spoon in his mouth, he didn't expect his cook to cater to his every culinary whim. "We've got plenty on our plates right now," she finished lamely. "Besides, we might get us another murder and then where would I be? Hamstrung"—she nodded vigourously—"that's what I'd be. I can't have my sources in and out of this kitchen with a gossiping old woman under my feet, now, can I?"

Mrs. Jeffries sighed inwardly. The cook had a point, but as they didn't have a murder to investigate, it was rather a weak argument. "But Mrs. Goodge," she pointed out, "we don't have anything to investigate right at the moment."

"More's the pity," Mrs. Goodge snapped impatiently. "But that doesn't mean we won't get one, does it? If you don't mind my saying so, I don't want to have to miss another one because of my auntie! A woman her age shouldn't be out gallivanting all over the place anyway. She should be safely home."

"So that's it then." Smythe laughed. "You're afraid that dear old Auntie Elberta'll diddle ya out of a murder."

"It wouldn't be the first time," the cook replied darkly.

"But Mrs. Goodge," Mrs. Jeffries said kindly, "it wasn't your aunt's fault she became ill. . . ."

"Never said it was." Mrs. Goodge set her chin stubbornly. "But the fact is, I'm one murder short on the lot of you and it isn't fair. If I hadn't had to go off to see her last year, I'd not have missed that Barrett murder. She only had a touch of bronchitis, and here she had me dashing about thinkin' she was at death's door and causin' me to miss my fair share of the investigatin'. Well, I'll not be taking a risk like that again. I've got a feeling in my bones that sure as rice needs water, the minute Elberta shows up on our doorstep, we'll have us a fine murder."

"But sayin' we do get us one." Wiggins thought he ought to add his opinion to the discussion. "Why would it matter if she was 'ere or not? You'd still be able to do yer part."

The cook snorted derisively. "With Elberta hangin' about and puttin' her oar in it every time I was entertaining one of my sources? You must be daft, boy."

The cook had a veritable army of sources trooping through her kitchen. Chimney-sweeps, costermongers, laundrymen, street urchins, bakers' boys, delivery men and even the men from the gas works if necessary. She plied them with hot tea, sticky buns, Madeira cake and trifle while pumping them ruthlessly for every single morsel of gossip to be had. Her help on the inspector's previous cases had been important, and on several occasions, it had been a tidbit of gossip she'd learned that had been paramount in solving the case. She was most proud of her contribution to the cause of justice. Despite the fact that she never left the kitchen, the cook knew everything there was to know about everyone who was anybody in the city of London.

"I'm afraid you've left it a bit late," Mrs. Jeffries said kindly. "Even if Wiggins goes out tonight to the telegraph office, I doubt a message would reach your aunt before she left in the morning. You did say she lives quite a ways out in the country."

Mrs. Goodge thought about it for a moment and then gave a sigh of defeat. "Oh, bother. You're right. Besides, Elberta would just ignore it anyway. But it's inconvenient, her coming now. Ruddy inconvenient."

Mrs. Jeffries understood why the cook was so upset, but there was nothing they could do about it. "It'll all work out," she said cheerfully. "Besides, if she doesn't come tomorrow, Inspector Witherspoon will be most disappointed. He's so looking forward to meeting her." She could think of no other household in the city in which an employer not only allowed, but positively delighted in the staff's relatives coming to visit.

But then again, Gerald Witherspoon was an exceptional man. He'd not been born to wealth. He'd acquired a fortune and this huge house when his Aunt Euphemia had died. He'd also acquired Smythe and Wiggins at the same time. Mrs. Jeffries, Mrs. Goodge and Betsy had been later additions.

They were all devoted to the inspector and they were equally devoted to his cases. Murder investigations. Not that he knew about their efforts on his behalf. That would never do. But they contributed greatly to his success. As a matter of fact, Mrs. Jeffries thought smugly, if it hadn't been for them, Inspector Witherspoon would still be a clerk in the Records room at Scotland Yard and not one of its best homicide detectives.

"Has the inspector decided who he wants to invite to his dinner party?" Betsy asked.

Mrs. Jeffries frowned. "Yes, I'm afraid it's worse than we feared."

There was a collective groan around the table.

"She's really comin', then?" Smythe asked.

The housekeeper nodded. "Unfortunately, yes. She's going to be in London buying her trousseau . . ."

You mean that man's really goin' to marry 'er?" Wiggins asked incredulously.

"As far as I know, yes," Mrs. Jeffries replied. "Otherwise, she wouldn't be coming to London. Since she is going to be in the city, the inspector can hardly ignore her."

"But that's not fair," Wiggins yelped. "Isn't this bloomin' party supposed to be for Lady Cannonberry?"

"Well, yes," Mrs. Jeffries said quickly. "She is the guest of honor." Lady Cannonberry was their neighbor, the widow of a peer and a thoroughly delightful friend to all of them. She was also a bit of a political radical, an enthusiastic helper on some of their investigations and very, very enamored of their dear employer. "I'm sure she'll not mind in the least that the inspector's cousin is invited as well."

"But she's only comin' for the dinner party, right?" Smythe asked anxiously. "She's not stayin'?"

"She's not staying," Mrs. Jeffries assured him. "We'll only have to put up with the woman for a couple of hours." She deliberately didn't tell them who else would be on the guest list for the evening. It would only depress them. Gracious, when Inspector Witherspoon asked her to send out *that* particular invitation, she'd been sorely tempted to rip it to shreds rather than pop it in the post-box. But good sense and integrity had prevailed against her personal prejudices and so she'd invited the odious man. But there was no need to share that information yet. "And it's only for a dinner party. We probably won't see her at all, except when we're serving. I hardly think she'll be coming down to the kitchen for a chat."

Betsy giggled. "I can't wait to see Luty's face when she hears. Maybe we ought to seat them next to each other."

"Oh no, lass," Smythe said. "That's not fair. That's no way to treat a friend. To be honest, I'd not stick Miss Edwina Livingston-Graves on my worst enemy."

"This isn't a toss," Chief Inspector Jonathan Barrows said quietly to the constable standing at his elbow. "This is murder. Cold-blooded, premeditated murder."

"Yes, sir," the constable, a young man who'd only been on the force two months, replied quickly. He glanced around the room and wondered what the Chief saw that he didn't. It sure looked as if the place had been burgled to him. There was a broken pane of glass in the window of the French door. Looked to him like that was how the thief had gotten into the house, but he wasn't about to argue with the Chief Inspector. No sir, not him. He knew what was what. Frowning, he stared through the open bedroom door on the other side of the room. The top drawers in the dresser were open and bits of clothing were sticking out, a silver hairbrush and a bottle of scent were lying on the carpet amidst the tangle of the lace runner and a lamp had been knocked over. He shook his head. Looked like a toss to him. He glanced quickly at the woman crumpled on the floor. She had a knife sticking out of her back. Seemed to Constable Jesse Sayers, the poor lady had had the bad luck to walk in on a thief.

Barrows looked down at the body and grimaced. "Stabbed." He grunted sympathetically. "Not a nice way to die. But hopefully, it was quick."

Constable Sayers cleared his throat. "Uh, sir, P.C. Meadows has already sent for Inspector Nivens. He should be here any minute now."

Barrows's mouth tightened. He didn't like Inspector Nivens. Few people did. But in all fairness, he didn't blame P.C. Meadows for sending for him. Nivens was a good enough man when it came to burglaries, but he knew sod-all about murder. "He'll not be any use to us, will he? I don't want him mucking up the evidence until Witherspoon sees it." Barrows, who normally would have been at home with his feet up and reading a good book instead of standing over a corpse, had just attended a dinner party next door to the Cameron house when the alarm was raised.

He and Mrs. Barrows had just come out to hail a hansom when they'd heard the Cameron butler shouting for the constable from up at the corner. He'd put Mrs. Barrows into a hansom and taken charge.

"I assure you, sir," a harsh voice said from the doorway, "I am properly trained enough not to 'muck up the evidence.'"

Barrows whirled around. "Ah, Nivens. Sorry, I didn't know you were there. But this isn't really your balliwick."

"I understood there'd been a murder and robbery here," Nivens said, stepping farther into the room. He nodded toward the body. "Is that the victim?"

Barrows sighed. That was the sort of question he expected from Nivens. Never could stick the man. Too much of a bootlicker to the politicians, he was. "Of course it's the victim. Not many people nap on their sitting-room floors with knives sticking out of their backs."

Nivens ignored the sarcasm and walked toward the bedroom. "The place has been tossed," he commented.

"No, it hasn't," Barrows said testily. Much as he disliked Inspector Nivens, he'd best be careful. All that bootlicking had paid off. Nivens had powerful friends. "Someone's tried to make it look like a toss. But if a pro did that"—he jerked his chin toward the tallboys—"I'll eat my hat."

"Not every toss is done by a pro." Nivens gave his superior a thin smile. "Did I hear you say you were calling Inspector Witherspoon in for this one?"

"I am," he replied firmly. Nivens might be right, but Barrows didn't think it likely. "I know full well that not all burglaries are done by pros, but someone went to a great deal of trouble to convince us that this one was. This isn't a burglary gone bad, it's murder." He nodded toward the victim. "Someone wanted that woman dead."

"Are you absolutely certain of that?" Nivens asked.

Barrows hesitated. In his heart, he knew he was right. He could smell a sham when he was standing in it. But he'd worked himself up from the ranks with good, honest police work and he wasn't a fool. Anyone with half a brain could tell that Nivens wanted this case. Scotland Yard was as riddled with politics and pressure as any department in Whitehall. Much as he disliked Nivens, he couldn't honestly say with one hundred percent certainty that this wasn't a burglary. Blasted inconvenient that one of the police constables had taken it upon himself to send for Nivens. "Well, it certainly looks that way to me and I have had a number of years of experience."

Nivens said nothing. He walked over to stand in the doorway between the two rooms, his gaze darting back and forth between them. "No professional would do the drawers like that," he admitted, "and there's plenty of valuables about that should have been grabbed first, but I don't think you can state with any absolute certainty that this is simply a case of murder."

Barrows said nothing.

"In which case," Nivens continued, "I'd venture to say that I'm far more experienced in this kind of case than Inspector Witherspoon is." He walked across the room and knelt down by the body.

Barrows watched him for a moment. Scotland Yard was organized quite rigidly, at least on paper. If he was really following regulations, he'd have called in whatever inspector was on duty and assigned to this district. But no organization was independent of politics or the latest headlines in the *Times*. The police were under constant pressure to solve crimes quickly, efficiently and with some assurance of actually catching the real culprits. Especially now. So organization or not, every chief inspector had his own way of making sure he got his fair share of collars. It was common knowledge that when a good copper was needed to sort out a burglary, Nivens, sod that he was, was the one who got it. By the same token, if one wanted a killer caught, the odds were that Gerald Witherspoon would catch the killer. And Barrows wanted a killer caught. But he didn't dare step too hard on Nivens's toes.

"You're right." Barrows grinned. "Oh, by the way, I shouldn't touch that body if I were you."

Surprised, Nivens looked up. "Why ever not?"

"Because I want Witherspoon to examine the victim."

Niven's eyes narrowed angrily but Barrows continued before he could protest. "I've decided to have you both on this one."

Niven's jaw dropped. "That's highly irregular, sir."

"Of course it is," Barrows said cheerfully, "but after the beating the force has taken over this wretched Ripper case, I'm not going to risk someone else getting away with murder." He turned to Constable Sayers.

"Get a lad over to Witherspoon's straight away. Tell him to get here quickly. He and Inspector Nivens will be working together on this one."

"It ought to be a fine day tomorrow," Smythe ventured softly.

Betsy looked up from the apron she was mending and smiled. Smythe was staring over her shoulder, at a spot on the far wall rather than at her. She knew what that meant. The poor man was working up the courage to ask her to go out with him again. She thought it was sweet the way the cocky, sometimes arrogant coachman could be as shy as a schoolboy. "Should be nice," she commented, putting the last stitch through the stiff cotton. "But it'll be cold."

"True," he said quickly, "but it's goin' to be sunny." He cleared his throat. "I'm takin' Bow and Arrow for a good run tomorrow with the carriage, and seein as it's yer day out, I was wonderin' if you'd like to come along?"

"I would," Wiggins volunteered from the doorway. Blissfully unaware of the scowl the coachman directed toward him, Wiggins and Fred, the household's mongrel dog, advanced into the warm, cozy kitchen. "I've not been out in ages. Where we goin' then?"

Betsy stifled a grin as she caught a quick peek at the thunderous expression on Smythe's face. "*We're* not going anywhere," she said tartly, taking pity on the coachman. "It's my day out, remember? Not yours. You've got to be here to help Mrs. Goodge get her Aunt Elberta settled in."

Wiggins opened his mouth to protest, but just then, Mrs. Goodge, a brown bottle in her hand, came bustling through the kitchen door. "This ruddy cap's stuck again," she cried, charging toward Smythe and thrusting the bottle under his nose. "See if you can get it unstuck. I don't know why they make them like that. Silly bottle makers, don't they know that people with rheumatism in their joints can't undo those wretched tops? If we could, we wouldn't need the ruddy stuff in the first place."

Smythe, wondering when, if ever, he'd get a chance to be alone with Betsy, took the bottle, gave the top a fast, hard twist and when he felt it give, handed it back to the cook. "There you are, Mrs. Goodge. All nice and open for ya. A good night's sleep and a bit of this on yer 'ands and you'll be right as rain tomorrow."

"Is your rheumatism bothering you again?" Mrs. Jeffries asked as she too stepped into the kitchen.

Blimey, thought Smythe, it's a ruddy train station in here. Doesn't this lot ever go to sleep? Blasted inconvenient it was, never havin' a moment to be alone with the lass.

"It's been actin' up a bit." Mrs. Goodge plopped down in the chair next to Betsy. Wiggins sat down next to her.

Smythe sighed inwardly. Maybe they'd all go to bed soon.

"Can we have some cocoa?" Wiggins asked.

Smythe shot the footman a savage frown, but Wiggins didn't see it. He was too busy scratching Fred's ears.

"It's gettin' kinda late," Smythe said quickly. "And with Mrs. Goodge's 'ands actin' up, I don't think we ought to be botherin' her with makin' a 'ot drink."

"Oh, I'll make it," Mrs. Jeffries said airily as she bustled toward the wet larder in the hall. "I've nothing else to do. The inspector's gone up already . . ." she broke off and cocked her head, listening.

From outside the kitchen window, the sound of heavy footsteps running up the stairs to the front door could be heard. A second later, they all heard the loud banging of the knocker.

"I wonder who that could be?" Mrs. Jeffries started for the stairs.

But fast as she was, Smythe headed her off. "I'll go up and see who it is," he said. "It's too late for you to be openin' that front door without knowin' who's doin' the knockin'"

Together, they went up and started down the hall. Inspector Witherspoon, dressed in only his trousers and an unbuttoned white shirt was just reaching for the handle.

"Let me, sir," Smythe called, charging past the housekeeper and making a mad dash for the front door. Blimey, didn't these two realize it weren't safe to be openin' that blooming door at this time of night?

"Oh, that's all right," Witherspoon replied. He slapped the latch back and turned the key. "I am, after all, a policeman."

"But sir." Smythe leapt toward the front door just as the inspector pulled it open. He elbowed his employer to one side and planted his big body directly in front of him. "That's what I'm afraid of, sir. You've put enough killers away to have plenty of enemies out there."

"Uh, excuse me." Constable Sayers blinked at the sight of the huge burly man standing like a mountain on the other side of the door. "But is this the home of Inspector Gerald Witherspoon?"

"It is," Smythe replied as he eased to his left. "And I take it ya want to see 'im?"

"It's a police constable, Smythe," Witherspoon said cheerfully. "I do believe it's quite safe to let him in."

"Sorry to bother you, sir," Constable Sayers apologized as he came in, keeping a wary eye on Smythe. "But Chief Inspector Barrows sent me round to get you, sir. There's been a murder."

"A murder?" Witherspoon repeated. He hated getting roused out at all hours for a murder. But then, murderers were not by nature the most thoughtful of people.

"Yes, sir," the young man replied. He noticed that both the woman, who he assumed was a housekeeper, and the big man, who looked more like a thug than a coachman, were still standing beside the inspector. "Chief Inspector Barrows thinks you should come quick, sir. That's why he sent me along to fetch you. A woman's been stabbed, sir."

Witherspoon stared at the young man for a moment. "Chief Inspector Barrows sent you?"

Constable Sayers nodded. "The Chief asked for you, sir, though Inspector Nivens was against it."

Mrs. Jeffries and Smythe looked at each other.

"Inspector Nivens?" the inspector repeated. Gracious, this was most odd. Most odd, indeed.

"Yes, sir. He's on the scene because we thought it was just a burglary. Then the Chief Inspector arrived and said it weren't, that it were murder and we'd best send for you. We've sent along for Constable Barnes as well, sir. He'll meet us there, sir."

"Thank you, Constable." Witherspoon decided to wait till he got to the scene of the crime before asking any more questions. "If you'll have a seat in the drawing room"—he gestured down the hall—"I'll be ready to go back with you in just a few moments."

But Mrs. Jeffries wasn't going to let a golden opportunity like this pass. "Inspector, it's quite cold outside. Why don't I take the constable down to the kitchen for a nice cup of tea or cocoa while you're getting ready?"

"How very thoughtful of you, Mrs. Jeffries," the inspector replied as he headed for the steps. "I'm sure the constable could use something warm to drink."

"Thank you, ma'am, I'd be most obliged," Constable Sayers replied honestly. Truth was, he was frozen to the bone.

"Come this way, then," she said, smiling cheerfully as she took his arm. "We'll have you fixed up in no time."

Smythe, following on their heels, grinned hugely. Mrs. Goodge would really get her apron in a twist now. It looked as if they had them a murder. Even better, if he knew Mrs. Jeffries as well as he thought he did, she'd grill this poor lad until she'd wrung every single little detail out of him.

Barnes was indeed waiting for the inspector when he and Sayers slipped past the police constable, who nodded smartly, and into the back sitting room of the elegant Mayfair home. So was Inspector Nivens.

Feeling a bit awkward, Witherspoon smiled faintly. "Good evening," he said. "I understand Chief Inspector Barrows wanted me to have a look in."

Nivens grunted in reply, so the inspector turned his attention to the scene of the crime.

The room was small, and in the daylight probably quite a cheerful little place. The floor was covered with a cream colored carpet. Bright yellow-and-white striped wall paper, adorned with colorful prints of pastoral scenes, graced the walls. A small but delicately carved mantel stood guard over the fireplace. A silver pitcher brimming with orange and yellow dried flowers sat atop the buttercup-colored fringed shawl on a table at the far side of the room. Clustered beside it in a nice, cozy circle was a deep brown horsehair settee and two mustard-coloured velvet balloon-backed chairs. On the opposite wall, a door was half open and Constable Barnes leaned against the doorjamb.

Nivens's lip curled when their gazes met. He jerked his head toward the French doors. "We'd best get cracking. The Chief Inspector wants this cleared up as soon as possible."

"Is he still here?" Witherspoon asked, taking care to avoid looking in the direction that Nivens indicated. He wanted to put off looking at the dead woman until the last possible moment. It was quite difficult to ignore her. She did have a rather large knife poking out of her back.

"He's having a quick word with the victim's husband," Nivens replied. "But he'll be back directly. Maybe you'll have this case solved by then." His voice dripped sarcasm but Inspector Witherspoon didn't appear to notice.

Constable Barnes, a craggy-faced man with a shock of iron-gray hair and a ruddy complexion, glared at Nivens's back and stifled a rude remark. Stupid git! He didn't like Inspector Nivens; most of the constables who'd worked with him didn't like him. But he had to tread carefully here; the man was assigned to this case. Thank goodness the Chief had had the good sense to call in Inspector Witherspoon. God knows what kind of muck up Nivens would have made of it.

"You'll want to have a look at the body, sir." Barnes directed his comment to Witherspoon. "The police surgeon should be here any moment now."

Witherspoon smiled briefly and steeled himself. He wished Constable Barnes wasn't so keen on always getting him to examine the corpse. But it was his duty, so he'd best get it over with. He stepped across the room and knelt down by the fallen woman. But he couldn't bring himself to look, not quite yet. He gazed out the window pane to the balcony and beyond that, to the vague outline of skeletal tree limbs and bushes. "Is that a garden?"

"Yes, sir," Barnes replied, "we've had the lads out there having a look round, tramping about in the darkness, but they've found nothing."

"We'll search it again tomorrow morning," Witherspoon said.

"I've already given those instructions," Nivens snapped. He'd come over and stood over them, his pale face set in a scowl, his mouth compressed into a flat, thin line. From the backlighting of the gas lamps on the wall behind him, Witherspoon could make out the sheen of hair oil on his dark blond hair.

"Uh, I say, did you want something?" The inspector didn't mind being a tad squeamish about corpses in front of Barnes, but he didn't wish to make a spectacle of himself in front of Inspector Nivens.

"I want you to tell me what you make of that." Nivens pointed to the body.

"What's the victim's name?"

"Hannah Cameron." Nivens tapped his foot impatiently. "Well, what are you waiting for? Get on with it."

Witherspoon, grateful that his dinner had been several hours ago, forced himself to look down. She lay slumped on her side directly inside of the door. Her hair was a faded blond, going gray at the temples, and her face, now deathly white, was long and narrow. Her eyes, open still, were blue. She'd been wearing a green velvet dress. She did not look like a happy woman. Even in death, there was an air of joylessness about her that filled Witherspoon with regret. But whatever she had been in life, whether harridan or saint, no one had had the right to shove a knife in her back and kill her. "She's dead."

"Of course she's dead," Nivens cried. "That's why you're here. For some odd reason, the Chief Inspector seems to think you're the only person capable of handling a simple homicide."

"I don't think it's simple," Witherpsoon muttered. They never were. He steeled himself and turned her shoulder so that he could see her back. He swallowed heavily and closed his eyes. The handle of the blade stuck out obscenely. The green velvet fabric was soaked with blood. There was more blood on the carpet, directly beneath where she'd lain. He eased her gently back down and stood up. His forehead creased in thought. "Has anyone touched the body?"

"No, sir," Constable Sayers said. "Her husband found her, sir, and he had sense enough not to touch anything."

"It looks as if she were standing looking out onto the garden and was struck from behind," the inspector commented.

"Yes, sir." Barnes had knelt down on the other side of the body. He too stood up. "That's one of the reasons I'm fairly sure it weren't a burglary."

Nivens snorted. "I didn't realize you were such an expert, Constable."

Witherspoon looked at him sharply. "Constable Barnes's observations are always most pertinent. I agree with him."

Barnes smiled, grateful that his superior had stood up for him. "I'm thinkin', sir, that if she were standin' looking out at the garden, the burglar"—he tossed a quick glance at Nivens—"would have already been in the room."

"Of course he would have," Nivens said quickly. "And that's the whole point. She came in and saw the window was broken, walked over to have a look at it and when she had her back turned, the killer, who was probably hiding in that bedroom"—he pointed toward the door on the other side of the room—"stabbed her and then escaped. This is a simple robbery gone bad. There was no reason for the Chief to call you out on this one. With my sources among the thieves of this city, I'll soon find who killed her."

"Do the doors open in or out?"

"In, sir," Barnes replied.

Witherspoon glanced down at the body again and noted that it was lying less than two inches from the door. "If that was the case, Inspector Nivens," he asked softly, "how did the burglar get out?"

Nivens looked confused. "I don't understand your question. Isn't it obvious? He walked out the way he got in."

"Through the French doors?"

"Yes," Nivens said, but his voice wasn't as certain as before.

Witherspoon looked down at the floor again, studying the carpet surrounding the body. He frowned, trying to recall some of the conversations he'd had with his housekeeper. Why, just last week they'd had quite an interesting discussion about blood. What was it she'd said? Then he remembered. "I don't think so. If he'd killed her in a panic, he'd have wanted to get out in a hurry. That means she'd have still been bleeding quite profusely."

"So?" Nivens asked sullenly, his gaze on the doorway in case the Chief Inspector toddled back in just as the brilliant bloody Witherspoon was expounding on one of his ridiculous theories.

"What I'm trying to say"—Witherspoon wasn't sure exactly how to put it. He wished he could remember the precise way Mrs. Jeffries had discussed the matter. "—is that if he tried to get out this door while the poor woman was still bleeding profusely, there'd be blood all over the carpet. He would have had to jostle her and shove her out of the way. As you can see, there's only blood directly beneath the body, which implies that she fell almost directly after she was struck down and that the body hasn't been moved at all. That means the killer couldn't have gone out these doors."

Nivens stared at him thoughtfully. Then he said, "That's the most ridiculous thing I've ever heard."

CHAPTER 2

"I knew it," Mrs. Goodge cried. "I just knew it. Here we finally have us a nice, ripe murder and I'm saddled with my daft old aunt."

"Stop yer frettin', Mrs. Goodge," Smythe said kindly. "It'll not be as bad as ya think. We'll find a way to keep yer auntie occupied."

"Doing what? She's eighty-five if she's a day," Mrs. Goodge muttered disgustedly. "I can hardly shove her into a hansom and send her down to Regent Street to look at the shops."

"Now, now," Mrs. Jeffries soothed. "We'll think of something. If she's that elderly, she'll probably spend a lot of time in her room, resting."

Betsy gave a worried glance at the clock. "Should we send for Luty and Hatchet? You know how Luty gets."

Mrs. Jeffries thought about it. Luty Belle Crookshank and her butler, Hatchet, were dear friends. They considered themselves almost a part of the inspector's household and as such, they were determined to be in on all of the inspector's cases. They were born snoops. Luty in particular got a bit testy when she wasn't directly informed that they had a killer to catch. "I honestly don't know." She hesitated. "It's awfully late."

"I don't think we ought to bother," Smythe said. "We'll none of us be able to get started until tomorrow. I can always nip out bright and early and bring them back 'ere for breakfast."

"No, you can't," Mrs. Goodge said darkly. "You'll not have time. You've got to help me move Aunt Elberta's bed into that little room next to mine and then you've got to go to Charing Cross to pick her up."

"Can't Wiggins do it?"

"I can't drive the carriage," Wiggins cried. He'd driven the carriage once before and the experience had left him so shaken, he'd sworn he'd never do it again.

"I know," the coachman replied, "and the 'orses know it as well. What I meant was, can't you move the ruddy bed?"

"It's too heavy for him," Mrs. Jeffries said. "As a matter of fact, it'll probably take both of you." She tapped her fingers on the top of the table as she considered a way around their problem. It was imperative they get an early start tomorrow and it was equally imperative that Luty and Hatchet be fully informed. "I'll tell you what," she said, as an idea struck. "The inspector won't be home for hours so there's no reason Smythe and Wiggins can't move the bed tonight. That'll free Smythe up to go fetch Luty and Hatchet early tomorrow morning. We can have our meeting then and we'll bring them up to date on everything we learned from Constable Sayers."

"He was a nice young man," Betsy murmured, remembering the way the constable's gaze had kept straying to her, even when he was talking to someone else.

"Bit of a nervous Nellie, if you ask me," Smythe grumbled. He too had noticed the way Sayers had been eyeing up Betsy. He hadn't liked it one bit. "Couldn't even hold his cocoa without 'is 'and shakin'"

"Only because he was cold." Betsy defended him. She'd felt sorry for him. As much as Constable Sayers had tried to hide it, he'd been rattled by seeing the dead woman's body.

"Who's going to fetch Aunt Elberta from the station?" Mrs. Goodge interrupted. She wanted to get this problem sorted out now so she wouldn't have to worry about it all night. "Her train is in early."

"I will," Mrs. Jeffries volunteered. "I'll pop over in a hansom. We'll bring her back, get her nicely settled in and then start our inquiries."

"But I wanted to get round to Mayfair early tomorrow," Betsy complained. "You know, before the police start snooping about the neighborhood."

"They're already snoopin' about," Smythe said. "Your getting there at ten o'clock instead of eight won't make any difference."

Betsy pursed her lips. "I don't know. We'll have to be really careful on this one. Inspector Nivens would love to catch one of us interfering."

"We'll just have to make sure he doesn't, won't we?" Mrs. Jeffries said firmly. But despite her bravado, she was concerned. Inspector Nivens had made no secret of the fact that he thought Gerald Witherspoon had help on his cases. If he so much as caught a glimpse of one of them, the jig would be up. What rotten luck that their dear inspector had gotten saddled with that odious man. They'd just have to make doubly sure they didn't get caught.

"Well, at least we found out a few things tonight," Wiggins said cheerfully. "We know who died and where she lived. That's a good start, in'n it?"

The tall, red-haired man with the handlebar mustache sat hunched in a wing-back chair. The collar of his white evening shirt was off and though he was decently dressed in proper black evening trousers and boots, he wore a heavy brown dressing gown over his clothes. His face was buried in his hands. "I can't believe she's dead," he murmured. "I simply can't believe it. Who would want to do such a thing? Why? Why hurt Hannah? Why didn't they just run when they saw her? Why kill her?"

Witherspoon stared at him sympathetically. This was one of the worst aspects of his job, talking to the loved ones of the victim. "I'm terribly sorry for your loss, sir," he said. "But if you're able, we'd like to ask you a few questions."

"Really, Inspector," a woman's voice said harshly, "have you no sense of decency? Mr. Cameron's just lost his wife. He's in shock. Can't this wait until tomorrow?"

Witherspoon raised his gaze and looked at the speaker. She'd been introduced as Fiona Hadleigh, a friend of the victim's who was staying overnight at the Cameron house. She stood next to Brian Cameron's chair, her thin, bony hand on the man's shoulder. A tall woman, she wore an evening dress of sapphire blue velvet fitted at the neck with a double layer of white lace. Matching blue velvet slippers peeked out from beneath the hem of her skirt. Her hair, upswept in an elaborate arrangement on top of her head, was circled with a bandeaux that had a flurry of white ostrich feathers. But despite her beautiful outfit, she was a homely woman, her brown hair streaked with gray at the temples, her face long and horsey and her mouth a thin wedge beneath a rather large nose.

"We're not insensitive to Mr. Cameron's shock," the inspector said softly, "but the sooner we start asking questions, the sooner we can catch the person who committed this foul murder."

"It's all right, Fiona." Brian Cameron raised his head and smiled at her. "The inspector's only doing his job. Please, do go up to bed. There's nothing you can do. Tell the others to go on up as well. There's no need for Kathryn or John to keep the vigil. I'll be all right."

"Nonsense, Brian," Fiona said briskly. "I wouldn't dream of leaving you alone." She walked across the drawing room and yanked at the bell pull. "I'll ring for some tea."

Witherspoon glanced at Barnes, who'd taken out his notebook and was busily scribbling away. Inspector Nivens had gone off to the Yard, no doubt to complain about the situation. Inspector Witherspoon didn't much blame the fellow. It was going to be decidedly awkward for both of them. But he had a duty to perform and, uncomfortable or not, he'd make the best of the situation. "Mr. Cameron, I understand your household is very upset and that it's getting very late. Your servants and your other guests can go up to their rooms as soon as they've made a statement to the police constable."

"P.C. Sayers and P.C. Meadows have taken statements from the staff. I've taken Kathryn Ellingsley's and John Ripton's statements," Barnes told Witherspoon. "The servants have all gone back to bed. But Miss Ellingsley and Mr. Ripton insisted on waiting up for Mr. Cameron. They're in the library if you'd like a word with them."

"Do you think that's necessary tonight?" Witherspoon asked him. He wondered if Nivens had bothered to talk to anyone.

"I think you could question them tomorrow, sir," Barnes replied. "Neither of them saw or heard anything."

Fiona finished giving instructions to the maid and stomped back to take up her post next to Brian Cameron. "Well," she snapped, "get on with it. We don't wish to stand about here all night."

"Then I suggest you have a seat, Fiona," Brian said, softening his words with a smile and a pat on her hand. "Please, Inspector, do sit down and make yourself comfortable. I'm sure you've a number of things you need to ask."

"Thank you, sir," he replied, walking over and sitting down on a hard-backed chair across from the settee. "I'll try to be as brief as possible. First of all, how many people were in the house tonight?"

Cameron thought about it a moment. "Other than the servants, there was my wife and myself, Fiona, of course, and John Ripton. The four of us had gone to dinner tonight. They'd decided to stay over."

"Anyone else?"

Cameron shrugged. "Just Kathryn and the children."

"Kathryn Ellingsley—she's the governess, I believe." Witherspoon stated.

"She's been with us for about six months," Cameron replied. "I've two children, Inspector. Edward and Ellen. Edward's ten and Ellen is eight. This will be very difficult for them to understand."

Witherspoon clucked his tongue sympathetically. "How dreadful for them to lose their mother so young."

"Mrs. Cameron was their stepmother," Fiona put in.

"But she's the only mother the children have ever known," Brian added. "We married when they were both babies. My first wife died of influenza right after Ellen was born."

"So you've been widowed twice, sir," Barnes commented quietly.

Fiona Hadleigh glanced at him sharply. "What's that supposed to mean? The first Mrs. Cameron died of influenza."

Barnes raised his eyebrows slightly. "It wasn't a question, Mrs. Hadleigh, just a comment."

"I'll thank you to keep your comments to yourself."

Witherspoon cleared his throat. "Can you tell me what happened this evening, sir?"

Cameron sighed wearily. "As I told you, the four of us had dinner together . . ."

"At a restaurant?" Witherspoon interrupted. He hated to be rude, but he'd found that if he didn't get a question out when he thought of it, he sometimes forgot it altogether.

Cameron nodded. "At Simpsons. We were to dine at eight, but the restaurant was crowded so it took quite a while to get served and have our meal. By the time we got home, it was so late that we invited Mrs. Hadleigh and Mr. Ripton to spend the night. They accepted the invitation. John and I had a glass of port before retiring and Fiona and Hannah kept us company. About eleven-thirty, we all went to bed. I read for a while and then just as I started to get undressed, Miriam, my wife's maid, knocked on the door. She asked if I'd seen Mrs. Cameron. She couldn't find her."

"So it was the maid who alerted you to the fact that Mrs. Cameron wasn't in her room?" Witherspoon said. He wanted to get the sequence of events clear in his own mind.

"That's correct."

The inspector thought about it for a moment. "How long was it from the time you went up until the maid came and knocked on your door?"

He shrugged. "Twenty minutes or so, perhaps a bit more, perhaps a bit less. I've really no idea. It's my habit to read before I retire. I remember I'd just put down my book when the maid knocked. But I didn't think to look at the clock."

"And then what happened?" Witherspoon prompted gently.

"Then I went back downstairs thinking that perhaps Hannah had forgotten something and gone to fetch it. But she wasn't in the drawing room or the library, so I had a look in the small back sitting room and . . . and . . ." His voice broke and he looked down at the floor.

"It's quite all right, sir," Witherspoon interrupted. "You needn't go on about that part of it. We know what you found."

"Had the maid searched for Mrs. Cameron?" Barnes asked.

"I don't know," he replied, shaking his head. "I assume not."

"Why?" the constable persisted. From what he knew of rich people, they didn't get off their backsides and hunt for someone if they had a servant to do it for them.

Brian Cameron seemed surprised by the question. "Why what? Why didn't the maid search? I've no idea. You'll have to ask her."

"Was there any reason that you can think of why your wife went into that room tonight?" Witherspoon asked.

Cameron closed his eyes and shook his head.

"Not that I know about. I've no idea why she went downstairs at all. The only thing I can think of is that she'd forgotten something and gone back downstairs to fetch it."

"But if she'd forgotten something, wouldn't she have sent her maid to get it?"

"Usually, yes."

"But this time, she went down herself," Witherspoon mused. He thought back to how the body had been situated in the room. "Is it possible she could have heard something out in the garden and gone down on her own to see what it was?"

"It's possible," Cameron replied. "Quite honestly, Inspector, I've no idea why my wife came downstairs. She only uses that sitting room in the mornings. But as it was, she did go down and it cost her dearly. She obviously surprised a thief and the cur murdered her."

Witherspoon knew he had to tread cautiously here. Apparently, Chief

Inspector Barrows hadn't informed the master of the house that his wife's murder might not be as simple as that. "Were any of the windows or doors opened when you came downstairs?"

"I don't know. I didn't think to look. As soon as I realized that Hannah was dead, I sent the butler out for help."

"The front door was open," Fiona Hadleigh volunteered. "I saw it standing wide open when I came downstairs to see what all the commotion was about."

"It was only open because Hatfield was so rattled he dashed out into the street shouting his lungs out for the police," Cameron replied. "It wasn't opened before that. It was locked. I checked that when I came down looking for Hannah." He looked up at Witherspoon. "The police searched the house earlier. They didn't find any windows open and the bolt was still on the back door when they looked. Why are you asking about the doors and windows?"

"If your wife surprised a burglar," Witherspoon replied, "I'm wondering how he got in and out?"

"Well, surely that's obvious. The French doors in the study. The glass was broken in one of them. That's how he must have gotten in."

Witherspoon thought about the position of the body again, about the way Hannah Cameron had been crumbled in a heap less than two inches from the door frame.

"Mr. Cameron," he began hesitantly, "I'm afraid there's a possibility your wife didn't surprise a thief."

Cameron's brows drew together. "But that's nonsense. She must have. Who else could have killed her?"

Witherspoon thought it prudent not to share all his information with someone who might be a suspect in this case. He was sorry now that he'd said anything. But if Hannah Cameron had surprised a thief, he'd eat his hat for breakfast. "I'm afraid, sir, that we can't rule out any possibilities. I'll have to ask everyone, including your servants, to make yourselves available for further questioning."

Mrs. Jeffries was at her wit's end. Getting Aunt Elberta safely ensconced in the household while at the same time trying to pry a bit of information out of a dreadfully tired Inspector Witherspoon had greatly taxed her resources, not to mention her stamina. But by ten o'clock the next morning,

Aunt Elberta was resting comfortably in her room upstairs and they were grouped around the kitchen table. Inspector Witherspoon, having come home very late, had gone to bed with only a weary smile at his housekeeper and then been up and out with only a cup of tea for his breakfast.

But Mrs. Jeffries had gotten some basic facts out of the man. Facts she was eager to share with the others, all of whom were chomping at the bit to get cracking.

"What's takin' Luty and Hatchet so long?" Wiggins asked. "Smythe left to get 'em 'ours ago."

"It's not been hours," Betsy corrected, but she too frowned at the clock.

At that moment, they heard the back door opening and the sound of voices.

"Howdy, everyone," Luty called as she dashed into the kitchen. "I'm sorry it took us so long to git here, but I had to get shut of some business before I could come." Luty Belle Crookshank was white-haired, dark-eyed and sharp as a razor despite her advanced years. She wore a bright blue bonnet with a plume of peacock feathers on the crest and carried a large mink muff. Her small frame was swathed in a heavy black coat which she shedded as she crossed the room. Tossing it on the coat tree, she smoothed the skirt of her outrageously bright green-and-blue striped day gown and hurried over to the others.

"I'd hardly call Sir William Marlin 'business to get shut of,'" Hatchet reproved his employer stiffly. He was a tall, distinguished looking man with a full shock of white hair, a carriage straighter than the Kaiser's and a ready smile that belied his always correct manner. "Good morning, everyone," he said formally as he pulled out a chair for his employer. "I must say, I was utterly delighted when your good man Smythe came round this morning and told us our services were needed."

"Glad you finally got here," Mrs. Goodge said testily. She whipped a quick glance over her shoulder toward the hall and the backstairs. No doubt she was still worried that Aunt Elberta would come bursting in on them.

"We got 'ere as quick as we could," Smythe said, dropping into the chair next to Betsy. "But Luty had some important business . . ."

"Piddle." Luty snorted. "Bill Marlin only wanted to badger me about givin' my money away. I told him it weren't none of his business who I give my cash to and sent him along. Stupid men, always tryin' to stick their noses in other people's business."

"You didn't have to be so rude to him." Hatchet sniffed disapprovingly. "Honestly, madam, you practically threatened to shoot the poor fellow."

"I never threatened him," Luty protested. "Can I help it if he turned tail and skedaddled just because I got my gun out?" Luty liked to carry a Colt .45 in her fur muff when they were on a case.

"Oh dear." Mrs. Jeffries cast a worried glance at the muff that lay innocently on the table in front of Luty. "I thought we'd agreed that perhaps carrying a loaded weapon in London wasn't such a good idea."

"Don't fret, Hepzibah." Luty laughed. "I only got the gun out to have a look at it. I'm not carryin' it. Hatchet claims it makes him nervous."

"It would make anyone nervous," Hatchet replied. "And you got the weapon out to terrorize Sir William . . ."

"It worked, didn't it?" Luty shot back. "Bill took one look at my peacemaker and suddenly remembered another appointment."

Hatchet harrumphed loudly. "*Bill* indeed! All he was doing was his proper job, madam. Your late husband did specifically request that Sir William act as your financial advisor."

"Let's argue about it later," Luty replied. "I want to hear what we've got on our plates." She turned to Mrs. Jeffries. "What do we know about this here killing?"

"We've learned enough to get started," Mrs. Jeffries said. "The inspector was too tired to talk when he came home and he was in a hurry this morning. But luckily, one of the constables on the scene was here last night and we got quite a bit out of him. The victim is a woman named Hannah Cameron. Whoever killed her tried to make it look as though she'd interrupted a burglary. She was stabbed in the back. Chief Inspector Barrows of Scotland Yard happened to be leaving the house next door when the alarm was raised and he took charge. The moment he saw the room the woman was found in, he knew it was a case of willful murder."

"Then I take it that someone, presumably the killer, deliberately tried to make it look as though the victim had surprised a burglar?" Hatchet ventured.

"Indeed." Mrs. Jeffries picked up her tea cup. "They went to a great deal of effort. There was a broken window in the pane of the French doors, some drawers were left open and a number of items were found on the floor. But apparently, whoever did it didn't know the first thing about how a real burglar would have behaved. It was the top drawers that were opened, you see," she explained. "And there were a number of small, expensive items in the bedroom that hadn't been touched. A true professional would have nabbed those before he'd even touched the drawers looking for valuables."

Luty's brows drew together. "I ain't followin' ya. What difference does it make which drawers were open?"

"A professional burglar would have started from the bottom up," Hatchet answered. "It's much faster that way. If you start from the top and work down, you have to take the time to close the drawer before you can properly see what's in the one below it. Oh, excuse me, Mrs. Jeffries, I didn't mean to interrupt."

She smiled in amusement. "That's quite all right, Hatchet. You are correct." She went on to tell them the rest of what they'd learned. "So you see," she concluded, "we must be extra careful. Not only is this case extremely puzzling, but we've got to contend with Inspector Nivens being very involved in it."

There was a collective moan from the others. Mrs. Jeffries smiled briefly and went on, "But we do have a list of suspects. Inspector Witherspoon thinks that the killer must have already been in the house. As there was no sign of a door or window being open, he's assuming that the killer either was already in the house or had a key."

"But didn't you just say that this Hadleigh woman noticed the front door standing wide open?" Betsy asked.

"I did," Mrs. Jeffries nodded. "And that's one of the things we'll need to confirm. Brian Cameron claims it was only opened when the butler dashed out to get a policeman."

"Was Cameron watchin' the door the whole time?" Smythe asked. "I mean, a lot of thieves are quick on their feet. If the burglar couldn't have gotten out the French doors in the sittin' room before the alarm was raised, he could have been hidin' and waitin' for a chance to slip out the front door."

"At this point," the housekeeper explained, "we simply don't know enough one way or the other. But if Chief Inspector Barrow and our inspector both think this wasn't a burglary, I believe we ought to go along with that assumption. At least until we have some facts in our possession which indicate differently."

"Who else was in the 'ouse?" Wiggins asked.

"A number of servants were there," Mrs. Jeffries replied, "but most of them were asleep, of course. Then there's the governess, Kathryn Ellingsley; the two guests, Fiona Hadleigh and a Mr. John Ripton; and, of course, Brian Cameron."

"What kind of knife was it?" Hatchet asked.

"Just a simple butcher knife," Mrs. Jeffries frowned. "According to Constable Sayers, there's no way to trace it. There's a lot we don't know, but there's plenty enough for us to get started."

Betsy got to her feet. "I'll get over to Mayfair straight away and start asking questions. By this time, the news of the murder will be all over the place."

"Excellent, Betsy." Mrs. Jeffries smiled in approval. "Concentrate on the shopkeepers and find out what you can about the victim and her family."

"Do you want me to try and make contact with a servant?" Betsy asked.

"Only if you can do so without running into Inspector Nivens," Mrs. Jeffries warned. "Remember, we've all got to keep a sharp eye out. He's actually helping the inspector with this case. They've both been assigned to it and I don't want him catching so much as a glimpse of any of us."

"'Old up, Betsy," Smythe called to the maid as he too got up. "We might as well go together. If it's all right with Mrs. J., I'll head over that way and begin talking to the cabbies and seein' what I can pick up at the pubs."

"That's a good idea," the housekeeper said. She watched in approval as the two of them put on their hats and coats and started for the back door. Both of them knew precisely what to do, precisely how to begin this investigation.

"I reckon you want me to start buzzin' my sources about information on Brian Cameron," Luty said.

"If you would, please. That would be most helpful," Mrs. Jeffries replied. Luty was rich. She knew a lot of bankers and financial people. Using charm, grace, tact, diplomacy, intimidation and stubbornness, she could find out how much a person was worth down to his last penny.

"I'll get the word out too," Mrs. Goodge said. She openly glared toward the hall. "With any luck, Aunt Elberta will sleep a few hours and leave me in peace. I've got a fair number of people stopping by today. Once I tell 'em about the murder, I might be able to learn all sorts of things."

"What do you want me to do?" Wiggins asked. "With Inspector Nivens hanging about and gummin' up the works, it'll not be easy for me to meet up with a servant from the Cameron 'ousehold."

Mrs. Jeffries had already considered that problem. "I know. I think that this time instead of trying to talk with one of them at the Cameron house in Mayfair, perhaps you ought to see if anyone leaves the household."

"You want me to follow 'em?" Wiggins's eyes widened. "You mean you want me to 'ang about waiting for someone to come out? But that could take all day. Besides, what if a copper spots me 'angin' about the place? They'll be combing the neighborhood asking questions."

"I know, Wiggins," Mrs. Jeffries said sympathetically. "Your task isn't going to be easy. Just do the best you can."

Wiggins looked doubtful. "Don't be surprised if I'm back 'ere pretty fast. We can't risk my gettin' caught."

"Use your noggin, boy." Luty reached over and patted his hand. "A clever lad like you ought to be able to give a few policemen the slip."

Hatchet put his elbow on the table and leaned forward. "I've heard the name Ripton before. I can't remember where. You say the man staying as a houseguest was named John. John Ripton?"

"That's right, though I don't know as yet what connection he has to the Camerons."

"Probably a pretty close one if he was spendin' the night there," Luty put in.

"Perhaps I'll start my inquiries with this gentleman," Hatchet said.

"Good. That'll keep you out of my hair," Luty rose to her feet. "I'm goin' to git started then. What time should we meet back here?"

"Four o'clock," Mrs. Jeffries replied. "That should give everyone time to learn something."

Inspector Witherspoon wished that Inspector Nivens would stop pacing. Just watching the man was making him tired. He stifled a yawn and promised himself that unless another corpse landed at his feet, tonight he was going to get a decent night's sleep. He wasn't used to trying to think on so little rest.

"Really, Witherspoon," Nivens said testily, "must you keep yawning?"

Constable Barnes, who was standing in the corner of the Cameron drawing room, shot Nivens a quick glare. "The inspector didn't get much sleep last night, sir," he said flatly. "Unlike you, sir, he was here at the crime scene until well after three o'clock."

"Don't be impertinent," Nivens snapped. His mouth clamped shut as the door opened and a young woman stepped inside.

Witherspoon smiled at her kindly. She was quite a lovely woman. Dark auburn hair neatly tucked up in a modest fashion, pale white skin and strikingly beautiful brown eyes. She was dressed in a black skirt and a high-necked gray blouse.

"I'm Kathryn Ellingsley," she said. "I understand you want to ask me a few questions."

Inspector Witherspoon introduced himself and the others. "Please sit down, Miss Ellingsley."

Her skirt rustled faintly as she walked to the settee and sat down. "I don't know what I can tell you about this dreadful thing," she began. "I was asleep. I generally go to bed right after the children."

"We understand that," Witherspoon replied. "But it's always helpful in a case like this to question everyone in the household."

"I've already been questioned," she said, but she sounded more confused than angry. "I don't understand."

"You don't really need to understand," Inspector Nivens said. "Just answer our questions. What exactly do you do here?" He stalked over and stood directly over the young woman. His posture, like his tone, was meant to be intimidating.

Kathryn shrank back against the cushions. "I'm the governess."

"How long have you worked for the Camerons?" Nivens demanded.

"Almost six months," Kathryn answered.

"What are your duties?" Nivens stared at her stonily, deliberately giving her the impression he didn't believe a word she said.

But she'd regained her composure. She straightened her spine and looked him directly in the eye. "I've already told you I'm the governess. I should think my duties would be obvious even to someone like . . ."

Infuriated by her tone, Nivens interrupted. "Don't be impertinent with me, girl."

"And I'm Brian Cameron's cousin," she finished.

Nivens was taken aback. It was one thing to browbeat the servant of a wealthy household; it was quite another to do it to a blood relation. Even a poor one. He stepped back, his expression softening. "I see," he said, giving her a quick smile. "Well, then, if you were asleep, we shan't bother you with any more questions. You may go, Miss Ellingsley."

Witherspoon, who didn't believe in browbeating anyone, gaped at Nivens. "Excuse me," he said. "But I do have a few questions for Miss Ellingsley."

"Don't be ridiculous, Witherspoon." Nivens waved at him dismissively. "Miss Ellingsley said she was asleep. What could she possibly tell us?"

"We'll never know if we don't ask," the inspector said. He turned and smiled at her. "I'm sorry to intrude on you at what must be a very difficult time, Miss Ellingsley, but if you wouldn't mind . . ."

Kathryn Ellingsley smiled and deliberately turned toward the Inspector. "Ask what you like, Inspector. I want you to catch the person who did this terrible thing."

"Do you know if Mrs. Cameron had any enemies? Anyone who wished her ill?"

Kathryn shook her head. "Hannah hadn't any enemies that I know about. There were people who didn't like her very much, but that's to be expected, isn't it? No one is well liked by everyone."

"Who didn't care for her?" Witherspoon pressed.

"Oh, you know, some of the neighbors weren't all that friendly to her, and she wasn't particularly popular with the servants."

"Was she a hard mistress, then?" Nivens put in. "Given to sacking people, was she?"

Kathryn turned and gave him a long, steady stare before answering. "Certainly not. But she was strict with the staff. It was her way."

"Could you be a bit more specific?" Witherspoon urged her.

Kathryn Ellingsley hesitated briefly and then looked quickly toward the door. "I shouldn't have said anything, Inspector. Mrs. Cameron was liked and respected by the entire household."

Witherspoon smiled faintly, appreciating the fact that the girl didn't wish to cause her cousin distress by being candid about his late wife. "Miss Ellingsley, you've just admitted she wasn't universally popular. Please, do tell us what you meant. I assure you that nothing you say in this room will get back to Mr. Cameron."

"I don't want to cause him any more grief," Kathryn said quickly. "He's enough to bear now and I don't think I ought to speak ill of the dead. It doesn't feel right."

"Of course it doesn't," the inspector agreed. "But murder victims can't be considered in that light. If we're going to catch the person responsible for taking Mrs. Cameron's life, we need to know as much about the victim as possible."

Kathryn looked down at her clasped hands. "I didn't mean to imply that Mrs. Cameron was unduly harsh or unfair. She wasn't. She was just strict. But no stricter than many other households."

Witherspoon leaned forward eagerly. "In what way was she strict?"

"She made the maids account for their day out, made them tell her where they were going and who they were going with," Kathryn said. "If Mrs. Cameron didn't approve, she wouldn't let them go out. She was very strict about morning prayers. None of us were allowed to be absent. But she was always there herself, so she never asked more from the staff than she asked of herself."

Witherspoon nodded slowly. "I see," he said. He wasn't sure what he saw, except he had the feeling that this young woman wasn't being all that truthful with him. He sensed she was holding something back.

"When was the last time you saw Mrs. Cameron alive?" Nivens suddenly asked.

"I guess it must have been about six o'clock. Yes, that's right. She came up to the nursery to say goodnight to the children after they had their tea."

"How was her manner?" Witherspoon asked. Kathryn stared at him blankly. "Her manner?"

"Was she upset or did she seem worried about anything?"

"No, she was quite ordinary," Kathryn replied. "She inspected the nursery, checked behind the children's ears and then sent them off to bed."

"What did she do then?" Barnes asked.

Nivens frowned at the constable, but for once had the sense to keep his mouth shut.

"She said goodnight and went out." The governess shrugged. "She was already dressed in her evening clothes. I didn't see her after that. I assumed she and Mr. Cameron had left for their engagement. I don't know what else I can tell you. As soon as the children were in bed, I had my supper and then went to my room."

"Thank you, Miss Ellingsley," Witherspoon said. "You've been most helpful."

She stood up. "I hope you find whoever did this to Hannah. She wasn't the most lovable person in the world, but she didn't deserve to die like that."

"We'll do our very best, Miss Ellingsley," the inspector promised her. "Would you be so kind as to ask Mr. Ripton to step in, please? We'd like a word with him."

"Of course, Inspector." She gave him a dazzling smile and exited gracefully from the room.

"We ought to keep an eye on that one," Nivens said softly, as soon as the door had closed behind Kathryn Ellingsley. "Too pretty for her own good, if you know what I mean."

Witherspoon didn't. "I'm afraid I don't."

Nivens stared at him in disbelief. "Good Lord, man, you've got eyes in your head." He jerked his chin in the direction the woman had gone. "Would you pay much attention to your wife if you had a bit of fluff like that about to play with?"

Witherspoon's jaw dropped. He was shocked to his core. He'd never in his entire life considered women "fluff" and he certainly didn't assume that a pretty woman in a man's household would turn a decent man away from his marriage vows. Nor did he have any reason to believe that Miss Ellingsley was anything less than an honorable woman. He knew there were some at the Yard who considered him a bit naive, but really, Nivens was being decidedly crass. It was only in the interests of interdepartmental cooperation that the inspector didn't speak sharply to the man.

CHAPTER 3

———◦⊱◦⊰◦———

Mrs. Goodge eyed her victim carefully through the back door. Tommy Mullins, the butcher's boy, stood there grinning at her foolishly, him and his chipped teeth. "Do you want me to leave it out here?" he asked, jerking his chin at the brown-wrapped package in his arms, "or should I bring it in and put it in the wet larder?"

Tommy was a skinny, runty fellow with stringy yellow hair sticking out of a stained porkpie hat. His shirt was dirty, his apron even dirtier and his shoes were speckled with clumps of a congealed brown-and-red substance that made the cook shudder. But this was a murder she was investigating, so filthy shoes or not, she'd have him in her kitchen. But she promised herself that arthritic fingers or not, she'd have a good go at the floor with a bottle of Condy's disinfectant as soon as he'd gone. Even though the stuff wasn't supposed to be used for anything but the pipes, if it could kill off the smell in the drains, it could certainly kill off whatever this boy tracked in on his wretched shoes. She hesitated for a fraction of a second and then took a deep breath. Tommy Mullins might look like something the cat dragged in on a particularly awful wet night, but he'd talk the head off a cabbage. More important, he had a twin who worked for a butcher in Mayfair. If Tommy's brother was anything like Tommy, he'd have already wagged his tongue about the Cameron murder.

Mrs. Goodge wasn't one to let a good opportunity slip through her fingers. "Bring it in to the wet larder for me, Tommy." She beamed at him. "And then come on in to the kitchen. I expect you could use a cuppa, couldn't you?"

He stared at her suspiciously as he stepped inside. Mrs. Goodge had a bit of the tartar about her oftentimes. He wondered what had her grinning like a cat which had just got the cream. But he did as she asked, carefully placing the bundle of wrapped meat on the larder shelf and then hurrying into the kitchen. His eyes widened as he saw the table. "Blimey, Mrs. Goodge, that's fit fer a king."

Mrs. Goodge smiled encouragingly as she patted the chair beside her. "It's only a few buns and a bit of cake. Come on, sit down and I'll pour you some tea. It's awfully cold outside."

Mouth watering, Tommy slipped into a seat and gratefully accepted the mug she handed him. He licked his lips as she filled a plate with a slice of cake, a mince tart and a hot cross bun and slid that across to him as well. "This is very nice of you," he said, stuffing a piece of cake in his mouth.

"You're a hard workin' lad," Mrs. Goodge said cheerfully. "Not like some I've known. How's your brother doin'?" It never hurt to prime the pump. Hector, the rag and bones man, was due soon and she wanted to get as much as she could out of Tommy before Hector's cart trundled up the road.

"Oh, you wouldn't believe it, Mrs. Goodge, but 'e got sacked last week."

Mrs. Goodge resisted the urge to snatch the plate out from under Tommy's nose. Tommy's brother sacked! Blast! Fat lot of good it would do her to pump Tommy for information now! Silly boy probably wouldn't know a ruddy thing.

"But 'e's ever so lucky, Tim is. Always was the lucky one in the family, not like me. If I got sacked it'd take me ages to find another position, but not Tim. Oh no, he got himself taken on as an undergardener right round the corner from where 'e worked." Tommy picked up the mince tart and demolished it in one bite. "Mind you, 'e didn't think 'e'd be doin' much work today, not with the police trampin' about the gardens and makin' a nuisance of themselves."

Mrs. Goodge's heart leapt into her throat. Goodness, was it possible? Could the boy have actually had the good sense to get a job right there at the scene of the crime, so to speak? "Police?" she echoed. "What were the police doin' there?"

"Didn't ya hear? There was this awful murder over where Tim works. A Mrs. Cameron. She got done in last night."

"Who got done in?" a ready voice asked from the door.

Tommy, his mouth full of mince tart, gaped at the figure stalking toward them. The woman was the oldest person he'd ever seen. Her hair was white and thin enough so that he could see her scalp, her face was a crisscross of wrinkles and she wore a high-necked black dress that had probably been new at Queen Victoria's christening. Bent over her cane, she thumped her way across the floor toward them.

"Aunt Elberta." Mrs. Goodge gasped. "You're supposed to be resting."

"Don't need to rest," Elberta said pleasantly, giving the lad a happy, if somewhat toothless grin. "Be plenty of rest waitin' fer me in the grave. Now, who's this fine boy?"

"He's the butcher's lad," Mrs. Goodge muttered.

"Huh." Elberta cupped a hand behind her ear as she sat down. "Speak up. I don't hear as well as I used to."

"I said, he's the butcher's boy. He brings the meat."

"I thought I heard him talkin' about murder. Who'd he do in?" She pointed a long, spindly finger at him. "He doesn't look like a killer. Mind you," she continued chattily, "you can't always tell by looking at someone. That Hiram McNally that murdered both his sons-in-laws and the house-maid looked like a nice man too."

"I'm not a killer," Tommy protested. He stuffed the last of the bun in his mouth and got to his feet. "I didn't do anyone in."

"Of course you didn't. Don't mind my auntie; sometimes her mind wanders." Mrs. Goodge said soothingly. "Now sit back down and finish your tea." She shoved the platter of food towards him. "Have another bun."

"I'll thank you to keep a civil tongue in your head," Elberta said tartly, giving her niece a good glare. "Tinkers wander, my mind does not."

"I've got to go." Tommy snatched the bun the cook had just put on his plate. "Thanks for the tea, Mrs. Goodge."

John Ripton pushed a hand through his thinning brown hair and sighed deeply. He was a man of medium height and build. Pale-skinned, with light brown eyes, he was one of those men who had a permanent beard shadow on their faces no matter how often they shaved. "This has been the most dreadful experience of my life, Inspector. Absolutely dreadful. Last night was a nightmare. Even after all the police left, I didn't sleep a wink."

Inspector Witherspoon thought it had been a bit more dreadful for

Hannah Cameron, but he did feel some sympathy for this man. It couldn't be pleasant to be someone's houseguest and then find that one's hostess has been murdered. "I'm sure it has, sir," he murmured. "And we'll try to make our inquiries as easy for you as possible. But you do realize we must ask you a few questions."

"But I don't understand why." Ripton complained. "I thought Hannah was killed by a burglar. What's that got to do with me?"

"We don't know who killed Mrs. Cameron," Witherspoon said patiently. "But we're doing our best to find out. Now, could you tell me how long you've known Mrs. Cameron?"

Ripton's brows drew together. "What on earth has that got to do with anything?"

"Absolutely nothing." The inspector smiled pleasantly, trying to put the man at ease. "However, I've found the more I know about the victim, the easier it is for me to investigate the circumstances of the crime."

Ripton stared at him for a moment, his expression clearly indicating his view of such a nonsensical notion. "I've known Hannah my entire life. She's my half-sister. Older half-sister," he explained quickly.

"I see," the inspector replied. He wondered why Brian Cameron hadn't mentioned this, stored the fact in the back of his mind and went on with his questioning. He might as well get the basic facts out of the way. "What is your profession, Mr. Ripton?"

"I work for Stoddard and Hart. Commerical builders. I'm the general manager."

"I've heard of them. They're quite a large firm, aren't they? Property redevelopment and that sort of thing." Witherspoon nodded. "Where do you live, sir?"

"In Pinner," he replied. "Moss Lane to be exact. That's one of the reasons I stayed over last night. By the time we got back here, it was too late to get a train home and I knew a hansom would take hours. So when Mr. Cameron—"

"Mr. Cameron invited you to spend the night," Barnes interrupted softly. "Not your sister?"

Ripton looked surprised by the question. "Brian asked me to stay," he said. "But I'm sure Hannah didn't mind. She seconded the invitation. As a matter of fact, she insisted."

Witherspoon surreptitiously stuck his hand in his coat pocket. The house was very cold. There was no fire in the fireplace and he wished he'd had the sense to hang on to his overcoat when he'd arrived today. John Ripton must have felt the cold as well; his neck was muffled in a heavy red scarf, an incongrous note against the somber black evening clothes he wore.

"Could you tell me what happened?" the inspector asked.

"You mean last night?"

At the inspector's nod, Ripton continued. "Nothing unusual, if that's what you mean. I'd been invited out to dinner with the Camerons and Mrs. Hadleigh. We met at eight o'clock at Simpsons, had dinner and then came back here for a glass of port. As I said, by the time we'd finished our drinks, it was so late they invited me to stay the night."

"What time did you retire?" Witherspoon wondered whether it would be proper to move the questioning into the kitchen. His feet were positively chilled.

"About half past eleven," Ripton replied.

"Did all of you go upstairs at the same time?"

Ripton thought for a moment. "As far as I can recall, Mrs. Hadleigh and Mrs. Cameron went upstairs first. Brian checked to make sure the front door was locked and then he and I followed the ladies."

"Where was your room, sir?" Witherspoon asked. Perhaps it would help to know where everyone was at the time of the murder.

"I stayed in one of the guest rooms on the second floor," he said.

"Where was your room in relation to Mr. and Mrs. Cameron's private quarters?" Witherspoon asked.

"At the opposite end of the hall." Ripton sighed. "Mrs. Hadleigh had the room next to Mrs. Cameron's. Brian's room is beside hers."

"Were the servants still awake when you went up?" Barnes asked.

Ripton frowned, as though it were a difficult question. "I don't know. I don't recall seeing any of them, so I suppose they'd been dismissed for the night."

"Mr. Cameron locked up, not the butler?" the inspector prodded. He'd learned in the past that details could be terribly important.

"Yes, I've already told you that." Ripton's voice rose slightly. "Look, Inspector, I've had a terrible shock and I'm dreadfully tired. Do you think you can hurry this along? I'd like to go home."

"Just a few more questions, sir," the inspector said kindly. But he noticed that the man seemed more annoyed than grieved over the loss of his sister. "Did you hear anything unusual after you went upstairs?"

He shook his head. "Nothing. I went straight to bed and was just falling asleep when the alarm was raised and the police were sent for. After that, it was bloody impossible to get any rest. The police were tramping all over the place, Fiona was having hysterics and well, after all, Brian is my brother-in-law. I felt I ought to stay up and help if I could."

"Did anything unusual happen while you were at the restaurant?" Barnes asked.

"The roast beef was tough," he replied casually, "and Hannah sent hers back to the kitchen. But I hardly think the chef followed us home to murder a complaining customer."

Witherspoon stifled a sigh. "Did you see anyone at the restaurant or on the way home that made you uneasy or suspicious? Any ruffians or odd-looking characters?"

"No, Inspector. There was nothing."

"And you're absolutely certain you heard nothing after you went upstairs?" he pressed. Surely someone must have heard something. If the glass in the window pane had been broken before Hannah Cameron entered the room, she'd have summoned a servant or her husband. Therefore, Witherspoon was fairly certain it had been smashed after she was killed. Gracious; were these people all deaf? This was a large house, but at that time of night, the streets would have been quiet and the sound of glass shattering should have carried quite a distance. "You didn't hear the sound of the glass being broken?"

"No, Inspector. I did not." Ripton rubbed his eyes.

But the inspector wasn't ready to give up. Even if one couldn't hear glass breaking from the second floor, surely someone must have heard a door open or the stairs squeaking when Mrs. Cameron came back downstairs. "How about someone walking about the house? Did you hear anything like that?"

"I heard nothing," Ripton said impatiently, "and I saw nothing. Now, may I please be allowed to get about my business?"

"Excuse me." Betsy smiled at the young man with more enthusiasm than was proper. "But I think you dropped this." She held a shilling in the center of her hand.

He was hardly more than a schoolboy, sixteen at most, and when he saw her dazzling smile, he blushed all the way to the roots of his wheat-colored hair. "That's not mine," he said, but he looked at the coin with

longing. "My master didn't give me no money, only told me to come down
and book the ticket."

They were standing in the center of the Albert Gate booking office of
the Great Northern Railway on William Street. Betsy had spotted the
young man leaving the house next door to the Cameron house and had
followed him. When he'd gone into the booking office, she'd hesitated for
a split second and then pulled open the heavy doors and stepped inside
herself. She'd hovered on the far side of the room, pretending to be studying a timetable while he worked his way to the front of the queue. The
moment he'd finished his business she'd waylaid him.

"I'm sorry to have bothered you, then." She gave him another dazzling
smile. "But I could have swore I saw you drop it." Sighing, she turned to
leave. The lad was after her like a shot.

"Uh, excuse me, miss," he said. He leapt in front of her and opened
the door. "I din't thank you properly for taking the trouble to ask if the
money were mine. Most people woulda just kept it."

"Not me. I'm an honest girl and it was no trouble at all." She stepped
out the door, confident that he would follow. He did. She watched him
from the corner of her eye as she pulled her coat tighter against the chill
air. "I was happy to do it."

"Uh, my name's Bill Tincher," he said, hurrying to keep pace with her
as she headed past the newstand towards Knightsbridge. "If I may be so
bold as to inquire, what's yours?"

"My name's Elizabeth"—she giggled—"but everyone calls me Betsy.
Have you finished with your business then?"

Surprised by her boldness and thanking his lucky stars, he nodded
eagerly. "Oh yes, I've booked Mrs. Loudon's ticket."

"Would you like to walk me to the omnibus stop on the Brompton
Road, then? I could do with the company," she said briskly. "A girl feels
better walking about with a strapping young man such as yourself beside
her." She was shamelessly flirting with him. But it couldn't be helped. She'd
spent half the day chatting up butchers, bakers and green grocers and she
didn't have a bit of information about the Camerons to show for her efforts.
So she wasn't above using what resources were available. So far, this lad
was the best she could do. Blast, she hoped he knew something about the
murder.

Beneath the gray material of his footman's jacket, his chest swelled.
"I'd be right pleased," he replied. "And you're right to be careful. These

days you can never tell what's goin' to happen. Why, just last night there was a horrible murder right next door."

"Really?" Betsy pretended to be shocked. "How awful. Who got killed?" Deliberately, she slowed her pace. Brompton Road wasn't all that far and she wanted to get as much information out of Bill Tincher as possible.

"Mrs. Cameron. She were murdered right in her own home," he replied, taking her elbow politely as they stepped off the pavement and started across Sloane Street. "It were terrible, just terrible."

"The poor woman." Betsy clucked sympathetically. "How was she killed?"

Bill gently pulled her back as a hansom clip-clopped past. "Stabbed, she was."

"You seem to know an awful lot about it."

"'Course I do," he bragged. "Chief Inspector Barrows was havin' dinner with Mr. and Mrs. Loudon last night. He were right there when the alarm was raised, went straight round, he did. Then he come back and told the Loudons what had happened. Warned them to be careful and all."

Betsy widened her eyes and tried to look impressed. "What did happen?"

"Seems some think Mrs. Cameron interrupted a thief that were burgling the place," he said eagerly, "but the Chief Inspector don't think that. He's called in some famous detective, some feller the Yard uses when they've got a real hard one to solve."

"Have the police been round to see you then?" Betsy asked.

"What could I tell them?" Bill grinned sheepishly. "I was sound asleep when it happened. No one, not even the Chief Inspector, heard a thing. Mind you, there's some that say there's plenty of strange goin' -ons at the Cameron house, and truth to tell, I've seen a thing or two."

"What kind of things?" she asked eagerly.

"Well, I really shouldn't be speakin' ill of the dead"—he dropped his voice to just above a whisper—"but there was some funny stories about Mrs. Cameron."

Betsy strained toward him to hear him over the roar of the traffic. "Stories," she repeated. "Oh, do tell me. It's ever so excitin', me meetin' you like this. Nothing ever happens where I live." The moment the words left her lips, she knew from the eager, pleased expression that flitted across his face that she'd made a tactical error.

"And where do you live, then?" he asked, patting her elbow in a proprietory fashion. "Close by, I hope."

She wanted his attention back on the murder, not on her. Perhaps she ought to tone down the flirting just a bit. Bill Tincher seemed like the sort to like the sound of his own voice. "Oh, that's not important." She waved her hand dismissively. "I'm just a housemaid to a gentleman who lives in Holland Park. But do go on with what you were sayin'. It's ever so interesting."

He hesitated a moment, his expression confused, then he shrugged his thin shoulders and continued. "Well, like I was sayin', there's plenty of gossip about the Camerons . . ."

"About both of them?"

"Oh yes," he said, "they've had some awful rows. This summer, when all the windows was open because of the heat, we could hear them shoutin' at each other something fierce. When I first heard she'd been murdered, I thought he'd done her in. Mind you, they hadn't been carrying on as much as they used to, at least not loud enough for us to hear."

Betsy was disappointed. During the heat wave in August, every temper in London had been frayed and strained. People had snapped, snarled and generally made themselves utterly miserable. Even she and Smythe had had a few harsh words. "Is that all? Most people get a bit het up when it's hot. I don't expect Mr. and Mrs. Cameron were any different from anyone else."

"That wasn't the only time they argued," he replied defensively. "I've heard 'em myself when they was goin' at it out in their back garden and I was outside cleaning the brasses on the back gate. Mrs. Cameron was havin' a real go at Mr. Cameron. Claimed he'd wasted all her money and they was goin' to be ruined because he didn't have no head for business."

"Really?" Betsy could tell her earlier comment had offended him and as they were quickly approaching the ominibus stop, she had to make amends in short order. "Gracious, you are a sly one, aren't you? You ought to go to work for the police. Seems to me you're a real clever lad."

He grinned proudly. "Well, there's a few things I could tell the police, not that they're likely to listen to me. But I know what I've seen."

She smiled coyly. "Are you going to tell me?"

"Are you goin' to tell me where you live?" He rocked back on his heels and stared at her boldly.

Betsy felt trapped. Over his shoulder, she could see the ominibus pulling around the corner. She didn't want to tell him, of course. Smythe would make mincemeat of this lad if he came around to Upper Edmonton

Gardens. On the other hand, she wanted to know what he knew. It could be important. She supposed she could lie to the boy, but that seemed so wrong. Her conscience would torment her for days.

The omnibus drew closer, the horses' hooves stomping hard against the pavement as they clomped toward the Brompton Road. Betsy tried to think of what to do.

"Well," he demanded, "where do you live, then?"

"You haven't told me where you live." she shot back, stalling for time. Perhaps she shouldn't take this ominibus. Maybe if she was clever enough, she could keep him here and talking until the next one came by.

"Mayfair," he said quickly. "I work for Mr. James Loudon. Now, it's your turn."

Betsy quickly made a decision. "Number twenty-two, Upper Edmonton Gardens."

"Is that in Holland Park, then?" he clarified. She nodded.

"And who do you work for?"

She gave him an innocent smile. "Inspector Gerald Witherspoon of Scotland Yard."

Fiona Hadleigh glared at the inspector. "Really, sir, I hardly think this is decent. Poor Hannah isn't even buried yet." She flounced across the room and plopped down on the settee. Crossing her hands in her lap, she continued to frown at all three of the policemen.

"I'm terribly sorry to intrude on your grief." Witherspoon began, though to be perfectly honest, the woman didn't look a bit grieved, merely irritated. "But we must ask questions. It's our duty."

"We could have waited until after the inquest, Witherspoon," Nivens said tartly. "I hardly think another twenty-four hours would make all that much difference to this investigation."

Fiona smiled at Nivens. He smiled back at her. Witherspoon glanced at Barnes and shrugged. Today had been most difficult. Most difficult, indeed. but Chief Inspector Barrows had assigned both men to this investigation, so he'd try his best to cooperate. "We've found that in murder cases . . ."

"This is hardly a murder case," Nivens interrupted. "It's a homicide in the course of a burglary. Your usual methods"—he almost sneered as he said the words—"won't find out the identity of the culprit. My methods will. I don't know why the Chief Inspector insisted on your coming in. If he'd let me take charge of everything, we'd have this case cleared up in no time."

"Of course Hannah was killed by a burglar," Fiona Hadleigh echoed. "And as I'm not a thief, I don't know why I have to be subjected to this ridiculous questioning. Nor do I think you ought to be bothering poor Brian."

Witherspoon wished he didn't have to question any of them. But duty was duty and he knew that Nivens was wrong. "Miss Hadleigh," he began.

"Mrs. Hadleigh," she snapped. "I'm a window. My husband died two years ago."

"Mrs. Hadleigh," he corrected, "could you please tell us what happened last night?"

She looked as through she wasn't going to reply for a moment, then she straightened her spine and took a deep breath. "We went out to dinner . . ."

"Did anything odd happen while you were at the restaurant?" Witherspoon interrupted.

Nivens sighed loudly.

"Nothing, Inspector. We had our meal and took a hansom back here so the gentlemen could share a glass of port."

"Did you notice if there was anything unusual or different about Mrs. Cameron's manner?" Witherspoon knew he was clutching at straws. But he honestly didn't know what else to ask.

Fiona hesitated briefly. "No, not really."

"Are you sure?" Witherspoon pressed.

"Well." she frowned. "Hannah was a bit preoccupied last night. I will grant you that."

"Preoccupied how?" Witherspoon surreptitiously rubbed his hands together to keep them warm.

"Oh, it was nothing, really." Fiona dismissed the matter. "I shouldn't have said anything."

"No, please," the inspector insisted, "you obviously noticed something odd in her behaviour."

"Really, Witherspoon," Niven scolded, "don't put words in the witness's mouth."

"I'm not," the inspector protested. "But Mrs. Hadleigh strikes me as being a most intelligent and perceptive woman. Witnesses like her are quite extraordinary. I'd like to hear what she has to say." He, of course, didn't believe anything of the sort, but he'd just remembered how his housekeeper had once told him that people would believe the most blatant lies about themselves as long as they were flattering. A happy person was frequently a chatty person. The inspector wanted Mrs. Hadleigh to be very happy. It might be the only way he could get the woman to talk.

"Why thank you, Inspector," Fiona said pleasantly. Her whole demeanour suddenly changed. She relaxed back against the settee and smiled. "How very astute of you to notice. Hannah was definitely preoccupied last night. She kept asking John for the time. It drove us all mad."

"Do you have any idea why?" Witherspoon asked.

"No, not really. But I had the impression she wanted to be home by a certain time. On the way back, she refused to let the hansom driver take the route through the park. When Brian protested, she claimed she was cold and wanted to get home. But I think there was more to it than that. Of course, it could be she merely wanted to annoy John."

"Why would Mrs. Cameron have wanted to irritate her half-brother?"

Fiona laughed. "Simply to be difficult. They've never gotten along very well. I think Hannah knew that John wanted to stay the night, and just to be contrary, she wanted to hurry them home so he'd have plenty of time to catch the train."

"Is there a particular reason she wouldn't want her brother to stay?" Witherspoon asked. He'd gotten the impression from Ripton that Mrs. Cameron had insisted he stay the night.

Fiona's thin shoulders moved in the barest hint of a shrug. "Not really. As I said, they didn't really get on that well. John is actually closer to Brian than he was to her. For some reason, she was a bit out of sorts with him last night. She'd snapped at him twice during dinner. I think she was tired of his company. He can be a most annoying man."

Barnes looked up from his notebook. "In what way?"

"He kept trying to bring up business at dinner," Fiona replied, looking disgusted by the memory. "It was revolting. How is one expected to enjoy one's food when every few minutes John would start badgering Hannah about some property she owns over near the Commercial Docks?"

"What was the nature of his . . . er . . . 'badgering'?" the inspector inquired eagerly. Now they were getting somewhere.

Fiona smiled cattily. "He wanted her to sell to him. I must say, Brian didn't help matters either. He kept encouraging John every time he brought up the subject. But the property belonged to Hannah, and she was adamant about keeping it herself." She laughed harshly. "Ironic, isn't it? Now that Hannah's dead, John will inherit it anyway."

"Mr. Ripton will inherit the property?" Witherspoon asked. "Not her husband?"

"Oh no, those two buildings have been in Hannah's family for generations. They were left to her with the provision that in the event of her death, they were to stay in the family. As she's no children of her own, they'll go to John. Now that she's dead, he's the only one left." She sighed. "Poor Hannah. She was in such a hurry to get home last night and look what happened."

Witherspoon's mind was reeling with new possibilities. Hannah Cameron had had words with her half-brother over dinner. She'd also been preoccupied and eager to get home. Why? Was it only because she found John Ripton annoying or was there another reason? She'd been found in a room by herself, stabbed as she'd stood at the doors leading to a balcony. Maybe she had an appointment with someone. Someone she let into the room and who then consequently killed her. The moment the thought entered his mind, he knew he was right. "Mrs. Hadleigh, in your opinion did Mrs. Cameron's wish to get home quickly have anything to do with her brother?"

"I don't know, Inspector," Fiona replied. "It's possible, of course. Sometimes she delighted in tormenting John." She paused, and her expression grew thoughtful. "But I don't think that was the case last night. She was too distracted to take any real pleasure in annoying him. Or perhaps she wanted to check on the children or wanted to make sure the servants had locked the house up." She shrugged. "I don't know. But I do know I thought it strange."

"According to what the servants have told us," Witherspoon said, "all of the servants, with the exception of Mrs. Cameron's maid, were in bed."

"That couldn't possibly be true." Fiona shook her head. "They're lying. Hannah never allowed all the servants to go to bed when the master and mistress were out. The butler and a kitchen maid were always to be up when they got home, in case Hannah wanted a hot drink from the kitchen."

"Yet last night, she specifically told them they could all retire." Witherspoon was sure about that point. He and Constable Barnes had questioned all the servants when they'd arrived that morning. The housemaids, the footman, the butler and the cook had said the same thing. They couldn't all be lying.

Fiona looked confused for a moment. "That certainly wasn't Hannah's habit."

Nivens had wandered over to stand in front of the fireplace. Witherspoon was aware of his eyes on him. It was making him slightly nervous. It was most inconvenient having the man hanging about while he tried to investigate. Most inconvenient, indeed."After you retired last night, did you hear anything unusual?"

She thought about it for a moment. "No, I was very tired. I went right to sleep."

"You didn't hear Mrs. Cameron go back down stairs?" he pressed. He'd trod those stairs himself earlier today and the two top ones definitely creaked. Quite loudly. The only way anyone could have gone down them without making a racket was if they deliberately avoided them.

"No, Inspector. I did not."

Witherspoon smiled happily. He was right. He knew it. Hannah Cameron hadn't wanted anyone to hear her going downstairs so she'd been as quiet as a mouse. That could only mean one thing. She didn't want anyone knowing she was leaving her room. But why would she have let her maid stay up? That question bothered him. She'd told everyone else to go to bed, but her maid had still been awake and waiting for her. He glanced at Barnes, hoping the constable would have a question or two of his own. But Barnes was scribbling madly in his notebook. "Thank you, Mrs. Hadleigh. I appreciate your cooperation. Could you ask the butler to send in Miriam?"

"Of course." She dismissed them with a nod as she left.

"Why do you want to question the maid?" Nivens barked. "I've already spoken to the girl and she's as thick as two short planks."

Barnes looked up from his scribbling, an expression of mild disgust on his face as he flicked a glance at Inspector Nivens.

Witherspoon, not wanting to offend his colleague, quickly said, "After speaking with Mrs. Hadleigh, I've thought of another question or two. I'm sure you questioned the girl most thoroughly, Inspector. Most thoroughly, indeed." He hoped Nivens hadn't been rude to the maid. He'd noticed the inspector was a bit brusque with servants and hansom drivers and others of that ilk. It rather annoyed Witherspoon. But he didn't wish to make a fuss.

"You wanted to see me, sir?" a timid voice said from the doorway.

Witherspoon smiled at the dark-haired young woman and waved her into the drawing room. "Come in, miss," he invited, gesturing to the settee. "Please have a seat. I'd like to ask you a question."

She looked hesitantly at the settee and then shook her head. "It wouldn't do for me to sit, sir. If it's all the same to you, I'll stand."

Though her voice was timid, she carried herself proudly as she advanced into the room. A slender girl, she was quite pretty, with dark brown eyes, full lips and a slightly turned up nose.

"As you wish, miss." Unwilling to sit while a lady stood, Witherspoon rose to his feet. "How long have you been ladies' maid to Mrs. Cameron?"

"A year, sir," she replied. She shot Nivens a malevolent glance.

"Did you like her?"

Miriam hesitated before answering. "She was as good a mistress as some," she replied honestly. "But no, I didn't like her. She was very demanding and most particular about how things was to be done."

"Did she specifically ask you to wait up for her last night?" Witherspoon asked.

Miriam looked surprised by the question. "No. As a matter of fact, she told me I could go to bed as soon as I finished tidying up her toilette."

"Then why did you wait up for her?" He was quite curious now. The maid had admitted she didn't like the woman, and from what Witherspoon had seen of this household, he'd have thought any of the servants would have taken any chance for a bit of extra rest when they could get it.

"I did go to bed, sir," Miriam explained. "But I came back down when I heard her moving about her bedroom, sir. My room's right above hers, sir. I knew she was in her room because I heard the door to her dressin' room squeakin'. I was afraid if I didn't come down and help her get undressed, she'd be a real tartar in the morning."

"Why would you think that?" Barnes asked softly. "She'd said you could go to bed."

Miriam's lips twisted in a bitter smile. "I didn't trust her. She might have said we could go to bed, but I knew if I didn't come down, it'd be the worse for me in the mornin'"

"When you went downstairs, did you find Mrs. Cameron in her room?" Witherspoon didn't even look in Niven's direction. This was important information and the inspector hadn't mentioned a word of it.

Miriam shook her head. "No sir, I didn't, and I thought it odd, because

I knew I'd heard her moving about. That dressin' room door squeaks something fierce."

"What did you do, then?" he asked.

"I looked about for her," Miriam replied. "Glanced in her dressin' room and checked the bath down the hall, but I couldn't find her. I thought she might have gone downstairs, so I decided to wait. I waited and waited but she never come up. That's when I went to Mr. Cameron."

"Why didn't you go downstairs and look for her?" Barnes asked.

Miriam shrugged. "Because I was in my night clothes, sir. Mrs. Cameron would have had a fit if she'd caught me movin' about the house like that."

CHAPTER 4

Smythe reached into his pocket, pulled out a shilling and slapped it on the counter of The Three Stags pub. "What'll you 'ave?" he asked, turning to the young man standing next to him. Smythe kept his voice casual; the bloke was really no more than a lad. Dark blond hair combed back haphazardly over a longish face, deep-set hazel eyes and a slightly protruding mouth.

"A pint of bitter, please." The young man grinned, revealing front teeth that stuck out. But despite the smile, his eyes were puzzled. Smythe knew he was wondering why a perfect stranger had befriended him and hustled him into the nearest pub.

"Two pints of bitter," Smythe called to the barman. He turned back to his companion. "You worked round 'ere long?"

"Two years."

"Got a name?"

"Harry Comstock. What's yours?"

"Joe Bolan," Smythe lied quickly. With Inspector Nivens sniffing around this neighborhood, it wouldn't do to use his own name when he was snooping about. "Well, 'arry, 'ow do you like the area? I'm thinkin' about tryin' to find work 'ere abouts."

"Neighborhood's posh, but the wages ain't. The rich are a tight-fisted lot with their money. Don't much like to share with a workin' man. But there's always a few jobs goin'"

"Where do you work?" Smythe knew very well where Harry Comstock worked. That's why he'd befriended the man.

"Communal garden for a block of Mayfair houses. I'm the gardener and the caretaker. Don't pay a lot, but it keeps the rent paid for the missus." Harry moved his bony shoulders in a shrug. "What kinda work you lookin' for?"

"I've been a coachman most of my life," Smythe said. He wondered how to get around to the subject of the murder. It was so long since he hadn't paid for information, he hoped he hadn't forgotten how to get someone talking. He shouldn't have used Blimpey Groggins so much on the last few cases. Cor blimey, he was getting as tongue-tied as a schoolboy. But that's what came of having money. Made you soft and dulled your wits. The thought of his money momentarily depressed him. Determinedly, Smythe pushed that problem to the back of his mind and concentrated on why he was here. Getting information from Harry Comstock. "But I was thinkin' about lookin' about for somethin' else. Not much call for private coachmen these days. I've done a bit of diggin' in my time. Any jobs goin' where you work?" He nodded to the publican as their drinks were shoved under their noses.

"Nah." Harry took a long swig from his mug. "The gardens ain't that big and they've just taken on another boy to help me. The residents'll not pay for three when they can get by on two."

"Give you a lot of grief, do they?" Smythe took a sip from his own mug.

"Just some of 'em." Harry suddenly laughed. "Odd thing is the worst one of the lot up and got herself murdered." He sobered just as suddenly when he realized what he'd said. "I don't mean to be disrespectful of the dead."

"Don't fret, 'arry," Smythe said easily. "I'm a workin' man myself. I know what puttin' up with the gentry is like. But tell me about this murder. Who got done in?"

"Well." Harry eagerly began to tell all he knew, which wasn't much. But he had a wonderful imagination and those facts that he didn't know, he easily made up.

Dutifully, Smythe listened to the bloke. Harry, interspersing his tale with quick sips of beer, got happier and happier the longer he talked. Perhaps it was the beer or perhaps it was just that the lad hadn't had anyone to talk to but a privet hedge or an elm tree in a while, but within moments, his tongue was moving faster than a steam engine. "And like I said, I'm not surprised she got herself killed. She's not got many friends."

"Uh . . ." Smythe tried to interrupt with a question, but Harry appeared to be deaf.

"No one likes that woman. Not even her husband. Mind you"—Harry took another quick swig of bitter—"he's not a particularly nice man, either. But at least he doesn't scream like a scalded cat just because I trimmed the hedges a bit too short." He paused to take a breath, and Smythe leapt at his chance, but he was too late. Harry's lungs apparently didn't need much air. "Mind you, I'm sure with these coppers trampin' all over the gardens lookin' for God knows what, I'll hear from Mrs. Masters about them ruddy summer roses." Harry shook his head.

"Who do they think did it?" Smythe asked quickly.

"Some say it was a burglar," Harry replied. He looked pointedly at his now empty mug. Smythe quickly nodded to the barman and Harry resumed talking. "But others say it were probably her husband. Or her half-brother, or even that woman who's always hangin' about moonin' over Mr. Cameron. Not that he's all that bad a bloke, not as tight-fisted as she was, that's for sure. Pay you a bob or two to do a few things for him, Mr. Cameron does. Give me a few bits when I run over to the post office for him last week."

Smythe's interest had perked up at the mention of "husband," "half-brother" and especially at "that woman who's always hangin' about." "What woman is this then, 'angin' about?" he asked.

"Mrs. Hadleigh." Harry snorted. "Claims to be Mrs. Cameron's friend and all that, but she didn't like Mrs. Cameron any more than I did."

"How do you know?"

"Any fool with eyes could see that Mrs. Hadleigh hated Mrs. Cameron. Pulled all sorts of ugly, sour faces at the woman's back whenever Mrs. Cameron wasn't lookin'. But then everyone in the 'ousehold did that exceptin' for Miss Ellingsley . . ." He broke off and sighed. "Now there's a lovely woman. Too bad she had to go to work for the Camerons. But that's what comes of bein' a poor relation. Mind you, I expect that Mrs. Hadleigh will do her best to get Miss Ellingsley sacked now that Mrs. Cameron is gone. She'll not want the master gettin' any fancy ideas in his head about a younger woman. Not that Miss Ellingsley is interested in Mr. Cameron. Good Lord, no. She's got other fish to fry, that one does."

Smythe's ears were ringing. Harry Comstock was like a blocked drain-pipe; one good clean-up and words gushed out like backed-up water. There were dozens of questions that he could ask, but he wouldn't be able to ask a single one of them if he couldn't get this fellow to slow up a bit.

"Uh, look," he interrupted sharply. Harry blinked owlishly. Smythe forced himself to smile. "Why don't we go and 'ave us a nice sit down." He jerked his head toward the table near the hearth. "I'll get us a couple of whiskies."

Betsy arrived back at Upper Edmonton Gardens before the others. She found Mrs. Goodge pacing the kitchen floor and muttering. "Silly old thing is going to ruin everything . . ."

"Who's ruining everything?" Betsy asked. She took her hat and coat off and hung them up.

"Aunt Elberta, that's who." Mrs. Goodge, her face flushed and her eyes flashing behind her glasses, stomped over to put the kettle on. "She's been here all day. You'd think someone her age would have to rest. But no, she's here hour after hour, interruptin' my sources, asking her silly questions . . ."

"Mrs. Goodge." Mrs. Jeffries's soft voice interrupted the cook's tirade. "Do lower your voice. She'll hear you."

"She's deaf as a post," the cook snapped. She picked a plate of buns up from the sideboard and slapped them down on the table. "I had half a dozen people through here today and I didn't learn a ruddy thing. It's all her fault."

Mrs. Jeffries and Betsy exchanged glances as they came toward the table. Both of them sympathized with Mrs. Goodge's plight, but they felt sorry for poor Aunt Elberta too.

"I had a bit of luck today," Betsy said cheerfully, hoping some good news might distract the cook.

Mrs. Goodge snorted.

Mrs. Jeffries drew her chair back when there was a loud knocking on the front door.

"I'll get it," Betsy said, dashing for the stairs.

Mrs. Goodge kept muttering under her breath as she got tea ready, and Mrs. Jeffries, wisely, held her peace. She'd let the cook fume for a few minutes, get the poison out of her system and then they'd have a nice little chat about the best way to deal with Aunt Elberta. Perhaps the others could take turns taking the old dear out to Holland Park.

Betsy returned clutching an envelope.

"Is that for the inspector?" Mrs. Jeffries asked.

"No, it's for Smythe." Curious, but not wanting to let it show, Betsy carefully placed the envelope at Smythe's usual place at the table. "I wonder who's writing to him? It's an awfully posh envelope . . ." She was interrupted by the sound of the back door opening.

Wiggins, accompanied by Fred, dashed into the room a few minutes later. "Am I late?"

"No, Wiggins," Mrs. Jeffries replied.

"Good." Wiggins slid into his chair and beamed at them. "I found out ever so much today . . ."

"I'm glad someone has," Mrs. Goodge interrupted, and then she too broke off as the back door opened again.

This time it was Smythe. He swaggered into the kitchen, a cocky grin on his face, and tossed off a jaunty salute to the others. "'Ello, 'ello," he said. "What a day I've 'ad. You'll not believe what all I've found out . . ."

"You'll not believe my day either," Mrs. Goodge complained.

"You've got a letter, Smythe," Betsy interjected hastily, hoping to get him to shut up about how much he'd accomplished before Mrs. Goodge worked herself up into a fit.

Smythe's cocky grin faded. "A letter?" He picked up the envelope. His eyes narrowed as he looked at the neat handwriting and he paled as he realized who it was who'd written him. Blast! He'd told that stupid sod not to contact him here. Conscious they were all staring at him, he slipped the letter into the pocket of his waistcoat, plopped down next to Betsy and busied himself pouring out a mug of tea.

"Is something wrong, Smythe? You've gone a bit white about the mouth," Betsy said. "Are you feeling all right?"

"I'm fine, lass." He tried to smile and knew he was doing a bad job of it. He'd kill that ruddy man when he got his hands on him. "Just a bit winded from gettin' back 'ere so fast."

"Aren't you going to open it?" she asked curiously. It wasn't often one of the staff got a letter, especially one in a posh envelope.

"There's no time to now," he explained quickly. "I saw Luty and Hatchet comin' right behind me. We've probably got a lot to get through, so I'll read it later."

"My turn won't last long," Mrs. Goodge said.

Mrs. Jeffries closed her eyes briefly and hoped they could get through this with a minimum of fuss. The cook was already out of sorts, Betsy was dying of curiosity about Smythe's letter, Wiggins probably wouldn't think to be tactful when he started bragging about what he'd learned and goodness knows what Luty and Hatchet had found out.

By the time Luty and Hatchet arrived a few moments later, the rest of the tea things were on the table, Mrs. Goodge's fury had dulled to a slow simmer and Smythe's color had returned to normal.

"Who would like to go first?" Mrs. Jeffries asked.

Luty waved her hand. "If'n it's all the same to everybody, I'd like to say my piece." She plunged straight ahead when no one objected. "I found out quite a bit about Brian Cameron. Seems he don't have much luck with wives. His first one died off from influenza right after she had a child. Brian up and married the second one less than a year after the first one died. Some said it weren't decent, but the man did have two orphan babies he told everyone they needed a mother."

"Was your source absolutely sure that the first Mrs. Cameron's death was due to natural causes?" Hatchet asked.

No one was surprised by the question. The same thought had crossed everyone else's mind.

Luty nodded vigorously. "He was sure. They was visiting one of Mr. Cameron's relatives up in Yorkshire when she took sick. But she weren't the only one to get sick—half the village had the flu. A lot of them died."

"Did you learn the name of the village?" Mrs. Jeffries asked. She was from Yorkshire.

"It's a place called Paggleston," Luty replied. "Brian Cameron's uncle still lives there."

Mrs. Jeffries nodded. "I believe it's quite near Scarborough. Yes, now I remember. There was a terrible outbreak of influenza a few years back."

"The first Mrs. Cameron died from the flu," Luty said firmly. "My source was sure about that. But that's not what's important. I found out that Brian Cameron inherited a lot of money from her, somewhere in the neighborhood of twenty thousand pounds. He got his hands on plenty when he married Hannah Cameron too, but—and this is the interesting part—seems ole Brian don't have much of a head for business, not that that keeps him from trying. So far, he's invested in a Malaysian tea plantation that got hit with a typhoon and a cattle ranch in Montana that lost every head of beef to hoof and mouth. He put up the money to have two ships built for the Australian trade and put a big lump of cash out on investin' in South American railroads. But it don't seem to matter what he puts his money in—he loses it sooner or later."

"What about the ships?" Wiggins asked.

"Sank. Both of 'em. One of 'em sank before she even left the English

Channel and the other made it all the way to Fremantle but got hit by a bad storm on the way home and was lost."

Smythe whistled softly through his teeth. "Cor, the poor blighter don't 'ave much luck."

"Not with money or wives," Luty said. "But as far as my source knew, he hadn't lost the money he'd put in the South American railroads."

"Will he inherit a lot of money now that Hannah Cameron's dead?" Betsy asked eagerly.

"I ain't sure," Luty admitted. "My source didn't know but he said he'd check on it for me. That was the first thing I thought of too."

"Excellent, Luty," Mrs. Jeffries said, then she caught herself as she saw Mrs. Goodge's shoulders slump.

"I'll have a go next," Betsy said brightly. "What I learned sort of goes along with what Luty told us. It seems that Mr. and Mrs. Cameron didn't get on too well. The footman from the house next door to them told me that he heard them arguing all the time." She went on to tell them everything she'd learned from Bill Tincher. "And one of the things they argued about was Mrs. Cameron telling Mr. Cameron he didn't have a head for business."

"Just because a bloke has a bit of bad luck at business don't mean 'e's a killer," Wiggins charged. "There's plenty others that didn't like Hannah Cameron."

"True," Betsy agreed. "But someone's been up to something funny at that house. Bill told me that last week he spotted someone slipping out of the house late one night. Whoever it was didn't go anywhere; they just crept into the shadows behind one of the trees and stood there for the longest time."

"Who's Bill?" Smythe asked.

"The footman from the house next door," she replied. "He's just a lad, but he's a sharp eye and I don't think he was making it up. He did see someone."

"Was it a man or a woman?" Luty asked.

"He couldn't tell," Betsy said. "They were swathed from head to foot in a hooded cloak. But it could have been Mr. Cameron."

"We don't know that, Betsy," Mrs. Jeffries said calmly. "It could have been anyone. Were any of the other suspects in the house that night?"

"I don't know," she said, "but it was on a Friday evening, not this past Friday, but the one before that."

"You'd best find out," Mrs. Jeffries instructed. The nighttime excursion may have nothing to do with the murder, but then again, it was possible. She turned her attention to the footman. "Why don't you tell us what you learned?"

"I think I know who it was that this footman saw that night," he boasted. "Kathryn Ellingsley 'as a sweetheart."

"Is her young man a tree, then?" Mrs. Goodge sniffed disdainfully.

"'Course 'e isn't," Wiggins shot back defensively. "But my source told me that she's been sneakin' out late at night to meet her feller. So it were probably Kathryn Ellingsley this Bill saw." Wiggins wasn't really sure his source could be trusted. He'd not even planned on telling the others what he'd found out, considering who his source was for the information. But the cook had niggled him enough so that he'd told all. He wished he hadn't. It would be shameful if the others knew the only person he managed to get talking today was an ten-year-old boy, and then only after he'd bribed the child with a packet of sweets. He wasn't sure the lad wasn't telling tales.

"Kathryn Ellingsley slips out of the Cameron house at night to see her sweetheart?" Mrs. Jeffries clarified.

"That's what the lad said," Wiggins admitted. "But 'e's just a little fellow and I think 'e was just repeatin' what 'e picked up 'ere and there."

"Who was this child?" Mrs. Goodge demanded.

"He's the son of the housekeeper at one of the 'ouses across the gardens from the Camerons," Wiggins explained. "I couldn't find anyone else to talk to. I was lucky I spotted this lad before the coppers spotted me."

"We understand, Wiggins," Mrs. Jeffries said. "It's going to be difficult for all of us to do our investigating, but we'll do the best we can. I think you've done quite splendidly today. Your source might be young and might well only be repeating gossip, but that doesn't mean it isn't true. Did you learn the name of Miss Ellingsley's sweetheart?"

"No, Davey didn't know the bloke's name." He shook his head. "But I think I can find out. If everyone on the gardens is gossipin' about it, someone must know the man's name."

Hatchet cleared his throat. "I don't think you'll have to bother your source again, Wiggins," he said. "His name is Connor Reese, Dr. Connor Reese, and he's Hannah Cameron's first cousin." He smiled sheepishly. "It seems, my boy, that you and I found out the very same thing today."

"Well, that's a bit of rotten luck," Betsy said.

"Not necessarily," Mrs. Jeffries interjected smoothly. "Hatchet's information apparently confirms what Wiggins learned."

"That's not all," Hatchet said. "I also found out that Dr. Reese hated Hannah Cameron. Unfortunately, I wasn't able to learn why. But I do know that he wasn't welcome in the Cameron household."

"Who's not welcome?" Aunt Elberta said from the doorway. She peered at the group gathered around the table. "Is it a tea party?" Eagerly, she scuttled toward the others, her cane thumping heavily enough to send Fred wiggling under Wiggins's chair. "I just love parties."

Mrs. Jeffries cornered the inspector the moment he came through the front door. She helped him off with his coat and hat and ushered him into the drawing room where she had a glass of his favorite sherry already poured and waiting for him. "Do sit down, sir. You look very tired."

Witherspoon sighed in satisfaction as he eased himself into his chair. "I have had a tiring day, Mrs. Jeffries, and I'm frozen to boot."

"Frozen, sir?"

"Yes, the Cameron house was very chilly, very chilly, indeed. Of course, I suppose one can't blame Mr. Cameron for not having seen to the fires; he has had a rather bad shock. But you'd think the butler would have taken care of it."

"Perhaps he forgot, sir," she ventured. There were a dozen good reasons why the house might have been cold and Mrs. Jeffries didn't want to discuss any of them. She wanted to find out what the inspector knew. The meeting downstairs had been cut short due to Aunt Elberta's arrival, and Mrs. Jeffries was annoyed about that. Goodness knows it was important that they share information. There were a dozen things she needed to know from the Inspector. "Why don't you tell me about your day, sir? You know how I do love hearing about your methods."

He gave her a brief smile. "I'm not sure my methods are going to work in this case. It's a bit of a muddle, I'm afraid. Inspector Nivens still seems to think it was a burglary gone awry and not murder. It's most awkward having him about while I try to question people. Most awkward, indeed."

"I'm sure it is, sir. But knowing you as I do, I'm sure you discharged your duty perfectly. Furthermore, I've every confidence in your methods. They've never failed you before."

Grateful for her confidence, he relaxed a bit and some of the tension left his face. "I did my best. But it's an odd household, Mrs. Jeffries. Very odd, indeed."

"In what way, sir?"

"In several ways. To begin with, no one seems to be very grieved by Mrs. Cameron's death. Even her own brother didn't seem overly upset by her murder." He leaned back, took a sip of sherry and unburdened himself to his housekeeper.

She was a wonderful audience. She listened carefully, asked questions in all the right places and made him feel ever so much better about his own abilities as a detective. By the time Betsy came in to announce that dinner was ready, he was feeling quite on top of things. There was something about discussing the case with his housekeeper that got his mind moving in the right direction. Yes, first thing tomorrow morning there were a number of inquiries he would make.

Smythe was in front of his bank the next morning before it even opened. He paced back and forth in front of the imposing building, his feet smacking hard against the pavement as he scanned the bustling street. He pulled a heavy gold watch out of his pocket and checked the time. Five minutes to nine. The blighter should be coming any minute now. Smythe leaned back against the gray stone building and crossed his arms over his massive chest and prepared to wait. He didn't have to wait long. Within a few minutes, a tall, white haired man with his nose in the air walked briskly toward the bank. He wore a dark gray greatcoat and an old fashioned black top hat and carried a cane.

Smythe leapt away from the building as the man drew abreast of him. Startled, the fellow stepped back. "Goodness, you gave me quite a start," he said, recovering quickly when he saw who it was who'd accosted him.

"I'm goin' to be givin' you more than that if you don't stop sendin' them fancy letters to me," Smythe snapped. "I told ya never to do that."

Mr. Bartholomew Pike, general manager of Breedlow and Bascombs Bank, wasn't in the least intimidated. "Mr. Smythe," he said calmly, "I realize I was acting against your explicit instructions. However, you left me no choice. As I've told you before, you've a number of important decisions to make. If you'll recall, sir, we were scheduled to have a meeting two days ago. When you did not come and you sent no word, I was forced to communicate with you." He took Smythe's arm and started for the front door. "Now, sir, if you'll come with me, we'll take care of business immediately."

Smythe shook him off and dug in his heels. "I don't have time to meet with you now—" he began, but he was cut off by his banker.

"You always say that, sir," Pike challenged, "and I simply must insist that you make time. We've serious business to discuss, sir. You've made another five thousand pounds on those American investments. You must make some decisions. You don't seem to understand, sir. You can't just leave your money sitting in a deposit account . . ."

"Isn't that what bleedin' banks is for?" Smythe yelped.

"Not when one has as much money as you do, sir," Pike insisted. "We're not simply your bankers, sir, we're your financial advisors as well. In good conscience, I simply cannot allow you to . . ."

"Look, mate." Smythe cut him off. He'd love to poke his banker in the nose, but the truth was, he was ruddy good at his job. In the past year, Pike's advice had fattened Smythe's fortune substantially. "I don't 'ave a lot of time just now. I only come to tell ya to stop sendin' them bloomin' letters . . ."

"Letters? I only sent one, Mr. Smythe," Pike said indignantly.

"That's one too many," Smythe snapped. "You've caused me no end of bother." It was more than just "bother." Smythe couldn't risk anyone else at the household finding out that he had money. At this point, they'd feel as if he'd been deliberately hiding the truth from them. Which, of course, he was.

"That certainly wasn't my intention," Pike countered. "But you must realize you have a responsibility. Money is serious business, sir . . ."

"It's my bleedin' money, is'n it?"

"That's not the point, sir," Pike insisted.

"It is the point," Smythe fired back. "It's for me to decide what to do with it and I'll thank you to just sit on it awhile longer until I've a mind to take care of it." Withe that, he turned and stalked down the street.

"I'll expect to see you next week, sir," Pike called after him. Smythe ignored him. "Bloomin' fool can wait till 'ell freezes over," he muttered as he stormed around the corner. "Blighter's caused me no end of trouble. I've 'alf a mind to pull my money out of that ruddy bank and bury it in the back garden." But he knew he wouldn't. And even if he did take his money from the hallowed vaults of Breedlow and Bascombs, he knew he'd run into the same problem wherever else he put it. Bankers just couldn't stop themselves from giving advice. It was as if they were personally insulted to see great big heaps of cash sitting in a vault minding its own business. Oh no, they were always saying that money had to earn its keep. Well, his money had brought him nothing but grief. He'd never meant to hide his wealth from the others; it had just happened that way. Euphemia, may she rest in peace, had made him promise to stay on at Upper Edmonton Gardens and keep an eye on her naive nephew, Inspector Witherspoon. Before Smythe knew it, Mrs. Jeffries and Mrs. Goodge had come and then Betsy and soon, they were solving murders and watching out for each other. He'd never told them about his money and now he couldn't. It would change things, make him different from them. Not that *he* felt that way, but that's the way they'd see it. They'd not like it. He couldn't stand the idea of losing the very people who'd come to mean more to him than anyone. Especially one particular person. Betsy.

"What's your 'urry, mate?" A familiar voice hailed him from behind.

Smythe whirled around. "As I live and breathe, Blimpey, what's the likes of you doin' in this neighborhood?"

Blimpey Groggins, a short, fat, red-haired man wearing a rust-colored porkpie hat, a dirty brown-and-white checkered waistcoat and a clean white shirt with a bright red scarf hanging around his neck, hurried toward him. A former petty thief and con man, Blimpey'd mended his ways when he'd discovered that his inordinant love of a good gossip and his phenomenal memory for detail could make him a much fatter profit than lifting the occasional silver candlestick or picking a pocket. He was a professional purveyor of information. If you wanted to find out anything about anyone in London, Blimpey was your man. What he didn't already know, he could find out in the blink of an eye. Smythe had used his services on more than one of the inspector's cases.

"Been to the bank," Blimpey wheezed. He lifted one end of the scarf and wiped his face. "Made a deposit."

Smythe raised his eyebrows. "You? Trustin' a bank?"

Blimpey shrugged. "Got to keep yer money somewheres, don't ya? What you doin' round 'ere?"

Smythe shrugged noncommittally. "A bit of this and that. You got time for a quick one?" He decided to spend a bit of his bloomin' money. It was ten times quicker for Blimpey to get the goods on someone than for him to waste hours trying to find a cabbie or publican who knew anything about the murder. He'd gotten blooming lucky yesterday with that gardener; he didn't think Lady Fortune would smile on him twice.

"You buyin?"

"Aren't I always?" Smythe started across the road. "Come on, there's a pub just over there."

Blimpey kept up a stream of chatter until they were seated in the back of the saloon bar at the Horse and Hound. He raised his glass of beer, took a long sip and then sighed in satisfaction. "That's good, mate. What'da ya need, Smythe? Same as always? Bit of information?"

"That's right."

Blimpey took another long swig of his bitter. "You've come to the right man fer it. What's the particulars?"

"I need to know somethin' about some people." Smythe picked up his whiskey and took a sip. He didn't usually drink spirits, especially in the daytime, but the confrontation with his banker had left a bad taste in his mouth.

Blimpey grinned. "That's my specialty, is'n it? Just give me the names and before you can spin yer granny, I'll find out what there is to know."

"One's a doctor by the name of Connor Reese. The other two are John Ripton and Brian Cameron."

"Cameron?" Blimpey's brows drew together as he concentrated. "He related to that woman that got herself knifed the other night?"

"Her husband," Smythe admitted. He'd given up any pretense of keeping his activities secret from Blimpey. The man knew he worked for Inspector Witherspoon and knew that the inspector had built quite a reputation for solving homicides. Blimpey knew everything, including, he suspected, that Smythe had more money than half the toffs in Mayfair. But Blimpey had a code and he lived by it. He didn't shoot off his mouth unless he was paid for his trouble.

"Papers said it were a burglary," Blimpey said conversationally.

Smythe knew he was fishing. "The papers were wrong. It weren't a burglary." No harm in tellin' him that much.

Satisfied, Blimpey nodded. "Didn't think so. No one's takin' credit for that toss. Besides, a pro wouldn'a a made such a muck up of it." He wiped his mouth with his sleeve. "Anyone else, or just them three men?"

"Just the three names I gave ya." Smythe noticed he didn't ask for addresses or anything else. Blimpey didn't need to. He had his own network of information. For a second, Smythe considered adding Fiona Hadleigh to the list and then decided against it. Betsy was tackling that one.

Right now wasn't the time to go poachin' on Betsy's patch. Her nose was still out of joint over his ruddy letter. She hadn't liked the fact that he'd ignored her hints for him to tell her who'd written to him.

"Anythin' in particular ya want to know?" Blimpey asked casually.

Smythe thought about it for a moment. "Find out if any of 'ems 'ard up for money and then see what ya can dig up in general about 'em."

"Want the gossip or just the facts?" Blimpey asked. He finished his drink and looked pointedly at his empty mug.

Smythe ignored the hint. He was going to be payin' Blimpey plenty for the information; he didn't intend to throw any more money down the man's throat. "Get it all for me," he said, tossing back the last of his whiskey and then getting to his feet. "I'll meet ya at the Dirty Duck tonight. That give ya enough time?"

Blimpey looked affronted. "Does a dog 'ave fleas? 'Course it gives me enough time. I'll be there at ten."

"I might be a bit late," Smythe said. The household had agreed to have their meeting after Aunt Elberta was safely tucked up for the night.

"That's all right. I'll wait fer ya." Blimpey grinned broadly. "Yer payin' fer me time."

Inspector Witherspoon peeked around the door of the drawing room and then breathed a sigh of relief.

"Inspector Nivens isn't here, sir," Barnes said softly as he and the inspector stepped into the room. "He's questioning the neighbors."

"But the police constables did that yesterday," Witherspoon said. "Inspector Nivens was given a complete report. Why's he doing it again?"

"He wasn't satisfied with the reports. Claimed they weren't done properly. Matter of fact, he had a couple of the lads in front of his desk and was tearin' a strip off 'em last night." Barnes looked disgusted. "There wasn't a ruddy thing wrong with those reports, sir. The lads did a fine job of it."

Witherspoon clamped his mouth shut. It wouldn't do to say anything rude about Inspector Nivens, but really, sometimes he was most undiplomatic. "I'm sure they did, Barnes. Perhaps Inspector Nivens is just being unduly cautious."

Barnes shrugged, turned away and muttered something under his breath that Witherspoon couldn't quite catch. He turned back to his superior and asked, "Exactly who are we questioning today, sir?"

"The servants."

Barnes looked surprised. "But we did that yesterday."

"Yes, I know," Witherspoon smiled brightly. "But after thinking about their statements, I realized there were one or two important things that hadn't been asked."

"Are you sayin' I left something out?" Barnes asked, his tone defensive. Good Lord, was Witherspoon turning into Nivens?

"Oh no, no," the inspector hastily assured him. "Your questions were, as always, excellent. But I realized last night that I'd neglected to find out the one thing that might be very important to this case."

Barnes brightened and was immediately ashamed of himself for thinking, even for a moment, that Inspector Witherspoon was anything like Nivens. "And what would that be, sir?"

Witherspoon beamed happily. He was rather proud of himself for having thought of it last night. "Something that can help us a great deal, Barnes. I'm assuming, of course, that the killer was in the house."

"Yes, sir, I agree."

"And I do hope you've plenty of paper in that notebook of yours."

"It's a new one, sir."

"Excellent, excellent." Witherspoon couldn't wait to begin. "Then let's have a go at the butler, shall we?" He started for the hallway.

"But sir, I don't understand. Exactly what is it we're doing?"

"Didn't I say? Goodness, I'm getting ahead of myself." Witherspoon stopped and turned to his constable. "We're going to do a timetable, Barnes."

CHAPTER 5

"A timetable, sir?" Barnes was really confused now. "You mean like the railways use?"

"That's it precisely." Witherspoon continued toward the hallway. "Only instead of trains, we're going to have people on ours. I say, I wonder where the maid's gone?" He stopped at the doorway and peered down the silent hall. "Do you think we ought to ring the bell-pull for someone?"

But then they heard footsteps on the staircase and a moment later, Kathryn Ellingsley appeared. Startled, she drew back a bit when she spotted the two policemen lingering by the drawing room door. She came closer, stopping just in front of a huge potted fern sitting on an elaborate mahogany table by the foot of the staircase. "Good day, Inspector. Are you looking for Mr. Cameron?" she asked.

"Actually, Miss Ellingsley, we were looking for the butler." He thought it best to conduct this area of the inquiry solely among the servants.

"Hatfield's downstairs in the kitchen," she replied, glancing briefly at the front door. "He's supervising the food preparations for after the funeral tomorrow."

"I see," Witherspoon murmured. Drat. He didn't relish the thought of dragging the butler away from his duties, especially that particular kind of task. But he needed to talk to the servants. Every one of them. Individually. Perhaps he ought to speak to Mr. Cameron after all. "Oh dear, this is a bit awkward. I'm afraid I'll have to interrupt the household even further. I suppose we ought to let Mr. Cameron know that we're here."

Kathryn gave him a strained smile. "He's not here. He and Mrs.

Hadleigh took the children to her estate in the country. It's just outside Tunbridge Wells."

"You mean he's left London?" Witherspoon didn't like the sound of that. They hadn't instructed any of the household to stay in town, but surely leaving before the victim's funeral was a bit much.

"He'll be back tonight," she said quickly. "As will Mrs. Hadleigh. Brian felt the children would be better off away from here. It's been a rather dreadful experience for them."

"Aren't they going to their stepmother's funeral?" Barnes asked.

"No." Kathryn shook her head. "Brian felt that considering the way she died, it would be better for the children not to go. He's only told them that she died. He didn't tell them how. After the funeral tomorrow, the house will be full of people. Brian doesn't want the children to overhear any of the ugly circumstances of her death."

The inspector felt a surge of pity for the little ones. Losing a mother, even a stepmother, must be very frightening.

"Were the children fond of Mrs. Cameron?" Barnes asked quietly.

Kathryn hesitated and then shrugged. "I think so. They were both very upset when they heard the news. But she was quite strict with them and though she was their stepmother, she was the only mother they'd really ever known."

"Will you be staying on?" Witherspoon wanted to make sure she wasn't planning on leaving town as well. "I mean, now that the children are gone, perhaps you'll go away for a time as well."

She smiled and shook her head. "I'm staying on, Inspector. My only other relation is in a little village in Yorkshire. I may go up to visit him. He's not been well lately and he's quite elderly. But the children will be coming back as soon as this is over, and Brian's asked me to stay on."

There was a knock on the front door. Kathryn moved quickly toward it as footsteps pounded on the back stairs. "Don't bother to come up," she called to the maid whose head bobbed up from the staircase. "I'll get it." She flung open the door and then stepped back. "Come in, Dr. Reese," she said formally.

"Miss Ellingsley." The man took off his bowler and stepped into the hall. He was about thirty, tall and neatly dressed in a dark gray suit with a white shirt and black tie. His hair was that shade of colour that's somewhere between brown and dark blond. He turned and stared at the two policemen out of cool blue eyes.

"This is Inspector Witherspoon and Constable Barnes." Kathryn introduced them quickly. "They're investigating Hannah's death."

"I'm Connor Reese." He stepped forward and offered his hand, first to the Inspector and then to the constable. "I came by to extend my condolences to Brian."

"Are you a friend of the family?" Witherspoon asked.

"Hardly, Inspector," Reese replied. "I'm Hannah Cameron's cousin."

Wiggins eyed the housemaid warily. She skittered about so quickly down the road, he was having a hard time keeping up with her. But he was determined not to go back to this afternoon's meeting empty-handed, so to speak.

The girl disappeared around the corner, and Wiggins dashed after her. Unfortunately, the maid had stopped smack in the middle of the pavement. Wiggins went flying into her, knocking her flat. "Oi . . ." she screamed.

Horrified by what he'd done, Wiggins quickly reached down to help her up. "I'm ever so sorry, miss," he sputtered.

"You stupid git," she snapped. "Why don't you watch where you're going?" She brushed off his assistance and got up.

"I'm sorry, miss." He tried again. Up close, he could see she was quite a pretty girl. Brown hair, neatly tucked up under her cap, scrubbed pink complexion and rather pretty blue eyes. "Please, miss. It were an accident . . ."

"Oh, bother, now me skirts are dirty." She brushed at the loose dirt on the gray broadcloth. Wiggins reached over and tried to help, but she smacked his hand before his fingers even brushed the fabric. "'Ere, keep your ruddy paws to yourself."

"I'm sorry." He apologized again. "I'm only tryin' to 'elp."

"You'd help more by takin' yourself off and lettin' me be about me business," she said, but her voice had softened a bit and there was a hint of a smile on her pretty face. She turned and started off.

But Wiggins wasn't about to let her get away. "Please, miss," he said, dogging her heels like Fred did when he was trying to get you to take him on walkies. "I am ever so sorry. Is there something I can do to make it up to you?"

"I'm in a hurry," she answered, taking his measure. "I've got to get this ruddy telegram sent."

"Can I walk with ya?" he asked.

She shrugged. As a maid, she didn't often get a chance to meet a young man. "I don't mind. It's a free country. You can walk where you like."

"A telegram, eh?" he said pleasantly.

She bobbed her head. "Right, like I don't have enough to do round that place. Still, it gets me out of the house and what with the police and then that ruddy butler worryin' himself to death over the funeral reception, I'm glad to 'ave an excuse to get out."

"There's police at your 'ouse?"

"Not my house," she corrected him. "I only work there. I'm the parlour maid. But there's been murder done where I live. The police think it were burglars. Fat lot they know."

Wiggins inhaled sharply. The girl was a talker, that was for sure. But he'd best be careful. It wouldn't do to be too nosy too quick. Put people off, that did. "Burglars? Cor blimey, ain't ya scared to stay in a such a place?"

"Weren't no thieves." She snorted derisively. "Besides, why should I be scared?"

"But you just said there was murder done," he said. He watched her carefully. Despite her brave words, he could see a flash of fear in her pretty eyes. "That'd scare me, all right. I'd be out of that 'ouse fast as I could."

She shrugged. "Got no place to go, do I?"

"Who got killed, then?" Wiggins thought this the strangest conversation he'd ever had.

"The mistress, Mrs. Cameron. She were knifed a couple of nights ago. We've had the house full of coppers ever since. God, they ask a lot of questions."

"That's their job, is'n it?"

"Bloomin' stupid, the lot of them," she charged. "Especially that smarmy lookin' one with the greased-back hair. Stupid git, don't have enough brains to see what's right under their noses, think that just because we're servants we ain't got eyes in our heads and treat us like dirt, they do."

Wiggins suddenly realized the girl wasn't particularly talking to him; she was just talking.

"Place was bad enough before the old cow got knifed," she continued, "now it's even worse with that Hadleigh woman flouncing about and givin' everyone orders. No talkin', no laughin', no doin' nothin' but waitin' on her hand and foot."

Wiggins stared at the girl in amazement. He had the impression that she'd be haranguing a lamppost by now if he hadn't happened along. Some people were like that. They simply had to get it all out. "Who you on about?"

"That ruddy Mrs. Hadleigh," she snapped. "Got her cap set for the master and the mistress not even buried yet." She lifted the hem of her dress and stepped onto the street.

Wiggins took her arm. "Allow me," he said graciously as they crossed the road.

"And the police poppin' in every few minutes with their silly questions . . . It's enough to blind a saint, I tell ya. Especially that one copper that kept on about who we talked to and did we have a feller and all sorts of silly things that weren't none of 'is business."

"So the police 'ave questioned you, 'ave they?"

"I wouldn't call it questions," she answered, "more like accusations."

That didn't sound like Inspector Witherspoon. "Accusations? What they accusin' you of?"

They waited for a dray to pass and then crossed to the other side before she answered. "Well, he didn't come right out and say it, but he kept on about did I have a feller and that sort of thing and it weren't just me—he asked all the maids the same thing. But none of us do have sweethearts—we'd have not kept our jobs if we did. I tried tellin' this Nivens feller that, but he wouldn't listen."

"Why did he want to know if you 'ad a young man?" Wiggins asked curiously.

"'Cause he's a ruddy copper," she snarled. "And if there's thievin' done, the first thing they think of is that it's some maid who's got a thief for a sweetheart. He practically accused every one of us of lettin' someone in the house that night."

Wiggins was incredulous. "Not all coppers is like that, surely?"

"Most of 'em is," she argued. "There's two of 'em seems to be in charge, but I don't think neither of 'em knows whats what, if you get me meanin'. 'Course the other one's nicer, treats us decent-like. But even the nice one don't know his arse from a hole in the ground. He ain't askin' the right questions either. But that's his problem, not mine."

For a housemaid, her language was very rough, almost crude, but Wiggins would worry about that later. "Do ya know somethin', then?"

"'Course I do," she said with a laugh. "Well, not really. It's just that I know a thing or two about what the coppers didn't ask and should have."

Wiggins stopped. The girl was so surprised by his movement she stopped too. He stared at her a moment, wondering if she was just having him on or if she really knew something. Her mouth quirked in a grin, her eyes were sparkling mischieviously and he thought she might just be paying him back for his knocking her down. Or she might just be tryin' to make herself seem important.

"I thought you was goin' to walk with me," she taunted.

She was teasing him, he was sure of it. But he couldn't take the risk. Maybe she really did know something. "Can I buy you a cup of tea?" he asked politely. "There's a tea house not far from 'ere."

"I've got to send this ruddy telegram off first," she replied, "but now that Mrs. Cameron's dead, I don't have to go rushin' back. God knows Mr. Cameron's not goin' to notice; he's not home. Tell you what, you come with me and then after I've sent it, you can take me fer tea."

At four o'clock, they were assembled around the table in the kitchen of Upper Edmonton Gardens. Mrs. Goodge was actually smiling as she put the teapot on the table.

"Where's Aunt Elberta?" Smythe asked.

"Gone to her room for a nice lay down," the cook replied. "That long walk she went on this morning really took the wind out of her sails. She could barely keep her head up at lunch."

"You let your poor old auntie go out for walk alone?" Wiggins asked.

"Lady Cannonberry kindly volunteered to take her out," Mrs. Jeffries said quickly. She didn't want anyone thinking the cook was derelict in her duty towards her elderly relative. "Ruth was distributing pamphlets for the Women's League for Equality and had to be out anyway. She took Aunt Elberta with her. Said she did a fine job too."

"Did Aunt Elberta know she was handing out pamphlets?" Betsy asked in amusement. Their neighbor, Lady Cannonberry, was a bit of a political radical. Not that they thought any less of her because of her activities. On the contrary, they all admired her for working so hard for her beliefs. At least the women admired her; the men thought she ought to be ashamed of herself, but didn't quite have the courage to bring the subject up anymore.

Mrs. Jeffries smiled. "I don't think so. But she enjoyed the walk and it did keep her out of the kitchen. Now, who'd like to start?"

"I would," Mrs. Goodge stated firmly. "I found out a bit of gossip about the Camerons. It seems that Mr. Cameron is a bit of a ladies' man and Mrs. Cameron suspected him of playing about, if you take my meaning."

"Half the husbands in London are suspected of that," Luty laughed. "But he ain't dead, she is."

Mrs. Goodge leaned forward eagerly. "Yes, but what if he wanted to get rid of her so he could get him a new wife? It wouldn't be the first time a man's done murder for that reason."

"It certainly isn't," Mrs. Jeffries said. "Do go on, Mrs. Goodge, tell us the rest."

"Not much more to tell. But the gossip I heard is that Fiona Hadleigh's rich and Brian Cameron's been seeing her on the sly. According to my sources, he's gone down to her country house more than once lately to see her and he didn't take his wife with him."

Mrs. Jeffries thought that most interesting. "Anything else?"

"Well." The cook dumped a teaspoon of sugar into her tea. "There was no love lost between the late Mrs. Cameron and her half brother, John Ripton. The two of them have never gotten along, and if it wasn't for Mr. Cameron's influence, Hannah Cameron wouldn't have allowed Ripton in the house."

"She didn't seem to like any of 'er family, then, did she?" Wiggins put in. "I found out today that she can't stand her cousin, either."

"Do you mind?" Mrs. Goodge asked archly. "I wasn't finished with my bit."

"Oh, sorry." Chastised, the footman sank back in his chair and waited his turn.

"As I was sayin', Hannah Cameron wouldn't have allowed Ripton in the house. Seems John Ripton spends it faster than he earns it. He's always resented the fact that Hannah inherited the family money and some valuable property and all he got was some poxy little stocks that don't earn more than a few pounds a year." Satisfied that she'd done her fair share, Mrs. Goodge settled back in her chair.

"Is that it, then?" Wiggins asked. "Can I go now?"

"Yes, Wiggins," Mrs. Jeffries said patiently. "Do tell us what you found out."

Wiggins told them about how he'd tracked the Cameron housemaid and pounced upon her when she was well out of range of any police

constable that might have recognized him. Naturally, he omitted any reference to knocking the poor girl flat on her backside. "Anyways," he continued, "I couldn't suss out why she was talkin' me 'ead off and me not
even askin' any questions." He took a sip from his mug. "But after I took
her fer tea, I realized why Helen was rattlin' on so. Seems the 'ousehold is
right strict. They 'ad to be quiet as mice when they was workin'. No natterin' in the kitchen in Hannah Cameron's 'ouse, that was fer sure. It was
like she'd been savin' up her words and when she 'ad someone to listen to
'er, she couldn't stop."

He didn't tell them the other reason the poor girl had talked his ear
off. It didn't have anything to do with the murder, and it would shame her
if he repeated it. But as they'd shared tea and cakes at Lyon's, he'd realized
that Helen was lonely. Desperately so. Because of her crude speech and
rough ways, the other servants in the Cameron house looked down on her.
Wiggins knew all about that. House servants were the biggest snobs in the
world. Before he came to work for the inspector's Aunt Euphemia, he'd
had plenty look down their noses at him too.

"Well, go on then. What did she tell ya?" Luty prodded.

"Really, madam," Hatchet said, "do let the lad tell it in his own
fashion."

"Helen said the police weren't askin' the right questions," Wiggins said.
"She said they should 'ave been askin' why people was still dressed in their
evening clothes when they shoulda been gettin' ready for bed."

"Why were they dressed in their evening clothes?" Betsy repeated.
"What did she mean?"

"That Fiona Hadleigh," Wiggins explained. "Helen said when she stuck
her head out to see what all the commotion was about, she saw Mrs.
Hadleigh, and the woman was still wearing all her evenin' clothes."

"But from what the inspector said, they'd only retired a half hour or
so before the body was discovered," Mrs. Jeffries pointed out. "Why did
Helen seem to think Mrs. Hadleigh's attire was important? I frequently
have my dress on a good hour after I go up to my room. Perhaps she was
reading or saying her prayers."

"She still had that thing in her hair," Wiggins explained.

"What thing?" Betsy asked curiously.

He frowned, trying to remember what Helen had called the blasted
thing. "That bandeau or maybe it was a hat . . . I don't know, but Helen
said it were funny, that even if she was readin'—'cause I did think to

mention that to 'er—she'd 'ave taken that ruddy thing out of her hair at the very least. But she 'adn't. 'Er 'air was still done up. Helen claims there weren't no books in the guest room either, so Mrs. Hadleigh couldn't have been reading."

"That's a good point, Wiggins. This girl sounds right sharp." Luty drummed her fingers on the tabletop. "I like to dress up. But when I'm wearin' fancy duds, I don't keep 'em on a minute more than I have to." She glanced at Mrs. Jeffries. "You wear a plain, sensible dress, Hepzibah. But if you was gussied up in an evening gown and yer head was loaded with baubles, you'd take that get-up off quicker than spit."

"Madam, really," Hatchet hissed. "Do watch your language."

"Oh, don't be such a priss, Hatchet." Luty waved at him dismissively. "I'm tryin' to make a point. It's the kinda detail a woman would notice, not a man. Besides, from what we know, the killin' took place a good twenty mintues or a half hour after they all went up to bed. No woman keeps her corset on that long if she don't have to. So why was this Hadleigh woman still gussied up like the dog's dinner?"

"Why indeed?" Mrs. Jeffries mused. "Had I been in full evening regalia, I would have taken them off as soon as I got to my room. But she didn't."

"That's not all I learned, either," Wiggins said proudly. "You know 'ow the inspector said the 'ouse was so cold the next day? Well, Helen told me they found one of the windows on the top floor wide open. But they didn't say nothin' to the police. Seems that the butler was scared they'd all get the sack because that must 'ave been 'ow the killer got out."

"How big is the house?" Betsy asked.

"Three floors and an attic."

"The killer climbed down from a third floor window?" Mrs. Goodge snorted delicately. "I'll believe that when I see it."

"It's possible, though," Smythe said quietly. "Some burglars make workin' second and third stories in a 'ouse their specialty."

Mrs. Jeffries thought about this new information. Could it be possible that Inspector Nivens was correct and this murder was a burglary gone wrong? No, she didn't believe it. Chief Inspector Barrows had taken one look at the scene of the crime and he'd known it was cold-blooded murder.

"But surely the police searched the house the night of the murder and they didn't notice any windows left open?" Hatchet said.

"Helen said that she doesn't think the constables looked all that carefully," Wiggins replied. "The window on the third floor has these right heavy velvet curtains that go all the way to the floor. The curtains cover the whole wall. Mrs. Cameron got 'em cheap from some estate sale last year and stuck them in this top bedroom. The room 'asn't been used properly in years. Helen said that a body could glance in that room and unless there was a right gale blowin' they wouldn't even notice the window were open."

"I cannot believe the police would be that negligent." Hatchet shook his head. "It doesn't make sense. The police were specifically looking for that kind of evidence. Is it possible this young woman was pulling your leg?"

Wiggins felt himself blush. "Well," he admitted, "it's possible, but I don't think so. We was gettin' along right good by the time she told me this. And why would she be 'avin' me on? She didn't know I was snoopin' about tryin' to find out about the murder. She's the one that brung the subject up in the first place."

"It's more likely someone in the household opened the windows the next day and then forgot to mention it to her," Betsy guessed.

But Mrs. Jeffries didn't think so. Nor did she think the police had overlooked an open window. Despite the very bad publicity the police had gotten in the last months over this wretched Ripper case, they weren't incompetent fools. But that was a matter she'd have to take up with the inspector. Now, she needed to get this meeting moving along. Time was running short. Aunt Elberta might come trundling in at any moment and she did have her own information to report. "Excellent, Wiggins," she said. "You've done a fine job."

"Right, my boy." Hatchet echoed her sentiments. "Good work. If you're quite through, I'd like to share what I've learned. I found out something very useful about John Ripton."

"Of course, Hatchet." Mrs. Jeffries forced a cheerful smile. Her turn would come soon enough.

"It seems Ripton isn't just a bit hard up for money these days," Hatchet began. "According to my sources, he's desperate enough that he swallowed his pride a few days ago and asked his sister for a loan."

"How the dickens did you find that out?" Luty demanded irritably. On their last few cases, her butler had gone positively mute on the subject of his sources.

Hatchet gave her a superior smile. "I have my ways, madam. But I assure you, my information is absolutely trustworthy."

"Did 'e get the money?" Smythe asked, even though he could guess the answer.

"My source wasn't sure," he replied with a faint frown. "But he's working on it for me. I ought to know by tomorrow."

"I'll bet ya she didn't give it to 'im," Wiggins said eagerly. "Accordin' to what Helen told me, Mrs. Cameron weren't the generous sort."

"Is that it, then?" Smythe asked.

Hatchet nodded. Mrs. Jeffries took a deep breath, but before she could get her mouth open to speak, Fred leapt up and started tearing for the staircase. A second later, they heard the front door open and footsteps coming down the hall.

"I'll see who it is," Betsy said, getting to her feet and dashing out of the kitchen. She returned a few moments later, her expression wary. "It's the Inspector," she hissed softly. "He's home for tea."

"Bloomin' inconvenient, that is," Mrs. Goodge mumbled as she got up and headed for the larder.

"We'd best be off." Luty sprang up and tapped Hatchet on the shoulder. "There's someone I want to talk to before it gets too late."

"When shall we meet again?" Hatchet asked politely as he too rose and pulled out Mrs. Jeffries's chair.

"Tomorrow afternoon," the housekeeper replied. She stifled a sigh. She'd so wanted to tell them her informaton. But it could wait a day or two. As a matter of fact, it might be even more effective if she kept this little tidbit to herself for a while.

As the others said their goodbyes, she hurried out of the kitchen and up the stairs. Not finding the inspector in the drawing room or the dining room, she looked into the study.

Inspector Witherspoon was sitting at his desk, his head bent over a sheet of paper. He was scribbling furiously.

"Excuse me, sir." She advanced into the room and stopped in front of his desk. "I didn't hear you come in."

Witherspoon looked up and beamed at her. "I thought I'd nip home and have a spot of tea."

"Mrs. Goodge is preparing a tray," she replied. Curious about what he was writing, she glanced at the paper. "Would you like it served in here?"

"That would be fine," he said.

She was now standing directly opposite him but she could see quite a bit. The paper was filled with straight lines, both vertical and horizontal. Along one edge, a list of names was written and along the top. . . . She cocked her head to one side to get a better view, but his handwriting was so small, she couldn't quite make it out.

"It's a timetable, Mrs. Jeffries," the inspector said.

Startled, she drew back. "Do forgive me, sir. I didn't mean to pry . . ." She let her voice trail off pathetically.

The ploy worked perfectly.

"Of course you weren't prying, Mrs. Jeffries," he said, putting his pen down. "Naturally, you were curious. Anyone would be and I know how interested you are in my methods. Well, I've come up with a new one. I do believe I'm onto something very important here. Very important, indeed."

"You're so understanding, sir," she murmured. "What is it, sir?"

"This is a timetable." He tapped the paper proudly. "I think you'll find this quite fascinating. Do sit down. I'll tell you all about it. I think it'll help me to clarify things in my own mind if I discuss it."

"Thank you, sir." She sat down in the maroon wing-back chair next to his desk and folded her hands in her lap expectantly.

The inspector took a deep breath and then leaned back in his chair. "As I said," he began, "this is a timetable. Only instead of trains or omnibuses, it's got people on it." He leaned forward, picked up the paper and shoved it toward her. "The names on the left are the people who were actually in the Cameron household when the crime took place."

"What's this on the top of the page?" she asked, though she could see perfectly well what it was.

"That's the time frame," he replied. "Quite clever, I think. As you can see, I've broken the time down into ten-minute increments. I think this is going to work beautifully, don't you?"

She hadn't a clue what he was talking about. All she saw was a list of names down one column and a list of times at the top. The neatly marked-off squares on the paper didn't tell her anything at all. "I'm afraid I don't quite understand, sir."

He looked disappointed. "Oh, really? I thought it quite self-explanatory." He jabbed his finger at the list of names. "It seems to me that if I can locate where everyone was from the time the Camerons and their guests arrived home until when the body was discovered, I'll know who the killer is." He sat back and waited for her reaction to his brilliant plan.

Mrs. Jeffries had no idea what to say. Knowing the movements of the suspects was one thing, but she didn't quite see how his timetable was going to tell them that. People lied. Especially someone who'd just shoved a knife in some poor woman's back. But she could hardly say that to the Inspector.

"Of course, sir." She smiled reassuringly. "Why, this is very clever, sir. Naturally, you'll corroborate all the statements of where the suspects were at any specific time with witnesses."

His bright smile faded. "Well, that might be a bit difficult . . ."

"Not for you, sir," she said bracingly. Actually, now that she thought about it, this timetable of his might be a good idea. "Now, don't be coy, sir. You know I'm onto you. Really, sir, you are becoming a bit of a tease. I know precisely how you'll verify the facts."

"You do?"

"Certainly." She broke off and laughed delightedly to give herself time to think. "When Mrs. Cameron was killed, the servants were all in bed, but I'll wager they weren't asleep. Now, sir, if the staff sleeps on the floor above the guest rooms . . ."

"They do," he interrupted eagerly. "All of them except the governess."

"Then they most probably heard the Camerons and their guests moving about. You know, sir, doors squeaking, floorboards moaning, that sort of thing. You've already decided to go back to the Cameron house tomorrow morning and have a word with each and every one of the servants about what they heard and, more importantly, when they heard it. Then, of course, you'll take a new statement from Brian Cameron and his two houseguests to verify what the servants say." It was weak and she knew it. But it was the best she could do on the spur of the moment. The servants probably hadn't heard any noise at all. In most households, the staff was worked so hard they slept like the dead the moment their heads hit the pillows. But his timetable might work with the suspects. Perhaps Cameron or one of his houseguests might let something slip. Furthermore, one never knew what the inspector would come up with when he was trying a new method. It just might work.

Witherspoon nodded happily. "You're onto me, Mrs. Jeffries," he said. "That's precisely what I'm going to do. I should have liked to do it this evening, but the Chief Inspector has called us in for a progress report." He sighed. "It'll be very interesting to see what Inspector Nivens has to say. I'm afraid I don't have much progress to report."

"Nonsense, sir, you've accomplished a great deal." She hesitated. "I mean, sir, look at all you've found out already."

"What have I found out?"

"Well," she hedged, "you've found out that Mr. and Mrs. Cameron weren't on the best of terms and you've learned that Mrs. Cameron was in a hurry to get home that night. And what about John Ripton, sir? You've found out that he wanted her to sell him her property and now that Mrs. Cameron is dead, he'll inherit it."

"Yes." Witherspoon cheered up. "I think you're right. We have learned a great deal." He patted his timetable. "We'll learn even more once I've completed this, too."

"It's all right, Fred." Wiggins reached over and pulled the dog closer against his side. It was as much to keep warm as it was a display of affection. "We'll not be much longer," he crooned. "We shouldna come out at all. But you know, Fred, I didn't want to get stuck with Aunt Elberta, and the way Mrs. Goodge was eyein' us up when her old auntie come thumpin' down them stairs, well, I knew we'd best make tracks."

He and Fred were sitting behind a privet hedge in the gardens behind the Cameron house. His back was up against the cold brick of the garden wall and it was almost dark, but he was well hidden from prying eyes even if it had been broad daylight.

The trees were bare of leaves, the ground was damp and his backside was getting numb. But he didn't want to miss the chance that he could find out something. He'd remembered what Mrs. Jeffries had told them when she'd brought the inspector's empty tea tray downstairs. The master of the house wasn't due home till late tonight. Wiggins had decided that if any of the staff was going to go out and have a bit of time to themselves, they'd do it while Brian Cameron was gone. "Maybe I'll get lucky and Helen will come out for a bit of fresh air," he said aloud. Fred snuffled softly and licked him on the ear. "Silly pup." He chuffed the dog under the chin. "You're a good feller, ain't ya? You know the real reason I'm sittin' 'ere. Not that we're likely to see 'er, but ya never know. She's a bit on the rough, but I liked 'er." He honestly didn't expect to see anyone come out of the house. Most of the windows were dark and the place was as silent as a tomb.

A cold blast of air shook the leaves and Wiggins dug his cold hands into the dog's fur. Fred cuddled closer. "Maybe we ought to pack it in," he mumbled. In truth, he was beginning to get right hungry, not to mention feeling a bit foolish. "No one's comin' out."

But just then, he saw a crack of light appear at the back door. Wiggins sat up and strained in the failing light to see what was going on. The light disappeared and a woman swathed in a long, dark cloak stepped out. She looked to the left and the right, then walked quickly across the gardens toward the small gate at one end.

Fred snuffled and sniffed. "Hush, boy," Wiggins whispered. "We don't want 'er to 'ear us." But the woman was struggling with the latch on the gate and didn't look toward the hedge. She yanked the gate open and went out.

Wiggins got up and motioned to the dog. Silently, they followed her. By the time they were through the gate, he saw her disappearing around the corner. "Let's ope she don't grab a 'ansom," Wiggins muttered to Fred.

He hurried after her, his footsteps moving lightly on the pavement. At the top of the road, the traffic both on the pavement and in the road was heavy.

The dark figure was moving more quickly now and he had almost to run to keep up with her. Fred, delighting in the chase, trotted along next to Wiggins as they scampered up the road, taking care to stay far enough back so that they'd not be noticed.

They seemed to walk for ages. She moved fast and soon they were moving toward the park. Wiggins had a moment's panic when she disappeared behind a four wheeler crossing Park Lane, but a second later she emerged in front of Stanhope Gate. She paused at the gate and looked around her. Then she went through the gate and into Hyde Park.

"Come on, Fred, let's not lose 'er." He and the dog made their way carefully through the heavy traffic on Park Lane. They cut through the pedestrians on the pavement and followed their quarry into the park. She was practically running now, and Wiggins had to do the same. Fred, clearly enjoying the game, soon flew ahead of his master. Wiggins whistled him back as they gained on her. Suddenly, she stopped and looked around her again.

Wiggins had no choice but to go past her. Her face was well hidden by the hood of her cloak so he couldn't see what she looked like. Nonchalantly, he wandered toward a bench and sat down on it. Fred jumped up and sat beside him. Pretending he was fixing his shoe buckle, Wiggins bent down and looked back the way he'd just come. The woman had been joined by a man.

"Blast," Wiggins mumbled. Fred woofed softly, sensing his master's distress. "I can't see who it is and I'm too bloomin' far away to get a better look."

But his luck suddenly changed, for the couple turned and started walking toward him. As they drew abreast of him, he pretended to be fixing the buckle of his other shoe. Keeping his head down, he cocked his ear to one side to see if he could suss out what they were saying.

"Don't worry, love," the man said in a soothing voice. "It's almost over now."

They continued on down the path. Wiggins looked up and bit his lip. Blast! He had to know more. He couldn't just let them disappear. He waited till they went a bit farther up the footpath. "Come on, Fred, let's follow 'em."

CHAPTER 6

Betsy frowned at the clock for the tenth time in as many minutes. "Where is he?" she said to the others sitting at the kitchen table. "For goodness' sakes, it's gone on twelve o'clock."

"Now lass," Smythe soothed, "I'm sure 'e's fine. Just lost track of the time is all." He hated seeing Betsy's face all pinched and riddled with fear. Even more he hated the dread clawing at his own belly. It wasn't like the lad to miss a meal. Wiggins wasn't one to stay out and worry the blazes out of the rest of the household either.

"But he's been gone since right after tea," Betsy wailed. "He didn't have his heavy coat with him, only that thin little jacket, so he's probably half frozen by now. And what would 'e be doin' till this time of night, anyway?"

"He might 'ave stopped into a pub," Smythe replied, "to warm 'imself up a bit. You know Wiggins. 'E mighta started chattin' with someone and then walked 'em 'ome and then lost track of what time it was and all." But even as he said the words, Smythe knew they sounded hollow. His mind flashed back to the pub he'd been in earlier tonight with Blimpey Groggins.

A right rough place it was too. In his mind's eye, Smythe could still see the ruffians lined up at the bar, pouring four-ale and gin down their throats and just itching for an excuse to put their fists in anyone's face. London was full of men like that. Thugs that would slit your throat for the price of a beer. He hoped Wiggins hadn't run in to anyone like that. He prayed the silly git had gotten lost or was stranded or was chasing Fred. The thought of the dog brought some small measure of comfort to him. "He's got Fred with 'im and 'e'll go fer anyone that tries to mess about with Wiggins."

"I'm going to box his ears when he gets here," Mrs. Goodge declared. "Stupid boy, worryin' us like this. He's probably out standing under some silly girl's window and tryin' to write one of those wretched poems of his."

Mrs. Jeffries didn't wish to add to the tension by voicing her own fears. And she was afraid. Wiggins hadn't ever been this late before. "I'm sure he'll be home any moment now," she said firmly, "and I'm equally sure he'll have a perfectly valid explanation as to where he's been this evening."

"I think we ought to tell the inspector he's gone missing." Betsy drew a deep, long breath into her lungs. "Wiggins is a bit silly at times, but he's never, ever done something like this. He knows we'd be worried sick about him. Something's happened to him."

"Nothing's happened to Wiggins," Mrs. Jeffries said firmly, hoping it was true. She'd never forgive herself if their involvement in the inspector's cases led to one of them getting hurt or worse. Sometimes, when the chase was on, she forgot they were dealing with killers. "He's really quite able to take care of himself. Let's give him a bit longer. If he's not home within the hour, I'll wake the inspector."

"I'm going to have his guts for garters," Mrs. Goodge hissed, but her voice was shaky and behind her spectacles, and her eyes were brimming with unshed tears. "If anything's happened to that silly boy, I'll—I'll . . ."

Her tirade was interrupted by a soft bark from outside the back door.

"That's Fred." Betsy leapt to her feet and flew down the hall toward the back door. The rest of them were right on her heels. Even Mrs. Goodge managed to move with a speed that belied her bulk.

"Let me get it," Smythe ordered as Betsy reached for the lock. He gently eased her aside, slid the bolt and threw the door open.

"Oh? Waited up for me, did ya?" Wiggins grinned at them cheerfully as he and Fred sauntered inside. "That's right nice of ya. Cor, it's right cold out tonight. I could do with a cup of cocoa."

For a long moment, everyone relaxed in intense relief that the lad was safe and home. Then the tongues started wagging.

"Cocoa! You daft boy," Mrs. Goodge snapped. "You've had us worried sick."

"Where have you been?" Betsy cried indignantly. "We were about to rouse the inspector and call out the constables."

"You've a lot to answer for tonight, lad," Smythe warned, "and from the way the ladies was all wringin' their 'ands and 'aving you floatin' face down in the Thames, you'd better 'ave a good story." As the others were quite happily tearing a strip off the lad, he decided to go easy on the boy.

"Come into the kitchen, everyone," Mrs. Jeffries instructed. "And we'll see what Wiggins has to say for himself."

"What's goin' on?" Wiggins asked anxiously, realizing at last that everyone was rather annoyed with him. "I know I'm a bit late, but when I tell ya what I've found out, you'll . . ."

"A bit late," Betsy snapped. "We've been walkin' the ruddy floor for hours worryin' about you." When she lost control of her temper, Betsy frequently lost control of her speech as well. Glaring at the hapless footman, she stalked to the table, yanked a chair out and plopped down. "You'd better have a good reason why you're so bloomin' late."

Wiggins swallowed nervously. Cor blimey, they were really het up. "Er, look," he began, "I didn't mean to be out this long. I didn't mean to worry anyone." But he was secretly pleased that they cared enough to be worried about him. "But I was stuck, ya see, and I couldn't get away."

"Stuck where?" Smythe asked.

Wiggins rubbed his hands together to get them warm and eyed Mrs. Goodge warily. She'd picked up a wooden spoon from the sideboard and was smacking it hard against her palm. He had a feeling she was pretending it was his backside she was walloping. "Hyde Park. I was 'idin' in some bushes and then when I followed 'em back to the Cameron 'ouse, I got stuck 'idin' in one of them nasty little side passages behind the dustbins because there was coppers all over the street and I didn't want 'em to see me. I only got away when the police constable dashed off to the corner 'cause a hansom 'ad run into a cooper's van . . ." He paused to take a breath.

"Wiggins," Mrs. Jeffries said, "please start at the beginning and tell us everything. Otherwise, we're going to be here all night."

"It's like this, ya see," he said slowly, "I went back to the Cameron 'ouse after tea. I was hopin' to get another go at talkin' to Helen."

"Humph," Mrs. Goodge exclaimed. "Didn't I tell you? He was out moonin' over a girl."

"But Helen never come out," he continued. "But just when I was about to give up and come 'ome, I seen a woman slip out the back door. I weren't sure what to do, but she come out so quiet and sly-like, I were sure she were up to something and I was right. She went to Hyde Park."

"Did she see you following her?" Smythe asked quickly.

Wiggins shook his head. "No, I kept well back and I was careful. Anyways, in the park, she met up with a man. I didn't know who he was at first, so I followed 'em, of course. I heard 'er callin' 'im Connor, so I sussed out it must be Connor Reese."

"Who was the woman?" Betsy asked. "I'll bet it was Kathryn Ellingsley."

"It was," Wiggins replied. "Looks like my source was right. She has been slippin' out to meet her feller. 'Course I was surprised to find out it were Dr. Reese she was sweet on . . ."

"Do get on with it, Wiggins," Mrs. Jeffries said impatiently. "It's very late and we've got to get up early."

Chastised, he nodded. "I couldn't 'ear what they was sayin' at first, but then they sat down on a bench, private like, near some bushes and started talkin' their 'eads of. Fred and me slipped round to one side and crept up real quiet-like so we could 'ear everything." He smiled proudly.

"What did they discuss?" Mrs. Jeffries prompted.

"That's the funny bit. She kept tellin' 'im that they couldn't go on the way they was and I thought maybe 'e were married or somethin', but that weren't it at all. Seems that this Connor Reese mighta been Hannah Cameron's cousin, but 'e didn't dare set foot in the Cameron 'ouse. There was real bad feelin' on 'is part toward Mrs. Cameron. 'E 'ated the woman. I 'eard 'im say so."

"We know that, Wiggins," Betsy said. "But did you find out why he hated her?"

"No, 'e never said, but I do know that 'e don't 'ave an alibi for the night of the killin'," he replied, "and 'e's scared the police is goin' to find out about the bad blood between 'im and 'is cousin and come to question 'im."

"Why would that worry him?" Mrs. Jeffries mused. "Many people dislike their relatives. He wasn't in the Cameron house that night. I don't see that his lack of an alibi makes him a real suspect."

"But that's just it, Mrs. Jeffries," Wiggins said hastily. "'E was in the 'ouse that night. 'E told Kathryn Ellingsley 'e' left when 'e 'eard the Camerons and their guests come in. Kathryn was supposed to 'ave nipped down and locked the French doors behind 'im. Only one of the children started to cry and she didn't. Reese let 'imself out and when Kathryn did try and get down there to lock the door, she saw Mrs. Cameron going into that room."

"Cor blimey," Smythe muttered, "that puts a different twist on things, don't it?"

"That's not all," Wiggins said. "When they was talkin', I heard somethin' else, too. Seems that the governess 'ad been sneakin' out lots o' times to be with Connor Reese. She'd wait till the children was asleep, slip out the French doors and then slip back in again before the Camerons come 'ome from wherever they was. But that night, she didn't slip out so 'e snuck in to see why she 'adn't come to meet 'im."

Mrs. Goodge leaned forward. "The girl has been sneaking out regularly?"

Mrs. Jeffries wasn't interested in the governess's morals. There was something far more important she needed to know. "Why didn't Kathryn go out that night?"

Wiggins smiled triumphantly. "Because she was sure Mrs. Cameron was on to 'er. I 'eard 'er tellin' 'im—that's why she didn't meet 'im. She was convinced Mrs. Cameron was layin' a trap to catch 'er out. When she saw Mrs. Cameron goin' into that room later, she knew she was right too."

"I wonder how she knew?" Betsy mused. "I mean, surely Mrs. Cameron wouldn't have told her anything, not if she was trying to trap her."

"She never said 'ow she found out." Wiggins shrugged nonchalantly.

"That would explain why Hannah Cameron was in the sitting room that night and why she was in such a hurry to get home from the restaurant," Mrs. Jeffries said thoughtfully. There was something about the situation that didn't make sense. "Let me see if I understand precisely what you've said, Wiggins. According to what you overheard tonight, Kathryn Ellingsley and Connor Reese are attached to one another . . ."

"They're in love," he corrected. "'E's wantin' to marry 'er straight away."

"Yes, yes." The housekeeper nodded. "I understand that part. Are you sure about the rest? About what you overheard?"

He looked offended. "'Course I am," he insisted. "Mind you, they didn't say it straight out, but from the way they was talkin', you could tell she'd slipped out to see 'im lots of times and that she was sure Mrs. Cameron were on to 'er."

"But why didn't she just see Connor Reese on her day out?" Betsy asked. "Why go to all the bother of sneakin' about? Even if Mrs. Cameron and her cousin disliked each other, that shouldn't have stopped Kathryn from seeing him on her free time."

"Of course it would," Mrs. Goodge declared "If she did, Hannah Cameron would have tossed her out on her ear." She said it so vehemently that everyone turned and stared at her.

"Don't you understand?" the cook continued. "Hannah Cameron was very, very strict. I've worked in those sorts of households. Let me tell you, if a maid or a governess or a cook so much as thinks about disobeying the mistress's wishes, she's out on her ear. You've all gotten spoiled, the right lot of you. This house isn't like most. Inspector Witherspoon is a kind, decent man that treats us like people. Mrs. Jeffries doesn't go poking her nose into our business, either. I've seen plenty of women like Hannah Cameron and they're all the same. Mean, miserable tyrants, so ruddy wretched with their own lives they can't stand to see anyone happy. Well, bully for Kathryn Ellingsley, that's what I say. If she is in love with this young man, I'm glad she took her chances and kept right on seein' him. I hope neither of them is the killer."

Mrs. Jeffries was very tired the next morning as she served the inspector his breakfast. Furthermore, she was deeply troubled by the progress on this case. She had a feeling she was missing something important, some clue that was right under her nose but that she hadn't taken notice of because she was too distracted by everything else. The distractions had to cease.

Nothing was going as it should. The household hadn't had a proper meeting about the case since it began; they'd been constantly interrupted by one thing or another. Everyone seemed to be dashing off in his or her own direction and not sharing what they'd learned. This simply wouldn't do. If they were going to catch this murderer, they needed to pool their information. But between Aunt Elberta popping into the kitchen at the most inappropriate moments, Wiggins worrying them to death and the inspector's unexpectedly late hours at the Yard, they weren't progressing well at all. She sighed.

"Are you all right, Mrs. Jeffries?" the inspector asked.

Turning away from the sideboard, she smiled brightly and lifted the pot. "I'm fine, sir. Would you like more tea?"

The inspector popped the last bite of egg into his mouth and shook his head. "I really don't have time. I've too much to do today. It'll probably take hours just to get my timetable filled out properly."

Mrs. Jeffries quickly put the pot down and then took a seat at the table. She didn't want him dashing off just yet. If they were going to get this investigation under proper control, there were one or two things she had to do. There was plenty of information to be had, but unfortunately time enough to sit down and dig it out of people was in short supply. That was going to stop too. Right now.

"You must eat a good breakfast, sir," she said calmly as she shoved the toast rack toward him. "You'll not do yourself nor your investigation any good at all if you don't eat and rest properly."

Witherspoon looked longingly at the two remaining slices. Mrs. Jeffries, seeing him weaken, tempted him further by pushing the marmalade pot next to the toast rack.

"Well"—he hesitated for a split second—"I suppose you're right. I must eat, keep my strength up. Goodness knows this case certainly requires an enormous amount of stamina. Chief Inspector Barrows had us in his office last night until after ten o'clock." He picked up a piece of toast as he spoke and slathered it with butter. "I gave him a full report of my progress and he seemed to think we were making some strides in the case. Then, of course, Inspector Nivens gave his report." He dug a spoonful of marmalade from the pot and dumped it onto his plate.

"Was Inspector Nivens able to contribute anything?" Mrs. Jeffries asked. She might as well find out what that one was up to. She wondered how she could share what they'd learned from Wiggins. And share it she must, because it could completely change the direction of the investigation. Additionally, she had to think of a way to let him know why the Cameron house was so cold the day after the murder. That open window could be important.

"Not really," Witherspoon said honestly. "Though perhaps I'm being unfair. He did report that his own inquiries had revealed that none of the criminal underworld knew of any burglars working the area. Even knowing that, he still doubled the police patrols along that street and had several constables doing duty in front of the Cameron house as well. Still, I mustn't be critical. Inspector Nivens is doing what he thinks best."

"I'm sure he is, sir," Mrs. Jeffries replied, deciding to take the bull by the horns. "But you know, sir, it's only to be expected that Inspector Nivens isn't much help on this case. He's nowhere as brilliant or experienced as you are."

"Dats mos kind of you . . ." Witherspoon smiled around a mouthful of toast. "Thank . . ."

She waved off his garbled attempts at modesty. There wasn't time for pleasantries. "Of course you're brilliant, sir," she continued briskly. "You're the only detective at Scotland Yard who realizes the value of a true investigation. I do believe, sir, that after this case is completed, you ought to speak to the Chief Inspector about training others in the force to use your methods."

"Do you really think I should?" he responded, looking both pleased and surprised by the suggestion.

"I do indeed, sir. Your methods get results."

He beamed appreciatively and then his smile vanished as quickly as it had come. "Er, Mrs. Jeffries, precisely which of my methods are we referring to here? I mean, sometimes I rely on my—well, one hates to use the term, but there's really no other to use—my inner voice. That's not the sort of method I could really teach anyone else to use, is it?"

Mrs. Jeffries kept her smile firmly in place. His "inner voice" had caused the staff no end of trouble on one of his previous cases, but she could hardly fault him for that as she was the one who'd invented the wretched idea. "Agreed, sir. Your unique abilities are precisely that—unique. They can't be taught. But you could teach other policemen about your additional methods. You know the sort of thing I'm referring to, sir. Your technique of never taking a first statement at face value."

Witherspoon looked puzzled. Mrs. Jeffries realized she was going to have to be far more specific.

"Take this case, for instance," she continued brightly. "I know good and well you'll take your timetable and go right back to the Cameron house. You'll question the staff again, just as you said you would when we spoke yesterday afternoon. But, sir, you'll not just repeat the same questions you've already asked. You'll get the staff talking freely and you'll do it with such tact, diplomacy and sensitivity, they'll remember a myriad of details about the night of the murder. Then you'll go over all the statements the uniformed lads have gotten from the neighbors, compare the new statements of the servants with what other witnesses say and from there, you'll leap hot-foot into a new direction. That's what you always do, sir.

You get people to talk and remember." She was laying it on a bit thick, but she didn't think he'd notice.

Witherspoon regarded her thoughtfully for a long moment. "Yes," he agreed slowly, "I do do that, don't I?"

"It's one of your many talents, sir," she replied. She was banking on the fact that if Hannah Cameron knew Kathryn Ellingsley was slipping out to meet her young man, someone else in the household knew it too. She was also hoping a few more chats with the servants would reveal the truth about the open window as well. Additionally, there was the chance that if he did get the servants talking freely, the inspector would learn about Brian Cameron's doomed business ventures, John Ripton's need for money and Connor Reese's hatred of the victim. She had no doubt that some of the servants knew about all these matters. Perhaps even all of them.

The inspector's expression was reflective as he finished his morning meal. Mrs. Jeffries busied herself clearing up the breakfast things. By the time the inspector had gone, she was quite sure in her own mind precisely what they had to do and more important, where the best place to do it would be. To that end, she put the dirty crockery on a large wooden tray and hurried down to the kitchen.

Aunt Elberta was still at the breakfast table. Betsy was sweeping the floor, Smythe was filling the coal shuttle, Mrs. Goodge was whisking cooking pots into the sink and Wiggins was in the corner, stuffing paper into the toes of his boots.

"Smythe, can you bring the carriage here, please?" she asked.

"I thought the inspector had already left," the coachman replied quizzically. He put down the bucket and brushed his hands together. "Is 'e wantin' me to take 'im somewhere?"

"It's not for the inspector," Mrs. Jeffries said blandly, "it's for us."

Betsy stopped and leaned on the top of the broom. Mrs. Goodge paused, her hands still in the soapy water and Wiggins looked up from his task, his mouth open in surprise. Before any of them could formulate a question, she continued. "We're going to Luty's."

"Who's Luty?" Aunt Elberta croaked. She'd forgotten she'd already met the woman.

"She's a dear friend." Mrs. Jeffries smiled brightly at the old lady. "You're coming with us. Betsy, go to Aunt Elberta's room and get her warmest wrap. Wiggins, pop upstairs and get my notepaper."

"How long are we going to be gone?" Mrs. Goodge asked darkly. She hated being away from her kitchen. The thought of missing one of her sources caused her genuine pain.

"Just for a couple of hours this morning," she assured the cook, "but don't fret. We're leaving a note on the back door telling anyone who comes calling to come back early this afternoon."

Smythe grinned hugely, as though he'd figured out what the housekeeper was up to. "Right, then, I'll get the carriage."

Betsy bustled back in with Aunt Elberta's coat, almost bumping into Smythe. He grabbed her arms to steady her. "Want to come with me, lass?"

"I've got to finish my chores—" she began but Mrs. Jeffries interrupted her.

"Nonsense. I'll finish the sweeping and Wiggins can help Mrs. Goodge with the pots and pans. You go with Smythe. By the time you get back, we'll be ready."

Wiggins tossed his boots down and stood up. "Why're we goin' to Luty's then? I thought she was comin' 'ere."

Mrs. Jeffries refused to tell him. She'd wait till they got there. It was time to get cracking on this case.

"Do please sit down, miss," Witherspoon said kindly to the young maid. He was aware that two sets of eyes watched his every move and that one set thought he was a fool. But he was equally aware that Mrs. Jeffries was right; he was a very good detective and he'd become so because of his methods. He was just going to ignore Inspector Nivens's sneering expression and carry on with his investigation. "If I remember correctly, you're named Helen Moore."

The girl bobbed her head politely, but her eyes swept the small sitting room, her gaze taking in Nivens, who was standing next to the fireplace with his arms crossed over his chest and a scornful look on his face. Barnes was sitting quietly in a chair with his notebook on his lap.

"Yes, sir, I am."

"Do you mind if I call you Helen?"

Her chin jerked up in surprise. "No," she replied, her expression confused. It wasn't like the gentry or the coppers to ask your permission to do anything. But Helen decided she liked this man. He had a kind face.

She'd noticed he seemed to treat everyone, gentry and servant, like they were important, not like they were dirt. Not like that other one. She gave Nivens a quick, disdainful glance and then looked back at Witherspoon. "You can call me what ya like, Inspector."

"Good. Now, Helen," the inspector began, "you seem to be a very bright young woman."

Nivens harrumphed in disbelief.

Witherspoon ignored him and carried on. "And I'm going to ask for your help with this dreadful murder."

"I'll do what I can, sir."

"Excellent," the inspector replied. "Would you like a cup of tea?"

Taken aback, Helen blinked and then nodded. The inspector smiled politely at Nivens. "Inspector Nivens, would you be so kind as to go to the kitchen and ask for a pot of tea?"

Nivens's mouth dropped open in shock. A funny cough emerged from Barnes's throat. It sounded suspiciously like a laugh. But before Nivens could gather his wits to protest the indignity of the request, Witherspoon carried on. "I do hate to ask," he said blandly, "but I've a lot of questions for this young woman and for the rest of the staff. I really don't want them coming in and out while I'm speaking with Helen. Nor do I want any other member of the household to interrupt us."

"Now see, here," Nivens sputtered.

"I would send the constable," Witherspoon said conversationally, "but I need Barnes to take notes. He's so very good at it, never misses a word. Most important, that. And as you so kindly told Chief Inspector Barrows last night, I know you're eager to do everything you can to help this investigation."

Nivens's nostrils flared with rage, but the mention of Barrows's name kept his mouth firmly shut. With one last, contemptuous glance at Witherspoon, he stomped out toward the back stairs.

"Now," the inspector said softly to Helen. "Let's talk about the night of the murder, shall we?"

"What are we doin' 'ere?" Wiggins asked as he opened the carriage door and helped Aunt Elberta out.

Mrs. Jeffries smiled serenely as she got out of the carriage and then turned to help Mrs. Goodge down the tiny metal step. "Don't worry, Wiggins, all will be revealed in a few moments."

Everyone got out and Smythe turned the carriage over to one of Luty's manservants, who'd come running when he saw them pulling up.

Luty Belle Crookshank lived in a three-story mansion in Knightsbridge. She was standing in the open front door as the household of Upper Edmonton Gardens descended upon her en masse. "Lands sakes, we was just fixin' to come over to your place," she said, ushering them inside.

The house was exquisite, with a parquet inlaid floor in the foyer, a mammoth crystal chandelier on the ceiling and a wide staircase sweeping up to the second story. No one took any notice of their surroundings; they'd all, save Aunt Elberta, who was gawking like a schoolgirl, been there before.

"Do forgive us for barging in like this," Mrs. Jeffries began, "but"—she glanced meaningfully at Elberta—"we have certain requirements that only you can fulfill."

Luty grinned. "I think I know what ya mean. Come on in to the drawin' room and we'll have us a nice sit-down."

"Where's Hatchet?" Betsy inquired. It was rare to see Luty without the butler hovering somewhere close.

"I'm right here, Miss Betsy," Hatchet said from the door of the library. "And, of course, like madam, I'm delighted to see you." But he looked as puzzled as the rest of them.

"Luty," Mrs. Jeffries said, "do you think Effie Beals could take Aunt Elberta out to the gardens? They're quite spectacular, even this time of the year. When she's finished with showing her the gardens, do you think she might take her down to the kitchen for some tea and cakes?"

Aunt Elberta was whisked away in very short measure, and soon they were all seated in Luty's sumptuous drawing room. Before the questions could start, Mrs. Jeffries began issuing orders like a general.

"We're going to need a lot of help, Luty," she said. "This case has gotten completely away from us. Between Aunt Elberta's visit and our constant interruptions, we've not even had time to have a good meeting to share our information or our ideas. Today, that's going to change."

"Tell me what ya need," Luty declared, "and I'll see that ya git it."

"First of all, I want you to ask your cook to whip us up something to take back for lunch and possibly dinner tonight. Mrs. Goodge may not have time to cook when we get home."

"But the inspector doesn't like fancy food," Mrs. Goodge protested. In truth, though, she was delighted at the thought of having the whole day to pump her sources.

Luty reached over and patted her arm. "Don't worry, I'll have him fix somethin' simple like roast beef or steak and kidney pie. He'll squawk like a scalded rooster, but he'll do it."

"Could 'e fix us some of them fancy cream cakes?" Wiggins asked eagerly.

"Wiggins," Mrs. Jeffries objected, "we mustn't take advantage of Luty's hospitality."

"Piffle, Hepzibah," Luty said stoutly, "it's no trouble. That lazy cook of mine spends half his time sittin' on his backside. He'll enjoy fixin' up something special for you all to take home."

"Thank you, Luty," Mrs. Jeffries replied gratefully.

"What else do you need, madam?" Hatchet asked.

"Well, if you could spare one of your maids or footmen, I'd like someone to take Aunt Elberta out during the days."

"Effie can keep her occupied," Luty answered. "She likes gettin' out and about. You want me to send her home with you today?"

"That would be fine," Mrs. Jeffries said. "And lastly, I want us to finally, have a decent meeting about this case."

"It's about time, I'd say." Luty stood up. "Fer the last couple of days, we've been runnin' around like a bunch of chickens with their heads cut off. I'll ring fer tea and we can find out what's what about this killin'"

"A pity Inspector Nivens didn't stay," Barnes said quietly to Inspector Witherspoon as soon as Helen had left to fetch Mrs. Cameron's maid. "He might have discovered something useful."

"I expect he's his own inquiries to take care of," the inspector replied, but he was sorry Nivens hadn't stayed as well. He was quite pleased with the inquiries so far. He'd be even more pleased when he had a moment to fill in his timetable—especially with the information he'd just received from Helen. But the timetable could wait until he was finished.

"Excuse me, Inspector." Brian Cameron stood in the doorway, a quizzical expression on his face. "If you've a moment, I'd like to speak to you."

"Certainly, sir," Witherspoon replied.

Cameron smiled fleetingly and stepped into the room. "I don't want to tell you your business, but I fail to understand what you're doing here. For God's sake, man. My wife's funeral is this afternoon."

"We're investigating your wife's murder," he answered, somewhat taken aback. "I do assure you, we won't be intruding upon you or your household while you're paying your last respects to your wife. We only wish to have a few words with your staff."

"My servants know nothing of this matter," Cameron exclaimed. "Why are you wasting time here? Shouldn't you be out trying to apprehend the monster that did this?"

Witherspoon didn't know what to say. What did the man expect him to do, ask people in the street if they'd recently stabbed some poor woman to death? But on the other hand, he could understand Cameron's point of view. "We're doing our best, Mr. Cameron. But these things take time."

"How much time?" Cameron whispered, his face a mask of anguish. "I've had to send my children away, I'm worried about my staff and if it wasn't for the support of my friends, I believe I'd go out of my mind."

"I'm sorry if we're upsetting your household routine, especially at a terrible time like this," the inspector said apologetically, "but it really can't be helped."

Cameron gestured impatiently. "I'm not concerned about our routine, Inspector. Under the circumstances it would hardly be normal in any case. I suppose what I'm really asking is if you've made any real progress. I'm sorry, I know I must sound half-demented. But when the butler told me you were here, I'd hoped you might have some good news for me. I don't think I'll be able to rest until Hannah's killer is brought to justice."

"Oh, give it to me." Fiona Hadleigh's voice sounded from outside the room. "I'll see that Mr. Cameron gets it."

She flounced in carrying an envelope. "This telegram just came for you," she said, ignoring the policemen.

"Thank you, Fiona." He took it and tore it open.

"Good day, Mrs. Hadleigh," Witherspoon said politely. Barnes merely bobbed his head at the woman.

"Back again," she said archly, but she was watching Cameron out of the corner of her eye. "I should have thought you'd be finished here."

It was Barnes who answered her. "We've a number of questions still to ask, Mrs. Hadleigh. As a matter of fact, now that you and Mr. Cameron are both here, would you mind going over a few things with us?"

Witherspoon blinked in surprise. Though he encouraged Constable

Barnes to participate fully in their investigations, he was a bit startled by his boldness. He hadn't planned on asking either of them anything until after he'd filled in his timetable.

Then again, Barnes was a most intelligent man. The inspector decided that if he had some questions to ask, they were probably very good ones.

CHAPTER 7

———◆———

"This room's much cozier," Luty said as she ushered them into a smaller sitting room down the hall from the drawing room. "The fire's already lit."

"This one's my favorite," Betsy said, smiling as she turned in a slow circle. The walls were painted the colour of thick cream, an exquisite Persian carpet was on the floor and the windows were hung with cheerful blue-and-cream flowered print drapes.

At one end of the room next to the cheerful fire, there was a round mahogany table and six chairs. Luty pointed. "You all have a seat," she instructed. "Tea'll be ready in a minute."

While they were taking their places, Hatchet arrived pushing a heavy silver cart loaded with a china rose teapot with matching cups, a tray of tea cakes and a Battenburg cake.

Wiggins licked his lips at the sight. "Cor blimey, this is right nice."

"You just help yerself," Luty ordered. She sat down next to the house-keeper and for a few moments, everyone busied themselves pouring tea and filling their plates with sweets.

"If no one has any objection," Mrs. Jeffries began, "I'd like to begin." This time she wasn't taking any chances, so she plunged straight ahead. "Actually, I've been trying to tell everyone this information for two days now and I haven't had much success. I'm not sure it's important, but it may be."

"What is it, then?" Betsy asked. "Have you figured out who the killer is already?"

"Not quite, my dear." The housekeeper smiled ruefully. "But I think I've found out something that eliminates one of our chief suspects. I don't think Brian Cameron's the murderer."

"Why not?" Luty demanded. "Seems to me he's the one with the strongest motive. Accordin' to what Mrs. Goodge heard, he's a real ladies' man. Lots of men like to rid themselves of an inconvenient wife so's they can be free to git another one. Besides, look at some of the other cases we've worked on. Husbands can't ever be ruled out. Not unless there's an eyewitness that saw 'em someplace else when the killin' was done." Luty, though she professed to have had a happy marriage to the late Mr. Crookshank, frequently took a dim view of the marital state.

"I don't think we ought to knock 'im out of the runnin' yet," Smythe added. "I found out that Cameron's already gone through all of his wife's money. My sources told me there was a fine settlement from her family when they got married and he's spent just about every bloomin' cent. What's more, that Mrs. Hadleigh is sweet on the man and she's got plenty of lolly."

"That may be true—" Mrs. Jeffries began again, only this time she was interrupted by Hatchet, of all people.

"Really, Mrs. Jeffries," he chided, "I do think it's a bit premature to start eliminating anyone as a suspect. Unless, as madam colorfully puts it, you've got an eyewitness that clears him."

"There's no eyewitness." Mrs. Jeffries took a deep breath. Really, sometimes they were most impatient. "But there is something just as good."

"And what's that, then?" Mrs. Goodge asked.

"A motive. Brian Cameron didn't have a motive to kill his wife," she said. "Unless, of course, you're willing to accept the premise that he murdered the woman on the off chance that he could find another wealthy woman to marry him. Namely, Mrs. Hadleigh."

"But she probably is fixin' to marry the bloke," Smythe protested. "She's got 'er cap set for the man and 'e probably knows it."

"That may be true," she replied calmly. "In which case, I'd be more likely to think Mrs. Hadleigh was the killer than Mr. Cameron. With Mrs. Cameron dead, Brian Cameron stands to lose everything, including the very house he lives in."

"You mean the 'ouse belonged to Mrs. Cameron?" Wiggins asked.

She nodded. "Not quite. The house belongs to Mrs. Cameron's *family*. She has a lifetime use of it, but upon her death, the actual property goes to John Ripton. So you see why I was inclined to eliminate her husband. Now, that doesn't mean he didn't do it, but it seems to me he's got less of a motive than some of the others that were there that night."

"John Ripton for one," Mrs. Goodge said thoughtfully. "Seems to me that he's goin' to do quite nicely. He not only gets his hands on those dockside properties but he gets the house as well."

"And the income that comes with the house," Mrs. Jeffries added. "The maintenance and upkeep on the property and the servants wages are paid out of a trust established by Mrs. Cameron's family before she married."

"And Ripton didn't much like his sister," Luty commented.

"But that don't mean 'e killed 'er." Wiggins hated the thought that a man could murder his own kin in cold blood. "And what about Kathryn Ellingsley and Dr. Reese? Seems to me that they didn't much like 'er either. Especially Dr. Reese. 'E's Mrs. Cameron's cousin. Does 'e inherit as well?"

"Hold yer horses, there," Luty said. "Just what about this Ellingsley woman and this here Reese feller?"

Mrs. Jeffries realized they hadn't brought Luty and Hatchet up to date on the latest developments in the case. She quickly filled them in on Wiggins's adventure of the night before.

Luty shook her head slowly. "All right, I'll give ya that the girl might not a liked Mrs. Cameron, but if she's in love with this feller Reese and fixin' to marry him, why would she kill the woman? Why not just marry Reese and get out of there?"

"Because she couldn't," Smythe replied. He smiled apologetically for stealing Mrs. Jeffries's thunder, but he'd learned quite a bit from Blimpey Groggins the other night. "Not yet, anyway. My sources give me some information about Reese. He's been studyin' to be a doctor, just got 'is degree from the Edinburgh Medical School a few months back. But 'e don't 'ave much in the way of a practise. 'E spends most of 'is time workin' with the poor over in the East End and that don't give 'im much of a wage to support a wife on." He hoped the killer wasn't Reese. From what Blimpey had told him, the good doctor sounded a right decent sort of bloke.

"If 'e can't support 'er," Wiggins asked curiously, "why's 'e trying so 'ard to talk 'er into marryin' 'im now? And I know 'e is. I 'eard it with my own ears."

Smythe shrugged. "I don't know, maybe 'e's got expectations of an inheritance or somethin'. But I do know that right now, Reese hasn't got two farthings to rub together."

"Perhaps that's something we ought to find out," Mrs. Jeffries murmured thoughtfully. "We've concentrated our efforts on finding out what we could about what Ripton stands to inherit. But as Wiggins pointed out, Dr. Reese was a relation as well."

"I think I can find out," Smythe volunteered. He already had Blimpey working on that very problem. "It may take a day or two, though. The family fortune seems to be muddled up with trusts and all sorts of complicated bits and pieces."

Mrs. Jeffries nodded. She was a bit disappointed that the others didn't agree with her reasoning about Brian Cameron. But then again, she told herself briskly, other points of view are most important. Besides, she had a few other things to tell them, but that could wait for a few moments. "Were your sources able to give you any other information?"

"Not really," Smythe admitted. "Just 'eard more about what we already knew, you know, that Ripton was 'ard up for cash and that Cameron was a bit of a ladies' man."

"You've done better than I have," Betsy said morosely. "All I found out was that the Cameron household's been sending a lot of telegrams to Yorkshire, but that's just because of his uncle being so ill."

"At least you found that out," Mrs. Goodge said. "With Aunt Elberta hovering around the kitchen like the Angel of Death, I haven't found out a ruddy thing."

"There's something I don't understand," Hatchet said with a frown. "If Hannah Cameron's money was all gone, why did John Ripton ask her for a loan?"

Mrs. Jeffries brightened and silently patted herself on the back for having had the foresight to learn that particular fact. "Her own capital might have been gone," she replied, "but she could borrow from the trust. As a matter of fact, from what I can tell, the trust was set up specifically to keep most of the family money out of her husband's hands. She can borrow from it whenever she pleases and, of course, it never has to be paid back."

"But is'n that the same as 'avin' the money?" Wiggins asked. "I mean, couldn't Mr. Cameron just get 'er to give 'im some whenever 'e needed it?"

"Of course," Mrs. Jeffries replied. "For the first few years of their marriage, that's precisely what she did. But as the marriage deteriorated, so did Hannah's willingness to dip into her money."

Hatchet nodded in satisfaction. "Yes, it makes sense now."

"What makes sense?" Luty asked irritably. "You're gettin' as tight-lipped as one of them mummys at the British Museum. Come on, tell us what ya mean."

"I was going to tell what I've learned, madam," Hatchet answered. "I was merely waiting my turn."

"All right, all right," Luty waved impatiently and looked around at the rest of them. "Everyone finished?" As they nodded in assent, she shot her butler a scathing glare. "There, happy now? It's your turn."

"Thank you, madam." Hatchet reached for a napoleon and laid it daintily on his saucer. "As I told you at our last meeting, I'd decided to look more closely at John Ripton. In doing so, I not only found out that he was hard-pressed for money, but that he'd asked his half-sister for a loan. Well, my sources confirmed yesterday that Ripton had gotten the loan from Mrs. Cameron. As a matter of fact, he and Mrs. Cameron had an appointment at her bank for the day after the lady was murdered. That's the real reason he stayed the night at the Cameron house. Mrs. Cameron was going to loan him two thousand pounds from the family trust."

"Cor blimey," Wiggins exclaimed. "I guess Ripton was right narked when she were killed."

"Bloomin' Ada," Smythe muttered. "That lets 'im out as the killer."

"Not so danged fast," Luty charged. She hated it when Hatchet got the goods before she did. "If Ripton's gonna inherit the family trust, then seems to me he'd have the best motive for killin' the woman. With her dead, he gits it all."

"No, he doesn't, Luty," Mrs. Jeffries said. "The trust was set up by Mrs. Cameron's family specifically for her. When she died, the ability to borrow from the trust died with her. All Ripton gets is the property and the means of upkeep for the house."

"So that means Ripton was better off with her alive than dead?" Betsy murmured.

"Correct, Miss Betsy." Hatchet grinned. "For all their dislike of one another, my sources confirmed that Mrs. Cameron frequently helped her half-brother financially."

"But them properties must be worth something," Luty charged.

"They are," Hatchet said. "No doubt Ripton will make a handsome profit off them."

"More than two thousand quid?" Wiggins asked.

"Probably," Hatchet answered. "There's rumors in the city that the area over by the Commercial Docks is scheduled for redevelopment . . ." His voice trailed off and he frowned thoughtfully. "Which means that

Ripton could stand to gain a lot more than what his half-sister was going to loan him."

"Then that gives 'im a motive to kill Mrs. Cameron," Wiggins exclaimed.

"Now, Mrs. Hadleigh, do you think you could be more specific as to the exact time you went upstairs on the night of the murder?" Barnes asked. He'd decided that if the inspector's timetable was going to be of any use at all, they ought to get another quick statement out of the houseguests before they questioned the servants again. He hoped the inspector didn't mind, but he hadn't had a chance to ask for permission.

"No, Constable," she said coldly. "I cannot. I wasn't all that aware of the time when I went upstairs, merely that it was late. The best I can tell you is what I've already said. I *think* it was close to half past eleven." She started for the door. "Now, if you don't mind, I must get ready to leave. The funeral's in less than an hour."

"Yes, Inspector," Brian Cameron added. "Your questions will have to wait. We simply don't have time to spare." With that, he joined Mrs. Hadleigh at the door, nodded brusquely and the two of them left.

"Sorry, sir," Barnes said hastily. "Didn't mean to overstep my authority . . ."

"It's quite all right, Constable." Witherspoon sighed. "I understand what you were doing and if I do say so myself, it was a jolly good idea. You were trying to pinpoint their movements before I spoke to the staff, weren't you?"

Pleased, Barnes nodded eagerly. "I thought it would be easier that way"—he glanced glumly at the closed door—"but it looks like they flummoxed us."

"Not to worry, Barnes," the inspector said kindly. "While they're gone, we'll have a nice chat with the staff. That'll give me a chance to fill out our timetable. By the time they're back from the funeral and the house is quiet, I'll have all sorts of questions for the lot of them. By the way, I wonder where Inspector Nivens is today? Do you think he's going to the funeral?"

"I shouldn't think so, sir." Barnes was in a quandary. Nivens wasn't planning on paying his respects to the dead today. The constable knew that for a fact. He had his sources of gossip at the Yard, and what he'd heard this morning when he'd run into Constable Griffith had confirmed his worst suspicions about Nivens. That's why he'd been so eager to ask his questions. But he didn't want to say anything to the Inspector. He could be wrong. There might be a perfectly good reason why Inspector Nigel Nivens had gone over everyone's head and gone off first thing today for a visit to the home office.

"Does everyone understand what they're to do?" Mrs. Jeffries asked.

"I'm to keep on digging about all of them," Mrs. Goodge said.

"And I'm to find out what I can about Fiona Hadleigh," Betsy clarified. "But, Mrs. Jeffries, her house is in the country."

"She spends a lot of time with the Camerons," Luty pointed out. "We already know that. Seems to me a resourceful gal like you ought to be able to get someone's tongue waggin' about the woman."

Betsy looked doubtful. "Well, I'll do my best . . ."

"You'll do fine." Smythe patted her on the shoulder and was rewarded with one of her beautiful smiles. If he had to, he could always set Blimpey on the problem of the Hadleigh woman. Of course, he'd have to figure a way to get the information to Betsy without her knowing what he'd done.

"You still want me to keep my eye on Connor Reese?" Wiggins asked. "Wouldn't you rather I try findin' out what I can about John Ripton?"

"I'm taking Ripton," Hatchet answered. "I've already got my sources digging further into the man's life. I fear changing at this late date will only delay our investigation."

"Is there some reason you're not interested in Reese?" Mrs. Jeffries asked. "I know it's a bit of a bother, having to go over to the East End . . ."

"It's not that I don't like the East End," Wiggins interrupted. Actually it was, only he didn't want the others to think him a coward. The police had never caught this Ripper fellow that had done in all those poor women. The bloke might still be about and maybe by now, he'd decided to start slicing up young men as well.

"I don't like the East End," Betsy said cheerfully, "and no one else who'd ever spent much time there would like it either." She'd grown up in that district and thanked her lucky stars daily that she'd managed to get out.

"It is a long ways for the lad," Smythe said thoughtfully. "Why don't I take Reese and let Wiggins have Brian Cameron? Cameron's 'ouse is close by and I can always use the carriage to get over to that part of town if I 'ave to."

"As long as the two of you think that's a good idea," Mrs. Jeffries said, "then I don't see why any of us should object. Luty, are you all right with your task?"

Luty nodded. "If there's anything to know about Kathryn Ellingsley, I'll find it. She's a suspect too, though it seems to me that exceptin' fer havin' to sneak out to meet Dr. Reese, she'd have no reason to want the woman dead."

"Oh, I don't think she could be the killer," Wiggins objected.

"You never think a pretty woman's capable of murder." Hatchet sighed, as though he couldn't remember what it was like to be taken in by a pretty face. "Despite much evidence to the contrary. The female of the species is frequently deadlier than the male."

Luty chuckled. "Too bad so many of you men keep forgettin' that."

"Excellent." Mrs. Jeffries smiled in satisfaction. "We all know what we're going to be doing. I'll keep prodding the inspector and in general picking up what I can, and all of you will be out there gathering clues."

Mrs. Goodge shifted in her seat. "Don't you think it's time we got back? That butcher's boy is due round and I'd like to have another go at him." She was going to get some information out of Tommy Mullins if she had to shake it out of him.

"Goodness," Mrs. Jeffries said, "you're right. We really ought to get going. We've a lot to do today. But before we go our separate ways, I just want to say that for the first time since this case began, I've a very good feeling about it. I just know we're going to be successful in bringing this killer to justice."

"Mrs. Hadleigh, I do realize you're tired," the inspector said politely, "but we really must trouble you to answer our questions. It'll only take a few moments."

They'd buried Hannah Cameron and the funeral reception was over and done with. Witherspoon and Barnes had spent the day questioning servants and generally trying not to make a nuisance of themselves while the family paid their last respects to the dear departed.

"Really, Inspector," Fiona Hadleigh snapped. "This is ridiculous. I don't see what it is you're trying to prove . . ."

"I've just another simple question or two," Witherspoon said quickly. "Do you think it would be accurate to say that you were in your room by eleven thirty-three?"

According to Miriam, Mrs. Cameron's maid, she was sure she heard movement in the Hadleigh guest room when she went looking for Mrs. Cameron. Miriam's estimate of the time had been just after eleven thirty, and if one correlated her statement with the butler's, who claimed he heard the guest room door close at approximately eleven thirty-five, then eleven thirty-three was a fair guess.

"You can say whatever you like, but that won't make it a fact." She jerked her chin toward the paper in his hand. "What is that thing?"

"A timetable," the inspector said proudly. "It's quite useful in ascertaining where everyone was at specific times during the evening of the murder." Unfortunately, so far it hadn't given him a clue as to who the killer might be, but he was a patient man. He'd keep right on digging.

Fiona Hadleigh said nothing. She simply stared at him for a moment and then she shook her head. "If you think that one of us murdered Hannah, you're very much mistaken. It was a burglar who killed her."

"We don't really know that, Mrs. Hadleigh," Witherspoon began, but he broke off as the door opened and Inspector Nivens came inside. "Good day, madam."

"Inspector." Her voice was frosty but Nivens didn't appear to care. He gave Witherspoon a smile and a nod.

"Good day, Inspector Nivens." The inspector wondered why the man looked so pleased with himself. "Have you come to lend us some assistance?" Perhaps Nivens wouldn't mind doing a quick round of the neighbors to see if any of them had anything to add to the timetable. One never knew what one would find out until one asked. It was quite possible some neighbor had seen a light go on in one of the rooms and had noted the time. That could be quite helpful, quite helpful indeed.

"No, Witherspoon, I haven't."

The inspector thought he heard Barnes groan softly.

"I've just had a chat with Chief Inspector Barrows," Nivens announced. "And after I told him about a certain fact that's come into my possession, he quite agrees with my previous assessment about the way this case should be handled."

"Fact?" Witherspoon queried. "What fact?"

"There was an open window on the third floor the night Hannah Cameron was killed," Nivens replied.

"What window?" Fiona demanded. "What are you talking about?"

Nivens's smile grew positively smug. "The window in one of the guest rooms was open that night. That's how the thief got out of the house. It seems our uniformed lads were in a bit of a hurry when they searched. They didn't take the time to properly examine the whole house. It happens sometimes. Especially when there's a great deal of confusion."

"That doesn't sound right, sir," Barnes protested. His expression was angry but his voice was calm. "Those lads aren't careless, especially when there's been murder done."

"Are you saying it wasn't open?" Nivens inquired mildly.

Barnes hesitated. He and Witherspoon had heard about the window being left open today. Curious, he'd nipped up to have a look for himself. The awful thing was, with those floor to ceiling curtains, the window really could have been overlooked. But still, it seemed wrong somehow. "No, sir. But it's a straight drop down."

"Don't be naïve." Nivens laughed. "There's a solid drain pipe less than a foot away from the thing. A good snakesman or second-story man could get down and out of the gardens in less than a minute."

Witherspoon couldn't argue with his colleague. Facts were facts and it was possible a burglar could have shimmied down that drainpipe. But even with the evidence of the open window, he was sure that murder, not burglary, had been done in this house. "I do agree that the evidence of the window is quite strong," he began.

Nivens cut him off. "Your agreement isn't necessary, Inspector," he said. "Chief Inspector Barrows's is. As of right now, this isn't going to be investigated solely as a homicide, but as a burglary. My balliwick"—he grinned—"wouldn't you agree?"

"Well, of course you've quite a bit of experience in burglary," the inspector answered, "but nonetheless, a woman was murdered."

"But not deliberately, Witherspoon," Nivens shot back. "Her death is the result of her being in the wrong place at the wrong time. The thief panicked. But don't worry. I'll catch the blighter."

"You'll catch him, sir," Barnes said softly, his heart sinking by the minute.

Nivens flashed them a broad smile. "Of course. Who else? I'm taking over this case. You're welcome to lend a hand, Witherspoon, but considering you haven't any experience, I don't really see that you'll be all that useful."

"I don't believe it, sir." Constable Barnes shook his head as he and Witherspoon trudged down the front stairs of the Cameron house. "The lads wouldn't have overlooked an open window. For goodness' sakes, that's exactly what they were looking for that night—the way the thieves—or killer, if you ask me—might have gotten out."

Witherspoon couldn't believe it either, but he wasn't one to question his Chief's orders. "Perhaps they made a mistake," he suggested glumly. "It's possible. You said yourself that with those curtains it was jolly difficult to even realize that room had windows." But he didn't think the constables had overlooked anything. He thought that for some odd reason, Chief Inspector Barrows was giving way to pressure. "But it is peculiar," he muttered. "Very peculiar, indeed."

"What is, sir?" Barnes asked as they turned onto the road and started walking toward the corner. "The fact that Inspector Nivens has now gotten charge of the case?"

"Well, yes . . ."

"Nothing odd about that, sir." Barnes snorted in disgust. "Nivens just called in some favors and had a bit of pressure applied to the Chief."

Witherspoon wished he could be shocked by such a statement, but the sad fact was that he wasn't. He knew he was a bit naive about such things, but one would have to have lived in a cave not to know that Scotland Yard was as subject to political pressure as any other social institution. It was clear, even to him, that Nivens had pulled his political strings and used the excuse of one open window to get the case classified as a burglary instead of a homicide. Murder, had, of course, been done, but once the powers that be decided it was done in the course of a break-in, then Nivens, not himself, was clearly the officer to put in charge.

He still didn't understand what was motivating the Chief Inspector. "Why, Barnes?" Witherspoon shook his head. "I don't understand why. Inspector Nivens knows that this isn't a burglary . . ."

"Of course he does, sir," Barnes interrupted angrily. "But he doesn't care. He wants you off the case, sir, for one reason and one reason only. He wants all the glory of solvin' this one. He don't want to have to share it with you. Let's face it, sir. His name will be on the front pages of every paper in the country if he brings someone in for this crime. The public isn't all that happy with the police these days, not after all that horror in Whitechapel. They haven't caught the Ripper yet, and from the gossip I hear, they're not likely to either. Nivens knows that. He knows the home office doesn't want another unsolved murder on their hands. The Ripper case has already cost Sir Charles Warren his job. There's more than a few more at the top that are worried about theirs too. Nivens is no fool. He knew what he was about and let's face it, sir, an unsolved burglary, even with a killing, is a sight better in the public's eye than a cold-blooded murder."

Barnes's analysis did shock the inspector. He didn't want to believe that even Inspector Nivens was so brutally ambitious. "Surely not . . ."

"I'm as sure of it as I am that my missus'll have Lancashire Hot Pot waiting on the dinner table on Thursday nights," Barnes cried, "and I'm just as sure that Nivens has as much chance of solvin' this one as I do of havin' dinner with the Prince and Princess of Wales. But that doesn't mean that he won't arrest someone for it. He'll find some poor sod to parade in front of Fleet Street."

Witherspoon wanted to protest but found that he couldn't. He feared Barnes could well be right. He hated the thought that justice might not be done in this case, that Hannah Cameron's killer might get away with it. There was nothing more abhorrent to him than the unlawful taking of human life. For that matter, though he was careful to keep his thoughts on the subject to himself, he didn't really believe that anyone, even lawfully constituted authorities like courts and judges, had the right to take a life. That was God's place, not man's. But the Inspector refused to give up hope. "Perhaps we do the man an injustice," he murmured. "Perhaps he will find the killer."

"Not in our lifetime, sir," Barnes said glumly. "The only chance Hannah Cameron had at justice disappeared when they took you off the case, sir, and that's a fact."

"Git out of my way," Luty hissed at Hatchet. She tried poking him with her parasol, but he wedged himself in the doorway of her elegant carriage and wouldn't budge.

"I'm not moving, madam," he shot back, "not until you come to your senses."

"There ain't a danged thing wrong with my reason, Hatchet," she snapped, "and the last time I looked, I was able to take care of myself. I've done it fer a number of years now."

"That isn't the point, madam," he said acidly. "It's ridiculous and foolhardy for you to go traipsing off to the East End of London on your own this time of the day." Hatchet wouldn't have liked her going to that part of town at any time of the day, but he was especially aggrieved that she'd taken it into her head to go now. It would be dark shortly.

She glared at him. "Well, I'm sorry that you're so het up over it, but my sources told me that Kathryn Ellingsley is goin' over that way to meet this Reese feller and I want to find out what she's up to."

"She's probably not up to anything except wanting to visit her sweetheart," he replied. He didn't know how the woman managed to find out so much information in so little time. They'd only finished their meeting with the others a few hours ago. If he were of a suspicious nature, he'd think the madam was bribing someone at the Cameron house for information. The moment his back was turned, the madam had taken it into her head to go careening off after her quarry. Luckily, John had tipped him as to madam's plans. Undignified as it was, he'd dashed out and leapt for the carriage just before she took off. "And all you'll do is waste your time and endanger yourself. In case you've forgotten, they haven't caught the Ripper."

"I've got my peacemaker." Luty dumped the parasol on the seat and patted her fur muff. "And Dickory's with me."

Hatchet rolled his eyes. Dickory, the coachman, was an excellent driver. But he, like most of Luty's household, was a stray she'd taken in when she found him cowering in a back alley after he'd been tossed out of a pub by a couple of sailors. "Dickory would be useless if you got into difficulties, madam," he said through clenched teeth. "You know I've an appointment so I cannot go with you." His own appointment involved one of his sources of information and he didn't want to miss it. On the other hand, he didn't trust the madam not to take off on her own the minute his back was turned. Dickory, unlike most of the others in the household, was totally cowed by her.

"Then you'll just have to take me with you." Luty grinned. "I figure we've got just about enough time fer you to talk to your source and then by the time you're done, we ought to be able to find Kathryn and her sweetheart." She pulled a man's gold watch out of the folds of her coat, flipped open the case and nodded. "It's just gone on four. If'n you can git a move on, we ought to be able to do what you need to and then git to the East End just about the time this Dr. Reese finishes fer the day."

Hatchet's eyes narrowed as he studied his employer. She settled back on the seat and smiled at him innocently. He didn't trust her for a moment. She was being too reasonable. That meant one thing. She was up to something.

"Well, you comin' or not?"

"Oh yes, madam," he replied. He eased his left side out of the carriage door and stuck his hand in his pocket. Taking care so that she wouldn't see, he pulled out a small metal object. "I'm coming."

"Good, I'll wait while you go git yer coat and hat."

She'd be off the moment he got out of the carriage.

"That won't be necessary, madam." He lifted the object to his lips and blew. The shrill blast of the whistle had the back door opening and John, a lanky twelve-year-old who was allegedly training to be a footman in the household but was really another stray that Luty was housing and educating, came bursting out. In his hands he carried the butler's cane, heavy greatcoat and formal black top hat. "Here ya are, Mr. Hatchet." He handed them to Hatchet inside the carriage. "I told ya she was up to somethin'" He bobbed his head at his employer and benefactress.

"You little traitor," Luty yelped. "See if I ever trust ya again."

"Sorry, madam." John's smile made it apparent he was anything but contrite. "But I couldn't let ya go off on yer own, not to the East End."

"Thank you, John," Hatchet said formally. "Your help has been most invaluable."

John waved and went back inside. Luty turned on her butler. "Where the dickens did ya get that?" she asked, glaring at his whistle.

"Never you mind, madam," Hatchet put it back in his pocket and then picked up his cane and rapped on the top of the carriage. "I always knew it would come in useful."

She snorted. "Where we goin'?"

"To the West End," he said.

"That where your source is?"

Hatchet was loathe to share this with her, but he really had no choice. "Yes. To be precise, madam, we're going to visit a man I used to work for."

Luty realized he'd said "man" and not "gentleman." "What's his name?" She was quite curious now.

"Newlon Goff." He sighed. "He was my first employer."

Luty cocked her head to one side and studied him. Hatchet's expression was sour enough to curdle cream. "What's wrong? Don't ya want to see this Goff feller?"

"Not particularly, madam." Hatchet coughed slightly. "However, I've found him to be a most enlightening source of information about some of the less than honest citizens of our fair city."

"He some kind of policeman?" Luty asked curiously. She couldn't imagine that her butler had ever worked for a lawman; he'd have told her.

"Hardly, madam." Hatchet tried to keep his face straight but failed. It had been most difficult to get just the right expression on his face when the madam had started asking her question, but the strain was worth it. But he honestly didn't know how long he could keep the pretense up. This was too delicious. In another moment, he'd be grinning from ear to ear.

Hatchet leaned closer to Luty. "But he's quite well known to the police force. One could say the inside of the Old Bailey is almost a second home to him."

Luty was getting suspicious now. Despite his expression, Hatchet's eyes were sparkling. "He a lawyer?"

"Oh no, madam, but he knows quite a number of them very well."

"Well, then what in the blazes is the man?" she demanded.

Hatchet broke into a wide smile. "A felon, madam."

"You mean a criminal . . ." Luty sputtered. She couldn't imagine that Hatchet even knew, let alone had been employed, by a crook. "a . . . a . . ."

"A thief, madam. He was only released from Pentonville a few months ago."

"You worked for a thief!" She was affronted that her boring, staid, impeccably correct butler had kept this interesting tidbit from her. "And you never told me!"

"Not just any old thief, madam." Hatchet was enjoying himself enormously. "But one of the best in the business."

CHAPTER 8

Mrs. Goodge hummed as she cleared up the last of the tea things. Without Aunt Elberta underfoot, Tommy Mullins's second visit to her kitchen had been quite a success, if she did say so herself. She couldn't wait to tell the others what all she'd learned. Pity that everyone, including Mrs. Jeffries, was still out.

She glanced out the window, noted that it was getting darker by the minute and decided to lay the table. Yet she wasn't rushed this evening. It was a godsend, not having to actually cook for the household when they were on a case. Thanks to Antoine, Luty's toff-nosed French cook, there was a casserole in the oven, fresh baked rolls and a lovely sponge and cream cake that would have Wiggins moaning in pleasure.

They should be in soon. Mrs. Goodge ceased humming and broke into the first verse of *Christ, the Lord, is Risen Today*. She'd gotten to the first Hallelujah when there was a soft cough from behind her. Startled, she dropped a spoon and whirled around. "Gracious, Inspector," she gasped, "you did give me a fright. We didn't expect you home so early."

"I'm dreadfully sorry, Mrs. Goodge," Witherspoon replied. "I didn't mean to scare you. But there was no one upstairs when I came in." His tone was vaguely curious.

Mrs. Goodge thought quickly. She could hardly announce that the rest of the staff was out investigating his murder. "No, sir, they're all out. Smythe's gone over to coddle those horses of yours," she lied and crossed her fingers behind her back. "Betsy's run a pound of sugar over to Lady Cannonberry's, Wiggins is out giving Fred a walk and Mrs. Jeffries is . . . is . . . ," she broke off as her mind went blank.

"Mrs. Jeffries is where?" the inspector prompted.

"Right here, sir," the housekeeper, still in her coat and hat, stepped into the kitchen, a calm smile on her face. "I'm sorry I wasn't home when you arrived, sir, but I had to dash over to the butcher's shop. The beef he sent over today wasn't what we ordered. But not to worry, sir, it's all straightened out now."

Witherspoon nodded distractedly. He was still somewhat depressed. The interview with his Chief Inspector had been very tedious. "That's nice," he murmured. "Ah, when's dinner to be served?"

"Whenever you like, sir." Mrs. Goodge spoke quickly. "It's in the oven."

"I'll bring it up to the dining room when you're ready, sir," Mrs. Jeffries said as popped her bonnet on the coatrack and removed her coat. She could tell he was upset. "But wouldn't you like to have a glass of sherry first?"

Witherspoon glanced at the tea kettle. "I'd like a cup of tea more," he said. The kitchen, with its cheerful warmth, was comforting. "If you don't mind, I'll just have a quick cup down here." He sat down at the head of the table.

Mrs. Jeffries and the cook exchanged quick, surreptious glances.

"Tea'll be ready in two shakes of a lamb's tail. Would you like a cup, Mrs. Jeffries?" Mrs. Goodge asked as she put the kettle on to boil.

"Yes, thank you." The housekeeper took a seat next to Witherspoon. "Is there something wrong, sir?"

"Wrong." He sighed and smiled wearily. "Not really. I mean, not officially."

"So the case is progressing," she prodded.

"Actually, well, I suppose one could say that. The truth is, Mrs. Jeffries, there isn't a case to progress. At least, not a murder case. Not for me."

Mrs. Jeffries went absolutely still. Surely, surely, she'd misunderstood him. "What do you mean, sir?"

"Chief Inspector Barrows and his superiors have decided that the case is to be investigated as a burglary, not a homicide. I've been taken off it. Inspector Nivens is now in charge."

Newlon Goff lived in some rented rooms off Drury Lane in the tawdry section of the West End. Hatchet kept a firm hand on Luty's elbow as they went inside the shabby two-story house and climbed the rickety stairs to the second floor. He rapped firmly on the door. From inside, a muffled voice yelled, "Look, I've already told you, you'll get your rent tomorrow."

"It's Hatchet," he called. "Not your landlord. Open up, Goff. We've business to discuss."

The door cracked open an inch and then widened further. "So it is you," said a tall, gaunt man with thinning iron-gray hair and piercing brown eyes. He wore a clean white shirt, dark tie and freshly pressed trousers. "Come in," he offered, his eyes sweeping them and lighting in amusement when he saw Luty. "I see you've brought a visitor."

"This is my er . . . associate, Mrs. Crookshank." Hatchet introduced them.

Goff bowed formally. "Newlon Goff, at your service, madam."

Luty grinned. "Pleased to meet you, Mr. Goff."

They stepped inside and Luty was surprised by how clean and well kept the place was, considering the house itself was one step above a tenement. The paint might have been cracked and peeling, but the day bed was neatly made; there were books stacked along the walls; a table and two chairs, both with missing spokes in the backrest, sat next to a lumpy green settee that had seen better days. But the oil-cloth on the table, though faded, was clean, and the chairs, though delapidated, were free of dust.

"Do sit down, Mrs. Crookshank." Goff gestured to the settee. "And you too Hatchet. Welcome to my home, such as it is."

"Thank you." Luty dropped onto the worn cushion and made herself comfortable.

"May I offer you some refreshment?" Goff asked as he sat down on one of the chairs.

"No, thank you," Hatchet said quickly, sitting down and then leaning forward, balancing part of his weight on his walking stick as the chair groaned in protest. "We don't have much time." He wanted to get this over and done with. He could tell by the glint in madam's eyes that she was enjoying herself far too much.

Goff raised his hand. "Of course, I quite understand. I'll get right to the point. I was able to find the information you requested." He stopped abruptly and smiled.

Hatchet sighed and dug out some notes from his pocket. He placed them on the table. Goff picked them up and started to count them.

"It's all there," Luty said testily. It was one thing for her to annoy her butler, but she wasn't going to stand for anyone else thinking he was a cheat. Though she would taunt him nicely for having to use bribery to get his information. That was too good a chance to pass up. "You jus' get on with it and tell us what ya know."

Goff grinned. "I didn't mean to be offensive, madam."

"None taken," Hatchet said quickly. The last thing he wanted was madam getting into a character debate with Newlon Goff. Both of them were far too fond of the sound of their own voices for that.

"As you surmised, Hatchet," Goff began, "if the Cameron house was burgled, it wasn't done by pros. Nobody, and I do mean nobody, is owning to that toss."

"Could it have been an amateur?"

"It would have had to have been. A pro wouldn't have stabbed that woman. They'd have just gotten out."

From the corner of his eyes, Hatchet noticed Luty nodding and looking very satisfied with herself. So far, Goff had only told them what they already knew. "Yes, we were very much aware of that fact."

Goff looked amused. "I'm sure you were, but isn't it nice to have it confirmed? But I'll bet you didn't know that this isn't the first break-in for the Cameron family."

"Are you sayin' they was robbed before?" Luty asked. She wondered why Mrs. Jeffries hadn't found that out from the inspector.

"Not directly," Goff said. "But Brain Cameron has an uncle. A Yorkshire man by the name of Neville Parrington. Six months ago, his London town house was burgled."

"Was someone killed?" Hatchet asked.

Goff shook his head. "No, no one was even there the night it happened. But I got curious about it and asked a few questions. What do you think? No one owns up to that toss either."

"How much was stolen?" Hatchet's chair creaked and he tightened his grip on the cane.

"As a matter of fact, the only thing taken from the townhouse was some papers."

"What kind of papers?" Luty demanded.

"No one really knows," Goff answered. "They were kept in a strong box in Parrington's study. The thieves took the box. My guess is they were after something inside it."

"Maybe the burglars were interrupted," Hatchet mused. He couldn't think why this would have anything to do with the Cameron case, but nevertheless, it was interesting.

"It's possible, I suppose," Goff said doubtfully. "But a pro wouldn't have walked out with just a box full of papers unless it contained the deed to Buckingham Palace. The place was ripe for picking. There were lots of silver trinkets laying about, not to mention a wad of notes stuffed in the bottom of the old man's desk."

"That's most curious," Hatchet said.

"Curious." Goff hooted with laughter. "Don't be stupid, Hatchet, it's more than that. It means whoever broke in was after something, and it wasn't a silver candlestick. The place was completely empty. Old man Parrington had gone to the theatre and given his servants the night off."

"What did the police think?" Hatchet asked.

Goff grinned slyly. "They didn't think anything. Parrington never reported the break-in. He just shut up the house and left."

"Then how the dickens did you find out?" Luty demanded.

"Oh, madam," Goff replied, "that was the easy part. Parrington may not have reported the burglary to the police, but his neighbors did. They were most alarmed and insisted the police patrols in that area be increased. Of course, my contacts are always interested when the peelers show up in any neighborhood in force."

"I can't believe this," Mrs. Goodge moaned. "Just when I'd found out a bit too. It isn't fair, I tell you. Just not fair."

"It's worse for the inspector," Wiggins said loyally. "He was so depressed 'e didn't eat 'ardly any of that nice casserole."

"He should have raised more of a fuss," the cook cried. She was actually quite enraged about the whole situation. For the first time since this case had begun, she'd found out something useful and now it didn't even matter. "He shouldn't have allowed them to toss him off the case. Anybody with half a brain in their heads can see this is a case of cold-blooded murder, not a bungled burglary."

"Of course it is, Mrs. Goodge," Hatchet agreed. "But I hardly think that even if the inspector had 'raised a fuss,' he'd not have been allowed to continue the investigation. As Mrs. Jeffries has already explained, politics is raising its ugly head. The police aren't anxious to have another unsolved murder on their hands. Especially a murder of a wealthy and prominent citizen."

"But murder was done," Betsy argued. "They can't pretend she wasn't stabbed."

"Yes," Hatchet agreed, "but a killing in the course of a burglary has far less of an impact on the public." He sighed. He too was bitterly disappointed.

"Silly fools," Luty muttered. "I can't believe they're so stupid. Besides, they didn't give the inspector time to solve the case."

"They don't want there to be a case to be solved," Mrs. Jeffries added. "That's really the point. I've no doubt that Chief Inspector Barrows was quite willing to continue investigating the case as a homicide, but, unfortunately, he was overruled when the evidence of that open window was found."

"They was just lookin' for an excuse," Smythe murmured. "And Nivens found it for 'em. Sneaky little sod."

"That woman was killed by someone in that house," Betsy said fervently, "and she might not have been a very nice woman, but she didn't deserve to get murdered that way. It makes my blood boil to think some killer's going to get away with it."

"I agree," Mrs. Jeffries said. "But I don't know what we can do about it. It would be difficult, if not impossible, to continue to investigate a case the inspector is no longer involved with."

"Are you sayin' we ought to give up?" Wiggins asked incredulously.

"Well," the housekeeper said, "I don't see that we can continue. . . ."

"Fiddlesticks," Luty interrupted. "Where's it written in stone that just because the inspector's off the case that we can't keep nosin' around?"

"But how could we hope to bring the murderer to justice if the inspector can't make an arrest?" Mrs. Jeffries pointed out. She didn't want them to be bitterly disappointed when and if they determined who the killer was. With the position the police were taking, unless they had incontrovertible proof of the identity of the murderer, she didn't think Witherspoon could act.

"Who says 'e can't make an arrest?" Smythe added his voice to the argument. "If'n we can figure out who the killer is, we can find the evidence, and once that 'appens, they'll 'ave no choice but to let the inspector make an arrest."

Mrs. Jeffries was sorely tempted. But there was one thing stopping her.

What if Inspector Nivens was right? What if it really had been a burglary gone bad? They'd spend the next few days or possibly even weeks, running all over London seeking clues and risking exposure of their activities. If it turned out that Nivens did make an arrest on the burglary, they'd not only be disappointed, but they could very well damage the inspector and themselves irreparably. Oh, she wished she'd had time for a good, long think about the situation. But as soon as the inspector had eaten his dinner, he'd gone up to bed. She'd sent Wiggins over to find Luty and Hatchet and then waited for the others to come in.

If Mrs. Jeffries had only had more time to think about the problem, if she'd only been able to stave off saying anything until tomorrow morning, she was sure things would be much clearer in her mind.

"Look," Smythe said reasonably, "what it boils down to is this: are we gonna stop our investigatin' just because the inspector's off the case or are we gonna keep on? I say we keep right on goin'"

Mrs. Jeffries looked around the table. She suddenly realized she was being rather arrogant. This wasn't just her decision. It belonged to all of them. "How do the rest of you feel?"

"Let's keep at it," Mrs. Goodge declared.

"I don't want to give up," Betsy said.

"Never could stand politicians stickin' their noses in where they don't belong." Luty sniffed disdainfully. "And they shoulda had better sense than to stick their noses in murder. I say we keep diggin'"

"I agree," Hatchet echoed.

Mrs. Jeffries folded her hands together in front of her as she looked at the faces around the table. Everyone looked determined to proceed. Everyone, that is, but Wiggins, who was staring down at the tabletop with a sad, almost wistful expression on his face.

"Wiggins," she prodded gently, "what do you think?"

He looked up slowly. "It's a bit 'ard to put into words, but I'm thinkin' we got no right to stop," he said earnestly. "I'm thinkin' that since we started it, we've got to finish it. I mean, like Betsy said, maybe Hannah Cameron weren't a very nice woman, but no one deserves to get a knife shoved into their back in their own 'ome. Besides"—he dropped his gaze again, as though he were embarrassed—"this might sound a bit funny, but I'm thinkin' if we don't do it, who will?"

There was a long moment of respectful silence. Wiggins's words had a most profound effect on them, especially on Mrs. Jeffries. She knew precisely what he was saying and he was absolutely right. Now that they'd started along this path, they had almost a moral obligation to keep going, regardless of what the consequences might be. As he'd said, if they didn't do it, no one would. "Well said, Wiggins," she said firmly. "We'll keep on. But do keep in mind that we'll have to be very, very careful and that even if we find out who the killer is, unless we can get proof, our efforts might be to no avail. Now, let's get cracking. Tomorrow . . ."

"Tomorrow," Mrs. Goodge squealed. "What about now! I've found out somthing and I'm goin' to burst if I don't tell it. It seems that there is some money in the Cameron family. It belongs to Brian Cameron's uncle."

"Neville Parrington," Luty mumbled.

Mrs. Goodge gasped. "How did you know that?"

"We found out he got burgled too," Luty explained. "Only it were six months ago and nothin' was taken exceptin' a box full of papers. Is that what you found out?"

"No. I just found out about Parrington being rich, and I mean very rich. Cameron, who's ignored the old man for the past five years suddenly started cozyin' up to him a year or so ago when his wife stopped handin' it out to him. He even went up to Yorkshire to visit him. That's how Kathryn Ellingsley happened to get her position as the Cameron governess. She was living with her uncle until Brian and Hannah Cameron brought her to London. They let their other governess go to give Kathryn the position."

"Why would she want to come down here and be a governess when she could stay in Yorkshire and not have to work?" Betsy asked. That didn't make sense to her at all. If she had a rich uncle, she'd certainly not be minding someone else's children.

"I know why," Wiggins interjected. "She wanted to come to London because she'd met Connor Reese and fallen in love with him." He smiled. "I 'ad another chat with Helen this afternoon."

"'Ow'd you manage that?" Smythe asked.

"She had to go and send another telegram," Wiggins replied. "I walked along with 'er. She told me all about 'ow Kathryn Ellingsley met Reese. Seems the girl 'ad come with her uncle to 'is town 'ouse about six months ago and they'd gone to 'ave dinner with the Camerons. Reese showed up to 'ave a go at Hannah Cameron over somethin' and they 'ad a right old dust-up. The next day, Reese went round to the uncle's 'ouse to apologize for disruptin' the dinner party. But Kathryn and the uncle were fixin' to leave for Yorkshire. So 'e wrote 'er a letter and she wrote 'im back." He smiled brightly. "Before you knew it, Kathryn 'ad agreed to come down to London with the Camerons and look after the children. But Helen's sure she only came so she could be near Dr. Reese. They started sneakin' out to be together almost as soon as she got into town."

Mrs. Jeffries's head was spinning. So much information. But did any of it have to do with Hannah Cameron's murder? She simply didn't know. Tonight, as soon as the others left and she could have some time alone in her room, she'd try putting the pieces together to see if any of them fit. "Goodness, you've all found out quite a bit today. Does anyone else have something to contribute?"

"I'm finished," Mrs. Goodge mumbled. She was a bit annoyed that everyone else seemed to have stolen her thunder.

"Madam's told you our news," Hatchet said, "except for one thing." He went on to tell them about Goff's certainty that the burglary at the Cameron house wasn't the work of professionals. Not that anyone was surprised.

"In that case," Mrs. Jeffries said a few moments later, "why don't we see what we can find out tomorrow? Everyone meet back here after supper and we'll see if we've learned any more."

Betsy pulled her heavy cloak tighter, stepped down off the train and onto the platform at Tunbridge Wells. She patted her pocket to make sure the small black purse containing her money was still safely on her person. She wasn't sure how far the Hadleigh house was from the station, and it was good to have money in any case. She swallowed nervously as she realized how far from home she was. A lot of people, one person in particular, would probably be a tad annoyed with her for taking off before breakfast and going off alone. But she was determined to learn what she could. Was it her fault that Fiona Hadleigh lived in Tunbridge Wells and not in London?

The platform had cleared of people and she noticed the conductor staring at her. Clutching her ticket, she hurried toward the small waiting room. Stepping inside, she looked around and spotted the schedule on the far wall next to the door. Betsy dashed over, checked the times of the afternoon trains and smiled. She wouldn't have to rush. There was a late afternoon train at four that would get her back to London before anyone even knew she was gone.

But it took her more than two hours to find the Hadleigh house. It was, indeed, out in the country. Betsy took refuge in a copse of trees directly across the road from the residence.

Betsy wearily leaned up against a trunk and stared at the large, red brick house through a pair of ugly, black wrought iron gates. The house sat well back from the road. A broad lawn enclosed completely by a high stone fence surrounded the place.

Now that she was here, she wasn't quite sure what to do. This wasn't like London. She glanced at the road. There weren't any houses or other buildings, only a small, narrow, unpaved lane leading toward the town. She looked back at the house. From here, it appeared to be empty. The place was deadly silent and there was no smoke coming from any of the chimneys. Where was everyone? There ought to be groundsmen and gardeners and people moving curtains as they dusted and cleaned. But she hadn't so much as seen a tradesman go up through the gates.

Supposedly, Brian Cameron had brought his children here to stay. But if they were here, she thought dismally, they were kept inside. Probably to keep from freezing to death, she thought morosely. Her feet were so cold she could hardly feel them.

A huge bank of clouds seemed to appear from nowhere, blocking the pale wintry sun. "Blast," she muttered aloud, "it'll probably be pouring soon. This turned out to be a silly idea."

But Betsy wasn't about to give up. Not yet, anyway. She'd come all this way and she was determined that the journey shouldn't be wasted. She kept to her shelter for more than two hours but she saw nothing. She was just about to give up and go back into town when a wagon, loaded with boxes and trunks, pulled around from the back of the house. Curious, she stepped closer. The wagon drew up to the gates and a young man nimbly jumped down, opened the gate and led the horses through.

Betsy knew this was her only chance. She waited till he was closing the gates and had his back to her before dashing out into the road. Taking a deep breath, she started back toward town, taking care to limp slightly as she walked.

Her ruse worked. Five minutes later, she was sitting next to the driver, a nice lad named Michael Hicks.

"It's ever so nice of you to give me a lift," she gushed. "I can't think what happened. I guess the agency must have made a mistake."

"Lucky for you I happened along," Michael Hicks replied. He was a slender young man with dark hair, a narrow face and deep set hazel eyes. He looked about twenty.

"Or you'd have been bangin' on that front door for hours," he continued. "The rest of the staff left this mornin' for London. Only reason I didn't go was because Mrs. Hadleigh needed me to bring her trunks into town."

Betsy smiled charmingly. "Well, I'm going to have a harsh word for the agency. Imagine sending me all the way to Tunbridge Wells to look after two children that aren't even there."

He clucked at the horses. "You lookin' for a position as governess, then?"

"Oh, yes," she replied brightly. "According to the agency, I was to interview with your Mrs. Hadleigh for the position." She crossed her fingers and hoped that her fibs in the course of justice wouldn't do anyone else any harm.

Michael Hicks looked confused. "That's funny. They've already got a governess. Nice young lady she is too." But then his expression cleared and he laughed. "Mind you, no doubt her nibs will send her packin' as soon as she and Mr. Cameron are married. I can't see Mrs. Hadleigh wantin' a pretty lass like that Ellingsley girl about the place. That's probably why you've had a wild goose chase." He snorted in derision. "Just like her to jump the gun and have you come all the way out here for nothing."

Betsy felt like she'd found pure gold. "I was told the lady of the house was a widow and that there were two children."

"She is, but not for long." He shook his head, his expression disgusted. "And there are two little ones, but they're not hers."

"What? Not her children?"

"They're not here anymore, either," he said. "They went back to London early this morning with their father."

"I don't understand." Betsy frequently found that playing stupid got her lots of information. "The agency specifically said I was to come and interview for a position as a governess. But if she doesn't have any children . . ." she let her voice trail off in confusion.

"Mrs. Hadleigh was only takin' care of the children for a few days. There was a tragedy in the family. Mind you, that won't stop her from usin' it to her own advantage." He clucked at the horses again. "Humph. She already has. Already rented a big house right in the same block as Mr.

Cameron's. Don't know how she found the time, what with the funeral and all. But I'll say one thing for the woman—she knows what she wants and don't let no grass grow under her feet while she's gettin' it. She's probably plannin' on bein' Mrs. Cameron before that other poor woman is cold in her grave."

"Gracious," Betsy cried, "this sounds most curious. Who, pray tell, is being buried?"

"Mrs. Cameron," he replied, giving her a quick, sympathetic look. "The mother of the two children. Well, she was actually their stepmother. She was stabbed to death a few nights back.

"How dreadful." Betsy was glad she'd gotten the East End out of her voice and learned the proper way of speaking from Mrs. Jeffries. She could tell that he believed her story, unlikely as it was. "Someone was killed? Perhaps it is best that I was unable to interview for a position. Though, I must say, it's very inconvenient having come out all this way."

"Better a bit of inconvenience than a blade in yer back," he said darkly. Then he shook his head quickly. "Forget I said that. It's no business of mine what the gentry get up to."

She didn't want him to dry up now. "Oh, please, Mr. Hicks," she implored, "do tell me what you know. I must report this to the agency. If something is amiss with this household, I can't let them send some other poor girl for the position. The agency is most respectable. They'll not like any of this. No, indeed they will not." She crossed her fingers, hoping he would rise to the bait.

"You can call me Michael," he said, giving her a quick grin. "And as you've come all this way, I reckon you do have a right to know what's what."

"Oh, thank you." She gave him her most dazzling smile. "Now, why don't you start at the beginning. I'm really most confused, and you do have such a nice way of speaking."

"He's well liked in the area," Blimpey Groggins declared. "I'll give 'im that much. Don't charge those that can't pay and won't turn anyone away."

Smythe nodded. He and Blimpey were standing on the steps of the Mile End Chapel staring at a run down building opposite them. The offices of one Dr. Connor Reese were on the ground floor of the structure, which was right next to a police station. The building leaned slightly to one side, the bricks were old and discolored and the neighborhood was rough. "'Ow's 'e pay his expenses, then?" Smythe asked. "Not many round these parts can afford to pay."

"But there's some that can," Blimpey said. "Not everyone in the East End is skint, you know. Plenty of shopkeepers and such that have a few bob to spare. But like I said, no one would say a word against the man. He's well liked. There's more than a few about this neighborhood that owe the man their lives. I also heard that Reese coulda worked in a practise over on Harley Street, but he chose to come work in this neighborhood. Good thing too. Not many want to take care of people over here."

"Yeah," Smythe muttered. "That's the truth. Any idea why Reese hated his cousin?"

Blimpey laughed. "Is that all ya want to know, then?"

"I want to know everything," Smythe replied. He watched a blond haired young woman come out of the doctor's front door. She clutched her shawl tightly about her thin shoulders and braced herself against the cold air. He felt sorry for the girl; she was thin and pale. But in her hand he noticed she had a brown bottle. Medicine, probably. Maybe it would do her good. It flashed through his mind that had fate not intervened, Betsy could well be the young woman leaving the doctor's office. He thanked his lucky stars she wasn't. If she had been, he'd never have met her. Then he wondered, for the hundredth time, where she'd gone off to so early this morning. She'd already left when he came down to breakfast. He didn't like it. Much as he respected her independence, he didn't like her goin' off without a word to anyone.

"The family used to be quite friendly, seein' each other at holidays and the like," Blimpey began. "But then Reese's father and Hannah Cameron's mother were killed in a carriage accident and some property that should have been Reese's unexpectedly went to Hannah Cameron. There was some kinda dispute about the death."

"What do ya mean? Dispute? They was either dead or they wasn't."

"Nah." Blimpey wrinkled his nose. "It weren't like that. It were somethin' to do with the time . . . Who died first and what have you. I'm checkin' into it, but sussin' out somethin' like that's not so easy. Anyways, when Reese's mother tried to take the Cameron woman to court, sayin' that there was somethin' funny about the whole thing, that the property belonged to her son, Hannah started a lot of vicious talk about the woman . . . and this was before the case was even heard." Blimpey stepped further back into the shadowed eaves of the chapel as a policeman from the station across the road stepped outside.

"Mrs. Reese was of a high-strung nature, and when the gossip and such started—and right old rotten gossip it was too," he continued, still keeping an eagle eye on the copper, "she started takin' laudanum for her nerves. A week or so before the case was to be heard, she took too much of it and died. The case was dismissed and Hannah inherited the lot."

"Why didn't the son fight fer the inheritance?" Smythe grinned as Blimpey flattened himself against the wall of the Chapel as the policeman sauntered past.

"He'd just gone away to Edinburgh, to school." Blimpey breathed a loud sigh of relief as the peeler turned the corner and disappeared. "He probably didn't have the lolly. Ruddy soliciters don't work fer free. Ask me, I've paid enough of 'em in my time."

"Do ya 'appen to know what property was in dispute?" Smythe asked. He'd heard about Hannah Cameron's wealth, about the trust set up when her own father died. But that had been eight years ago, before she married Brian Cameron.

"A couple of pieces of property over on the docks," Blimpey replied. "I can get ya the addresses if ya want me to."

"I do." He was curious now. Really curious. That property was also a bone of contention between the victim and her half brother, John. Smythe was becoming increasingly certain that Hannah Cameron was killed because she owned those buildings.

"Fair enough," Blimpey said. "I can get that information fer ya by tonight."

"Can ya get it any sooner?" Maybe he ought to take a quick run over there and have a look at them.

Blimpey looked surprised. "I can do it now, if ya want."

"Good." Smythe gave him a cocky grin. "As a matter of fact, if ya don't mind, I'll come with ya."

"It's gettin' a bit late, isn't it?" Smythe drummed his fingers on the table and tried not to look at the clock for the hundredth time. "Betsy shoulda been back by now."

"I'm sure she'll be here any moment," Mrs. Jeffries replied, but she too was concerned. "She's rarely, if ever, late for the evening meal."

"Should I go ahead and serve?" Mrs. Goodge asked. "I've already taken Aunt Elberta her dinner on a tray. She regrets she'll be unable to eat with us, but she's too tired." She grinned. "Effie took her to Kew Gardens today. Poor old woman's dead on her feet. She's going right to bed as soon as she eats."

"Why don't we wait just a few more minutes?" Mrs. Jeffries replied. "The inspector's gone over to Lady Cannonberry's and Luty and Hatchet aren't due for another hour."

"Maybe I ought to go out and look for her," Smythe said. Blast, he was goin' to give her the sharp edge of his tongue when she came home. What was she thinkin', worryin' him like this?

"Where would you go lookin'?" Wiggins asked. "She never said where she were goin'"

Smythe glared at him, not liking the reminder that she was out there with night comin' and not one of them knew where she was.

"She'll be here any moment now," Mrs. Jeffries said. "I'm sure of it."

"Sorry I'm late," Betsy called as she came in the back door and rushed into the kitchen. She skidded to a halt, her smile evaporating as she came face to face with Smythe. He towered over her, his hands on his hips and his face set in a scowl that could strip the polish off the floor. "But it really couldn't be helped."

CHAPTER 9

Betsy swallowed nervously. Smythe looked ready to spit nails. She knew she was a bit late, but she'd figured that the gossip she'd gotten out of Michael Hicks was worth it. Now she wasn't so sure. "Uh, listen," she began, but he cut her off.

"No, you listen," Smythe said, trying hard to keep a lid on his temper. "It's dark. You didn't tell anyone where the blazes you was goin', and you've been gone since before breakfast. We've been worried sick, lass. Remember how it felt when you was worried about Wiggins?"

"But that was different," she protested. "He didn't get home till after midnight."

"It isn't different, Betsy," Mrs. Jeffries said firmly. "We've all been just as concerned about you. Mainly because you left so early and said nothing as to your plans."

In fact, no one but Smythe had really been too anxious, but the housekeeper had decided to intervene to keep this incident from becoming a fullout spat between the two of them. The last thing the household needed was Betsy and Smythe feuding.

"But you're home now," she continued briskly. "Safe and sound. So let's have our meal and by then, Luty and Hatchet will be here and we can all share what we've learned today."

"That's a good idea," Betsy said as she scurried past Smythe, who was still scowling like a fiend. She took off her coat and hat and quickly took her place at the table.

"Let's talk about something other than the case," Mrs. Jeffries said. "Give ourselves a bit of break from thinking about it all the time. How are the preparations for Inspector Witherspoon's dinner party coming along?" she asked the cook.

Mrs. Goodge looked unconcerned. "It's done. The meat's been ordered and the fishmonger's getting us a nice bit of haddock for the evening."

"The silver's polished and all the linens have been pressed," Betsy put in.

"And I've dusted out them dining room curtains all right and proper," Wiggins added. "And washed the windows inside and out. Seems to me the only fly in our ointment is the inspector's cousin bein' one of the guests."

"She'll only be here for few hours," Mrs. Jeffries said matter-of-factly, "and considering she's only in London to buy her wedding clothes, I don't think she'll be all that interested in us." She sincerely hoped that Edwina Livingston-Graves wouldn't take it into her head to stay for a visit. That would be most unfortunate.

"Let's hope not," Mrs. Goodge said fervently. "Don't relish the thought of her hanging about the place. I don't care if she is the inspector's relation; she's more trouble than she's worth. Most inconvenient woman, she is."

"What did you say?" Mrs. Jeffries asked, putting down her fork.

"I just said she's a most inconvenient woman," Mrs. Goodge repeated, "and I was bein' kind by just callin' her 'inconvenient' and not a few other names I could think of if I wasn't so polite. Why? Is it important?"

The cook's statement niggled something at the back of Mrs. Jeffries's mind, but before she could grasp the notion and wring any sense out it, it was gone. She shook her head. "No, it's nothing," she said, reaching for her fork and slicing a bite off her roast potatoes. But she promised herself she'd think about it later. Tonight, when she was alone.

They finished eating quickly and cleared up. The last of the dishes had just been put into the drying rack when they heard the distinctive sound of the carriage pulling up outside. A few moments later, Luty and Hatchet were sitting at the table with the others.

"I hope you all have somethin' decent to report," Luty began testily. She shot her butler a disgruntled look. "Because I ain't found out nothin'"

"I have something to report." Hatchet smiled smugly.

"Only because you snuck out before I was up this mornin'," she charged.

"He weren't the only one sneakin' out at the crack of dawn." Smythe shot Betsy an evil look. He still wasn't ready to forgive her for causing a few more gray hairs in his head.

"I found out a few things," Wiggins said cheerfully. "And if it's all the same to the rest of ya, I'd like to go first."

"By all means," Mrs. Jeffries said.

"Well, I 'ad another chat with Helen today . . ."

"Another one," Smythe interrupted. "Cor blimey, Wiggins, unless the girl's dafter than a mad dog, she'll know you're up to something if you keep after 'er."

"She likes me," he said defensively. "And she's not mad. Besides, ya told me to keep an eye on Brian Cameron, but 'e don't go nowhere. All 'e does is stay in that 'ouse with that Mrs. Hadleigh fussin' all over 'im. It's not my fault that Helen's the only one I can get at, and what's more, she trusts me. She told me somethin' today she's afraid to tell the police."

Mrs. Jeffries leaned forward eagerly. "What did she tell you?"

"It were somethin' about John Ripton," he said slowly. "Accordin' to Helen, 'e didn't go right up to 'is room when 'e said 'e did. She says she knows 'cause she saw 'im comin' upstairs right before all the shoutin' started."

"Why didn't she tell Inspector Witherspoon?" Betsy demanded.

"Where was she when she saw Ripton?" Smythe challenged. "I thought everyone except Mrs. Cameron's maid 'ad gone to their rooms."

"She were peekin' down the back stairs," Wiggins stated, "and she didn't tell the inspector because she was afraid 'e'd give 'er away to the Camerons and she were scared of losin' 'er position. But she saw Ripton, saw 'im plain as day. Helen 'ad just reached the landing to the third floor, when she 'eard 'is footsteps comin' up the front stairs. You can see the front stairs if you go to the bottom of the servants stairs and peek around the corner. She did and she saw Ripton comin' up as plain as day."

"Why would she be frightened of losing her position?" Hatchet asked. "For goodness' sakes, the Cameron house isn't a prison. People are allowed out of their rooms, I presume."

"But it is a bit like bein' in stir," Wiggins protested. "And she were scared to say anything 'cause she didn't want anyone knowin' what she was doin' roamin' about the house that time of night."

"And what was she doing?" Betsy asked suspiciously.

"She were hungry," he explained. "The other girl she shared the room with 'ad gone to sleep and so she went down to the kitchen to pinch a bit of food. All she took was a sausage and a bit of bread. But she were afraid that if she said anythin' and the Camerons found out, they'd think she was a thief and toss 'er out on 'er ear."

Mrs. Jeffries considered this new information carefully. "Was she absolutely sure about who it was she saw coming up the front stairs?" she asked.

"She saw Ripton as plain as day," he replied.

"Ripton does have a good motive," Hatchet added. "That property he inherited on the Commercial Docks is going to be redeveloped. Now he can sell it and make an enormous profit."

"How the blazes do you know that?" Luty yelped.

"My sources, madam, aren't all former convicts." He sniffed disdainfully. "Some of them are quite informed about the financial community."

"Former convicts?" Wiggins looked at Hatchet with disbelief. "You? You know someone who's done time?"

Hatchet realized that everyone was staring at him. "It's not quite what you think," he sputtered.

"Oh, fiddlesticks, Hatchet." Luty waved dismissively. "Don't get yer trousers in a twist. It ain't no crime to know someone who's been in jail. But we ain't got time to discuss it now." She turned to the housekeeper. "What are we gonna do now? Seems to me that Ripton's got to go to the top of our suspect list."

"I agree," Mrs. Jeffries replied. "We know that Ripton needed money now. That's why he'd asked his sister for a loan."

"But she was goin' to loan him the money," Betsy charged. "So why would he kill her? Even if he does inherit that property, if it were cash he needed, and he needed it quick, he'd have to wait for all the legal things to be over. I mean, even when you inherit, it takes a bit of time to get things sorted out. You don't just get the deed to a piece of property the next morning."

"I think 'e was scared she'd changed her mind," Wiggins said. "Remember 'ow she acted when they was all at dinner? She were right upset with him because 'e kept badgerin' her to sell to 'im. Maybe he figured she'd changed her mind about loanin' the money, so 'e decided to do 'er in instead and get what was 'is once and for all."

Mrs. Jeffries thought about that. Wiggins did have a point. From what the inspector had said about the victim's behaviour on the night of the murder, she could well have changed her mind. The problem was, they simply didn't know. "Whether she changed her mind or not is unknown," she said, "but it's important that we figure out a way to get Helen to tell the inspector that she saw John Ripton coming up the stairs that night. If, indeed, she saw him right before 'all the commotion,' then there is a possibility he's the killer. In any case, he can't be counted out."

"'Ow we gonna do that?" the footman asked. "I don't think Helen's goin' to be too eager to say anythin'"

But Mrs. Jeffries already had an idea. "Wiggins, go up to the inspector's study. You'll find his timetable on his desk. Bring it down and bring down the bottle of India ink and his pen."

"Back in a tick." The footman dashed off. Fred, who was bored, followed right at his heels.

"What are you plannin' on doin?" Smythe asked her.

"I'm not sure," she said. "It will depend."

Wiggins was true to his word and returned a moment later, the requisite items clutched in his hand. He sat them down in front of Mrs. Jeffries. "'Ere you are. They was right where you said they'd be."

No one said anything as Mrs. Jeffries studied the sheet in front of her. She ran her finger down one column while scanning the top with her gaze. "Yes, here it is—Helen. And here's the square for eleven forty-five. We're in luck. It's empty. She claims to have been asleep since half past nine. Now, let's look at the same time square for Ripton. Ah, as I thought, he claimed to have been in his room."

She looked up and smiled. "Is anyone here any good at copying?"

"'Ow do ya mean, Mrs. J.?" Smythe asked curiously. He thought he knew what she wanted from them. "If ya mean what I think ya do, it's a bit risky."

"It's very risky," she agreed, "but we've really no choice. Not if we're to give the inspector the means to bring the murderer to justice."

"I don't see what Mrs. Jeffries is up to," Wiggins cried.

"It's very simple, Wiggins," Mrs. Jeffries replied. She tapped the empty square under Helen's name. "We've got to fill in this space."

Hatchet leaned over and stared hard at the paper. "The inspector's handwriting is very distinct. It might be difficult to duplicate it."

"Someone's got to try," the housekeeper persisted.

"Excuse me," Mrs. Goodge said, "but like Wiggins, I don't understand what's going on."

"Well," Mrs. Jeffries said hesitantly, "the only way to get this information to the inspector is to let him know what Helen saw, or in this case, what she heard. If instead of leaving that square blank because the girl was sleeping, we can fill in the square with something like 'heard footsteps/ front stairs.' That will get the inspector to thinking. Especially when I point it out to him. Because we've only written that she 'heard footsteps,' hopefully the inspector will start asking more questions. At that point, Helen might own up to what she actually saw that night."

"Won't he remember that he didn't fill it in himself?" Betsy asked.

"That's the risk we're takin'," Smythe said, "but I think it's worth takin'. Remember, the inspector got tossed off the case before 'e 'ad much of chance to really examine his timetable."

"That's what I'm counting on." Mrs. Jeffries smiled brightly. "Who wants to have a go at it?"

"Not me," Wiggins declined. "Me 'andwritin's not anythin' like 'is."

"Don't look at me," Smythe echoed. "You can barely read my writin'"

Betsy stared at the small, elegant handwriting of her employer and shook her head, as did Mrs. Goodge.

"I know I can't do it," Luty declared.

"If I must," Mrs. Jeffries said hesitantly, "I suppose I can try . . ."

"That won't be necessary." Hatchet picked up the pen and reached for the bottle of ink. Mrs. Jeffries quickly shoved the paper over to him. Opening the ink carefully, he dipped the pen in, gave it a slight shake as he lifted it out and then looked at the housekeeper. "Shall I write 'heard footsteps/front stairs'?"

"That will do nicely."

They watched in fascinated silence as he slowly, carefully began to write. When he was finished, he leaned back, stared at his handiwork for a moment and then smiled. "I think this ought to do it," he said, shoving the paper out to the middle of the table where everyone could see it.

"Oh, it's ever so like the inspector's," Betsy crooned.

"Cor blimey, Hatchet, you're ruddy good at this," Smythe agreed.

"Excellent work," Mrs. Jeffries murmured. "Really excellent."

"Nells Bells, Hatchet," Luty cried. "Did ya use to work for a forger?"

Mrs. Jeffries closed the door of her room softly. Pulling her shawl tighter, she turned down the light and went to sit in her chair by the window. Sitting quietly in the darkened room, staring out at the sleeping city, helped her to think. Tonight, she thought, she had much to think about.

They had so much information. Unfortunately, their meeting had been cut short by Aunt Elberta coming into the kitchen in search of a cup of cocoa. But they had had time to hear most of the important news. Betsy had told them that she'd found out that Fiona Hadleigh had rented a house

on the same block as the Cameron house. Apparently, the woman had told
her personal maid that this time she wasn't going to sit back and wait for
Cameron to get over his grief. Fiona Hadleigh was bound and determined
to marry the man. Mrs. Jeffries wondered how badly Mrs. Hadleigh
wanted him. Badly enough to kill? Betsy had been a bit reticent about
where she'd come by her information and it was only the arrival of Aunt
Elberta that had kept Smythe's questions in check. But was Betsy's news
anything more than Fiona Hadleigh's "jumping the gun," as it were? Or
was it a motive for murder?

The only facts Betsy really had were that the woman was moving into
a rented house close to the Cameron house and that if Hannah Cameron
had not come along right after Cameron's first wife died, he would have
married Mrs. Hadleigh.

Mrs. Jeffries shifted in her chair and stared out at the quiet street. A
pale yellow fog had drifted in and now wafted eerily among the gas lamps.
She thought about Smythe's report on Connor Reese. Like the coachman,
she found herself hoping that Reese wasn't the killer. She rather liked the
good doctor herself. Anyone who worked among the poor and destitute
of the East End had her admiration. She shook her head, cautioning herself
against prejudgment. Reese had a strong motive to kill Hannah Cameron.
He hated her and blamed her for his own mother's death. Furthermore,
he'd been in the house that night. Reese could easily have slipped the knife
into the victim's back and then slipped out the front door. But Cameron
claimed the front door was locked and bolted until his butler had raised
the alarm. So how did Reese get out? She sighed. There was only one logi-
cal answer to that question. Reese must have had help. Namely, Kathryn
Ellingsley. She lived in the house. That night, she assumed that everyone
was asleep. She could easily have unbolted a door and slipped her lover
out. Add to that the fact that Reese was a doctor and would therefore have
no trouble knowing the precise spot to stab someone in order to perforate
her heart. Death had been instantaneous. The killer had either been very
lucky or very knowledgeable. Dr. Reese might have been both.

But Mrs. Jeffries didn't like that idea either. It didn't really make sense.
Why would the governess help commit murder? Kathryn Ellingsley knew
that Hannah Cameron was going to try and trap her that night. That's
why she didn't go out in the first place. Instead, Reese came in. Surely,
then, if she was frightened of losing her position . . . Mrs. Jeffries went
still as another thought occurred to her. Why would Kathryn Ellingsley

be frightened? If the Camerons sacked her, she could always go back to her uncle in Yorkshire. Or could she?

Mrs. Jeffries stood up. Gracious, she'd been such a fool. Two different pieces of the puzzle tumbled into her mind. Neville Parrington and a stolen box of papers.

She walked over and lit the small lamp she kept on her desk. Sitting down, she pulled open a drawer, drew out her writing paper and picked up her pen. When she'd finished, she looked at the short message and nodded in satisfaction. Tomorrow morning, she'd send this by telegram to her old friend Constable Trent in York. If anyone could find the answer to her questions and find them quickly, it would be him.

Inspector Witherspoon stared at his fried eggs and bacon with something less than his usual enthusiasm. Being taken off the case had quite lost him his appetite.

"Would you like tea, sir?" Mrs. Jeffries asked cheerfully.

"Yes, thank you," he mumbled.

"Here you are, sir," she said, placing his tea next to his plate. "I'm delighted you're taking the time to eat a proper breakfast this morning. It's quite cold outside and I know you've a lot to do today."

Witherspoon looked at her over the rim of his spectacles. "A lot to do today?" he echoed.

"Why, yes, sir." She smiled brightly and drew his timetable out of her pocket. Unfolding the paper, she put it down next to his teacup. "I hope you don't mind, sir, but I was quite curious about this . . ."

"I've been taken off the case, Mrs. Jeffries," he said wearily.

"I know that, sir," she said crisply, "but just because you've been taken off the case doesn't mean you've stopped being a brilliant detective and a true agent of justice in this great land of ours." She watched him carefully as she spoke, hoping her words would perk him up a bit.

He straightened his spine and lifted his chin. She noted that his expression was no longer glum. Instead, he looked puzzled. "I'm afraid I don't follow you." He gave her a brief smile and then slumped back down in the chair. "But thank you for your kind words."

"I'm sorry, sir." She sighed dramatically. "Perhaps I've overstepped my bounds. I shouldn't bother you with this." She started to reach for the paper but he shot back up and snatched it up himself.

"Bother me with what?" he asked, his attention now on the timetable.

She knew she had to be careful here. Their dear Inspector, despite seeming to be a bit muddled at times, wasn't a fool. "Well, sir, I was so very curious, you see. So when I was dusting your desk, sir, I happened to glance at it . . . and well, I must say I was quite astounded. Absolutely flabber-gasted, to tell you the truth."

"Flabbergasted? About what?"

"About your plan, sir. Your timetable." She walked over to stand by his chair. "It worked. You did find something. That's what made me so curious. I don't quite understand why Chief Inspector Barrows took you off the case. It seems to me, sir, he ought to be thanking his lucky stars that he had you on the hunt, so to speak. If not for your magnificient efforts, a grave miscarriage of justice could happen."

Witherspoon squinted at the paper. "Er, thank you, Mrs. Jeffries, but I don't quite see what you're getting at."

"You don't?" She contrived to sound confused. "But right here, sir." She pointed to the square that Hatchet had altered. "Look. Eleven forty-five . . ."

"Oh yes, I see now," Witherspoon interrupted. "Gracious, I don't remember this. How odd. 'Heard footsteps/front stairs'—that was reported by the maid, Helen." He shook his head. "Honestly, I don't remember writing that down, and you're right, of course—it's quite pertinent. Quite pertinent, indeed. That's the precise time, according to my calculations on the timetable, that the killer would have been moving about the house."

"I know sir," Mrs. Jeffries said enthusiastically. "And I shouldn't worry about not remembering writing it, sir. I'm sure your inner voice prompted you to do it almost by rote. You know how you are, sir. When you're on a case, your instincts take over, so to speak. Besides, sir, you've been under a great deal of strain since your discussion with Chief Inspector Barrows. It's no wonder that a few things have slipped your mind."

Witherspoon nodded vigorously. "You're absolutely right, Mrs. Jeffries. I must pursue this. I'll go and see the Chief Inspector straight away . . ."

"But sir," she interrupted quickly. "Wouldn't it be easier for you to just go and see this maid"—she made a great show of peeking at the timetable again—"Helen. Wouldn't it be far easier politically to do your investigation on the . . . oh dear, what's the right word to describe this situation?"

"Sly?"

"No, no, sir," she replied. "You're far too honorable a man for that. What I was trying to say was perhaps it would be best to be a bit discreet. Until you have some real evidence, that is."

He looked doubtful. "But this is real evidence," he said. "But perhaps you're right. The situation is delicate." He sighed deeply. "Politics, Mrs. Jeffries. I must be careful here. I don't wish to go against my superiors. But in this case, I've a feeling they are terribly, terribly wrong. Perhaps a bit of discretion wouldn't be amiss. Perhaps I'll just nip out and get Constable Barnes and we'll see what we can find out without stepping on anyone's toes or upsetting any applecarts."

"Do finish your breakfast before you go," she said happily. "I believe you'll need your strength."

"Want me to go with ya?" Wiggins asked Helen as he held open the back garden gate for the maid.

"How'd you know I'd be comin' out?" Helen asked. But she was smiling.

He grinned. "I figured 'e'd be sendin' you out with another telegram today."

"Right you are, you cheeky lad." She laughed and linked her arm with his as they started up the street. "Where's Fred?"

"I left 'im 'ome today," he admitted. Fred had stared at him mournfully when Wiggins had left that morning. But it had been ever so early and he'd not wanted to take the dog with him when he went to the post office to send that telegram for Mrs. Jeffries. He didn't reckon the post office much liked dogs. "You seem ever so much 'appier today. 'Ow come?"

Helen laughed again and then sobered. "I shouldn't be laughin', not really. But the truth is, that household is a lot happier now that her nibs is dead. I know it sounds wicked. I mean, she were stabbed and no one ought to die like that. But she were a right old mean hag and that's the truth. Ever since she's been dead, everyone's breathin' a right sight easier. Especially the governess." She giggled. "She can see her young man now without sneakin' about like a thief in the night. Not that she was foolin' anyone . . . We all knew she was sneakin' out to see that Dr. Reese."

Wiggins looked at her. "You mean all the servants knew?"

She shook her head. "Not just us. Mr. Cameron knew too. He's known for months, since right after Miss Ellingsley come to work there."

"'Ow do you know that?" Wiggins wasn't sure this was important, but it might be.

"'Cause I saw 'em," she declared.

"You saw 'em? 'Ow?"

"What do you mean, 'ow? With me eyes." Helen gave him a sharp look. "You don't believe me?"

"'Course I do," he soothed. "I'm just curious, that's all."

She stared at him as though debating whether or not to take offense. Then she shrugged. "Well, if you must know . . ."

"I must, I must. I love the way ya tell things. So much more interestin' than when I try and tell somethin'. Go on, what 'appened, then?"

"Well." She smiled happily. "It were one night just a few weeks after Miss Ellingsley come there. She's ever such a nice one, she is. Not at all stuckup or mean like Mrs. Cameron, despite bein' one of the gentry herself."

"And what 'appened?" he prodded.

"It were one night late like, and . . . uh . . . well, I got a bit hungry . . ."

"That's all right, Helen," Wiggins said kindly. "Don't be embarrassed. I've been 'ungry myself a few times."

"Yeah, I expect you have." She sighed and closed her eyes briefly, then continued. "But like I was sayin', I got hungry and the girl I share with always sleeps like the dead, so I slipped down to the kitchen. Mrs. Cameron was always so stingy with how much we could eat, ya see, and I'd not had much so as soon as Hazel were asleep, I slipped down to the kitchen and got a bit of bread and cold sausage. I'd just nipped back upstairs when I heard footsteps comin' up the stairs behind me. I run lickety split right up to the top landin' and then I nipped in behind the post and stuck me head round to see who it was. I couldn't think who it were and I were scared to death it were Mrs. Cameron. But it weren't. It were Kathryn Ellingsley. I watched her slip up the back stairs and then go on down the hall to her room on the second floor. Below me, then just as she disappeared, I heard more footsteps and it were Mr. Cameron. He were followin' Miss Ellingsley. I stood there, my knees shakin', hopin' he didn't look up and catch me peekin' out from behind that top post, but he didn't. He just stood there staring in the direction where she'd gone, a funny little smile on his face. A few days later, I found out from one of the other servants that Kathryn was sneakin' out at night to meet that nice Dr. Reese."

"You like Dr. Reese, then?" Wiggins asked. He found her story quite startling.

"Oh, yes, he's ever so nice. He treated Hazel for bronchitis, you know. Didn't charge her, neither." Helen made a face. "She was ever so sick, she was, and that bloody Mrs. Cameron was goin' to sack her. But Miss Ellingsley slipped Dr. Reese in one night when the Camerons were out with that stupid Hadleigh woman, and he give her some medicine. Hazel were right as rain in a few days."

They'd come to the entrance of the post office. Wiggins opened the door for Helen. "Allow me," he said, bowing gallantly. He really did like this girl. He hoped he could still see her once this case was over.

"Thank you." She smiled happily and stepped inside. "I'll only be a minute. It's only Mr. Cameron's telegram up to Yorkshire to see how his old uncle's gettin' on. Won't take more than a few moments. Are you goin' to wait fer me?"

"Right 'ere," he replied. "I've time to walk ya back."

Walking her back would give him a chance to see what, if anything, he could find out about Brian Cameron. He thought it awfully strange that the man knew a woman in his household was slipping out regularly and did nothing to stop it. It didn't seem right, somehow.

Constable Barnes lived in a neat little house on Brook Street near the Hammersmith Bridge. Witherspoon knocked softly on the pristine white door, hoping the constable hadn't already left for the station.

He wasn't sure he was doing the right thing, but he didn't honestly see that he had any choice. His inner voice had told him all along that this wasn't a burglary. But on the other hand, he knew he was taking a great risk by disobeying a direct order to stay off the case. It was a risk he was prepared to take, but did he have the right to involve Constable Barnes? Barnes didn't have a fortune and a big house. Barnes lived on his policeman's salary. Furthermore, he had a wife to support. Witherspoon had just about talked himself into leaving when the door flew open.

"Goodness, Inspector," Barnes said in surprise. "I didn't expect to see you." He was in his shirt-sleeves and braces.

"Oh, well," Witherspoon muttered. "I didn't really expect to be here."

"Come in, sir." He ushered the inspector inside and closed the door. "Would you like a cup of tea? The wife and I are just havin' breakfast."

Witherspoon opened his mouth to answer, to say that he was sorry to have bothered the good constable, that it was all a mistake, when before he could get a word out, a woman's voice came from the room at the end of the hall. "Who is it, dear?"

"It's Inspector Witherspoon, lovey," Barnes replied, gesturing at the inspector to proceed him. "Come to have a cuppa with us."

"Oh, dear," Witherspoon murmured. "I didn't mean to interrupt your breakfast."

"Not to worry, sir." Barnes chuckled. "You didn't and we've plenty of tea."

They entered a small, cheerful room with white walls adorned with shelves of knickknacks and china, a tiny fireplace and bright yellow-and-white lace curtains at the windows. An oak sideboard sat against the wall, and a round table, covered in a white lace tablecloth and set for breakfast, was square in the middle of the room. A woman with gray hair neatly tucked up in a bun and enormous blue eyes smiled up at him. "Do sit down, Inspector," she said, patting the empty chair next to her. "I'm Adelaide Barnes."

He bowed formally. "It's very nice to meet you, Mrs. Barnes. Do forgive me for interrupting your meal."

"We were just finishing, sir. Have a sit down and I'll pour you some tea. Then you two can have a nice natter about this murder you've been working on."

She got up, went to the sideboard and took out a pink-and-white flowered china cup and matching saucer, then poured the tea.

Not knowing what else to do, the inspector sat down. "Er, your house is very nice, Mrs. Barnes."

"Thank you, sir." She put his tea down in front of him. "Would you like some toast?"

"No, thank you, I've eaten."

"Good." She smiled at her husband. "A man needs a decent breakfast. That's what I always tell my husband. Sometimes he rushes off with nothing more in his stomach than a bite of bread."

"Now Addie." Barnes chuckled. "I've only done that a time or two. I like my food as well as the next man."

"That's a time or two too many," she countered. "I know your work is important, but so is your health. Isn't it, Inspector?"

"Uh, well, yes, of course." Witherspoon smiled warily. "I expect it's been my fault that Constable Barnes occasionally misses a meal. I do sometimes drag him off at the oddest times."

Adelaide Barnes laughed. "And are you here to drag him off again this morning?"

"Er, yes," the inspector admitted.

She turned to her husband, a triumphant gleam in her eyes. "It looks like I've won this wager, now, doesn't it? I told you he'd be round."

Barnes laughed. "That you have, Addie, and come Saturday night, I'll pay up fair and square."

"You told your husband I'd be round?" the inspector repeated. "But how could you possibly know that?"

"How could I not know it?" she said as she reached for her husband's empty plate. "Alfred's told me all about you."

"All about me?" The inspector wasn't certain whether he should be complimented or insulted.

"He's only said nice things, sir," she said. She stacked her own plate on top of her husband's. "That's how I knew you'd be round. I knew you'd not give up on this murder. I told him you'd be here by noon today. I was right, wasn't I, Alfred?"

"Yes, dear." Barnes sighed. "You're always right."

CHAPTER 10

Inspector Witherspoon struggled mightily with his conscience as they approached the Cameron house. Despite Constable Barnes's assurances that he was quite willing to come along and do his bit in the interest of justice, the inspector couldn't stop thinking about whether this action could damage Barnes.

They reached the front of the house. Witherspoon took a deep breath and turned to Barnes. "Constable, I think you ought to reconsider going in with me. I don't wish to put you in an awkward position. Inspector Nivens may come along at any moment and I don't want him getting you into trouble because we've disobeyed an order."

"No, we haven't, sir," Barnes said calmly. "We was told that Nivens was now in charge of the case. But if I recall, sir, the Chief Inspector himself said we was welcome to help. Seems to me, sir, that's what we're doin'. Helpin' a bit. That's all. Come along now, sir, you've a few questions to ask." Not giving the inspector time to argue the point, he turned on his heel and marched to the front door.

Witherspoon had no choice but to follow.

Hatfield, the butler, let them in, sniffed in disapproval and escorted them into the drawing room. "If you'll wait here," he said, "I'll see if Mr. Cameron is available to see you." He left them standing awkwardly by the settee.

"Do you think we ought to sit down, sir?" Barnes asked. "It might look a sight better, make him think we've a perfect right to be back here if Inspector Nivens . . ." His voice trailed off as they heard footsteps approaching.

Kathryn Ellingsley, a book in her hand, stepped inside. She started nervously when she saw the two policemen. "Oh, I didn't know anyone was here." Her tone was flustered and she didn't look well. There were dark circles under her eyes and her fair skin was pale.

"We've come to ask a few more questions, Miss Ellingsley," Witherspoon smiled briefly. "We're waiting for Mr. Cameron."

"He's in the study," she said, edging back toward the door, "I'll just get him for you."

"That won't be necessary." Witherspoon wondered what on earth was wrong with the girl. She looked like she wanted to bolt. "The butler's gone for him. We're sorry to interrupt him while he's working . . ."

"He's not working," she said quickly, nervously. "Oh, do forgive me, Inspector. I'm not myself today. We've had more bad news. My uncle in Yorkshire has taken a turn for the worse."

"I'm so sorry to hear that," the inspector said sympathetically. "Especially at what must already be a most upsetting time for both you and Mr. Cameron."

She seemed to relax. "Thank you, sir. You're most kind. It's difficult for Brian, of course, considering what's happened recently, but he was never as close to Uncle Neville as I was. I lived with him before I came to London. To be perfectly frank, I'm very concerned, though Brian tells me I'm making too much of it. But Uncle Neville's not a young man."

"You wanted to see me, Inspector?" Brian Cameron strode into the room.

"Yes, I'm so sorry to intrude. Miss Ellingsley has just told me about your concern over your uncle."

Brian smiled at Kathryn. "I've just sent a telegram, dear. They'll let us know straight away if you need to go up to him."

"But Brian, I really think I ought to go . . ."

"Nonsense," Cameron said briskly. "Neville's going to be all right. He's a tough old bird. Besides, my dear, you really must have a bit of a rest before you go up to do sick-room duty. You've had quite a trying time lately. We all have." He turned his attention to the inspector. "Thank you for your concern, Inspector, but I'm sure it's a bit of a tempest in a teapot. As I've told Kathryn, our uncle is quite a sturdy fellow for his years. He's only got a touch of bronchitis. Now, what can I do for you?"

"We'd like to have a word with one of your staff," he replied. "The maid, Helen."

Cameron nodded. "Kathryn, could you run along and get the girl, please? Ask her to step in here."

As soon as she'd gone, Cameron asked, "Would you mind telling us why you want to speak to her? I was under the impression that your Inspector Nivens was out there trying to find a burglar."

Witherspoon was prepared for this question. He'd thought about it all morning. He only hoped his answer made sense to anyone other than himself. "You're correct, sir. Inspector Nivens is doing just that. The constable and I are only helping to tidy a few things up. We have reason to believe that the maid may have heard someone that night but was too frightened to say anything."

Cameron raised his eyebrows. "Why on earth would one of the servants be frightened?"

"She's scared they'll be back," Barnes said calmly, before the inspector could say anything. "It's a common enough reaction," he continued. "A murder's been done and young women get frightened. Sometimes they think it's safest not to say too much. So don't be hard on the girl, Mr. Cameron."

"Brian, what on earth are these policemen doing here?" Fiona Hadleigh, her face set in an unflattering scowl, stormed into the room. "I thought we were done with all this. Honestly, are we to have no peace here at all? First Kathryn insists on talking to that wretched Mr. Drummond, though why she feels it's necessary for a young woman her age to trouble him about her will, I'll never know. Then you shut yourself up in your study all morning . . ."

"Don't upset yourself, Fiona," he interrupted, reaching over and patting her on the arm. "Everything will be fine. There's nothing wrong."

"Then why are they here?" she pointed in the direction of Witherspoon and Barnes. "I'll not have you tied up all day answering their stupid questions. You promised to accompany me to Regent Street this morning . . ."

"It's all right, dear," he soothed, giving Witherspoon an imploring look for understanding. "They're only doing their job. They've just a couple of things to clear up with one of the servants and then they'll be on their way."

"I should hope so." She sniffed. "We've enough bother here as it is without having policemen under foot all day. I do want your opinion on those curtains I'm thinking of getting for my drawing room."

"Mrs. Hadleigh," Barnes asked suddenly, "now that you're here, there's a question I'd like to ask you."

"Again?"

"Yes, ma'am," Barnes answered as he dug out his notebook. He flipped it open and leafed through the pages. The inspector wondered what he was up to.

"Ah, here it is," the constable said. He glanced up at Mrs. Hadleigh. "In your statement, you said you went up to bed at eleven thirty. Is that correct?"

"As well as I can remember, it was about then." She didn't sound quite so haughty now. "Why?"

"And when you retired, did you read or write a letter perhaps?" he prodded.

Fiona's brows drew together. "That's most impertinent, but if you must know, I got ready for bed."

"I see," Barnes said. He flipped a page over. "According to both Mr. Cameron's and Mr. Ripton's statements, they retired at little past eleven thirty."

"What are you getting at, Constable?" Cameron interrupted.

Witherspoon wondered the same thing, but he trusted that Barnes knew what he was doing.

Unruffled, Barnes merely said, "Just tryin' to get a few facts straightened out, sir. You and Mr. Ripton did go up a little past eleven thirty, right?"

Cameron nodded.

"And both of you said that Mrs. Cameron and Mrs. Hadleigh had retired a few minutes earlier. Would it be fair to say they went upstairs at eleven twenty-five?"

"All right, Constable, so we went up to bed at eleven twenty-five," Fiona said curtly. "What of it?"

"Actually, dear." Brian smiled at her fondly. "It was closer to eleven-fifteen when you and Hannah retired."

"Eleven-fifteen," Barnes mused. "Mrs. Hadleigh, my question is this: if you'd gone up to bed at eleven-fifteen and gotten ready to go to sleep, then why were you fully dressed, still in your evening clothes, when the body was discovered a good forty minutes later."

"Are ya sure I said that?" Helen peered closely at the timetable, her pretty face confused. "I don't remember tellin' ya that."

"But I'm sure you did," Witherspoon insisted. Actually, he wasn't, but he thought his inner voice must have had some reason for prompting him to fill in the square. "Are you saying you didn't hear anyone on the front stairs?"

Helen licked her lips and shot a quick glance at the open drawing room door. "No, not exactly. I mean, I did hear someone."

Witherspoon beamed at her approvingly. "Excellent, excellent. I was sure you had."

"I did, but ya see, I didn't exactly hear footsteps . . . but . . . uh . . . well—" She broke off, her face an agony of indecision.

Wisely, the inspector decided not to interrupt this time. He simply looked at her.

Finally, she took a deep breath. "It were a bit more than just hearin' someone, sir," she blurted. "I saw 'im as well."

Witherspoon's spirits soared. His inner voice was right. "Who did you see?" he prompted gently.

"It were Mr. Ripton, sir," she whispered. "I saw him comin' up the front stairs. It were dead on eleven-forty-five too. I know 'cause I looked at the clock in the kitchen when I left to come upstairs."

"Why didn't you tell us this when we spoke to you before?" Barnes asked.

Helen looked down at the carpet. "I guess I was scared, sir. I didn't want anyone to know what I was doin'. You know, roamin' about the house that time of night."

"Exactly what were you doing, Helen?" Witherspoon asked.

Helen twisted her hands together. "Do I have to tell?"

"We can't force you to tell us anything," the inspector said gently, "but I think it would be best if you did."

Helen swallowed heavily. "I were ever so hungry, sir, and so when I thought everyone was asleep, I went down to the kitchen to get something to eat. I only took a bit of bread and sausage. Please don't tell on me, sir. I'll not do it again."

Witherspoon and Barnes exchanged glances. After what they'd seen of this household, neither of them could really blame the girl for holding her tongue.

"We won't say a word," the inspector assured her. "It's no crime to be hungry. Were you afraid you'd be sacked if Mrs. Cameron knew you were taking food?"

She nodded. "Then after I heard she was dead, I was scared someone might think I 'ad somethin' to do with killin' her. I mean, I wasn't in me room when she were gettin' murdered."

"We don't think anything of the sort," Witherspoon said honestly. Of all the people who disliked the late Mrs. Cameron, this frightened girl was one of the least likely people to have killed the woman. "Is there anything else you'd like to tell us?"

"No, sir, that's the only unusual thing that happened. May I go now?"

"Yes, Helen, and thank you for your help."

Hatfield materialized in the doorway as the girl was leaving. "Mr. Cameron would like to see you," he told her.

Helen's eyes got as big as saucers. "He wants to see me?"

"Right now," Hatfield replied. "He's in the study."

The girl, her face paling, nodded and hurried out.

Barnes and Witherspoon exchanged glances and then, without speaking, took off right behind her. Both men feared the same thing, that the butler had run tattling to Cameron about the girl taking food. She was probably going to get the sack.

"He only wants her to take a telegram for him," Hatfield said, stopping both of them in their tracks. "She's not in any trouble."

Witherspoon turned and stared at the butler. His thin face was creased in worry and his shoulders slumped dejectedly. "We're not monsters, you know," he said. "I'd not let the girl lose her position for taking a little food."

"Then you were listening?" Witherspoon charged gently. "You overheard what she told us."

He nodded. "I did. I was curious because you wanted to speak to her." He cleared his throat. "I know I shouldn't have eavesdropped, but some of us here don't like the way this whole situation's been handled. Mrs. Cameron wasn't killed by any burglar, despite what that other policeman says."

"I see," the inspector replied. He was a bit puzzled. He didn't know whether he ought to press the man for more information or not. "Did you hear everything she told us?"

"Yes, sir. But if you're thinking that Mr. Ripton stayed downstairs that night to murder his sister, you're mistaken."

"Mistaken?"

Hatfield shook his head vehemently. "He did come back downstairs. I've no doubt of that, sir. But that was only so he could pinch the rest of the port, sir. I ought to know; the bottle was missing the next day. I found the empty in Mr. Ripton's room."

"You're saying that Ripton stole a bottle of port?" Witherspoon couldn't believe it.

"Oh, yes, sir. He does it every time he stays the night."

"Telegram, Mrs. Jeffries." Mrs. Goodge eagerly handed the housekeeper the small envelope. "You was out when it come so I took it."

"I hope it's a reply from Yorkshire," Mrs. Jeffries said. She ripped the small brown envelope open and pulled out the thin paper. "It is my reply," she said cheerfully. "I do hope it helps clarify things a bit."

But the message really didn't clarify anything.

Parrington in poor health but no sign of foul play. Large estate. Heir is his niece, Kathryn Ellingsley. Hope this helpful.

"What's it mean, then?" asked Mrs. Goodge, who was reading over her shoulder.

"I'm not sure, Mrs. Goodge," she admitted. "I quite expected a different answer."

"What were you expecting?" the cook asked curiously.

"To be frank, I was actually thinking that Brian Cameron would be the heir, not Kathryn Ellingsley. I mean, Hannah Cameron's murder would make sense if he were expecting to inherit a fortune from a dying uncle. But as it is . . . " She shook her head, unwilling to say more until she'd had time to think the situation through. She'd obviously made a grave mistake in her reasoning. But she'd been so sure, so very sure. Part of her still was. It was the only thing that made sense. She tucked the telegram in her pocket and started for the coatrack. Taking down her bonnet, she slipped it on and then grabbed her coat.

"Where are you off to, then?" the cook asked. Her curiosity overcame her desire to have her kitchen empty in case one of her sources came by.

"To the post office," Mrs. Jeffries declared. "To send another telegram."

"What do you make of Mrs. Hadleigh's statement?" Barnes asked the inspector as they went down the hall to the front door.

"I suppose she could be telling the truth," Witherspoon replied. "Some people are very devout. But I personally don't think the Almighty cares whether one says one's nightly prayers fully dressed or in one's nightclothes."

Barnes snorted. "I can't see that one down on bended knees in an evening dress for a good halfhour, sir," he said. "She just doesn't strike me as bein' that religious a woman."

But that's precisely what she'd claimed to be doing from the time she went to her room until she heard the commotion downstairs. Praying. With all her clothes on. She'd told them quite haughtily that she didn't think it proper to pray in one's night-clothes.

Like the constable, Witherspoon found it difficult to believe, but even with his timetable, he'd no evidence to dispute her.

They'd reached the front door when the subject of their conversation suddenly stopped them in their tracks.

"I'd like a word with you, if you please," Fiona Hadleigh demanded. Witherspoon dropped his hand from the doorknob and turned. "Yes, Mrs. Hadleigh," he said politely. "What can I do for you."

"There's something you ought to know," she said as she stalked toward them. "It's about Kathryn."

"Miss Ellingsley?" Witherspoon said. "What about her?"

"She isn't quite what she appears to be," she replied. She stopped directly in front of them and took a deep breath. "Brian didn't want me to mention it, but I feel it's my duty . . ."

"Oh, for God's sake, Fiona." Brian Cameron's voice thundered down the hall. "Leave it alone. Kathryn's my cousin. She's family. I'll not have you telling tales to all and sundry about her."

"I'm sorry it displeases you, Brian." Fiona's cheeks turned red. "But it really is our duty to tell the police everything."

"Kathryn has nothing to do with any of this."

"But we don't know that," Fiona insisted. "Hannah was murdered."

"She was killed by a burglar," Cameron shot back. He glared at his guest, his eyes glittering with rage. "And I'll thank you to mind your own business . . ."

"Excuse me." Witherspoon thought he ought to take control of the situation. "But why don't we all sit down and sort this out."

"There's nothing to sort out," Cameron snapped. "Fiona doesn't know what she's talking about."

"I most certainly do," Fiona charged. She lifted her chin and looked at Witherspoon. "Kathryn Ellingsley has been slipping out of the house at night to meet her paramour. Furthermore, she always went out through the small sitting room. The one Hannah was murdered in."

Inspector Witherspoon's head was spinning by the time he got home that evening. He hung up his coat and hat and started down the hall to the drawing room just as Mrs. Jeffries came up the back stairs.

"Good evening, sir," she said cheerfully.

"Good evening, Mrs. Jeffries. I do believe I'll have a sherry before dinner. It's been a most extraordinary day."

She followed him into the drawing room and went right to the cupboard. Pulling out a bottle of Harvey's she poured him a glass and took it over. Sitting it down next to him, she said, "Extraordinary, you say. Well, sir, I'll venture to guess that your continued investigation has been successful."

Witherspoon reached for his drink, took a sip and sighed happily. "I think you may be right, but it's all a bit muddled so far." He'd learned far more than he expected today, but he wasn't quite sure what it all meant.

"Not to worry, sir." She plopped down in the chair opposite him and settled herself comfortably. "You'll sort everything out in no time. You always do. Now, sir, tell me all about it."

At the meeting that night, Mrs. Jeffries didn't waste any time. Before anyone else could start, she told them everything she'd learned from the inspector. She was glad she'd found out such a wealth of information from him. None of the others had found out a thing.

"I still don't think Ripton ought to be let off the hook just because of what the butler says," Luty complained. "Seems to me he's doin' quite nicely now that his sister's dead."

"We're not letting him off the hook," Mrs. Jeffries replied. "But the inspector felt that Hatfield had no reason to lie for John Ripton."

"Well, at least the inspector knows about Kathryn Ellingsley slippin' out of the 'ouse now," Wiggins put in.

"But Kathryn hadn't slipped out that night," Betsy said. "She'd let Dr. Reese in. Seems to me we ought to be thinking of a way to let the inspector know about that."

"I don't think 'e's a killer," Wiggins said defensively. "The only motive 'e's got is that 'e 'ated 'is cousin. But it weren't nothin' new. 'E'd 'ated the woman for years. Why would 'e take it into 'is 'ead to kill that night?"

"He could have done it to protect Kathryn," Hatchet suggested.

Wiggins stubbornly shook his head. "If she sacked Kathryn, Dr. Reese woulda gotten what 'e wanted. 'E'd have just married the girl. Seems to me, that 'e 'ad less of a reason for wantin' the Cameron woman dead than any of 'em."

"Well, I agree with Betsy. It was downright mean of that Hadleigh woman to tattle on her the way she did," Luty declared. "Hate tattlers. Always did. It's obvious she's tryin' to make the girl look bad. How the dickens did she find out about Kathryn slippin' out anyway?"

"Probably from one of the other servants," Hatchet ventured.

"I don't think so," Mrs. Jeffries replied. "I think the ones that knew Kathryn's secret kept it to themselves. Remember, Kathryn had slipped Dr. Reese into the house one other time when one of the maids was ill. His care kept that girl from being sacked. No, I think Mrs. Hadleigh found out accidentally. Perhaps from Brian Cameron."

"Funny, isn't it?" Betsy said. "But everyone in that house except Hannah Cameron knew about Kathryn. She didn't find out until right before she was killed."

"I think Mrs. Hadleigh did it," Mrs. Goodge declared. "She's the one that's really benefitting. She'll finally get her hooks into Brian Cameron, though why the woman wants the man, I'll never know. And that silly excuse she gave the inspector for being fully dressed.." She *harrumphed* indignantly. "Praying, indeed. Twaddle, that is. The Archbishop of Canterbury doesn't stay on his knees for that long in prayer. Especially not on a cold, hard floor."

"I still think we ought to keep an eye on Ripton," Smythe mused. "It don't take more than a minute or two to pinch a bottle. What was 'e doin' downstairs that whole time?"

"Maybe he wasn't," Luty said. "Maybe he went upstairs with Brian Cameron, waited till he thought the coast was clear and then went back down to get his liquor."

As the others argued and debated, Mrs. Jeffries let her mind drift. Suddenly, something Betsy said a few moments ago popped into her head. She looked at the maid. "What did you just say about Hannah and Kathryn?"

"Me?" Betsy looked at her in surprise. "I just said that everyone but

Hannah Cameron knew about Kathryn slipping out at night. Why? Is it important?"

"Yes, yes, I think it could be," Mrs. Jeffries replied. She didn't quite see how that piece of the puzzle fit, but she was suddenly certain that it was very important. She hoped the telegram she'd sent might give her an answer, but it would only if her basic assumption was correct. Was she right? That was the question. But there was another avenue of inquiry she could take. It was dangerous, but it might provide the one piece of evidence she needed.

She realized that all of them were looking at her expectantly. "Hatchet," she said. "Are you dreadfully tired?"

Hatchet, to his credit, didn't so much as raise an eyebrow at the odd question. "Not at all, Mrs. Jeffries. Why? Is there something I need to do tonight?"

She hesitated. What she was going to request was totally wrong. Practically immoral. Patently illegal. But it might be the only way to catch the killer. She had to know this information. It was imperative and impossible at the same time. If she could have found a way to have the inspector get it, she would have. But there simply wasn't enough evidence for him to seek a search warrant.

Yet she couldn't bring herself to put someone else in harm's way. If this was going to be done, she'd do it herself. "No," she replied as she got to her feet, "there's nothing you need to do. I'm going to do it."

Alarmed, Smythe got up. "What are you up to, Mrs. J.?"

"Nothing, Smythe," she replied airily. "Besides, the less you know about it, the better you'll be. But if I could trouble you to call me a hansom . . ."

"If you need to go out tonight," he interrupted, "you'll be takin' me with ya. You're up to somethin'"

"And me." Hatchet rose as well. "Whatever you're planning, you'll have to let us in on it."

Luty leapt to her feet. "Is it dangerous? I'll go home and git my gun. Oh, lordy, I can tell, this is goin' to be fun."

"You'll not be leaving me here, either," Betsy declared. "Whatever it is you're planning, I'm going to be right there."

Exasperated, Mrs. Jeffries didn't know whether to laugh or to box their collective ears. "I'm trying to protect you all," she cried. "For goodness' sakes, I could be absolutely, positively wrong about this whole matter."

"I don't care if you is wrong," Wiggins said staunchly. "You ain't get-tin' outta this 'ouse tonight without me and Fred."

Fred, upon hearing his name, jumped up from his warm spot by the stove and dashed over to the table. He bounced excitedly at Wiggins's feet, hoping everyone getting up meant he was going to go out.

"Where are you planning on going, Mrs. Jeffries?" Hatchet asked calmly. "And more importantly, what do you want us to do?"

She had two choices. Either let them in on her scheme or give it up altogether. But if she did that, a murderer might go free. More important, if she was right, someone else—someone innocent—might die. She stood there for a moment in indecision.

"I'm not sure precisely where the place is," she replied. "But I think it should be quite simple to find that information."

"What information?" Smythe pressed.

"The address of a solicitor," she replied. "You see, it's quite imperative that I have a look at someone's will."

In the end, it was Hatchet and Smythe who went. Armed with various small kitchen utensils, a pocket knife, and Inspector Witherspoon's old policeman's lantern, they went out into the night with assurances to the ladies that they'd be fine.

Luty, Mrs. Goodge, Betsy, Wiggins and Mrs. Jeffries prepared to wait.

Mrs. Goodge put on the kettle and got out her knitting.

Wiggins got his pen and paper and set to work writing a poem for Helen.

Luty pulled out a pack of playing cards and started playing Patience.

Mrs. Jeffries went up to her room to have a nice long think and Betsy began to pace.

"This is it," Hatchet murmured. He glanced over his shoulder at Smythe. They were in the back of a block of offices on Connaught Street. The alley was quiet; the area was deserted at this time of night. Hatchet reached for the door handle, gave it a turn and wasn't in the least surprised to find the thing locked solid. "It's locked."

But Smythe wasn't listening. He was standing on an overturned wooden crate he'd found and had a wicked-looking knife out. He was busy prying open a smallish window on the far side of the door. "This is'n," he muttered, "but it'll be a tight job for us to get through it. It's right small, but I think we can manage."

Hatchet looked doubtful.

"Ah, there she goes," Smythe murmured as he wedged the bottom of the window open far enough to get his fingers under. With a grunt, he shoved it all the way up, tossed Hatchet a quick grin and then shoved his head inside.

Hatchet watched in amazement as the rest of the big man followed. He heard a loud thump.

"Are you all right?" Hatchet whispered.

"Yeah. I landed on me 'ead. It's a bit of a drop. Do you think you can make it through?"

"I'll give it try," he replied. He stepped up on the box, grasped the side of the window and emulated Smythe by just diving straight in, putting his arms straight out in front of him as soon as his torso had cleared the frame.

He was saved from a nasty bump on the head by Smythe, who grabbed him before his forehead connected solidly with the floor.

Getting up, Hatchet brushed his coat off.

Smythe was already moving down the hall. He'd switched the lantern on and was shining the dim light on the doors as he walked. Hatchet hurried to catch up with him.

"This is it." Smythe stopped and handed the lantern to Hatchet. "'old this." He pulled his pocket knife out, eased it between the lock and the door and then applied pressure. There was a faint click as the lock disengaged.

Impressed, Hatchet asked, "Where did you learn to do that?"

"Picked it up 'ere and there." Smythe shrugged. "Not much to it, really. Wouldn't work on a decent lock. Lucky for us this 'ere's a cheap one. You ready?"

"As ready as I'll ever be." Hatchet took a deep breath, thanked his lucky stars there wasn't a night watchman in this building and opened the door.

"What's takin' them so long?" Betsy wailed. "They've been gone for hours."

"They've only been gone for two and a half hours," Mrs. Jeffries assured her. "And I'm sure they're just fine."

"But what if they got caught?" she moaned.

Mrs. Jeffries was thinking the same thing. They'd be ruined. All of them. And it would all be her fault.

"They ain't gonna get caught," Luty said. "Hatchet's too smart and fer that matter, so is that feller of yours."

"Mine?" Betsy stopped pacing and stared at Luty. "What are you talking about?"

Luty chuckled. "We ain't blind, ya know. Everyone can see you two are sweet on each other. 'Course he's not much to look at . . ."

"I think he's fine to look at," Betsy said indignantly. "His appearance isn't ordinary, but I think he's quite handsome."

"You think Smythe is 'andsome?" Wiggins exclaimed. "Our Smythe?"

"Yes, our Smythe," Betsy shot back. "And furthermore, if you repeat one word of this to him, I'll have your guts for garters."

From the flaming red in her cheeks and the glint in her eyes, Wiggins was sure she meant what she said. "I can keep a secret," he retorted. "I've kept 'em for Smythe often enough. You should ask me what 'e says about you."

"What does he say?" she demanded.

Wiggins grinned. "Can't tell ya. It's a secret."

Mrs. Jeffries smiled at Luty, grateful the woman had distracted everyone with her remarks. Luty winked at her.

They continued the vigil.

Mrs. Goodge yawned. Wiggins scribbled. Luty played another hand of Patience and Betsy continued to pace. Mrs. Jeffries's thoughts swirled around the case. What if she was wrong? What if Smythe and Hatchet got caught?

The clock had just struck the half hour when they heard the back door open. Betsy almost cried in relief when the two men, grinning like they'd just conquered a mountain came into the kitchen.

"Did you have any difficulties?" Mrs. Jeffries asked anxiously.

"Not a one, madam," Hatchet said. "No one will even know we were ever there." That wasn't quite the truth. Someone might notice the scratches on the window, but he didn't think it likely.

"You were right, Mrs. Jeffries," Smythe said as they all took their seats at the table. "She did have a will. Lucky for us she'd seen her solicitor recently too. It were right on 'is desk."

"Unfortunately, we did waste some time looking for the wretched thing in the file cabinets," Hatchet added. "Until I suggested we have a look at Drummond's desk."

"I'd a sussed that out eventually," Smythe told him testily.

"Were you able to determine who her heir is?" Mrs. Jeffries said quickly. She crossed her fingers. The suspense was killing her. "Is it Brian Cameron?"

Smythe looked Hatchet, waited for him to nod and then said. "Sorry to disappoint ya, Mrs. J., but you were off the mark with that one."

She stared at him in disbelief. She simply couldn't believe it. "Are you certain?" she whispered.

"Quite sure," Hatchet said. "The will is very simple. I'm sorry to say the heir is Connor Reese. On her death, everything goes to him."

CHAPTER 11

Mrs. Jeffries didn't sleep well. How could she? She'd been wrong. Dreadfully so. She got up the next morning grumpy and still angry at herself for being so foolish as to think that only her solution was the right one. She'd put Hatchet and Smythe in terrible danger and she wasn't going to forgive herself easily.

But as she puttered about the drawing room, halfheartedly running a feather duster over the mantel, she couldn't help thinking that she couldn't have been that wrong. She was sure she knew who murdered Hannah Cameron. She sighed as she glanced at the clock, wondering if the inspector was having a better day than she was.

He'd been so excited by his discoveries yesterday that he'd not even had a proper breakfast this morning. He'd just grabbed a slice of toast and dashed off.

Her shoulders slumped and she put the duster down on the table. In a short while, she'd have to tell the others. Admitting she was wrong wasn't going to be pleasant, but she owed them the truth. Luckily, it had been so late last night when Hatchet and Smythe had returned, she'd been able to get everyone to hold their questions until today. They were due to meet back here at four for tea. Everyone, except herself, was out snooping about, doing their very best to bring this case to a just conclusion. She sighed again and shook her head. Too bad she hadn't a clue about how to go about it.

"Dr. Reese," Witherspoon said, "we're sorry to bother you, but we've a few questions to ask."

"Can you be quick about it?" Reese looked pointedly at his waiting room, which, as the inspector and Barnes knew because they'd come in that way, was filled with patients wanting to see the doctor. "Some of those people out there are very ill. I don't like to keep them waiting."

They were in the doctor's surgery—in his examination room to be precise. It was quite small. There was a privacy screen in one corner. A table covered with a clean linen cloth stood in the center of the room and beyond that was a desk beside a glass cupboard filled with medical texts. Next to the door was a cupboard and a sink. The room smelled heavily of disinfectant. But despite its size, the inspector was quite impressed. The surgery was obviously clean and well equipped. Not really what one would expect for an East End practise.

"We won't keep you long, sir," Witherspoon assured him. "Uh, this is a bit awkward, Doctor, but can you tell me where you were on the night your cousin was murdered?"

Reese hung his coat in the cupboard and pulled out a clean, white apron. He slipped it over his head. He looked surprised, but not unduly alarmed by the question. "May I ask why you want to know?"

"We've had it on good authority that you're . . . uh . . . er . . ."

"You're courting Miss Ellingsley." Constable Barnes took pity on Witherspoon and interrupted. "We've heard that she's been sneakin' out at night to see you. Is this true?"

"It is," Reese replied. He walked over to the table, pulled a drawer open and began taking instruments out. "I imagine you know all about Kathryn and I. Otherwise you wouldn't be here."

Witherspoon nodded.

"I imagine you also know that I loathed my cousin," he continued. "But I've loathed her for years. I'd hardly bother to murder her now."

"Nevertheless, she was murdered," Barnes said.

"Kathryn and I had nothing to do with Hannah's death," Dr. Reese stated flatly.

"But it was because of Mrs. Cameron that you had to sneak about to see each other," Barnes charged. "Seems to me that gives you a bit of a motive, sir."

"Hannah tried to make it impossible for us to see one another," he said curtly. "But that didn't stop us. We started meeting secretly. That was Kathryn's idea. I wanted her to marry me. But Kathryn felt she should stay on at the Cameron house for awhile longer for the children's sake. She was hoping that Brian would send them away to boarding school next term."

"Even the little girl?" Witherspoon asked. He thought eight years old was quite young to send a child away from her home.

"Ellen would be better off at school than she was living with that woman," he said disgustedly. "But that's not the issue, is it? I'm just explaining why we met secretly. Why Kathryn didn't just chuck the position and marry me. She's devoted to those children."

Witherspoon wondered how a devoted governess could sneak out and leave her charges unattended. "Wasn't she worried about the children when she slipped off to be with you? I mean, what if one of them woke up and needed her?"

"Ellen and Edward sleep very well," he replied, going to the sink and turning on the water. He picked up a bar of carbolic soap and started scrubbing his hands. "They never wake up. But please don't think Kathryn is in any way negligent. Hazel, one of the housemaids, would slip up and stay in Kathryn's room by the nursery. The children were always well looked after."

"How often did you and Miss Ellingsley see one another?" Witherspoon asked. He had no idea what prompted the question, but he felt he ought to ask something. He was rather surprised by the doctor's candor. He'd expected the man to hem and haw and deny everything.

"Not often enough to suit me." Reese dried his hands. "Look, Inspector. Kathryn and I are going to be married. I'll not have you thinking she's loose or doesn't have the highest of morals. When we did manage to see one another, all we ever did was walk and talk."

"You're engaged?" Witherspoon asked. That probably wasn't pertinent either, but it never hurt to ask.

"Yes." Reese sighed. "We were going to announce it last week, but then Kathryn's uncle took ill and she didn't want to announce our engagement publicly till she told him privately. Now, if there's nothing else, I've a room full of patients."

"You haven't answered the question, sir," Barnes reminded him. "Where were you on the night that your cousin was murdered?"

Reese smiled. "I think you already know the answer to that question. I was visiting Kathryn. Only this time, instead of her slipping out to meet me, she'd let me into the house."

• • •

"This come for ya, Mrs. Jeffries," Wiggins said as he came into the kitchen. He handed her a small brown envelope, the twin to one the housekeeper had received yesterday.

"Thank you, Wiggins," Mrs. Jeffries replied. She dreaded this meeting. She wasn't sure what to say. One part of her was still convinced she had to be correct.

"Been a lot of telegrams today," Wiggins continued cheerfully. "Helen was tellin' me that Kathryn Ellingsley's 'ad one as well. 'Ers was bad news, though. Her uncle's not expected to last through the night."

"Who's not going to last?" Aunt Elberta, wrapped in her coat and hat, thumped into the kitchen and headed purposely toward the table. "Thought I'd find the lot of you here," she continued, not waiting for an answer to her question. "Can't see how you get any work done. Every time I come in here you're sittin' around drinking tea."

"Aunt Elberta," Mrs. Goodge cried in alarm. "What are you doing here? You're supposed to be at the British Museum with Effie!"

She waved her hand dismissively. "Got boring, that did. Told Effie to bring me home." She stopped beside the cook. "I'm tired. That girl's dragged me all over London."

"Would you care for a cup of tea?" Mrs. Jeffries asked.

Aunt Elberta shook her head. "No, I'm going to go lay down for a bit. I just come in to let you know I'll be goin' home tomorrow."

"But I thought you were staying the week," the cook said.

"Changed my mind," Aunt Elberta replied with a yawn. "No offense meant, but I've decided I'm too old for sightseein'" She smiled wearily. "Now, if you don't mind, I'll go have a nap before I start my packing."

"Really." Mrs. Goodge sniffed as soon as the woman left the room. "This is a bit of a surprise. She seems quite anxious to leave."

"Not to worry, Mrs. Goodge," Mrs. Jeffries said. "I think she's had a nice visit. But when a person gets to be your aunt's age, they like their own home."

"At least Effie'll stop complainin' about havin' to ride herd on the woman," Luty commented. Then she looked at the envelope in the house-keeper's hand. "Well? Ain't ya gonna open it?"

"Oh, yes, of course." Mrs. Jeffries smiled bravely and tore the ruddy thing open, though she didn't expect that this answer would be much better than the one she'd had last night. She pulled the paper out and stared at the brief message.

"Who's it from?" Betsy asked curiously.

"Constable Trent," Mrs. Jeffries murmured. Her mind was racing with questions. "He's a family friend. He used to work with my late husband."

"What's it say, then?" Luty demanded.

But Mrs. Jeffries paid no attention to her friend. Instead, she looked at Wiggins. "You say Kathryn Ellingsley got a message that her uncle isn't expected to last through the night?"

"Right," Wiggins said. "She and Mr. Cameron are fixin' to go to Yorkshire tonight. They're leavin' for the station in a bit. Helen told me the 'ouse was in an uproar, that Mrs. Hadleigh were 'avin' fits about 'im goin' off with Miss Ellingsley . . ."

"Do you know what time?" Mrs. Jeffries interrupted. "Think, Wiggins. It's very important. A life might depend on it."

Wiggin's gaped at her for a moment. "I think Helen said they was leavin' on the six o'clock train. But truth to tell, Mrs. Jeffries, I really wasn't payin' all that much attention. Helen does rattle on a bit and I was more concerned with gettin' back 'ere on time than listenin' to 'er."

"What's goin' on, Mrs. J.?" Smythe asked.

"Get the horse and carriage," she told him. "Get back here as quickly as you can."

She knew the answer now. But unless they moved quickly, someone else was going to die.

Smythe didn't question her. He leapt to his feet and bolted for the back door. "I'll be back in 'alf an 'our," he promised.

"Thank goodness the inspector is upstairs," Mrs. Jeffries muttered. "At least now I won't have to track him down. Wiggins, run upstairs and get my notepaper. Hurry, and don't let the inspector see you."

Sensing her urgency, he nodded and moved quickly to do her bidding.

"Hatchet," Mrs. Jeffries said, "I'm going to need your services again. I want you to write a note, and here's precisely what I want it to say. We'll have to move quickly and we'll have to take some risks. If we don't, an innocent person is going to die tonight."

• • •

"Do you know, Mrs. Jeffries, he admitted it straight out," Witherspoon told his housekeeper. "Dr. Reese made no pretenses whatsoever. He said he was in love with the girl and he was going to marry her. They were going to announce their engagement last week, but then her uncle became ill so they postponed it."

Mrs. Jeffries was only half listening. Her eye was on the clock and her head was cocked toward the front door. Two minutes to go. Then Wiggins would pound on the knocker and run for all he was worth. She crossed her fingers, hoping that none of their neighbors would see the lad and mention it to the inspector later.

"At least Dr. Reese didn't lie to you, sir."

There was a loud pounding on the front door. Mrs. Jeffries leapt to her feet. "I'll get it sir." Wiggins was a bit premature, but it really didn't matter.

She flew down the hall, threw open the door and blinked in surprise. "Hello? Can I help you?"

The tall, white-haired man inclined his head slightly. "My name is Bartholomew Pike and I'd like to see Mr. Smythe if he's available."

"He's not," she said quickly, wanting to get rid of him. "But I'll be happy to tell him you called around."

He frowned in disappointment. "Please ask him to contact me immediately. The matter is most urgent."

Mrs. Jeffries saw Wiggins hotfooting it down the street towards the front door. "I'll do that, Mr. Pike."

He nodded brusquely, turned and left, passing Wiggins as the lad dashed up the stairs. Mrs. Jeffries snatched the note out of his hand and hurried back into the house.

"Who was it?" the inspector asked.

"I don't know, sir." Mrs. Jeffries took a long, calming breath. "But it was a gentleman, sir. He didn't give his name but he did ask me to give you this." She handed the inspector the note and watched while he unfolded it.

Witherspoon's mouth opened as he read. "Gracious! Mrs. Jeffries, what sort of man was it who gave you this?"

"He looked like a gentleman, sir. Quite respectable, really. Why, sir? What's wrong?"

Witherspoon waved the note in the air. "This note says that if I don't get to the Cameron house immediately, Kathryn Ellingsley will die."

"Then you'd better go, hadn't you?" She was itching to grab his coat and hat for him, but held herself in check. It wouldn't do to look too anxious.

"But what if it's someone's idea of a joke?"

"I shouldn't think the man who brought it was playing a joke, sir. He looked as somber as a banker. Perhaps, sir, you'd best go. Isn't it lucky that Smythe just happened to pick today to give the horses a good run? He's got the carriage right outside."

"I do hope this isn't someone's idea of a prank," the inspector muttered as he climbed out of the elaborate carriage in front of the Cameron house. Wiggins held the door open for him. Fred, who'd jumped into the carriage before anyone could stop him jumped down and began to prance excitedly at the footman's feet.

A hundred feet up the road, a hansom had stopped in the middle of the street and was picking up a man and a woman. Witherspoon started for the front door.

"Excuse me, sir," Wiggins hissed, "but isn't that Mr. Cameron and Miss Ellingsley getting into that cab?"

The inspector squinted through his spectacles. Night had fallen and he couldn't see very well. The man was helping the woman inside. "I do believe you're right, Wiggins. I say." Witherspoon raised his voice. "Mr. Cameron, we need to have a word with you."

Cameron looked back at them and then quickly jumped into the cab and slammed the door. "Drive on," he cried. The hansom took off.

"Well, really," Witherspoon snapped. "I know the fellow heard me. This is terrible. I've got the most dreadful feeling about this . . ."

But Wiggins wasn't listening. He was bolting after the cab. The inspector watched in stunned amazement as his footman nimbly grabbed the back of the thing and leapt on.

Fred, barking his head off, took off after his beloved friend.

"Get in, sir," Smythe shouted. "We'll catch them up."

They raced after the hansom, thundering through the streets at a breakneck pace. Witherspoon, his head stuck out the window, kept his eye on the running dog as they careened around a corner and into the heavy traffic of Park Lane. But a heavy carriage was no match in speed for a lightweight hansom and they soon lost sight of their quarry completely. Inspector Witherspoon feared the worst.

Wiggins breathed a sigh of relief as the hansom slowed to a reasonable pace. It felt like he'd ridden for hours, though in fact, they'd only come down to the docks. The vehicle turned onto a small, dark street. Wiggins shivered. In the distance, he could hear a dog barking. The hansom slowed further and finally pulled up aross the street from a building next to a wharf.

"Here's an extra five for your trouble," he heard Brian Cameron say to the driver. "Thank you."

Wiggins dropped off the back and, taking care to stay out of sight, dashed behind an empty coopers van parked by the side of the road. He watched as Cameron got out and then turned and helped Kathryn Ellingsley down. "But why are we stopping here?" he heard her ask her cousin. "We'll be late for the train."

"We've plenty of time, my dear," Cameron replied. "And I must pick up some important papers. Uncle Neville wanted me to bring them to him."

They crossed the road as soon as the hansom pulled away. Wiggins started to follow them. But instead of going toward the front door of the building, Cameron suddenly grabbed the girl's arm and started pulling her toward the wharf.

"Brian," she cried, "what are you doing?"

Wiggins froze.

"Let's go have a look at the water," Cameron said. "It's quite lovely. I think you'll enjoy the view."

"Are you mad?" Kathryn tried to free her arm, but he held fast. "Let me go, I tell you."

"I'm sorry it has to be this way." Cameron grabbed her around the waist and dragged her further out onto the wharf. "But you're in the way. You've got to die before Uncle Neville does. It's most inconvenient. You should have been in that room that night. Not Hannah."

"Let me go," Kathryn cried, struggling in earnest now. "Brian, what are you doing?"

Wiggins started across the street at a dead run. But they were almost across to the end of the wharf now.

Kathryn Ellingsley was fighting him, fighting hard, but it wasn't doing her any good. Cameron grabbed her around the neck and drug her toward the water. She flailed at him with her fists and tried to kick, but he slapped her hard and picked her up.

"Hey," Wiggins yelled as they got to the edge of the dock. "Leave her alone, I tell ya." He charged across the wood pilings.

Cameron, with one frantic look at his pursuer, dropped her into the river. Kathryn screamed as she hit the water.

Wiggins leapt for the edge.

But Cameron was ready for him. He grabbed him around the knees and pulled him back, throwing him onto the wharf hard enough to knock the wind out of his lungs. Wiggins kicked out with one leg, catching the man on the thigh and toppling him over. He landed smack on Wiggins. The two men rolled across the wharf. Cameron smashed a fist into Wiggins's face. Wiggins tried punching him in the stomach, but his arm was held down by the bigger man's weight. Cameron's hand shot up and grabbed Wiggins's throat. He squeezed hard. Wiggins finally got his own hand free and clawed at Cameron's arm. But his own strength was failing and the pressure increased, choking the life out of him. His vision clouded and the night turned blacker and blacker.

Suddenly, the pressure was gone as sixty pounds of furious dog leapt onto Brian Cameron's back. Fred, snarling and barking, clamped his jaws onto the arm squeezing the life out of his master.

Cameron screamed and rolled to one side, trying desperately to get away from the enraged beast. Witherspoon and Smythe raced across the wharf. "Are you all right, Wiggins?" the inspector shouted.

Wiggins tried to sit up and point to the river. "Drownin', she's drownin'!"

Smythe didn't hesitate. He continued running. Wiggins slumped back as he heard the sound of a body hitting water. He prayed the coachman would be in time to save the drowning woman.

"I've got 'er," Smythe called.

Witherspoon blew hard on his police whistle and then dropped to his knees beside his fallen footman. "Dear God, Wiggins. Are you all right?"

"I'm fine. Don't let him get away," Wiggins moaned. He lifted his head and looked over at his dog. Then he smiled.

Fred, still snarling dangerously, had driven Cameron back against the side of the building. The man cringed there, held at bay by the animal who lunged at him every time he moved.

Witherspoon jumped up and rushed to the edge of the wharf. "Is she all right?"

Smythe nodded. "She's alive, but this water is freezin'. We've got to get her out of here."

Heavy footsteps pounded across the wharf as two police constables responded to Witherspoon's whistle. One of them recognized the inspector.

"Over here," the inspector shouted.

Within moments, they had Kathryn and Smythe out of the water and wrapped in blankets while the inspector tended to Wiggins.

As soon as the inspector realized that Wiggins was really going to be all right, he got up and walked over to Brian Cameron.

He wasn't in the least worried that Cameron would try to make a run for it. Not with Fred standing guard. The man had flattened himself against the building, his face a mask of terror as the dog snarled viciously at him.

"It's all right, Fred," he told the dog. "You've done a good job, but we'll take over now." Fred didn't budge.

"Here, boy," Wiggins called softly, and the animal, with one last snarl at the cowering man, trotted over and began licking the footman's cheek.

"Brian Cameron," the inspector said firmly, "you're under arrest for the murder of Hannah Cameron and the attempted murder of Kathryn Ellingsley and Cuthbert Wiggins."

It was very late by the time they were all gathered around the kitchen table. The inspector was still at the station, but Wiggins, wrapped in one of Mrs. Goodge's knitted afghans and with a cup of cocoa in front of him, was quite happily enjoying being the center of attention.

Smythe, who'd very much liked the way Betsy had fussed when he'd arrived home in wet clothes and wrapped in a blanket, was quite content to sit back and enjoy a glass of fine Irish whiskey while the footman retold the tale several times over.

"All right." Luty put down her glass and stared at Mrs. Jeffries. "Tell us how ya figured it out."

"Actually"—she smiled briefly—"there was one fact that kept bothering me. It was something Betsy said yesterday. Namely, that everyone in that household except Hannah Cameron knew that Kathryn Ellingsley went out at night."

"I don't follow ya," Smythe said. "What does that 'ave to do with anythin'?"

"But that was the key to the puzzle," she replied. "Don't you see, Brian Cameron didn't know his wife knew about Kathryn. He'd no idea she was in the room. He wanted to murder Kathryn Ellingsley all along. I figured it out yesterday, but then when I found out who Kathryn's heir was, I wasn't sure I was right. You see, I'd gotten the inheritance sequence wrong."

"What does that mean?" Wiggins asked.

"It means that we were confused from the start," she replied. "We kept focusing on Hannah Cameron . . ."

"She was the one that was murdered," Hatchet interrupted, somewhat testily. He and Luty were both annoyed that they'd missed the action down on the wharf.

"Yes, I know," Mrs. Jeffries said. "But that was a mistake. You see, Cameron knew about Kathryn. He went into that room that night, expecting to find Kathryn slipping in. Instead, his wife was standing by the door waiting to catch the girl in the act, so to speak. In the darkness, he stabbed her. But she was the wrong one."

"I still don't understand why 'e'd want to kill a nice girl like Miss Ellingsley," Wiggins said.

"He wanted her dead so that he could inherit their uncle's fortune," Mrs. Jeffries said. "That's why he kept sending all those telegrams to Yorkshire. He was running out of time. But I got confused. I thought his plan was to murder Kathryn and then wait until their uncle died and then inherit her share of the estate. Last night, when you found out who her heir was, that it was Connor Reese, I still didn't understand until it was almost too late."

"I'm confused," Mrs. Goodge complained. "I can't make heads nor tails of it."

"It's very simple, really," Mrs. Jeffries said. "Neville Parrington had a burglary six months ago." She pulled the telegram out of her pocket and read it to the them.

ELLEN AND EDWARD CAMERON INHERIT AFTER K.E.
PARRINGTON'S WILL STOLEN IN LONDON BURGLARY SIX
MONTHS AGO.
HOPE THIS HELPFUL AND KEEP UP THE GOOD WORK.
CHEERS, EDWIN TRENT

She shook her head disgustedly. "But even with this, it still didn't make sense because I was still focusing on the wrong thing. You see, I didn't realize until Wiggins came along and told us today that Neville Parrington was on his deathbed. It was then that the shoe dropped."

"I'm glad you know what you're talkin' about." Mrs. Goodge sniffed. "I don't. What does Parrington's burglary have to do with our murder?"

"I'm not explaining it very well." She sighed. "And I've no proof, but I'm sure that Brian Cameron was the one that stole his uncle's will. The circumstances were very much the same."

"That's true," Hatchet said. "According to my source, that burglary wasn't done by a professional. Neither was the one at the Cameron house."

"No, both of them were done by Cameron. He stole his uncle's will to find out one thing—who was Parrington's heir? I expect he was a bit annoyed to find out it was Kathryn Ellingsley and not himself."

"But why'd Cameron wait six months to kill her?" Betsy asked.

"He didn't want to arouse suspicion," Mrs. Jeffries stated. "We know he fired his governess to give her a position in his house and I expect he was absolutely delighted when she fell in love with Dr. Reese. If you'll recall, Kathryn and Dr. Reese met at the Cameron house."

"But Dr. Reese had gone there to 'ave a go at Mrs. Cameron," Wiggins interjected. "It's not like 'e were a guest."

"True." Mrs. Jeffries grinned. "But I'll wager that Cameron noticed they were attracted to each other and I'll bet if you asked Dr. Reese, you'd find out that it was Brian Cameron who gave him Kathryn's Yorkshire address so that Reese could correspond with her."

"You mean he connived to get the girl to come?"

"That's it precisely. He wanted Kathryn in London. I expect that he was planning on her having an unfortunate 'accident." Let's remember what we know about Brian Cameron. He needs money. But it wouldn't do him any good to kill his wife. He'll not get anything from her estate, but he would get quite a bit of money if Kathryn Ellingsley were dead. And she had to die before Neville Parrington did. Don't you see, she'd left her estate to her fiancé, Dr. Reese. If Parrington died before Kathryn did, she'd inherit. There was no point in killing her then. All the money would go to Reese. If she died before Parrington, the estate would go to Cameron's children. Essentially, he'd have control of a huge amount of money to do with it what he pleased." She sat back and smiled.

They looked at her blankly.

"Oh, I know it's a bit muddled. But I'm certain of it."

"But why were you so confused when you found out Reese and not Cameron was her heir?" Betsy asked. "You looked ready to spit nails last night when Hatchet and Smythe come in."

"Because, like most people, I'd assumed that Kathryn left her money to her family. If not to Cameron then to his children. That's all the family she had. It was only when I thought about it and found out from Wiggins today that Cameron was taking Kathryn to Yorkshire that I realized what he was up to. He had to kill her before Neville Parrington died. Otherwise, Cameron would get nothing. I'd suspected he was the killer, but I was a bit confused as to the details. But not to worry. We sorted it out in the end."

Luty shook her head. "I'm still confused."

"Me too," Smythe muttered, but he didn't mind all that much. Good Irish whiskey could take the edge off anything. That and the fact that Betsy had kissed him when the others weren't looking.

"I still think it shoulda been that Hadleigh woman," Mrs. Goodge muttered.

"She was a strong suspect," Mrs. Jeffries said, "but she really had a very flimsy motive. She hated Hannah Cameron, but from what we learned, she'd hated her for a long time. Besides, I didn't think it was her because she was still fully dressed when the inspector arrived."

Wiggins cocked his head to one side. "Huh?"

"Remember, the victim was stabbed. That means the murderer probably got blood on his clothes. Even the cleanest of stabbings involves some blood spurts. There wasn't any blood on her clothes when the inspector got there. Brian Cameron was wearing a heavy dressing gown over his clothing. I expect there was a drop or two of blood on that shirt of his. But he didn't dare take it off in case the police searched the house, so he did the cleverest thing possible. He kept the shirt on and put on a dressing gown."

"'E was takin' a bit of a risk," Smythe commented.

"Not really," Mrs. Jeffries said. "He'd done his best to make it look like a burglary. If Chief Inspector Barrows hadn't come onto the scene so quickly and spotted that it was murder, Cameron would have gotten away with it. Can you really see Inspector Nivens asking a gentleman to remove his dressing gown?"

"Gracious, are you all still up?" Inspector Witherspoon, smiling broadly, stepped into the kitchen. "Oh, I'm so glad to see that Wiggins and Smythe are all right. I can't tell you how worried I've been."

"We didn't hear you come in, sir." Mrs. Jeffries wasn't sure what to do.

"Oh, that's all right. I expected to be at the station all night." Witherspoon ambled over to the table and pulled out a chair. "But Chief Inspector Barrows insisted I come home. I think he could tell I was a bit concerned about Wiggins and Smythe. By the way, he sends his heartiest regards to you two." He nodded at them. "If not for your bravery, that young woman would be dead now. You should be very proud of yourselves. Very proud indeed."

Wiggins grinned foolishly.

Smythe blushed. "It weren't nothin'," he muttered.

"It was so." Betsy chided the coachman. "Just ask Miss Ellingsley."

"Is that whiskey?" Witherspoon peered over his spectacles at the open bottle sitting smack in the middle of the table.

"Uh, yes, sir, it is," Mrs. Jeffries admitted.

"Hatchet and I are right lucky we come by to visit," Luty said quickly. "Otherwise we'd a missed hearin' all about yer excitin' evenin'. When I heard this one"—she jerked her thumb at Smythe—"had been swimmin' in the Thames and that this one"—she nodded at the footman—"had almost had the life squeezed outta him, I talked Hepzibah into breakin' out a bottle of yer best whiskey. I didn't think you'd mind. Celebratin', ya know. They ain't dead."

"Excellent idea, Mrs. Crookshank." The inspector shuddered at the memory. He'd come close to losing two people who were very dear to him. "May I have some too?"

"I'll get another glass," Betsy said, getting up.

"What happened at the station, sir?" Mrs. Jeffries asked.

"Brian Cameron's refused to make any statement at all," he replied. "Thank you, Betsy," he said as she put the glass of whiskey in front of him.

"Oh, dear, sir," Mrs. Jeffries commented. "That will make it difficult for you."

"Not really. We've a lot of evidence against him. Miss Ellingsley managed to make a statement. Cameron's references to her possible inheritance from her uncle give him quite a strong motive. We're sure he meant to murder Kathryn that night, instead of Mrs. Cameron. But even if we can't convict him of his wife's murder, and I think we can, we've got the evidence of his attempted murder of Miss Ellingsley and Wiggins, of course." He tossed the whiskey down his throat and then coughed. "Oh dear, this isn't at all like sherry. Quite strong, isn't it?"

"Is Miss Ellingsley all right?" Wiggins asked anxiously. He still felt bad that he hadn't been able to prevent Cameron from tossing her into the Thames.

"She's fine, Wiggins," Witherspoon assured him. "She managed to keep from drowning by grabbing a piling. But if Smythe hadn't jumped in and pulled her out when he did, she probably would have died. We've a number of heroes in this house." He paused and looked curiously around the room. "Where's Fred? Surely he should be here too."

"He's in the larder eatin' a beefsteak," Mrs. Goodge said. "A great big thick one I got from the butcher this mornin'. I figured he deserved it."

"He most certainly does," Witherspoon agreed with a laugh. Then he sobered and looked at Smythe and Wiggins. "Now that I know you two aren't suffering any ill effects from our adventure, I can rest easy." He yawned widely.

"Inspector." Mrs. Jeffries had to ask. "Was Inspector Nivens at the station?"

"He did come by," the inspector replied. "He didn't seem at all pleased that we'd solved the case, either. As a matter of fact, he quite rudely told me he wasn't coming to my dinner party."

"What a pity, sir." She fought hard to keep from smiling.

"Yes, isn't it?" Witherspoon murmured. "Too bad, really. I was going to seat him next to cousin Edwina. But she's not coming either."

Knowing that she couldn't keep a straight face, Mrs. Jeffries looked down at her half-empty glass.

"'Ow come she's not comin'?" Wiggins asked.

"Oh, she's decided to buy her clothes in Edinburgh so she won't be coming to London to shop for her trousseau. But not to worry; we'll have plenty of guests," Witherspoon said cheerfully. "I've invited Chief Inspector Barrows and his wife. They're quite looking forward to it." He started to get up, frowned and popped back down in his seat. "But there is one thing I'm still very puzzled about."

"What's that, sir?" Mrs. Jeffries asked.

"I can't help wondering who that man was who came with the note."

"I've no idea, sir." Mrs. Jeffries shrugged. "As I told you"—she glanced at Smythe—"he looked very much like a banker."

Smythe, who'd just taken a sip of whiskey, had the good grace to choke.

MRS. JEFFRIES REVEALS HER ART

CHAPTER 1

"I don't care what kind of a report you've had," Neville Grant snapped impatiently. "No one here knows that person. Now kindly take yourself away and don't bother me or my household again."

"I'm sorry to disturb you, sir," said Constable Theodore Martin—Teddy to his friends—swallowing nervously. Just his rotten luck that the master of the house himself would answer the door and not the ruddy butler. "But we must make inquiries. It's our duty. Are you sure none of your servants have seen this woman?"

Grant glared at the pale-faced lad who dared to continue questioning him. The fact that the man was a policeman didn't intimidate him in the least. "Are you deaf, young man? I've already told you. Some incompetent has made a mistake or, more likely, is playing the police for fools, which, by the look of you, isn't difficult to do. This household is hardly likely to be issuing invitations to women like that."

"We've still got to inquire, sir," the constable said quickly. "Someone's filed a report. She's gone missing. This house is the last known place where she was, sir. That's why we've got to make sure no one here's seen her."

"You've the wrong address." Grant stamped his cane against the parquet floor for emphasis. "She wasn't here. Now go away."

Martin hesitated indecisively. He didn't like to make a fuss, but if he went back to the station without even setting foot in the house, his sergeant would have his guts for garters. Ever since the ruddy Whitechapel killings, the police had to be extra careful—even if it was some flitty artist's model that had gone missing. More likely this old tartar was right—the woman probably hadn't come here at all. But if the missing girl turned up with

her throat slashed or her guts torn out and the newspapers found out that
the police hadn't even bothered to make inquiries when she'd been reported
missing—Constable Martin didn't even want to think about that! "It is
the right address, sir," he insisted.

Grant's wrinkled face reddened in rage. "How dare you contradict
me," he yelped, stamping his cane again and coming within a hair's breath
of smashing the constable's toe. "I don't care what address you've got."
Grant started to close the door. "And I don't care if the girl has been kidnapped by white slavers. Someone's made a mistake. No one here knows
anything about a missing woman."

"If I could just speak to the rest of the household, sir," Martin persisted
desperately. It wasn't just his superiors he worried about facing if he went
back without any information. It was that French woman. She'd raised
such a ruckus down at the station this morning that even his hardened old
sergeant had stepped back a wary pace or two when she was ranting and
raving like a she-demon.

"Don't be ridiculous. We have guests this afternoon," Grant snapped.
"I'm not having you bother my wife or anyone else with this silly
matter."

"Then if I could have a word with your servants," the constable asked.
"Maybe one of them invited her."

"My servants are hardly in the habit of inviting their friends for social
calls."

"But one of them might know something."

"They've already been spoken to, you fool," Grant shouted, his complexion deepening to crimson. "The butler made inquiries amongst the
staff yesterday after that other constable came round bothering us with
this ridiculous tale. None of them know what the blazes you're on about
either. You've bothered us twice now and we've been very patient. But
enough is enough. Now get off with you and leave us in peace." With that,
he slammed the door in Martin's face.

The constable sighed and trudged down the three steps to the paved
walkway. As he went out the ebony wrought-iron gate that surrounded
the property, he glanced back over his shoulder. Blooming toffs, he thought
as he glared at the handsome three-story brick house, just because they're
rich they think they don't have to answer to the law. Well, they'd find out
soon enough that they did. Constable Martin knew in his bones that this
wasn't the end of things.

• • •

"Zhey do nothing!" Nanette Lanier banged her dainty fist against the tabletop hard enough to rattle the china. "She's been gone now for a week and still zhey do nothing. Zee English police," she cried. "Useless."

Mrs. Hepzibah Jeffries, housekeeper to Inspector Gerald Witherspoon of Scotland Yard, would normally have challenged such a statement, but considering the highly excitable state of her guest, she thought it best to let the comment pass.

"Miss Lanier," she began, only to be interrupted.

"Please call me Nanette."

"Very well, Nanette," she replied. She glanced at the clock. Almost three. The others should be back any moment. This would go a good deal easier if the rest of the staff were here. Smythe, the coachman, had taken everyone, even Mrs. Goodge, the cook, out for a drive in the inspector's carriage. "I quite sympathize with your position. I don't quite understand . . ." She paused, relieved, as she heard the back door open and the muted sound of several voices talking all at once. Good, the others were back. Now she wouldn't have to deal with this on her own.

Nanette's expression of indignation turned to alarm. "Is zat zee inspector?" she asked.

"No, no," Mrs. Jeffries assured her. "It's the rest of the staff. They've been out this afternoon."

"I told ya you'd like it," Wiggins, the footman, exclaimed.

Mrs. Goodge, her hat somewhat askew and her spectacles slipping down her nose, bustled into the kitchen with Wiggins right on her heels. Fred, the mongrel dog the household had adopted, trotted in after them.

"Smythe drove too fast," the cook groused, but her round cheeks were flushed and despite her grumbling she was smiling. She stopped dead when she saw Mrs. Jeffries had a guest.

"He weren't goin' that fast," Wiggins said defensively. "Not like that time he made it all the way to the . . ." He broke off in mid-sentence as he spotted the beautiful woman sitting next to the housekeeper. He stumbled to his left to avoid ramming into the cook's broad back.

"Good afternoon," Mrs. Jeffries said calmly. "As you can see, we have a guest. This is Miss Lanier." She gestured at Nanette, who nodded politely. "Miss Lanier," she continued, "this is Mrs. Goodge, our cook, and Wiggins, our footman."

"Pleased to meet you," Mrs. Goodge said.

"Likewise," Nanette said with a regal incline of her head.

"Miss Lanier is joining us for tea," Mrs. Jeffries explained.

"I'll just put my hat away." Mrs. Goodge shot the housekeeper a curious look as she bustled off toward the hallway and her room.

Wiggins, who was still staring at the woman like a lovestruck cow, started for a chair, tripped over his own feet, blushed bright red and then managed to seat himself without further ado.

"Where are Betsy and Smythe?" the housekeeper asked him. Nanette Lanier's arrival wasn't a social call. Mrs. Jeffries wanted everyone here before the woman went any further with her story. She forced herself to stay calm, deliberately keeping a tight lid on her rising excitement. She didn't want to get her hopes up. Nanette's problem might be a tempest in a teapot. But she hoped not. She hoped that soon the household would be out and about doing what they did best. Snooping. Seeking answers. Solving a mystery. They were very good at it too. But then, they should be. They'd done it often enough in the past. As the household staff for Inspector Gerald Witherspoon of Scotland Yard, they'd had plenty of practise. Not that their inspector had any inkling they regularly assisted him in his cases. Oh no, that would never do. But the point was, they did. Why, if not for them, their dear inspector would probably still be a clerk in the records room.

"They're just coming," Wiggins answered absently, his gaze still on their guest. He was the perfect picture of a love-struck youth. His eyes had gone all soft and dreamy, a half smile played around his mouth and a rosy blush had swept across his cheeks. Mrs. Jeffries ducked her head to hide a smile. Wiggins would be mortified when he looked in a mirror. Several tufts of his dark brown hair were sticking up at the back of his head.

The cook returned and took her regular chair at the table just as the back door opened again and the muted voices of the maid and the coachman drifted down the hallway. A moment later they came into the kitchen.

They made a striking contrast. Betsy, pretty and slender with blue eyes and blond hair, walked daintily next to a dark-haired hulk of a man. "Oh!" she exclaimed. "We've got company." She poked her companion in the arm. Smythe looked toward the table. His features were strong enough and brutal enough to intimidate a bear, but he'd not noticed they had a visitor because his eyes had been gazing adoringly at the maid.

Mrs. Jeffries repeated the introduction and then said, "Miss Lanier has come here for our help. It seems she has a problem." Her voice was calm and her expression serene, but there was something in her tone that caught all their attention.

Smythe's lips curved in a smile.

Mrs. Goodge grinned.

Betsy's eyes sparkled.

Even Wiggins jerked his gaze away from the Frenchwoman to look at the housekeeper in pleased surprise.

Mrs. Jeffries knew good and well what was going on in their minds. The same thing she'd thought when she'd opened the back door fifteen minutes ago and seen Nanette standing there. They had a case. A mystery to solve.

"What kind of a problem?" the cook asked eagerly.

"Before we go into that," Mrs. Jeffries said, "I'd like to remind everyone that Miss Lanier was involved in one of our first cases."

"But of course," Nanette said quickly. "It was when zat awful Dr. Slocum was murdered. I was working as a maid to Mrs. Leslie. We were Dr. Slocum's neighbors."

"It were that Knightsbridge one?" Wiggins exclaimed eagerly.

"*Oui,*" Nanette replied, giving him a dazzling smile. "*C'est* correct. I remember, you see. I remember very well what I saw when zee police were trying to find out who killed Slocum. If it had not been for all of you, zee real killer would have gotten away with it. Zat's why I come here when zee police do nothing. I zink all of you are very good at finding answers."

No one was quite sure how to respond to her statement, so no one said anything. Save for the faint ticking of the carriage clock on the cupboard shelf, the room was silent as they all drifted back to the memory of the first case they'd knowingly worked on together. It hadn't been their first case; there had been those horrible Kensington High Street murders. But on that one, they'd each worked separately, under Mrs. Jeffries's guidance and without even knowing what they were doing. But the murder of Dr. Bartholomew Slocum had been different. Mrs. Jeffries had realized they not only enjoyed and were good at snooping about but were just as devoted to the inspector as she was, and that they could work together as a team.

It had been the Slocum murder that had really brought them together. Mrs. Jeffries smiled at the memory. Now they were a family.

Misinterpreting the continued silence, Nanette quickly said, "I can keep a secret. If you help me, I won't say a word to anyone, especially not to your Inspector Witherspoon."

"Well," Mrs. Jeffries said thoughtfully, glad the woman had given them this promise freely, "that would put us more at ease. Now as to whether or not we can help you, we can't determine that until we know precisely what it is you need."

"My friend is missing," Nanette said. She plucked a pristine white handkerchief out of the pocket of her elegant green spring jacket and dabbed at her eyes. "She's been gone for a week."

Mary Grant's serene expression didn't change as she watched her husband come out the French doors and stamp across the lawn to where she was entertaining his wretched business guests. Her eyes narrowed slightly as she saw Neville deliberately smash an early blooming daffodil with his cane. They'd discuss that later, she thought before casting her gaze back to their visitors. Tyrell and Lydia Modean weren't friends but business acquaintances. And though they'd been foisted upon her by her husband, she was far too proud a hostess to ever do less than her best. She smiled warmly at the tall man standing behind his wife, who was seated directly across from her. "Have you had time to visit many galleries?" she inquired politely. Modean was quite an attractive man, even if he was an American.

"Quite a number of them," Tyrell Modean replied. He laid a hand on his wife's shoulder. He'd been standing here now for ten minutes and was hoping they'd go in to tea soon. "We took in the Japanese Gallery on New Bond Street this morning. Some of the work was exquisite, wasn't it, Lydia?"

But it wasn't Lydia Modean who replied. It was the man sitting across from their hostess. James Underhill was also a guest, but one who'd been invited by Arthur Grant, Neville's son, who was slouched in a chair across the table. "Exquisite? Do you really think so?" Underhill said doubtfully. He opened a tin of mints and popped one in his mouth.

"Yes," Modean replied, not bothering to look at the Englishman. "I do." He deliberately moved so that he was turned away from Underhill. The snub was obvious to everyone seated at the table. Helen Collier, Mary Grant's sister, leveled an outraged frown at the American.

"Mrs. Grant," Modean continued calmly, "I understand the Caldararos were originally part of your family's collection."

Underhill shot a fierce glare at the American's broad shoulders. God, he hated him. He snapped the lid shut on his mints and started to put them back in his coat pocket.

"James," Mary ordered. "Could you go and get Mr. Modean a chair? Take Arthur with you to help carry it. They're quite heavy."

James Underhill was outraged. The witch was treating him like a servant. Well, by God, she'd pay for that. He glared quickly at the others around the table. Arthur practically trembled as Underhill's gaze raked him. Helen gave him her mewling calf's smile that for some odd reason she thought was attractive and Mary merely stared at him imperiously, daring him to object. Modean and his slut of a wife didn't even bother to look in his direction.

Underhill slapped the tin onto the table. "Of course, Mrs. Grant," he replied coldly. "I'll be delighted to get Mr. Modean a chair. Come along, Arthur. I could use a hand."

"Have you told the police?" Mrs. Goodge asked. Her tone was polite, but behind her spectacles, her eyes were suspicious. She'd never had much liking for foreigners. Especially the French.

"Zee police!" Nanette snorted. "Useless fools! I went to them zee morning after Irene did not come home! Zhey claimed zhey'd make inquiries. But zhey did nothing. A rich man says he knows nothing of Irene and zhey are cowed like zee dog."

"I'm not quite followin' ya," Smythe said softly. "Why don't ya start at the beginnin' and tell us everythin'?"

"But I've already told Mrs. Jeffries," Nanette wailed. "I don't want to waste time. Something has happened to Irene. I know it. I can feel it in my liver."

"Liver?" Wiggins echoed. "That's a funny place to feel somethin'"

Nanette waved her hand impatiently. "Not my liver—what's zat other word . . ." She tapped her chest.

"Heart?" Betsy suggested.

Nanette nodded. "Zhat's it. I can feel it in my heart. Sometimes I get my English mixed up when I'm excited or upset and now I am very upset."

"Then I suggest you drink your tea and calm down," Mrs. Jeffries said. "You'll need to have all your wits about you when you tell us the facts of this matter."

Nanette nodded and took a deep breath. "But of course. You are right. I must be calm. It happened last week. My friend Irene Simmons came to take tea with me. A charming custom, is it not? Afternoon tea . . . but forgive me, I'm wandering off zee point. Irene lives in zee flat upstairs from my shop. She lives with her *grandmère*. Pardon, I mean grandmother."

"You own a shop?" Betsy asked curiously.

"A hat shop," Nanette replied proudly. "We carry all zee latest designs from Paris. We also carry a full line of gloves, scarves, fans and shawls."

"Go on," Mrs. Jeffries prompted. She too was curious how someone who only a few years ago was a lady's maid had acquired the capital to open her own business. But she wasn't going to ask that question now. She'd learned it was better to find some answers indirectly. "Do tell us about Miss Simmons."

"She's an artists' model," Nanette continued. "But Irene is a good girl, a decent girl. She is from a good family. They once had a bit of money, but when her parents died, she and her grandmother lost everything. I gave her a job working for me in zee shop . . ."

"I thought you said she was an artists' model," Wiggins asked.

"She is. But she only got her first modeling position a few months ago. A Spanish artist named Gaspar Morante happened to come into zee shop. He took one look at Irene and asked her to pose for him. He didn't offer her much money, but I told her to do it because I knew it might lead to other work. To be honest, my own business hadn't been so good."

"So she doesn't work for you now?" Smythe asked.

"Only occasionally," Nanette replied. "Her *grandmère* is quite ill. Irene needed to make money to pay for her medicines and zee doctor."

"So now she's makin' a livin' posin' for pictures?" Mrs. Goodge asked, her tone clearly indicating her thoughts on that kind of employment.

"She is a decent woman," Nanette declared with a sniff. "She does not pose in zee nude even though zat ridiculous Englishman offered her a hundred pounds."

Mrs. Jeffries reached over and patted Nanette's arm. "No one is saying your Miss Simmons isn't a perfectly nice woman . . ."

"That's right," Wiggins interrupted. "And even if she took all her clothes off, we'd still go out and look for her."

"Really, Wiggins," the cook snapped. "Please watch your tongue."

Wiggins blushed a fiery red. "Sorry. What I meant to say was that no matter what Miss Simmons does for employment, we'd look for 'er if she's missin'. No one deserves to be ignored just because they might be poor or different or . . . well." He looked helplessly at the housekeeper. "You know what I mean, Mrs. Jeffries."

"Of course we do, Wiggins, and I must say, you're absolutely right." She smiled approvingly at him and then turned to Nanette. "Do continue with your story. Miss Simmons came to have tea with you last week," she prompted.

"It was quite late in zee afternoon. Irene, she was excited because she'd received an offer of employment. She was to go zat night and discuss the terms with zee artist. I walked her to zee corner, to zee omnibus stop, and waited with her till it came. Zat was the last time I saw her."

"Do you know where she was going?" Betsy asked. "Do you have an address?"

"To a house on Beltrane Gardens. Zat's why Irene was so excited. The address was very fashionable, and she was sure she'd get a good wage," Nanette explained. "But she never came home. Zee next morning, her *grand-mère* came down to zee shop and told me Irene's bed hadn't been slept in."

"What did you do?" Betsy asked.

"As I told you, I went to zee police. I was afraid there'd been an accident. But Irene, she wasn't in any of zee hospitals and zee police hadn't found any bodies without zee names."

"Huh?" Wiggins said.

"She means unidentified bodies," the housekeeper clarified.

"Zat's right. There were no unidentified bodies." Nanette pursed her mouth in disgust. "I even gave them zee address of zee house Irene went to, but zhey did nothing. Zee man who owns zee house told zem Irene never arrived. He is lying."

"Why do you think 'e's lyin'?" Smythe asked.

"Because I know Irene," Nanette declared. "I know she went to zat house. She needed zee work so badly she wouldn't have dared not gone. Zat's how I know he is lying . . . zat stupid old man. He's lying about Irene and zee police will do nothing . . ." Nanette broke off and launched into French with such speed and fury that everyone around the table was rather glad they couldn't understand what she was saying.

When the storm had passed, she got a hold of herself, wiped her wet eyes and said, "Please forgive me, but Irene is very dear to me, like a sister. I'm alone in zhis country. She and her *grandmère* aren't just my neighbors, but my family. I know zat Mr. Grant is lying. Why, he even claimed he hadn't sent zee note asking Irene to come. But he had sent it . . . I saw it with my own eyes."

"You saw it?" Mrs. Jeffries said. There were a dozen different explanations as to why the girl hadn't arrived at the house, but for now, they'd accept Nanette's assumption that the girl had indeed arrived at her destination that evening.

"*Oui,*" Nanette cried, "and there is nothing wrong with my eyes. Irene did not write zat note to herself."

"So you're suspicious of this, er . . . Mr. Grant because you think he lied to the police," Mrs. Goodge said.

"He is lying! It was his notepaper. It had his name and address on it. Neville Grant. Thirty-four Beltrane Gardens, Holland Park."

Smythe sucked in his breath. "Cor blimey, that's right near 'ere."

"Does Irene have a sweetheart?" Betsy asked softly.

"*Non.*" Nanette shook her head. "There is no one. Several young men have been interested, but Irene is devoted to her *grandmère*. She would never desert her to run off with someone."

"Maybe somethin' 'appened to 'er after she left the Grant 'ouse?" Wiggins suggested. "You said yourself it were evenin'. Maybe somethin' 'appened to 'er after she come out?"

"I don't believe zat," Nanette said emphatically. "If she'd been there and gone, zhen why would zis man keep lying to zee police? He claims she was never there at all and I know she was."

"Perhaps someone was playing a trick on her?" Mrs. Jeffries suggested.

"I thought of zat," Nanette replied, "but zhen again, why wouldn't Grant admit she'd come to the door and zhey'd sent her off? But he said she was never there. I know she was. I saw her get on zee omnibus."

"That doesn't mean Irene didn't get off somewhere between the stop and the Grant house," Betsy pointed out. "Perhaps she stopped off to buy something at the chemist's?"

"Impossible," Nanette insisted. "She hadn't enough money."

"None at all?" Mrs. Goodge asked suspiciously.

"None." Nanette snorted delicately. "I had to loan her zee fare for zee omnibus. Zee next day, Madam Farringdon, one of my customers, came into zee shop. She mentioned zat she'd seen Irene on zee omnibus zee night before. Of course I questioned her, because I knew by zat time zat Irene hadn't come home. Madam said zat Irene and she had gotten off zee omnibus together and even walked up Holland Park Road. Madame left her at zee corner of Beltrane Gardens. That's only a very leetle distance from zee Grant house. What could have happened to Irene? It was a public street and she only had to walk a leetle ways to her destination."

"Had it gone dark by then?" Smythe asked.

Nanette nodded. "Yes, but when Madam Farringdon left Irene, she didn't have far to go."

"'Ow was Miss Simmons plannin' on gettin' 'ome?" Wiggins asked.

Nanette shrugged. "I lent her money for a hansom. I didn't want her on zee streets too late at night. Why?"

"I was just wonderin'," he mumbled.

"Will you help me?" the Frenchwoman pleaded. "Her *grandmère* is frantic with worry, and so am I. I can pay you for your trouble."

There was an immediate chorus of protests. But it was Smythe's harsh tones that stood out. "We 'elp people because it's right, not because we're wantin' to make a bob or two."

"We're not a private inquiry firm." Mrs. Goodge sniffed.

"Please excuse me." Nanette's pretty blue eyes filled with tears. "I didn't mean to offend."

"None is taken," Mrs. Jeffries said calmly. There were a number of things to consider before they leapt into this venture. The main one being that they might not have any more luck in locating this poor woman than the police had. "But before we can agree to assist you, we really must discuss it among ourselves."

Nanette leapt to her feet. "I'll step outside in zee garden for a few minutes. Will zat give you enough time?"

Taken aback, Mrs. Jeffries could only nod. She'd rather thought they might have the whole evening to discuss the matter, but as Nanette was already scurrying toward the back door, there wasn't much she could do about it. She waited till she heard the door close before turning to the others. "What do you think?"

"We should 'elp 'er," Wiggins said quickly. "Poor lady's in a state, worryin' about 'er friend."

Mrs. Goodge sighed. "Well, it's not a murder," she began, "but finding this model is better than sittin' around here twiddling our thumbs."

"I don't know." Betsy glanced toward the back hall and shook her head. "We've never really done anything like this and if the girl's been gone a week . . ."

"You think she's already dead?" Smythe said bluntly.

"I'm not saying that," Betsy explained. "But there's something funny about the whole thing."

Mrs. Jeffries rather agreed with the maid's assessment. But she didn't want to give her opinion until everyone had been heard from. "Smythe, what do you think?"

Smythe leaned back and folded his arms across his massive chest. "Betsy's right. Somethin' strange is goin' on. But I don't think the girl's dead. I think someone's got 'er."

"You don't think she's dead? Goodness. Why?" Mrs. Jeffries was curious as to his reasoning.

"Because Nanette's already been to the police about this and even though she claims they ain't doin' nothin' about it, they probably are. Since this awful Ripper case, they're under a lot of pressure when it comes to missin' young women. Maybe they haven't brought this Grant feller in for questionin', but you can bet your last farthin' they're watching the morgues and the 'ospitals." Smythe shrugged. "Probably watchin' 'im, as well."

"What are you sayin'?" Wiggins scratched his chin.

"I'm sayin' 'er body 'asn't turned up," Smythe replied softly. "And there's not many places in a crowded city to hide a corpse."

"What about the river?" Mrs. Goodge put in quickly. "That's a good place to get rid of it."

Smythe shook his head. "It woulda floated up by now and someone would've seen it."

"So what do you think's happened?" Betsy prodded.

"I think she's been kidnapped," he said seriously.

Mrs. Jeffries wasn't sure she would go that far, but there was enough to Nanette's tale to warrant a futher look. "What do you all think? Should we agree to help find this young woman?" She looked around the table at the others.

"I think we ought to," Betsy declared. "We can find out if she went into the Grant house if nothing else."

"I'm for it," Smythe agreed. "Mind you, I don't think we're goin' to have much more luck than the police . . ."

"Of course we will," Mrs. Goodge scoffed. "We've got ways of findin' things out that the police don't."

"That's true," Mrs. Jeffries murmured. They were quite good at digging out information. Even Mrs. Goodge, who never left the kitchen, could find out just about anything about anyone who was important in the city. But then, the cook had a veritable army of people marching through her domain. Tradesmen, delivery boys, costermongers, chimney sweeps and laundrymen. She kept them well supplied with sweet cakes and tea while she ruthlessly pumped them for every morsel of information there was to be had. "We're agreed, then. We're going to help?"

Everyone nodded. Wiggins got to his feet. "I'll just nip out and get Miss Lanier."

Mrs. Jeffries raised her hand. "Not yet. I think we ought to bring the inspector into this."

"What for?" Mrs. Goodge demanded. "He'll not be able to do anything the police haven't already done."

"On the contrary. According to what Nanette told me earlier, a police constable has gone to the Grant house twice requesting information. They didn't even get inside the place."

"So what good would it do to get the inspector involved?" Smythe asked.

Mrs. Jeffries smiled. "Ah, but he's not a constable, is he? It's a far different matter when an inspector shows up on your doorstoop and starts asking questions. If nothing else, it will put the cat among the pigeons . . ."

Smythe chuckled. "I see what you're gettin' at."

"I don't," the cook demanded.

"Simple, Mrs. Goodge. If someone in that house knows anything about Irene Simmons, the inspector showin' up and askin' a few questions might loosen a few tongues."

"I say, Mrs. Modean is quite a lovely lady, isn't she?" Arthur Grant said to his companion as they paused at the top of the stairs and watched the couple below entering the drawing room.

James Underhill shrugged and patted the pocket of his elegant black jacket, checking to see that he had his box of mints handy. Damn, they were gone. He'd probably left them out in the garden earlier. "She's beautiful, but hardly a lady. She was a model before Modean married her. I ought to know. I'm the one who introduced them."

Grant gave Underhill a knowing smirk. "I fancy you wouldn't say something like that within earshot of her husband." He was satisfied when he saw a quick flush creep up Underhill's cheek. The man didn't like being reminded of their earlier meeting with the American. "Modean doesn't appear to like you very much."

"We've had dealings before," Underhill muttered. He started down the stairs, one well-manicured hand clasped lightly onto the polished mahogany banister.

"He seems a cultured sort, for an American." Arthur fell into step next to Underhill.

"Don't be absurd." Underhill stopped. His fingers tightened against the wood. "Modean's nothing. He's just a stupid, colonial upstart who thinks because he's made a bit of money he can buy art and culture the same way he buys mining shares or bonds. The man can barely read. No real education, no breeding, no family. Nothing but money. That's all they care about in America. Money." He continued down the stairs.

"Then it's fortunate for Modean that he has so much of it." Arthur said gleefully, taking such momentary delight in reminding Underhill of today's humiliation that he forgot Tyrell Modean and his American money were causing him a lot of trouble as well. "But rather unfortunate for us," he amended quickly, hoping that Underhill hadn't quite realized he was deliberately trying to bait him. Sometimes, Arthur lamented, he frequently let his mouth loose without thinking.

Underhill was no fool. He shot Arthur a withering glare as they reached the bottom of the stairs. Across the wide hall, they could hear the muted voices of the others.

Arthur swallowed nervously and stepped back a bit. "Sorry," he mumbled. "I didn't mean . . ."

"Stop trying to goad me," Underhill warned. "You haven't the wit for it. In any case, without me, you're in very deep trouble. Don't forget that, my friend."

Grant's pale face turned even whiter. "But you will help me," he pleaded, casting a quick glance toward the drawing room. "He'll toss me out if he finds out. Yee gods, he'll probably kill me. You promised . . ."

"I promised nothing," Underhill interrupted. He was beginning to enjoy himself. The momentary shame at being reminded of Modean's snub was washed away as he saw Grant cringing like a whipped pup. "This really isn't my problem at all, is it?"

"It will be if it all comes out," Grant blustered, his hazel eyes shifting between the drawing room and the man standing in front of him. "If I go down, you go down."

"Do you really think he'll believe you?" Underhill sneered, somewhat taken aback that the cowed pup had the nerve to fight back, even a little.

"Perhaps he won't believe me, but the police will." Grant appeared to gain courage as he spoke. "It's not the first time you've done it. I know that much."

Underhill watched him for a moment, his expression amused. "What you know is one thing. What you can prove is something else entirely. You weren't complaining when you got your money, little man. I suspect the police will be interested in that too."

Grant's bravado deserted him completely. He lifted his hand and ran it nervously through his thin, blond hair. "Look, let's not get silly over this. It's in both our interests to cooperate with each other."

Underhill's lip curled in derision. "You really are a cowardly little whelp, aren't you? Well, lucky for you I happen to need money. Otherwise, you'd be on your own. We made a deal and I kept my part of it. So if you want my help now, I suggest you keep your mouth shut and do precisely as I say."

"Arthur." Mary Grant's voice interrupted their conversation.

The two men turned and saw the elegant middle-aged woman with graying blond hair and cool blue eyes standing in the doorway of the drawing room. "We do have guests, Arthur," she said. "Would you and Mr. Underhill like to join us now or will you be having your tea in the hall?"

Arthur gulped. "We'll be right there, Mama."

She nodded regally and turned away. Underhill snickered. "You're more scared of her than you are of him."

Arthur would have dearly liked to deny it, but he couldn't. He was frightened of his father. But he was positively terrified of his stepmother. "We'd better go in. She hates to be kept waiting."

Underhill laughed aloud. He was going to enjoy annoying Mary Grant today. He owed her that much for the way she'd helped humiliate him earlier. But perhaps the pup was right; perhaps he oughtn't annoy the lady too much. Not just yet, anyway.

Together, the two men went into the drawing room just as a maid came up the hall pushing an elaborate tea trolley.

"Girl," Underhill said to the maid, "go out in the garden and see if my mints are there. I think I left them on the table. They're in a red-and-white tin."

"Yes, sir," the maid answered. She placed the trolley carefully in front of where Mary Grant was sitting and scurried off.

"Will your husband be joining us for tea, Mrs. Grant?" Tyrell Modean asked.

"Of course. He only went into his study for a moment. I believe he's gone to get *The Times*. I think there's a notice he'd like you to see. There are some old tapestry panels being offered for sale. Neville thought you might be interested in acquiring them for your museum." She smiled warmly at the handsome American. Her smile slipped a bit when she glanced at Modean's wife.

Lydia Modean was too beautiful to be liked and too rich to be ignored, despite the fact that she'd once made her living posing for half the artists in Soho.

A thumping came from down the hallway and Mary steeled herself to continue being gracious as her husband, deliberately slamming his cane against the floor, banged into the room.

His thinning white hair was disheveled, his watery eyes glittering with rage. "Call the police," he thundered. "Someone's stolen my paintings. My Caldararos. They're gone!"

CHAPTER 2

⸺⸱⸲⸱⸺

Inspector Gerald Witherspoon hoped he was doing the right thing. He slowed his pace as he walked up Holland Park Road. Perhaps he ought to have sent Wiggins or Smythe over to fetch Constable Barnes? But as the constable was off duty, he hadn't wanted to bother him at home. Especially for something like this. So he'd decided to bring his coachman and footman along with him—unofficially, of course.

Still undecided, because what he was doing was highly irregular, Witherspoon stopped in the middle of the pavement. His two companions stopped as well.

"Is somethin' wrong, Inspector?" Smythe inquired politely.

"No, no. I just needed to have a bit of a think. Was Miss Lanier absolutely certain of the address?" he asked. Perhaps he ought to have sent Miss Lanier to the police station, but she'd been so desperate, so distraught. He really hadn't had the heart to refuse her request. Especially when she'd gone on and on about what a brilliant detective he was and how she'd remembered his kindness and sensitivity from that awful Slocum murder. Then she'd started to cry and—well, to be honest, he'd have agreed to anything to get her to stop. So here he was, trotting along to some man's house and preparing to ask a few uncomfortable questions. He hoped this Mr. Grant would be civil about it. Witherspoon brushed his doubts aside. Surely he wasn't stepping out of line merely by making a few inquiries. After all, he was a police officer and a young woman had gone missing.

"Miss Lanier was certain of the address, sir," Smythe replied. He hoped they'd done the right thing in having Nanette throw herself upon the inspector's good nature. Cor blimey, he'd hate to see the inspector get the sticky end of the wicket over this, especially as it was really their problem, not his.

But none of the household had been able to resist, as Mrs. Jeffries had put it, "putting the cat amongst the pigeons." If nothing else, it would get the servants at the Grant house gossiping and speculating. Always a handy situation when it came to solving cases, Smythe reckoned. "Number thirty-four, Beltrane Gardens. It's just up there, sir," he said.

Witherspoon stiffened his spine and charged ahead. Best to get this over with.

"No one's stolen anything, Neville," Mary said calmly. She smoothed the folds of her elegant brown tea gown. "Arthur suggested I send the Caldararos out to be cleaned before Mr. Modean's expert has a look at them."

"Who told you to do that?" Grant grumbled, more out of habit than anger. Mary, for all her shortcomings as a woman, was a jolly fine household manager. The paintings had become a bit scruffy. He was just surprised that his half wit of a son had the foresight to suggest it.

Mary was unperturbed. "The frames were getting quite dirty. Now do sit down and have tea. Cook has surpassed herself this afternoon." She surveyed the loaded trolley with a critical eye. There were two kinds of sandwiches, tongue and ham. Tea, of course, in the silver-plated pot as well as a smaller silver pot of coffee. A plate of balmorals sat beside a tray of fancy biscuits. Next to that was an urn of heavy cream, a perfect madeira cake and a Victorian sponge. She nodded, satisfied that her kitchen wouldn't shame her in front of her guests.

"Everything certainly looks lovely," Lydia Modean said quickly. She glanced at the others in the room. Nobody looked like they were having a very nice time.

Arthur Grant was perched on the edge of a chair, his fingers nervously scratching the silk lapels of his elegant gray frock coat. Neville Grant, dressed less formally in a black morning coat and wing-tipped collar, had thumped over and flopped down on the settee. Mary Grant was sitting behind the tea cart, her mouth curved in a slight smile, her eyes glittering coldly.

Lydia avoided looking at Underhill. Watching the man smirk at her when they'd been outside had been bad enough.

"Have you enjoyed your visit?" Arthur Grant asked timidly.

"Very much," Tyrell replied graciously, though he'd already answered that same query out in the garden. "London is a beautiful city." He patted his wife's hand. "I do believe that Johnson was correct when he wrote, 'When a man is tired of London, he is tired of life, for there is in London all that life can afford.'"

"You've read Samuel Johnson?" Underhill inquired archly. "How fascinating. I hadn't realized one could acquire a classical education in your part of the world."

Refusing to rise to the bait, Tyrell merely shrugged. "San Francisco has many fine educational establishments. Unfortunately, I never had the opportunity to acquire much formal education. I'm basically self-educated. Like so many *successful*"—he stressed the last word ever so slightly—"men of my country, I relied upon myself, not my family, to make my way in the world."

Underhill flushed angrily as the barb struck home. Everyone in the room knew he'd dissipated the fortune his family had left him. A series of disastrous investments had forced him to sell the once extensive Underhill art collection as well as the family estate. The only thing left was a small cottage out in some unfashionable part of the countryside. Underhill now made a living using the only skill he had. An eye for art. He hung about the fringes of the art world, brokering deals and acting as an art agent.

"And you, Mrs. Modean?" Arthur inquired hastily. "Are you enjoying your visit?"

"Yes," she replied. "But I'm anxious to go home."

"You don't miss England, then?" Underhill asked. "I should think you'd miss your old friends."

"My wife loves San Francisco," Tyrell interjected smoothly.

Underhill ignored Modean and kept his attention fully on Mrs. Modean. "But surely you must miss the cultural aspects of our great city. I believe you were once quite involved with the art world yourself."

Lydia stared at him for a moment, debating on whether or not to be openly rude. "I was an artists' model," she replied calmly, giving her husband a quick look. He gave her a warm smile. "And to be perfectly honest, I'm afraid I'm not as enamored of London as Tyrell. I prefer the 'cultural aspects' of San Francisco. Last Saturday we went to a sale of supposed 'Old Masters' at Christie's. There wasn't anything worth mentioning in the whole lot."

"I don't know, my dear," her husband said, his eyes sparkling with amusement. "I would have liked to have had that Morland."

"Why?" Lydia countered bluntly. "You didn't like it."

"No," he agreed, "but Morland's work has continued to rise in value and it would have made a nice addition to the collection for the museum. Too bad that other fellow got his hands on it."

"Did it sell for a lot of money?" Arthur asked.

Tyrell shook his head. "Not really. A few hundred pounds."

"Three hundred and thirty-six pounds," Underhill muttered. He knew precisely what everything in that collection had sold for. He'd been there. "If it wasn't much money, why didn't you buy it?"

"I didn't want it that badly," Tyrell answered, looking him straight in the eye, "and the other fellow did."

"So your trip here is business more than pleasure," Mary said conversationally.

"As you've probably guessed, it's a bit of both." Tyrell patted Lydia's arm. "Lydia does have some old friends and relations she likes to stay in touch with. But basically we're here to acquire for the museum. That reminds me. I got a cable from the other board members. They're delighted your husband has agreed to sell the Caldararos."

"I understand the paintings were originally from your family's collection?" Lydia said.

Mary nodded. "They'd been in my family for over two hundred years when I married Neville." She reached for the teapot. "How do you take your tea, Mrs. Modean?"

"Plain, please," Lydia replied.

"When will the paintings be ready?" Tyrell asked.

The maid came back holding a small red-and-white tin. She skirted around the group of guests and handed them to Underhill. "Your tin of mints, sir," she whispered, giving him a quick curtsy and then hurrying out.

Underhill gave the tin a small shake, flipped the lid open and frowned. Two left. Bloody girl. She'd no doubt helped herself. He'd make a fuss but he didn't want to give that wretched American an excuse for thinking him ill-mannered. He'd show them what good breeding was, by God. He popped the last two in his mouth and slapped the lid down.

"In a few days," Mary replied. "Why? Are you in a hurry for them? I understood you weren't leaving until the end of next week."

"It's not that we're in a rush, Mrs. Grant," he explained. "It's that Mr. Marceau, the expert we've hired to authenticate the paintings, is going to Paris on Monday next. I'd hoped to have everything concluded by then."

"Oh, I'm dreadfully sorry. I didn't mean to be so late." This comment was uttered by Helen Collier, Mary Grant's sister. Her face was long and bony, her hair a light brown and worn in a girlish style. Frizzed at the front and plaited low on the neck in a rolled braid, the coiffure was not suited to one of her middle years. She hurried into the drawing room, an apologetic smile on her thin lips. "Do forgive me."

"How's your headache?" Mary asked. "Any better?"

"Much. Thank you for asking." Helen smiled coquettishly at Underhill as she took the chair next to him. He gave her a nod in return and raised his hand to cover his mouth as he coughed.

"It's amazing what having even a little lay down can do for one," she said airily.

"I'm glad you're feeling better," Tyrell said gallantly. He thought females who developed sick headaches from a few minutes in the miserably weak English sun were poor excuses for women. "We were just having the most interesting discussion about English art."

Underhill's coughing got louder, but everyone politely ignored it.

"I'm so sorry to have missed it," Helen said enthusiastically. "Art is one of my great loves."

A peculiar, strangling gasp suddenly filled the quiet room. It took a moment or two before anyone realized the strange sound was actually coming from Underhill. He gasped again and then again before opening his mouth completely, as if he were going to scream. But only great, choking, wheezing croaks were emitted from his thin throat.

Modean was the first to realize something was seriously wrong. He leapt to his feet and dashed to the stricken man. "Good God, what's wrong with you, man?"

Underhill's eyes bulged and his pale skin flushed as he struggled to drag air into his chest.

"He must be choking on those damned mints," Modean cried, lifting his hand and slapping the man's back.

But it didn't help. Underhill began thrashing about on the cushions, his hands clawing at the tight collar of his white silk shirt.

Helen screamed. "Oh, God. Someone do something."

By this time everyone, even Neville Grant, had moved toward the man flailing about on the settee. Underhill slipped off his seat and landed on the carpet with a thud, his legs kicking so wildly he clipped Helen on the arm. She screamed again and Lydia Modean pulled her back out of the way.

"Give them some space," Lydia ordered.

Tyrell wrestled Underhill onto his back and yanked off the tight buttons of his collar, freeing his throat. But that made no difference. His face turned white, so white it was almost bluish in color.

"For God's sake, what's wrong with him?" Mary demanded. "Is he having a fit?"

Suddenly the thrashing stopped.

James Underhill went completely still.

Modean bent down and put his ear to the man's chest. He raised his hand for silence as he listened. For a moment the room was quiet. But then Modean straightened and looked up at the others. He shook his head.

"Well, what's wrong with the fellow?" Neville Grant asked brusquely. "Is he sick? Should we call a doctor?"

"That's not going to do him any good now," Modean replied as he rose to his feet. "He's dead. I think you'd better call the police."

"Dead?" Neville poked at the lifeless form with his cane. "Are you sure?"

"For God's sake, Neville, stop that," Mary snapped.

"Dead? But that's impossible," Helen Collier wailed.

Lydia Modean closed her eyes.

Arthur Grant slumped into the nearest chair.

Mary Grant stiffened her spine, strode to the bell pull and gave it a hard tug. Almost immediately the doors opened and the butler appeared. His gaze swept the room, his eyes widening as he espied Underhill lying in front of the settee.

Before any of the Grants could issue an order, Tyrell Modean spoke. "Send for the police," he instructed the surprised servant. "We've a dead man here."

"That won't be necessary, sir." The butler swallowed nervously. "They're already here."

"The police? Here?" Neville Grant stomped past the butler and into the hallway. Standing by the front door, he spotted three men. "Don't just stand there," he called. "Come on. It's in here."

Witherspoon stared at the apparition at the opposite end of the hall. The gentleman seemed to be talking to them.

"I say," he murmured to Smythe. "This looks like it might be a tad easier than I thought. The fellow certainly seems eager to answer questions."

"Do get a move on," the elderly man shouted, waving at them impatiently with his cane. "Why aren't you in uniform? You'd better be the police or I'll have your . . ."

"I am a policeman," Witherspoon assured him, "and these gentlemen"

—he gestured at Smythe and Wiggins—"are from my household. Now, if you don't mind, I'd like to ask you a few questions."

"For God's sake, Neville," Mary shouted from the open door of the drawing room. "Bring them here."

"This way, this way." Grant turned on his heel and started back the way he'd just come.

"Cor blimey," the coachman muttered, "what's goin' on 'ere?"

"I don't know," Witherspoon replied honestly. "But I do believe he wants us to follow him." He hurried after the man, and after a moment's hesitation, Wiggins and Smythe trotted after him.

Witherspoon stopped short when he entered the drawing room. A group of elegantly dressed people stood staring down at a man lying on the carpet. The inspector, thinking the man was injured, flew across the room and dropped to his knees. "What's happened here?"

"We've no idea," a woman replied archly.

Witherspoon felt for a pulse. There was none. But that didn't mean the fellow was gone. He looked at Wiggins. "Run and fetch the constable on the corner. Tell him to find a doctor and get here right away."

"That won't do any good," a man with an American accent said. "He's dead."

"How long?"

"A few moments ago," the American continued. "He choked to death. He was eating those hard confectionaries. Mints, I think. They must have lodged in his throat."

"Fetch a doctor anyway," Witherspoon ordered Wiggins. "It might not be too late." The footman took off at a run.

"Poor bloke," Smythe muttered. He dropped down next to the inspector. "What 'appened?"

"We just told you. He choked to death," Mary Grant replied. "We were sitting here having tea when all of a sudden, he started gasping for air and then he simply keeled over."

"Oh, no," Helen wailed. "He can't be gone, he simply can't."

Mary ignored her sister and kept her gaze on the two men kneeling by Underhill. One of them looked like a brutal street thug and the other, though far more respectably dressed, looked like a bank clerk. "You say you're from the police?"

Witherspoon nodded slowly but didn't look up. "I'm Inspector Gerald Witherspoon."

Helen continued to sob. As no one else in the room took any notice of the woman, Lydia Modean put an arm around her and led her away. "I'll just take her up to her room," she murmured to her husband.

"What should we do now, sir?" Smythe asked the inspector.

Witherspoon wasn't sure. There was something decidedly odd about this situation. He swallowed hard and forced himself to continue examining the body. The inspector was a bit squeamish about corpses. Then he wondered if this one could really count as a corpse. After all, the poor man had only just died a few moments ago.

"What was his name?" he asked. He had the strangest feeling the man hadn't choked to death. For one thing, the fellow's mouth was gaping open and he could see two small, round, white objects stuck to the roof of his mouth.

"James Underhill," a male voice replied.

Smythe cleared his throat. "Uh, sir . . ."

"Oh, sorry, Smythe." He looked up and gave his coachman a weary smile. Then he looked at the imposing woman standing over him. "Madam, would you be so kind as to take everyone to another room? I'd like to have a few moments of privacy to examine this gentleman."

"We'll go into the morning room," she said. "It's just down the hall."

Smythe waited till they were alone and then said, "Is something wrong, sir?"

"I don't think this fellow choked to death, Smythe," Witherspoon said. He took a deep breath, forced the man's jaws further open and stuck his hand into the dead man's mouth.

"What are you doin', sir?" Smythe hissed, shocked to his very core.

Witherspoon jerked his fingers out and exhaled the breath he'd been holding. "Checking to see if there was any obstruction in his throat." He gasped. "There isn't. Would you please reach into my coat pocket and grab my handkerchief?" His hands were covered with spittle and he didn't want to get it on his clothing.

Perplexed, the coachman did as instructed and pulled a clean, white cotton hankie out of the inspector's inside pocket.

"Could you open it, please," Witherspoon directed, "and hold it firmly on the sides?" He took another deep breath and stuck his fingers between the corpse's lips.

Smythe spread the material as instructed. He felt his stomach contract as the inspector slowly eased his hand out—and there on the tip of his finger was a small, round, white object.

"He couldn't choke on this if he'd not swallowed it," Witherspoon murmured, carefully depositing the object in the center of the outspread handkerchief.

Smythe still couldn't believe what he'd just seen. "Shouldn't we wait for the doctor before we go pokin' at the poor feller?"

"Normally, yes." Witherspoon hoped he wouldn't faint. "But in this case, I want to make sure our evidence doesn't melt."

"Cor blimey, sir." Smythe shook his head as he saw the inspector repeating what he'd just done. "You've a stronger stomach than I do."

"No, I don't." Witherspoon hoped he'd keep his dinner down. "I assure you, this is quite the most difficult thing I've done in a very long time." It was his duty that forced him to do such an abominable thing. But duty was duty and despite his revulsion, he had to know the truth. "Despite what the witnesses said, I've an idea this man didn't choke to death."

Smythe's heavy brows creased. "What are ya thinkin', sir?"

"Well . . ." The inspector didn't wish to "jump the gun," so to speak. But his "inner voice," that instinct that Mrs. Jeffries was always reminding him to listen to, was prompting him along a certain course of action. "I'm thinking he couldn't have choked if the confectionaries were on the roof of his mouth and not obstructing a breathing passage. Furthermore, he's a young man, probably not past his thirtieth year. His limbs appear to be straight." The inspector examined the man's hands. "His skin isn't discolored and there's no sign of blood or any other injury. Except for being dead, he looks to be in relatively good health. He's not particularly fat or diseased looking . . ." He paused, not quite sure to put what he was thinking into words.

"Right, sir," the coachman agreed. "Except for him bein' dead and all, he looks right healthy to me too."

"So it seems to me if he keeled over in the middle of tea, he might have been"—he hesitated—"poisoned."

"He's been poisoned." Dr. Bosworth rose to his feet and nodded at the constable. "Go ahead and take him away," he instructed. "I'll do the full postmortem at the hospital."

"Are you certain?" Witherspoon pressed.

"As sure as I can be without doing an autopsy," Bosworth replied. He was a tall man with a thin, serious face and red hair. "But if I were a betting man, I'd say that poor fellow had ingested potassium cyanide."

"What, precisely, makes you think so?" Witherspoon wanted to be as certain as possible before he started asking questions.

Bosworth hesitated only briefly. "There's a faint scent of bitter almond on the man's lips. From the color of his skin, I'd say he died of asphyxiation. As no one admits to choking the life out of the poor fellow, I'd wager he must have ingested something to cause such a reaction."

"Could it have been on one of these?" Witherspoon opened the handkerchief he'd been holding and held it out so the doctor could see it clearly. "Mints, I believe. I took them out of the victim's mouth."

"May I?" Bosworth asked. He brought the open handkerchief close to his face. His face was a mask of concentration as he took a long, deep breath. "Hum . . . yes, unless I'm very much mistaken, underneath the mint scent is bitter almonds." He looked at the inspector. "Have you touched these?"

"Only with the tip of my finger."

"Then you'd best go wash your hands soon. Ask one of the servants to show you to a cloakroom and be sure to use plenty of soap." Bosworth waved the constables carrying a stretcher into the room.

While the inspector hurried off to wash up and the doctor supervised getting the body moved, Smythe took a few moments to suss out the lay of the house. He tiptoed out into the hallway and peeked into a room a little further up the hall. They were all in there. The old gent with the cane was stomping about muttering something under his breath. The American was sitting next to his wife, his arm draped around her shoulders. The other two women were standing next to the window. The one with the frizzy brown hair had stopped crying and was talking in a low, hissing whisper. Smythe thought she looked mad enough to spit nails. The tall, regal-looking one didn't seem to be paying any attention to her. She just stood there, tapping her foot and shooting glares at the pale-faced young man. He sat on the chair, looking like he'd just lost his best friend.

"Oh, there you are, Smythe." The inspector appeared from around the corner.

"What are you goin' to do, sir?" Smythe was itching to get back and tell the others, but at the same time, he was loathe to leave the inspector. He didn't want to miss anything.

"I'm not sure, Smythe," Witherspoon admitted. "Officially, this isn't a murder investigation yet, only a death under suspicious circumstances. I'm not certain I ought to do anything except trot along to the station and make a report."

"But if it is a murder," the coachman pressed, "probably one of them"—he jerked his head toward the room the others were in—"had something to do with it. If you let 'em loose without questionin' 'em, they might muck up or destroy any evidence that's 'ere."

"I know."

"You can at least question 'em, sir," Smythe persisted. "Like ya said, it is a death under suspicious circumstances."

"Of course it is," Witherspoon decided. Turning, he called to the constable standing beside the open front door. "Constable, sent to the police station and inform the duty sergeant that there's been a suspicious death at this house. After that I'd like you to fetch Constable Barnes. He's off duty, but you can get his address."

"I'm already here, sir." A tall man with a craggy face stepped through the front door. "Wiggins fetched me, sir. He thought you might need me."

"I 'ope I did right, sir," Wiggins said cautiously.

"Yes, Wiggins, you did."

"What've we got, sir?" Barnes asked as he advanced toward his superior.

"A suspicious death," Witherspoon replied. "Luckily, Dr. Bosworth happened to be available." He stepped back to let the constables carrying the stretcher move past him towards the front door.

"There was nothing lucky about it," Bosworth commented as he stepped into the hall. "I was on my way to see you, Inspector. I'd just gotten off the omnibus on the Holland Park Road when your lad came dashing up to the constable. He spotted me and told me there was a possible death here." Dr. Bosworth wasn't telling the whole truth. As a matter of fact, he'd been on his way to the inspector's house, but it was Mrs. Jeffries he'd wanted to visit, not the inspector. But as his association with Mrs. Jeffries generally involved one of the inspector's cases, and as he was now part of the conspiracy of silence surrounding the household's help in those cases, he was in a bit of a quandry.

"You were on your way to see me?" Witherspoon said, somewhat perplexed.

"I wanted to invite you to dine with me one evening next week,"

Bosworth replied. "A colleague of mine from New York is in London. I thought you might be interested in meeting him. He works very closely with the New York police. Like myself, he's a doctor." The invitation was quite genuine. But Bosworth had meant it for Mrs. Jeffries. She was someone whose abilities rather astonished him.

"Oh." Witherspoon was quite flattered. "How very kind of you, Dr. Bosworth. I'd like that very much."

Bosworth smiled absently and started toward the door.

"Excuse me, sir." One of the constables came out of the drawing room. "I've found this, sir." He hesitated, not knowing whether to give the object in his hand to the doctor or the inspector. "It's a tin of peppermints. I saw it under the settee when we moved the body."

Witherspoon nodded for the constable to relinquish the tin to Bosworth, who took it and flipped open the lid. Holding it to his nose, he sniffed. "Ah ha." He shoved the tin under Witherspoon's nose. "Can you smell it?"

Witherspoon took a deep breath. Even though the tin was empty and all he was smelling was the inside paper wrapper, the scent was unmistakable. Faint, perhaps, but definitely there despite being masked by the overpowering mint scent. "Almonds," he said, raising his eyes to meet the doctor's. "Bitter almonds. Do you think it's cyanide?" He didn't want to make any rash accusations. But he didn't wish to ignore evidence either.

"Probably," Bosworth replied. "I'll run an analysis. Unfortunately, there aren't any mints left, only the paper, the half-eaten mints and a few grains of residue powder. Still, there should be enough to give us a definite answer one way or another."

"By all means, Doctor," Witherspoon agreed quickly. "Run the tests. Be sure and mark it into evidence with the constables."

"I know the procedure, Inspector." Bosworth grinned cheerfully. "Even if I'm not on my own patch tonight. Well, I'd best be going. I'll get started on the PM early tomorrow morning. We ought to know something definite straight away."

"You'll not have any difficulty with the local police surgeon, will you?" Witherspoon asked. Bosworth's comment had made him realize this whole procedure was highly irregular. The postmortem was supposed to be done by the local doctor assigned to this district.

Bosworth shook his head. "I'm assigned to Westminster, Inspector. So I'm having the body taken to St. Thomas's. There shouldn't be any difficulty. The local doctor for this district is a colleague of mine and a friend. He'll not make a fuss. He's enough on his plate as it is." He nodded goodbye and left.

"What do we do now, sir?" Barnes asked.

"I'd best send Smythe and Wiggins home," Witherspoon muttered. But when he turned around, neither one of them was anywhere to be found.

"I knew that once Constable Barnes arrived, we'd not 'ave much of an excuse to keep 'angin' about," Smythe explained. "So I 'ot footed it back 'ere to let you know what was goin' on so we could get crackin' on it."

Smythe and Wiggins had told the household everything that occurred since they'd left the house with the inspector in tow.

"Are we sure it's a murder, then?" Betsy asked suspiciously. She didn't want to get her hopes up and then find out the man had dropped dead from something else.

"We won't know for sure until tomorrow," Smythe replied, "but Dr. Bosworth seemed to think it was poison."

Mrs. Jeffries had a dozen different questions to ask, but right now, she didn't have the time. If this was a case of deliberate poisoning, then the sooner they got started, the better. "I think we ought to proceed on the assumption that it is murder. Did you manage to find out the names of the people present at the Grant house?" she asked hopefully, looking at Smythe.

"I didn't 'ave time," he admitted.

"I did," Wiggins volunteered.

Smythe slanted him a suspicious glance. "'Ow'd you manage that with all yer toin' and froin'?"

"I'm fast when I want to be," he said proudly. "And I nipped down to the kitchen after I brung the constable. Two of the 'ousemaids was natterin' on about what 'ad 'appened. They named names, if ya know what I mean. Seems the fellow who died was named Underhill. The woman doin' all the screamin' when we come in was Helen Collier. She's sister to Mr. Neville Grant's wife, Mary. She was glarin' like a tartar and actin' like the bloke dyin' was a personal insult. Neville Grant was an old bloke with a cane and there was a pale-faced feller that looked like he'd just lost his best friend—that was Arthur Grant, Neville's son. The two others were an American couple by the name of Modean."

Awed, they all stared at him. Wiggins shrugged. "The 'ousemaids was natterin' like a couple of magpies. I'da 'eard more but that stick of a butler come by and chased 'em both about their business."

"So at least we've a few names to start with," Mrs. Goodge said triumphantly.

"We'd best send for Luty and Hatchet," Betsy said. "You know how they get when we don't send for them right away."

Smythe looked at Mrs. Jeffries. "Should I go?"

"The inspector might take it upon himself to start asking questions tonight," she said thoughtfully. "On the other hand, he might come home quite soon."

"I think Smythe ought to go straight away," Mrs. Goodge said stoutly. "The worst that can happen is the inspector comin' in and finding them here. But he'd think nothing of it. They're good friends."

"Go ahead, Smythe," Mrs. Jeffries instructed. "See if you can get them here quickly. We've much to discuss."

As soon as Smythe had disappeared, she turned to Wiggins. "Was there any sign of Irene Simmons at the Grant house?"

Wiggins shook his head. "Nothin'. That's one of the reasons I nipped down to the kitchen. I wanted to 'ave a bit of a look about the place. But I didn't see anything."

"Do you think this man dyin' and Irene Simmons might be connected?" Betsy asked.

Mrs. Jeffries wasn't sure. "I don't know. It would be so much simpler if we knew for certain this man was murdered."

"For the sake of argument, let's say he was," Mrs. Goodge suggested.

"Then I'd say the disappearance of Irene Simmons is connected in some way with the dead man," she replied.

"Good." Mrs. Goodge lit the fire on the stove. "That'll make it nice and simple-like. I'll just put some water on to boil. We might as well have tea when Luty and Hatchet get here. It'll help us keep our wits about us."

"I'll get the cups," Betsy volunteered.

They kept themselves busy tidying up and setting the table. Finally, after what seemed like hours, they heard the sound of a carriage pulling up outside.

"They're here," Mrs. Jeffries said as she took her seat at the head of the table.

"Land o' Goshen," Luty cried, "thank goodness Smythe got there when he did. We was fixin' to go out."

She was an elderly American woman with sharp black eyes, white hair and a penchant for bright clothes. Her small frame was swathed in a deep crimson evening jacket decorated with ostrich feathers. Tossing her handbag onto the table, she snatched out the chair next to the housekeeper and flopped down.

"Good evening, everyone," Hatchet, her tall, white-haired, dignified butler said as he followed his mistress into the kitchen. He was dressed as always: pristine white shirt, black frock coat and trousers. "It is rather fortunate that Smythe arrived when he did. We were about to leave for Lord Staunton's dinner party." He tossed a malevolent glance at Luty. "Unfortunately, Madam didn't have time to send her regrets to Lord Staunton."

"Piddle." Luty waved a hand dismissively. "That old windbag has so many people cluttering up his place he'll not notice if I'm there or not. I ain't missin' me a murder to go have supper with a bunch of people I don't even like. I would'na accepted the invitation in the first place if you hadn't nagged me into it."

The American woman was rich, eccentric and had a heart as big as the country that had spawned her. Her butler was smart, devoted to his mistress and a bit of a martinet. They were dear friends of the household, having worked with them on a number of the inspector's cases.

Hatchet raised one eyebrow and drew out a chair for himself. "I never nag, madam. However, like you, I didn't want to risk missing out either."

"We ready, then?" Smythe asked, dropping into the chair next to Betsy.

"Yes," Mrs. Jeffries replied. "If no one objects, I'll start." She told the newcomers everything, beginning with Nanette Lanier's unexpected visit. "So you see," she finished, "we may have called you out under false pretenses. We don't know that we do have a murder here. Underhill might have died from natural causes."

"If he did, then I'm the Queen of Sheba," Luty declared. "A disappearin' woman and a dead man in the same house within days of each other." She snorted. "Somethin' funny's goin' on, that's for sure."

"I quite agree," Hatchet added. "One extraordinary event might be explainable, but two? No, Mrs. Jeffries, you were right to send for us. Something strange is indeed going on in that household."

"So what do we do now?" Mrs. Goodge asked. She glanced anxiously in the direction of her larders. Her provisions were low and she had to do a bit of baking to feed her sources. People loosened their tongues better over a slice of cake or a good currant bun.

"Well," Mrs. Jeffries said slowly, "I think we ought to proceed as we usually do. Though there is something we must keep in mind."

"What's that?" Wiggins asked, picking up his mug and taking a sip.

"We did promise Nanette we'd find her friend."

"But you said they was probably connected," Smythe declared.

"Might be connected," she corrected. "Then again, one thing may have nothing to do with the other. We did make a promise. We must honor our word."

"Does that mean we can't get crackin' on this 'ere murder?" Wiggins asked the question that all of them were thinking.

"It means," Mrs. Jeffries said firmly, "that we might have to do both."

CHAPTER 3

"We'd best take statements tonight," Inspector Witherspoon said to Barnes. "I think we'd better have a quick word with the members of the household."

"Right, sir," Barnes agreed. He stifled a yawn and cast a longing glance at the loaded tea trolley. Tea would be nice right about now. Then he remembered the victim might have been poisoned and suddenly he wasn't quite so thirsty. "Do you want to speak to everyone together or should I bring them in one at a time?"

"One at a time, I think," Witherspoon said. "This is, after all, a suspicious death. Start with the elderly gentleman. We might as well hear what he's got to say so he can get to bed. People that age need their rest. Have the police constables take statements from the servants."

"Yes, sir," Barnes said, moving smartly toward the door. As soon as he'd disappeared, the inspector took a few moments to study his surroundings. No shortage of money here, he thought, as his gaze flicked about the huge room.

An elegant crystal chandelier, ablaze with light, cast a bright glow over the exquisite furnishings. Oil paintings in ornate gold frames and family portraits were beautifully set off by the pale, wheat-colored walls. Dark panelling, its wood shining in the reflected glow of the chandeliers, covered the lower half of the walls. The furnishings were as elegant as the house itself: settees in heavy blue and gold damask, two groupings of high-backed upholstered velveteen chairs and tables covered with silk-fringed shawls. Heavy royal-blue curtains were draped artistically across the windows.

His gaze came to rest on the tea trolley. He wondered if he ought to take it into evidence.

"What's all this nonsense, then?"

Witherspoon whirled about just as Barnes and the elderly gentleman entered the drawing room. "What's the matter?" the man snapped at the inspector. "Cat got your tongue? Why are you still here and why does this person"—he pointed his cane at Barnes—"insist I make a statement like I'm some kind of a criminal? Underhill choked on one of those wretched mints he was always popping in his mouth. That's all I've got to say on the subject."

"And you are?" Witherspoon asked politely.

"Neville Grant. I own this house."

"I'm sorry to inconvenience you, Mr. Grant," the inspector said apologetically, "but there is some question as to how Mr. Underhill met his death."

"What do you mean?" Grant sputtered. "There's no question as to how he died. He choked to death. I saw it with my own eyes."

"Then you'll make an excellent witness, sir," Witherspoon assured him. "Now, I suggest we all sit down. Constable, will you be so kind as to take notes?"

"That'll not be so 'ard," Wiggins said cheerfully. "We can keep a lookout for Miss Lanier's friend while we're sussin' out who killed this Underhill bloke."

"Seems to me if the two things are connected," Betsy added thoughtfully, "we shouldn't have any problems getting information about Irene Simmons while we're digging for clues on the murder."

"Should be dead easy," Smythe agreed.

"Could be the girl's run off with some artist," Luty put in. "Could be she ain't missin' at all."

Mrs. Jeffries was afraid she wasn't making her point. "It could be that the two events aren't at all linked," she said firmly, "and it might be quite difficult to do both investigations at once. I must remind you, we did agree to help Nanette find her friend."

A heavy, guilty quiet descended on the kitchen. Everyone tried to pretend they didn't really understand what Mrs. Jeffries was trying to tell them. Finally, Smythe cleared his throat. "What are ya tryin' to tell us?"

"I'm simply trying to point out that we have a prior obligation."

"You want us to find out who snatched Miss Simmons before we can start trackin' Underhill's killer?" Wiggins asked incredulously.

"I didn't say that," Mrs. Jeffries objected. "But it may be necessary for us to divide our resources. Some of us might need to work on the Underhill matter and some of us might need to investigate Miss Simmons's disappearance. There's no reason we can't do both at the same time. There are"—she swept her arm out in an arc, a gesture that encompassed the entire group—"rather a lot of us. We can easily handle both tasks."

Again, no one said anything. The silence spoke volumes about what they were thinking. The mystery surrounding Irene Simmons's disappearance was definitely second fiddle to a possible murder case. Everyone wanted to investigate the murder. But no one wanted to be the first to admit it.

Hatchet broke the impasse. "I'll be quite happy to lend my efforts to locating the girl," he volunteered. "After all, Underhill is already dead. This young woman may still be alive."

"I'll help find Irene too," Betsy added. Her conscience had gotten the best of her as well. "I mean, I like investigatin' murder and all, but Hatchet's right. Irene Simmons might be alive and needing help."

Satisfied, Mrs. Jeffries smiled. She'd been fairly sure they'd do what was right. If need be, she'd been quite prepared to take on the task of locating Irene Simmons herself. "Excellent. I, of course, shall be assisting in both matters. Now, let's see what we can come up with for tomorrow. Betsy, why don't you use your resources to find out if anyone in the Grant household knew the girl."

"All right," Betsy replied brightly. While she was at it, she'd suss out a few things about this murder too. "I'll have a go at the local shopkeepers tomorrow as well. Perhaps one of them saw Irene."

"There ain't no shops on Beltrane Gardens," Wiggins told her, trying to be helpful.

Betsy shot him a frown. "Well, someone might have seen her walking on Holland Park Road. There's shops along there. Just because Nanette claims the girl never came out of the Grant house, that doesn't make it a fact. Someone might have seen her and we won't know for certain unless we ask."

"You're right, Betsy," Mrs. Jeffries interjected. "As we've learned from our past cases, we mustn't take everything we're told at face value. Nanette Lanier could easily be mistaken about the real facts surrounding Irene's disappearance." She knew good and well that Betsy wasn't one to let a chance pass her by. The maid would do her utmost to find the missing girl, but while she was at it, Mrs. Jeffries knew she'd get as much information as possible about the Grant household and James Underhill.

"As I shall be using my rather considerable resources to locate the girl," Hatchet declared, "and Miss Betsy will be using her own exceptional detecting and observation skills, I'm sure we'll have the young woman home safe and sound in no time." He beamed encouragingly at the maid, who smiled in return.

"What do ya mean, 'resources'?" Luty demanded suspiciously. It galled her that her own butler constantly got the jump on her when it came to hunting down clues. The man had more sources to tap for information in this city than a dog had fleas. She wasn't fooled for one minute by his pronouncement, either. She knew good and well he'd be snooping about looking for Underhill's killer at the same time he was trying to find the Simmons girl.

Hatchet allowed himself a small smirk. "I believe, madam, we agreed on a previous occasion that some of our resources were to be kept secret. Even from one another. If you don't mind, I'd rather not say what or who I'll be using in my investigations."

"Use whatever means you have at your disposal," Mrs. Jeffries said quickly. Luty and Hatchet, despite their devotion to one another, were fierce competitors when it came to investigations. "And the rest of you, please, don't feel that because Betsy and Hatchet are taking the primary responsibility for locating Miss Simmons that the rest of you won't be expected to do your fair share. All of us must do our best to find her."

"Of course we will," Mrs. Goodge agreed stoutly. Mentally, she made a list of people she could drag into her kitchen tomorrow. It wouldn't hurt to ask a few questions about missing models while she was at it.

Hatchet leaned forward on one elbow. "Before I forget, Mrs. Jeffries, would you please give me a brief description of Miss Simmons?"

Mrs. Jeffries cringed, disgusted at herself for overlooking such an important detail. "Oh my goodness, I never thought to ask Nanette Lanier. Gracious, how silly of me."

"None of us thought of it, either," Smythe said, seeing the housekeeper's stricken expression. "Don't be so 'ard on yerself. Guess we was all so excited about gettin' somethin' to do, we forgot one of the most important bits. Findin' out what she looked like." He shook his head in disbelief.

"I know what she's like," Wiggins announced cheerfully. "She's got dark brown hair, green eyes and she's about my height."

"Cor blimey, 'ow'd you know that?" Smythe demanded.

"I asked Miss Lanier when I walked 'er out to get a 'ansom," he explained. "She told me Miss Simmons was wearing one of her old dresses too. It were a dark blue wool with white piping on the jacket."

"Excellent, Wiggins," Mrs. Jeffries congratulated him.

"I thought it might be important," he replied modestly.

"And it is important." Hatchet clapped the footman on the back. "Well done, lad. Well done. Armed with that pertinent information, Miss Betsy and I will really be able to get cracking on finding our missing lady."

"Humph." Luty contented herself with giving Hatchet a good frown and then turned her attention to Mrs. Jeffries. "What do ya want me to start on?"

Mrs. Jeffries had already thought about that. Luty was one of the wealthiest women in London. She socialized with stockbrokers, bankers and industrial leaders. Her contacts in the city were legendary, and, most important, Luty knew who would talk and who wouldn't. "Find out what you can about the victim's financial situation."

"What about this Neville Grant feller?" Luty queried. "Underhill was killed at his house."

"By all means, Luty," Mrs. Jeffries said. "Find out what you can about all of them."

"Includin' the visitin' Americans?"

"Oh yes, we mustn't leave anyone out," she replied.

"Do ya want me to start on the pubs and the cabbies?" Smythe asked.

"Actually, I'd prefer you find out what you can about the victim. It's too bad we don't know where he lived or anything else about the man, but I think it's important we find out as much as possible."

Smythe drummed his fingers lightly on the table, thinking. "I can nip out tonight and find out a bit about 'im from the locals. Believe me, the news of a suspicious death like that'll already be makin' the rounds of the local pubs."

"You just want an excuse to go out drinking," Betsy charged. "It's not fair, either. The women in the household can't go out looking for information at night—"

"Oh yes, we can," Luty declared. "I've got my peacemaker out in the carriage—"

"Really, madam," Hatchet interrupted. "I do wish you'd leave that wretched gun at home. We're not in the Old West. Carrying a weapon is illegal here. This is a civilized country."

Luty snorted. "Civilized? Cow patties! If you're so dang blasted civilized, how come we always got murders to solve? You ain't any more civilized than I am. You've just got a fancier accent."

"That's not true, lass," Smythe said earnestly, paying no attention to anyone but Betsy. "I only 'ave a pint or two when I go out. But it's important we get started on this—"

"We are gettin' started," Mrs. Goodge interrupted, "and as we don't even know for sure that Underhill's been murdered, I agree with Betsy. It isn't fair that the men can go out and about at night lookin' for clues and we can't."

"But you never leave the kitchen," Wiggins protested.

"That's not the point," the cook replied stoutly.

"Really, everyone," Mrs. Jeffries said firmly. "Let's calm down a moment. There's no need for us to be interrupting one another and making accusations. Betsy"—she looked at the maid—"I quite agree with Smythe. It is important that we get started right away. We are investigating two possibly separate matters. If he can find out a few more facts about either situation, I think he ought to go." She glanced at Wiggins. "But I quite agree with Mrs. Goodge as well. It isn't fair that a female can't walk the city streets at night the way a man does. Now, can we please put our attention back to the immediate problems at hand?"

"I know what I'll be doin' tomorrow," the cook said. "I'll be getting my sources primed and while I'm at it, I'll find out what I can about Irene Simmons."

"What do ya want me to do?" Wiggins asked.

"Get as much information as you can from the servants in the Grant house. Find out who was there, what their relationships to one another are and if any of them had a reason for wanting Underhill dead," she said crisply. "Also, see if any of the staff knows anything about Irene Simmons."

"Cor blimey." Wiggins blinked in surprise at the enormity of his task. Then he saw the teasing glint in the housekeeper's eyes. "Oh, I get it. Find out what I can."

"That's right." She laughed.

"What'll you be doin', Hepzibah?" Luty asked curiously.

"To begin with, I shall wait up for the inspector and find out what he's learned this evening," Mrs. Jeffries said. "Tomorrow, I do believe I'll make a couple of calls."

"To who?" Smythe asked.

"Dr. Bosworth and Nanette Lanier."

"I can see why you want to talk to the good doctor," Hatchet said, "but why are you going to see Miss Lanier? Hasn't she already told you everything she knows about Miss Simmons's disappearance?"

"Indeed she has." Mrs. Jeffries smiled. "But I want to find out what she knows about James Underhill."

Witherspoon's ears were ringing by the time he finished taking Neville Grant's statement. The man didn't believe in speaking below a roar. He winced as the drawing room door slammed shut violently behind Grant.

"He wasn't very helpful, was he, sir?" Barnes asked, glancing down at his notebook. "Perhaps one of the others will be more forthcoming."

"Excuse me, sir." Constable Martin stuck his head into the room. "But the American gentleman wants to know if he and his wife can leave now."

"Could you just send them in here, please?" the inspector instructed. "I'd like to take their statements before they go."

"Yes, sir," the constable replied.

"You're going to interview them together, sir?"

"I'm not sure I ought to be questioning them at all." Witherspoon rubbed his eyes and fought back a yawn. "They've probably got nothing to do with the fellow's death, even if it is a murder. Neville Grant told us they only arrived from America recently, so I don't see how they could have disliked Underhill enough to poison the fellow."

A few moments later, Constable Martin ushered in the Modeans. The inspector introduced himself and Barnes. Tyrell Modean—a tall, dark-haired man with gray sprinkled at his temples and a rugged, tan complexion—was a good ten years older than his beautiful, auburn-haired wife. Lydia Modean wore a bronze-colored day gown that rustled faintly as she crossed the room. The dress was simple with only a decorative fichu of cream lace at the base of her slender throat. But from the cut of the fabric and the way it fitted against her slender frame, it was obviously expensive, even to Witherspoon's less-than-experienced eyes. She wore no jewelry save for an ornately filagreed gold wedding band. The inspector noted her husband wore one just like hers.

When she spoke, his surprise was obvious. "You're English?" he asked. He'd assumed that, like her husband, she was from America.

"Born in Bristol," she replied with a slight smile.

"Excuse me, Inspector, but how long is this going to take?" Tyrell asked. "It's been quite an ordeal for both of us."

"I appreciate that," Witherspoon answered, "but there are a few questions I need to ask. I'll be as quick as possible. Why don't you both have a seat?" He gestured towards the settee.

Modean looked for a moment as though he were going to refuse, then he sighed, took his wife's arm and gallantly seated her before sitting down himself. "What do you want to know? All we can tell you is what we saw."

"That'll be fine, sir. Do go ahead."

"We'd just sat down to have tea when all of a sudden, Underhill started making these noises, kind of a coughing sound. At first I thought he'd swallowed the wrong way or was just coughing to clear out his throat. Then I realized the poor devil was choking. I jumped up and tried to help." He shrugged defeatedly. "Slapped him on the back and got his collar undone, but nothing seemed to do any good. He just kept wheezing and coughing and making these god-awful noises. I thought he must be having a fit of some kind. His body was jerking so hard he fell off the settee. We got him onto his back, but that didn't do any good either. He just thrashed about for a few minutes and then died."

"I see," Witherspoon said slowly. "Was today the first time you'd met James Underhill?"

"No." Modean shook his head. "I'd met him a number of years ago. We didn't really travel in the same circles, but I had run across him before."

"James Underhill introduced the two of us," Lydia Modean put in quickly. "It was several years ago. Tyrell bought some Flemish watercolors from him."

"You're an art dealer, sir?" Witherspoon asked, thinking him a gallery owner from America.

Modean laughed. "I'm a businessman, Inspector. I've a number of irons in the fire back home. Banking, hotels, investments. My vocation is making money, but my great love is art. That's why we're here. I'm negotiating with Mr. Grant to buy three Caldararos."

"Mr. Underhill was an art dealer?" the inspector commented.

"I wouldn't really say that." Modean leaned back against the cushions.

"I think 'art dealer' is a bit more formal for what he actually did. The man didn't own a gallery or anything like that, Inspector. He's more what one would call an art broker. By that I mean that he seemed to always know who was buying and who was selling."

"Was Mr. Underhill involved in your negotiations with Mr. Grant?" Witherspoon asked.

"Absolutely not," Modean replied bluntly. "I don't know why Underhill was here today, but it had nothing to do with us." He shot his wife a quick glance. "I just assumed he was a guest of the Grants."

"I see," the inspector murmured. "You were invited for tea?"

"Right. But as Grant and I had business to discuss, Mrs. Grant asked us to come early."

"Exactly what time did you arrive, sir?" Barnes asked.

"I'm not sure."

"Four o'clock, dear," Lydia said. "You and Mr. Grant joined us in the garden about four-fifteen."

Witherspoon wasn't sure precisely what he ought to be asking. It was decidedly awkward questioning people when one wasn't even sure a murder had taken place. "So Mr. and Mrs. Grant were there, as were the two of you. Anyone else?"

It was Lydia who answered. "Helen Collier, Mrs. Grant's sister, was also there, as was Arthur Grant and, of course, Mr. Underhill."

"Arthur Grant?" The inspector vaguely recalled seeing a pale, fidgety young fellow when he'd first arrived. "Is he Mr. Grant's grandson?"

Lydia's eyes sparkled with amusement. "Arthur is his son, Inspector. By his first wife."

"Ah, I see. Well, I suppose Mr. Arthur Grant's antecedents are really neither here nor there."

"Inspector," Tyrell said, "I don't really know what else my wife or I can tell you. We arrived here at about four, I spent ten minutes in the study with Mr. Grant discussing business, then we sat in the garden with the others until tea was served. We'd only been in the drawing room a few moments before Underhill died. It was a perfectly ordinary, civil, if somewhat boring afternoon. Now, if you don't mind, it's been a rather trying day. I'd like to take my wife back to the hotel."

Witherspoon concentrated hard, trying to think if there was something else he ought to ask, but nothing came to mind. "Of course, sir."

Modean and his wife stood up. She sagged against him gently and he put his arm around her shoulders. "If you need to ask us anything else, we'll be at your disposal. We're at the Alexandra in Knightsbridge."

It was quite late by the time the inspector came home that night, but Mrs. Jeffries waited up for him. She took his hat and coat. "I dare say, sir, you must be exhausted. Wiggins and Smythe told us what happened."

"I am a bit tired," he admitted.

"Would you care for some tea before you retire, sir?" she asked. "I've just made a fresh pot."

"That would be lovely, Mrs. Jeffries," Witherspoon agreed eagerly.

"Let's go into the drawing room, shall we?" The housekeeper led the way, clucking sympathetically as she ushered him into his favorite chair and poured his tea.

"I say, Mrs. Jeffries, I went out in such a rush after Miss Lanier's visit that I forgot to ask if there was any word from Lady Cannonberry."

Lady Ruth Cannonberry was their neighbor—a very special friend of the household and, most important, the inspector. She'd been gone now for more than a week on a duty visit to relatives. Inspector Witherspoon missed her dreadfully. "We had a short note saying she'd arrived safely but her plans hadn't changed." Mrs. Jeffries replied. "She'll be back next week."

Mrs. Jeffries continued. "Now, sir. What do you think has happened? Wiggins and Smythe both seemed to think you'd decided this Mr. Underhill had been murdered."

"I'm not certain of that," Witherspoon replied. "But the death was suspicious enough that I began an immediate investigation."

"Yes," she agreed, watching him carefully. "Wiggins told us about Dr. Bosworth's idea. What do you think, sir? Was the man poisoned?" She was quite certain that Bosworth was right, but her main goal right at the moment wasn't to establish the facts in the case—it was to get her employer talking.

"We won't know for sure until after the postmortem." Witherspoon took a sip of tea, sighed in satisfaction and leaned back in his chair. He closed his eyes.

Alarmed, Mrs. Jeffries quickly said, "What do your instincts tell you, sir?" She firmly squashed the nagging guilt that crept up on her. The poor man was tired. His face was pale, his thin brown hair disheveled and behind his spectacles, his eyes were red-rimmed with fatigue. Even his mustache seemed to droop in weariness.

"Huh?" He blinked. "Oh, sorry, must have dozed off. What did you say?"

"I asked what your instincts told you about this case, sir."

He hesitated. Unlike his housekeeper, he wasn't certain he trusted his instincts all that much. Sometimes they played him false.

"Come now, sir, you mustn't be modest with me. I know you must have some feel for what happened to James Underhill. You're far too brilliant a detective not to have sensed something from the atmosphere surrounding the man's death. Please do tell me."

Pleased by her faith in him, he smiled. Perhaps he was simply tired tonight. It had been rather a long day. His "inner voice" or instincts were really quite sound. Quite sound, indeed. After all, as she'd just reminded him, he was a brilliant detective. One of Scotland Yard's finest. He'd solved any number of tricky murders. "Perhaps I shouldn't say this, but it's my considered opinion that the man was murdered. As a matter of fact, I'm sure of it."

"How very astute of you, sir." She reached for her cup. "Do go on."

Suddenly, the inspector wasn't as tired as he'd been only a few moments ago. "Well, I must say, one of the things that led me to my conclusion was the way the rest of the guests in the house behaved," he explained eagerly. "Not one of them seemed in the least upset that he was actually dead. As a matter of fact, they were more annoyed at being inconvenienced than anything else. That's always a pertinent clue, I think. Whether or not people actually cared about the victim. I sensed that no one really liked James Underhill and it's often been my experience that people who aren't well liked frequently end up murdered."

"So you questioned everyone?"

"I took statements from the guests and had the police constables question the servants."

Mrs. Jeffries took a sip from her own cup. "According to those statements, exactly what happened this afternoon?"

Witherspoon yawned. "Well, just as Mrs. Grant was getting ready to pour the tea, James Underhill popped some peppermints in his mouth and then appeared to choke. By the time the others in the room realized the man was having serious difficulties, it was too late to do anything for him.

Though mind you, if Dr. Bosworth is correct, there wouldn't have been anything anyone could do for the poor chap."

"I see," she said softly. There were a dozen questions she needed to ask, but she couldn't decide what was the best way to proceed.

The clock struck the hour and she started, realizing that one of the reasons she couldn't think straight was that it was late. When she glanced over at the inspector, he was slumped back against the seat, his cup and saucer rested precariously on his lap, and his eyes were closed.

Rising quietly, she plucked the china out of harm's way and placed it on the table beside the inspector's chair. Gently, she shook him. "Sir," she whispered. "I do believe you'd better retire for the evening."

Mrs. Jeffries was up and gone from the house before the others had stirred. The hansom let her out at the junction where Newgate Street meets Cheapside. She smiled at the statue of Sir Robert Peel, the founder of the police force, and fancied for a moment that he smiled back at her, approving her actions. Then she straightened her spine, nimbly stepped off the hackney island and made her way down Cheapside.

The area was quiet at this time of the morning, though shortly it would be swarming with pedestrians hurrying to work, hacks vying for fares and omnibuses disgorging shoppers and clerks. She drew her cloak tighter against the morning chill as she walked toward Cutters Lane. Turning the corner, her footsteps slowed as she surveyed the shops lining both sides of the ancient, narrow lane. Nanette's shop was on the other side of the street, halfway down the block.

The shop itself was still dark and the awning rolled back against the building. But on the floor above, Mrs. Jeffries noticed the windows were open and the blinds up.

Moving quickly but quietly, Mrs. Jeffries crossed the road and stopped in front of the shop. LANIER'S was written in delicate script lettering on the front door. She turned and stared at the goods displayed in the front window.

Elegant hats were exhibited artfully on a three-tiered brass hatstand. Below them a display of gloves, both two-button and four-button and one spectacular twelve-button pair embroidered with red silk, were artfully displayed on a bed of white velvet. The window itself was draped with a mantle of blue crepe de chine, puffed elegantly around the edges to give one the sensation of looking at a painting. From the looks of things, Mrs. Jeffries thought, Nanette Lanier was doing quite well.

She glanced along the building front, looking for the entrance into the flats above the shop. A door, the same gray color as the stone of the building, was at the far end.

As there was no knocker or bell, Mrs. Jeffries made a fist and banged on the wood. Several times.

"A moment, *s'il vous plait*!" an irritated voice shouted.

Footsteps sounded on stairs and then the door was flung open. "I have told you a thousand times . . ." Nanette's voice trailed off as she saw Mrs. Jeffries standing in front of her. "*Mon dieu*, I thought you were someone else," she apologized quickly and moved back. "You have zee news already! Please, tell me it is good news you bring me."

"We haven't found your friend yet," Mrs. Jeffries said calmly as she stepped inside. The foyer was so small there was barely room for the two women. "But I must talk with you."

"But of course. Please, let's go upstairs," Nanette said. "It's more comfortable."

Mrs. Jeffries followed her up the narrow, steep stairs to the first-floor landing. Nanette led the way through an open door into a small sitting room. Like its owner, the room was elegant, unusual and decidedly French. There was very little furniture—only a love seat upholstered in pale green damask and a matching chair. A small table, polished to a high gloss and holding only a crystal vase with a rose sat next to it. An exquisite blue-and-green woven rug covered the floor. Nanette gestured to the love seat. "Please sit down. Would you like some café au lait?"

"No, thank you," Mrs. Jeffries said politely. She sat down on the settee.

Nanette's expression was speculative as she took a seat in the chair. "Why have you come?"

"Do you know a man named James Underhill?" Mrs. Jeffries asked. She watched her quarry carefully.

Nanette's body jerked ever so slightly. "I have heard zhis name, yes. Why? What has he to do with Irene's disappearance?"

"He was murdered yesterday afternoon."

Nanette gasped involuntarily. "He is dead?"

"Oh yes, he's quite dead. According to witnesses, he may have been poisoned," Mrs. Jeffries said briskly. She'd deliberately been blunt. The fact that she still wasn't certain Underhill's death was a murder hadn't deterred her from seeing what kind of reaction she'd get from Nanette. "He died at the Grant house."

"*Mon dieu,*" Nanette whispered. "*C'est impossible.*"

"I'm afraid it's quite possible," Mrs. Jeffries said. "He popped a peppermint in his mouth and a few moments later, he was gone. Now I want to know what's going on. What, precisely, is your relationship to this man and, most important, when was the last time you saw him?" She was certain she was right. It wasn't that Mrs. Jeffries didn't believe in coincidences. She did. She'd seen them happen all the time, but she didn't think there was anything coincidental between the death of James Underhill and the alleged disappearance of Irene Simmons. At first, she'd not been sure that Nanette had even known the dead man. But after seeing her reaction to his name and glimpsing the wariness in her eyes, she realized that the events were connected.

Nanette said nothing for a moment. Finally, she sighed and looked toward the open window. "I used to love him."

"Used to love him?"

Nanette nodded slowly, her gaze still locked on the window, her eyes unfocused. "Zhen I found out what kind of a man he really was"—her voice trembled—"and I stopped loving him. I made myself stop loving him." She wiped at a tear that rolled down her cheek.

"When was the last time you saw him?" Mrs. Jeffries asked again.

"Yesterday afternoon." Nanette sniffed and wiped her cheeks. "He was here right after zee noon meal."

"Why?" Mrs. Jeffries queried. "It certainly doesn't sound like you had any love left for the man."

"I didn't," Nanette said hastily. "I hated him. I've hated him for a long time."

"Then why was he here?"

"Because I had no choice. If I wanted any peace, I had to see him. He came to get his payment . . . it was already a week late." She leapt to her feet and began pacing the room.

Mrs. Jeffries ignored the histrionics. This was starting to sound interesting. Despite what the romantics would have one believe about love making the world go round, it had often been Mrs. Jeffries's experience that as a motive for murder, money was usually the culprit more often than affairs of the heart. "What kind of payment might this be?" she asked. "A loan, perhaps?"

"A loan? From Underhill?" She stopped next to the window and laughed bitterly. "*Mais, non.* He was too mean to loan anyone money." Nanette turned and stared out onto the street. Her back was ramrod straight and her arms held stiffly against her sides. Her hands were balled into fists so tightly her knuckles turned white.

Sensing that the Frenchwoman was waging some terrible internal battle, Mrs. Jeffries simply waited patiently, saying nothing.

Nanette sighed deeply. "James was blackmailing me."

"How long has it been going on?"

"Almost from the day I opened zhis shop." She turned and shrugged. "I've told you now. I suppose you'll want to tell zee inspector. Underhill is dead. I had a reason to kill him, *non*?"

"Nanette," Mrs. Jeffries said gently, "why don't you tell me the whole story?"

"I'm afraid it's an old one, madam. A foolish young girl. A clever man and voilà, I am in chains for zee rest of my life." Nanette smiled wearily. "Two years ago, I was uh . . . given a painting by a gentleman friend. It was a nice oil painting. Quite old and very pretty. It was a picture of a city along a river somewhere in Italy. I didn't zink it was very valuable, but I liked it. My friend died. He was quite an . . . er, elderly gentleman. At his funeral, I met James Underhill. We were immediately attracted to one another, or so I thought." She shrugged her shoulders. "I was alone in zee world. I wanted to leave my employment and make a better life for myself. James and I began seeing each other. Within a short while, he began asking questions about zee painting. He told me it was worth a lot of money and he offered to sell it for me." She waved her arm in a wide arc. "Zat's where I got zee money for all zhis, zee shop, zee lease hold on zee building. Zee money for zee stock. I was so happy. I opened my shop and I had my lover."

"Selling one painting got you that much money?"

Nanette laughed bitterly. "The painting was a Caldararo."

"Ah, now I understand." Mrs. Jeffries was no expert, but even she knew the value of a Genoa Caldararo painting. The great sixteenth-century Florentine artist had done fewer than a dozen canvases before his untimely death. His work was valuable not simply because of its brilliance, but because of its scarcity.

"A few months after I'd opened," Nanette continued, "after I'd spent every *sou*, James took me to dinner at a beautiful restaurant. There was wine and music and fresh flowers on zee table. I thought he was going to propose. I know such a thing is unusual. A man usually asks for a lady's hand in private, after zee formalities are completed with zee family. But I had no family, no papa for James to ask permission. So when he took such care to make zee dinner so special, so . . . so . . . well, I was a silly, romantic fool. He took me to zhat restaurant not to please me, but to make sure I wouldn't make a public scene. As you've guessed, James didn't ask me to marry him. Instead, he announced zat zee painting I'd sold was a forgery. An excellent one, but a forgery nonezeeless. It was worthless."

"But that wasn't your fault," Mrs. Jeffries exclaimed.

"Zat didn't matter," Nanette replied. "If zee new owner of zee Caldararo found out it was worthless, he would sue me. Perhaps even have me arrested. James had made sure it was my name on zee bill of sale."

"But he'd been the one to broker the painting."

"He'd merely claim he'd been duped as well," Nanette replied. "I am a foreigner, Mrs. Jeffries. I was a maid before I opened my shop. James Underhill was from an ancient and honorable family. That makes a difference in zhis world. Believe me, Mrs. Jeffries, if I could have found a way to put zee blame on him, I would have. But zee truth was, I couldn't afford a lawsuit. Zee man who bought zee Caldararo was a rich collector. He could ruin me."

"I take it Underhill wanted money for his silence."

Nanette nodded. "He said he wasn't going to be unreasonable," she said. "He'd take monthly payments. Every bit of profit zhis place has earned has gone into his pocket, not mine. I've paid well for his silence."

"And now he's dead."

"Yes," Nanette admitted. "He's dead. I won't have to pay him again. So, as you can see, I had a reason to want him dead."

"I've a suspicion you weren't the only one," Mrs. Jeffries mused thoughtfully. She considered the method used to murder Underhill. Nanette could have done it. Easily. But had she? "Nanette, there's one more thing I need to know. What connection did Irene Simmons have with Underhill?"

CHAPTER 4

———◆◆◆———

"It were murder, all right," Wiggins told the others. They were gathered around the table at Upper Edmonton Gardens. As planned, they'd met back there for an early mid-day meal.

"I done just like you told me, Mrs. Jeffries," he said to the housekeeper. "I went straight into the station. The copper at the desk tried to stop me, but Constable Barnes was comin' down the stairs and when he 'eard me natterin' on with that tale of needin' to give the inspector 'is spectacles, he took me straight up. The inspector had just come back from a meetin' with the chief inspector." He leaned forward, his expression as solemn as an undertaker's. "Underhill was poisoned. Our inspector's got the case."

"Pinched the inspector's spectacles, did ya, Hepzibah?" Luty cackled. "You ain't pulled that trick in a long while."

"I did think it rather prudent to have an excuse at hand so that one of us could see the inspector this morning," she replied. "Admittedly, I haven't had to use that particular ruse in a good while. But it has stood us in good stead. We now know that Underhill's death really was murder." She turned her attention back to the footman. "Were you able to find out anything else?"

Wiggins frowned. "No. Right after I gave him 'is spectacles, he 'ad to dash off with Constable Barnes. I 'eard 'im tellin' the sergeant they was goin' back to the Grant house to ask some more questions."

"Excellent work, Wiggins," Mrs. Jeffries said. "I'm delighted our assumptions were correct."

"Before you lot start on about your precious murder," Betsy said hastily, "I've got something to report. I've found out a bit about Irene Simmons. It's right interestin' if I do say so myself."

"'Ow'd you do that?" Wiggins demanded. "It's not even gone on eleven o'clock."

"I was up and out early," Betsy retorted.

"And you left without a bite of breakfast," Smythe chided. "You'll make yourself ill if you start missin' meals, lass. Besides, I don't know that you ought to be dashin' off anywhere without lettin' someone know where you're goin'"

"Betsy did let me know where she was going," Mrs. Jeffries said quickly. She didn't want an argument to break out between Smythe and Betsy. The maid was an independent sort and the coachman, for a variety of reasons, tended to be ridiculously overly protective of her. "Please do go on, Betsy. What have you found out today?"

"Well, I was going to go over to the Grant house and have a go at the servants there, see if any of them might have seen Irene. But when I got there the place was dark as a tomb. It was still so early, you see. I didn't want to waste the morning so I nipped over to the Battersea Bridge and walked up the river a bit."

Smythe, who'd just taken a drink of tea, choked. "You was walkin' along the river? By yourself? At the crack of dawn?"

"Oh, Smythe, don't be such an old wo—silly," she sputtered, quickly changing the last word from "woman" to "silly" before she could cause offense to any of the three elderly ladies at the table. "I was perfectly safe. There's police constables about on Cheyne Walk."

"What put it into your head to do that?" Mrs. Goodge asked curiously.

"There's artists there," Betsy explained, ignoring the disapproving scowl on Smythe's face. "They go to paint the river in the morning light. I've seen them. This morning there was two of them. One was down by the Chelsea Pier, but he was useless. He'd never heard of anyone called Irene Simmons. Got a bit nasty when I asked him too." She snorted delicately. "He didn't much like having his painting interrupted, not that there was all that much to interrupt if you ask me. Fellow wasn't very good. The river looked like an oily old fat snake with a bad case of the pox, and that's what I told him when he got all shirty with me too," she said indignantly. "But the second painter was a bit more useful."

"He knew Irene?" Mrs. Jeffries asked.

"No, but he knew where I might find out something. He sent me along to a cafe in Soho. I had some really good luck there. The first person I spoke to was able to tell me something. Seems Irene's quite well known as a model. Anyway, Harriet—she's the woman who works the counter at the cafe—told me that Gaspar Morante had been in a few weeks earlier. He had some sketches with him which he was showing to another artist. Harriet couldn't remember exactly what the sketches were, but they had a woman in them. Harriet picks up a bit of money every now and then posing, so she asked Morante if he was going to do a painting of the picture he'd sketched and if he was, did he need a model." She leaned forward eagerly. "And you'll never guess what Morante told her. He said he was going to use the model that had posed for the sketches."

"I take it the model was Irene Simmons," Hatchet finished.

Betsy nodded. "Right."

"Gaspar Morante. Sounds like a foreigner," Mrs. Goodge muttered. "Probably one of them dark, swarthy types that are up to no good. Where have I heard that name before?"

"He's the one that give Irene her first job," Betsy replied eagerly. "And that's what's important. According to Harriet, Morante would probably know everyone who'd ever hired Irene." She paused to take a breath and realized that the others at the table were gazing at her blankly. "Don't you understand? Morante might have some idea of who wrote her the note."

"Betsy," Mrs. Jeffries warned. "The note luring Irene to the Grant house was probably quite bogus. We've no idea why it was written. It might not have anything to do with an artist . . ." She faltered as she realized the maid's reasoning might be right on the mark. Whoever wrote that note knew that Irene was a model. That might be common knowledge at a cafe in Soho, but it probably wasn't information that was known outside of a rather small circle. Irene Simmons didn't advertise herself as a model. She obtained work through word-of-mouth. Besides, Betsy needed to be encouraged, not discouraged. She and Hatchet didn't have all that much to work with in the way of clues. This idea, weak that it might be, was certainly better than nothing. "On the other hand, you're probably on to something here. Whoever wrote Irene that note knew she was available for work."

"That's what I thought," Betsy agreed. "I know it's not much. This man might not have seen Irene in weeks and probably won't know anything about her at all. But unless Hatchet's come up with some more ideas, it's all I've got."

"I'm afraid I haven't," Hatchet admitted.

"So what are you going to do now?" Mrs. Goodge asked. "Track down this Spaniard?"

"Morante's got a studio in Soho," Betsy replied. "It's right near the cafe. I'll go there right after we finish up here."

"By yourself?" Smythe blurted out before he could stop himself.

Betsy rolled her eyes. "It'll be broad daylight. I'll be just fine. Now stop interrupting or we'll be here all morning. I'm not the only one who's got something to report. Mrs. Jeffries has been to see Nanette. I want to hear what she found out." She pretended to be more annoyed than she really was. She loved her independence, but she also liked knowing that there were people who cared about her.

"Would you like me to come with you to the man's studio?" Hatchet offered.

Luty snickered. "What's the matter, Hatchet, you worried that Betsy's gittin' the jump on ya?"

"Don't be absurd, madam." Hatchet sniffed. "That would be childish."

Betsy thought about it for a moment. If she said yes, then she'd be admitting that going out in the middle of the afternoon was too dangerous for a woman to handle on her own. That could cause lots of future problems with a certain overly protective male of her acquaintance. On the other hand, she hadn't liked the way some of the men at the cafe had looked at her this morning. "No, that's all right. I'll take care to be cautious. I always do. But thank you for offering."

"That's quite all right." Hatchet inclined his head formally. "However, do let me know if you need my assistance. I'm well aware that there are some parts of this city where it isn't safe for a young woman to be alone, even in broad daylight."

"Did you find out anything else?" Luty asked.

"Not really." Betsy covered her mouth as she stifled a yawn.

"I think you've done quite well." Mrs. Jeffries reached for the teapot. "As Betsy mentioned, I went along to see Nanette Lanier this morning."

"Is her shop nice, then?" Wiggins asked eagerly. He didn't give a fig about women's hats, but he did want to know everything he could about the lovely Frenchwoman.

"Very." With a wry smile, Mrs. Jeffries picked up her cup and took a dainty sip. "I'd rather expected a more modest establishment."

Mrs. Goodge, noting the half-smile on the housekeeper's lips, eyed her speculatively. "Just how posh is this shop?"

"Let me put it this way, if I may," Mrs. Jeffries said. "The cost of one pair of evening gloves would be enough to provide you or I with clothing for the entire year. Nanette wasn't jesting when she told us she had the latest hat styles directly from Paris. She does. With French prices too, I might add."

"Cor blimey," Smythe exclaimed. "'Ow in a month of bloomin' Sundays did a maid get the capital to open a fancy place like that? She must be rich as sin."

"She's not rich," Mrs. Jeffries remarked.

"Doesn't the shop do well?" Hatchet asked.

"Very. If it weren't for one minor detail, I suspect Nanette would be making a handsome living from the place. As it is, she can barely make ends meet." Mrs. Jeffries smiled grimly. "Despite the success of her business, Nanette Lanier's financial position is quite precarious. You see, she's being blackmailed."

"Blackmailed!" Luty echoed eagerly. "By who?"

"James Underhill."

Smythe whistled softly. Betsy's pretty mouth parted in surprise, Wiggins's eyes widened to the size of treacle tarts and even Hatchet was taken aback.

The only one who didn't appear shocked was Luty. "I ain't surprised," she commented. "Never did much believe in coincidences. I figured Underhill dyin' and Irene Simmons disappearin' had to be all muddled up together somehow or other."

"How very astute of you, madam," Hatchet said sarcastically. "Unfortunately, the rest of us aren't nearly as perceptive as yourself, so if you don't mind, can we let Mrs. Jeffries go on with her report?"

Luty, to her credit, didn't respond to her butler's sarcasm, though she did snicker a little as soon as he'd turned his attention back to the housekeeper.

"Now, as I was saying," Mrs. Jeffries continued briskly, "Underhill was blackmailing Nanette."

"Why didn't Nanette tell us?" Betsy asked, feeling horribly confused. Pity, really, she had a lot of plans of her own for doing some discreet digging about both the murder and Irene.

"Because she didn't think her problem of being blackmailed by Underhill had anything to do with Irene's disappearance," Mrs. Jeffries explained.

"Did Underhill know Irene?" Wiggins asked.

"Oh, yes. As a matter of fact, Underhill got Irene her first modeling position."

"But Nanette told us that Irene got started 'cause Gaspar Morante 'ad walked in and seen 'er behind the counter." Smythe raised an eyebrow. "She's changin' 'er story now?"

"Morante was the artist," Mrs. Jeffries said. "But he didn't walk into the shop. As far as Nanette knows, he's never been in. It was Underhill who got Irene the work. He spotted the girl when he went to collect his money from Nanette."

"Why didn't she tell us the truth right from the start?" Wiggins complained. "All this lyin' is gettin' me confused."

"It is annoying," Mrs. Jeffries agreed. "But I think you'll understand when you hear the rest."

Inspector Witherspoon didn't like to be unkind, but Arthur Grant reminded him a bit of a nervous rabbit. The fellow couldn't seem to sit still for more than two seconds. His behaviour was in marked contrast to his stepmother's.

Regal as a queen, Mary Grant sat on the settee next to her sister. She hadn't so much as batted an eyelash when the inspector had told them that their late guest had been poisoned. Her expression had softened momentarily at Helen's involuntary gasp upon hearing the news. But after a quick, sympathetic glance at her sister, she'd turned back to stare at the inspector and Barnes, her expression calm and composed. "How very unfortunate," she murmured. "What kind of poison was it?"

Witherspoon hesitated. There was no reason not to tell them. All three of them had witnessed the victim's death. They'd seen how fast he'd died. As there were very few poisons that acted that quickly, there was no point in trying to keep it a secret. "Cyanide."

"I don't see why you've come back." Arthur whined and chewed on his lower lip. "We told you everything last night."

"I'm sure you did, sir," Witherspoon said patiently, "but at the time, we didn't know Mr. Underhill was a victim of foul play."

"Are you sure you're not mistaken?" Mary Grant asked.

"I assure you, madam," Witherspoon said. "The post-mortem was quite thorough. Cyanide is not difficult to detect."

"I don't doubt that, Inspector," she replied. "What I meant was, are you sure it was foul play? Underhill could just as well have committed suicide as been murdered."

"James would never have taken his own life." Helen sobbed. "He had too much to live for. We were going to announce our engagement."

"Don't be ridiculous, Helen," Mary chided her sister, gentling her expression a fraction. "Your engagement was hardly official. I don't think you ought to be telling all and sundry you were his fiancée. It doesn't look very nice, especially as he had the bad taste to die in our drawing room during high tea."

"You don't understand. I loved him." Helen shoved a handkerchief over her mouth. "And he loved me."

Witherspoon looked at Barnes, hoping the constable could give him some clue as to what to do next. A woman crying always made him feel he ought to help in some way. But Barnes appeared unperturbed and merely continued scribbling in his little brown notebook.

Mary sighed patiently, the way one did when dealing with a foolish child who refused to believe that three pieces of cake would make one ill. "I'm sure it's nice for you to think he was in love with you," she said. "But dearest, do be sensible. You didn't really know him all that well. The poor man might have been upset or depressed about any number of things."

"I've known him since before Papa died," Helen cried. "So I think I would know whether or not he was depressed, and he wasn't. He was happy."

Mary's anguish for her sister was reflected on her face. "Please, Helen, don't upset yourself . . ."

"Upset myself! Don't be absurd. My fiancé is dead. Of course I'm upset. Anyone would be. Anyone except you, and that's because you've no feelings," Helen flung at her sister. "None at all. James and I were going to be married. He told me so right before he died." With that, she leapt to her feet and ran from the room.

Mary Grant sighed and turned her attention back to the police. "You'll have to forgive Miss Collier," she said formally. "She's not herself today. Now, sir, will you please answer my question? Helen's hysterics aside, isn't it possible that Mr. Underhill chose to take his own life?"

The police had considered and rejected the idea of suicide.

"It's a bad way to go, ma'am," Barnes supplied. "If he wanted to kill himself, he'd have likely chosen an easier way of doing it." The constable could think of a half dozen better ways of dying other than choking your life out with cyanide.

"I see." Mary swallowed heavily. "All right, Inspector, perhaps you'd better get on with this. Ask your questions."

"Er, if you don't mind," Witherspoon ventured, "I'd quite like to speak to young Mr. Grant first."

Confused, Mary stared at him, then smiled slightly as she realized precisely what he meant. "Oh, I understand. You want to question him alone."

"That's right." Witherspoon was too much of a gentleman to ask her to leave. "Is there another room we can use? Perhaps your husband's study?"

She got to her feet and started for the door. "That won't be necessary. You can speak to him here." With that, she nodded and swept out of the room, slamming the door ever so slightly as she left.

Witherspoon turned his attention to the young man, searching for just the right words to calm the fellow so he could get some answers out of him.

But apparently, Arthur had gotten over his nervousness.

He was grinning from ear to ear. "You got the old girl ruffled." He chuckled.

"Ruffled? I'm afraid I don't understand, sir."

"She tried to hide it, but she was as angry as a scalded cat." Arthur snickered. "She didn't like being asked to leave. Hurt her pride, that did."

"I assure you, that wasn't my intention, sir." Gracious, the inspector thought, was everyone in this household peculiar? "Now, if you don't mind, I'd like to get this over with. How long have you known James Underhill?"

The mention of the dead man wiped the grin off Arthur's thin face. "A good number of years. I don't know exactly." He began drumming his fingers against the sides of his thighs.

"How did you meet him, then?"

"I didn't," Arthur sputtered. "I mean, he's the sort of person who's always been about the place."

"I'm sorry," the inspector pressed. "But I don't understand."

"He was a friend of the family," Arthur said quickly. "He's been around for ages. Absolutely ages."

"But I got the distinct impression from your mother . . ."

"Stepmother," Arthur corrected, interrupting. "She's my stepmother."

Witherspoon raised a placating hand. "All right, your stepmother—that Mr. Underhill was merely a business acquaintance."

"He is," Arthur explained worriedly. "I mean, he was. Oh, dash it all, I'm not explaining it very well."

The inspector agreed. The young man was explaining nothing.

"But you see," Arthur began, "this is deucedly awkward. He's from quite a good family. But they've no money, not anymore. So James had to resort to actually earning his living. Quite awful for him, really."

Witherspoon closed his eyes briefly. "I'm sorry, sir. But what does Mr. Underhill having had to earn a living have to do with how long you'd known the poor man?"

"But I'm telling you," Arthur exclaimed. "That's how we knew him. He's sort of an art dealer. My stepmother first met him a number of years ago. He helped her sell off some very valuable paintings that had been in her family for years. When she married Papa, she recommended he use Underhill to act as a broker when he bought or sold. Papa does dearly love his collection."

"So Mr. Underhill was more an employee of the family rather than a friend?"

Arthur shook his head. "No . . . well . . . but as I said, it was quite awkward sometimes. I mean, before they lost all their money, his family was quite well connected. Quite well off as well." He sighed. "Poor old James was the last of them and now he's dead too."

"Was he here as a friend or an art advisor?" Witherspoon asked. He'd no idea why he thought that point worth clarifying, but he did.

"Yesterday he was here as my guest," Arthur admitted.

"So he is a friend of yours, then?"

"Well, yes, you could say that." Arthur clasped his hands together in his lap. "But we weren't particularly close friends."

"Then why did you invite him for tea?" Barnes asked dryly.

Arthur hesitated a moment before answering. "He asked me to."

"He asked to be invited?" Witherspoon wanted to make sure he understood correctly. This young man was a bit muddled in his answers. In his thinking, as well.

"Oh, yes," Arthur said brightly. "He waylaid me at my club yesterday morning and specifically asked me to invite him to tea."

Witherspoon stared at him speculatively. "Did he tell you why? Did he give you a reason?"

Arthur shrugged. "Not especially." He leaned forward and dropped his voice to a whisper. "But just between you and me, sir, I think he wanted to see Mrs. Modean. He was quite taken with her."

Betsy quietly opened the back door and slipped out. She glanced around her, making sure that one of the others wasn't lurking about on the small, square back terrace or in the communal gardens directly ahead of her. Satisfied that she was unobserved, she scurried to the side of the house, crept along the walk and out the gate leading to the street. She wasn't being secretive, just cautious. She wouldn't put it past Smythe to try to come with her. Or failing that, she wouldn't put it past the man to put Wiggins up to trailing her. Betsy didn't want or need either of them dogging her heels. She could handle this on her own.

Coming out onto the pavement, she cast one fast look over her shoulder and hurried down the street. She patted the pocket of her short gray wool jacket, making sure she had money enough for a hansom cab if her business kept her out after dark. Reassured by the hefty weight of the coins, she smiled and picked up her step. She had a plan. A plan to find out precisely what had happened to Irene Simmons. Perhaps, she thought, as she hurried to the omnibus stop, she'd find out who murdered James Underhill while she was at it.

Smythe stood in the kitchen and scowled. "What do ya mean, ya don't know where she's gone?"

Wiggins, who was pulling on his boots, shrugged. "But I don't," he said. "After we finished our meetin' I nipped upstairs to get me jacket and when I come down again, everyone was gone."

"I'm still here," Mrs. Goodge said as she came out of the cooling pantry carrying a bag of flour. "And I'll thank you two to get on your way. The grocer's lad should be here any time now and I want to find out if he knows anything. After that I've got a costermonger and the rag and bones man stopping in."

"Have you seen Betsy?" Smythe asked as he and Wiggins edged toward the back hall. "She didn't say she was goin' out so soon, and I was wantin' to make sure she didn't nip off to Soho on 'er own."

Mrs. Goodge allowed a soft smile to play about her lips for a moment. The man was crazy in love with the girl, that was certain. Betsy, whether she'd admit it or not, was just as balmy about him. Too bad the two of them were so pigheaded and stubborn about it. Sometimes Mrs. Goodge felt like giving them both a good cuff around the ears. For every step forward they took, they went two steps back. Love really was wasted on the young. "Don't fret, Smythe. Soho's not the black pit of sin. She'll be fine. Betsy's got a good head on her shoulders. Go on, now, out with the two of you. We've a murder to solve, and my sources will be here any minute. They'll not talk much with you lot hangin' about. Off with you."

Smythe, knowing when he was beaten, scowled and headed for the back door. "When Betsy gets 'ome," he called over his shoulder to the cook, "ask her to stay put, will ya? I'd like to ask 'er somethin'"

"Are you goin' to ask 'er to the Crystal Palace?" Wiggins asked excitedly. "I 'eard it's the last week for the Photographic Exhibition. I bet she'd love to go. I sure would," he hinted. "There's a diorama and a military band and . . . and . . ."

"Yes, I'm goin' to ask 'er." Smythe grunted irritably as he stepped out the back door. Blast, he didn't like the idea of her going to some studio in Soho. Annoyed that she'd slipped out before he could talk to her, he was also wracked with guilt. He'd planned on taking Betsy to the Palace alone. But he knew how badly Wiggins wanted to go. The lad had talked about the exhibition for days now. Only the boy probably hadn't the money to go before it closed. Wiggins put a good portion of his wages in his post office savings account. Mrs. Jeffries had seen to that, and it was a good thing too. Money slipped through the footman's fingers like water. Smythe was torn. He wanted an evening or an afternoon alone with Betsy, but if he didn't take Wiggins, the boy wouldn't get to go. Blast, Smythe thought as he stomped toward the gate at the side of the house, what good did it do him being rich as sin if he couldn't help his friends? "Why don't ya come with us?"

"Ya mean it?" Wiggins yelped, his face bright with pleasure. "But I really shouldn't . . . it'll cost . . ."

"Don't worry about the cost, lad," Smythe said brusquely as he opened the gate. "I've had a good turn or two at the races lately. It'll be on me. Now, where ya off to?"

Wiggins grinned. "I'm goin' back to the Grant house to see if I can find one of them 'ousemaids. The red-haired one was right nice lookin'. 'Ow about you?"

"Me? Oh, I'll try the pubs and the cabbies in the area," he lied. "See what I can pick up. What time are we meetin' back 'ere?"

"Mrs. Jeffries said right after supper," Wiggins replied. "Luty and Hatchet are supposed to be here too."

They swung around a corner. Smythe started to cross the road. He stopped when Wiggins called to him. "I thought you said you was goin' to the pubs?"

Smythe jerked his chin toward the hansoms lined up on the other side of the busy intersection. "I'm just goin' to 'ave a quick word over there," he replied. "I'll see you back at 'ome tonight."

Wiggins waved and continued on his way, his mind already on the red-haired housemaid.

Smythe waited till the footman was well up the road before crossing over to one of the hansom cabs. "Do ya know a pub called The Dirty Duck?" he asked the cabbie.

The driver laughed and looked Smythe up and down. "Reckon I do, mate. But it'll cost a bit. It's over by the docks."

"That's all right." Smythe swung himself inside. "I know where it is. But if ya can get me there quick, there'll be an extra bob or two for yer pocket."

Mary Grant regarded the two policemen calmly. If, as her stepson claimed, she'd been "ruffled," the inspector thought, there was certainly no sign of it now.

"Mrs. Grant," he began, "I'd like to ask you a bit about your relationship with Mr. Underhill. I understand from your son . . ."

"My stepson," she corrected. "He's Neville's son, not mine. As to my relationship with James Underhill . . ." She shrugged. "It was purely business."

"Business? But young Mr. Grant claims Underhill had known you and your sister since before you were married to Mr. Neville Grant."

"That's correct," Mary replied. "But it was still basically a business relationship. He helped dispose of my father's art collection when he died."

"Yet he was an invited guest in your house," Witherspoon reminded her.

"Only because Arthur asked me to invite him," she replied. "In any case, it wasn't really a social occasion. The Modeans were only here for business reasons. They're hardly the sort of people I would consider friends."

"But I was under the impression"—the inspector cleared his throat—"that Mr. Underhill was your sister's fiancé."

Mary Grant smiled grimly. "This is rather awkward, Inspector. I'm not in the habit of discussing personal business with the police, but given the conversation you've already witnessed between Helen and I, I suppose I've no choice but to explain."

The Inspector wished someone would. His interview with Arthur Grant hadn't made much sense either.

"James Underhill was not Helen's fiancé," Mary said bluntly. "She would like to think they were engaged, but I assure you, they were not."

"How can you be so sure?" Barnes asked softly. He flipped back through the pages of his notebook. "Miss Collier clearly stated that Mr. Underhill and she had discussed the matter of marriage when they were out in the garden yesterday afternoon. And that she'd agreed to wed the man."

She sighed dramatically. "I don't doubt that she said just that. She may actually believe it happened. But the truth is, James hardly spoke to her when we were out in the gardens. Oh, they may have vaguely discussed marriage. James may have even dropped a hint or two about it yesterday afternoon. But an official engagement? No. As I said, our relationship with the man was one of business."

"What about Miss Collier's relationship?" the inspector pressed. She'd been most adamant on the subject, although not particularly coherent. She had been very difficult to question. She'd kept dissolving into tears. Still, the one thing they had managed to get out of her was that she and James Underhill had decided to marry. Yesterday afternoon. Right before Underhill was murdered. The inspector had rather admired the way she'd popped into the drawing room as soon as they'd finished questioning Arthur. Red faced and teary eyed, she'd demanded they listen to her.

"Relationship?" Mary smiled sadly. "The only relationship Helen had with James Underhill was in her imagination. My sister makes her home with us. But she comes and goes as she pleases. I don't particularly know how or why she developed this affection for Mr. Underhill, but I assure you, it wasn't mutual. He wouldn't have proposed to her. Not under any circumstances."

Witherspoon thought that a rather harsh assessment. Miss Collier was past the first blush of youth, but that didn't mean she was unmarriageable. "Why ever not?"

"Because she's no money," Mary replied bluntly. "No dowry, no property, nothing but a small yearly income which wouldn't be enough to keep her if she didn't live with Neville and I."

"Perhaps Mr. Underhill planned to support her," Barnes suggested dryly.

Mary stared at him a moment and then laughed. "James Underhill loved only one thing in this world, Constable, and it wasn't my sister. It was art. He'd never have married a virtually penniless woman, even if he was in love with her. James was like one of those dreadfully pathetic opium eaters. Only instead of opium, his need was for beauty."

"Not money?" Witherspoon queried.

"Money was only useful to him as a means of acquiring art," she replied.

"Does he have an extensive art collection?"

"Not really." She shrugged. "He couldn't afford any truly valuable paintings, but he fancied himself talented at spotting undiscovered genius in others. James was always picking up pieces here and there on the cheap. His collection is quite extensive in size, but nonetheless quite worthless in value, I assure you."

Witherspoon made a mental note to have a look at Underhill's collection himself. "You've stated your relationship with Mr. Underhill was strictly business, correct?"

"Correct."

"Did you acquiesce to your stepson's request to invite Mr. Underhill to tea because of the pending sale to Mr. Modean?" Witherspoon asked.

"When Arthur asked if he could invite James to tea, I thought it a good idea to have him come. James knows much about what a piece is really worth. Actually, I wanted Neville to have a chat with James before he sold the paintings," Mary explained. "I wasn't sure the American was going to pay what they were really worth. My husband is a bit naive when it comes to art."

Witherspoon tried to hide his surprise. Neville Grant didn't look in the least naive about anything. "Did your husband talk with Mr. Underhill?"

"No," Mary admitted with a sad smile. "There wasn't time. James was late. By the time he arrived, my husband and Mr. Modean had already come to an arrangement."

"You mean that Mr. Modean now owns the paintings?" Witherspoon asked.

"I'm not sure." She stiffened slightly. "Neville refused to discuss it with me."

The inspector didn't know what to ask next. He was getting very muddled, very muddled indeed. But, mindful of his housekeeper's always sound advice, he trusted his "inner voice" and pressed on, asking any question that popped into his head. "Do you know if Mr. Underhill had any enemies?"

"Enemies?" Mary looked amused by the question. "I dare say, sir, he probably had many of them. He wasn't a particularly charming man. I don't think Mrs. Modean liked him all that much, and I'm quite certain her husband had no use for him. He virtually snubbed him yesterday afternoon."

"Did you know that James Underhill was in the habit of eating peppermints?" Witherspoon asked.

"Everyone knew it, Inspector. He was continually popping those wretched things in his mouth. He never offered them to others, either."

"Did he eat any when you were out in the garden before tea?"

"I'm not sure," she said, her expression thoughtful as she cast her mind back. Finally, she shook her head. "I don't know. Frankly, I was too busy being a proper hostess to Mr. and Mrs. Modean to pay much attention to James."

"If you weren't watchin' him, ma'am," Barnes asked softly, "how can you be so certain he didn't become engaged to your sister?"

She cast the constable a glance that would wither apples. "It's a perfectly reasonable question, Mrs. Grant," the inspector said defensively.

"It's not at all reasonable," she argued. "I wasn't paying much attention to him, but Helen was sitting right next to Mrs. Modean and I most assuredly was paying attention to her. The woman was my guest."

"Couldn't Miss Collier and Mr. Underhill have slipped off for a few moments without your realizing it?" Witherspoon persisted. He'd no idea why he was pressing this particular point so hard, but for some odd reason, he was compelled to find out if Helen Collier's engagement was a figment of her imagination or a reality. It might have some connection to why someone had killed Underhill.

"I suppose so, Inspector," she admitted, "but I don't think it's likely."

"But you don't know for sure that it's impossible," he pressed.

"Of course not, Inspector. As I said, Helen is a grown woman, not a two year old. I don't watch her every moment of the day. However, my sister came out to the gardens a few moments after I'd taken Mrs. Modean out there to enjoy the sunshine. That was about five past four in the afternoon. James Underhill arrived with Arthur a few minutes after that. As far as I recall, Helen didn't get up from her chair until we came into the house for tea. So unless she and James discussed and agreed to marry in the few moments between my escorting Mrs. Modean out of the drawing room and Helen's arrival out in the garden, I don't see how this proposal could have taken place."

"But Miss Collier says she came inside before the rest of you," Witherspoon said. "She had a headache. She also said that Underhill escorted her to the bottom of the front staircase and that it was during this time that they finished making their plans to marry."

CHAPTER 5

Despite the directions she'd been given at the cafe, it took Betsy half the afternoon to find what she hoped was the right street. Morante, apparently, didn't much care that none of his friends appeared to know his exact address.

Taking a deep breath, Betsy stepped off the pavement and onto busy Dean Street. Nimbly dodging a whitechapel cart, she ignored the shouts of the driver and plunged straight toward the entrance to the alley. Gaining the other side, she stopped and peered down the narrow, dark lane. A shiver climbed her spine as she read the small sign attached to the side of the building. Adders Row. Shaking her head, she wondered why an artist, someone who captured beauty, would have a studio in such an ugly, mean-looking place. She supposed it must be because it was cheaper to live here than in most other places in the city.

She headed in, her gaze darting quickly along the row of tiny, derelict houses looking for the one with the "henna-colored window sills." The fellow at the cafe, the one who'd given her the directions to Morante's studio, hadn't had a proper house number. Betsy only hoped sending her along to this nasty little street wasn't his bohemian idea of a good joke. He'd gotten a lot less friendly when she'd told him flat out she wasn't interested in posing for him.

But then she saw the house. It was halfway down the alley, propped against its neighbor like a drunken sailor. The once-white paint was a dull gray, the brickwork along the tiny footpath leading to the front door was crumbling and the windows were covered with a thick layer of grime.

Except the ones on the top floor. Betsy noticed they were sparkling clean. And they had bright henna-colored sills. Taking another fortifying breath, Betsy went up the walk, made a fist and banged on the door.

Nothing.

She pounded again and then plastered her ear to the wood listening for the sound of movement.

"He's gone, dearie."

Startled, Betsy leapt back so fast she stumbled, righted herself and then whirled around to see who'd spoken. Shocked, she gasped and was instantly ashamed of herself. A woman, practically bald, old and pink-eyed like an albino, stood grinning at her. She was bent almost to her waist from age. One gnarled hand clasped a heavy walking stick. "Scared ya, did I? There's no use yer knockin' anymore. He's gone."

"Who?" Betsy asked. She knew who she'd been seeking, but she'd found in the past that pretending to be a bit stupid frequently got a lot of information out of people.

"Whoever it is yer lookin' for," the woman cackled. She moved her stick forward a few inches and followed that action with a tiny step.

"What makes you think I'm lookin' for anyone? Maybe I was just lost," Betsy said.

The old woman shook her head, dislodging the motley shawl from her shoulders and sending it skittering onto the dirty cobblestones. "If ya was lost you'da stayed out there"—she pointed toward Dean Street—"and asked one of them peelers for directions. He not pay ya, then? You wouldn't be the first to come round lookin' for what she's owed and I don't reckon you'll be the last."

Betsy decided to try another tactic. "That's right." She deliberately shifted her accent back to the one she'd been born with, the one she'd worked so hard to lose. "'E's not paid me a bloomin' bob and I'm tired of waitin' for 'im. You know where 'e's gone?" She jerked her head at the house and put her hands on her hips.

The woman cocked her head to one side and examined Betsy speculatively, her gaze taking in the clean wool jacket and neat broadcloth dress. "Come here." She motioned her toward her, keeping her gaze lowered to Betsy's feet as she walked over to the old woman. "Don't look to me like you're hurtin'," the woman mumbled. "Them shoes cost a pretty bob or two."

Unable to stop herself, Betsy glanced at the woman's feet. She grimaced in disgust. They'd once been a sturdy pair of proper black walking shoes. But now they were old, scruffed and badly cracked. The sole of the right shoe was tied with a piece of dirty string to keep it attached to a cracked leather upper. She bit her lip, wondering how much money she had with her. Too bad she hadn't taken the time to count it properly. Instead she'd just snatched it out of her top drawer in her hurry to get out of the house unnoticed. She silently debated with herself for a moment and then glanced up at the afternoon sky. The day was gray and overcast, though it was still mid-afternoon; the dark would come quickly. Now though, it was still light and Betsy needed information. She wasn't *that* far from home. She could always take an omnibus. "I'm not 'urtin'," she said, "but I want what's mine. I worked for it." She smiled slyly at the old woman. "I tell ya what, ya look like ya could use a bit o' coin. If ya tell me where 'e's gone, I'll make it worth yer time."

"How much?"

"'Ow much ya want?" Betsy shot back.

"No reason to give me coin," the woman said thoughtfully.

Betsy's spirits soared.

"He'll only take it off me afore I kin spend it," she mumbled. "Likes his drink, he does, and me daughter's bringin' by a meat pie for me supper, so I don't need no food." She glanced down at Betsy's feet again and then raised her chin, her face split in another toothless grin. "So I don't really need yer coin, but I sure could use me a pair of decent shoes."

The Dirty Duck public house was dark, dank and very much in keeping with its name. Filthy if one bothered to look. Not that seeing the grime was all that easy, Smythe thought, as he stepped into the public bar. The place was too dark to see much of anything at all. Even in the middle of the afternoon. Smythe didn't consider himself all that picky. He'd lived rough plenty when he was a young man out in Australia, but he'd only set foot in this place for one reason. Luckily, that reason was sitting as big as life smack in front of the poxy little fireplace to one side of the bar.

Smythe made his way across the wooden floor, his feet crunching on the sawdust as he walked toward the table where one man sat alone, a tankard in front of him. The air was musty with the scent of stale beer, cheap gin and unwashed bodies.

"Afternoon, Smythe." Blimpey Groggins smiled amiably and motioned at the empty bench on the other side of the rough hewn table. "Have a seat. Ain't seen you in a while."

Smythe looked at the barman. "Two more over 'ere, please," he called and then sat down at the publican's nod. "Afternoon Blimpey. Don't mind if I buy ya a pint, do ya?"

Blimpey laughed. A round-cheeked fellow with ginger-colored hair, he wore an old, dirty porkpie hat and a ready smile. His brown-and-white checked jacket was topped by a bright red scarf tossed jauntily over his shoulder. "I'm not one to look a gift 'orse in the mouth, son. Ya know that. So, how ya been keepin'?"

"Same as always," Smythe replied, digging some coins out of his pocket as the barman brought them their beer. "Ta," he said and handed over the money. He waited till the man left then reached for his glass. "To yer 'ealth, Blimpey."

"I'll drink to that." Blimpey raised his glass and tossed back a mouthful. But he kept his eyes on the coachman. Lowering his glass, he said, "What da ya need, son?"

Smythe grinned. "That's one of the things I like about ya, Blimp, ya get right down to business."

"It's what makes the world go round," Blimpey replied. "Now, what do you want this time?"

Smythe winced inwardly. One part of him felt downright guilty about this, but another part of him, the practical part, didn't see a blooming thing wrong with using his money to do what was right. It wasn't that he couldn't find out information about this case all on his own—he could and would. But using Blimpey's considerable resources was faster and, if he were honest, easier. Besides, if he could help an old friend out with a few extra bob, where was the harm? "Same as always," he replied.

Blimpey Groggins bought and sold information. He'd once been a thief and a pickpocket. But he'd discovered he could make far more money selling knowledge. As he'd been born with a phenomenal memory and a genuine fear of incarceration or even worse, transport to Australia, he'd changed his occupation when he'd almost been caught helping himself to a few pounds he'd found lying about in a silversmith's till.

Blimpey took another swig. "Figured that when you walked in here. What kind ya need this time?"

"Just some general bits and pieces for right now," Smythe said. "Fellow was poisoned—name was James Underhill. I want ya to find out what ya can about 'im," Smythe began.

Blimpey raised his eyebrows. "Underhill's dead?"

"Ya know 'im?"

Blimpey shrugged. "Course not, but I've heard the name." He stroked his chin, his expression thoughtful. "Can't remember where, but I know I've heard it a time or two."

Smythe reconsidered. Blimpey having heard of the dead man cast the victim in a whole new light. "In that case, I'll need to know all ya can find out and I'll need it right quick. 'E's supposed to be some kind of art broker or some such thing—"

"Art!" Blimpey slapped the top of the table. "That's it, then. That's where I've heard of Underhill. His name come up when Jiggers tried to fence some paintings from a toss over in Mayfair."

"Cor blimey, Blimpey, 'ave a care what ya say to me. I do work for a peeler," Smythe warned. "As much as I appreciate yer ways of doin' business, I'd just as soon not know the details of any out and out . . . bloomin' Ada, you know what I mean."

"Don't get yer shirt in a twist, mate," Blimpey replied. "Sometimes I forget who ya works for. How is the inspector?"

"'E's fine. Now go on with what you were sayin'," Smythe ordered. "What about Underhill?"

"Let me think how to say it now." He grinned wickedly. "All right, then. Let's say a friend of mine was tryin' to sell some lovely paintin's that had come into his possession. Imagine his surprise when he found out they wasn't what he thought they was. Instead of bein' some very valuable pictures what were done by some famous Italians a couple a hundred years ago, they was nothin' but forgeries. Well, my friend, who'd gone to a great deal of trouble to acquire these wonderful works of art, was right narked about them bein' nothin' more than copies and so 'e did a bit of checkin'" Blimpey picked up his drink and took a quick sip. "Seems this weren't the first time somethin' like this had happened. After a bit more checkin', the name of Underhill cropped up."

Smythe frowned. "You mean this thief was narked because he'd stolen forgeries?"

Blimpey nodded. "Narked enough to dig about and see what's what. That's when Underhill's name come up. But as I remember it, no one could really find out all that much. I mean, let's face it, Smythe, who ya gonna complain to? The police?" He laughed heartily at his own joke.

"I see what ya mean," Smythe muttered.

"I'll see what more I can find out about the fellow," Blimpey said easily. "Anything else ya need?"

"Quite a bit," Smythe said. He didn't completely understand whether Underhill was supposed to be a forger or a thief but decided it would be better to let Blimpey sniff about a bit before he worried about it anymore.

"Good. Nice to know I can count on you to give me a bit of business." Blimpey finished off his drink and looked pointedly at his empty glass. "If we're goin' to be here awhile, I could use another round."

"Order us another," Smythe said, "because there's a lot I've got to tell ya yet."

"It's goin' to be complicated, is it?" Blimpey waved at the publican. "Complicated costs."

"Don't worry about the lolly," Smythe replied. "I'm good for it."

"I wasn't questionin' that," Blimpey assured him. "I was just wonderin' how fast you're goin' to be wantin' some answers. I might have to put one of me boys on it and that'll cost a bit more, that's all."

"Put whoever ya need to on it." Smythe waved a hand dismissively. "'Cause I want answers quick and there's a whole bunch of people I need to know about."

"Which one of them do you believe, Inspector?" Barnes asked softly.

"I'm not sure," Witherspoon replied. He kept his eye on the closed drawing room door, not wanting either Miss Collier or Mrs. Grant to pop in while he and the constable were trying to decide which one of them was a liar. "What do either of them have to gain by lying? That's the question, Barnes." He sighed. "But, of course, at this point in the investigation, it's too soon to answer that question."

"Well, you can have another go at Miss Collier," Barnes said. "Why did you want to question her again?"

"Because she was so hysterical this afternoon, I wasn't able to get a complete statement out of her." He frowned anxiously. "I do so hope she's calmed down a bit."

"We'll know in a moment," Barnes whispered as footsteps sounded in the hallway.

Helen Collier swept into the drawing room. Her face was swollen from weeping, she carried a crumpled handkerchief in her hand and her mouth trembled as she struggled to hold back her tears.

Witherspoon cringed. Drat. She didn't look in the least calmed. Perhaps speaking to her now wasn't such a good idea after all. "I'm sorry for your loss, ma'am," he said gently, "but, as I'm sure you realize, there are a few questions I neglected to ask when we spoke earlier today. But perhaps it would be best if I came back another time. Tomorrow, perhaps?"

"No, Inspector." She wiped her eyes and lifted her chin. "That won't be necessary. I want to help. I'll do whatever I can to bring James's killer to justice. Ask me anything you like." She took a deep breath, straightened her spine and then walked over to the settee. Sitting down, she folded her hands in her lap and looked up at him expectantly.

For a moment, the inspector couldn't think of one single thing to ask.

It was the constable who came to his rescue. "Could you tell us if you know of anyone who disliked your . . . uh . . . fiancé?"

Grateful, Witherspoon nodded at Barnes and then focused his attention on Helen Collier. It wouldn't do to be swayed too much by pity. But she was either genuinely distressed by the man's death or one of the best actresses in the world. In the past few years he'd learned to be a bit careful of believing in appearances. Gracious, he'd seen murderers weep and wail over the corpses of their victims and then turn right around and do it again. Not that he thought everyone was prone to such behaviour. Oh no, but he'd learned to be cautious in his judgments. Miss Collier might appear to be most distraught, but that didn't mean she could be eliminated as a suspect.

"Disliked him? You mean socially?"

"Did he have any enemies?" the inspector clarified.

"James had no enemies," she declared.

"None?"

"None, Inspector," she replied. "I've no idea why anyone would want to kill him. He was a gentleman."

"Your sister insists that your relationship with Mr. Underhill was a business—not a social—relationship."

"Must we go over this again?" Helen sighed wearily. "That is how we first met. James took care of selling my father's art collection when he passed away. I'll admit that Mary dealt with him more than I did. But the relationship wasn't merely business, despite what my sister would have you believe. For God's sake, he's escorted the both of us to galleries and museums. He's been here a dozen times for dinner or tea. I don't know why Mary keeps insisting it was only a business relationship. That's simply not true. We stopped at his country house a few weeks back on our way back from the north. I don't understand it."

"It's quite natural for people to try and distance themselves from murder victims," Witherspoon said softly. "Did you know that your sister wouldn't approve of your engagement to Underhill?"

"It made no difference whether Mary approved or not," Helen declared. "I live in this house, Inspector, because it's convenient. But I've my own money. Papa made sure of that."

Witherspoon tried to keep from looking as surprised as he felt. Mary Grant had specifically claimed that her sister lived here because she had no money. Now Helen was saying just the opposite. But which of them was telling the truth? As he'd have to do some more digging to know the answer to this query, he decided to try another tactic. "Could you tell us what happened yesterday afternoon?"

"I've already made a statement."

The inspector didn't want to remind her that she'd been so hysterical she'd not made any sense. "We'd like you to go over it again," he said tactfully. "There might be a detail or two that you can recall now."

"The Modeans had been invited to tea." She shrugged. "Neville wanted to sell his three Caldararo paintings to Mr. Modean. They were going to make the final arrangements yesterday afternoon."

"So you went out into the garden when the Modeans arrived?" he persisted, hoping to get her to speak freely.

"No, Mary took Mrs. Modean into the garden," she replied calmly. "Mr. Modean went into the study with Neville. I went out into the garden a few minutes after Mary and Mrs. Modean and then James and Arthur came out."

"Why didn't you go out with your sister and Mrs. Modean?" Witherspoon asked.

"Because I wanted to wait and have a private word with James," Helen replied. "I knew James had been invited, you see. But Arthur met him at the front door and took him straight into the drawing room. As I didn't wish to be rude, I went on outside. We'd been out there enjoying the fresh air for about ten minutes when Arthur and James came out. It was rather awkward. Mary wasn't all that pleased to see James and she didn't bother to hide it."

"She was rude to him?"

"Hardly, Inspector. My sister is never blatantly rude. She was merely cold, distant." Helen's eyes flashed with resentment. "She ordered him about like he was a common servant. James was far too much a gentleman to make a scene, so he did what she asked and got that upstart American a chair. Not that the man appreciated it. He virtually snubbed him."

"Snubbed him? How?" Witherspoon pressed. This was getting quite interesting.

"Oh, you know." Helen shifted, her eyes narrowed angrily. "It wasn't anything he actually said, it was the way he barely acknowledged James. For a moment, I was afraid he wasn't even going to speak to James."

The inspector tucked that bit of knowledge into the back of his mind. Americans were generally quite friendly. But he had other questions to ask, other ideas that needed checking. "Did you see Mr. Underhill take out his tin of peppermints?"

She hesitated for a moment, her expression thoughtful. "It's difficult, Inspector. James did love his mints. He always had a tin or two in his pocket. I honestly can't remember whether I saw him take them out or whether I was just so used to seeing him with them that I'm imagining I did." Her forehead wrinkled in concentration. "He took the tin out and ate one. I remember because it was right when Mary asked him to get Mr. Modean a chair . . . that's right. He put the tin down on the table."

Barnes looked up from his notebook. "Why didn't he put it in his pocket?"

The Inspector nodded approvingly. Excellent question. Obviously his methods were beginning to wear off on his constable. "Yes, why didn't he?"

"I've no idea, Inspector. But I remember the entire sequence of events now. James had just put a mint in his mouth when Mary asked him to get a chair for Mr. Modean. Of course, as he's a gentleman, he complied with her request immediately and instead of putting the tin back in his inside coat pocket . . ."

Witherspoon interrupted. "His overcoat?"

"That's where he generally carried them," she replied. "But as I was saying, he simply laid them down on the table and went over to the terrace. Yes, that's right, because I was going to remind him not to forget them when we went inside for tea." Her voice faltered and her eyes filled with tears. To give her her due, she took a deep breath and straightened her spine. "But of course, I didn't. I quite forgot all about the mints."

"You're sure the tin was still on the table when you left?" Barnes asked.

"Absolutely."

Witherspoon asked, "Did Mr. Underhill offer them to the rest of you?"

Helen smiled uneasily, as though she were a bit embarrassed. "Well, no, not exactly. I know it sounds silly, Inspector, but everyone is entitled to one fault. James was just a bit selfish with his mints. So, no, he didn't offer them around. He never did."

Witherspoon glanced at Barnes and saw by the knowing expression on the constable's face that he grasped the significance of what Helen Collier had just told them.

"Did you see how many mints were in the tin when he opened it?" Witherspoon asked.

Helen considered the question. "No, I can't say that I did. Is it important?"

The inspector wasn't sure. It could be. Unfortunately, there wasn't any way to really know. It was very possible that the mints had been poisoned while they were out on the table, or considering what Helen had told them about his habit of not offering them to others, they could have been poisoned at any time with the killer banking on the fact that Underhill never shared them with others. Drat. "It could be very important, Miss Collier. Er, this is a rather delicate question. You told us earlier that you and Mr. Underhill agreed to become engaged when you came into the house a few moments before tea. Is that correct?"

"Yes," she said. "I told the others I had a headache from the sun and needed to lie down. But that was just an excuse for James and I to have a few moments of privacy. He escorted me inside and proposed to me. It wasn't unexpected, Inspector," she explained dryly. "When you get to be my age, you don't play the simpering miss. He proposed at the foot of the staircase and I accepted. I then went upstairs to check on my appearance. We were going to announce the engagement at tea and I wanted to look my best."

"When you say it wasn't unexpected . . ." Witherspoon hesitated. This was decidedly an awkward question. "What, precisely, led you to believe Mr. Underhill was going to propose? Had he mentioned it to you?"

Helen crossed her arms over her chest. "I fail to see how that's any of your concern."

Witherspoon sighed inwardly. "Ma'am, I assure you, under any other circumstances it wouldn't be the concern of the police. However, your fiancé was poisoned."

"Well, I didn't do it," she snapped.

"We're not implying you did, ma'am," he said hastily. "We're merely trying to learn as much as we can about everything that happened yesterday. There appears to be some question as to whether or not your engagement was real—"

"Of course it was real," she interrupted. "If you must know, he asked me yesterday morning."

"Mr. Underhill was here yesterday morning?" Witherspoon exclaimed. Egads, why hadn't someone mentioned that before?

"No, he wasn't," she corrected. "I went to see him."

"You went to his house?" the inspector asked.

"To his rooms, yes." She glanced down at the carpet and then lifted her chin definatly. "James doesn't have a house here in town. He has lodgings in a private home in Bayswater. It's not that he can't afford a home—he most certainly can. I mean, he could. But there wouldn't be any point to it, surely. After we'd married, we were going to move to his cottage out in the country, so there wasn't any reason for him to go to the trouble and expense of finding a house here in town,"

"Yes, yes, of course," Witherspoon said quickly. "I quite understand." He was amazed that rather than the woman being embarrassed about admitting she went to a gentleman's rooms alone, she appeared to be mortified because the man she'd consented to wed lived in lodgings. "And he asked you to marry him then? What time was this?"

"It was early, just after eight in the morning. I went out right after breakfast."

"Did his landlady see you?" Barnes asked.

"No, James was just leaving when I arrived. He was in a hurry for a business appointment. He proposed to me right then, I accepted and then we caught a hansom."

"Together?"

"No, separately. I came home. James went on about his business."

"Did he say where he was going?" Witherspoon asked.

"As a matter of fact, he did," she said proudly. "He was going to Soho. There was some artist or other he wanted to see."

Mrs. Jeffries stood on the south side of the Thames Embankment staring at the Houses of Parliament across the river. Traffic on the river moved briskly, barges and flat boats, some of them so loaded with goods they rode low in the water, chugged and skimmed alongside steamers and ferries belching black smoke into the gray afternoon. Every few seconds, she cast her gaze over her shoulder, watching for her prey. She spotted him coming out of St. Thomas's Hospital.

"Good day, Doctor," she called gaily, waving her umbrella to get his attention.

Preoccupied, he looked around vaguely and then his face broke into a huge grin when he saw her. "Good day, Mrs. Jeffries," he said, hurrying toward her. "I've been expecting you."

"Of course you were," she agreed with a chuckle. They were old collaborators. Dr. Bosworth frequently advised her on the inspector's homicides. He had a way of looking at corpses that frequently shed light on the hows, whys and wherefores of the crime itself. Most of his medical colleagues didn't share some of his rather radical views about what one could and couldn't learn from a dead body, but that made no difference to the good doctor. Except when he was helping Mrs. Jeffries, he kept his observations quiet around others in the medical establishment. Perhaps when he was very old and ready to retire, he'd publish the notebooks he kept on his work.

"I'm afraid I don't have much time this afternoon," he said apologetically as he took her arm. "I've an appointment at the medical school in fifteen minutes. Perhaps you'd care to walk with me? It's just down there." He pointed to the buildings at the other end of the hospital.

"You know why I've come," she said.

"James Underhill," he replied. "Poisoned. Cyanide in the peppermints. They were impregnated with the stuff."

"Impregnated how?"

He steered her around a lollygagging group of young men, medical students by the look of them, and in no hurry to reach their destination. "I'm not sure. I suspect the poison was, however it was obtained, soaked in a small amount of water and then the water dropped onto the individual mints. There wasn't much left to analyze, only the inside wrapping paper and a few granules."

"Are you absolutely certain the poison was in the mints and not something else?" she asked. It was essential to clarify how the victim had ingested the lethal dose.

Amused by the question, Bosworth smiled. "Mrs. Jeffries, take my word for it. It was the mints. Cyanide kills so quickly that if he'd ingested it any other way, he'd have dropped dead before he had that last mint."

She felt a bit foolish. "You're right, of course. Silly of me to ask."

"Not at all," he said gallantly. "Perfectly reasonable question."

They'd reached their destination. Mrs. Jeffries glanced at the groups of students cluttered along the walkway leading to the front door of the medical school. Dressed for the most part in thick black overcoats and stiff collared white shirts, they all looked much alike. "You're very kind, Doctor," she murmured. "Look at all of them." She swept her hand at a knot of students huddled at the far end of the building. "All male. What a pity. There's no reason at all a woman couldn't be a physican or a surgeon."

"I agree," Bosworth replied with a grin. "Several of them are. It's fairly rare, though, and they meet with a lot or resistance."

She clucked her tongue in disgust. "One day, perhaps even in my life-time, women will march up to this building and take their rightful place."

"If it's any comfort to you," Bosworth said, "not every country is as rigid about educating women as Britain. In Pennsylvania they actually have a medical college to train women doctors. I must be off, Mrs. Jeffries. Is there anything else you needed to ask me?"

"No, but do let me know if you think of anything that might be helpful."

"Right." He turned toward the building then whirled back around. "I really would like you to meet an American colleague of mine who's in town for a few days . . ." He paused, not quite sure how to tell her about having had to invite the inspector.

"Is it the person who Inspector Witherspoon said you wanted him to meet?" she asked sweetly.

"Yes, but I only said that because your Wiggins ran into me in your neighborhood last evening—I was on my way to see you, but I could hardly tell that to your employer, so I said I was coming to see him. But the point is"—Bosworth blushed a fiery red—"I'd really like you to meet this man. He's quite an expert on pathology . . . he's a number of ideas about what the dead can tell us."

Heads swiveled at Bosworth's words. But he ignored the odd stares cast his way. "I'll send you a note," he called to Mrs. Jeffries as he turned and hurried into the building.

He was gone before she had a chance to say goodbye.

• • •

Betsy's feet were freezing. She got out of the hansom at the junction of Addison Crescent and Holland Park Road. Wincing, as the pavement was cold, she told herself she'd not far to walk. But she hadn't dared take the hansom all the way home. Wiggins or Smythe or Mrs. Goodge or *someone* would have seen and started asking why she was using a cab when it wasn't even dark out.

But it had been worth it. Betsy flinched as her stockinged feet hit a rough spot on the uneven pavement. These stockings would never be the same, that was for sure. But the loss of a pair of shoes and stockings was nothing compared to what she'd gained.

Betsy nodded at a maid sweeping the front door stoop of a house she hurried past. She hunkered down slightly, hoping the girl wouldn't notice her feet. The less said about it the better. There were some, she thought, that would get right nasty about what she'd done. One in particular who would have a fit if he knew she'd been traipsing about London like this. She quickened her pace, glad the day was overcast and that there weren't many people out. Luckily, her dress was on the longish side, so she reckoned she could make it into the house and up to her room without running into any of her friends.

Betsy breathed a sigh of relief as she turned the corner and saw that the road leading to the inspector's house was clear. "Ow," she yelped as a sharp pain lanced straight into her right heel. She yanked her foot up, which caused her to lurch to one side. "Ow, ow, ow," she mumbled, trying to regain her balance without actually having to put her foot back down. She managed to steady herself by grabbing onto the wrought iron fence of the house a few doors down from the inspector's. Leaning over, she dug a pebble out of her flesh, gave it a good glare and tossed it onto the road.

"Betsy? What's goin' on 'ere?"

The familiar voice rattled her to the quick. Betsy whirled around, forgetting that one of her feet was still a good two inches off the ground. She stumbled heavily to one side. Smythe lunged for her, catching her before she completely crumbled.

"Bloomin' Ada," he cried, "what's 'appened? Are you all right?"

"I'm fine." She struggled to regain her footing, but he kept a tight grip on her waist.

"Ya don't look fine," he accused, frightened that she was ill. He examined her closely, his gaze starting at the top of her head and moving slowly down her slender figure. "Cor blimey," he yelled, "where in the ruddy blue blazes is yer shoe?"

Betsy tried to think of how to answer. "Well, it's a bit complicated."

He reached over and tugged the hem of her dress up. "Where's the other one? Betsy, you've no shoes on!"

"Yes, I know that," she replied.

"What in the blazes is ya doin' out 'ere without yer shoes?" he demanded. "It's not the dead of winter, but it ain't 'igh summer either. Now you just wait 'ere and I'll nip along to the 'ouse and fetch 'em for ya."

"They're not in the house," she admitted.

He studied her for a moment and then his eyes narrowed. "Then where are they?"

"Well . . ." She hesitated. "If you really must know, they're in Soho. I gave them to an old lady in exchange for information."

CHAPTER 6

———◆———

"Would you care for a glass of sherry before dinner, sir?" Mrs. Jeffries asked the inspector as soon as he'd taken off his coat and hat. "Mrs. Goodge said it'll be a few minutes yet."

She wanted to find out what he'd learned before he sat down to eat. Sometimes, she'd noticed, he tended to get a bit drowsy on a full stomach.

"A lovely idea," he said, heading for the drawing room. He plopped down in his favorite chair while Mrs. Jeffries poured them both a glass of Harveys. The custom of sharing a glass of sherry with his housekeeper helped him to relax after a day's work. From the inspector's point of view, it was absolutely necessary. Talking about the case did so help him to clarify matters in his own mind. Sometimes he wondered how he'd actually solved so many murders, but as Mrs. Jeffries frequently pointed out when he began to doubt his abilities, he'd been born with an "instinct" or "inner voice" when it came to catching murderers. But inner voice or not, it really did help to have someone to talk with.

"How did your investigation go today?" she asked cheerfully.

"Very well," he allowed. Then he admitted, "Actually, I don't know if I learned anything important or not. As you know, this early in an investigation I tend to get a bit muddled, but I'm sure I'll make sense of it eventually."

"You always do, sir," she assured him. Gracious, she was going to have to dig it out of him tonight. "Did you go back to the Grant house?"

"Oh, yes," he said, taking a quick sip. "I got full statements from everyone, even the servants. Mind you, Mr. and Mrs. Modean weren't there." He frowned. "They weren't at the hotel either, but Constable Barnes and I shall have another go at seeing them tomorrow morning. We intend to get there quite early, before they go out for the day."

"They haven't left the hotel?" she asked.

"No, no. We've a man on duty there. The manager would let us know if they'd tried to check out. They were merely out when I went there, that's all."

"Do you expect them to be able to shed any light on this matter?"

"I'm not sure," he replied. "On the surface it would appear that they simply had the misfortune to be in the wrong drawing room at the wrong time. But after what I found out today, I'm not so sure that's the case."

"Indeed? I take it, then, you were able to learn something useful, sir?"

"I do think so, Mrs. Jeffries." He put his glass down on the table next to him and, leaning forward slightly, told her every little detail about the interviews with everyone from the Grant household.

Mrs. Jeffries was a skillful listener. It was one of her greatest talents. She never interrupted and never asked questions before he'd finished speaking. By the time he'd completed his narrative, her own mental list of questions was at the ready. She fired her first shot. "So the tin was out in the garden for at least ten minutes," she said. "Anyone could have tampered with it."

"True." He pursed his lips. "But I'm not so sure it would be as easy as it sounds. According to the kitchen staff, none of the guests went back to the garden after they'd all come inside."

"Meaning that none of them would have had the opportunity to poison the mints," she said slowly. "But surely there's more than one way out to the garden."

"There is a side door," he acknowledged, "but it was locked tight and no one seems to know where the key is."

Her mind whirled at the possibilities. "I see," she replied thoughtfully. "Is it your opinion, then, that the mints were tampered with while they were still in Mr. Underhill's possession?"

"What do you mean?"

"Do you think someone waited till he'd set them on the table and then added the poison, or was the deed done some other way?" she suggested. "Perhaps the tin was switched when the victim wasn't aware of it?"

Witherspoon pondered the idea for a moment and sighed. "Frankly, Mrs. Jeffries, I don't know. I suppose it could have happened either way. We simply don't have enough information yet. The servants insist none of the guests went back out to the garden and the side door was locked."

"Which means that for someone to have tampered with the mints while they were outside, the staff would have had to be lying or not noticed one of the guests going out. Or, the killer would have had a key to the side door."

"That's right." Witherspoon took another sip of sherry. "And I don't think the servants are lying. Why should they? They've nothing to gain by keeping quiet. The staff was preparing a high tea, Mrs. Jeffries. There were half a dozen of them working. Scullery maids, a cook, the butler, a footman. I simply can't believe all of them would lie about whether or not one of the guests had trotted back out to the garden."

"What about the key, sir?" she pressed.

"There isn't one," he said. "I mean, there was one, but apparently, it's been lost for years."

She got up and reached for his empty glass. "Another one, sir?" At his nod, she walked slowly to the sideboard and the bottle of sherry. "Did you have a look at the lock, sir?"

"Oh yes, Mrs. Jeffries. It's old and rusty looking. I don't believe that door has been opened in years." He shrugged. "I'm afraid this case is going to be quite complex. Quite complex, indeed."

"They always are, sir." She smiled reassuringly. "And you always solve them."

Luty and Hatchet arrived just as they finished cleaning up the kitchen. Betsy put the last of the supper dishes in the cupboard, dusted her hands off and, ignoring Smythe's glinty-eyed look of disapproval, took her usual place with the others at the kitchen table. Obviously, he was still upset over their argument earlier that afternoon. To put it mildly, they'd had words.

"I'm so glad you and Luty got here early," Mrs. Jeffries said. "We've a lot to talk about this evening."

"Good thing I had the kettle on the boil," Mrs. Goodge said, setting the brown teapot down and then taking her own seat. "We'll need a cuppa or two by the time we're all done here. I've got a might lot to say tonight."

"What did you git out of the inspector?" Luty asked eagerly.

"Quite a bit." Mrs. Jeffries smiled. "But I think before I tell you what he found out, we ought to see what everyone else has learned."

"'Ow come?" Wiggins demanded. "Usually we 'ear the inspector's bits first." He wasn't all that keen to report on the day's activities. He'd not learned a blooming thing.

"Actually, the inspector's made rather good progress," she announced. "Who wants to go first?"

"I didn't hear much today," Smythe said. "But I've got me feelers out and I should 'ave somethin' tomorrow."

"I found out that Neville Grant's not near as rich as you'd think," Luty said proudly. "That's why he's sellin' his paintings to Tyrell Modean. He needs the cash."

"How badly?" Smythe inquired.

"Bad enough to sell them Caldararos," Luty replied seriously. "And he loves them more than just about anythin'. He wanted 'em bad enough to marry just so's he could git his hands on 'em."

"Disgusting, isn't it?" Mrs. Goodge put in. "That's what I found out today as well. That's the only reason he married the poor woman. She owned those paintings and he wanted them. They were her dowry."

"Why'd she want to marry 'im?" Wiggins asked. "'E's old as the hills and not very nice."

"Because she was sick and tired of bein' an old maid," Mrs. Goodge said bluntly. "She and her sister spent most of their life taking care of their father. About ten years ago, old Mr. Collier finally died. But the estate they lived on was entailed so it went to some distant cousin. All Mary and Helen got was their father's art collection. Helen put hers in a bank vault. Mary gave hers to Neville Grant in return for a proposal of marriage."

"Cor blimey, that's right cold-blooded." Smythe made a face. He couldn't imagine spending his life with someone he didn't truly care about. "Was Neville Grant the best the poor woman could do?"

"Yes," Luty replied. "For a woman of her class and background, I expect he was the best she could hope for. She's fifty-five if she's a day. Ten years ago she'd have been pushin' forty-five. When you git to be that old, there ain't much for a woman to choose from. Most of the men of her own age are already hitched. If they ain't and they got money, they could git 'em a young woman." She snorted derisively. "Course it seems to me if she'd had any sense she'd a sold them paintin's and taken off for some fun and adventure."

"I suspect," Hatchet said smoothly, "that Mrs. Grant may have had a number of reasons for wanting to wed Mr. Grant."

"What reasons?" Luty asked indignantly. "He's mean, he's ugly and he ain't rich."

"But perhaps he was less mean, less ugly and a good deal richer ten years ago." Hatchet smiled slyly.

Luty eyed him suspiciously, wondering what he knew. "And just what do you mean by that?"

Hatchet smiled benignly. "All in good time, madam. All in good time."

"How bad is Grant's financial position?" Mrs. Jeffries asked.

"About as bad as it kin git," Luty said. "He owes just about everyone. The butcher, the baker, the bank, his wife's dressmaker. Everyone. Some of 'em are startin' to press him pretty hard for what they're owed too. Sellin' those Caldararos to Modean came just in the nick of time. Otherwise, he'd probably be losin' his house. Seems most of Grant's investments have gone sour in the last few years. He's been livin' on borrowed money to keep up that fancy house and all them servants."

"The whole town knows about it too," Mrs. Goodge added eagerly. "It's common gossip. But the Grants, Mrs. Grant in particular, has expensive taste and they've been livin' above their means for years. Guess it finally caught up with them. According to what I heard, they're so hard up for money that Mrs. Grant was pressing her sister to sell her art collection as well."

"Maybe that's why she was so set against Helen Collier's engagement to Underhill," Mrs. Jeffries mused, remembering the information she'd gotten out of the inspector. "If the marriage took place, she'd never get her hands on those paintings. Oh dear, I'm getting ahead of myself again. Does anyone have anything else to contribute?"

Wiggins cleared his throat. "Like I said, I don't 'ave much to say. With the inspector and the police bein' at the Grant 'ouse today, I couldn't get too close. There might 'ave been a bit of comin' and goin' amongst the servants, but the only one I got near enough to talk to was a shirty little footman who weren't 'alf full of 'imself. But 'e didn't know much. 'E weren't even there when the murder 'appened. Mrs. Grant 'ad sent 'im off on an errand." He gave an embarrassed shrug. "It's not much, but it were the best I could do today."

"Not to worry, lad," Smythe said kindly. "We all 'ave our bad days. I didn't find out much either. But tomorrow'll be better for both of us."

"Right then," Mrs. Jeffries said briskly. "Before I get on to the inspector's bits and pieces, I want to tell you what I learned from Dr. Bosworth." She told them of her meeting that day with the doctor, omitting only that she'd been invited to dinner. Then she charged right in to the rest of what she'd gotten out of their employer.

"I don't quite understand." Hatchet frowned. "Didn't you just tell us that the servants said no one had come through the kitchen?"

"True," she replied. "But there is a side door. It was locked when the inspector tried it, but that doesn't mean it was locked yesterday afternoon. The inspector said he looked at the lock and it didn't appear to have been opened recently, but can one really tell? Even a rusty lock can be opened with the right key."

"I'm gittin' confused," Luty muttered. "The servants didn't see anyone go out to the garden, the key to the side door is missin', Tyrell Modean snubbed Underhill, Mary Grant or Helen Collier is lyin' about whether she was or wasn't engaged to the victim . . . land o' Goshen, this is gittin' too muddled for a body to know whether they're comin' or goin'. Why don't we take this one suspect at a time?"

"I don't think we ought to bother," Mrs. Goodge put in. "We're putting the cart before the horse. We don't know that any of the people at the Grant house when Underhill died really are suspects. We don't know for a fact that the mints were tampered with at the Grant house. They coulda been doctored well before that afternoon."

"That'd be a bit risky," Wiggins muttered.

"Not really. Underhill never shared," the cook insisted. "We just heard that. He was famous for not handin' them mints around. Seems to me the killer must have known this. Them mints coulda been poisoned ages ago. When you think of it, it's a real good way of murderin' someone. All the killer had to do then was wait until Underhill ate the right one."

Nanette Lanier locked the outside door and hurried off toward the intersection, her expression preoccupied. As soon as she'd turned the corner, a figure stepped out of the shadows and crossed over to unlock the door Nanette had so carefully locked.

Moving quickly, he stepped inside and shut the door. The hallway was in total darkness. He stepped onto the bottom stair, wincing when it creaked in the quiet of the night. But there was no choice. None at all. It had to be done.

He took a long, calming breath and climbed to the first floor landing. Pausing there, he scanned the area, making sure that no one was in Nanette's flat. But behind the closed door of her quarters there was nothing but silence.

He continued up the stairs. On the third floor, he stopped and listened, wanting to see if he could hear anyone following him. He still wasn't sure it was safe, even with Underhill dead. But he heard nothing.

He moved to the door. There was a faint light coming from underneath it. But he'd expected that. She slept with the lamp burning now. Taking a key out of his pocket, he gently eased it into the lock, turned it slowly and grasped the handle when he heard the faint click of the mechanism sliding into place. Cautiously, he eased into the room, sticking his head in first to make sure it was empty.

There was no one inside the tiny drawing room. To his left was a small kitchen and on the far side of the room, behind the shabby settee, was the door that led to the bedroom. Without giving himself time to think about what he was doing, he closed the door and tiptoed quietly into the kitchen.

There, on the rickety old table next to the cooker, sat the bottle. He gave it a shake. As expected, it was almost empty. He cast a quick glance at the bedroom door. He didn't want her coming in and catching him.

He put the bottle down and reached into his pocket, taking out another, identical bottle to the one on the table. He put it down and then removed the stoppers from both of them. He poured the contents of the one he'd brought with him into the other, almost empty bottle.

By the time he'd finished his task and returned both bottles to their rightful place, the one on the table now full and the one in his pocket now almost empty, his face was covered in a sheen of sweat.

By the time he made it safely back down the stairs and out into the chilly night, his whole body was drenched.

"I found out something today," Betsy said when they'd finally finished nattering on about the wretched mints. "And I know it's not about the murder, but we are still supposed to be lookin' for Irene Simmons."

"Of course, Betsy," Mrs. Jeffries said cheerfully. "We're all most interested."

"Especially me." Hatchet gave her a wide smile. "As I too have learned something that may shed some light on the young lady's disappearance."

Betsy cleared her throat. "Well, I started thinkin' that maybe we ought to backtrack a bit here."

"Yes, yes, of course, Betsy. How very clever of you," Mrs. Jeffries said. She wished Betsy would get on with it and then immediately felt ashamed of herself. Irene's disappearance was every bit as important as finding Underhill's killer. "Presumably that's why you're trying to track down this Spanish artist. Were your efforts today fruitful?"

"I'm not really sure. But I went to his studio in Soho." Betsy paused and waited. All eyes were on her. She wanted their complete attention for her next revelation. "And I found out he disappeared the same day that Irene did."

"Actually, it was the very same evening," Hatchet added. "And under most unusual circumstances."

Betsy gasped involuntarily. She'd sacrificed a pair of shoes to find out this information and here Hatchet not only knew it, but he'd got the better of her to boot. Well, blow me for a game of tin soldiers, she thought resentfully. She shot Smythe a quick glance and her eyes narrowed angrily as she saw the grin dancing around his mouth. Unable to stop herself, she kicked him under the table.

"Ouch!" Smythe yelped. "Oh, sorry," he said, not wanting to embarrass Betsy even though the minx blooming well deserved it, "got a sudden cramp in me foot. Go on with what you were tellin' us, Hatchet."

Hatchet, to his credit, seemed to realize that he'd stolen Betsy's thunder. "Forgive me, Miss Betsy," he said gallantly, "I interrupted you."

"Ya interrupt me all the time," Luty muttered. "I don't hear ya askin' for my forgiveness."

"Really, madam." Hatchet sniffed disdainfully. "That charge is so uncalled for it does not even merit a response. Now, Miss Betsy, please go on."

"Thank you," Betsy said primly. "Well, as I was saying, I went to Soho and found out that this Gaspar Morante had taken himself off most unexpectedly. And what's more, I wasn't the only one who's been round looking for him, either. Seems that several people have been trying to find him, and one of them was James Underhill."

"Underhill," Mrs. Jeffries said. "Are you sure?"

Betsy nodded. "Oh, yes. He was there on the day he was murdered. That morning. When Morante didn't answer the door, Underhill went round asking the neighbors if they knew where he'd got off to. But no one did, of course. My source says Underhill was right upset too, tried to break into Morante's house but a couple of lads threatened to go get the policeman from over on Dean Street if he didn't leave."

"I'm glad to see your information tallys somewhat with mine," Hatchet began. "I—"

Enjoying her moment in the limelight, Betsy continued eagerly. "Did you find out about Morante? You know, how he was asking questions about Irene Simmons on the night before she disappeared?"

"What kind of questions?" Mrs. Goodge asked.

"He wanted to know where the girl lived," Hatchet put in. He'd restrained himself admirably, or so he thought, but really, he'd something to contribute here as well.

"Right," Betsy agreed. "And then the next day, Morante's gone and she's gone. I think it's a bit more than a coincidence. I think if we can find him, we'll find her."

"If she's still alive," Luty said darkly.

"Thanks for not tattling on me," Betsy said softly as she and Smythe cleared up the last of the tea things. The kitchen was empty save for Fred, who refused to go up even with Wiggins as long as there was a chance a morsel of food might come his way.

"Humph." Smythe snorted faintly. "It's one thing for me to get irritated with you, lass. But I'll not have the others tearin' a strip off ya. Though it were foolish, Betsy, givin' that woman yer shoes."

Betsy smiled. "I've seen you do almost the same."

He bit his tongue to keep from telling her it was different for him. He could afford it. She couldn't. He knew her gesture hadn't just been done to get information out of an old woman. Betsy had done it as much out of pity as anything else. But now the lass hadn't a decent pair of work shoes left. Only her Sunday best and a pair of old ones that he knew had holes in the soles.

Blast it anyway, he thought grimly, he'd money enough to buy her a whole shop full of shoes and he couldn't. Sometimes he despaired of being able to tell her the truth. Or any of the others, for that matter. He was a rich man. He'd come back to England five years ago with a blooming fortune. On a whim, he'd stopped in to see Euphemia, Inspector Witherspoon's late aunt and a dear friend of his. Euphemia, God rest her soul, had known she was dying. She'd willed her house and fortune to her only living relative, the incredibly naive Gerald Witherspoon. She'd begged Smythe to stay on in her home and keep an eye on her nephew. Smythe, under the guise of being a coachman, had agreed. Then Mrs. Jeffries and Betsy had come and everything had changed. Before you could snap your fingers, they were investigating murders and looking out for one another and becoming almost like a family. In the meantime, his fortune had grown like weeds in a flower bed and he was even richer than before. But he couldn't say one word about it—all he could do was secretly help the others when they needed it. If he told them the truth, everything would change. They'd feel differently about him. They wouldn't treat him the same. He wouldn't be one of them. Smythe wouldn't risk that. He wouldn't lose the only family he'd known in years. Most especially, he wouldn't risk losing Betsy. He clenched his hands into fists, frustrated because the woman he cared about would be trotting about London with blooming holes in her shoes. "I've done things like that before," he admitted, "but it isn't always wise."

"Don't go on about it," she said wearily. She didn't regret what she'd done. Well, perhaps just a bit. But she didn't want to talk it to death either. After all, she was the one who'd be wearing her old, worn out shoes till she got her next quarter's salary.

"All right, lass, I'll not say another word." He'd find a way to buy her some new shoes.

"Good." She favored him with one of her wan smiles. "What are you going to be up to tomorrow?" She wished she were working on the murder too. Despite Luty's dark predictions, she had a feeling that Irene Simmons was fine. She didn't know why, but that's how she felt. Not being really involved in the murder investigation was beginning to niggle her a bit. Not much, but a bit.

"Oh, just out and about diggin' up what I can," he replied. "I'm trying to find out more about Underhill's dealings. Seems to me like we don't know much about the bloke. Not even what kind of a 'ouse 'e lives in."

"Wiggins said he'd take a gander at Underhill's lodgings."

"I thought 'e were goin' back to the Grant 'ouse."

"He is," Betsy replied. "But then he's going to have a snoop around Underhill's rooms." She sighed. "It feels a bit strange not being involved like the rest of ya is."

"You're doin' somethin' important," he pointed out. "As we said before, Underhill's dead. This girl might still be alive."

"I know," she replied. "I know it's important. But it still feels a bit odd. I guess I'll have another go at Soho tomorrow. Talk to a few more artists. This time, though, I'll hang onto my shoes."

"Betsy," he began and then hesitated. "Be careful. I mean, Soho isn't the best area of London."

Betsy laughed. "I'm always careful, Smythe. You know that."

As they'd arranged, Witherspoon met Constable Barnes at the hotel early the next morning. This was most definitely an establishment that catered to the rich.

Settees and balloon-backed chairs, upholstered in rich brown and green leather, were placed comfortably around the huge lobby. Long velvet curtains festooned the windows, dampening the noise from the busy street outside. A long oak-paneled reception area, behind which an army of smartly uniformed young men worked busily, stretched along the length of one wall. Bellmen and housemaids, laden with silver trays and hoisting huge carpet bags, went back and forth willy-nilly across the elegant rose-and-green patterned carpet.

Witherspoon started for the lift. But he'd not taken two steps when a soft voice called his name.

"Inspector Witherspoon."

Turning, he saw Lydia Modean standing next to a potted fern. Quite a large fern, he thought. He was sure she hadn't been standing there a moment ago.

"Good morning, Mrs. Modean," he said politely. "The constable and I were just on our way up to see you."

"I know," she replied. "The manager said you'd been by yesterday. I'm sorry we missed you." She cast a nervous glance towards the lift. "I knew you'd be back this morning. That's why I came down. I'd like to have a word with you before you speak to my husband."

"Of course, madam," he said.

She gestured toward the settee behind her. "If you'd be so kind, Inspector. We can sit here."

As they sat down, the inspector noticed that Mrs. Modean had positioned herself in such a way that she could see anyone coming down the central staircase or getting out of the lift. Barnes took a seat on the chair opposite and whipped out his notebook.

"Do you have to write it down?" she asked quietly.

Witherspoon was rather perplexed. They didn't *have* to write anything down. "The constable is taking notes, Mrs. Modean," he said gently, "not writing an official report."

She looked relieved. "Good. I mean, I don't even know if what I'm going to tell you has anything to do with this dreadful business."

"Why don't you just tell us, madam?" he said, giving her a reassuring smile. "And then we'll decide if it needs to be 'official.'"

Lydia drew a short, sharp breath and looked away. "I've known James Underhill for a long time," she said, turning back to the inspector. "Since I was eighteen. I hated him."

Witherspoon deliberately kept his expression blank. Though it was jolly difficult to think of this delicate creature hating anyone. "I see, madam. Would you tell me why?"

"This is hard, Inspector. Very hard." She swallowed. "To understand my feelings, you have to understand my circumstances."

"The same could be said for all of us," he said gently. "But please do go on."

"I came to London when I was eighteen. I had a job as a governess to a family in St. John's Wood. My own family was poor but well educated. That's why I was able to obtain the position. My father had been a schoolmaster before he became too ill to work, and I had to make my own way in the world. But I digress, sir. You're not interested in my personal misfortunes. As I said, I worked as a governess to a family named Peake. They were decent people, not unkind, but not unduly generous either. But I was very young, Inspector, and like many young women, I was silly and vain. My head was easily turned." She smiled sadly. "One day I was taking my charge for a walk in the park. A man approached me. He said I was the most beautiful woman he'd ever seen and asked if I would be willing to consider taking a position as an artists' model. Naturally, I told him no. I thought that was the end of the matter. But I was a fool. I should have told my employer about being accosted in the park the moment I got home. I shouldn't have even allowed this man to speak to me." She closed her eyes briefly.

"Gracious, madam, I don't see how you could have prevented it," Witherspoon said.

"I could have walked away," she said. "And I should have. The least I should have done was to go before he spoke to me in such intimate terms. Because my charge, Charlotte, told her mother what had happened. Oh, she was just a child of nine. She wasn't being malicious or deliberately trying to get me into trouble. But Mr. and Mrs. Peake were very angry. They told me in no uncertain terms that I was never, ever to carry on that kind of conversation with a strange man while in their employ. Especially when I had their daughter in my care. If I was approached again, I was to walk away."

"I take it you were accosted a second time?" Witherspoon asked, though he was fairly sure he could guess the answer.

"The following week. He came right up to me and started chatting like we were old friends." She laughed bitterly. "I told him to go away. But he didn't. To make matters worse, he followed me home."

"But surely your employers couldn't hold you responsible for this man's ungentlemanly behaviour," Witherspoon exclaimed.

"Oh, but they could and did." She shrugged. "I suppose I should have been flattered. When they sacked me they did tell me it wasn't my fault I was pretty. But that's neither here nor there." She waved a hand dismissively. "The end result was that I found myself alone in London with very little money and very little prospects of getting another position as a governess."

"But surely they gave you a reference," Barnes blurted.

"They did," she replied. "But I'd gotten the job through the post, due to my father's influence. They'd never seen me before they hired me." She blushed selfconsciously. "Mrs. Peake told me privately that if she'd seen me she'd never have given me the position."

"Please don't be embarrassed, Mrs. Modean," Witherspoon said gallantly. "You are a very beautiful woman. I suppose you were in a position where your appearance tended to be an obstacle to gainful employment." They both knew to what the inspector referred. Most wives would take one look at Lydia Modean and immediately find a dozen reasons not to hire her, regardless of how qualifed or well educated she was. Odd, the inspector thought, it was really the first time in his life he'd realized that being too attractive could cause one terrible difficulties.

"That's correct." She smiled, grateful for his understanding. "I couldn't go home. My father had died and my mother had been taken in by relatives. There wasn't room for me. So I tried to find work. But there was nothing, absolutely nothing. Of course, I ran out of money. I was just about to be turned out of my lodgings when the man who'd been the cause of all my troubles accosted me again. Only this time, when he asked if I was interested in a position, I told him yes. It was James Underhill. He got me jobs. Lots of them. I've posed for dozens of artists. That's how I met Tyrell."

"So your husband knows about your er . . . former occupation?"

She nodded. "Oh yes, he knows. He's bought a number of the paintings in which I was the model."

"Then I don't see why . . ." Witherspoon trailed off, not sure precisely what the right phrase should be.

"Why I wanted to meet you down here? Why I'm telling you all this? Why I don't want Tyrell to hear? It's very simple, Inspector. James Underhill was trying to blackmail me."

"But you've been living in America."

"He contacted me the day after we arrived here," she stated. "He demanded ten thousand pounds or he'd tell Tyrell about my past."

This time it was Barnes who asked, "But ma'am, you've just told us your husband knew. I'm assumin' that means he didn't much mind."

"He didn't mind," she insisted. "At least he didn't mind the legitimate artists. Not even the nudes."

"Nudes?" The word escaped the inspector's lips before he could stop it. "Oh, gracious, excuse me, Mrs. Modean. I meant no offense."

"None is taken," she replied.

"Then if your husband wasn't concerned about the uh . . . unclothed modeling jobs . . ." Witherspoon dithered ridiculously.

"He was going to tell Tyrell about the other one. The job I took when I was absolutely desperate." She closed her eyes and sobbed softly. "I posed for . . . for . . ."

The inspector was a policeman. He knew precisely what kind of pictures Mrs. Modean had posed for. "I think I know what you're trying to tell us, madam. Er, were the uh . . . pictures photographic plates or paintings?"

"It was only one and it was a plate. Underhill had it." She closed her eyes briefly. "It would hurt Tyrell unbearably if he found out. He's been so good to me. I love him so much. I'd do anything to spare him pain."

"Did you pay Underhill?" Barnes asked. He'd recovered faster than the inspector.

"No, I don't have that kind of money," she admitted. "But I was going to give him all the cash I had in exchange for the plate. But he was killed before I had the chance."

CHAPTER 7

Wiggins knew he was taking a terrible risk, but he didn't think he had much choice. He stopped at the edge of the strip of pavement on the side of the Grant home and peered down its gloomy length. If the layout of this house was like most Wiggins had seen in this part of London, then the kitchen, scullery, storerooms and the larders probably butted onto this side of the house. Halfway down the length of the walk, he could see an open door.

Wiggins took a hesitant step, grasped the package in his arms tighter and told himself not to be such a lily-livered coward—he was here to do a job and thanks to his own ingenuity, he had the means to get himself inside. If he was real lucky, he could do a bit of chatting with whoever happened to be about the place. If his luck run out, then the worst that could happen was he'd be given the boot. No, he reminded himself, getting booted off the premises wasn't the worst that could happen. Running into a copper that knew him or even, Wiggins gulped, running into the inspector himself made that pale in comparison. He'd just have to take care and look sharp.

Moving briskly, he started down the walkway. Coming to the doorway, he stuck his head in and saw that it opened into the scullery. A young woman, hardly more than a girl, was standing at a double sink just to the left of the doorway. She didn't notice Wiggins as she was up to her elbows in washing the mountain of pots, pans and crockery in the stone sink. He waited till she'd rinsed a bowl and sat it carefully on the wooden rack. He cleared his throat. "Excuse me, miss," he said.

Startled, the girl jumped back. "Who are you?"

"Sorry." He gave her his best smile. "I didn't mean to sneak up on ya. My name's Wiggins."

She cocked her head to one side and studied him. "If you're lookin' for work, it's not on. There's nothin' goin' here."

"I'm not lookin' for a position," he said. She was quite a pretty girl. Her hair, neatly plaited and tucked up under her maid's cap, was a lovely shade of brown, her eyes green and her skin, nicely flushed from the steam rising from the sink, a creamy shade of ivory. "I'm lookin' for someone."

"You'd best go round to the back door," she said, jerking her head toward the back garden. "The butler'll help you."

"I thought I was at the back door," Wiggins said. "I tried the one on the other side but it was locked tight."

"Not the side door." She shook her head. "That one's never used. There's a big door right round the back. It leads straight into the hall and the butler's pantry."

Shifting to one side, he deliberately brushed the brown paper wrapping of the parcel in his arms against the open door, drawing the girl's attention to it. "Can't you 'elp me?" he complained. "This is awfully 'eavy." He looked down at the package. "I'm lookin' for a . . ." He squinted, pretending he couldn't read the label."

"Well, who you looking for?" she demanded.

Helplessly, he glanced back up at her. "I can't read the blasted name. It's rubbed off the paper. What are the names of the girls that work 'ere?"

"My name's Cora," she began, "and there's a Rose and an Edith."

"That's it," he cried. "The one this is for! It's for you." As he'd doctored the name on the paper himself, he was quite sure that even if she could read, she'd not see through his ruse.

"What is it?" she asked suspiciously. But she took her arms out of the sink and reached for a tea towel. "And who'd be sending me somethin'?"

"I think it's from yer secret admirer," Wiggins said. "A feller paid me to bring it 'ere and gave me strict instructions not to give it to anyone but Cora."

Flattered, she broke into a huge smile. But she sobered instantly as she glanced at another closed door on the far side of the room. Through there was the kitchen. "I don't know." She hesitated. "This is a right strict house. I'll get into trouble if I accept presents. You know how some people are about a girl havin' 'followers.'"

"But I think this is a nice tin of sweets," he persisted. "It'd be a shame to let 'em go to waste. Besides, the feller'll box me ears if I don't give it to ya."

She bit her lip in an agony of indecision. Then she brightened suddenly. "It's my afternoon out today. Can I meet ya somewhere? Then ya can give me the package?"

Wiggins pretended to consider the idea. But as he already knew from his chatting up the baker's delivery boy earlier today that it was some of the staff's day out today, he thanked his lucky stars he'd stumbled onto a girl who was going to be of some use to him. What he was doing wasn't very nice, pretending that this poor girl had a secret admirer and all, but it wasn't so awful either. And she would be getting a nice box of chocolates in the bargain. "Well, I don't rightly know. I'm busy, ya see . . . but still, ya look like a nice girl." He smiled brightly. "All right, then. Where do ya want me to meet you?"

"Do you know the Addison Station? It's just up the road a ways." Another worried glance at the kitchen. "I'll be there at half past two. Is that all right with you?"

Unable to believe his good luck, Wiggins nodded. "See ya then," he promised.

Wiggins spent the time before he was to meet Cora talking to the shopkeepers in the neighborhood. Chatting them up wasn't risky at all. Everyone in the neighborhood was talking about the murder and everyone had an opinion about it too.

"Well, we weren't at all surprised there was murder done there," the stout shopkeeper said, jerking her head in the direction of the Grant house. "Mind you, my first thought was that it was probably some poor, honest merchant trying to collect his money. But of course, it wasn't, was it? It was some artist fellow or some such nonsense." She snorted in disgust. "Just like the Grants, isn't it? Always puttin' on airs and actin' like gentry. Well, I say gentry pays their bills. But they've not paid us what they owe, have they, Bert?" she yelled to a skinny man who was busy refilling the potato bins. "All toffee-nosed she is too, that Mrs. Grant. Not at all like her sister, Miss Collier. She's a nice one, she is. But that Mrs. Grant, she's no better than she ought to be, is she, Bert?" Bert didn't appear to feel it necessary to answer his wife's questions. he picked up a basket of cabbages and began plopping them into the bin next to the spuds.

"Do you know she actually had the nerve to come in here and have a go at me because I refused to send any more vegetables to the house?" the shopkeeper continued. "The nerve of the woman."

"Really?" Wiggins pretended to be shocked.

"Well, I told her she had to pay her bill, didn't I, Bert? But did she? Oh no, too good to pay the likes of us, isn't she?"

"Maybe she didn't have the money," Wiggins suggested, more to keep the greengrocer talking than for anything else.

She scoffed. "Don't be daft, boy. The likes of her always has money. She's got enough to be out flouncing about in hansom cabs and toing and froing with all them fancy pictures she and her husband collect. Well, I say let 'em sell a few of them off and pay her bills. That's what I say, don't I, Bert?"

Wiggins's ears pricked. "When did you see Mrs. Grant out in a hansom?"

The woman pursed her lips, her round face creased in concentration. "It was the day that poor bloke got poisoned." She leaned closer and poked him in the chest with one short, sausage-shaped finger. "That very morning, in fact. Isn't that so, Bert?"

"What do you think, sir?" Barnes asked the inspector as they climbed the carpeted stairs to the second floor of the hotel. Mrs. Modean, after bringing herself under control, had gone upstairs a few moments earlier. It had been tacitly understood that none of them would allude to the earlier meeting.

Witherspoon winced visibly. "I don't quite know what to think," he admitted. "She certainly had a motive for wanting Underhill dead."

"But she claims she was going to pay him off," Barnes commented. "If she was going to pay him, why would she kill him? It's not like he could blackmail her indefinitely. She and her husband are going back to San Francisco soon and Underhill knew that."

"We only have her word that she was going to pay." Witherspoon gulped air into his lungs as they reached the top of the stairs. "And, of course, it's one thing to say it—it's quite another to actually have the money to do it."

"But she's rich."

"Her husband's rich," the inspector corrected. "For all we know, she has to account for every penny she spends."

They walked briskly down the hall, their footsteps making little noise against the thick maroon carpet.

"There it is." Barnes pointed to the door of room number twenty-two, then walked over and rapped lightly on the glossy wood.

From inside, they heard the soft murmur of voices. A second later Tyrell Modean, his lean, handsome face somber but not unfriendly, opened the door wide. "Good day, gentlemen," he said in his soft American drawl. "Come in. We've been expecting you." He moved back and ushered them into an elegant sitting room.

Lydia Modean, as composed as the Queen herself, sat on a cream-and-maroon striped settee next to the fireplace on the other side of the large room. "Hello, Inspector, Constable," she said politely.

"Good day, madam," Witherspoon replied, impressed by her composure. Barnes nodded.

"Please sit down," she said, pointing to a matching love seat and pair of chairs opposite the settee. "There's no reason we can't be civilized about this."

"We're only going to be asking you a few questions," the inspector said. "I don't think we'll be taking up too much of your time."

"That's very good of you, sir." Modean sat down on the settee next to his wife. He took her hand. "But we're prepared to give you as much time as you need. I apologize for not being here yesterday, but we had some rather important things to do. But you're not interested in my personal business, Inspector, and I'll get right to the point. I'll admit straight out that I didn't have much liking for James Underhill, but he didn't deserve to die like that."

"No one deserves to be murdered, sir," Witherspoon agreed. "Now, I know you've given us a statement already, but I've a few more details I'd like clarified. Was Mr. Underhill present when you arrived at the Grant house?"

Tyrell thought about it for a moment. He looked at his wife. "I don't remember seeing him, do you?" She shook her head negatively. "I think our answer has to be no, Inspector," he said, "unless he was there and in another room."

Witherspoon expected that reply. But he'd wanted to ask anyway. Sometimes asking obvious questions got surprising answers. "Do you recall what time Mr. Underhill did arrive?"

"Not really." Tyrell let go of his wife's hand and crossed his arms over his chest. "I was probably in the study with Neville Grant and I think Lydia had already gone outside with Mrs. Grant."

"How long were you in Mr. Grant's study?" Barnes asked.

"No more than ten minutes, when we went out to the garden. James Underhill was there with Arthur Grant. But I had the impression they'd only just arrived."

Barnes, who'd brought out his notebook, flipped back a few pages. "When you were in Mr. Grant's study, did you hear anyone coming in the front door?"

Modean looked surprised by the question. "Not that I recall," he began. "Why?"

"Because, sir"—Barnes frowned at his own handwriting—"according to the servants, no one remembers letting James Underhill in that afternoon."

"You mean he didn't come in with Arthur Grant?" Lydia asked.

"Arthur Grant was home that afternoon," Witherspoon replied. "He'd been up in his room since lunch, sleeping. He remembers hearing the door knocker twice. Once, earlier in the afternoon, when a police constable arrived asking for the whereabouts of a young woman, and again when the two of you arrived."

"I'm afraid I'm very confused," Lydia said. "Are you saying a police constable was at the Grant house before Underhill was murdered?"

The inspector had no idea why he was telling them this bit of information. There was no evidence whatsoever that the alleged disappearance of Irene Simmons had anything to do with James Underhill's murder. But evidence or not, as his housekeeper had pointed out that morning at breakfast, a murder and a disappearance at the same house in the same week was stretching coincidence a bit too far. Besides, his conscience had been bothering him something terrible about that young woman. Since Underhill's murder, he'd completely pushed it to the back of his mind. Witherspoon wondered if he ought to speak so freely in front of what were possible suspects. At least in the Underhill matter. "Before I answer that," he said to them, "I need to ask you a question. Where were you a week ago yesterday? Around six o'clock in the evening."

Modean's jaw gaped. "Where were we?"

"That's right." He nodded encouragingly. "Were you here in London?"

"We were in Bristol," Lydia answered. "I don't have much family left, but there were a few people I wanted to see while I was here. You can check with the manager of the hotel. It was the Great Western Hotel. Inspector, could you please tell us what's going on?"

Witherspoon felt much better. If the Modeans were telling the truth, and he could find that out quickly enough, it meant they couldn't have had anything to do with Irene Simmons's disappearance. They weren't even in London when it was alleged to have taken place.

"I'm sorry to be so mysterious," he said. "But the reason I happened to be 'on the scene' so quickly the afternoon that Mr. Underhill was murdered is because I was on my way to the Grant house. You see, we've had a report that a young woman has gone missing. The last place where she was supposed to have gone was the Grants'"

Lydia and Tyrell looked at each other in disbelief. Finally, Tyrell asked, "Was this young woman a friend of the family?"

"No, actually, no one in the Grant house seems to have heard of her," he replied. "And all of them, including the servants, insist she was never there that evening."

"You think this woman's disappearance has something to do with the murder, don't you?" Lydia guessed. "That's why you asked us where we were last week."

"I'm afraid so," the inspector replied. "But the two events may not have anything to do with one another."

"That would be a pretty strange coincidence, don't you think?" Tyrell drawled.

"It would indeed," Witherspoon agreed quickly. "And though I know coincidences do happen, in this case, I feel the two events are connected."

"She was a model, wasn't she?" Lydia said.

Surprised, the inspector raised his eyebrows. "How did you know that, ma'am?"

She smiled knowingly. "It wasn't at all hard to figure out, Inspector. As a matter of fact, if I were a gambler, I'd wager that she went there after receiving a note promising her work. What's more, I know who sent her that note."

"Lydia," Tyrell warned. "Be careful of what you say. These men are policemen. I don't want them to get the wrong impression."

"Please, Mr. Modean," Witherspoon ordered. "Do let your wife finish."

He looked at her. "Go on, please. A young woman's life may very well be at stake here." He turned to look at her. "Who sent her the note?"

Lydia smiled reassuringly at her husband and then turned her attention to the inspector. "James Underhill. It was one of his tricks. Believe me, I know. He did the same thing to me."

Wiggins spotted her as she hurried up the road toward the train station. He stepped away from the lamppost he'd been leaning on and dashed out to meet her. "I was afraid you'd changed yer mind," he said.

"Not likely." She shrugged. "I like my days out. Don't get 'em often enough if you ask me." As she spoke, her gaze was glued to the parcel in his hand. "Can I have it?"

From the eager expression on her face, Wiggins was afraid she'd snatch it and run off before he had a chance to talk to her. "Let's move over there," he said, jerking his head toward the railway station. "We're in the middle of the pavement 'ere."

"It's mine, isn't it?" Cora's eyes narrowed suspiciously.

"Course it is."

"Then just give it to me," she demanded. "I can take it with me."

"But won't they ask you questions if you come in with a nice package like this?" Wiggins's heart was sinking. The girl obviously wanted to be off.

"No. The household is strict, but they don't go snoopin' about in my parcels." She held her hand out.

"'E said I was to watch ya open it," Wiggins fibbed. He didn't like lying to the girl. She was suspicious and he didn't much blame her. Lots of bad things could happen to a girl if she wasn't careful. "Come on, let's just step over there and ya can open it and I'll be able to tell 'im what 'e wants to 'ear and then everybody'll be happy as larks."

"All right." She turned and flounced over to stand next to the station building, taking care to keep to one side of the steps to stay out of the way. "Can I have it now?"

"'Ere," he said, handing it to her. Frantically, he tried to think of something to keep her from leaving. He had to talk to her. He couldn't go back to this evening's meeting with nothing. And that little bit he'd gotten out of the shopkeeper wasn't worth repeating.

She stared at the parcel for a moment and then ripped off the paper.

Her somber expression changed as the last of the wrapping came away and the delicate pink roses on the top of the tin came into view.

"Oh, my," she breathed, "these are lovely. I've never had anything like it."

Wiggins was delighted she liked them, so delighted that for a brief moment, he almost forgot their true purpose. "Good, I'm glad you're pleased . . ." He amended his sentence as she looked up at him, her expression sharp: "I mean, I can tell 'im you like 'em. He spent a pretty penny on 'em, that 'e did." Well, he thought, it was true, they had cost plenty. Not that he begrudged them. Thanks to their own mysterious benefactor at Upper Edmonton Gardens, he wasn't short of cash anymore.

"Who sent them?" she asked.

"Well," he said, "I don't rightly know."

"What do ya mean, you don't know?" she demanded.

"I didn't know the bloke, he just come up and give me a bob to bring 'em to ya." He stepped away from the building. "Now that I've done it, I've got to be off."

She took the bait. "Here, wait a minute. I've a few more questions for you. I thought you said he wanted you to watch me open it? Made a big fuss about it, you did. How's he goin' to know you watched me if you don't even know who he is?"

"I'm meetin' him at the pub this evening."

"Which pub?" she persisted. A mysterious suitor who had the money to buy a girl expensive chocolates was worthy of a few more minutes of her time.

"I've got to go," he insisted. He started purposefully down the road. "You can walk with me if you'd like," he called over his shoulder.

She hesitated for a fraction of a second. Then her curiosity got the better of her and she fell into step beside him. "What did this fellow look like?"

"He was about my height and my colorin'," Wiggins said cheerfully. "'Andsome bloke, he was."

"It'll cost you a shilling, miss," the man said politely. "But it's well worth it."

Betsy gave him her best smile. She'd come all the way over to King Street, specifically to this art gallery, for one reason and one reason only. Information. She didn't mind spending a shilling to get it, either. But if the old woman had been right, she wouldn't have to. Her quarry was right in front of her. "I'm sure it is. Are you an artist?"

The man behind the counter blushed. He was quite young, but his light brown hair had already started to recede, his skin was pale and he had a goatee. "Well, yes, I am. I'm only working here so I can earn enough to buy my paint and canvas."

"Then your paintings aren't on exhibition?" She feined disappointment.

He laughed. "Me? At Mr. J. P. Mendoza's St. James Gallery? Not yet. Maybe one day."

She smiled brightly. "Is Mr. Morante's work on view today?"

The boy-man gaped at her in surprise. "Morante?"

"Gaspar Morante," she replied. "Surely you've heard of him. He's a Spanish artist. Quite talented, I'm told."

"I've heard of him, all right," he shot back. "He's a friend of mine. I'm just surprised you've heard of him—"

"Why?" she interrupted, needing to keep control of the conversation. "Isn't he any good?"

"I didn't mean that," he said quickly, shaking his head in confusion, which was exactly the state Betsy wanted him in. "Alex is real good. He'll probably be famous one day, but he's not done much exhibiting."

"I was told his work was on display here"—she pointed to the door of the gallery—"and that the artist himself would be here as well. It's important that I speak to him. I've a commission for him."

"A commission? For Alex?" His eyes narrowed angrily. "Look, I don't know who you've been talkin' to, but he doesn't do that kind of thing anymore."

Betsy hid her surprise. "Well, I've been told he does," she countered, playing the situation by instinct. "If the price is right, that is."

"You've been talking to the wrong people, then. Because it's not true."

"Why don't you let him decide that?" Betsy hoped she wasn't making a terrible fool of herself.

"I know what you want," the man sneered, "but you're not going to get it. Not this time. Now shove off before I call the police."

"Call the police? For what? Asking a few simple questions?"

"Don't act the innocent," he hissed. He leaned toward her menacingly, lifting the wooden partition that separated him from the customers.

"Hey, what're ya doin'?" Betsy jumped back a pace. She could make a run for it if she had to, but not before she got the most out of this fellow.

With the partition half raised, he hesitated and looked behind him toward the double front doors of the gallery. Obviously, leaving his post wasn't what he really wanted to do. "If you know what's good for you, you'll leave him alone," he warned. Slowly, he lowered the partition back into place. Betsy breathed a little easier.

"Like I said," he continued, his voice harsh with menace, "he doesn't do it. He never did. Those other times were accidents. He didn't know what was going on. He didn't do it deliberately. So go back and tell whoever it is you're working for that it's not on. Now get out of here."

Betsy suspected she'd gotten all she could get out of the man. He'd calmed down too much and seemed to have more control over his emotions. She backed away. "All right, all right. Just tell him there's a job for him if he's interested."

"He's not. Now get off." He snarled.

"Why don't you let him speak for himself?" she challenged again. Maybe she could goad the man into telling her where he was.

He laughed harshly. "Do you think I'm a fool? Now get out of here and don't come back."

Betsy turned and walked away.

But she didn't go far. Only to the next corner where she ducked around a lamppost, whirled back toward the direction in which she'd just come and then planted herself there firmly. From where she stood, she could see the front of the gallery. She stood there for a moment, taking deep breaths and thinking about what had just happened.

Alex? Who was that? It had to be Gaspar Morante. Betsy rolled her hands into fists in an agony of indecision. She might be barking up the wrong tree. She'd no real proof that Morante had anything to do with Irene's disappearance. But she was tired of coincidences. Morante had disappeared from his lodgings on the same day Irene had. And now this. All she'd done was make a few casual remarks and Morante's friend had gone from being friendly to threatening. That was odd.

No, she thought, the fellow's behaviour was more than odd. He'd been scared. She'd seen it in his eyes even when she'd been backing up and getting ready to make a run for it herself. But why was he frightened? What did it mean?

She mentally debated what the wisest course of action would be. She could go back to Upper Edmonton Gardens and tell the others . . . yes, that's what she ought to do. Then she glanced up at the sky. The sun was moving steadily westward. It was getting late and the gallery closed at six. She couldn't make it all the way back home, explain what had happened and then get back here before her quarry got away. She couldn't risk it.

Betsy took a deep breath and made her decision. There was really only one sensible course of action. Surely Smythe and the others would understand.

A woman's life might be at stake.

"Can't say that there's many mournin' the feller," Blimpey said casually as he lifted his tankard and took a long sip. "Underhill weren't popular."

Smythe nodded, encouraging Blimpey to go on.

"Bit of a toff," Blimpey continued, "but as crooked a gent as has ever walked this earth. Came from a right good background," he said eagerly. "Like I said, a toff he was. This is where it gets interestin'—that's usually who he was swindling. His own kind."

"He was a swindler?" Smythe said.

"Not in the sense that ya normally think of it. He was kinda special in what 'e did." Blimpey wiped his mouth with the sleeve of his jacket. "Let me tell ya what I found out. Seems he was an artist's agent of some sort."

"I already knew that," Smythe said dryly. He forced himself to concentrate on his companion. But it was ruddy hard. His mind kept wandering back to Betsy. What was she up to now? She'd been blooming secretive about what she was doing today and he didn't like it.

"Yeah, well, what you don't know is that he wasn't exactly on the up-and-up. Most of his clients or customers or whatever didn't know it, either. But some of 'em did." Blimpey grinned and leaned forward eagerly. "And that's why his services were in such demand. The word is there's more than a few of 'em that asked the late Mr. Underhill to procure them a picture, and sometimes it's a picture just like one they already own . . . if you're gettin' my drift."

Smythe wasn't sure that he was. "You mean they want to buy a copy of their own painting from him?"

"No, no." He waved his hand impatiently. "Look, here's the way it works. Say you've got a nice painting and it's worth a lot of lolly. Then say you want to sell that painting but you don't really want to sell it 'cause you like it and it's worth so much cash. More importantly, it's likely to be worth even more if you can hang onto it for a few years. That's where Underhill came in. Seems he knew how to make sure you could sell your painting and keep it too."

"He forged paintings."

"*He* didn't," Blimpey replied. "He wasn't that good. He hired it done. Seems there's more than a few toffs that breathed a sigh of heartfelt relief when old Underhill got it. Now they don't 'ave to worry about him spillin' the beans over one toff sellin' one of his friends copies and not the real thing."

"Cor blimey, if what you're sayin' is true . . ."

"It is." Blimpey frowned, offened to the core. "I don't give bad information. Not for what you're goin' to be payin' me."

"Sorry." Smythe apologized for the slur on the man's professional dignity. "But there's somethin' I don't understand. If I was to sell ya a paintin' that's worth a lot of money and then give ya a forgery of that picture, what good would that do me? I couldn't sell the paintin' to someone else. People'd find out right quick if I was doin' things like that."

"That's what I thought," Blimpey said. "But art's not like other stuff . . . seems people don't ask a lot of questions sometimes. If I was to sell to you and then give you a fake, that means I could keep the real one. But let's say you was a foreigner, one of them Argentinians or Australians, and let's say I sold ya the fake and you quite happily took it back to WoggaWogga land or whatever and hung it up on yer wall to show off to all yer friends. None of them could tell the difference now, could they? And if I've got the real paintin' sittin' in a bank vault or an attic, I can put it in me will that the paintings to stay in the family. A generation or two passes and who's the wiser? The picture just keeps gettin' more and more valuable and the people with the fake think they've got the real thing too. By the time anyone sorts it out, odds are the toff what commissioned the forgery is dead and buried and not havin' to worry about it. And don't forget this—if you owned the forgery and you found out it was a fake, would you tell anyone?"

"I don't know," Smythe replied honestly. "What good would havin' a fake do ya?"

"Plenty." Blimpey grinned. "You could pass it on to someone else. People don't bother gettin' forgeries done of paintings that ain't worth a lot of money. And that ain't all," he continued. "Seems that Underhill didn't do it just for the lolly. Rumor has it that he was a bit of an odd duck about paintings and such." he snorted. "Seems to me the feller was downright daft. Some claim that he kept more than he'd sold and had it stashed away somewhere." He laughed. "Sounds to me like he was buildin' a nest egg. Probably goin' to make one last, grand bunco and then take off. Maybe the bloke wasn't so daft after all. Art usually goes up in value. A few paintings sold on the sly could keep a fellow in clover for a long time. Course, playin' about a bit with a paintin' or two ain't the worst of the man."

"There's more?" Smythe said incredulously.

"You can bet your front teeth there is," Blimpey said. He looked quickly over his shoulder to make sure they weren't being overheard and then, just to be doubly safe, he leaned across the small table. "Word 'as it that he'd hired some thugs to do a killin'"

Smythe went utterly still for a few moments. "Are ya sure?"

Blimpey, his expression somber, nodded. "Sure as you and I are sittin' 'ere havin' this nice little chat," he said. "I double-checked that bit, I can tell ya that. Underhill did it, all right. Word is he hired a couple of Mordecai's boys along about ten days ago. Paid a fair amount for it too. They was supposed to stab a woman and make it look like it was the work of that Ripper fellow." Blimpey grimaced. "Ugly, that was. Now, there was one I would'na minded seein' swing by his neck. Too bad the coppers was too ruddy stupid to catch 'im."

Smythe swallowed heavily. He had to ask. He had to know. "Did they do it? Did they murder her?"

Blimpey chuckled and leaned back. "Nah, they was goin' to, but somethin' went wrong. Far as I know the girl's still alive."

"What's her name?"

"Now that, I can't tell ya," Blimpey said. He held up his hand quickly as he saw Smythe open his mouth. "And I ain't trying to squeeze any more lolly out of ya," he protested. "I don't hold with murder, especially women. If I knew the girl's name I'd not only tell ya, I'd tell 'er too. I may have been a thief and a pickpocket once, but that don't mean I got no morals. I know what's right. Separating a toff from 'is coin and sellin' a bit of information is one thing, but murder is somethin' else."

Smythe shut his mouth. Blimpey would tell him the girl's name if he knew it. Too bad he didn't. "Can you find out?"

Blimpey looked offended. "Is the Thames a river? Of course I can find out. I just couldn't find out before I had to meet ya 'ere now." His eyes narrowed to slits. "For yer information, I'm already workin' on it. It's not goin' to cost you a ruddy bob. As soon as I know who the lass is, you'll know too, and for that matter, so will the coppers."

Taken aback, Smythe stared at him with something akin to admiration. "Fair enough," he murmured. "Is there anythin' else?"

"Not yet." Blimpey downed the last of his drink. "I'll have more by tomorrow. Got to be on me way," he said, getting to his feet. "I'll send one of me lads with a message when I've more for ya." He nodded brusquely and turned toward the door.

"Blimpey." Smythe stopped him.

"What?"

"Be careful. Mordecai's boys are a pretty rough lot." They were worse than rough, Smythe thought. They were killers. Most of them did it for money, but some of them did it because they liked it.

Blimpey grinned. "I'm always careful, Smythe. That's why I'm still alive and kickin'. Don't worry. I can handle Mordecai and his lot."

"They're killers, Blimpey," he warned.

"And for the most part, they're dumber than tree stumps." Blimpey laughed. "Don't worry, me friend. When the day comes that I can't outsmart a thug like Mordecai, I'll give up the game and retire to me country cottage."

CHAPTER 8

Betsy missed supper, but she did manage to make it back to Upper Edmonton Gardens before the meeting started.

Smythe, his face thunderous, was pacing the back hall. "Just where in the bloomin' blue blazes 'ave you been?" he demanded.

"I've got a good reason for being late," she told him tartly as she took off her hat and coat and dashed for the kitchen, "and I'll thank you not to glare at me like that."

"You missed supper," he hissed, outraged that not only was she late, but she didn't look in the least repentant for worrying him half to death.

"I'm the one who's going hungry tonight," she shot back, "so don't fret about it."

"Fret about it?" he snapped. "I'm not frettin', lass, I'm ruddy furious. I've been worried sick about ya."

The look in his eyes took the wind out of her sails. Suddenly contrite, she dropped her voice as they came in to the kitchen proper. "I didn't mean to be late," she explained, "and I'd not have you concerned for me, Smythe. But it couldn't be helped."

"Good evening, Betsy," Mrs. Jeffries called. She, like the others, was already seated around the table. "Mrs. Goodge has kindly kept a plate of food in the oven for you. Would you like to eat while we have our meeting?"

"No." Betsy smiled in relief. The thought of going without supper had been a bit depressing. She was hungry. "I can wait till afterward. I'm ever so sorry to keep everyone waiting, but it couldn't be helped. I think I might have a clue as to Irene's whereabouts."

"Excellent, Miss Betsy." Hatchet beamed. "I too learned something interesting which may help us to find the young lady. Which of us should go first, do you think?"

"Hold yer horses, now," Luty chimed in. "Who says you get to go first? I've found out plenty today too and it's about the murder."

"Well, I've got my bits and pieces to tell as well," Mrs. Goodge put in, "and if I do say so meself, they're pretty interestin'"

"So do I," Wiggins added.

From the eager expressions on everyone's faces, Mrs. Jeffries suspected they all had something to report. "Why don't we take it in turns," she suggested. "As we've all agreed that there is a strong possibility the murder and Irene's disappearance are linked, I suggest we hear what Betsy and Hatchet have to say first." She smiled at Betsy. "Why don't you start? We're all rather curious as to why you were so late."

"All right. You know how yesterday I found out that that artist who first hired Irene, Gaspar Morante, had up and disappeared?" she began. "Well, what I forgot to mention was that I had a clue as to how I might find out where he'd got to."

Smythe snorted. "Forgot to mention it, did ya?"

Betsy ignored him. "Anyway, today I found out a bit more. Not just about him disappearin', but about the way he'd disappeared as well. He left his studio about five o'clock on that day, took off in a ratty old Bachelors Brougham and hasn't been seen since."

"Was it his carriage?" Smythe asked, getting interested in her information in spite of bein' so niggled at the girl that he couldn't think straight.

"He doesn't own it." Betsy shook her head. "That's why the neighbors noticed it when he drove off. Wasn't much of a driver, either."

"What's so odd about him goin' off in a brougham?" Mrs. Goodge asked. "Lots of people do that, even ones that aren't all that rich. Carriages can be hired, you know."

"But Morante's as poor as a church mouse," Betsy objected. "He barely makes ends meet. Then all of a sudden he up and takes off in a carriage of all things, even a ratty old one like the one he was driving that night. What's more, he left with people owing *him* money. Two days after he went, a gallery owner showed up at his studio wanting to pay Morante for selling one of his paintings."

"Did anyone have any idea where Morante went?" Hatchet asked.

"No, but that brings me to where I was today," Betsy said. "The old woman I talked to gave me the name of one of his friends, another artist. But when I went to see him today, he got all het up and started acting right strange. He kept going on about someone called Alex and saying that 'Alex doesn't do that anymore.' So I decided the fellow was acting so odd and rattled that maybe I ought to keep an eye on him."

"Keep an eye on 'im 'ow?" Smythe asked.

"I waited till he left work," Betsy clarified eagerly, "and then I followed him. That's why I was so late this evening. He didn't get off till six. I know something odd's going on too, because he kept looking over his shoulder and acting like he was expecting to be followed."

"You *were* following him," Mrs. Jeffries pointed out.

"But he didn't know that." Frustrated, Betsy frowned. "I made out that he'd scared me off."

"Scared ya off?" Smythe yelped. "What'd 'e do to ya?"

"Nothing, just got a bit shirty when I started asking about Morante." Betsy waved at him impatiently. "It wasn't me he was afraid might be following him, I know that. He never saw me, I made sure. But he was still walking like a man keeping one eye out for the grim reaper."

"What makes you think this man will help you find Irene?" Luty asked. "Seems to me there could be half a dozen reasons why this Morante skedaddled out of town."

"His name isn't Gaspar Morante," Hatchet said smoothly, his full attention focused on Betsy. "Well, it is, but that's only part of it. His real name is Alessandro Gaspar Morante de Montoya. That's probably why the man you spoke with referred to him as Alex."

"How did you find that out?" Betsy was impressed.

Hatchet grinned. "The same way you do, Miss Betsy, with my wits and my brain."

Luty snorted.

"I also found out that Morante seems to have come into some money recently," Hatchet continued seriously.

"From sellin' his paintings?" Wiggins guessed.

"Well, one could say that." Hatchet hesitated. "The rumor I heard was that Morante copied old masters, which were then sold as the genuine article." He sat back and folded his arms over his chest. "The man he worked for was James Underhill."

There was a long moment of silence as everyone digested that piece of information.

"And now that Underhill's dead," Smythe mused, "Morante's back to bein' as poor as a church mouse. That lets him out as a suspect. A man doesn't kill the goose that's layin' the golden egg."

"In most cases, your reasoning would be quite accurate," Hatchet said. "But we can't eliminate Morante as a suspect . . ."

"I didn't even know he was on the list," Mrs. Goodge grumbled.

" . . . because according to my sources," Hatchet continued, "Morante had no idea he was doing forgeries."

"No idea? But how is that possible?" Mrs. Jeffries asked. This case was certainly getting complex. If it took any more twists or turns, she might be reduced to writing out a cast of characters and a full complement of motives just to keep everything straight in her own mind.

"Underhill had duped Morante into doing the forgeries," Hatchet explained. He leaned his elbows on the table and steepled his hands together. "Supposedly, he went to Morante and told him he had a client who wanted copies of several paintings done. The client was going to put the originals in a bank vault for safekeeping and hang the copies up in his home. It sounds a reasonable enough sort of plan. Especially as Underhill was a broker known to have wealthy clients."

"But why would Morante agree?" Wiggins asked. "Didn't 'e 'ave 'is own paintin' to worry about?"

"Morante was desperate for money," Hatchet clarified. "His own work wasn't selling very well, so he agreed to do the copying."

"And he didn't know what he was doin' was forgery?" Luty said incredulously.

"I suppose he ought to have known"—a smile flitted around Hatchet's mouth—"but as it's quite common for artists to train in their craft by copying the old masters, somehow I imagine that they don't quite see it in that light. Be that as it may, Morante did the paintings and took the money. But when Underhill came to him again, about two weeks ago, with another client who wanted to do the same thing, he got suspicious."

"About what?" Mrs. Goodge yelped. "Sounds like good sense to put a valuable painting in the bank vault and hang a copy on the wall."

"It is," Hatchet said softly. "But Morante was suspicious that Underhill's clients weren't the rightful owners of the paintings at all. In short, he accused Underhill of having him paint forgeries and either selling them outright to unsuspecting buyers or using the forgeries while he stole the originals."

Smythe's breath hissed sharply through his teeth. Now it was starting to make a bit of sense. "How long ago was it that Irene Simmons last posed for Morante?"

Puzzled, Betsy shrugged. "I don't know. Why?"

"It was just over two weeks ago," Mrs. Jeffries said. "I found that out today when I went back to Nanette's for another chat. As a matter of fact, her posing for Morante was the last job she had before she received the mysterious note summoning her to the Grant house on the night she disappeared."

"Maybe she overheard somethin' she should'na?" Wiggins suggested somberly. "Maybe she overheard Morante and Underhill havin' a go at each other over forgin' them paintings?"

Mrs. Jeffries eyed the footman speculatively. She'd been thinking along those very lines herself. "I think you might be on to something," she mused, half thinking aloud as she spoke. "If Morante knew that Irene had overheard his conversaton with Underhill, that would give him not only a motive to kidnap her, but also a reason for getting rid of Underhill. Irene Simmons could go to the police. I don't know what the penalty for art forging is, but I expect it's most unpleasant. But more importantly, if it was ever learned that he'd copied paintings, his own work would be impossible to sell. No reputable gallery or agent would have anything to do with him."

"But how could he have gotten the poison into that tin of mints?" Mrs. Goodge asked. "I know we've already agreed that the killer didn't have to be at the Grant house the day that Underhill ate the mints, but he'd have to be able to get close enough to Underhill to tamper with his mints somehow. I don't see how Morante could have done that, not if he was openly squabbling with Underhill."

"But maybe he wasn't openly at odds with him," Mrs. Jeffries continued, her voice reflecting her growing enthusiasm for this solution. "Perhaps he pretended that all was well between them; perhaps he even apologized for their 'argument.' Then, all he had to do was buy a tin of mints, doctor a few of them with a solution of cyanide and then slip them into Underhill's coat pocket whenever he pleased."

"But when could he have done it?" Betsy asked. "Morante disappeared the same day Irene did and that was a week before the murder."

"He could have done it at any time," the housekeeper replied, absently brushing an errant bread crumb off the tabletop. "Underhill carried his mints in his coat pocket. All Morante would have had to do was find an opportunity to make the switch. It could have happened anywhere—a restaurant, an art gallery, anywhere. No one would be any the wiser. Then, all Morante had to do was wait until Underhill ate the poisoned mints. That would explain the time gap between his kidnapping of Irene and the death of Underhill."

Luty angled her head to one side and sighed dramatically. "I hate to be drapin' crepe on yer idea, Hepzibah, but like you've said yerself, hadn't we better git us some facts before we go makin' wild guesses that might have us runnin' around chasin' our tails and not the killer?"

Taken aback, Mrs. Jeffries simply stared at her. "You think my theory is flawed?"

"It's jest fine, for a theory," Luty replied. "But hadn't we better stick to facts? First of all, we don't know for sure Irene heard anything when she was at Morante's, and even if she did, seems to me a lot of time passed between the eavesdroppin' and the disappearance."

"But I've explained the time gap," Mrs. Jeffries protested, though Luty made a valid point. Perhaps she oughtn't be so eager to accept a theory just because it made sense on the surface.

"You've explained why there was a week between the kidnapping and the murder," Luty agreed, "but that don't explain why Morante waited to git his hands on Irene. If I recall rightly, you all said Irene was supposed to have overheard this conversation two weeks ago. That would mean that Morante, knowing that model had heard everythin' and had the power to ruin him, let her flit about London free as a bird while he did nothing. Then almost a week after her hearin' this damagin' information, he decides to kidnap her. Seems to me that's a bit like closin' the barn door after the horses have run off."

Mrs. Jeffries's shoulders slumped. Luty was right. The theory, lovely as it was, simply had too many holes in it. "I see your point. I'm basing my theory on unproven assumptions. Furthermore, my theory doesn't explain why Morante would kidnap Irene. Why not just murder her as well?"

"That don't mean you ain't right," Luty said quickly. "Jest because it's dumb don't mean people don't do it. Could be this here Morante feller's as thick as two short planks and it took him a week to do his plottin' and his plannin' to git his hands on the girl. I'm jest sayin' we've got to be careful, that's all. As to why he'd kidnap Irene and not kill her . . ." She shrugged. "Well, lots of men are kinda squeamish about doin' somethin' like that to a woman."

"You're being very kind, Luty," Mrs. Jeffries said. "But you've no need to try and spare my feelings. My idea is really quite silly. Morante may know something about the murder and Irene's disappearance. I believe it's in our interest to try and find him, but other than that, well, we'll just have to wait and see what he knows."

"This information does provide the necessary link between the murder and the disappearance,' Hatchet said. "I think we can safely assume the two events are definitely connected. But I agree with you, Mrs. Jeffries. I think we'd better wait until we locate Morante before we make anymore theoretical assumptions."

"I'm not so sure about that," Smythe said flatly. He was as confused as everyone else. But he wasn't going to worry about it yet. They'd sort it out in the end. They always did. "Seems to me Mrs. Jeffries might be on the right track after all."

"And how do you know that?" Mrs. Goodge asked. She was a bit put out because the bits and pieces she'd picked up today were beginning to pale into insignificance compared to the others.

"Because I found out from my sources that James Underhill is a killer himself," he replied, his tone disgusted. "'E 'ired a couple of thugs to murder a woman. Paid plenty for it too, only somethin' went wrong and the woman's not dead. That's why I'm thinkin' there might be somethin' to Mrs. Jeffries's theory. Seems to me that this Morante feller could've found out the same."

"Do you know who this woman was?" Mrs. Jeffries asked.

"Not yet," the coachman replied, "but I'm workin' on it."

"It's probably Irene Simmons," Wiggins guessed.

"That's what I'm thinkin'," Smythe agreed, "but I won't know for sure until tomorro—" He broke off as footsteps sounded on the back stairs. Everyone turned toward the hall just as the inspector, with Fred at his heels, bounded into the kitchen. "Gracious," he said, coming to a halt at the doorway. "I didn't know we had company."

Mrs. Jeffries rose quickly. "Luty and Hatchet only stopped in a few moments ago, sir."

Witherspoon's face mirrored his delight. He quite liked the eccentric American and her butler. "I say," he said cheerfully as he hurried toward the table, "do you mind if I join you? I could do with some company this evening. This horrid case I'm working on just won't let me relax."

Inspector Witherspoon was in fine form the next morning as he stepped out of the hansom in front of James Underhill's lodging house. He'd slept like a baby, eaten a huge breakfast and was brimming with new ideas about this case. Odd, how just an hour or two spent in convivial conversation with one's household could send the mind moving in so many interesting directions. Why, he thought, as he marched up the walkway to the front door, he'd not have considered coming back here if it hadn't been for an odd comment made by Wiggins.

Witherspoon knocked on the front door. Of course, Smythe's information was also important, the inspector told himself while he waited for someone to answer the door. Between his coachman and his footman, he'd come up with quite a number of things to do this morning.

The door opened and a middle-aged woman, her face set in grim lines, peeked out. "Yes?"

He doffed his bowler hat. "Good morning, madam. I'm Inspector Witherspoon. Are you the landlady of this establishment?"

"I am." She opened the door wider. "The police have already been here," she accused. "They said they were finished and I could rent his rooms out."

"Oh dear," Witherspoon replied. "You haven't cleaned them out yet, I hope?" There was no need to clarify what they were talking about. Both of them knew it was Underhill.

"I've been up there," she said, jerking her chin toward the staircase behind her, "but that lazy Feniman hasn't come round yet and I can't move that stuff without him. He claimed he'd be here at eight, and just look, it's gone past nine and the shiftless fool still isn't here."

Silently thanking the hapless Feniman for his tardiness, the inspector stepped past the landlady into the foyer. "If you don't mind, I'd like to have a quick look around before you remove his things."

"Help yerself." She shrugged. "Though I don't know why you coppers can't get it right the first time."

Witherspoon started up the stairs. "I'll try not to inconvenience you, madam."

"You've already inconvenienced me," she snapped. "Feniman was here the second time your lot come around to search and he had his wagon with him. If that peeler hadn't wasted the whole afternoon, I'da had them rooms cleaned and rented by now."

He stopped and turned to look at her. "Second time, madam?" he queried. "But the police have only been here once."

She shook her head in denial. "There was one here the other day, claimed he was with Scotland Yard."

"What did he look like?"

She shrugged. "Scrawny feller. Pale skinned, he was. Had wispy blond hair. He was here searchin' them rooms for a good two hours. Jumpy, he was. He about went through the ceiling when I come in to ask him if he was finished."

Witherspoon's heartbeat accelerated. He quickly cast his mind to the faces of those involved with this case. After a moment, he suspected he knew who had been in the victim's rooms. "Thank you, madam," he said. "You've been most helpful. However, in the future, if someone else claims they are the police, would you please be so kind as to send for me before you allow them into the late Mr. Underhill's rooms?"

"How many more coppers do you expect'll be around?" she yelped. "I'm wantin' to rent them rooms out."

"I don't think anyone else will come," he said hastily. "But in the event someone does, please contact me immediately."

She shrugged and wandered off down the hallway, still muttering about the lazy Feniman and the bloody coppers. The inspector continued up the stairs. The door leading to Underhill's quarters was open. He stepped inside and slowly let his gaze survey the sitting room.

The room was quite beautiful. Not just nicely appointed or adequately decorated, but stunningly lovely.

Brilliant jewel colors of a large Persian carpet covered polished hardwood floors. The settee and love seat grouped invitingly around a small rosewood table were upholstered in a deep, rich rose fabric that went beautifully with the color of the flowers in the cream-and-pink chintz curtains. In the far corner a Queen Anne armchair stood next to a dainty seventeenth-century single drawer desk, the top of which was bare. But it wasn't the elegance of the quarters that made one stop and take pause. It was the paintings. Dozens of them—they covered the walls so thickly one couldn't really make out what color the wallpaper might be. There were large ones in glittering gilt frames, small watercolors surrounded by simple wood and some that had no frames at all.

Shaking his head in wonder, the inspector advanced into the room. There was no one particular style or period to the collection. Bright, colorful landscapes hung next to somber portraits from the eighteenth century. Pastoral scenes, sailing ships, raging seas, Italian madonnas and even one or two nudes that made the inspector blush hung in uneven rows along all four walls. The room had been aesthetically designed to appeal to both the eye and the mind.

Witherspoon shook his head sadly. James Underhill, for all his faults as a human being, had been a man who'd understood the compelling lure of visual beauty.

"Excuse me, sir."

Witherspoon started and whirled around. "Oh, hello, Constable," he said to Barnes. "I see you got my message."

Barnes, his mouth gaping in wonder and his expression awed, stepped further into the room. "Yes sir," he muttered. "I got here as quickly as I could. Have you ever seen the like, sir?"

"Not outside a museum," Witherspoon replied honestly. "It's quite a spectacle, isn't it?"

"Are they all real, sir?" Barnes asked. "I mean, are they valuable . . . or copies or what?"

"I'm not sure," Witherspoon replied. "But from what we know of our investigation into Mr. Underhill's finances, I can't quite see them being valuable. According to both his solicitor and his bank manager, he'd not much money."

"Maybe this is why," Barnes said, grinning and jerking his head toward the far wall. "Could be the man loved art more than anything." He sobered quickly. "What are we doin' here, sir? The lads have already searched the place. They found nothing of interest, sir. No notes, no threatening letters, nothing which gives—"

"Precisely," Witherspoon interrupted with relish. "That's the whole problem. There should have been. Underhill conducted his business from here—he didn't have a proper office and he was a broker or an agent of some sort. At least enough of one to make a living at it and be able to afford all this." He swept his arm in an arc that included the paintings.

"I see what you're gettin' at, sir." Barnes nodded in understanding. "There should have been ledgers and bills of sales or invoices. But there aren't." He slowly turned and surveyed the room, and then he walked quickly to the desk in the corner. He opened the drawer, reached inside and pulled out a slender sheaf of pristine white notepaper. "Nothing here but his stationary. How did the man conduct his business?"

"That's what we have to find out," Witherspoon said cheerfully, remembering what Wiggins had inadvertently said the night before. "There's also another matter we need to investigate." His manner darkened perceptibly as he remembered the rather frightening message that Smythe had given him. Really, he wasn't sure he liked his staff being the recepients of such terrifying information. Even if they were just passing it along to him. He'd never forgive himself if one of his household were ever hurt or endangered by Witherspoon's profession. But right now wasn't the time to concern himself with that matter. It would be investigated thoroughly as soon as he and the constable finished here. Then again, he thought, maybe there was nothing to it. Perhaps his coachman had merely been accosted by one of those odd people who seem to come out from everywhere whenever they read about a murder.

"What other matter, sir?" Barnes asked.

"Huh? Oh." He smiled apologetically at the constable. "Nothing, Barnes. I mean, I'll tell you all about it on our way to the Grant house."

"We're going back there, sir?"

"Yes, we've got to have a word with Arthur Grant. But before we do that, I suggest we look for a key."

"To what, sir?" Barnes asked.

"To Underhill's office," the inspector replied.

"But he didn't have one, sir."

"That's just it, Constable. He has to have kept his paperwork somewhere. There has to be a room or a cupboard or a file cabinet or something."

"Maybe he kept it in his head," Barnes suggested.

"I doubt that, Barnes," Witherspoon replied, his attention caught by a lovely painting of a windswept beach. "His clients would no doubt have demanded receipts and invoices."

Barnes wasn't so sure. But nevertheless, he and the inspector set about looking for a key.

Mrs. Jeffries absently picked up her teacup and took a sip. Behind her, Mrs. Goodge closed the oven door with a bang. The housekeeper smiled to herself. The cook was still sulking because of the inspector's interruption last night. She'd been the only one of them who hadn't been able to get her information out in the open with their dear employer sitting there.

Mrs. Jeffries was actually quite proud of the staff. They'd done splendidly. Betsy, her eyes innocently wide, had asked the inspector how the hunt for Irene Simmons was proceeding. Witherspoon, after blustering a moment, had finally admitted that it wasn't going well at all. The murder of James Underhill was taking all of his time.

"Oh well, sir," Betsy had said, "I suppose then the bit of gossip I've picked up won't do you any good."

"Gossip?" Witherspoon had popped up in his chair like a marionette having his string pulled. He was well aware of the importance of gossip. "About Irene Simmons? By all means, Betsy, do tell me what you've heard."

The maid had outdone herself, making up a convuluted tale of back-fence whispers, shop assistants who'd heard this and that and delivery boys who'd stopped her on the high street because she worked for the inspector. Betsy had managed to get the whole tale of Morante's disappearance and connection to Irene straight into the inspector's listening ears.

"You see, sir," she'd concluded brightly, "everyone knows you're the most brilliant detective in all of Scotland Yard. That's why they're always stopping me and telling me things. You know how it is, sir. They want to be important but none of them wants to come to you themselves. They're afraid of looking foolish."

Mrs. Goodge slapped a round of bread dough onto the flour-covered marble slab on the far end of the table. Making a fist, she punched it hard enough to rattle the teapot.

Mrs. Jeffries winced. "Now, now, Mrs. Goodge, we're going to have another meeting this evening. You'll be able to tell us your bits and pieces then. You mustn't upset yourself."

"Who says I'm upset?" She rolled half the dough on top of itself and kneaded it with the palm of her hand. "It just seems to me the inspector didn't have to go runnin' up to bed before I had a chance to say my piece."

"But it was after ten o'clock. He was getting very tired."

"Humph." She snorted, taking another whack at the dough. "He had plenty of time to listen to Wiggins goin' on about Arthur Grant and Smythe's tale of Underhill's murder plot."

"Only because Wiggins's information dovetailed so very nicely with Smythe's," the housekeeper replied calmly. Really, it had been quite remarkable how the coachman had managed to get his information said. He'd been quite bold about it, claiming that he'd been stopped on his way out of the stables and told by a man that James Underhill had plotted a woman's murder. Witherspoon had been amazed. Of course he'd asked Smythe what this informant looked like. Smythe, always a fast thinker, said he couldn't say. The informant had kept to the shadows of the stable. The only other thing the alleged informant said was that he'd followed Smythe deliberately because he knew he worked for the inspector.

"My information would have dovetailed nicely too." Mrs. Goodge picked the entire round of dough up, turned it over and slapped it back on the marble. "If I'd had a chance to tell it. And Wiggins's bits didn't have anything to do with what Smythe told us," she continued, taking another swing at the hapless mound in front of her. "He just pretended like it did. All he said was that some silly maid at the Grant house had told him that Arthur Grant was all het up about something on the day that Underhill was killed." She snorted again. "If I'd had a chance, I could have told him what's what. I know what Grant was up to. That's what my sources told me."

Mrs. Jeffries put the cup she'd just picked up back down. She knew she should wait for the others, but this might be important. "What?"

"You want me to tell you now?" the cook asked. "Without the others?"

The housekeeper hesitated, but finally couldn't resist the temptation. "Yes. The day is still young. Tell me what you know. It may influence where I go and who I talk with today."

Mrs. Goodge smiled slowly. "All right, then. If you think it's important."

"I do," Mrs. Jeffries assured her. "I think it's very important."

"Well, there's two things, actually." Mrs. Goodge plopped the battered dough into a bowl. Wiping her hands on her apron, she sat down next to the housekeeper. "The first was that Mary Grant's family once had one of the best art collections in the country, but it was sold off piece by piece to keep a roof over their heads."

"When was this?" Mrs. Jeffries didn't remind the cook that she'd already shared this information. She didn't wish to hurt her feelings or interrupt her.

"Years ago, well before she married Mr. Grant. By the time he come along, all that was left was the paintings she used as a dowry."

"Strange that she'd use such valuable paintings to marry a man like Neville Grant," the housekeeper mused. "From what the inspector said, Mrs. Grant isn't hideously ugly."

"No, she's not hideous," the cook said, "but she's sharp tongued and a bit of a shrew. There weren't many that would have her, dowry or not. And she was tired of bein' a spinster. You'd think that would make her more understanding about her sister, wouldn't you? I mean, she wanted to marry so why shouldn't Helen want to marry too?"

"Perhaps she didn't wish her sister to get her hopes up," Mrs. Jeffries suggested. "The inspector did say that Mary Grant was convinced that Helen's engagement was all a figment of Helen's imagination."

"I don't think that's true," Mrs. Goodge said. "Not after what Wiggins told us."

Puzzled, the housekeeper looked at her. She couldn't recall Wiggins making any comment about Helen Collier. "I'm afraid I don't know what you mean."

"Don't you remember what the lad said Cora had told him?" Mrs. Goodge said. "Cora said that a couple of days before the murder, Miss Collier bumped into Underhill at her bank. Well, that proves it, doesn't it?"

"Oh, that." Mrs. Jeffries nodded. "Yes, I remember now. But I'm afraid I still don't understand. What does that have to do with Helen's alleged engagement?"

"Everything," Mrs. Goodge exclaimed. "My sources told me that Helen Collier goes to her bank once a month to withdraw the money she'll need. She also goes to have a look-see at her paintings. She owns three Caldararos as well. Underhill met her there but I'd bet my next quarter's wages it wasn't an accident. I think he met her there so he could see those paintings for himself. Having seen them, I think he made up his mind to marry her so he could get his hands on 'em."

Mrs. Jeffries stared at her for a long moment. "My goodness, you might be right. Of course, knowing what we know of the dead man, he'd want to make sure the paintings were real before he committed himself to marriage. If, of course, he was genuinely considering marriage to the woman."

"No reason for him not to," Mrs. Goodge said bluntly. "Underhill wasn't any spring chicken himself. Man gets to be his age, probably starts wondering who's going to be taking care of him and doin' his fetchin' and carryin' for him when he gets old. Remember, he was gentry too. But gentry with no money. It's not like he'd have been welcomed by many women of his own class. Not as poor as he was. Helen Collier did have a small income and three very valuable paintings to her credit. More importantly, she was willing."

"Yes, quite." Mrs. Jeffries was quite impressed with the cook's analysis. "And the second thing you learned?"

"Oh, that." She waved her hand impatiently. "I heard some gossip that Arthur Grant needed something from Underhill. Needed it desperately. That's why he invited him around to tea that day. He was waiting for Underhill to broker some kind of deal for him."

CHAPTER 9

This time, Betsy was prepared. She dodged behind a cooper's wagon as her quarry crossed the wide pavement of the railway station. He walked right on past the entrance to the cloakroom, stopped in front of the door to the station proper, glanced once over his shoulder and then ducked inside.

She gave him a few moments to get ahead and then dashed in after him. He was heading for the platforms. Betsy started to follow, realized she didn't have a ticket and then glanced anxiously around looking for the notice board. It was over the ticket kiosk. Lifting her skirts, she rushed toward it, praying a train wasn't just now pulling out with her prey already on it.

There were three trains leaving in the next half hour, two locals and an express. She dithered for a moment, wondering which he'd be on and then made up her mind. She bought a ticket for the one leaving right away and raced for the platform at a run, telling herself that the worst that could happen is she'd have to go through this again tomorrow if she was wrong. But to her way of thinking, he'd been in an awful hurry to get out to the platform and this was the only train there.

After boarding, Betsy cautiously made her way down the length of the cars. She spotted him in the next to last carriage. Holding a bundle on his lap, he sat in the seat closest to the window, his nose buried in a newspaper.

Betsy smiled as she took a seat not far away. Now that she knew where he was, keeping him in her sights should be easy.

• • •

"What kind of deal?" Mrs. Jeffries prodded.

"That's the funny part," Mrs. Goodge said eagerly. "Arthur Grant doesn't have any money, so he couldn't be doin' any buyin'"

"Maybe he was selling one," the housekeeper suggested.

"He doesn't own any of 'em," the cook replied promptly. "I found that out when I was checkin' with my sources about the family in general. There's a valuable art collection, all right," she continued, "but it belongs to Neville Grant. None of it belongs to his son."

"His mother didn't leave him anything?"

"Nothing." Mrs. Goodge pursed her lips. "Not so much as a picture frame. She didn't share her husband's passion for art. As a matter of fact, she and Neville Grant were reported to be at odds over his spending the family money on buying paintings. One of the rumors I heard claimed that they was squabblin' about it so much that if Arthur's mother hadn't up and died when she did, Neville was goin' to divorce her."

"'Ello, 'ello," a singsong voice cried from down the hall. "Are you in there, Mrs. Goodge? It's me, Gavin. I've got a delivery for ya."

The cook brightened immediately and leapt to her feet. "Come on in, lad," she cried, lunging for the kettle and snatching it up. "It's the grocer's boy," she hissed at the housekeeper as she plopped the kettle on the burner. "He's always got heaps of gossip."

Mrs. Jeffries nodded and got up. "I'll leave you to it," she murmured as a young man carrying a huge covered wicker basket lumbered into the kitchen. She smiled at him and left.

As she climbed the back stairs to her room, Mrs. Jeffries began going over precisely what they'd learned so far. But it was still most confusing.

By the time she reached her room she was almost convinced that it was the most convoluted case they'd ever had. She walked over and sat down in her chair next to the window. Staring blindly out the window, she let her mind go blank. That was a neat trick she'd picked up over the past few years. Sometimes she did her best thinking by not thinking at all. She kept staring out at the rooftops of London, letting her brain leap willy-nilly where it would. Ideas, thoughts, unrelated bits of information—it all whirled about in her head in a rush of nonsense. But Mrs. Jeffries wasn't overly concerned. She'd sort the pieces out later. Right now, all she was really concerned with was a pattern, a connection of some kind. There was always a common thread in every case they'd had. It was like having a hundred keys to unlock one door. Difficult, yes, but not impossible. Especially if one had learned to pay attention to the kind of lock on the door. That's what she did now—tried to find what kind of lock this door had.

Smythe stood under the TO LET sign of the empty building on busy Villiers Street. He wondered why Blimpey had sent a street Arab to tell him to meet him here instead of at the pub. The street was quite busy with hansoms, pedestrians and shopkeepers all trying to get about their business. Smythe pulled out his watch, noted the time and then glanced at the facade of Gattis Restaurant across from where he stood. He blinked, amazed, as Blimpey Groggins, no cleaner than he ever was, emerged from the front door.

Blimpey spotted him immediately. Lifing his arm, he waved, motioning him over.

"Eat 'ere regularly, do ya?" Smythe asked. Gattis was one of London's most elegant restaurants. Smythe had the money to buy the place, but actually setting foot in it as a customer would never occur to him. He didn't like to think he'd be intimidated by a bunch of toffs—he wouldn't. Well, not too intimidated. But he couldn't for the life of him think of what Blimpey Groggins, disheveled and dirty, was doing here.

Blimpey laughed. "Not hardly, mate. Just was inside havin' a chat with one of the staff. The maître d' here owes me a couple of favors and I was collectin'"

Smythe wondered what kind of favors Blimpey was cashing in, but didn't like to ask. Sometimes it didn't pay to be too curious about someone like Groggins. "How come you wanted me to meet ya 'ere?"

"I'm bit pressed for time today," Blimpey replied. He jerked his head toward the end of the road. "There's a decent pub down there. Let's have a quick one. I do my best talkin' over a glass."

Smythe eyed his companion speculatively as they headed off. "You weren't too busy to get my information, were ya?" the coachman asked.

"Don't be daft," Blimpey said. "Have I ever failed ya?" They were abreast of the pub now. He reached out and yanked open the door. "Trust me, Smythe. Trust me. I might be busy, but that don't mean I'm not giving ya good service."

"The best that money can buy." Smythe stepped past his companion and into the pub. He was relieved to see it was an ordinary, plain sort of place with benches and tables and a bored-looking publican behind the bar. "Two bitters," he ordered quickly, knowing that the sooner he got beer pouring down Blimpey's throat, the faster he'd get his information.

A few minutes later, they were seated at a table. Blimpey took a long sip from his glass and then gave a loud, satisfied sigh. "Ah. That's good."

"Now that you've wet yer whistle," Smythe said, "what did ya learn?"

"You're an impatient sort, Smythe," Blimpey commented. "You ought to slow down a bit, take time to sniff the air and enjoy yerself. But seein' as we're both in a bit of a hurry today, I'll get right to it." His expression sobered. "It ain't very pretty. But ya know that already. The woman that Mordecai's boys was paid to kill is named Irene Simmons. She's an artist's model."

"I thought that might be 'er." Smythe kept his face impassive. "She's disappeared."

"But I bet no one's found her body, 'ave they?" Blimpey replied. "Like I told ya yesterday, it went wrong. They didn't do it. Mordecai himself is rumored to be havin' a fit, thinkin' his good name's been ruined."

"Why'd it go wrong? Were ya able to find out?" Smythe decided that getting as many details as possible just might help them track down Irene Simmons, especially as it looked like she hadn't been murdered—at least not by this particular set of hired killers.

"Story I got—and I've no doubt it's true"—Blimpey took a quick drink—"is that two of Mordecai's boys was going to be waiting for the woman when she walked down the street."

"You mean they was just standing on the street, waiting for 'er?" Smythe didn't think so, not in that neighborhood. "That can't be right. She disappeared from a posh area. Thugs like Mordecai's scum woulda stuck out like a sore thumb. Someone woulda spotted 'em and called the police."

"They weren't just standin' on the street," Blimpey corrected. "They was waiting at the top of the mews. It connects with Beltrane Gardens a half a dozen houses down from where this woman was supposed to be goin'. Anyway, as I was sayin', they was to grab her as she was walkin' toward Holland Park Road."

"She was supposed to be goin' to the Grant house," Smythe said. "The same 'ouse where Underhill 'imself got murdered a week later."

"I know." Blimpey grinned. "Knowin' things is me business, remember. Now do ya want to hear the rest of it or not?"

"Go on," Smythe said irritably.

"Anyways, like I was sayin', the thugs was to grab her when she reached the mouth of the alley. But she never got to 'em," Blimpey explained. "They waited and waited and waited, but she never come."

"Do they know for sure she went into the Grant house?" Smythe asked. He wanted to make good and sure that these thugs, who apparently weren't the smartest lads about, actually knew what they were on about.

"Oh, yes," Blimpey affirmed. "They had their eyes on 'er from the time she got off the omnibus and walked up Holland Park Road. She walked with a woman as far as Beltrane Gardens and then continued on by herself to the Grant house. It was at that point, after she was almost there, that they took off for the mouth of the mews and tucked themselves back out of sight. Like ya said, Mordecai's boys would stick out right smart in a posh neighborhood like that. They couldn't afford to be seen by too many people."

"Maybe the girl did spot them," Smythe suggested. "Maybe she came out of the house and went in another direction?"

"There isn't any other way," Blimpey said. "Not unlessin' yer goin' through someone's back garden, and I don't think a young woman would be up to that. Besides, if that were the case, why didn't she go on home or go to the police?"

He had a point, Smythe conceded silently. "Do these thugs 'ave any idea what 'appened?" he asked. "A woman doesn't just disappear into thin air."

"They figure she either never left the Grant house," Blimpey said, "or that she got nabbed before she reached the mouth of the mews."

"They see anything?"

"One of 'em claimed there was a carriage pulled up in front of the house." Blimpey shrugged. "But that don't mean much. It was gettin' toward evening and there was a lot of traffic. A neighborhood like that would have plenty of carriages and hansoms goin' in and out."

"So no one really knows what happened."

"All they know is what didn't happen."

"Do you believe yer sources are tellin' the truth?" Smythe motioned impatiently with his hand. "No, that's not what I mean. Do ya think that

Mordecai's boys is tellin' the truth? Now that Underhill is dead, could be they just want to put the word out that they didn't kill someone for 'im."

"It's the truth all right." Blimpey shook his head vehemently. "Underhill was furious with Mordecai for botching the murder. They had a blazin' row about it the next day. Underhill, stupid bugger, wanted his money back. Mordecai said he didn't give refunds and told him he'd get the job done as soon as they could find the girl. That's the strange part—they can't find her either. She's plum disappeared."

Smythe's brows drew together in an ominous frown. "They're not still lookin' for 'er, are they?"

"Nah. Mordecai don't take *that* much pride in his work. With Underhill dead, he's not goin' to care one way or another about Irene Simmons. The girl means nothing to him."

Smythe leaned forward, his expression grim. "I wonder if Mordecai murdered Underhill."

Blimpey laughed again. "With poison? Not bloody likely. He wouldn't be that neat about it. When scum like him do their work, they don't bother to be tidy. Besides, why would he want Underhill dead? He was a customer."

"I see yer point," Smythe muttered. "But it don't make sense."

"Who says life has to make sense?" Blimpey shrugged philosophically. "All I know is she didn't get carved up by Mordecai's thugs and she ain't been heard from since."

"So she's either still in the house," Smythe mused, "or she was kidnapped before she reached the mews."

"Or she was grabbed right before she went into the house," Blimpey corrected. "The thugs took off just as they saw her reaching the Grant house. They didn't see her go inside."

"I wonder what kind of a carriage it was?" he murmured, remembering what Betsy had told them.

"I don't know and I ain't sure I can find out. Mordecai's thugs don't usually talk to the likes of me." Blimpey belched softly. "Get me another, will ya? Then I'll tell ya the rest of it."

"Rest of it?" Smythe half rose and waved at the barman, gesturing for another round when he had the man's attention. "You mean there's more?"

"Course there's more," Blimpey bragged. "I always give ya yer money's worth."

• • •

Betsy's lungs hurt as she hurried to keep her quarry in sight. He'd gotten off the train at Reigate and she, keeping well behind him, had followed suit.

But he must have been feeling quite confident he wasn't being followed, because he never once looked over his shoulder as he left the station. Since leaving the town proper, Betsy had trailed him a good half mile now, first down a country lane and then onto a footpath through a copse of trees. The trees grew close enough together that she couldn't see all that far ahead, but she could still hear his footsteps echoing in front of her.

She stumbled over a tree root snaking across the foot path, righted herself and plunged onward, scrambling none too delicately toward a point ahead where the trees had started to thin. She stopped suddenly as she realized she couldn't hear his footfalls against the path. Her heart pounded in her ears. Her breathing sounded loud enough to wake the dead as she stood still and listened. A moment later, she heard him start to move.

Betsy's whole body sagged in relief. She'd feel a right fool if he'd suddenly turned tail and come back this way. She'd feel even more foolish if it turned out he wasn't leading her anywhere except his own home.

"Maybe someone was playing a joke on your coachman," Barnes said softly. He and the inspector were back at the Grant house, waiting in the living room while the butler went to fetch Arthur Grant. The inspector had just told the constable the disturbing information he'd learned from Smythe.

"That's certainly possible, I suppose," Witherspoon replied. He kept one eye on the entrance to the drawing room. "But Smythe seemed quite convinced the man was sincere. True or not, though, we must investigate it."

"Too bad it's Mordecai." Barnes grimaced. "None of his lot will ever turn on him. Too many that've tried are dead."

"Well, we can't prosecute on rumors," Witherspoon said dejectedly, "but on the other hand, according to what Smythe was told, this young woman wasn't murdered."

"But she's still missin'" Barnes didn't like that. He didn't like it one bit. Unlike the inspector, he wasn't too sure that Mordecai's boys had failed in their mission. As a gang leader, Mordecai wasn't quite as stupid as some of the others operating out of the east end or the docks. The constable wouldn't put it past the thug to put the word out that they'd failed when in reality, there was some poor woman at the bottom of the Thames trussed up like a Christmas goose.

"The butler said you wanted to see me," Arthur Grant said as he entered the drawing room. "I can't think why. I've already told you everything I know about this dreadful business." He stalked across the room and came to a halt right in front of Witherspoon.

The inspector noticed the man's face was haggard and thin, his pale complexion now almost a dead white, and there was a decided twitch in his right eye. "I'm afraid we've a few more questions we must ask you," he told him.

"Questions? That's ridiculous. What else could I tell you?"

"Where did Mr. Underhill conduct his business?" Witherspoon asked, thinking he might have to be careful in how he broached this interview. Arthur Grant looked as though he might faint.

"Conduct his business?" Arthur stammered. "I'm afraid I don't understand the question."

"He couldn't have done business out of his lodgings, sir," the inspector explained. "When his premises were searched there weren't any invoices or records or ledgers or anything at all to support the notion that he made his living as an artists' agent or broker."

Arthur stepped back a pace. "Why are you asking me? I didn't have anything to do with Underhill's business. His coming round here on the day he died was purely a social call. We were social acquaintances, nothing more. I know nothing of his business affairs, absolutely nothing." As he spoke he stepped farther and farther away from the two policemen.

"I'm afraid that's not true, sir," Witherspoon said, his gaze shifting slightly to one side as he spied Neville and Mary Grant standing in the drawing room door. "We know for a fact that you were doing business with Mr. Underhill. That's the reason you invited him here that day. Have you ever been to Mr. Underhill's lodgings?"

Grant hesitated briefly. "Only once."

"When was that, sir?" Barnes asked, looking up from his notebook.

"A few months ago." Arthur's eye spasmed furiously. "I went round for tea one afternoon. James had some new paintings he wanted to show me."

"Only once, sir?" Witherspoon shook his head. "Are you sure?"

"Of course I'm sure," Arthur insisted, his voice rising shrilly. "Why shouldn't I be sure?"

"Have you been there since Mr. Underhill was murdered?" Barnes asked calmly.

"No," Arthur cried. "Absolutely not. Who told you I was there? If it was that pie-faced old hag of a landlady of his, she's lying."

"But she isn't lying, sir," Witherspoon said mildly. "Why would she? She's no reason to tell us anything except the truth. Now, why don't you tell the constable and I why you claimed to be a policeman and then spent the afternoon searching James Underhill's lodgings? What were you looking for?"

"Nothing," he blurted out. Then he clamped his hand over his mouth. "I wasn't looking for anything."

"But you admit you were there?"

"I'm not sure," Arthur wailed. "Maybe I was. I don't know. I'm confused."

"Should we bring the landlady here to identify him, sir?" Barnes asked the inspector.

Arthur looked from one policeman to the other, his expression frantic. He still hadn't noticed his father standing behind him. "You don't have to do that. All right, I'll admit it. I was there. I did tell her I was a policeman. But that's all I did. I didn't kill him."

"Then what were you looking for, sir?" the inspector pressed. "Why would an innocent man go to a dead man's lodgings under false pretenses unless he had something to hide? What were you looking for that day, sir?"

"I don't know," Arthur cried passionately. "He told me he hadn't kept them in his rooms but I didn't believe him. Then when I saw he'd been telling the truth, that they weren't there, you see, I knew they had to be somewhere. I knew I had to find them. I've got to find them. So I thought there might be a key. If I don't, I'm ruined. Absolutely ruined."

Neville stepped into the room, for once not thumping his cane loud enough to rattle the windows. But his son wasn't aware of his father's entrance. Arthur's gaze was focused on the two policemen in front of him.

"Ruined, sir?" Barnes said gently. "In what way? Why don't you just tell us the truth, sir? It'll go easier on you in the long run."

Arthur blanched at the constable's comment. "I didn't kill him," he screamed. "I didn't kill him. I don't care what anyone says. I didn't do it.

I was going to pay him what he wanted. I had the money. I'd borrowed it from Aunt Helen."

"For God's sake, boy, shut up!" Neville thundered, poking his son in the back with his cane. "Don't say another word."

Arthur let out a squawk and whirled around. "Father? You've got to believe me. I didn't do it."

"Shut up!" Neville banged his cane against the floor. "Do you hear me, boy? Be quiet." He looked at the inspector. "Are you arresting my son?"

Witherspoon was quite taken aback. All he'd planned on doing was asking a few questions. "No. But we would like to ask him some more questions."

Neville stared at the policeman speculatively, as though he was weighing his choices. "Does he have to answer them?"

"Your son cannot be forced to answer our questions," the inspector replied. He'd no idea why the Grants were reacting like this, but both the father and the son now appeared almost frantic with worry. Witherspoon couldn't readily see that he had any evidence to connect them to Underhill's murder, but considering their suspicious behaviour, he decided to carry on. "However, we can ask him to accompany us to the station to help us with our inquiries."

Everyone in the room knew what that meant. Arthur would, in fact, end up under arrest.

"I see." Neville flashed a quick look at his son. "Tell them the truth, boy. Tell them now."

"The truth?" Arthur's voice shook. "I've no idea what you're talking about, Father . . ."

"Arthur, don't be such an imbecile," Neville snapped. He gestured at Witherspoon and Barnes. "They already know you were cooking up some silly scheme with Underhill. Now go ahead and tell them what it was so they'll go away and leave us in peace. Whatever it was you were planning can't be nearly as serious as a murder charge."

Arthur's mouth opened and closed, as though he were trying to speak, but no words came out.

Betsy dodged behind a tree and stared at the clearing. Two hundred feet ahead she watched the man she'd been following disappear through the door of a cottage—quite a large cottage, double storied and possibly with an attic on top, but nevertheless a cottage. A wooden fence, boards missing in spots, encircled an overgrown garden. The lawn was tufted with tiny hillocks, weeds sprouted in the flower beds and the stone walkway was cracked in several places.

The outside had once been white but was now a dull, dismal gray. Shutters, one of them hanging askew, banked the windows on either side of the door. No smoke came out of either of the chimney pots on the roof.

Betsy's heart thumped against her chest as she tried to decide what to do. Walking boldly up to the door and demanding entrance might not be too smart, she thought, casting a quick glance around at the surroundings. This place was all by itself out in the middle of nowhere. If the man got stroppy, she might be in trouble. Goodness knows, she'd not passed another living soul for a good half hour, so if she got in trouble, screaming her head off wouldn't do any good.

But she had a feeling about this place. Following the man from the gallery had been a risk, but now that she was here, she was almost certain she was on to something important. But what to do about it? Betsy surveyed the area. The clearing was a good two hundred feet long and at least that much wide. She couldn't sneak up to the house from the front, but maybe there would be a bit more shelter from the back.

Betsy moved quietly from tree to tree, making her way around the house and keeping her eyes peeled to make sure she wasn't seen. When she found herself standing directly in line with the corner of the house, she decided to move closer. The trees were thinning off up the hillside, useless as hiding places. Taking a deep breath, she lifted the hem of her skirt and dashed across the clearing toward the side of the house.

Reaching it, she flattened herself against the wood and took a long, deep breath of air into her lungs. Along the side, there were two more windows. Both of them were shut, but even from where she stood, she could see that the curtains on the one closest to where she stood were wide open.

Betsy eased away from the building and edged closer to the window. She kept her head cocked to one side, listening hard for the sound of voices. Her foot hit a patch of mud and made an ugly squishing sound as she crept down the side.

Finally, she reached the window. She bent her knees and ducked down so that her head was under the sill. Slowly, carefully, Betsy raised up until she could see over the edge.

Her eyes widened and her heartbeat quickened. She'd been right to follow him. She'd been right all along. It had been a kidnapping and the proof of it was right in front of her.

Irene Simmons. A young, dark-haired woman sat less than five feet from where she stood. Betsy was sure it was her. The description they had of Irene matched this woman completely.

What to do now?

Through the window, Betsy heard the telltale squeak of a door opening. Then footsteps as someone came into the captive's room.

Betsy pulled back out of view, flattening herself against the wall. What was she going to do? She had to do something. That poor woman was at the mercy of some fiend.

Holding her breath, she took another quick peek. Her mouth gaped open in surprise at what she saw.

Irene Simmons, kidnap victim, appeared to be locked in a passionate embrace with a tall, dark-haired man. Irene wasn't resisting the man. As a matter of fact, from where Betsy stood, it looked as if the girl was participating wholeheartedly.

"Well, I never," Betsy mumbled. She started to back away, thinking she'd got everything completely wrong. Mainly, she was concerned that the woman in the house wasn't Irene, but some perfectly innocent lady giving her husband a perfectly natural embrace. Retreating backward and shaking her head in disgust at her own stupidity, Betsy didn't see the man step out from the side of the house. She stumbled into him. Whirling around, she found herself face to face with the fellow she'd trailed from the St. James gallery. "Oh no," she cried. "Look, there's a good explanation . . ."

He grabbed her arm and yanked her towards him. "I told you to leave us alone," he snarled. "But no, you had to follow me, had to keep sticking your pretty little nose in where it weren't wanted." He pulled her toward a door at the back of the house.

"Let me go." Betsy tried to jerk her arm free, but he held on fast. "I told you, there's a good explanation . . ."

"I'll bet there is," he said.

The back door flew open and the dark-haired man came out. The woman, her eyes wide with fear, was right behind him. "George? What's going on?" he asked. His voice was tinged with a faint accent.

"This is the girl I told you about," George said, tugging Betsy forward none too gently. "The one who came round asking all those questions yesterday. She must have followed me. We'd better bring her inside, quickly." He started for the door as the other two stepped back a pace. "I don't know if she brought any of Underhill's thugs with her."

Betsy dug her heels into the ground and resisted with all her might. "No one followed me," she said before she could stop herself. She looked at the woman standing behind the dark-haired man. "Are you Irene Simmons?"

"Why, yes," she replied.

"We'll ask the questions," the man holding her arm said. He tried tugging her forward again.

Betsy had had it. This man talked like a thug, but he wasn't really very good at it. For starters, now that they'd stopped, she could feel his hand trembling as he hung onto her. She yanked her arm out of his grasp, made a fist with her other hand and cuffed him smartly on the shoulder.

"Ow," he yelped.

"Keep your hands off me, you silly fool," she ordered. She put her hands on her hips and looked directly at the woman. "You'd better listen. Nanette Lanier sent me."

"Nanette." The woman's eyes widened.

"Be careful, darling," the dark-haired man warned. "It might be a trick."

"Oh, for goodness' sake," Betsy grumbled. Now that she'd had a moment to calm down, she'd decided these three were the least likely looking bunch of hoodlums she'd ever seen. The one called George was shaking in his boots, Irene was pale with fear and even the dark-haired man, the calmest of the lot, was wide-eyed and anxious with worry. They weren't going to hurt her. "Let's go inside and talk like civilized people. We're not going to settle a ruddy thing standing out here."

"I'm afraid we're going to have to search your rooms, Mr. Grant," Witherspoon told the trembling young man. "If needed, I'm sure we can get a warrant."

"You've already searched the house once," Neville complained.

"It was only a cursory search, sir," Witherspoon said. "Do I have your permission to search your son's rooms again, or shall I get a warrant?" He held his breath and tried to remember what the judge's Rules said about a situation like this.

"That won't be necessary," Neville Grant said. "Go ahead and search. You won't find anything. My boy may be a fool but he's not a killer."

"Really, Neville," Mary snapped. "This is intolerable. We will not be treated like common criminals."

"I'm only trying to get at the truth, ma'am," the inspector said.

Mary Grant ignored him. From the expression on her face as she glared at her husband, she was more furious at him than she was at the inspector. "I won't have policemen stomping through my home. I demand that you send for our solicitor at once."

"Why?" Neville asked. "Arthur's got nothing to hide. He didn't kill James Underhill. Why should he? Now go ahead, boy, tell the inspector what kind of silly scheme you were cooking up with Underhill so we can have some peace in this house."

"Arthur, don't say a word," Mary ordered. "If your father won't do anything to protect you, I'll send for our solicitor myself."

"I know how to take care of my son. Stay out of this, Mary," Neville commanded. "Arthur's got no reason not to talk to the police. Now go on, boy, tell them the truth."

Mary stared at her husband and her stepson with an expression of utter contempt on her face. Without saying another word, she turned on her heel and stalked out.

Arthur moaned softly. "I didn't mean to do it, Father, but I was short of money and they were going to toss me out of the club if I didn't pay up my gambling debts."

Neville drew back a bit. "What didn't you mean to do?"

Arthur swallowed hard. "I meant to get them back," he said softly. "I really did. James promised he wouldn't sell them. He'd bought them for himself, you see. He'd come into some money so he wanted them for himself. But then you were going to sell them and that American, well, they act like they're so friendly, but really they're quite a suspicious bunch, aren't they? Well, he insisted they be authenticated. I couldn't let that happen, could I? I mean, they're good forgeries but an expert could tell in an instant they weren't the real thing."

Neville Grant had gone utterly pale.

"Forgeries," Witherspoon said. He cast a quick, worried glance at the old man. Fellow didn't look well. "Precisely what forgeries are you referring to?"

"Well." Arthur tried a sickly smile. "I mean, it wasn't really a forgery.

Like I said, I was going to buy them back. James promised I could, you know. He kept them out at his country cottage. He promised he'd send for them. I thought they might be at his lodgings, but they weren't there and they're not at the cottage either. But they must be somewhere."

"What are you talking about, boy?" Grant whispered. "Which paintings did you have forged?"

Arthur looked surprised by the question. "Oh, didn't I say? The Caldararos, of course."

Neville's mouth opened and closed. He jerked spasmodically, clutched at his heart and collapsed. He'd have fallen flat on his face if the inspector and Barnes hadn't grabbed him.

CHAPTER 10

"I'm sure Betsy will be here any moment now," Mrs. Jeffries said with a calmness she didn't feel. She glanced at the anxious faces around the table and forced herself to smile reassuringly. It was almost nine. Dinner had come and gone. Everyone was gathered back at Upper Edmonton Gardens for their meeting and Betsy wasn't home.

Smythe had gone beyond being worried. He'd stopped pacing the floor and ranting and raving a good half hour ago. Now he just sat staring at the carriage clock on the cupboard, almost as though he were willing time to stop. "When's the inspector due?" he asked.

"I don't know," Mrs. Jeffries replied. "He didn't come home for dinner and as he hasn't sent a message, I can only assume that means he's tied up on this case."

Smythe got to his feet. He knew what he had to do. "I'm going to find him. He can get every copper in London lookin' for 'er." It was either do that or slowly go insane.

Everyone looked at Mrs. Jeffries. They were all worried but no one was really sure that bringing the inspector in at this point was such a good idea.

"Give her a bit more time, Smythe," Hatchet said conversationally, though he was distraught as well. "Miss Betsy is a highly intelligent and most capable young woman. I'm sure nothing has happened to her."

"But what if somethin' 'as?" Smythe shook his head vehemently. "What if she's been 'urt or . . . or . . . ." He stopped, unable to put his greatest fear into words.

"She's not been hurt and she ain't dead," Luty declared confidently.

She hated seeing the pain on her friend's face, but she knew that if she sympathized the least little bit, he'd fall to pieces. "Betsy's on the hunt and she's just fine. Why, if she was a man, we'd not think a thing of her bein' a few hours late like this. There's been times when you and Wiggins have been out half the night and worryin' the rest of us sick. We didn't go runnin' to the inspector." But they'd been tempted to, Luty remembered.

Smythe closed his eyes briefly and clenched his hands into fists. "All right. I'll give it another 'alf 'our . . ."

"I don't think you'll 'ave to," Wiggins said. He'd wandered over to the far side of the kitchen and was peeking out the window that looked out onto the road. "There's a carriage pulling up outside and . . ." He stood on tiptoe to get a closer look. "Cor blimey, it's her. It's Betsy, and she's got three other people with her."

"Go let them in the front door," Mrs. Jeffries ordered the footman. "The inspector's not home and it'll save them coming around to the back." It would also give the coachman a few moments to get his emotions under control.

Wiggins raced off to do as he was bid.

Mrs. Goodge got up and turned her back on the others as she headed for the sink. "I'll put the kettle on," she mumbled, hoping that no one would notice the tears of relief that were running down her cheeks. "I think we could all do with a cup of tea."

"I think you'd better have a look at this." Barnes motioned the inspector into the bedroom. "We found it under the mattress." He held a small glass vial between his fingers. "Have a whiff, sir."

The inspector took a deep breath. The scent of bitter almonds drifted up his nostrils. "Oh, dear. We'd better send this along to Dr. Bosworth to be analyzed," he said. "But I've no doubt what it is."

Barnes put the stopper back inside. "Stupid of him to keep it under his mattress. Why didn't he get rid of it?"

"That's a bit more difficult to do than one might think," Witherspoon said. But the constable had made a valid point. Why hadn't Arthur gotten rid of the damaging evidence? The man wasn't the brightest chap, of course. But he wasn't a complete half-wit, either. "Perhaps he meant to but hadn't gotten around to it yet."

"Yes, sir. But leaving cyanide under your mattress"—Barnes put the vial in his pocket—"that really is idiotic, sir. Almost deliberately so, if you know what I mean. Are we going to arrest him now?"

"I'm afraid I'm going to have to." Witherspoon sighed. "Pity about his father. But let's keep our fingers crossed that Mr. Grant will be all right. Is the doctor still with him?"

"Yes." Barnes nodded. "When I poked my head in a few minutes ago, Mr. Grant had regained consciousness."

"Oh, dear." Witherspoon was in a quandry. "I didn't mean that the way it sounded. Of course I'm glad the elder Mr. Grant is conscious, but now I'm not sure what we ought to do. It would be so much easier to arrest Arthur if his father were asleep. I don't want to risk the poor old chap having another attack or fit or whatever it was he had."

"Well, sir, that can't be helped. Arthur's admitted to conspiring with Underhill. Forgery is a felony, sir. With the physical evidence of the cyanide, we've no choice but to arrest him."

"That's true," Witherspoon mused. "But conspiring in a forgery is a far cry from murder. Besides, if what Arthur says is true, why would he kill Underhill? He needed him alive. Underhill appears to be the only one who knows where the genuine Caldararos might be."

"We've already dispatched a telegram to Kent, sir," Barnes pointed out. "Maybe the local police will find them when they search Underhill's cottage."

"Let's hope so, Constable." Witherspoon sighed. "For some reason, I've a feeling those missing paintings are important to this case. But I can't quite determine precisely how."

"You'll suss it out in the end, sir," Barnes said. "Should I go and get young Mr. Grant now?"

Witherspoon hesitated. Drat. "He's upstairs in his father's room, isn't he?"

"Both he and Mrs. Grant are at Mr. Grant's bedside."

"Then we'll wait until tomorrow morning to arrest him. I won't run the risk. My conscience would torment me if in arresting Arthur we inadvertently harmed his father. We'll leave a constable on duty here and come back tomorrow morning. Perhaps the elder Mr. Grant will be stronger then and more able to cope."

"What if Arthur tries to scarper?"

"I don't think Arthur will be going anywhere," Witherspoon replied. "He's far too nervous a disposition to try making a run for it."

Barnes stared at his superior for a moment, his expression speculative. "You don't think he's guilty, do you, sir?"

The inspector smiled faintly. "You're very perceptive, Constable. And also quite correct. I don't think the fellow murdered anyone."

Witherspoon couldn't explain it, even to himself. But he had a feeling the young man wasn't a killer. "I know the evidence looks bad, but I can't quite see him doing the planning it would take to kill James Underhill with poisoned mints. Frankly, he seems far too much a bumbler."

"It could be an act, sir," Barnes suggested. "Perhaps he's not quite the fool everyone thinks."

"Well, his father seems to think him a fool," the inspector pointed out. "And he ought to know."

Every female in the room was staring at Alex Morante, as he asked to be addressed, like they'd never seen a man before. All right, Smythe thought, so he's not a bad-lookin' bloke. Even Mrs. Jeffries, who ought to have known better, was hanging on the fellow's every word. Just because Morante was as handsome as the devil and had courage and bravery oozing from his pores, the women were all atwitter over him. Smythe hated him. He glanced at Hatchet and Wiggins. They looked like they hated him too.

"I kidnapped Irene to save her life," Morante claimed.

"That's right. He did," Irene added. She gave him an adoring smile. "If it wasn't for Alex, I'd be dead. James Underhill had hired people to kill me. They were going to kidnap me that night."

"But instead 'e kidnapped you?" Wiggins jerked his head toward the Spaniard.

"I'm afraid I don't quite understand," Mrs. Jeffries said. She looked at the artist. "How did you know that Underhill was going to harm Miss Simmons?"

"Irene had come by my studio about two weeks ago. She was posing for me," he explained. "I'd sent her into the next room to put an apron on over her dress when Underhill stormed into my studio. He demanded I forge a painting for him—a Caravaggio, to be precise. He had a client who wanted a forgery to foist off on some banker as collateral for a loan. I told him I didn't do that sort of thing . . ."

"Why would Underhill want you to do it, then?" Smythe asked. "I mean, did he pick yer name out of a hat or somethin'?"

"Smythe," Betsy hissed. "Don't be so rude."

"No, it's a fair question." Alex held up his hand. "He asked me to do it because I'd done it before. I'd forged three Caldararos last year—but I thought they were to be known as copies only. I didn't know he was going to foist them off as the real thing. When I found out what he'd done, I was furious."

"How did you find out?" Mrs. Jeffries asked.

"Underhill told me." Alex smiled bitterly. "The man had no shame. He admitted what he'd done. After I'd painted the Caldararos, I started hearing rumors about him, about some of the scams he pulled on his clients and on the artists he dealt with."

"So you started askin' questions?" Wiggins guessed.

"That's right." Alex shrugged. "And I didn't like the answers I got. I'm not a saint, but I'm not a criminal."

"All right, go on with yer tale now," Luty commanded. "Underhill arrived at yer studio. Then what happened?"

"When I told him to leave, told him I wasn't interested, he got angry. He told me I'd no choice, that I had to forge the Caravaggio or I'd be sorry." Alex raised one eyebrow. "I don't like being threatened. I told him to get out and said if he came back I'd go to the police. But he laughed at me and said that I couldn't, that I was the one who had actually done the forging. If I told the police what he'd done, I'd be arrested. It would be my word against his. He was from an old, respectable family and I was a foreigner. Who would the police believe? Him or me?" His mouth curved in a cynical smile. "Underhill made his point and then he left. But I'd forgotten about Irene. She came back into the room and she was as pale as a ghost. I knew she'd overheard everything. She was scared and I don't blame her. She told me she couldn't pose, grabbed her shawl and ran out."

"So how did Underhill know she was there?" Wiggins asked.

"I ran after her. Underhill was waving down a hansom and saw her leaving my studio. He guessed that she'd overheard everything," Alex said. "I hoped everything would be all right, that Underhill wouldn't do anything. But then a few days later, I heard a rumor that someone had hired some thugs to kill Irene."

"It wasn't a rumor," Smythe said.

"But why?" Mrs. Goodge asked. "I mean, why murder just Irene?" She pointed at the Spaniard. "You knew what he was up to. You could ruin him just as easily. Why just kill the one of you?"

"But I couldn't tell," Morante explained. "Not without ruining myself. Even if the police believed I'd been duped into doing those forgeries, my career as an artist would be ruined. No respectable gallery or broker would handle my work. Underhill knew his secret was safe with me, but he didn't want Irene knowing it. So he was determined to silence her."

"How'd you find out about the bogus note that Underhill sent to Irene luring her to the Grant house?" Luty asked.

"I knew I had to do something to protect her," he said. "So I did the only thing I could. I went to Underhill's lodgings. I told him I'd changed my mind about doing the forgery. I told him I was broke and needed the money."

"And he believed you?" Hatchet asked.

"Oh, yes." Morante smiled cynically. "I can be quite convincing. I demanded some cash immediately, a kind of down payment on the forgery. I knew that he kept his money in the bedroom and I wanted a chance to search his desk. When he went to get the cash, I had a quick look. The note he'd written to Irene, the one luring her to the Grant house, was on his desk."

"Just sittin' there right where you could see it?" Smythe's tone was disbelieving.

"No," Morante replied. "I had to hunt for it. It was under a telegram Underhill was sending to someone in Kent. But as soon as I saw the note, I knew what he was planning. Why else would he have someone else's stationery in his desk? I made a note of the time of the appointment and the address, waited till Underhill came back into the room, took his money and left." His dark eyes sparkled with amusement. "I used Underhill's own money to rent the house in the country."

"The place he took me to be safe," Irene said, giving him a warm smile.

"Then what happened?" Luty asked.

"I knew that Irene would be going to Beltrane Gardens at six o'clock on the eighth." He nodded at his friend, who'd sat quietly through the entire narrative. "With George's help, we managed to foil the murder."

"George lent us the carriage." Irene flashed a grateful smile at George, who blushed a fiery red.

"That's right," Morante agreed. "George lent me his brougham . . ."

"It's an old one," George put in. "It used to belong to my father. But he's dead so he doesn't drive it anymore."

"Then what happened?" Hatchet asked.

"Then we waited outside the Grant house. I spotted a couple of thugs at the mouth of the mews so I knew we'd better grab her before she went inside." He smiled apologetically at Irene. "When she started up the walk, I called her. She turned, recognized me and came towards the carriage. Before she knew what happened, I pulled her inside and George took off."

"Why didn't you scream?" Mrs. Goodge demanded.

"I couldn't. Alex put his hand over my mouth." She didn't look as though she were still annoyed at Alex. "By the time we were on our way out of London, Alex had convinced me of the terrible danger I was in. I didn't know what to do. I couldn't get a message to my grandma, and I didn't dare send one to Nanette. Underhill and Nanette have some kind of relationship, and Alex wasn't sure we could trust her."

"But yer poor old granny was worried sick about you," Luty groused. "What if she'd needed something? What if she'd gotten sick . . ."

"We took care of that," Irene said quickly. "Alex slipped into the flat and refilled her medicine bottle when she was asleep. Besides that, George has kept an eye on her."

"Why didn't you come back when Underhill was murdered?" Hatchet asked.

"We didn't know if it was safe." Alex shrugged. "We knew he'd paid to have her murdered, but not being familiar with that sort of thing, we weren't sure if whoever had taken his money would still feel he had to do it."

"It took me quite a bit of talking to convince them it was safe to come here," Betsy said. She looked pointedly at Smythe. "That's one of the reasons we was so late."

"What do you know about Underhill's killin'?" Smythe asked them bluntly.

All three of them looked surprised by the question.

"What could we possibly know about it?" Alex asked. "We were in the country when he was killed."

"Yeah, but you've admitted you were in 'is flat. If ya knew Underhill at all, ya knew he was always chewin' them mints. It woulda been dead easy for ya to pop a tampered tin of mints into the man's coat pocket and then sit back and wait for yer problem to be solved permanently."

Morante stared at Smythe for a moment, then flicked a quick speculative glance at Betsy. He grinned. "Agreed. I could have done that. But"—he looked the coachman dead in the eye—"I didn't. I'm not a murderer. If that had been my solution, I wouldn't have gone to all the trouble of kidnapping Irene, involving my friend and hiding out in the country. I would have simply killed him the day I went to his lodgings."

The two men stared at one another, taking each other's measure. Smythe leaned back and folded his arms across his massive chest. "I reckon there's some merit to what you're sayin'"

"So what do we do now?" Irene asked.

"I suggest you all go home," Mrs. Jeffries said calmly. She looked at Irene. "I'm sure Nanette will be delighted to see that you're alive and well."

As soon as they were gone, Betsy turned to the others. "I'm ever so sorry I worried you," she said, "but I didn't know what else to do."

"Don't fret about it, Betsy," Mrs. Jeffries said. "We all occasionally have to make a decision. You did the best you could."

"We'll git over our scare," Luty said. "I'm just glad you're all right."

"All's well that ends well," Hatchet agreed.

"Thank goodness you're 'ome in one piece," Wiggins said. "That's 'ow I feel about it."

"I'll fix you a nice hot cuppa cocoa to make up for all the runnin' about you've had to do today," Mrs. Goodge said.

Smythe just glared at her.

Mrs. Jeffries met the inspector when he came in the front door. Within minutes, she had him in the drawing room, a glass of sherry in hand.

"I'll only have a quick one." He yawned. "I'm really very tired. It's been a most distressing day."

"You look exhausted, sir," she told him, clucking her tongue sympathetically. "How did the investigation go today?"

The inspector told her everything. By the time he put down his second glass of Harveys and got to his feet, Mrs. Jeffries knew every detail of the day's events.

The inspector went up to bed and Mrs. Jeffries double-checked that the front door was locked. As she climbed the stairs to her own room, she was deep in thought. She quite admired the way the inspector had decided not to arrest Arthur Grant. Like her employer, she didn't see him as the murderer either. But then, who had done it?

She went into her room and walked over to the window. The darkness blanketed her softly as she sat down in the chair and stared out into the night.

Mrs. Jeffries let her mind float free. Bits and pieces of conversations, facts and clues popped in and out of her consciousness willy-nilly. She made no move to sort anything, to categorize or to analyze. She'd already done that with no success whatsover. For a long time, she sat staring out at the London night. This case was absurdly muddled. Nothing was coming to her, nothing at all.

She sat up straighter in her chair and marshalled her thoughts. Perhaps, after all, she ought to try thinking about it in a more rational manner.

"Hadn't you better hurry, sir?" Mrs. Jeffries asked anxiously. The others were due to come by for a meeting this morning, and if she didn't get the inspector out of the house and on his way, their schedule would be thrown off completely. There were any number of things that she wanted to take care of today. Why, her little session in the dark last night had come up with half a dozen things that needed clarifying. "It's almost nine o'clock."

The inspector speared the last bite of egg with his fork. "Oh, I've plenty of time," he replied. "Constable Barnes is picking me up here and not at the station." He eyed the last piece of toast in the rack consideringly and then reached for it.

"Would you care for more tea, sir?" she asked. She cocked her head as she heard a faint knock on the front door. A moment later, footsteps sounded in the hallway, and Constable Barnes was ushered in by Betsy.

"Good morning, Inspector, Mrs. Jeffries." He nodded politely to both of them.

"Good morning," Witherspoon said. "Do sit down, Constable, and have a cup of tea."

"Thank you, sir." Barnes took a chair. "I believe I will."

Mrs. Jeffries poured him a cup and placed it in front of him. She was rather annoyed, but, of course, would never let it show. But now she had both of them camped out in the dining room and Luty and Hatchet would be here any minute. Perhaps if she began clearing up the breakfast things. Turning, she reached for the empty tray from the sideboard.

"We got an answer to our inquiry, sir," Barnes said to Witherspoon. "The police in Kent searched his cottage. There's lots of paintings there, but none that fit the description we gave 'em of the Caldararos."

Mrs. Jeffries picked up the tray and slowly, slowly turned back to the table.

"Gracious," the inspector said. "That was quick."

"Not really, sir," Barnes replied. "You see, they'd already been to Underhill's house. They'd searched it when we notifed them he'd been murdered."

Mrs. Jeffries put the tray down on the end of the table.

"Yes, yes, of course," Witherspoon muttered. He looked at his housekeeper. "Gracious, you're trying to clear up and we're in your way."

"Not at all, sir," she said hastily. "Do take your time."

"Where on earth could those paintings have got to?" Witherspoon said plaintively. "They couldn't have just disappeared into thin air."

Barnes smiled slyly. "Well, sir, I think we might have an answer to that question. Seems they've got a fairly bright young copper down in Kent. After our telegram askin' about the paintings, he took it upon himself to start askin' a few questions. Seems on the day before the murder a local delivery van was seen going to the Underhill cottage. He took a large parcel away with him."

Witherspoon brightened considerably. Now they were getting somewhere. "Where did he take it?"

"He took it, as instructed, to the train station and gave it to the station master." Barnes took a quick sip of tea. "The station master put it on the next train for London and it arrived that day, sir."

"Then Underhill must have picked it up and taken it somewhere other than his lodgings."

"But that's just it, sir," Barnes said. "He didn't. The parcel wasn't picked up till the next day—the day that Underhill was killed."

"Perhaps he got it early in the day, before he went to the Grant house?" the inspector suggested.

"No, sir. He didn't. That's why I was a bit late, sir. I nipped along to Victoria myself this morning and had a chat with the clerk in the freight office. That parcel got picked up late in the afternoon on the day of the murder. The clerk remembers it clearly. It was fetched by a footman in uniform. That means it was picked up after Underhill was already dead."

Mrs. Jeffries went absolutely still. Something niggled at the back of her mind. Something someone had said, something mentioned casually and then forgotten. For she knew instinctively that these misplaced paintings were the key to why James Underhill had been murdered.

CHAPTER 11

———⋅∞⋅———

"Are you going to arrest Arthur Grant?" Mrs. Jeffries asked the inspector.

"I'm afraid I must," the inspector replied. He and Barnes both got to their feet.

"But what about the parcel, sir?" she asked. She knew he was getting ready to make a big mistake. "You said yourself that these missing paintings were the key to finding Underhill's killer."

"I did?" Witherspoon's brows rose. "Really? When?"

"Last night, sir," Mrs. Jeffries said hastily. She fervently hoped that between his exhaustion and the sherry, he wouldn't remember precisely what all he'd said. "Right before you retired for the night, sir. You said, 'Mark my words, Mrs. Jeffries, those Caldararos are the key to this.' Well, sir, as you've so brilliantly deduced, the missing paintings are probably in that parcel."

Witherspoon smiled fondly at his housekeeper. She was so very devoted to him. Obviously, she hung on his every word. Quite fortunate that she did too. He couldn't remember all that much about last night. He'd been dead tired. "Yes, well, I do believe I'm right, Mrs. Jeffries," he said. "The missing paintings are the key to this whole business. But as the constable has just told us, the parcel is gone."

Mrs. Jeffries almost lost her nerve. If she was wrong, she'd be making a terrible fool of herself and worse, making an even bigger one of the inspector. An error at this junction could ruin everything. But if she did nothing, then the evidence—the only real evidence of the crime—could be destroyed.

"I know, sir," she said slowly. "But surely you know how to find it. Oh please, sir. Do let me in on it. Do let me see if I'm right."

"Pardon?"

She stared at him for a moment. "Oh, dear. I'm so sorry, sir. I quite forgot myself." She threw her hand up in a supplicating gesture. "I know you can't really tell me what you've planned. Please forgive my boldness, sir. I'm afraid I got carried away. I know I'm just your housekeeper, just a silly woman . . ."

"Really, Mrs. Jeffries," Witherspoon said in alarm. "You're not in the least silly and you're not just my housekeeper—you're a very valued friend. Er . . . what uh . . . what kind of plan did you think I had in mind?"

Mrs. Jeffries glanced at Barnes. She was treading on thin ice here, very thin ice indeed. The constable was no fool. But when their gazes met, the only thing she saw in his eyes was a faint amusement and perhaps, just perhaps, a bit of admiration.

"Well, sir, I naturally assumed you'd carry on along the lines of what we discussed last night." She smiled innocently. "You know, when we were talking about your list of suspects and how everyone, but most especially Arthur Grant, all needed Underhill alive and not dead." They had mentioned that aspect of the case, but only in passing.

"Yes, I recall saying that." Witherspoon nodded encouragingly.

"And you also mentioned that no one at the Grant house could remember letting Underhill into the house that day," she continued. "Well—I mean, it's quite obvious, isn't it, sir? There's only one person who could have let him in, and that person deliberately met him at the door, deliberately ushered him inside before any of the servants could answer the door. That person then searched his pockets and found the freight bill for the parcel. Having done that, that person gave the freight bill to a footman with instructions to pick up the parcel and take it somewhere safe."

Witherspoon stared at her in amazement. "I'm afraid I don't recall saying any of that," he admitted. But the idea did make a bizarre kind of sense. If a servant had answered the door, they'd have taken the man's coat and hung it up. But none of them had done it. Yet someone had hung Underhill's overcoat up in the cloakroom. Furthermore, in this investigation, there was only one household with a uniformed footman in it.

"You didn't say it, sir," she said briskly, "but you certainly implied it during our chat last night." She snatched up the tray. "But perhaps I misunderstood . . ."

"No, no, Mrs. Jeffries," Witherspoon said quickly. "I didn't mean any such thing."

She gave him a cheerful smile, praying he'd understand what the next obvious step might be. She couldn't push any further. "Thank you, sir. I'm glad I'm not completely wrong in these things. I do rather like to think I've learned a bit from you, sir."

"If I might make a suggestion, sir," Barnes said softly. "I think that before we arrest Arthur Grant, we might have a word with the footman at the Grant house."

Mrs. Jeffries gave the constable a dazzling smile.

"Would you pass me the jam pot, please?" Betsy asked Smythe. She didn't really want any. It was just an excuse to speak to him. Except for a grunt or two when she'd said goodnight before going up to bed last night, he'd not spoken to her. Betsy thought he was being awfully silly, but it bothered her nonetheless.

Wordlessly, he pushed the earthenware bowl in front of Betsy's plate.

"Thank you," she said. He grunted in reply.

"You're not in a 'appy mood this mornin', are ya?" Wiggins asked the coachman. He looked up as the housekeeper flew into the kitchen.

"Quick," she said, looking at Wiggins. "I want you to follow the inspector to the Grant house. Don't let him see you, but stay with him. He may go somewhere else. Go with him if he does, but do stay out of sight."

"I'll get the carriage," Smythe offered. "If he's on the move, he may try to grab a hansom. I'll make sure I'm there instead. I can always tell 'im I was takin' Bow and Arrow out for their exercise and 'appened to be passin'"

She was touched by their faith in her. Neither man bothered asking questions. They simply got up and prepared to do precisely what she'd asked. If she was wrong, she'd feel awful. Worse, she'd feel as though she'd let them down. "Excellent idea, Smythe," she said.

"Is things comin' to a head, then?" Mrs. Goodge asked eagerly. "Is there goin' to be an arrest?"

"Either that," Mrs. Jeffries admitted, "or I've made the world's worst mistake."

The footman wasn't a man at all, but a lad who looked to be about sixteen. His name was Horace Weatherby. Dark haired, pale skinned and small for his age, he stood next to a locked cupboard in the butler's pantry and stared at the inspector out of wary, pale blue eyes. "Mrs. Grant said you wanted to see me, sir?" he began. "But I can't think why. I wasn't even here when that Mr. Underhill got himself murdered."

"We know that," the inspector assured him. "We understand that you'd been sent out on an errand. Is that correct?"

"That's right," Horace replied.

"Where was this errand?" Witherspoon asked kindly. He knew what the butler had told him the boy had been sent to do, but he wanted to hear it from the lad's own mouth.

"I went to take Miss Collier's book back to Mudies Library," he replied.

"But according to the butler, you were gone for several hours," Barnes said. "Mudies is only over on New Oxford Street. Surely it didn't take that long to get there and back. Now why don't you tell us the truth? You went somewhere else that day, didn't you?"

Panic crossed the lad's face. "I'm not supposed to tell," he whined. "It'll cost me my job, ya know. She told me she'd sack me if I told anyone."

"This is murder you're involved in, lad," Barnes said sternly. "So you'd best tell us the truth."

"Murder," he squawked. "I didn't have nothin' to do with that. I just done what she told me and went to the station to get that parcel."

"Where did you take it?" Witherspoon pressed. "Did you bring it back here?"

"All I did was what she told me." He twisted his hands together. "I picked it up at Victoria, hopped a hansom and took it to the Great Northern Railway booking office."

"Is the parcel still there?" Barnes asked.

"I think so," he sputtered. "She ain't hardly left the house. Not since the murder, not since you coppers have been all over the place."

"Sit down, Hepzibah," Luty said calmly. "You're goin' to walk a hole in the floor."

"But what if I'm wrong?" Mrs. Jeffries suppressed a shudder. "What if I'm completely off the mark and the inspector is making a fool of himself at this very moment?"

"He's not makin' a fool of himself," Mrs. Goodge declared stoutly. She flopped a cut of veal onto the chopping block and began trimming off the fat. "He's a smart man, our inspector."

"But what if my reasoning is faulty?" She closed her eyes and wished she could turn back the clock. She'd sent them off on the flimsiest of evidence. Yet this morning, in one of those tremendous flashes of insight that make one so very certain, she'd been sure she was right. "It wouldn't be the first time I'd been wrong."

"No," Hatchet agreed. "But in all the cases we've solved, you've been correct far more often than you've been wrong. Besides, you've explained your reasoning to us. I think it makes perfect sense. As a matter of fact, I congratulate you on seeing what should have been obvious to all of us from the start."

"So do I," Betsy said. "Like you told us, every one of the others had a good reason for wanting Underhill alive." She held up her hand and began ticking off the fingers. "First, Arthur Grant needed him to get the original Caldararos back so his father'd not disinherit him when he found out the ones on his wall were fakes. Lydia Modean needed him alive so she could get the photographic plate back, Helen Collier wanted to marry him and Neville Grant and Tyrell Modean didn't have a reason to want him dead. That only leaves one person."

"It was lucky Smythe happened to be driving up Holland Park Road when we were trying to find a hansom," Barnes said dryly.

"Oh, there was nothing in the least lucky about it," Witherspoon said. He leaned forward on the seat and dropped his voice, though with the rattle of the carriage and the noise of the horses it would be impossible for anyone to overhear him. "Smythe deliberately drove up this way," he said conspiratorially. "My staff are always so very keen to learn whatever they can about my cases. They're always hanging about when I'm out on the hunt. I pretend not to notice. Though I must admit, having them about has come in handy a time or two. But as I said, I pretend not to notice them. I don't wish to make them feel awkward. I know they only do it because they're devoted to me. That, of course, and a very mild case of well . . . shall we say, hero worship."

"That's very good of you, sir," Barnes said.

"Not at all." Witherspoon waved his hand. "I'm a very fortunate man. Not many people have a staff as loyal and devoted as mine."

Barnes smiled. "That's true, sir. You are a very lucky man."

The carriage pulled around the corner into Lower Regent Street.

Witherspoon leaned out the window, trying to gauge how far they were from the Great Northern Railway booking office.

"I don't like the fact that she left the house right after sending the footman in to see us," Barnes commented. He scanned the pavement on the other side of the carriage.

"Yes, it's a pity it was her and not the butler who opened the front door," Witherspoon replied soberly. "We'd no choice but to ask her to send the footman to us. I do hope we didn't give the game away."

"Well, sir, we'll know if we get there and the freight clerk tells us the parcel was picked up just a few minutes earlier by a woman matching her description," Barnes said. "She'll not be able to get far. Not lugging a bloomin' great package."

The carriage pulled up in front of the booking office and the two policemen got out. Smythe stayed atop the carriage, ever alert and at the ready. Wiggins, who'd told the inspector he'd tagged along for the ride, jumped down and stood impatiently by the lamppost on the corner, eager to see what would happen next.

"I'll go in, shall I?" Barnes started for the door of the booking office.

"We'll both go . . ." Witherspoon paused, his eyes narrowing as his attention was caught by something on the other side of the carriage. "Gracious, there she is!" He pointed at the pedestrian island in the middle of the road. "We're too late. She's got the parcel. Quick, Barnes, come on. She's getting in a hansom."

He started across the road, only to be halted in his tracks by someone yanking hard on his jacket from behind. "Gracious," the inspector yelped just as an oncoming carriage thundered past.

"Sorry, sir," Wiggins said, "but that coach was comin' so fast I didn't think you'd 'ave time to get out of the way."

"Thank you, my boy," the inspector said gratefully. "I was in such a hurry, I wasn't paying attention to where I was going. If you'd not grabbed me, I'd have been crushed."

"Oh look, sir," Barnes cried. "She's gettin' away."

They watched in dismay as the hansom took off down the road.

Smythe whipped up the reins and in moments had turned the inspector's carriage around. "Hop in, sir," he called. "We can catch up."

Wiggins jumped on and scrambled up beside the coachman while the inspector and Barnes leapt inside. "I don't think we've a hope of catching her," the constable complained. "And if she manages to get rid of those paintings, we've no evidence." Actually, Barnes wasn't sure even catching her with the parcel would lead to anything. He hadn't a clue as to what was going on, but he was sure the inspector did.

Witherspoon stuck his head out the window. "I can see the hansom. We'll catch her, all right," he called. "Smythe is an excellent driver."

They raced through the busy London streets as fast as they dared. In what seemed like minutes to Barnes, but was in reality a bit longer than that, they'd covered well over a mile. From out the window, the murky waters of the Thames lay just ahead.

Smythe, using every ounce of skill and ingenuity at his command, kept the hansom in sight, but couldn't manage to get close enough to get directly behind it.

"The hansom's stopped," the inspector shouted, pointing ahead toward the water.

"She's gettin' out, sir," Wiggins cried.

Barnes stuck his head out and saw the hansom pulling away and a woman, a parcel clutched in her hands, racing for the side of the river. "She's goin' to toss it, sir," he warned.

But Smythe had seen too. Whistling through his teeth, he spurred his horses on even faster. They raced for the embankment. He didn't pull up. He didn't even slow. He simply kept on going right up to the concrete buttresses that held back the waters of the Thames.

She saw them as they jumped out of the carriage.

Instead of tossing the parcel over the edge of the embankment, she turned and started running along the pavement, the parcel clutched under her arm.

They started after her. The inspector was in the lead, but Wiggins was by far the fastest. "I'll get her," he called as he flew past the two policemen. But fast as he was, he didn't gain on her very quickly.

Driven by fear, she was a good deal swifter than one would expect from a woman of her age and background.

Wiggins put on more speed.

"Stop in the name of the law," Witherspoon gasped, but she paid no attention. She just kept running.

Wiggins finally began to gain on her. She looked back over her shoulder and saw him closing the gap between them. He was now only twenty or so yards away. She stopped and threw the parcel over the buttress.

"Oh, no," Wiggins cried as he saw it disappear over the side. He skidded to a halt beside her. She stared at him stonily, but didn't try to run. Wiggins was grateful for that. He wasn't quite sure what to do. Luckily, Barnes got there a second later, and right on his heels was the inspector.

"Out for a walk, Inspector?" she said calmly.

"Mary Grant," he replied breathlessly, "you're under arrest for the murder of James Underhill."

She smiled then. "But you won't be able to prove it, will you? And by the time you drag the Thames and find those paintings, the water will have ruined your precious evidence, I'm afraid. Even an expert won't be able to help you then."

"We won't have to drag the river," Wiggins said cheerfully. He pointed toward the river. "Look, there's a barge moored right below us. The parcel's sittin' right atop of it plain as the nose on yer face."

It was well past ten o'clock by the time the inspector got home that night. When he came into the kitchen he wasn't in the least surprised to see his entire household, as well as Luty and Hatchet, sitting at the table.

"Good evening, sir," Mrs. Jeffries said cheerfully. "Luty and Hatchet happened to drop by after supper, sir. Once they heard about all your excitement this afternoon, they were determined to stay and hear what happened."

"I don't mind in the least," he said. He reached down and patted Fred on the head. "There's a good boy, now. Just be a patient fellow and I'll take you walkies after I've had a cup of tea."

"Do tell us everything," Mrs. Jeffries urged him. She poured him a cup of steaming hot tea. "What happened?"

"Well, luckily, as I'm sure Wiggins told you, the parcel didn't go in the water." He picked up his cup and took a sip. "We took it back to the station and opened it and, of course, the Caldararos were inside." He winced. "It was at this point that I almost made a dreadful mistake, you see. Fortunately, Constable Barnes had the good sense to send for the Modeans. They came at once and brought their art expert with them." He shook his head. "It's a very good thing he did too. Otherwise, I'd have arrested the right person but the motive would have been all wrong and then she'd never have confessed."

"She confessed?" Mrs. Jeffries said.

"Oh, yes," the inspector said, "as soon as we brought in the art expert and the other set of Caldararos, the ones she'd sent out to be cleaned. We'd got those too, you see. So both sets were at the station. As soon as she saw all that, she told us everything."

"Ya gonna tell us why she murdered Underhill?" Luty demanded.

"To stop him from selling the original Caldararos back to Arthur Grant," Witherspoon explained. "Mary Grant knew all about how Arthur had sold the ones she'd brought to the marriage—the ones she'd used for a dowry—to Underhill. That was fine by her too. The last things she wanted was Underhill bringing those back to be authenticated."

"But why?" Betsy asked. "If they was the ones she brung to the marriage, why would she want Underhill to have them?"

"She didn't. But she didn't want an art expert authenticating them either," Witherspoon said. "You see, they were forgeries too. But, of course, that's where I'd made my mistake. I thought she'd murdered Underhill because she was angry at him."

"Angry at him?" Mrs. Goodge repeated.

"Oh, yes. I thought she'd poisoned him because she was in love with him. Gracious, I oughtn't to admit this, but I really had got it wrong. I thought that's why she refused to admit to us that her sister was going to marry Underhill. She was in love with him herself."

"But sir," Mrs. Jeffries asked softly, "if she murdered him out of jealousy, why would she have wanted to get her hands on the parcel so badly?"

Witherspoon gave an embarrassed shrug. "I thought those paintings belonged to her sister, Helen Collier. It occurred to me that Mary Grant had bought herself a husband with her paintings so why shouldn't her sister?"

"All right, Hepzibah," Luty said as soon as the inspector had taken Fred outside. "Tell us how ya figured it out."

"As I told you earlier, no one seemed to really benefit from Underhill's death," she explained. "No one liked him very much, but most of them weren't better off with the man dead. I couldn't see how anyone benefitted from his death except Irene Simmons. But she was completely out of the picture as she'd disappeared well before he ate those fatal mints. Last night, when the inspector told me that the poison had been found under Arthur's mattress, I realized that the mints must have been tampered with that very day. That meant that Irene and Morante couldn't have done the killing."

"But 'ow'd ya figure it was her?" Smythe asked.

"I wasn't sure until this morning," Mrs. Jeffries said. "It was when the constable told us about the parcel coming up by train from Underhill's cottage in Kent that it all fell into place. I understood then that there was only one thing that could be in that package—the paintings. The ones Arthur Grant had paid Underhill to give him back. Then I asked myself who wouldn't want the original paintings back—after all, if the originals were back in place and authenticated, the sale could go through and the Grants could pay off their creditors. Then I realized that Underhill might have been murdered to stop that from taking place. But why? Who would benefit from those paintings not being authenticated? There could be only one person. The person who'd originally brought them into the Grant household. Mary Grant. She didn't want an expert seeing them because she knew they were fakes. She knew they were worthless. And she'd do anything, anything at all, to make sure her husband never found out."

"But the ones she sent out to be cleaned were fakes as well," Betsy said.

"But that worked to her advantage," Mrs. Jeffries pointed out. "Once Neville Grant found out what his son had done, he'd disinherit him. That was one of the things she wanted. Her husband is a very sick man. He probably won't live much longer. He has nothing of value except his art collection. An art collection of real paintings she wanted to inherit. I'll wager Mary Grant knew full well what Arthur had done. She probably encouraged James Underhill to set up the whole scheme. The last thing she wanted was Underhill sending her paintings back here. If it ever came out that she'd bought her way into this marriage with forged paintings, Neville Grant would have divorced her in an instant." She smiled quickly at the cook. "We found out from Mrs. Goodge's excellent sources that Mr. Grant wasn't adverse to divorce. He was on the verge of divorcing his first wife, Arthur's mother, before she so conveniently died."

"Cor blimey." Wiggins gazed at her in admiration. "You're really somethin'. Figurin' all that out with just a few bits and pieces."

"Don't give me too much credit," she told him. "Without the information all of you worked so hard to get, we'd have never discovered the truth. Don't forget, Wiggins, it was you who told us about the footman who wasn't at the house on the afternoon of the murder. That was on the day when you were sure you'd not found out anything worthwhile and that turned out to be a vital clue."

"But how did you know that Mrs. Grant had searched Underhill's pockets?" Betsy asked.

"I was guessing there," she said. "But I remembered how the inspector had told me that none of the servants could recall letting Underhill into the house that day." She faltered a bit and hoped she wasn't blushing. "And, well, I've done the same thing myself with the inspector."

"Mrs. Jeffries, you're goin' all red in the cheeks," Wiggins pointed out.

Luty snickered. "Met him at the door so you could search his pockets, huh?"

"Only because I needed to borrow his spectacles," she explained. "You know, for when we need a good excuse to go to the station or the scene of the crime the next day. But that's what made me think that might be what happened. When you want to have a good look through someone's pockets, you make sure you get to the door before the butler does."

"Absolutely, madam," Hatchet concurred. "No selfrespecting butler would let the lady of the house take a gentleman's coat."

They talked about the case for another half hour, until the inspector, with a very tired Fred at his heels, came in from his walk and went up to bed.

Luty and Hatchet said their good nights after promising to come back the next morning for the delightful task of reliving the case from start to finish. Mrs. Jeffries went to make sure the back door was locked, Wiggins took Fred up to his room and Mrs. Goodge started to clear the table.

"I'll do that," Betsy volunteered. "You and Mrs. Jeffries go onto bed. I can tidy up."

"Thanks, dear," the cook said gratefully as she headed for her room. "I'll tell Mrs. Jeffries you're finishin' up down here. She could do with a good night's sleep herself."

Betsy cleaned off the table, rinsed out the cups and saucers and emptied the last of the tea down the drain.

She'd just reached over to turn down the lamp when she heard footsteps on the stairs. "Oh, it's you. I thought you'd gone to bed."

"I come down to see if you needed any 'elp," Smythe said. "It didn't seem fair for you to 'ave to do all the tidyin' up."

"I don't mind." Betsy picked up the small lantern the household used at night.

"Betsy, I'm sorry I've been so . . . so . . ."

"Cold?" she supplied. "Is that the word you're lookin' for?"

"I didn't mean it," he said, desperate to make things up with her. "But I was so scared when ya didn't come 'ome, lass. It took me a day or two to get over it."

She stared at him in the semidarkness. The way he'd acted towards her had hurt her feelings. Hurt her worse than she'd like to admit, and one part of her wanted to get him back. But on the other hand, she hated being at odds with him.

"Look, I know you're right annoyed with me," he began.

"I'm not annoyed anymore," she interrupted. "I can even understand a bit how you felt. I wouldn't like walkin' the floor and worrying myself sick over you, either."

He broke into a broad grin.

"But I've done it a time or two and I've not treated you like you've got the plague just because you made me a bit anxious."

He spread his hands helplessly. "I said I was sorry."

"I don't want you making a habit of this," she warned, raising her hand to stop him. "The next time I might not be so forgiving."

"I won't," he promised. He reached for the lantern. "'Ere, let me get that for ya. Would you like to go out with me tomorrow?"

"Out where?" But it was a silly question. She'd go anywhere with him.

"To the photographic exhibit at the Crystal Palace," he said, taking her elbow and heading for the hall. "But there's just one thing."

"What's that?" she asked.

"We have to take Wiggins with us."